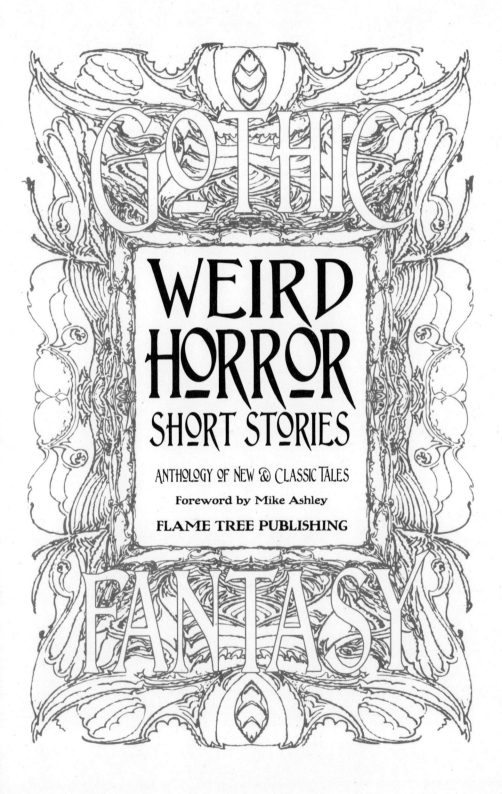

GOTHIC

WEIRD HORROR SHORT STORIES

ANTHOLOGY OF NEW & CLASSIC TALES

Foreword by Mike Ashley

FLAME TREE PUBLISHING

FANTASY

This is a FLAME TREE Book

Publisher & Creative Director: Nick Wells
Project Editor: Gillian Whitaker
Editorial Board: Catherine Taylor, Josie Karani, Taylor Bentley

Publisher's Note: Due to the historical nature of the classic text, we're aware that there may be some language used which has the potential to cause offence to the modern reader. However, wishing overall to preserve the integrity of the text, rather than imposing contemporary sensibilities, we have left it unaltered.

FLAME TREE PUBLISHING
6 Melbray Mews, Fulham,
London SW6 3NS, United Kingdom
www.flametreepublishing.com

First published 2022

ISBN: 978-1-83964-935-6
Special ISBN: 978-1-80417-166-0

The cover image is created by Flame Tree Studio
based on artwork by Slava Gerj and Gabor Ruszkai.

A copy of the CIP data for this book is available from the British Library.

Printed and bound in China

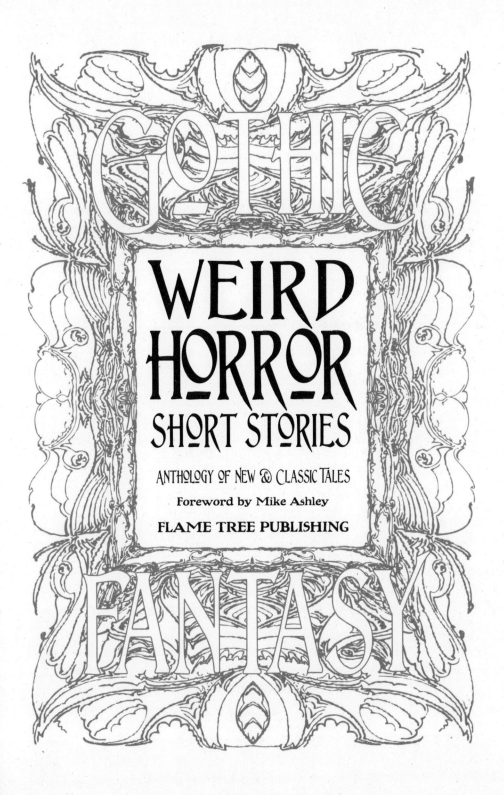

GOTHIC

WEIRD HORROR

SHORT STORIES

ANTHOLOGY OF NEW & CLASSIC TALES

Foreword by Mike Ashley

FLAME TREE PUBLISHING

FANTASY

Contents

CONTENTS

Foreword: Weird Horror Short Stories

EVER HAD that dream when you're running from something, you don't know what, but no matter how fast you run you cannot escape? That feeling that whatever you do, there are forces over which you have no power and that they will win.

That threat may be relatively simple, perhaps a beautiful woman who is deadly to the touch or something evil lurking behind a curtain. Or it may be on a cosmic scale, where our minds become a gateway for Outer Monstrosities from space or alien creatures from aeons past.

Whatever the threat, the fear is tangible and we have no way of fighting back. We are totally and utterly helpless.

That fear has been with us from childhood – the fear of being left alone in a dark room with strange sounds and no one to help. Many of the fairy tales that we enjoyed as children actually built upon our fears, such as being lost in the woods and encountering a fearsome old lady intent upon eating you, as in 'Hansel and Gretel', or the fear of being devoured by a wolf as in 'Little Red Riding Hood'. Lucy Clifford, who wrote several unusual fairy tales, produced perhaps the most frightening in 'The New Mother', included here, where children who have disobeyed find that their mother leaves them and is replaced by something frightening and grotesque.

Fears stay with us all our lives – phobias, perhaps of spiders, birds or the dark. Or such uncontrollable fears that manifest as OCD, obsessive-compulsive disorder, where we have to double-check things or make sure everything is okay and orderly.

Ultimately there is the fear of death – the one thing we cannot control. Or what happens if we try? Edgar Allan Poe, as far back as 1845, thought perhaps the new power of mesmerism might allow the mind to outlive the body. Then he considered the consequences as his story here reveals.

We cannot escape our fears but perhaps one way we can deal with them is to experience them second-hand in stories and maybe, just maybe, they will help us feel that perhaps we do have a little control. But therein lies another danger. By meddling and seeking to exert control we open up the horrors that lay hidden.

Throughout history, science has found ways where perhaps we can control our fears. Imagine when our cave-dwelling or hunter-gatherer ancestors mastered fire, which gave them some control over the dark and the fearsome creatures beyond the shadows. Science began to find cures for illnesses or how to treat wounds and our life expectancy increased. But science is a double-edged sword. In curing one illness do we release another? The purported medicines in the stories by Louisa May Alcott and Arthur Machen, for example, achieve something far more frightening than an intended cure.

Even if we feel we may be mastering our worst fears, others lie in wait. Perhaps the most dreaded is an encounter with a being that is not of Earthly origin – not a ghost but a completely different life form. In 'The Willows', based on Blackwood's own experiences, two men are at the mercy of forces on a remote island, forces that are unearthly and do not want the men there. The forces manifest in sounds and vibrations. Just imagine being trapped in a place with a constant, repetitive sound. Shiel's 'The House of Sounds' develops the menace even further.

H.P. Lovecraft, who was the master of describing the indescribable, considered how we might become victims of powerful beings that existed long ago and can project their psyche into the far future. If we dwell too long imagining the sheer immensity of time – the 'vertiginous cycles of time' as Lovecraft called it – it can turn our minds.

The stories included here deal with a wide range of fears and phobias and our limited abilities to control or evade them. How real are our fears, and how do we avoid becoming their victim? How much of our fears are in our imagination and how much are reality, but a reality we have no way of understanding? It is when we realise that not just the human race, but every living thing on this planet, is at the mercy of forces beyond their control, that we know that not all of our fears are of our own creation. After all, you don't have to be paranoid to think the world is out to get you. As the following stories reveal.

Mike Ashley

Publisher's Note

THIS LATEST instalment in our Gothic Fantasy series follows on from *Lovecraft Mythos*, widening the theme further to encompass a range of fiction where the boundaries of nature, science and sanity distort. Enter 'the tentacle', elemental slugs, fungoid creatures, and all manner of oozing entities that fascinate. We've chosen classic stories that cover these, but that also explore the separation of mind and matter, the intrigue of in-between spaces, and the limits of human knowledge. Within, characters encounter vast inescapable wildernesses ('The Willows', 'The Moonstone') and voids ('The Distortion out of Space', 'The Hill and the Hole'), the feeling of hurtling towards 'some dreadful unknown Horror' (as in Hodgson's 'The Hog'), and suspenseful explorations of swamps, ancient caverns and tombs.

Alongside these, we're excited to present a number of new stories, plus some excellent reprints on a theme that continues to stretch the imagination. The selections from submissions are always tough, and this time was no different. We're very proud of the included stories though, which we believe all demonstrate exactly what makes weird horror so captivating. From mysterious curses to experimental science, confrontations with greater forces in both the modern and classic visions here lend credence to the oft-cited idea from Lovecraft, and one of the central tenets of this genre, that 'the oldest and strongest kind of fear is fear of the unknown'.

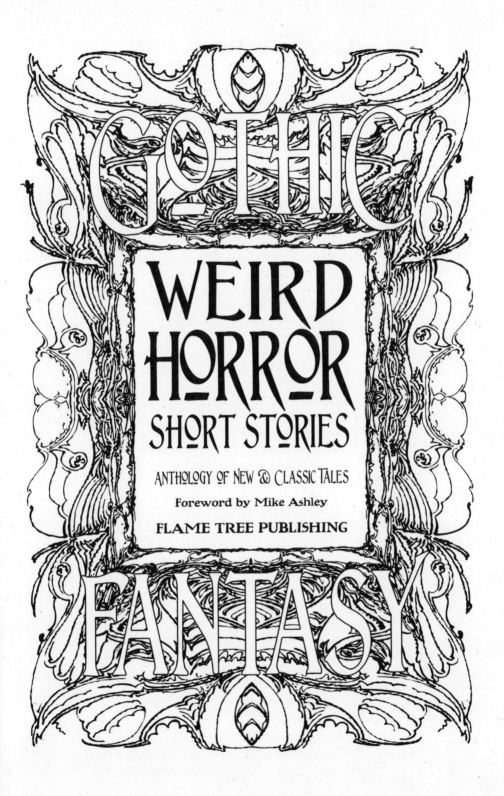

GOTHIC

WEIRD HORROR

SHORT STORIES

ANTHOLOGY OF NEW & CLASSIC TALES

Foreword by Mike Ashley

FLAME TREE PUBLISHING

FANTASY

Lost in a Pyramid

Louisa May Alcott

Chapter I

"AND WHAT are these, Paul?" asked Evelyn, opening a tarnished gold box and examining its contents curiously.

"Seeds of some unknown Egyptian plant," replied Forsyth, with a sudden shadow on his dark face, as he looked down at the three scarlet grains lying in the white hand lifted to him.

"Where did you get them?" asked the girl.

"That is a weird story, which will only haunt you if I tell it," said Forsyth, with an absent expression that strongly excited the girl's curiosity.

"Please tell it, I like weird tales, and they never trouble me. Ah, do tell it; your stories are always so interesting," she cried, looking up with such a pretty blending of entreaty and command in her charming face, that refusal was impossible.

"You'll be sorry for it, and so shall I, perhaps; I warn you beforehand, that harm is foretold to the possessor of those mysterious seeds," said Forsyth, smiling, even while he knit his black brows, and regarded the blooming creature before him with a fond yet foreboding glance.

"Tell on, I'm not afraid of these pretty atoms," she answered, with an imperious nod.

"To hear is to obey. Let me read the facts, and then I will begin," returned Forsyth, pacing to and fro with the far-off look of one who turns the pages of the past.

Evelyn watched him a moment, and then returned to her work, or play, rather, for the task seemed well suited to the vivacious little creature, half-child, half-woman.

"While in Egypt," commenced Forsyth, slowly, "I went one day with my guide and Professor Niles, to explore the Cheops. Niles had a mania for antiquities of all sorts, and forgot time, danger and fatigue in the ardor of his pursuit. We rummaged up and down the narrow passages, half choked with dust and close air; reading inscriptions on the walls, stumbling over shattered mummy-cases, or coming face to face with some shriveled specimen perched like a hobgoblin on the little shelves where the dead used to be stowed away for ages. I was desperately tired after a few hours of it, and begged the professor to return. But he was bent on exploring certain places, and would not desist. We had but one guide, so I was forced to stay; but Jumal, my man, seeing how weary I was, proposed to us to rest in one of the larger passages, while he went to procure another guide for Niles. We consented, and assuring us that we were perfectly safe, if we did not quit the spot, Jumal left us, promising to return speedily. The professor sat down to take notes of his researches, and stretching myself on the soft sand, I fell asleep.

"I was roused by that indescribable thrill which instinctively warns us of danger, and springing up, I found myself alone. One torch burned faintly where Jumal had struck it, but Niles and the other light were gone. A dreadful sense of loneliness oppressed me for a moment; then I collected myself and looked well about me. A bit of paper was pinned to my hat, which lay near me, and on it, in the professor's writing were these words:

"I've gone back a little to refresh my memory on certain points. Don't follow me till Jumal comes. I can find my way back to you, for I have a clue. Sleep well, and dream gloriously of the Pharaohs. N N.

"I laughed at first over the old enthusiast, then felt anxious then restless, and finally resolved to follow him, for I discovered a strong cord fastened to a fallen stone, and knew that this was the clue he spoke of. Leaving a line for Jumal, I took my torch and retraced my steps, following the cord along the winding ways. I often shouted, but received no reply, and pressed on, hoping at each turn to see the old man poring over some musty relic of antiquity. Suddenly the cord ended, and lowering my torch, I saw that the footsteps had gone on.

"'Rash fellow, he'll lose himself, to a certainty,' I thought, really alarmed now.

"As I paused, a faint call reached me, and I answered it, waited, shouted again, and a still fainter echo replied.

"Niles was evidently going on, misled by the reverberations of the low passages. No time was to be lost, and, forgetting myself, I stuck my torch in the deep sand to guide me back to the clue, and ran down the straight path before me, whooping like a madman as I went. I did not mean to lose sight of the light, but in my eagerness to find Niles I turned from the main passage, and, guided by his voice, hastened on. His torch soon gladdened my eyes, and the clutch of his trembling hands told me what agony he had suffered.

"'Let us get out of this horrible place at once,' he said, wiping the great drops off his forehead.

"'Come, we're not far from the clue. I can soon reach it, and then we are safe'; but as I spoke, a chill passed over me, for a perfect labyrinth of narrow paths lay before us.

"Trying to guide myself by such landmarks as I had observed in my hasty passage, I followed the tracks in the sand till I fancied we must be near my light. No glimmer appeared, however, and kneeling down to examine the footprints nearer, I discovered, to my dismay, that I had been following the wrong ones, for among those marked by a deep boot-heel, were prints of bare feet; we had had no guide there, and Jumal wore sandals.

"Rising, I confronted Niles, with the one despairing word, 'Lost!' as I pointed from the treacherous sand to the fast-waning light.

"I thought the old man would be overwhelmed but, to my surprise, he grew quite calm and steady, thought a moment, and then went on, saying, quietly:

"'Other men have passed here before us; let us follow their steps, for, if I do not greatly err, they lead toward great passages, where one's way is easily found.'

"On we went, bravely, till a misstep threw the professor violently to the ground with a broken leg, and nearly extinguished the torch. It was a horrible predicament, and I gave up all hope as I sat beside the poor fellow, who lay exhausted with fatigue, remorse and pain, for I would not leave him.

"'Paul,' he said suddenly, 'if you will not go on, there is one more effort we can make. I remember hearing that a party lost as we are, saved themselves by building a fire. The smoke penetrated further than sound or light, and the guide's quick wit understood the unusual mist; he followed it, and rescued the party. Make a fire and trust to Jumal.'

"'A fire without wood?' I began; but he pointed to a shelf behind me, which had escaped me in the gloom; and on it I saw a slender mummy-case. I understood him, for these dry cases, which lie about in hundreds, are freely used as firewood. Reaching up, I pulled it down, believing it to be empty, but as it fell, it burst open, and out rolled a mummy. Accustomed as I was to such sights, it startled me a little, for danger had unstrung my nerves. Laying the little brown chrysalis aside, I smashed the case, lit the pile with my torch, and soon a light cloud of smoke drifted down the three passages which diverged from the cell-like place where we had paused.

"While busied with the fire, Niles, forgetful of pain and peril, had dragged the mummy nearer, and was examining it with the interest of a man whose ruling passion was strong even in death.

"'Come and help me unroll this. I have always longed to be the first to see and secure the curious treasures put away among the folds of these uncanny winding-sheets. This is a woman, and we may find something rare and precious here,' he said, beginning to unfold the outer coverings, from which a strange aromatic odor came.

"Reluctantly I obeyed, for to me there was something sacred in the bones of this unknown woman. But to beguile the time and amuse the poor fellow, I lent a hand, wondering as I worked, if this dark, ugly thing had ever been a lovely, soft-eyed Egyptian girl.

"From the fibrous folds of the wrappings dropped precious gums and spices, which half intoxicated us with their potent breath, antique coins, and a curious jewel or two, which Niles eagerly examined.

"All the bandages but one were cut off at last, and a small head laid bare, round which still hung great plaits of what had once been luxuriant hair. The shriveled hands were folded on the breast, and clasped in them lay that gold box."

"Ah!" cried Evelyn, dropping it from her rosy palm with a shudder.

"Nay; don't reject the poor little mummy's treasure. I never have quite forgiven myself for stealing it, or for burning her," said Forsyth, painting rapidly, as if the recollection of that experience lent energy to his hand.

"Burning her! Oh, Paul, what do you mean?" asked the girl, sitting up with a face full of excitement.

"I'll tell you. While busied with Madame la Momie, our fire had burned low, for the dry case went like tinder. A faint, far-off sound made our hearts leap, and Niles cried out: 'Pile on the wood; Jumal is tracking us; don't let the smoke fail now or we are lost!'

"'There is no more wood; the case was very small, and is all gone,' I answered, tearing off such of my garments as would burn readily, and piling them upon the embers.

"Niles did the same, but the light fabrics were quickly consumed, and made no smoke.

"'Burn that!' commanded the professor, pointing to the mummy.

"I hesitated a moment. Again came the faint echo of a horn. Life was dear to me. A few dry bones might save us, and I obeyed him in silence.

"A dull blaze sprung up, and a heavy smoke rose from the burning mummy, rolling in volumes through the low passages, and threatening to suffocate us with its fragrant mist. My brain grew dizzy, the light danced before my eyes, strange phantoms seemed to people the air, and, in the act of asking Niles why he gasped and looked so pale, I lost consciousness."

Evelyn drew a long breath, and put away the scented toys from her lap as if their odor oppressed her.

Forsyth's swarthy face was all aglow with the excitement of his story, and his black eyes glittered as he added, with a quick laugh:

"That's all; Jumal found and got us out, and we both forswore pyramids for the rest of our days."

"But the box: how came you to keep it?" asked Evelyn, eyeing it askance as it lay gleaming in a streak of sunshine.

"Oh, I brought it away as a souvenir, and Niles kept the other trinkets."

"But you said harm was foretold to the possessor of those scarlet seeds," persisted the girl, whose fancy was excited by the tale, and who fancied all was not told.

"Among his spoils, Niles found a bit of parchment, which he deciphered, and this inscription said that the mummy we had so ungallantly burned was that of a famous sorceress who bequeathed her curse to whoever should disturb her rest. Of course I don't believe that curse has anything to do with it, but it's a fact that Niles never prospered from that day. He says it's because he has never recovered from the fall and fright and I dare say it is so; but I sometimes wonder if I am to share the curse, for I've a vein of superstition in me, and that poor little mummy haunts my dreams still."

A long silence followed these words. Paul painted mechanically and Evelyn lay regarding him with a thoughtful face. But gloomy fancies were as foreign to her nature as shadows are to noonday, and presently she laughed a cheery laugh, saying as she took up the box again:

"Why don't you plant them, and see what wondrous flower they will bear?"

"I doubt if they would bear anything after lying in a mummy's hand for centuries," replied Forsyth, gravely.

"Let me plant them and try. You know wheat has sprouted and grown that was taken from a mummy's coffin; why should not these pretty seeds? I should so like to watch them grow; may I, Paul?"

"No, I'd rather leave that experiment untried. I have a queer feeling about the matter, and don't want to meddle myself or let anyone I love meddle with these seeds. They may be some horrible poison, or possess some evil power, for the sorceress evidently valued them, since she clutched them fast even in her tomb."

"Now, you are foolishly superstitious, and I laugh at you. Be generous; give me one seed, just to learn if it will grow. See I'll pay for it," and Evelyn, who now stood beside him, dropped a kiss on his forehead as she made her request, with the most engaging air.

But Forsyth would not yield. He smiled and returned the embrace with lover-like warmth, then flung the seeds into the fire, and gave her back the golden box, saying, tenderly:

"My darling, I'll fill it with diamonds or bonbons, if you please, but I will not let you play with that witch's spells. You've enough of your own, so forget the 'pretty seeds' and see what a Light of the Harem I've made of you."

Evelyn frowned, and smiled, and presently the lovers were out in the spring sunshine reveling in their own happy hopes, untroubled by one foreboding fear.

Chapter II

I HAVE a little surprise for you, love," said Forsyth, as he greeted his cousin three months later on the morning of his wedding day.

"And I have one for you," she answered, smiling faintly.

"How pale you are, and how thin you grow! All this bridal bustle is too much for you, Evelyn." he said, with fond anxiety, as he watched the strange pallor of her face, and pressed the wasted little hand in his.

"I am so tired," she said, and leaned her head wearily on her lover's breast. "Neither sleep, food, nor air gives me strength, and a curious mist seems to cloud my mind at times. Mamma says it is the heat, but I shiver even in the sun, while at night I burn with fever. Paul, dear, I'm glad you are going to take me away to lead a quiet, happy life with you, but I'm afraid it will be a very short one."

"My fanciful little wife! You are tired and nervous with all this worry, but a few weeks of rest in the country will give us back our blooming Eve again. Have you no curiosity to learn my surprise?" he asked, to change her thoughts.

The vacant look stealing over the girl's face gave place to one of interest, but as she listened it seemed to require an effort to fix her mind on her lover's words.

"You remember the day we rummaged in the old cabinet?"

"Yes," and a smile touched her lips for a moment.

"And how you wanted to plant those queer red seeds I stole from the mummy?"

"I remember," and her eyes kindled with sudden fire.

"Well, I tossed them into the fire, as I thought, and gave you the box. But when I went back to cover up my picture, and found one of those seeds on the rug, a sudden fancy to gratify your whim led me to send it to Niles and ask him to plant and report on its progress. Today I hear from him for the first time, and he reports that the seed has grown marvelously, has budded, and that he intends to take the first flower, if it blooms in time, to a meeting of famous scientific men, after which he will send me its true name and the plant itself. From his description, it must be very curious, and I'm impatient to see it."

"You need not wait; I can show you the flower in its bloom," and Evelyn beckoned with the *méchante* smile so long a stranger to her lips.

Much amazed, Forsyth followed her to her own little boudoir, and there, standing in the sunshine, was the unknown plant. Almost rank in their luxuriance were the vivid green leaves on the slender purple stems, and rising from the midst, one ghostly-white flower, shaped like the head of a hooded snake, with scarlet stamens like forked tongues, and on the petals glittered spots like dew.

"A strange, uncanny flower! Has it any odor?" asked Forsyth, bending to examine it, and forgetting, in his interest, to ask how it came there.

"None, and that disappoints me, I am so fond of perfumes," answered the girl, caressing the green leaves which trembled at her touch, while the purple stems deepened their tint.

"Now tell me about it," said Forsyth, after standing silent for several minutes.

"I had been before you, and secured one of the seeds, for two fell on the rug. I planted it under a glass in the richest soil I could find, watered it faithfully, and was amazed at the rapidity with which it grew when once it appeared above the earth. I told no-one, for I meant to surprise you with it; but this bud has been so long in blooming, I have had to wait. It is a good omen that it blossoms today, and as it is nearly white, I mean to wear it, for I've learned to love it, having been my pet for so long."

"I would not wear it, for, in spite of its innocent color, it is an evil-looking plant, with its adder's tongue and unnatural dew. Wait till Niles tells us what it is, then pet it if it is harmless. Perhaps my sorceress cherished it for some symbolic beauty – those old Egyptians were full of fancies. It was very sly of you to turn the tables on me in this way. But I forgive you, since in a few hours, I shall chain this mysterious hand forever. How cold it is! Come out into the garden and get some warmth and color for tonight, my love."

But when night came, no-one could reproach the girl with her pallor, for she glowed like a pomegranate-flower, her eyes were full of fire, her lips scarlet, and all her old vivacity seemed to have returned. A more brilliant bride never blushed under a misty veil, and when her lover saw her, he was absolutely startled by the almost unearthly beauty which transformed the pale, languid creature of the morning into this radiant woman.

They were married, and if love, many blessings, and all good gifts lavishly showered upon them could make them happy, then this young pair were truly blest. But even in the rapture of the moment that made her his, Forsyth observed how icy cold was the little hand he held, how feverish the deep color on the soft cheek he kissed, and what a strange fire burned in the tender eyes that looked so wistfully at him.

Blithe and beautiful as a spirit, the smiling bride played her part in all the festivities of that long evening, and when at last light, life and color began to fade, the loving eyes that watched her thought it but the natural weariness of the hour. As the last guest departed, Forsyth was met by a servant, who gave him a letter marked 'Haste'. Tearing it open, he read these lines, from a friend of the professor's:

DEAR SIR – Poor Niles died suddenly two days ago, while at the Scientific Club, and his last words were: "Tell Paul Forsyth to beware of the Mummy's Curse, for this fatal flower has killed me." The circumstances of his death were so peculiar, that I add them as a sequel to this message. For several months, as he told us, he had been watching an unknown plant, and that evening he brought us the flower to examine. Other matters of interest absorbed us till a late hour, and the plant was forgotten. The professor wore it in his buttonhole – a strange white, serpent-headed blossom, with pale glittering spots, which slowly changed to a glittering scarlet, till the leaves looked as if sprinkled with blood. It was observed that instead of the pallor and feebleness which had recently come over him, that the professor was unusually animated, and seemed in an almost unnatural state of high spirits. Near the close of the meeting, in the midst of a lively discussion, he suddenly dropped, as if smitten with apoplexy. He was conveyed home insensible, and after one lucid interval, in which he gave me the message I have recorded above, he died in great agony, raving of mummies, pyramids, serpents, and some fatal curse which had fallen upon him.

After his death, livid scarlet spots, like those on the flower, appeared upon his skin, and he shriveled like a withered leaf. At my desire, the mysterious plant was examined, and pronounced by the best authority one of the most deadly poisons known to the Egyptian sorceresses. The plant slowly absorbs the vitality of whoever cultivates it, and the blossom, worn for two or three hours, produces either madness or death.

Down dropped the paper from Forsyth's hand; he read no further, but hurried back into the room where he had left his young wife. As if worn out with fatigue, she had thrown herself upon a couch, and lay there motionless, her face half-hidden by the light folds of the veil, which had blown over it.

"Evelyn, my dearest! Wake up and answer me. Did you wear that strange flower today?" whispered Forsyth, putting the misty screen away.

There was no need for her to answer, for there, gleaming spectrally on her bosom, was the evil blossom, its white petals spotted now with flecks of scarlet, vivid as drops of newly spilt blood.

But the unhappy bridegroom scarcely saw it, for the face above it appalled him by its utter vacancy. Drawn and pallid, as if with some wasting malady, the young face, so lovely an hour ago, lay before him aged and blighted by the baleful influence of the plant which had drunk up her life. No recognition in the eyes, no word upon the lips, no motion of the hand – only the faint breath, the fluttering pulse, and wide-opened eyes, betrayed that she was alive.

Alas for the young wife! The superstitious fear at which she had smiled had proved true: the curse that had bided its time for ages was fulfilled at last, and her own hand wrecked her happiness for ever. Death in life was her doom, and for years Forsyth secluded himself to tend with pathetic devotion the pale ghost, who never, by word or look, could thank him for the love that outlived even such a fate as this.

The Striding Place

Gertrude Atherton

WEIGALL, continental and detached, tired early of grouse-shooting. To stand propped against a sod fence while his host's workmen routed up the birds with long poles and drove them towards the waiting guns, made him feel himself a parody on the ancestors who had roamed the moors and forests of this West Riding of Yorkshire in hot pursuit of game worth the killing. But when in England in August he always accepted whatever proffered for the season, and invited his host to shoot pheasants on his estates in the South. The amusements of life, he argued, should be accepted with the same philosophy as its ills.

It had been a bad day. A heavy rain had made the moor so spongy that it fairly sprang beneath the feet. Whether or not the grouse had haunts of their own, wherein they were immune from rheumatism, the bag had been small. The women, too, were an unusually dull lot, with the exception of a new-minded débutante who bothered Weigall at dinner by demanding the verbal restoration of the vague paintings on the vaulted roof above them.

But it was no one of these things that sat on Weigall's mind as, when the other men went up to bed, he let himself out of the castle and sauntered down to the river. His intimate friend, the companion of his boyhood, the chum of his college days, his fellow-traveller in many lands, the man for whom he possessed stronger affection than for all men, had mysteriously disappeared two days ago, and his track might have sprung to the upper air for all trace he had left behind him. He had been a guest on the adjoining estate during the past week, shooting with the fervor of the true sportsman, making love in the intervals to Adeline Cavan, and apparently in the best of spirits. As far as was known there was nothing to lower his mental mercury, for his rent-roll was a large one, Miss Cavan blushed whenever he looked at her, and, being one of the best shots in England, he was never happier than in August. The suicide theory was preposterous, all agreed, and there was as little reason to believe him murdered. Nevertheless, he had walked out of March Abbey two nights ago without hat or overcoat, and had not been seen since.

The country was being patrolled night and day. A hundred keepers and workmen were beating the woods and poking the bogs on the moors, but as yet not so much as a handkerchief had been found.

Weigall did not believe for a moment that Wyatt Gifford was dead, and although it was impossible not to be affected by the general uneasiness, he was disposed to be more angry than frightened. At Cambridge Gifford had been an incorrigible practical joker, and by no means had outgrown the habit; it would be like him to cut across the country in his evening clothes, board a cattle-train, and amuse himself touching up the picture of the sensation in West Riding.

However, Weigall's affection for his friend was too deep to companion with tranquillity in the present state of doubt, and, instead of going to bed early with the other men, he determined to walk until ready for sleep. He went down to the river and followed the path through the woods. There was no moon, but the stars sprinkled their cold light upon the pretty belt of water flowing placidly past wood and ruin, between green masses of overhanging rocks or sloping banks tangled with tree and shrub, leaping occasionally over stones with the harsh notes of an angry scold, to recover its equanimity the moment the way was clear again.

It was very dark in the depths where Weigall trod. He smiled as he recalled a remark of Gifford's: "An English wood is like a good many other things in life – very promising at a distance, but a hollow mockery when you get within. You see daylight on both sides, and the sun freckles the very bracken. Our woods need the night to make them seem what they ought to be – what they once were, before our ancestors' descendants demanded so much more money, in these so much more various days."

Weigall strolled along, smoking, and thinking of his friend, his pranks – many of which had done more credit to his imagination than this – and recalling conversations that had lasted the night through. Just before the end of the London season they had walked the streets one hot night after a party, discussing the various theories of the soul's destiny. That afternoon they had met at the coffin of a college friend whose mind had been a blank for the past three years. Some months previously they had called at the asylum to see him. His expression had been senile, his face imprinted with the record of debauchery. In death the face was placid, intelligent, without ignoble lineation – the face of the man they had known at college. Weigall and Gifford had had no time to comment there, and the afternoon and evening were full; but, coming forth from the house of festivity together, they had reverted almost at once to the topic.

"I cherish the theory," Gifford had said, "that the soul sometimes lingers in the body after death. During madness, of course, it is an impotent prisoner, albeit a conscious one. Fancy its agony, and its horror! What more natural than that, when the life-spark goes out, the tortured soul should take possession of the vacant skull and triumph once more for a few hours while old friends look their last? It has had time to repent while compelled to crouch and behold the result of its work, and it has shrived itself into a state of comparative purity. If I had my way, I should stay inside my bones until the coffin had gone into its niche, that I might obviate for my poor old comrade the tragic impersonality of death. And I should like to see justice done to it, as it were – to see it lowered among its ancestors with the ceremony and solemnity that are its due. I am afraid that if I dissevered myself too quickly, I should yield to curiosity and hasten to investigate the mysteries of space."

"You believe in the soul as an independent entity, then – that it and the vital principle are not one and the same?"

"Absolutely. The body and soul are twins, life comrades – sometimes friends, sometimes enemies, but always loyal in the last instance. Some day, when I am tired of the world, I shall go to India and become a mahatma, solely for the pleasure of receiving proof during life of this independent relationship."

"Suppose you were not sealed up properly, and returned after one of your astral flights to find your earthly part unfit for habitation? It is an experiment I don't think I should care to try, unless even juggling with soul and flesh had palled."

"That would not be an uninteresting predicament. I should rather enjoy experimenting with broken machinery."

The high wild roar of water smote suddenly upon Weigall's ear and checked his memories. He left the wood and walked out on the huge slippery stones which nearly close the River Wharfe at this point, and watched the waters boil down into the narrow pass with their furious untiring energy. The black quiet of the woods rose high on either side. The stars seemed colder and whiter just above. On either hand the perspective of the river might have run into a rayless cavern. There was no lonelier spot in England, nor one which had the right to claim so many ghosts, if ghosts there were.

Weigall was not a coward, but he recalled uncomfortably the tales of those that had been done to death in the Strid.

This striding place is called the 'Strid',
A name which it took of yore;
A thousand years hath it borne the name,
And it shall a thousand more.

Wordsworth's Boy of Egremond had been disposed of by the practical Whitaker; but countless others, more venturesome than wise, had gone down into that narrow boiling course, never to appear in the still pool a few yards beyond. Below the great rocks which form the walls of the Strid was believed to be a natural vault, on to whose shelves the dead were drawn. The spot had an ugly fascination. Weigall stood, visioning skeletons, uncoffined and green, the home of the eyeless things which had devoured all that had covered and filled that rattling symbol of man's mortality; then fell to wondering if anyone had attempted to leap the Strid of late. It was covered with slime; he had never seen it look so treacherous.

He shuddered and turned away, impelled, despite his manhood, to flee the spot. As he did so, something tossing in the foam below the fall – something as white, yet independent of it – caught his eye and arrested his step. Then he saw that it was describing a contrary motion to the rushing water – an upward backward motion. Weigall stood rigid, breathless; he fancied he heard the crackling of his hair. Was that a hand? It thrust itself still higher above the boiling foam, turned sidewise, and four frantic fingers were distinctly visible against the black rock beyond.

Weigall's superstitious terror left him. A man was there, struggling to free himself from the suction beneath the Strid, swept down, doubtless, but a moment before his arrival, perhaps as he stood with his back to the current.

He stepped as close to the edge as he dared. The hand doubled as if in imprecation, shaking savagely in the face of that force which leaves its creatures to immutable law; then spread wide again, clutching, expanding, crying for help as audibly as the human voice.

Weigall dashed to the nearest tree, dragged and twisted off a branch with his strong arms, and returned as swiftly to the Strid. The hand was in the same place, still gesticulating as wildly; the body was undoubtedly caught in the rocks below, perhaps already halfway along one of those hideous shelves. Weigall let himself down upon a lower rock, braced his shoulder against the mass beside him, then, leaning out over the water, thrust the branch into the hand. The fingers clutched it convulsively. Weigall tugged powerfully, his own feet dragged perilously near the edge. For a moment he produced no impression, then an arm shot above the waters.

The blood sprang to Weigall's head; he was choked with the impression that the Strid had him in her roaring hold, and he saw nothing. Then the mist cleared. The hand and arm were nearer, although the rest of the body was still concealed by the foam. Weigall peered out with distended eyes. The meagre light revealed in the cuffs links of a peculiar device. The fingers clutching the branch were as familiar.

Weigall forgot the slippery stones, the terrible death if he stepped too far. He pulled with passionate will and muscle. Memories flung themselves into the hot light of his brain, trooping rapidly upon each other's heels, as in the thought of the drowning. Most of the pleasures of his life, good and bad, were identified in some way with this friend. Scenes of college days, of travel, where they had deliberately sought adventure and stood between one another and death upon more occasions than one, of hours of delightful companionship among the treasures of art, and others in the pursuit of pleasure, flashed like the changing particles of a kaleidoscope. Weigall had loved several women; but he would have flouted in these moments the thought that he had ever loved any woman as he loved Wyatt Gifford. There were so many charming women in the world, and in the thirty-two years of his life he had never known another man to whom he had cared to give his intimate friendship.

He threw himself on his face. His wrists were cracking, the skin was torn from his hands. The fingers still gripped the stick. There was life in them yet.

Suddenly something gave way. The hand swung about, tearing the branch from Weigall's grasp. The body had been liberated and flung outward, though still submerged by the foam and spray.

Weigall scrambled to his feet and sprang along the rocks, knowing that the danger from suction was over and that Gifford must be carried straight to the quiet pool. Gifford was a fish in the water and could live under it longer than most men. If he survived this, it would not be the first time that his pluck and science had saved him from drowning.

Weigall reached the pool. A man in his evening clothes floated on it, his face turned towards a projecting rock over which his arm had fallen, upholding the body. The hand that had held the branch hung limply over the rock, its white reflection visible in the black water. Weigall plunged into the shallow pool, lifted Gifford in his arms and returned to the bank. He laid the body down and threw off his coat that he might be the freer to practise the methods of resuscitation. He was glad of the moment's respite. The valiant life in the man might have been exhausted in that last struggle. He had not dared to look at his face, to put his ear to the heart. The hesitation lasted but a moment. There was no time to lose.

He turned to his prostrate friend. As he did so, something strange and disagreeable smote his senses. For a half-moment he did not appreciate its nature. Then his teeth clacked together, his feet, his outstretched arms pointed towards the woods. But he sprang to the side of the man and bent down and peered into his face. There was no face.

Negotium Perambulans

E.F. Benson

THE CASUAL TOURIST in West Cornwall may just possibly have noticed, as he bowled along over the bare high plateau between Penzance and the Land's End, a dilapidated signpost pointing down a steep lane and bearing on its battered finger the faded inscription 'Polearn 2 miles', but probably very few have had the curiosity to traverse those two miles in order to see a place to which their guide-books award so cursory a notice. It is described there, in a couple of unattractive lines, as a small fishing village with a church of no particular interest except for certain carved and painted wooden panels (originally belonging to an earlier edifice) which form an altar-rail. But the church at St. Creed (the tourist is reminded) has a similar decoration far superior in point of preservation and interest, and thus even the ecclesiastically disposed are not lured to Polearn. So meagre a bait is scarce worth swallowing, and a glance at the very steep lane which in dry weather presents a carpet of sharp-pointed stones, and after rain a muddy watercourse, will almost certainly decide him not to expose his motor or his bicycle to risks like these in so sparsely populated a district. Hardly a house has met his eye since he left Penzance, and the possible trundling of a punctured bicycle for half a dozen weary miles seems a high price to pay for the sight of a few painted panels.

Polearn, therefore, even in the high noon of the tourist season, is little liable to invasion, and for the rest of the year I do not suppose that a couple of folk a day traverse those two miles (long ones at that) of steep and stony gradient. I am not forgetting the postman in this exiguous estimate, for the days are few when, leaving his pony and cart at the top of the hill, he goes as far as the village, since but a few hundred yards down the lane there stands a large white box, like a sea-trunk, by the side of the road, with a slit for letters and a locked door. Should he have in his wallet a registered letter or be the bearer of a parcel too large for insertion in the square lips of the sea-trunk, he must needs trudge down the hill and deliver the troublesome missive, leaving it in person on the owner, and receiving some small reward of coin or refreshment for his kindness. But such occasions are rare, and his general routine is to take out of the box such letters as may have been deposited there, and insert in their place such letters as he has brought. These will be called for, perhaps that day or perhaps the next, by an emissary from the Polearn post-office. As for the fishermen of the place, who, in their export trade, constitute the chief link of movement between Polearn and the outside world, they would not dream of taking their catch up the steep lane and so, with six miles farther of travel, to the market at Penzance. The sea route is shorter and easier, and they deliver their wares to the pier-head. Thus, though the sole industry of Polearn is sea-fishing, you will get no fish there unless you have bespoken your requirements to one of the fishermen. Back come the trawlers as empty as a haunted house, while their spoils are in the fish-train that is speeding to London.

Such isolation of a little community, continued, as it has been, for centuries, produces isolation in the individual as well, and nowhere will you find greater independence of character than among the people of Polearn. But they are linked together, so it has always seemed to me, by some mysterious comprehension: it is as if they had all been initiated into some ancient rite, inspired and framed by forces visible and invisible. The winter storms that batter the coast, the vernal spell of the spring, the hot, still summers, the season of rains and autumnal decay, have made a spell which, line by line, has been communicated to them, concerning the powers, evil and good, that rule the world, and manifest themselves in ways benignant or terrible…

I came to Polearn first at the age of ten, a small boy, weak and sickly, and threatened with pulmonary trouble. My father's business kept him in London, while for me abundance of fresh air and a mild climate were considered essential conditions if I was to grow to manhood. His sister had married the vicar of Polearn, Richard Bolitho, himself native to the place, and so it came about that I spent three years, as a paying guest, with my relations. Richard Bolitho owned a fine house in the place, which he inhabited in preference to the vicarage, which he let to a young artist, John Evans, on whom the spell of Polearn had fallen, for from year's beginning to year's end he never left it. There was a solid roofed shelter, open on one side to the air, built for me in the garden, and here I lived and slept, passing scarcely one hour out of the twenty-four behind walls and windows. I was out on the bay with the fisher-folk, or wandering along the gorse-clad cliffs that climbed steeply to right and left of the deep combe where the village lay, or pottering about on the pier-head, or bird's-nesting in the bushes with the boys of the village. Except on Sunday and for the few daily hours of my lessons, I might do what I pleased so long as I remained in the open air. About the lessons there was nothing formidable; my uncle conducted me through flowering bypaths among the thickets of arithmetic, and made pleasant excursions into the elements of Latin grammar, and above all, he made me daily give him an account, in clear and grammatical sentences, of what had been occupying my mind or my movements. Should I select to tell him about a walk along the cliffs, my speech must be orderly, not vague, slip-shod notes of what I had observed. In this way, too, he trained my observation, for he would bid me tell him what flowers were in bloom, and what birds hovered fishing over the sea or were building in the bushes. For that I owe him a perennial gratitude, for to observe and to express my thoughts in the clear spoken word became my life's profession.

But far more formidable than my weekday tasks was the prescribed routine for Sunday. Some dark embers compounded of Calvinism and mysticism smouldered in my uncle's soul, and made it a day of terror. His sermon in the morning scorched us with a foretaste of the eternal fires reserved for unrepentant sinners, and he was hardly less terrifying at the children's service in the afternoon. Well do I remember his exposition of the doctrine of guardian angels. A child, he said, might think himself secure in such angelic care, but let him beware of committing any of those numerous offences which would cause his guardian to turn his face from him, for as sure as there were angels to protect us, there were also evil and awful presences which were ready to pounce; and on them he dwelt with peculiar gusto. Well, too, do I remember in the morning sermon his commentary on the carved panels of the altar-rails to which I have already alluded. There was the angel of the Annunciation there, and the angel of the Resurrection, but not less was there the witch of Endor, and, on the fourth panel, a scene that concerned me most of all. This fourth panel (he came down from his pulpit to trace its time-worn features) represented the lych-gate of the church-yard at Polearn itself, and indeed the resemblance when thus pointed out was remarkable. In the entry stood the figure of a robed priest holding up a Cross, with which he faced a terrible creature like a gigantic slug, that reared itself up in front of him. That, so ran my uncle's interpretation, was some evil agency, such as he had spoken about to us children, of almost infinite malignity and power, which could alone be combated by firm faith and a pure heart. Below ran the legend *Negotium perambulans in tenebris* from the ninety-first Psalm. We should find it translated there, 'the pestilence that walketh in darkness', which but feebly rendered the Latin. It was more deadly to the soul than any pestilence that can only kill the body: it was the Thing, the Creature, the Business that trafficked in the outer Darkness, a minister of God's wrath on the unrighteous...

I could see, as he spoke, the looks which the congregation exchanged with each other, and knew that his words were evoking a surmise, a remembrance. Nods and whispers passed between them, they understood to what he alluded, and with the inquisitiveness of boyhood I could not rest till I had wormed the story out of my friends among the fisher-boys, as, next morning, we sat basking and naked in the sun after our bathe. One knew one bit of it, one another, but it pieced together into a truly alarming legend. In bald outline it was as follows:

A church far more ancient than that in which my uncle terrified us every Sunday had once stood not three hundred yards away, on the shelf of level ground below the quarry from which its stones were hewn. The owner of the land had pulled this down, and erected for himself a house on the same site out of these materials, keeping, in a very ecstasy of wickedness, the altar, and on this he dined and played dice afterwards. But as he grew old some black melancholy seized him, and he would have lights burning there all night, for he had deadly fear of the darkness. On one winter evening there sprang up such a gale as was never before known, which broke in the windows of the room where he had supped, and extinguished the lamps. Yells of terror brought in his servants, who found him lying on the floor with the blood streaming from his throat. As they entered some huge black shadow seemed to move away from him, crawled across the floor and up the wall and out of the broken window.

"There he lay a-dying," said the last of my informants, "and him that had been a great burly man was withered to a bag o' skin, for the critter had drained all the blood from him. His last breath was a scream, and he hollered out the same words as passon read off the screen."

"*Negotium perambulans in tenebris,*" I suggested eagerly.

"Thereabouts. Latin anyhow."

"And after that?" I asked.

"Nobody would go near the place, and the old house rotted and fell in ruins till three years ago, when along comes Mr. Dooliss from Penzance, and built the half of it up again. But he don't care much about such critters, nor about Latin neither. He takes his bottle of whisky a day and gets drunk's a lord in the evening. Eh, I'm gwine home to my dinner."

Whatever the authenticity of the legend, I had certainly heard the truth about Mr. Dooliss from Penzance, who from that day became an object of keen curiosity on my part, the more so because the quarry-house adjoined my uncle's garden. The Thing that walked in the dark failed to stir my imagination, and already I was so used to sleeping alone in my shelter that the night had no terrors for me. But it would be intensely exciting to wake at some timeless hour and hear Mr. Dooliss yelling, and conjecture that the Thing had got him.

But by degrees the whole story faded from my mind, overscored by the more vivid interests of the day, and, for the last two years of my outdoor life in the vicarage garden, I seldom thought about Mr. Dooliss and the possible fate that might await him for his temerity in living in the place where that Thing of darkness had done business. Occasionally I saw him over the garden fence, a great yellow lump of a man, with slow and staggering gait, but never did I set eyes on him outside his gate, either in the village street or down on the beach. He interfered with none, and no one interfered with him. If he wanted to run the risk of being the prey of the legendary nocturnal monster, or quietly drink himself to death, it was his affair. My uncle, so I gathered, had made several attempts to see him when first he came to live at Polearn, but Mr. Dooliss appeared to have no use for parsons, but said he was not at home and never returned the call.

* * *

After three years of sun, wind, and rain, I had completely outgrown my early symptoms and had become a tough, strapping youngster of thirteen. I was sent to Eton and Cambridge, and in due course ate my dinners and became a barrister. In twenty years from that time I was earning a yearly income of five figures, and had already laid by in sound securities a sum that brought me dividends which would, for one of my simple tastes and frugal habits, supply me with all the material comforts I needed on this side of the grave. The great prizes of my profession were already within my reach, but I had no ambition beckoning me on, nor did I want a wife and children, being, I must suppose, a natural celibate. In fact there was only one ambition which through these busy years had held the lure of blue and far-off hills to me, and that was to get back to Polearn, and live once more isolated from the world with the sea and the gorse-clad hills for play-fellows, and the secrets that lurked there for exploration. The spell of it had been woven about my heart, and I can truly say that there had hardly passed a day in all those years in which the thought of it and the desire for it had been wholly absent from my mind. Though I had been in frequent communication with my uncle there during his lifetime, and, after his death, with his widow who still lived there, I had never been back to it since I embarked on my profession, for I knew that if I went there, it would be a wrench beyond my power to tear myself away again. But I had made up my mind that when once I had provided for my own independence, I would go back there not to leave it again. And yet I did leave it again, and now nothing in the world would induce me to turn down the lane from the road that leads from Penzance to the Land's End, and see the sides of the combe rise steep above the roofs of the village and hear the gulls chiding as they fish in the bay. One of the things invisible, of the dark powers, leaped into light, and I saw it with my eyes.

The house where I had spent those three years of boyhood had been left for life to my aunt, and when I made known to her my intention of coming back to Polearn, she suggested that, till I found a suitable house or found her proposal unsuitable, I should come to live with her.

"The house is too big for a lone old woman," she wrote, "and I have often thought of quitting and taking a little cottage sufficient for me and my requirements. But come and share it, my dear, and if you find me troublesome, you or I can go. You may want solitude – most people in Polearn do – and will leave me. Or else I will leave you: one of the main reasons of my stopping here all these years was a feeling that I must not let the old house starve. Houses starve, you know, if they are not lived in. They die a lingering death; the spirit in them grows weaker and weaker, and at last fades out of them. Isn't this nonsense to your London notions...?"

Naturally I accepted with warmth this tentative arrangement, and on an evening in June found myself at the head of the lane leading down to Polearn, and once more I descended into the steep valley between the hills. Time had stood still apparently for the combe, the dilapidated signpost (or its successor) pointed a rickety finger down the lane, and a few hundred yards farther on was the white box for the exchange of letters. Point after remembered point met my eye, and what I saw was not shrunk, as is often the case with the revisited scenes of childhood, into a smaller scale. There stood the post-office, and there the church and close beside it the vicarage, and beyond, the tall shrubberies which separated the house for which I was bound from the road, and beyond that again the grey roofs of the quarry-house damp and shining with the moist evening wind from the sea. All was exactly as I remembered it, and, above all, that sense of seclusion and isolation. Somewhere above the tree-tops climbed the lane which joined the main road to Penzance, but all that had become immeasurably distant. The years that had passed since last I turned in at the well-known gate faded like a frosty breath, and vanished in this warm, soft air. There were law-courts somewhere in memory's dull book which, if I cared to turn the pages, would tell me that I had made a name and a great income there. But the dull book was closed now, for I was back in Polearn, and the spell was woven around me again.

And if Polearn was unchanged, so too was Aunt Hester, who met me at the door. Dainty and china-white she had always been, and the years had not aged but only refined her. As we sat and talked after dinner she spoke of all that had happened in Polearn in that score of years, and yet somehow the changes of which she spoke seemed but to confirm the immutability of it all. As the recollection of names came back to me, I asked her about the quarry-house and Mr. Dooliss, and her face gloomed a little as with the shadow of a cloud on a spring day.

"Yes, Mr. Dooliss," she said, "poor Mr. Dooliss, how well I remember him, though it must be ten years and more since he died. I never wrote to you about it, for it was all very dreadful, my dear, and I did not want to darken your memories of Polearn. Your uncle always thought that something of the sort might happen if he went on in his wicked, drunken ways, and worse than that, and though nobody knew exactly what took place, it was the sort of thing that might have been anticipated."

"But what more or less happened, Aunt Hester?" I asked.

"Well, of course I can't tell you everything, for no one knew it. But he was a very sinful man, and the scandal about him at Newlyn was shocking. And then he lived, too, in the quarry-house... I wonder if by any chance you remember a sermon of your uncle's when he got out of the pulpit and explained that panel in the altar-rails, the one, I mean, with the horrible creature rearing itself up outside the lych-gate?"

"Yes, I remember perfectly," said I.

"Ah. It made an impression on you, I suppose, and so it did on all who heard him, and that impression got stamped and branded on us all when the catastrophe occurred. Somehow Mr. Dooliss got to hear about your uncle's sermon, and in some drunken fit he broke into the church and smashed the panel to atoms. He seems to have thought that there was some magic in it, and that if he destroyed that he would get rid of the terrible fate that was threatening him. For I must tell you that before he committed that dreadful sacrilege he had been a haunted man: he hated and feared darkness, for he thought that the creature on the panel was on his track, but that as long as he kept lights burning it could not touch him. But the panel, to his disordered mind, was the root of his terror, and so, as I said, he broke into the church and attempted – you will see why I said 'attempted' – to destroy it. It certainly was found in splinters next morning, when your uncle went into church for matins, and knowing Mr. Dooliss's fear of the panel, he went across to the quarry-house afterwards and taxed him with its destruction. The man never denied it; he boasted of what he had done. There he sat, though it was early morning, drinking his whisky.

"'I've settled your Thing for you,' he said, 'and your sermon too. A fig for such superstitions.'

"Your uncle left him without answering his blasphemy, meaning to go straight into Penzance and give information to the police about this outrage to the church, but on his way back from the quarry-house he went into the church again, in order to be able to give details about the damage, and there in the screen was the panel, untouched and uninjured. And yet he had himself seen it smashed, and Mr. Dooliss had confessed that the destruction of it was his work. But there it was, and whether the power of God had mended it or some other power, who knows?"

This was Polearn indeed, and it was the spirit of Polearn that made me accept all Aunt Hester was telling me as attested fact. It had happened like that. She went on in her quiet voice.

"Your uncle recognised that some power beyond police was at work, and he did not go to Penzance or give information about the outrage, for the evidence of it had vanished."

A sudden spate of scepticism swept over me.

"There must have been some mistake," I said. "It hadn't been broken..."

She smiled.

"Yes, my dear, but you have been in London so long," she said. "Let me, anyhow, tell you the rest of my story. That night, for some reason, I could not sleep. It was very hot and airless; I dare say you will think that the sultry conditions accounted for my wakefulness. Once and again, as I went to the window to see if I could not admit more air, I could see from it the quarry-house, and I noticed the first time that I left my bed that it was blazing with lights. But the second time I saw that it was all in darkness, and as I wondered at that, I heard a terrible scream, and the moment afterwards the steps of someone coming at full speed down the road outside the gate. He yelled as he ran; 'Light, light!' he called out. 'Give me light, or it will catch me!' It was very terrible to hear that, and I went to rouse my husband, who was sleeping in the dressing-room across the passage. He wasted no time, but by now the whole village was aroused by the screams, and when he got down to the pier he found that all was over. The tide was low, and on the rocks at its foot was lying the body of Mr. Dooliss. He must have cut some artery when he fell on those sharp edges of stone, for he had bled to death, they thought, and though he was a big burly man, his corpse was but skin and bones. Yet there was no pool of blood round him, such as you would have expected. Just skin and bones as if every drop of blood in his body had been sucked out of him!"

She leaned forward.

"You and I, my dear, know what happened," she said, "or at least can guess. God has His instruments of vengeance on those who bring wickedness into places that have been holy. Dark and mysterious are His ways."

Now what I should have thought of such a story if it had been told me in London I can easily imagine. There was such an obvious explanation: the man in question had been a drunkard, what wonder if the demons of delirium pursued him? But here in Polearn it was different.

"And who is in the quarry-house now?" I asked. "Years ago the fisher-boys told me the story of the man who first built it and of his horrible end. And now again it has happened. Surely no one has ventured to inhabit it once more?"

I saw in her face, even before I asked that question, that somebody had done so.

"Yes, it is lived in again," said she, "for there is no end to the blindness... I don't know if you remember him. He was tenant of the vicarage many years ago."

"John Evans," said I.

"Yes. Such a nice fellow he was too. Your uncle was pleased to get so good a tenant. And now—"

She rose.

"Aunt Hester, you shouldn't leave your sentences unfinished," I said.

She shook her head.

"My dear, that sentence will finish itself," she said. "But what a time of night! I must go to bed, and you too, or they will think we have to keep lights burning here through the dark hours."

* * *

Before getting into bed I drew my curtains wide and opened all the windows to the warm tide of the sea air that flowed softly in. Looking out into the garden I could see in the moonlight the roof of the shelter, in which for three years I had lived, gleaming with dew. That, as much as anything, brought back the old days to which I had now returned, and they seemed of one piece with the present, as if no gap of more than twenty years sundered them. The two flowed into one like globules of mercury uniting into a softly shining globe, of mysterious lights and reflections. Then, raising my eyes a little, I saw against the black hillside the windows of the quarry-house still alight.

Morning, as is so often the case, brought no shattering of my illusion. As I began to regain consciousness, I fancied that I was a boy again waking up in the shelter in the garden, and though, as I grew more widely awake, I smiled at the impression, that on which it was based I found to be indeed true. It was sufficient now as then to be here, to wander again on the cliffs, and hear the popping of the ripened seed-pods on the gorse-bushes; to stray along the shore to the bathing-cove, to float and drift and swim in the warm tide, and bask on the sand, and watch the gulls fishing, to lounge on the pier-head with the fisher-folk, to see in their eyes and hear in their quiet speech the evidence of secret things not so much known to them as part of their instincts and their very being. There were powers and presences about me; the white poplars that stood by the stream that babbled down the valley knew of them, and showed a glimpse of their knowledge sometimes, like the gleam of their white underleaves; the very cobbles that paved the street were soaked in it… All that I wanted was to lie there and grow soaked in it too; unconsciously, as a boy, I had done that, but now the process must be conscious. I must know what stir of forces, fruitful and mysterious, seethed along the hillside at noon, and sparkled at night on the sea. They could be known, they could even be controlled by those who were masters of the spell, but never could they be spoken of, for they were dwellers in the innermost, grafted into the eternal life of the world. There were dark secrets as well as these clear, kindly powers, and to these no doubt belonged the *negotium perambulans in tenebris* which, though of deadly malignity, might be regarded not only as evil, but as the avenger of sacrilegious and impious deeds… All this was part of the spell of Polearn, of which the seeds had long lain dormant in me. But now they were sprouting, and who knew what strange flower would unfold on their stems?

It was not long before I came across John Evans. One morning, as I lay on the beach, there came shambling across the sand a man stout and middle-aged with the face of Silenus. He paused as he drew near and regarded me from narrow eyes.

"Why, you're the little chap that used to live in the parson's garden," he said. "Don't you recognise me?"

I saw who it was when he spoke: his voice, I think, instructed me, and recognising it, I could see the features of the strong, alert young man in this gross caricature.

"Yes, you're John Evans," I said. "You used to be very kind to me: you used to draw pictures for me."

"So I did, and I'll draw you some more. Been bathing? That's a risky performance. You never know what lives in the sea, nor what lives on the land for that matter. Not that I heed them. I stick to work and whisky. God! I've learned to paint since I saw you, and drink too for that matter. I live in the quarry-house, you know, and it's a powerful thirsty place. Come and have a look at my things if you're passing. Staying with your aunt, are you? I could do a wonderful portrait of her. Interesting face; she knows a lot. People who live at Polearn get to know a lot, though I don't take much stock in that sort of knowledge myself."

I do not know when I have been at once so repelled and interested. Behind the mere grossness of his face there lurked something which, while it appalled, yet fascinated me. His thick lisping speech had the same quality. And his paintings, what would they be like…?

"I was just going home," I said. "I'll gladly come in, if you'll allow me."

He took me through the untended and overgrown garden into the house which I had never yet entered. A great grey cat was sunning itself in the window, and an old woman was laying lunch in a corner of the cool hall into which the door opened. It was built of stone, and the carved mouldings let into the walls, the fragments of gargoyles and sculptured images, bore testimony to the truth of its having been built out of the demolished church. In one corner was an oblong and carved wooden table littered with a painter's apparatus and stacks of canvases leaned against the walls.

He jerked his thumb towards a head of an angel that was built into the mantelpiece and giggled.

"Quite a sanctified air," he said, "so we tone it down for the purposes of ordinary life by a different sort of art. Have a drink? No? Well, turn over some of my pictures while I put myself to rights."

He was justified in his own estimate of his skill: he could paint (and apparently he could paint anything), but never have I seen pictures so inexplicably hellish. There were exquisite studies of trees, and you knew that something lurked in the flickering shadows. There was a drawing of his cat sunning itself in the window, even as I had just now seen it, and yet it was no cat but some beast of awful malignity. There was a boy stretched naked on the sands, not human, but some evil thing which had come out of the sea. Above all there were pictures of his garden overgrown and jungle-like, and you knew that in the bushes were presences ready to spring out on you...

"Well, do you like my style?" he said as he came up, glass in hand. (The tumbler of spirits that he held had not been diluted.) "I try to paint the essence of what I see, not the mere husk and skin of it, but its nature, where it comes from and what gave it birth. There's much in common between a cat and a fuchsia-bush if you look at them closely enough. Everything came out of the slime of the pit, and it's all going back there. I should like to do a picture of you some day. I'd hold the mirror up to Nature, as that old lunatic said."

After this first meeting I saw him occasionally throughout the months of that wonderful summer. Often he kept to his house and to his painting for days together, and then perhaps some evening I would find him lounging on the pier, always alone, and every time we met thus the repulsion and interest grew, for every time he seemed to have gone farther along a path of secret knowledge towards some evil shrine where complete initiation awaited him... And then suddenly the end came.

I had met him thus one evening on the cliffs while the October sunset still burned in the sky, but over it with amazing rapidity there spread from the west a great blackness of cloud such as I have never seen for denseness. The light was sucked from the sky, the dusk fell in ever thicker layers. He suddenly became conscious of this.

"I must get back as quick as I can," he said. "It will be dark in a few minutes, and my servant is out. The lamps will not be lit."

He stepped out with extraordinary briskness for one who shambled and could scarcely lift his feet, and soon broke out into a stumbling run. In the gathering darkness I could see that his face was moist with the dew of some unspoken terror.

"You must come with me," he panted, "for so we shall get the lights burning the sooner. I cannot do without light."

I had to exert myself to the full to keep up with him, for terror winged him, and even so I fell behind, so that when I came to the garden gate, he was already halfway up the path to the house. I saw him enter, leaving the door wide, and found him fumbling with matches. But his hand so trembled that he could not transfer the light to the wick of the lamp.

"But what's the hurry about?" I asked.

Suddenly his eyes focused themselves on the open door behind me, and he jumped from his seat beside the table which had once been the altar of God, with a gasp and a scream.

"No, no!" he cried. "Keep it off!…"

I turned and saw what he had seen. The Thing had entered and now was swiftly sliding across the floor towards him, like some gigantic caterpillar. A stale phosphorescent light came from it, for though the dusk had grown to blackness outside, I could see it quite distinctly in the awful light of its own presence. From it too there came an odour of corruption and decay, as from slime that has long lain below water. It seemed to have no head, but on the front of it was an orifice of puckered skin which opened and shut and slavered at the edges. It was hairless, and slug-like in shape and in texture. As it advanced its fore-part reared itself from the ground, like a snake about to strike, and it fastened on him…

At that sight, and with the yells of his agony in my ears, the panic which had struck me relaxed into a hopeless courage, and with palsied, impotent hands I tried to lay hold of the Thing. But I could not: though something material was there, it was impossible to grasp it; my hands sunk in it as in thick mud. It was like wrestling with a nightmare.

I think that but a few seconds elapsed before all was over. The screams of the wretched man sank to moans and mutterings as the Thing fell on him: he panted once or twice and was still. For a moment longer there came gurglings and sucking noises, and then it slid out even as it had entered. I lit the lamp which he had fumbled with, and there on the floor he lay, no more than a rind of skin in loose folds over projecting bones.

The Willows

Algernon Blackwood

Chapter I

AFTER LEAVING VIENNA, and long before you come to Budapest, the Danube enters a region of singular loneliness and desolation, where its waters spread away on all sides regardless of a main channel, and the country becomes a swamp for miles upon miles, covered by a vast sea of low willow-bushes. On the big maps this deserted area is painted in a fluffy blue, growing fainter in colour as it leaves the banks, and across it may be seen in large straggling letters the word *Sümpfe*, meaning marshes.

In high flood this great acreage of sand, shingle-beds, and willow-grown islands is almost topped by the water, but in normal seasons the bushes bend and rustle in the free winds, showing their silver leaves to the sunshine in an ever-moving plain of bewildering beauty. These willows never attain to the dignity of trees; they have no rigid trunks; they remain humble bushes, with rounded tops and soft outline, swaying on slender stems that answer to the least pressure of the wind; supple as grasses, and so continually shifting that they somehow give the impression that the entire plain is moving and alive. For the wind sends waves rising and falling over the whole surface, waves of leaves instead of waves of water, green swells like the sea, too, until the branches turn and lift, and then silvery white as their underside turns to the sun.

Happy to slip beyond the control of the stern banks, the Danube here wanders about at will among the intricate network of channels intersecting the islands everywhere with broad avenues down which the waters pour with a shouting sound; making whirlpools, eddies, and foaming rapids; tearing at the sandy banks; carrying away masses of shore and willow-clumps; and forming new islands innumerably which shift daily in size and shape and possess at best an impermanent life, since the flood-time obliterates their very existence.

Properly speaking, this fascinating part of the river's life begins soon after leaving Pressburg, and we, in our Canadian canoe, with gipsy tent and frying-pan on board, reached it on the crest of a rising flood about mid-July. That very same morning, when the sky was reddening before sunrise, we had slipped swiftly through still-sleeping Vienna, leaving it a couple of hours later a mere patch of smoke against the blue hills of the Wienerwald on the horizon; we had breakfasted below Fischeramend under a grove of birch trees roaring in the wind; and had then swept on the tearing current past Orth, Hainburg, Petronell (the old Roman Carnuntum of Marcus Aurelius), and so under the frowning heights of Thelsen on a spur of the Carpathians, where the March steals in quietly from the left and the frontier is crossed between Austria and Hungary.

Racing along at twelve kilometers an hour soon took us well into Hungary, and the muddy waters – sure sign of flood – sent us aground on many a shingle-bed, and twisted us like a cork in many a sudden belching whirlpool before the towers of Pressburg (Hungarian, Poszóny) showed against the sky; and then the canoe, leaping like a spirited horse, flew at top speed under the grey walls, negotiated safely the sunken chain of the Fliegende Brucke ferry, turned the corner sharply to the left, and plunged on yellow foam into the wilderness of islands, sandbanks, and swamp-land beyond – the land of the willows.

The change came suddenly, as when a series of bioscope pictures snaps down on the streets of a town and shifts without warning into the scenery of lake and forest. We entered the land of desolation on wings, and in less than half an hour there was neither boat nor fishing-hut nor red roof, nor any single sign of human habitation and civilization within sight. The sense of remoteness from the world of humankind, the utter isolation, the fascination of this singular world of willows, winds, and waters, instantly laid its spell upon us both, so that we allowed laughingly to one another that we ought by rights to have held some special kind of passport to admit us, and that we had, somewhat audaciously, come without asking leave into a separate little kingdom of wonder and magic – a kingdom that was reserved for the use of others who had a right to it, with everywhere unwritten warnings to trespassers for those who had the imagination to discover them.

Though still early in the afternoon, the ceaseless buffetings of a most tempestuous wind made us feel weary, and we at once began casting about for a suitable camping-ground for the night. But the bewildering character of the islands made landing difficult; the swirling flood carried us in shore and then swept us out again; the willow branches tore our hands as we seized them to stop the canoe, and we pulled many a yard of sandy bank into the water before at length we shot with a great sideways blow from the wind into a backwater and managed to beach the bows in a cloud of spray. Then we lay panting and laughing after our exertions on the hot yellow sand, sheltered from the wind, and in the full blaze of a scorching sun, a cloudless blue sky above, and an immense army of dancing, shouting willow bushes, closing in from all sides, shining with spray and clapping their thousand little hands as though to applaud the success of our efforts.

"What a river!" I said to my companion, thinking of all the way we had travelled from the source in the Black Forest, and how he had often been obliged to wade and push in the upper shallows at the beginning of June.

"Won't stand much nonsense now, will it?" he said, pulling the canoe a little farther into safety up the sand, and then composing himself for a nap.

I lay by his side, happy and peaceful in the bath of the elements – water, wind, sand, and the great fire of the sun – thinking of the long journey that lay behind us, and of the great stretch before us to the Black Sea, and how lucky I was to have such a delightful and charming travelling companion as my friend, the Swede.

We had made many similar journeys together, but the Danube, more than any other river I knew, impressed us from the very beginning with its aliveness. From its tiny bubbling entry into the world among the pinewood gardens of Donaueschingen, until this moment when it began to play the great river-game of losing itself among the deserted swamps, unobserved, unrestrained, it had seemed to us like following the growth of some living creature. Sleepy at first, but later developing violent desires as it became conscious of its deep soul, it rolled, like some huge fluid being, through all the countries we had passed, holding our little craft on its mighty shoulders, playing roughly with us sometimes, yet always friendly and well-meaning, till at length we had come inevitably to regard it as a Great Personage.

How, indeed, could it be otherwise, since it told us so much of its secret life? At night we heard it singing to the moon as we lay in our tent, uttering that odd sibilant note peculiar to itself and said to be caused by the rapid tearing of the pebbles along its bed, so great is its hurrying speed. We knew, too, the voice of its gurgling whirlpools, suddenly bubbling up on a surface previously quite calm; the roar of its shallows and swift rapids; its constant steady thundering below all mere surface sounds; and that ceaseless tearing of its icy waters at the banks. How it stood up and shouted when the rains fell flat upon its face! And how its laughter roared out when the wind blew up-stream and tried to stop its growing speed! We knew all its sounds and voices, its tumblings and foamings, its unnecessary splashing against the bridges; that self-conscious chatter when there were hills to look on; the affected dignity of its speech when it passed through the little towns, far too important to laugh; and all these faint, sweet whisperings when the sun caught it fairly in some slow curve and poured down upon it till the steam rose.

It was full of tricks, too, in its early life before the great world knew it. There were places in the upper reaches among the Swabian forests, when yet the first whispers of its destiny had not reached it, where it elected to disappear through holes in the ground, to appear again on the other side of the porous limestone hills and start a new river with another name; leaving, too, so little water in its own bed that we had to climb out and wade and push the canoe through miles of shallows.

And a chief pleasure, in those early days of its irresponsible youth, was to lie low, like Brer Fox, just before the little turbulent tributaries came to join it from the Alps, and to refuse to acknowledge them when in, but to run for miles side by side, the dividing line well marked, the very levels different, the Danube utterly declining to recognize the newcomer. Below Passau, however, it gave up this particular trick, for there the Inn comes in with a thundering power impossible to ignore, and so pushes and incommodes the parent river that there is hardly room for them in the long twisting gorge that follows, and the Danube is shoved this way and that against the cliffs, and forced to hurry itself with great waves and much dashing to and fro in order to get through in time. And during the fight our canoe slipped down from its shoulder to its breast, and had the time of its life among the struggling waves. But the Inn taught the old river a lesson, and after Passau it no longer pretended to ignore new arrivals.

This was many days back, of course, and since then we had come to know other aspects of the great creature, and across the Bavarian wheat plain of Straubing she wandered so slowly under the blazing June sun that we could well imagine only the surface inches were water, while below there moved, concealed as by a silken mantle, a whole army of Undines, passing silently and unseen down to the sea, and very leisurely too, lest they be discovered.

Much, too, we forgave her because of her friendliness to the birds and animals that haunted the shores. Cormorants lined the banks in lonely places in rows like short black palings; grey crows crowded the shingle-beds; storks stood fishing in the vistas of shallower water that opened up between the islands, and hawks, swans, and marsh birds of all sorts filled the air with glinting wings and singing, petulant cries. It was impossible to feel annoyed with the river's vagaries after seeing a deer leap with a splash into the water at sunrise and swim past the bows of the canoe; and often we saw fawns peering at us from the underbrush, or looked straight into the brown eyes of a stag as we charged full tilt round a corner and entered another reach of the river. Foxes, too, everywhere haunted the banks, tripping daintily among the driftwood and disappearing so suddenly that it was impossible to see how they managed it.

But now, after leaving Pressburg, everything changed a little, and the Danube became more serious. It ceased trifling. It was halfway to the Black Sea, within seeming distance almost of other, stranger countries where no tricks would be permitted or understood. It became suddenly grown-up, and claimed our respect and even our awe. It broke out into three arms, for one thing, that only met again a hundred kilometers farther down, and for a canoe there were no indications which one was intended to be followed.

"If you take a side channel," said the Hungarian officer we met in the Pressburg shop while buying provisions, "you may find yourselves, when the flood subsides, forty miles from anywhere, high and dry, and you may easily starve. There are no people, no farms, no fishermen. I warn you not to continue. The river, too, is still rising, and this wind will increase."

The rising river did not alarm us in the least, but the matter of being left high and dry by a sudden subsidence of the waters might be serious, and we had consequently laid in an extra stock of provisions. For the rest, the officer's prophecy held true, and the wind, blowing down a perfectly clear sky, increased steadily till it reached the dignity of a westerly gale.

It was earlier than usual when we camped, for the sun was a good hour or two from the horizon, and leaving my friend still asleep on the hot sand, I wandered about in desultory examination of our hotel. The island, I found, was less than an acre in extent, a mere sandy bank standing some two or three feet above the level of the river. The far end, pointing into the sunset, was covered with flying spray which the tremendous wind drove off the crests of the broken waves. It was triangular in shape, with the apex up stream.

I stood there for several minutes, watching the impetuous crimson flood bearing down with a shouting roar, dashing in waves against the bank as though to sweep it bodily away, and then swirling by in two foaming streams on either side. The ground seemed to shake with the shock and rush, while the furious movement of the willow bushes as the wind poured over them increased the curious illusion that the island itself actually moved. Above, for a mile or two, I could see the great river descending upon me; it was like looking up the slope of a sliding hill, white with foam, and leaping up everywhere to show itself to the sun.

The rest of the island was too thickly grown with willows to make walking pleasant, but I made the tour, nevertheless. From the lower end the light, of course, changed, and the river looked dark and angry. Only the backs of the flying waves were visible, streaked with foam, and pushed forcibly by the great puffs of wind that fell upon them from behind. For a short mile it was visible, pouring in and out among the islands, and then disappearing with a huge sweep into the willows, which closed about it like a herd of monstrous antediluvian creatures crowding down to drink. They made me think of gigantic sponge-like growths that sucked the river up into themselves. They caused it to vanish from sight. They herded there together in such overpowering numbers.

Altogether it was an impressive scene, with its utter loneliness, its bizarre suggestion; and as I gazed, long and curiously, a singular emotion began to stir somewhere in the depths of me. Midway in my delight of the wild beauty, there crept, unbidden and unexplained, a curious feeling of disquietude, almost of alarm.

A rising river, perhaps, always suggests something of the ominous; many of the little islands I saw before me would probably have been swept away by the morning; this resistless, thundering flood of water touched the sense of awe. Yet I was aware that my uneasiness lay far deeper than the emotions of awe and wonder. It was not that I felt. Nor had it directly to do with the power of the driving wind – this shouting hurricane that might almost carry up a few acres of willows into the air and scatter them like so much chaff over the landscape. The wind was simply enjoying itself, for nothing rose out of the flat landscape to stop it, and I was conscious of sharing its great game with a kind of pleasurable excitement. Yet this novel emotion had nothing to do with the wind. Indeed, so vague was the sense of distress I experienced, that it was impossible to trace it to its source and deal with it accordingly, though I was aware somehow that it had to do with my realisation of our utter insignificance before this unrestrained power of the elements about me. The huge-grown river had something to do with it too – a vague, unpleasant idea that we had somehow trifled with these great elemental forces in whose power we lay helpless every hour of the day and night. For here, indeed, they were gigantically at play together, and the sight appealed to the imagination.

But my emotion, so far as I could understand it, seemed to attach itself more particularly to the willow bushes, to these acres and acres of willows, crowding, so thickly growing there, swarming everywhere the eye could reach, pressing upon the river as though to suffocate it, standing in dense array mile after mile beneath the sky, watching, waiting, listening. And, apart quite from the elements, the willows connected themselves subtly with my malaise, attacking the mind insidiously somehow by reason of their vast numbers, and contriving in some way or other to represent to the imagination a new and mighty power, a power, moreover, not altogether friendly to us.

Great revelations of nature, of course, never fail to impress in one way or another, and I was no stranger to moods of the kind. Mountains overawe and oceans terrify, while the mystery of great forests exercises a spell peculiarly its own. But all these, at one point or another, somewhere link on intimately with human life and human experience. They stir comprehensible, even if alarming, emotions. They tend on the whole to exalt.

With this multitude of willows, however, it was something far different, I felt. Some essence emanated from them that besieged the heart. A sense of awe awakened, true, but of awe touched somewhere by a vague terror. Their serried ranks, growing everywhere darker about me as the shadows deepened, moving furiously yet softly in the wind, woke in me the curious and unwelcome suggestion that we had trespassed here upon the borders of an alien world, a world where we were intruders, a world where we were not wanted or invited to remain – where we ran grave risks perhaps!

The feeling, however, though it refused to yield its meaning entirely to analysis, did not at the time trouble me by passing into menace. Yet it never left me quite, even during the very practical business of putting up the tent in a hurricane of wind and building a fire for the stew-pot. It remained, just enough to bother and perplex, and to rob a most delightful camping-ground of a good portion of its charm. To my companion, however, I said nothing, for he was a man I considered devoid of imagination. In the first place, I could never have explained to him what I meant, and in the second, he would have laughed stupidly at me if I had.

There was a slight depression in the center of the island, and here we pitched the tent. The surrounding willows broke the wind a bit.

"A poor camp," observed the imperturbable Swede when at last the tent stood upright, "no stones and precious little firewood. I'm for moving on early tomorrow – eh? This sand won't hold anything."

But the experience of a collapsing tent at midnight had taught us many devices, and we made the cosy gipsy house as safe as possible, and then set about collecting a store of wood to last till bedtime. Willow bushes drop no branches, and driftwood was our only source of supply. We hunted the shores pretty thoroughly. Everywhere the banks were crumbling as the rising flood tore at them and carried away great portions with a splash and a gurgle.

"The island's much smaller than when we landed," said the accurate Swede. "It won't last long at this rate. We'd better drag the canoe close to the tent, and be ready to start at a moment's notice. I shall sleep in my clothes."

He was a little distance off, climbing along the bank, and I heard his rather jolly laugh as he spoke.

"By Jove!" I heard him call, a moment later, and turned to see what had caused his exclamation. But for the moment he was hidden by the willows, and I could not find him.

"What in the world's this?" I heard him cry again, and this time his voice had become serious.

I ran up quickly and joined him on the bank. He was looking over the river, pointing at something in the water.

"Good heavens, it's a man's body!" he cried excitedly. "Look!"

A black thing, turning over and over in the foaming waves, swept rapidly past. It kept disappearing and coming up to the surface again. It was about twenty feet from the shore, and just as it was opposite to where we stood it lurched round and looked straight at us. We saw its eyes reflecting the sunset, and gleaming an odd yellow as the body turned over. Then it gave a swift, gulping plunge, and dived out of sight in a flash.

"An otter, by gad!" we exclaimed in the same breath, laughing.

It was an otter, alive, and out on the hunt; yet it had looked exactly like the body of a drowned man turning helplessly in the current. Far below it came to the surface once again, and we saw its black skin, wet and shining in the sunlight.

Then, too, just as we turned back, our arms full of driftwood, another thing happened to recall us to the river bank. This time it really was a man, and what was more, a man in a boat. Now a small boat on the Danube was an unusual sight at any time, but here in this deserted region, and at flood time, it was so unexpected as to constitute a real event. We stood and stared.

Whether it was due to the slanting sunlight, or the refraction from the wonderfully illumined water, I cannot say, but, whatever the cause, I found it difficult to focus my sight properly upon the flying apparition. It seemed, however, to be a man standing upright in a sort of flat-bottomed boat, steering with a long oar, and being carried down the opposite shore at a tremendous pace. He apparently was looking across in our direction, but the distance was too great and the light too uncertain for us to make out very plainly what he was about. It seemed to me that he was gesticulating and making signs at us. His voice came across the water to us shouting something furiously, but the wind drowned it so that no single word was audible. There was something curious about the whole appearance – man, boat, signs, voice – that made an impression on me out of all proportion to its cause.

"He's crossing himself!" I cried. "Look, he's making the sign of the Cross!"

"I believe you're right," the Swede said, shading his eyes with his hand and watching the man out of sight. He seemed to be gone in a moment, melting away down there into the sea of willows where the sun caught them in the bend of the river and turned them into a great crimson wall of beauty. Mist, too, had begun to ruse, so that the air was hazy.

"But what in the world is he doing at nightfall on this flooded river?" I said, half to myself. "Where is he going at such a time, and what did he mean by his signs and shouting? D'you think he wished to warn us about something?"

"He saw our smoke, and thought we were spirits probably," laughed my companion. "These Hungarians believe in all sorts of rubbish; you remember the shopwoman at Pressburg warning us that no one ever landed here because it belonged to some sort of beings outside man's world! I suppose they believe in fairies and elementals, possibly demons, too. That peasant in the boat saw people on the islands for the first time in his life," he added, after a slight pause, "and it scared him, that's all."

The Swede's tone of voice was not convincing, and his manner lacked something that was usually there. I noted the change instantly while he talked, though without being able to label it precisely.

"If they had enough imagination," I laughed loudly – I remember trying to make as much *noise* as I could – "they might well people a place like this with the old gods of antiquity. The Romans must have haunted all this region more or less with their shrines and sacred groves and elemental deities."

The subject dropped and we returned to our stew-pot, for my friend was not given to imaginative conversation as a rule. Moreover, just then I remember feeling distinctly glad that he was not imaginative; his stolid, practical nature suddenly seemed to me welcome and comforting. It was an admirable temperament, I felt; he could steer down rapids like a red Indian, shoot dangerous bridges and whirlpools better than any white man I ever saw in a canoe. He was a grand fellow for an adventurous trip, a tower of strength when untoward things happened. I looked at his strong face and light curly hair as he staggered along under his pile of driftwood (twice the size of mine!), and I experienced a feeling of relief. Yes, I was distinctly glad just then that the Swede was – what he was, and that he never made remarks that suggested more than they said.

"The river's still rising, though," he added, as if following out some thoughts of his own, and dropping his load with a gasp. "This island will be under water in two days if it goes on."

"I wish the *wind* would go down," I said. "I don't care a fig for the river."

The flood, indeed, had no terrors for us; we could get off at ten minutes' notice, and the more water the better we liked it. It meant an increasing current and the obliteration of the treacherous shingle-beds that so often threatened to tear the bottom out of our canoe.

Contrary to our expectations, the wind did not go down with the sun. It seemed to increase with the darkness, howling overhead and shaking the willows round us like straws. Curious sounds accompanied it sometimes, like the explosion of heavy guns, and it fell upon the water and the island in great flat blows of immense power. It made me think of the sounds a planet must make, could we only hear it, driving along through space.

But the sky kept wholly clear of clouds, and soon after supper the full moon rose up in the east and covered the river and the plain of shouting willows with a light like the day.

We lay on the sandy patch beside the fire, smoking, listening to the noises of the night round us, and talking happily of the journey we had already made, and of our plans ahead. The map lay spread in the door of the tent, but the high wind made it hard to study, and presently we lowered the curtain and extinguished the lantern. The firelight was enough to smoke and see each other's faces by, and the sparks flew about overhead like fireworks. A few yards beyond, the river gurgled and hissed, and from time to time a heavy splash announced the falling away of further portions of the bank.

Our talk, I noticed, had to do with the faraway scenes and incidents of our first camps in the Black Forest, or of other subjects altogether remote from the present setting, for neither of us spoke of the actual moment more than was necessary – almost as though we had agreed tacitly to avoid discussion of the camp and its incidents. Neither the otter nor the boatman, for instance, received the honor of a single mention, though ordinarily these would have furnished discussion for the greater part of the evening. They were, of course, distinct events in such a place.

The scarcity of wood made it a business to keep the fire going, for the wind, that drove the smoke in our faces wherever we sat, helped at the same time to make a forced draught. We took it in turn to make some foraging expeditions into the darkness, and the quantity the Swede brought back always made me feel that he took an absurdly long time finding it; for the fact was I did not care much about being left alone, and yet it always seemed to be my turn to grub about among the bushes or scramble along the slippery banks in the moonlight. The long day's battle with wind and water – such wind and such water! – had tired us both, and an early bed was the obvious program. Yet neither of us made the move for the tent. We lay there, tending the fire, talking in desultory fashion, peering about us into the dense willow bushes, and listening to the thunder of wind and river. The loneliness of the place had entered our very bones, and silence seemed natural, for after a bit the sound of our voices became a trifle unreal and forced; whispering would have been the fitting mode of communication, I felt, and the human voice, always rather absurd amid the roar of the elements, now carried with it something almost illegitimate. It was like talking out loud in church, or in some place where it was not lawful, perhaps not quite *safe*, to be overheard.

The eeriness of this lonely island, set among a million willows, swept by a hurricane, and surrounded by hurrying deep waters, touched us both, I fancy. Untrodden by man, almost unknown to man, it lay there beneath the moon, remote from human influence, on the frontier of another world, an alien world, a world tenanted by willows only and the souls of willows. And we, in our rashness, had dared to invade it, even to make use of it! Something more than the power of its mystery stirred in me as I lay on the sand, feet to fire, and peered up through the leaves at the stars. For the last time I rose to get firewood.

"When this has burnt up," I said firmly, "I shall turn in," and my companion watched me lazily as I moved off into the surrounding shadows.

For an unimaginative man I thought he seemed unusually receptive that night, unusually open to suggestion of things other than sensory. He too was touched by the beauty and loneliness of the place. I was not altogether pleased, I remember, to recognize this slight change in him, and instead of immediately collecting sticks, I made my way to the far point of the island where the moonlight on plain and river could be seen to better advantage. The desire to be alone had come suddenly upon me; my former dread returned in force; there was a vague feeling in me I wished to face and probe to the bottom.

When I reached the point of sand jutting out among the waves, the spell of the place descended upon me with a positive shock. No mere 'scenery' could have produced such an effect. There was something more here, something to alarm.

I gazed across the waste of wild waters; I watched the whispering willows; I heard the ceaseless beating of the tireless wind; and, one and all, each in its own way, stirred in me this sensation of a strange distress. But the *willows* especially; for ever they went on chattering and talking among themselves, laughing a little, shrilly crying out, sometimes sighing – but what it was they made so much to-do about belonged to the secret life of the great plain they inhabited. And it was utterly alien to the world I knew, or to that of the wild yet kindly elements. They made me think of a host of beings from another plane of life, another evolution altogether, perhaps, all discussing a mystery known only to themselves. I watched them moving busily together, oddly shaking their big bushy heads, twirling their myriad leaves even when there was no wind. They moved of their own will as though alive, and they touched, by some incalculable method, my own keen sense of the *horrible*.

There they stood in the moonlight, like a vast army surrounding our camp, shaking their innumerable silver spears defiantly, formed all ready for an attack.

The psychology of places, for some imaginations at least, is very vivid; for the wanderer, especially, camps have their 'note' either of welcome or rejection. At first it may not always be apparent, because the busy preparations of tent and cooking prevent, but with the first pause – after supper usually – it comes and announces itself. And the note of this willow-camp now became unmistakably plain to me; we were interlopers, trespassers; we were not welcomed. The sense of unfamiliarity grew upon me as I stood there watching. We touched the frontier of a region where our presence was resented. For a night's lodging we might perhaps be tolerated; but for a prolonged and inquisitive stay – No! by all the gods of the trees and wilderness, no! We were the first human influences upon this island, and we were not wanted. *The willows were against us.*

Strange thoughts like these, bizarre fancies, borne I know not whence, found lodgment in my mind as I stood listening. What, I thought, if, after all, these crouching willows proved to be alive; if suddenly they should rise up, like a swarm of living creatures, marshalled by the gods whose territory we had invaded, sweep towards us off the vast swamps, booming overhead in the night – and then *settle down!* As I looked it was so easy to imagine they actually moved, crept nearer, retreated a little, huddled together in masses, hostile, waiting for the great wind that should finally start them a-running. I could have sworn their aspect changed a little, and their ranks deepened and pressed more closely together.

The melancholy shrill cry of a night-bird sounded overhead, and suddenly I nearly lost my balance as the piece of bank I stood upon fell with a great splash into the river, undermined by the flood. I stepped back just in time, and went on hunting for firewood again, half laughing at the odd fancies that crowded so thickly into my mind and cast their spell upon me. I recalled the Swede's remark about moving on next day, and I was just thinking that I fully agreed with him, when I turned with a start and saw the subject of my thoughts standing immediately in front of me. He was quite close. The roar of the elements had covered his approach.

"You've been gone so long," he shouted above the wind, "I thought something must have happened to you."

But there was that in his tone, and a certain look in his face as well, that conveyed to me more than his usual words, and in a flash I understood the real reason for his coming. It was because the spell of the place had entered his soul too, and he did not like being alone.

"River still rising," he cried, pointing to the flood in the moonlight, "and the wind's simply awful."

He always said the same things, but it was the cry for companionship that gave the real importance to his words.

"Lucky," I cried back, "our tent's in the hollow. I think it'll hold all right." I added something about the difficulty of finding wood, in order to explain my absence, but the wind caught my words and flung them across the river, so that he did not hear, but just looked at me through the branches, nodding his head.

"Lucky if we get away without disaster!" he shouted, or words to that effect; and I remember feeling half angry with him for putting the thought into words, for it was exactly what I felt myself. There was disaster impending somewhere, and the sense of presentiment lay unpleasantly upon me.

We went back to the fire and made a final blaze, poking it up with our feet. We took a last look round. But for the wind the heat would have been unpleasant. I put this thought into words, and I remember my friend's reply struck me oddly: that he would rather have the heat, the ordinary July weather, than this 'diabolical wind'.

Everything was snug for the night; the canoe lying turned over beside the tent, with both yellow paddles beneath her; the provision sack hanging from a willow-stem, and the washed-up dishes removed to a safe distance from the fire, all ready for the morning meal.

We smothered the embers of the fire with sand, and then turned in. The flap of the tent door was up, and I saw the branches and the stars and the white moonlight. The shaking willows and the heavy buffetings of the wind against our taut little house were the last things I remembered as sleep came down and covered all with its soft and delicious forgetfulness.

Chapter II

SUDDENLY I found myself lying awake, peering from my sandy mattress through the door of the tent. I looked at my watch pinned against the canvas, and saw by the bright moonlight that it was past twelve o'clock – the threshold of a new day – and I had therefore slept a couple of hours. The Swede was asleep still beside me; the wind howled as before; something plucked at my heart and made me feel afraid. There was a sense of disturbance in my immediate neighbourhood.

I sat up quickly and looked out. The trees were swaying violently to and fro as the gusts smote them, but our little bit of green canvas lay snugly safe in the hollow, for the wind passed over it without meeting enough resistance to make it vicious. The feeling of disquietude did not pass, however, and I crawled quietly out of the tent to see if our belongings were safe. I moved carefully so as not to waken my companion. A curious excitement was on me.

I was halfway out, kneeling on all fours, when my eye first took in that the tops of the bushes opposite, with their moving tracery of leaves, made shapes against the sky. I sat back on my haunches and stared. It was incredible, surely, but there, opposite and slightly above me, were shapes of some indeterminate sort among the willows, and as the branches swayed in the wind they seemed to group themselves about these shapes, forming a series of monstrous outlines that shifted rapidly beneath the moon. Close, about fifty feet in front of me, I saw these things.

My first instinct was to waken my companion, that he too might see them, but something made me hesitate – the sudden realisation, probably, that I should not welcome corroboration; and meanwhile I crouched there staring in amazement with smarting eyes. I was wide awake. I remember saying to myself that I was not dreaming.

They first became properly visible, these huge figures, just within the tops of the bushes – immense, bronze-coloured, moving, and wholly independent of the swaying of the branches. I saw them plainly and noted, now I came to examine them more calmly, that they were very much larger than human, and indeed that something in their appearance proclaimed them to be not human at all. Certainly they were not merely the moving tracery of the branches against the moonlight. They shifted independently. They rose upwards in a continuous stream from earth to sky, vanishing utterly as soon as they reached the dark of the sky. They were interlaced one with another, making a great column, and I saw their limbs and huge bodies melting in and out of each other, forming this serpentine line that bent and swayed and twisted spirally with the contortions of the wind-tossed trees. They were nude, fluid shapes, passing up the bushes, within the leaves almost – rising up in a living column into the heavens. Their faces I never could see. Unceasingly they poured upwards, swaying in great bending curves, with a hue of dull bronze upon their skins.

I stared, trying to force every atom of vision from my eyes. For a long time I thought they must every moment disappear and resolve themselves into the movements of the branches and prove to be an optical illusion. I searched everywhere for a proof of reality, when all the while I understood quite well that the standard of reality had changed. For the longer I looked the more certain I became that these figures were real and living, though perhaps not according to the standards that the camera and the biologist would insist upon.

Far from feeling fear, I was possessed with a sense of awe and wonder such as I have never known. I seemed to be gazing at the personified elemental forces of this haunted and primeval region. Our intrusion had stirred the powers of the place into activity. It was we who were the cause of the disturbance, and my brain filled to bursting with stories and legends of the spirits and deities of places that have been acknowledged and worshipped by men in all ages of the world's history. But, before I could arrive at any possible explanation, something impelled me to go farther out, and I crept forward on the sand and stood upright. I felt the ground still warm under my bare feet; the wind tore at my hair and face; and the sound of the river burst upon my ears with a sudden roar. These things, I knew, were real, and proved that my senses were acting normally. Yet the figures still rose from earth to heaven, silent, majestically, in a great spiral of grace and strength that overwhelmed me at length with a genuine deep emotion of worship. I felt that I must fall down and worship – absolutely worship.

Perhaps in another minute I might have done so, when a gust of wind swept against me with such force that it blew me sideways, and I nearly stumbled and fell. It seemed to shake the dream violently out of me. At least it gave me another point of view somehow. The figures still remained, still ascended into heaven from the heart of the night, but my reason at last began to assert itself. It must be a subjective experience, I argued – none the less real for that, but still subjective.

The moonlight and the branches combined to work out these pictures upon the mirror of my imagination, and for some reason I projected them outwards and made them appear objective. I knew this must be the case, of course. I took courage, and began to move forward across the open patches of sand. By Jove, though, was it all hallucination? Was it merely subjective? Did not my reason argue in the old futile way from the little standard of the known?

I only know that great column of figures ascended darkly into the sky for what seemed a very long period of time, and with a very complete measure of reality as most men are accustomed to gauge reality. Then suddenly they were gone!

And, once they were gone and the immediate wonder of their great presence had passed, fear came down upon me with a cold rush. The esoteric meaning of this lonely and haunted region suddenly flamed up within me, and I began to tremble dreadfully. I took a quick look round – a look of horror that came near to panic – calculating vainly ways of escape; and then, realising how helpless I was to achieve anything really effective, I crept back silently into the tent and lay down again upon my sandy mattress, first lowering the door-curtain to shut out the sight of the willows in the moonlight, and then burying my head as deeply as possible beneath the blankets to deaden the sound of the terrifying wind.

Chapter III

AS THOUGH further to convince me that I had not been dreaming, I remember that it was a long time before I fell again into a troubled and restless sleep; and even then only the upper crust of me slept, and underneath there was something that never quite lost consciousness, but lay alert and on the watch.

But this second time I jumped up with a genuine start of terror. It was neither the wind nor the river that woke me, but the slow approach of something that caused the sleeping portion of me to grow smaller and smaller till at last it vanished altogether, and I found myself sitting bolt upright – listening.

Outside there was a sound of multitudinous little patterings. They had been coming, I was aware, for a long time, and in my sleep they had first become audible. I sat there nervously wide awake as though I had not slept at all. It seemed to me that my breathing came with difficulty, and that there was a great weight upon the surface of my body. In spite of the hot night, I felt clammy with cold and shivered. Something surely was pressing steadily against the sides of the tent and weighing down upon it from above. Was it the body of the wind? Was this the pattering rain, the dripping of the leaves? The spray blown from the river by the wind and gathering in big drops? I thought quickly of a dozen things.

Then suddenly the explanation leaped into my mind: a bough from the poplar, the only large tree on the island, had fallen with the wind. Still half caught by the other branches, it would fall with the next gust and crush us, and meanwhile its leaves brushed and tapped upon the tight canvas surface of the tent. I raised a loose flap and rushed out, calling to the Swede to follow.

But when I got out and stood upright I saw that the tent was free. There was no hanging bough; there was no rain or spray; nothing approached.

A cold, grey light filtered down through the bushes and lay on the faintly gleaming sand. Stars still crowded the sky directly overhead, and the wind howled magnificently, but the fire no longer gave out any glow, and I saw the east reddening in streaks through the trees. Several hours must have passed since I stood there before watching the ascending figures, and the memory of it now came back to me horribly, like an evil dream. Oh, how tired it made me feel, that ceaseless raging wind! Yet, though the deep lassitude of a sleepless night was on me, my nerves were tingling with the activity of an equally tireless apprehension, and all idea of repose was out of the question. The river I saw had risen further. Its thunder filled the air, and a fine spray made itself felt through my thin sleeping shirt.

Yet nowhere did I discover the slightest evidence of anything to cause alarm. This deep, prolonged disturbance in my heart remained wholly unaccounted for.

My companion had not stirred when I called him, and there was no need to waken him now. I looked about me carefully, noting everything; the turned-over canoe; the yellow paddles – two of them, I'm certain; the provision sack and the extra lantern hanging together from the tree; and, crowding everywhere about me, enveloping all, the willows, those endless, shaking willows. A bird uttered its morning cry, and a string of ducks passed with whirring flight overhead in the twilight. The sand whirled, dry and stinging, about my bare feet in the wind.

I walked round the tent and then went out a little way into the bush, so that I could see across the river to the farther landscape, and the same profound yet indefinable emotion of distress seized upon me again as I saw the interminable sea of bushes stretching to the horizon, looking ghostly and unreal in the wan light of dawn. I walked softly here and there, still puzzling over that odd sound of infinite pattering, and of that pressure upon the tent that had wakened me. It *must* have been the wind, I reflected – the wind bearing upon the loose, hot sand, driving the dry particles smartly against the taut canvas – the wind dropping heavily upon our fragile roof.

Yet all the time my nervousness and malaise increased appreciably.

I crossed over to the farther shore and noted how the coastline had altered in the night, and what masses of sand the river had torn away. I dipped my hands and feet into the cool current, and bathed my forehead. Already there was a glow of sunrise in the sky and the exquisite freshness of coming day. On my way back I passed purposely beneath the very bushes where I had seen the column of figures rising into the air, and midway among the clumps I suddenly found myself overtaken by a sense of vast terror. From the shadows a large figure went swiftly by. Someone passed me, as sure as ever man did…

It was a great staggering blow from the wind that helped me forward again, and once out in the more open space, the sense of terror diminished strangely. The winds were about and walking, I remember saying to myself, for the winds often move like great presences under the trees. And altogether the fear that hovered about me was such an unknown and immense kind of fear, so unlike anything I had ever felt before, that it woke a sense of awe and wonder in me that did much to counteract its worst effects; and when I reached a high point in the middle of the island from which I could see the wide stretch of river, crimson in the sunrise, the whole magical beauty of it all was so overpowering that a sort of wild yearning woke in me and almost brought a cry up into the throat.

But this cry found no expression, for as my eyes wandered from the plain beyond to the island round me and noted our little tent half hidden among the willows, a dreadful discovery leaped out at me, compared to which my terror of the walking winds seemed as nothing at all.

For a change, I thought, had somehow come about in the arrangement of the landscape. It was not that my point of vantage gave me a different view, but that an alteration had apparently been effected in the relation of the tent to the willows, and of the willows to the tent. Surely the bushes now crowded much closer – unnecessarily, unpleasantly close. *They had moved nearer.*

Creeping with silent feet over the shifting sands, drawing imperceptibly nearer by soft, unhurried movements, the willows had come closer during the night. But had the wind moved them, or had they moved of themselves? I recalled the sound of infinite small patterings and the pressure upon the tent and upon my own heart that caused me to wake in terror. I swayed for a moment in the wind like a tree, finding it hard to keep my upright position on the sandy hillock.

There was a suggestion here of personal agency, of deliberate intention, of aggressive hostility, and it terrified me into a sort of rigidity.

Then the reaction followed quickly. The idea was so bizarre, so absurd, that I felt inclined to laugh. But the laughter came no more readily than the cry, for the knowledge that my mind was so receptive to such dangerous imaginings brought the additional terror that it was through our minds and not through our physical bodies that the attack would come, and was coming.

The wind buffeted me about, and, very quickly it seemed, the sun came up over the horizon, for it was after four o'clock, and I must have stood on that little pinnacle of sand longer than I knew, afraid to come down to close quarters with the willows. I returned quietly, creepily, to the tent, first taking another exhaustive look round and – yes, I confess it – making a few measurements. I paced out on the warm sand the distances between the willows and the tent, making a note of the shortest distance particularly.

I crawled stealthily into my blankets. My companion, to all appearances, still slept soundly, and I was glad that this was so. Provided my experiences were not corroborated, I could find strength somehow to deny them, perhaps. With the daylight I could persuade myself that it was all a subjective hallucination, a fantasy of the night, a projection of the excited imagination.

Nothing further came in to disturb me, and I fell asleep almost at once, utterly exhausted, yet still in dread of hearing again that weird sound of multitudinous pattering, or of feeling the pressure upon my heart that had made it difficult to breathe.

Chapter IV

THE SUN was high in the heavens when my companion woke me from a heavy sleep and announced that the porridge was cooked and there was just time to bathe. The grateful smell of frizzling bacon entered the tent door.

"River still rising," he said, "and several islands out in mid-stream have disappeared altogether. Our own island's much smaller."

"Any wood left?" I asked sleepily.

"The wood and the island will finish tomorrow in a dead heat," he laughed, "but there's enough to last us till then."

I plunged in from the point of the island, which had indeed altered a lot in size and shape during the night, and was swept down in a moment to the landing-place opposite the tent. The water was icy, and the banks flew by like the country from an express train. Bathing under such conditions was an exhilarating operation, and the terror of the night seemed cleansed out of me by a process of evaporation in the brain. The sun was blazing hot; not a cloud showed itself anywhere; the wind, however, had not abated one little jot.

Quite suddenly then the implied meaning of the Swede's words flashed across me, showing that he no longer wished to leave post-haste, and had changed his mind. "Enough to last till tomorrow" – he assumed we should stay on the island another night. It struck me as odd. The night before he was so positive the other way. How had the change come about?

Great crumblings of the banks occurred at breakfast, with heavy splashings and clouds of spray which the wind brought into our frying-pan, and my fellow-traveller talked incessantly about the difficulty the Vienna-Pesth steamers must have to find the channel in flood. But the state of his mind interested and impressed me far more than the state of the river or the difficulties of the steamers. He had changed somehow since the evening before. His manner was different – a trifle excited, a trifle shy, with a sort of suspicion about his voice and gestures. I hardly know how to describe it now in cold blood, but at the time I remember being quite certain of one thing – that he had become frightened?

He ate very little breakfast, and for once omitted to smoke his pipe. He had the map spread open beside him, and kept studying its markings.

"We'd better get off sharp in an hour," I said presently, feeling for an opening that must bring him indirectly to a partial confession at any rate. And his answer puzzled me uncomfortably: "Rather! If they'll let us."

"Who'll let us? The elements?" I asked quickly, with affected indifference.

"The powers of this awful place, whoever they are," he replied, keeping his eyes on the map. "The gods are here, if they are anywhere at all in the world."

"The elements are always the true immortals," I replied, laughing as naturally as I could manage, yet knowing quite well that my face reflected my true feelings when he looked up gravely at me and spoke across the smoke:

"We shall be fortunate if we get away without further disaster."

This was exactly what I had dreaded, and I screwed myself up to the point of the direct question. It was like agreeing to allow the dentist to extract the tooth; it *had* to come anyhow in the long run, and the rest was all pretence.

"Further disaster! Why, what's happened?"

"For one thing – the steering paddle's gone," he said quietly.

"The steering paddle gone!" I repeated, greatly excited, for this was our rudder, and the Danube in flood without a rudder was suicide. "But what—"

"And there's a tear in the bottom of the canoe," he added, with a genuine little tremor in his voice.

I continued staring at him, able only to repeat the words in his face somewhat foolishly. There, in the heat of the sun, and on this burning sand, I was aware of a freezing atmosphere descending round us. I got up to follow him, for he merely nodded his head gravely and led the way towards the tent a few yards on the other side of the fireplace. The canoe still lay there as I had last seen her in the night, ribs uppermost, the paddles, or rather, *the* paddle, on the sand beside her.

"There's only one," he said, stooping to pick it up. "And here's the rent in the base-board."

It was on the tip of my tongue to tell him that I had clearly noticed *two* paddles a few hours before, but a second impulse made me think better of it, and I said nothing. I approached to see.

There was a long, finely made tear in the bottom of the canoe where a little slither of wood had been neatly taken clean out; it looked as if the tooth of a sharp rock or snag had eaten down her length, and investigation showed that the hole went through. Had we launched out in her without observing it we must inevitably have foundered. At first the water would have made the wood swell so as to close the hole, but once out in mid-stream the water must have poured in, and the canoe, never more than two inches above the surface, would have filled and sunk very rapidly.

"There, you see an attempt to prepare a victim for the sacrifice," I heard him saying, more to himself than to me, "two victims rather," he added as he bent over and ran his fingers along the slit.

I began to whistle – a thing I always do unconsciously when utterly nonplussed – and purposely paid no attention to his words. I was determined to consider them foolish.

"It wasn't there last night," he said presently, straightening up from his examination and looking anywhere but at me.

"We must have scratched her in landing, of course," I stopped whistling to say. "The stones are very sharp."

I stopped abruptly, for at that moment he turned round and met my eye squarely. I knew just as well as he did how impossible my explanation was. There were no stones, to begin with.

"And then there's this to explain too," he added quietly, handing me the paddle and pointing to the blade.

A new and curious emotion spread freezingly over me as I took and examined it. The blade was scraped down all over, beautifully scraped, as though someone had sand-papered it with care, making it so thin that the first vigorous stroke must have snapped it off at the elbow.

"One of us walked in his sleep and did this thing," I said feebly, "or – or it has been filed by the constant stream of sand particles blown against it by the wind, perhaps."

"Ah," said the Swede, turning away, laughing a little, "you can explain everything."

"The same wind that caught the steering paddle and flung it so near the bank that it fell in with the next lump that crumbled," I called out after him, absolutely determined to find an explanation for everything he showed me.

"I see," he shouted back, turning his head to look at me before disappearing among the willow bushes.

Once alone with these perplexing evidences of personal agency, I think my first thoughts took the form of "One of us must have done this thing, and it certainly was not I." But my second thought decided how impossible it was to suppose, under all the circumstances, that either of us had done it. That my companion, the trusted friend of a dozen similar expeditions, could have knowingly had a hand in it, was a suggestion not to be entertained for a moment. Equally absurd seemed the explanation that this imperturbable and densely practical nature had suddenly become insane and was busied with insane purposes.

Yet the fact remained that what disturbed me most, and kept my fear actively alive even in this blaze of sunshine and wild beauty, was the clear certainty that some curious alteration had come about in his *mind* – that he was nervous, timid, suspicious, aware of goings on he did not speak about, watching a series of secret and hitherto unmentionable events – waiting, in a word, for a climax that he expected, and, I thought, expected very soon. This grew up in my mind intuitively – I hardly knew how.

I made a hurried examination of the tent and its surroundings, but the measurements of the night remained the same. There were deep hollows formed in the sand I now noticed for the first time, basin-shaped and of various depths and sizes, varying from that of a tea-cup to a large bowl. The wind, no doubt, was responsible for these miniature craters, just as it was for lifting the paddle and tossing it towards the water. The rent in the canoe was the only thing that seemed quite inexplicable; and, after all, it *was* conceivable that a sharp point had caught it when we landed. The examination I made of the shore did not assist this theory, but all the same I clung to it with that diminishing portion of my intelligence which I called my 'reason'. An explanation of some kind was an absolute necessity, just as some working explanation of the universe is necessary – however absurd – to the happiness of every individual who seeks to do his duty in the world and face the problems of life. The simile seemed to me at the time an exact parallel.

I at once set the pitch melting, and presently the Swede joined me at the work, though under the best conditions in the world the canoe could not be safe for travelling till the following day. I drew his attention casually to the hollows in the sand.

"Yes," he said, "I know. They're all over the island. But *you* can explain them, no doubt!"

"Wind, of course," I answered without hesitation. "Have you never watched those little whirlwinds in the street that twist and twirl everything into a circle? This sand's loose enough to yield, that's all."

He made no reply, and we worked on in silence for a bit. I watched him surreptitiously all the time, and I had an idea he was watching me. He seemed, too, to be always listening attentively to something I could not hear, or perhaps for something that he expected to hear, for he kept turning about and staring into the bushes, and up into the sky, and out across the water where it was visible through the openings among the willows. Sometimes he even put his hand to his ear and held it there for several minutes. He said nothing to me, however, about it, and I asked no questions. And meanwhile, as he mended that torn canoe with the skill and address of a red Indian, I was glad to notice his absorption in the work, for there was a vague dread in my heart that he would speak of the changed aspect of the willows. And, if he had noticed *that*, my imagination could no longer be held a sufficient explanation of it.

At length, after a long pause, he began to talk.

"Queer thing," he added in a hurried sort of voice, as though he wanted to say something and get it over. "Queer thing. I mean, about that otter last night."

I had expected something so totally different that he caught me with surprise, and I looked up sharply.

"Shows how lonely this place is. Otters are awfully shy things—"

"I don't mean that, of course," he interrupted. "I mean – do you think – did you think it really was an otter?"

"What else, in the name of Heaven, what else?"

"You know, I saw it before you did, and at first it seemed – so *much* bigger than an otter."

"The sunset as you looked up-stream magnified it, or something," I replied.

He looked at me absently a moment, as though his mind were busy with other thoughts.

"It had such extraordinary yellow eyes," he went on half to himself.

"That was the sun too," I laughed, a trifle boisterously. "I suppose you'll wonder next if that fellow in the boat—"

I suddenly decided not to finish the sentence. He was in the act again of listening, turning his head to the wind, and something in the expression of his face made me halt. The subject dropped, and we went on with our caulking. Apparently he had not noticed my unfinished sentence. Five minutes later, however, he looked at me across the canoe, the smoking pitch in his hand, his face exceedingly grave.

"I *did* rather wonder, if you want to know," he said slowly, "what that thing in the boat was. I remember thinking at the time it was not a man. The whole business seemed to rise quite suddenly out of the water."

I laughed again boisterously in his face, but this time there was impatience, and a strain of anger too, in my feeling.

"Look here now," I cried, "this place is quite queer enough without going out of our way to imagine things! That boat was an ordinary boat, and the man in it was an ordinary man, and they were both going down-stream as fast as they could lick. And that otter *was* an otter, so don't let's play the fool about it!"

He looked steadily at me with the same grave expression. He was not in the least annoyed. I took courage from his silence.

"And, for Heaven's sake," I went on, "don't keep pretending you hear things, because it only gives me the jumps, and there's nothing to hear but the river and this cursed old thundering wind."

"You *fool!*" he answered in a low, shocked voice, "you utter fool. That's just the way all victims talk. As if you didn't understand just as well as I do!" he sneered with scorn in his voice, and a sort of resignation. "The best thing you can do is to keep quiet and try to hold your mind as firm as possible. This feeble attempt at self-deception only makes the truth harder when you're forced to meet it."

My little effort was over, and I found nothing more to say, for I knew quite well his words were true, and that *I* was the fool, not *he*. Up to a certain stage in the adventure he kept ahead of me easily, and I think I felt annoyed to be out of it, to be thus proved less psychic, less sensitive than himself to these extraordinary happenings, and half ignorant all the time of what was going on under my very nose. *He knew* from the very beginning, apparently. But at the moment I wholly missed the point of his words about the necessity of there being a victim, and that we ourselves were destined to satisfy the want. I dropped all pretence thenceforward, but thenceforward likewise my fear increased steadily to the climax.

"But you're quite right about one thing," he added, before the subject passed, "and that is that we're wiser not to talk about it, or even to think about it, because what one *thinks* finds expression in words, and what one *says*, happens."

That afternoon, while the canoe dried and hardened, we spent trying to fish, testing the leak, collecting wood, and watching the enormous flood of rising water. Masses of driftwood swept near our shores sometimes, and we fished for them with long willow branches. The island grew perceptibly smaller as the banks were torn away with great gulps and splashes. The weather kept brilliantly fine till about four o'clock, and then for the first time for three days the wind showed signs of abating. Clouds began to gather in the south-west, spreading thence slowly over the sky.

This lessening of the wind came as a great relief, for the incessant roaring, banging, and thundering had irritated our nerves. Yet the silence that came about five o'clock with its sudden cessation was in a manner quite as oppressive. The booming of the river had everything in its own way then; it filled the air with deep murmurs, more musical than the wind noises, but infinitely more monotonous. The wind held many notes, rising, falling always beating out some sort of great elemental tune; whereas the river's song lay between three notes at most – dull pedal notes, that held a lugubrious quality foreign to the wind, and somehow seemed to me, in my then nervous state, to sound wonderfully well the music of doom.

It was extraordinary, too, how the withdrawal suddenly of bright sunlight took everything out of the landscape that made for cheerfulness; and since this particular landscape had already managed to convey the suggestion of something sinister, the change of course was all the more unwelcome and noticeable. For me, I know, the darkening outlook became distinctly more alarming, and I found myself more than once calculating how soon after sunset the full moon would get up in the east, and whether the gathering clouds would greatly interfere with her lighting of the little island.

With this general hush of the wind – though it still indulged in occasional brief gusts – the river seemed to me to grow blacker, the willows to stand more densely together. The latter, too, kept up a sort of independent movement of their own, rustling among themselves when no wind stirred, and shaking oddly from the roots upwards. When common objects in this way become charged with the suggestion of horror, they stimulate the imagination far more than things of unusual appearance; and these bushes, crowding huddled about us, assumed for me in the darkness a bizarre *grotesquerie* of appearance that lent to them somehow the aspect of purposeful and living creatures. Their very ordinariness, I felt, masked what was malignant and hostile to us. The forces of the region drew nearer with the coming of night. They were focusing upon our island, and more particularly upon ourselves. For thus, somehow, in the terms of the imagination, did my really indescribable sensations in this extraordinary place present themselves.

I had slept a good deal in the early afternoon, and had thus recovered somewhat from the exhaustion of a disturbed night, but this only served apparently to render me more susceptible than before to the obsessing spell of the haunting. I fought against it, laughing at my feelings as absurd and childish, with very obvious physiological explanations, yet, in spite of every effort, they gained in strength upon me so that I dreaded the night as a child lost in a forest must dread the approach of darkness.

The canoe we had carefully covered with a waterproof sheet during the day, and the one remaining paddle had been securely tied by the Swede to the base of a tree, lest the wind should rob us of that too. From five o'clock onwards I busied myself with the stew-pot and preparations for dinner, it being my turn to cook that night. We had potatoes, onions, bits of bacon fat to add flavor, and a general thick residue from former stews at the bottom of the pot; with black bread broken up into it the result was most excellent, and it was followed by a stew of plums with sugar and a brew of strong tea with dried milk. A good pile of wood lay close at hand, and the absence of wind made my duties easy. My companion sat lazily watching me, dividing his attentions between cleaning his pipe and giving useless advice – an admitted privilege of the off-duty man. He had been very quiet all the afternoon, engaged in re-caulking the canoe, strengthening the tent ropes, and fishing for driftwood while I slept. No more talk about undesirable things had passed between us, and I think his only remarks had to do with the gradual destruction of the island, which he declared was not fully a third smaller than when we first landed.

The pot had just begun to bubble when I heard his voice calling to me from the bank, where he had wandered away without my noticing. I ran up.

"Come and listen," he said, "and see what you make of it." He held his hand cupwise to his ear, as so often before.

"*Now* do you hear anything?" he asked, watching me curiously.

We stood there, listening attentively together. At first I heard only the deep note of the water and the hissings rising from its turbulent surface. The willows, for once, were motionless and silent. Then a sound began to reach my ears faintly, a peculiar sound – something like the humming of a distant gong. It seemed to come across to us in the darkness from the waste of swamps and willows opposite. It was repeated at regular intervals, but it was certainly neither the sound of a bell nor the hooting of a distant steamer. I can liken it to nothing so much as to the sound of an immense gong, suspended far up in the sky, repeating incessantly its muffled metallic note, soft and musical, as it was repeatedly struck. My heart quickened as I listened.

"I've heard it all day," said my companion. "While you slept this afternoon it came all round the island. I hunted it down, but could never get near enough to see – to localise it correctly. Sometimes it was overhead, and sometimes it seemed under the water. Once or twice, too, I could have sworn it was not outside at all, but *within myself* – you know – the way a sound in the fourth dimension is supposed to come."

I was too much puzzled to pay much attention to his words. I listened carefully, striving to associate it with any known familiar sound I could think of, but without success. It changed in the direction, too, coming nearer, and then sinking utterly away into remote distance. I cannot say that it was ominous in quality, because to me it seemed distinctly musical, yet I must admit it set going a distressing feeling that made me wish I had never heard it.

"The wind blowing in those sand-funnels," I said determined to find an explanation, "or the bushes rubbing together after the storm perhaps."

"It comes off the whole swamp," my friend answered. "It comes from everywhere at once." He ignored my explanations. "It comes from the willow bushes somehow—"

"But now the wind has dropped," I objected. "The willows can hardly make a noise by themselves, can they?"

His answer frightened me, first because I had dreaded it, and secondly, because I knew intuitively it was true.

"It is *because* the wind has dropped we now hear it. It was drowned before. It is the cry, I believe, of the—"

I dashed back to my fire, warned by the sound of bubbling that the stew was in danger, but determined at the same time to escape further conversation. I was resolute, if possible, to avoid the exchanging of views. I dreaded, too, that he would begin about the gods, or the elemental forces, or something else disquieting, and I wanted to keep myself well in hand for what might happen later. There was another night to be faced before we escaped from this distressing place, and there was no knowing yet what it might bring forth.

"Come and cut up bread for the pot," I called to him, vigorously stirring the appetising mixture. That stew-pot held sanity for us both, and the thought made me laugh.

He came over slowly and took the provision sack from the tree, fumbling in its mysterious depths, and then emptying the entire contents upon the ground-sheet at his feet.

"Hurry up!" I cried; "it's boiling."

The Swede burst out into a roar of laughter that startled me. It was forced laughter, not artificial exactly, but mirthless.

"There's nothing here!" he shouted, holding his sides.

"Bread, I mean."

"It's gone. There is no bread. They've taken it!"

I dropped the long spoon and ran up. Everything the sack had contained lay upon the ground-sheet, but there was no loaf.

The whole dead weight of my growing fear fell upon me and shook me. Then I burst out laughing too. It was the only thing to do: and the sound of my laughter also made me understand his. The strain of psychical pressure caused it – this explosion of unnatural laughter in both of us; it was an effort of repressed forces to seek relief; it was a temporary safety-valve. And with both of us it ceased quite suddenly.

"How criminally stupid of me!" I cried, still determined to be consistent and find an explanation. "I clean forgot to buy a loaf at Pressburg. That chattering woman put everything out of my head, and I must have left it lying on the counter or—"

"The oatmeal, too, is much less than it was this morning," the Swede interrupted.

Why in the world need he draw attention to it? I thought angrily.

"There's enough for tomorrow," I said, stirring vigorously, "and we can get lots more at Komorn or Gran. In twenty-four hours we shall be miles from here."

"I hope so – to God," he muttered, putting the things back into the sack, "unless we're claimed first as victims for the sacrifice," he added with a foolish laugh. He dragged the sack into the tent, for safety's sake, I suppose, and I heard him mumbling to himself, but so indistinctly that it seemed quite natural for me to ignore his words.

Our meal was beyond question a gloomy one, and we ate it almost in silence, avoiding one another's eyes, and keeping the fire bright. Then we washed up and prepared for the night, and, once smoking, our minds unoccupied with any definite duties, the apprehension I had felt all day long became more and more acute. It was not then active fear, I think, but the very vagueness of its origin distressed me far more that if I had been able to ticket and face it squarely. The curious sound I have likened to the note of a gong became now almost incessant, and filled the stillness of the night with a faint, continuous ringing rather than a series of distinct notes. At one time it was behind and at another time in front of us. Sometimes I fancied it came from the bushes on our left, and then again from the clumps on our right. More often it hovered directly overhead like the whirring of wings. It was really everywhere at once, behind, in front, at our sides and over our heads, completely surrounding us. The sound really defies description. But nothing within my knowledge is like that ceaseless muffled humming rising off the deserted world of swamps and willows.

We sat smoking in comparative silence, the strain growing every minute greater. The worst feature of the situation seemed to me that we did not know what to expect, and could therefore make no sort of preparation by way of defence. We could anticipate nothing. My explanations made in the sunshine, moreover, now came to haunt me with their foolish and wholly unsatisfactory nature, and it was more and more clear to us that some kind of plain talk with my companion was inevitable, whether I liked it or not. After all, we had to spend the night together, and to sleep in the same tent side by side. I saw that I could not get along much longer without the support of his mind, and for that, of course, plain talk was imperative. As long as possible, however, I postponed this little climax, and tried to ignore or laugh at the occasional sentences he flung into the emptiness.

Some of these sentences, moreover, were confoundedly disquieting to me, coming as they did to corroborate much that I felt myself; corroboration, too – which made it so much more convincing – from a totally different point of view. He composed such curious sentences, and hurled them at me in such an inconsequential sort of way, as though his main line of thought was secret to himself, and these fragments were mere bits he found it impossible to digest. He got rid of them by uttering them. Speech relieved him. It was like being sick.

"There are things about us, I'm sure, that make for disorder, disintegration, destruction, our destruction," he said once, while the fire blazed between us. "We've strayed out of a safe line somewhere."

And, another time, when the gong sounds had come nearer, ringing much louder than before, and directly over our heads, he said as though talking to himself:

"I don't think a gramophone would show any record of that. The sound doesn't come to me by the ears at all. The vibrations reach me in another manner altogether, and seem to be within me, which is precisely how a fourth dimensional sound might be supposed to make itself heard."

I purposely made no reply to this, but I sat up a little closer to the fire and peered about me into the darkness. The clouds were massed all over the sky, and no trace of moonlight came through. Very still, too, everything was, so that the river and the frogs had things all their own way.

"It has that about it," he went on, "which is utterly out of common experience. It is *unknown*. Only one thing describes it really; it is a non-human sound; I mean a sound outside humanity."

Having rid himself of this indigestible morsel, he lay quiet for a time, but he had so admirably expressed my own feeling that it was a relief to have the thought out, and to have confined it by the limitation of words from dangerous wandering to and fro in the mind.

The solitude of that Danube camping-place, can I ever forget it? The feeling of being utterly alone on an empty planet! My thoughts ran incessantly upon cities and the haunts of men. I would have given my soul, as the saying is, for the 'feel' of those Bavarian villages we had passed through by the score; for the normal, human commonplaces; peasants drinking beer, tables beneath the trees, hot sunshine, and a ruined castle on the rocks behind the red-roofed church. Even the tourists would have been welcome.

Yet what I felt of dread was no ordinary ghostly fear. It was infinitely greater, stranger, and seemed to arise from some dim ancestral sense of terror more profoundly disturbing than anything I had known or dreamed of. We had 'strayed', as the Swede put it, into some region or some set of conditions where the risks were great, yet unintelligible to us; where the frontiers of some unknown world lay close about us. It was a spot held by the dwellers in some outer space, a sort of peep-hole whence they could spy upon the earth, themselves unseen, a point where the veil between had worn a little thin. As the final result of too long a sojourn here, we should be carried over the border and deprived of what we called 'our lives', yet by mental, not physical, processes. In that sense, as he said, we should be the victims of our adventure – a sacrifice.

It took us in different fashion, each according to the measure of his sensitiveness and powers of resistance. I translated it vaguely into a personification of the mightily disturbed elements, investing them with the horror of a deliberate and malefic purpose, resentful of our audacious intrusion into their breeding-place; whereas my friend threw it into the unoriginal form at first of a trespass on some ancient shrine, some place where the old gods still held sway, where the emotional forces of former worshippers still clung, and the ancestral portion of him yielded to the old pagan spell.

At any rate, here was a place unpolluted by men, kept clean by the winds from coarsening human influences, a place where spiritual agencies were within reach and aggressive. Never, before or since, have I been so attacked by indescribable suggestions of a 'beyond region', of another scheme of life, another revolution not parallel to the human. And in the end our minds would succumb under the weight of the awful spell, and we should be drawn across the frontier into *their* world.

Small things testified to the amazing influence of the place, and now in the silence round the fire they allowed themselves to be noted by the mind. The very atmosphere had proved itself a magnifying medium to distort every indication: the otter rolling in the current, the hurrying boatman making signs, the shifting willows, one and all had been robbed of its natural character, and revealed in something of its other aspect – as it existed across the border to that other region. And this changed aspect I felt was now not merely to me, but to the race. The whole experience whose verge we touched was unknown to humanity at all. It was a new order of experience, and in the true sense of the word *unearthly*.

"It's the deliberate, calculating purpose that reduces one's courage to zero," the Swede said suddenly, as if he had been actually following my thoughts. "Otherwise imagination might count for much. But the paddle, the canoe, the lessening food—"

"Haven't I explained all that once?" I interrupted viciously.

"You have," he answered dryly; "you have indeed."

He made other remarks too, as usual, about what he called the "plain determination to provide a victim"; but, having now arranged my thoughts better, I recognised that this was simply the cry of his frightened soul against the knowledge that he was being attacked in a vital part, and that he would be somehow taken or destroyed. The situation called for a courage and calmness of reasoning that neither of us could compass, and I have never before been so clearly conscious of two persons in me – the one that explained everything, and the other that laughed at such foolish explanations, yet was horribly afraid.

Meanwhile, in the pitchy night the fire died down and the wood pile grew small. Neither of us moved to replenish the stock, and the darkness consequently came up very close to our faces. A few feet beyond the circle of firelight it was inky black. Occasionally a stray puff of wind set the willows shivering about us, but apart from this not very welcome sound a deep and depressing silence reigned, broken only by the gurgling of the river and the humming in the air overhead.

We both missed, I think, the shouting company of the winds.

At length, at a moment when a stray puff prolonged itself as though the wind were about to rise again, I reached the point for me of saturation, the point where it was absolutely necessary to find relief in plain speech, or else to betray myself by some hysterical extravagance that must have been far worse in its effect upon both of us. I kicked the fire into a blaze, and turned to my companion abruptly. He looked up with a start.

"I can't disguise it any longer," I said; "I don't like this place, and the darkness, and the noises, and the awful feelings I get. There's something here that beats me utterly. I'm in a blue funk, and that's the plain truth. If the other shore was – different, I swear I'd be inclined to swim for it!"

The Swede's face turned very white beneath the deep tan of sun and wind. He stared straight at me and answered quietly, but his voice betrayed his huge excitement by its unnatural calmness. For the moment, at any rate, he was the strong man of the two. He was more phlegmatic, for one thing.

"It's not a physical condition we can escape from by running away," he replied, in the tone of a doctor diagnosing some grave disease; "we must sit tight and wait. There are forces close here that could kill a herd of elephants in a second as easily as you or I could squash a fly. Our only chance is to keep perfectly still. Our insignificance perhaps may save us."

I put a dozen questions into my expression of face, but found no words. It was precisely like listening to an accurate description of a disease whose symptoms had puzzled me.

"I mean that so far, although aware of our disturbing presence, they have not *found* us – not 'located' us, as the Americans say," he went on. "They're blundering about like men hunting for a leak of gas. The paddle and canoe and provisions prove that. I think they *feel* us, but cannot actually see us. We must keep our minds quiet – it's our minds they feel. We must control our thoughts, or it's all up with us."

"Death, you mean?" I stammered, icy with the horror of his suggestion.

"Worse – by far," he said. "Death, according to one's belief, means either annihilation or release from the limitations of the senses, but it involves no change of character. *You* don't suddenly alter just because the body's gone. But this means a radical alteration, a complete change, a horrible loss of oneself by substitution – far worse than death, and not even annihilation. We happen to have camped in a spot where their region touches ours, where the veil between has worn thin" – horrors! he was using my very own phrase, my actual words – "so that they are aware of our being in their neighbourhood."

"But *who* are aware?" I asked.

I forgot the shaking of the willows in the windless calm, the humming overhead, everything except that I was waiting for an answer that I dreaded more than I can possibly explain.

He lowered his voice at once to reply, leaning forward a little over the fire, an indefinable change in his face that made me avoid his eyes and look down upon the ground.

"All my life," he said, "I have been strangely, vividly conscious of another region – not far removed from our own world in one sense, yet wholly different in kind – where great things go on unceasingly, where immense and terrible personalities hurry by, intent on vast purposes compared to which earthly affairs, the rise and fall of nations, the destinies of empires, the fate of armies and continents, are all as dust in the balance; vast purposes, I mean, that deal directly with the soul, and not indirectly with mere expressions of the soul—"

"I suggest just now—" I began, seeking to stop him, feeling as though I was face to face with a madman. But he instantly overbore me with his torrent that *had* to come.

"You think," he said, "it is the spirit of the elements, and I thought perhaps it was the old gods. But I tell you now it is – *neither*. These would be comprehensible entities, for they have relations with men, depending upon them for worship or sacrifice, whereas these beings who are now about us have absolutely nothing to do with mankind, and it is mere chance that their space happens just at this spot to touch our own."

The mere conception, which his words somehow made so convincing, as I listened to them there in the dark stillness of that lonely island, set me shaking a little all over. I found it impossible to control my movements.

"And what do you propose?" I began again.

"A sacrifice, a victim, might save us by distracting them until we could get away," he went on, "just as the wolves stop to devour the dogs and give the sleigh another start. But – I see no chance of any other victim now."

I stared blankly at him. The gleam in his eye was dreadful. Presently he continued.

"It's the willows, of course. The willows *mask* the others, but the others are feeling about for us. If we let our minds betray our fear, we're lost, lost utterly." He looked at me with an expression so calm, so determined, so sincere, that I no longer had any doubts as to his sanity. He was as sane as any man ever was. "If we can hold out through the night," he added, "we may get off in the daylight unnoticed, or rather, *undiscovered*."

"But you really think a sacrifice would—"

That gong-like humming came down very close over our heads as I spoke, but it was my friend's scared face that really stopped my mouth.

"Hush!" he whispered, holding up his hand. "Do not mention them more than you can help. Do not refer to them *by name*. To name is to reveal; it is the inevitable clue, and our only hope lies in ignoring them, in order that they may ignore us."

"Even in thought?" He was extraordinarily agitated.

"Especially in thought. Our thoughts make spirals in their world. We must keep them *out of our minds* at all costs if possible."

I raked the fire together to prevent the darkness having everything its own way. I never longed for the sun as I longed for it then in the awful blackness of that summer night.

"Were you awake all last night?" he went on suddenly.

"I slept badly a little after dawn," I replied evasively, trying to follow his instructions, which I knew instinctively were true, "but the wind, of course—"

"I know. But the wind won't account for all the noises."

"Then you heard it too?"

"The multiplying countless little footsteps I heard," he said, adding, after a moment's hesitation, "and that other sound—"

"You mean above the tent, and the pressing down upon us of something tremendous, gigantic?"

He nodded significantly.

"It was like the beginning of a sort of inner suffocation?" I said.

"Partly, yes. It seemed to me that the weight of the atmosphere had been altered – had increased enormously, so that we should have been crushed."

"And that," I went on, determined to have it all out, pointing upwards where the gong-like note hummed ceaselessly, rising and falling like wind. "What do you make of that?"

"It's *their* sound," he whispered gravely. "It's the sound of their world, the humming in their region. The division here is so thin that it leaks through somehow. But, if you listen carefully, you'll find it's not above so much as around us. It's in the willows. It's the willows themselves humming, because here the willows have been made symbols of the forces that are against us."

I could not follow exactly what he meant by this, yet the thought and idea in my mind were beyond question the thought and idea in his. I realised what he realised, only with less power of analysis than his. It was on the tip of my tongue to tell him at last about my hallucination of the ascending figures and the moving bushes, when he suddenly thrust his face again close into mine across the firelight and began to speak in a very earnest whisper. He amazed me by his calmness and pluck, his apparent control of the situation. This man I had for years deemed unimaginative, stolid!

"Now listen," he said. "The only thing for us to do is to go on as though nothing had happened, follow our usual habits, go to bed, and so forth; pretend we feel nothing and notice nothing. It is a question wholly of the mind, and the less we think about them the better our chance of escape. Above all, don't *think*, for what you think happens!"

"All right," I managed to reply, simply breathless with his words and the strangeness of it all; "all right, I'll try, but tell me one more thing first. Tell me what you make of those hollows in the ground all about us, those sand-funnels?"

"No!" he cried, forgetting to whisper in his excitement. "I dare not, simply dare not, put the thought into words. If you have not guessed I am glad. Don't try to. *They* have put it into my mind; try your hardest to prevent their putting it into yours."

He sank his voice again to a whisper before he finished, and I did not press him to explain. There was already just about as much horror in me as I could hold. The conversation came to an end, and we smoked our pipes busily in silence.

Then something happened, something unimportant apparently, as the way is when the nerves are in a very great state of tension, and this small thing for a brief space gave me an entirely different point of view. I chanced to look down at my sand-shoe – the sort we used for the canoe – and something to do with the hole at the toe suddenly recalled to me the London shop where I had bought them, the difficulty the man had in fitting me, and other details of the uninteresting but practical operation. At once, in its train, followed a wholesome view of the modern skeptical world I was accustomed to move in at home. I thought of roast beef, and ale, motor-cars, policemen, brass bands, and a dozen other things that proclaimed the soul of ordinariness or utility. The effect was immediate and astonishing even to myself. Psychologically, I suppose, it was simply a sudden and violent reaction after the strain of living in an atmosphere of things that to the normal consciousness must seem impossible and incredible. But, whatever the cause, it momentarily lifted the spell from my heart, and left me for the short space of a minute feeling free and utterly unafraid. I looked up at my friend opposite.

"You damned old pagan!" I cried, laughing aloud in his face. "You imaginative idiot! You superstitious idolater! You—"

I stopped in the middle, seized anew by the old horror. I tried to smother the sound of my voice as something sacrilegious. The Swede, of course, heard it too – the strange cry overhead in the darkness – and that sudden drop in the air as though something had come nearer.

He had turned ashen white under the tan. He stood bolt upright in front of the fire, stiff as a rod, staring at me.

"After that," he said in a sort of helpless, frantic way, "we must go! We can't stay now; we must strike camp this very instant and go on – down the river."

He was talking, I saw, quite wildly, his words dictated by abject terror – the terror he had resisted so long, but which had caught him at last.

"In the dark?" I exclaimed, shaking with fear after my hysterical outburst, but still realising our position better than he did. "Sheer madness! The river's in flood, and we've only got a single paddle. Besides, we only go deeper into their country! There's nothing ahead for fifty miles but willows, willows, willows!"

He sat down again in a state of semi-collapse. The positions, by one of those kaleidoscopic changes nature loves, were suddenly reversed, and the control of our forces passed over into my hands. His mind at last had reached the point where it was beginning to weaken.

"What on earth possessed you to do such a thing?" he whispered with the awe of genuine terror in his voice and face.

I crossed round to his side of the fire. I took both his hands in mine, kneeling down beside him and looking straight into his frightened eyes.

"We'll make one more blaze," I said firmly, "and then turn in for the night. At sunrise we'll be off full speed for Komorn. Now, pull yourself together a bit, and remember your own advice about *not thinking fear!*"

He said no more, and I saw that he would agree and obey. In some measure, too, it was a sort of relief to get up and make an excursion into the darkness for more wood. We kept close together, almost touching, groping among the bushes and along the bank. The humming overhead never ceased, but seemed to me to grow louder as we increased our distance from the fire. It was shivery work!

We were grubbing away in the middle of a thickish clump of willows where some driftwood from a former flood had caught high among the branches, when my body was seized in a grip that made me half drop upon the sand. It was the Swede. He had fallen against me, and was clutching me for support. I heard his breath coming and going in short gasps.

"Look! By my soul!" he whispered, and for the first time in my experience I knew what it was to hear tears of terror in a human voice. He was pointing to the fire, some fifty feet away. I followed the direction of his finger, and I swear my heart missed a beat.

There, in front of the dim glow, *something was moving*.

I saw it through a veil that hung before my eyes like the gauze drop-curtain used at the back of a theatre – hazily a little. It was neither a human figure nor an animal. To me it gave the strange impression of being as large as several animals grouped together, like horses, two or three, moving slowly. The Swede, too, got a similar result, though expressing it differently, for he thought it was shaped and sized like a clump of willow bushes, rounded at the top, and moving all over upon its surface – "coiling upon itself like smoke," he said afterwards.

"I watched it settle downwards through the bushes," he sobbed at me. "Look, by God! It's coming this way! Oh, oh!" – he gave a kind of whistling cry. *"They've found us."*

I gave one terrified glance, which just enabled me to see that the shadowy form was swinging towards us through the bushes, and then I collapsed backwards with a crash into the branches. These failed, of course, to support my weight, so that with the Swede on top of me we fell in a struggling heap upon the sand. I really hardly knew what was happening. I was conscious only of a sort of enveloping sensation of icy fear that plucked the nerves out of their fleshly covering, twisted them this way and that, and replaced them quivering. My eyes were tightly shut; something in my throat choked me; a feeling that my consciousness was expanding, extending out into space, swiftly gave way to another feeling that I was losing it altogether, and about to die.

An acute spasm of pain passed through me, and I was aware that the Swede had hold of me in such a way that he hurt me abominably. It was the way he caught at me in falling.

But it was the pain, he declared afterwards, that saved me; it caused me to *forget them* and think of something else at the very instant when they were about to find me. It concealed my mind from them at the moment of discovery, yet just in time to evade their terrible seizing of me. He himself, he says, actually swooned at the same moment, and that was what saved him.

I only know that at a later date, how long or short is impossible to say, I found myself scrambling up out of the slippery network of willow branches, and saw my companion standing in front of me holding out a hand to assist me. I stared at him in a dazed way, rubbing the arm he had twisted for me. Nothing came to me to say, somehow.

"I lost consciousness for a moment or two," I heard him say. "That's what saved me. It made me stop thinking about them."

"You nearly broke my arm in two," I said, uttering my only connected thought at the moment. A numbness came over me.

"That's what saved *you!*" he replied. "Between us, we've managed to set them off on a false tack somewhere. The humming has ceased. It's gone – for the moment at any rate!"

A wave of hysterical laughter seized me again, and this time spread to my friend too – great healing gusts of shaking laughter that brought a tremendous sense of relief in their train. We made our way back to the fire and put the wood on so that it blazed at once. Then we saw that the tent had fallen over and lay in a tangled heap upon the ground.

We picked it up, and during the process tripped more than once and caught our feet in sand.

"It's those sand-funnels," exclaimed the Swede, when the tent was up again and the firelight lit up the ground for several yards about us. "And look at the size of them!"

All round the tent and about the fireplace where we had seen the moving shadows there were deep funnel-shaped hollows in the sand, exactly similar to the ones we had already found over the island, only far bigger and deeper, beautifully formed, and wide enough in some instances to admit the whole of my foot and leg.

Neither of us said a word. We both knew that sleep was the safest thing we could do, and to bed we went accordingly without further delay, having first thrown sand on the fire and taken the provision sack and the paddle inside the tent with us. The canoe, too, we propped in such a way at the end of the tent that our feet touched it, and the least motion would disturb and wake us.

In case of emergency, too, we again went to bed in our clothes, ready for a sudden start.

Chapter V

IT WAS my firm intention to lie awake all night and watch, but the exhaustion of nerves and body decreed otherwise, and sleep after a while came over me with a welcome blanket of oblivion. The fact that my companion also slept quickened its approach. At first he fidgeted and constantly sat up, asking me if I "heard this" or "heard that." He tossed about on his cork mattress, and said the tent was moving and the river had risen over the point of the island, but each time I went out to look I returned with the report that all was well, and finally he grew calmer and lay still. Then at length his breathing became regular and I heard unmistakable sounds of snoring – the first and only time in my life when snoring has been a welcome and calming influence.

This, I remember, was the last thought in my mind before dozing off.

A difficulty in breathing woke me, and I found the blanket over my face. But something else besides the blanket was pressing upon me, and my first thought was that my companion had rolled off his mattress on to my own in his sleep. I called to him and sat up, and at the same moment it came to me that the tent was *surrounded*. That sound of multitudinous soft pattering was again audible outside, filling the night with horror.

I called again to him, louder than before. He did not answer, but I missed the sound of his snoring, and also noticed that the flap of the tent was down. This was the unpardonable sin. I crawled out in the darkness to hook it back securely, and it was then for the first time I realised positively that the Swede was not here. He had gone.

I dashed out in a mad run, seized by a dreadful agitation, and the moment I was out I plunged into a sort of torrent of humming that surrounded me completely and came out of every quarter of the heavens at once. It was that same familiar humming – gone mad! A swarm of great invisible bees might have been about me in the air. The sound seemed to thicken the very atmosphere, and I felt that my lungs worked with difficulty.

But my friend was in danger, and I could not hesitate.

The dawn was just about to break, and a faint whitish light spread upwards over the clouds from a thin strip of clear horizon. No wind stirred. I could just make out the bushes and river beyond, and the pale sandy patches. In my excitement I ran frantically to and fro about the island, calling him by name, shouting at the top of my voice the first words that came into my head. But the willows smothered my voice, and the humming muffled it, so that the sound only travelled a few feet round me. I plunged among the bushes, tripping headlong, tumbling over roots, and scraping my face as I tore this way and that among the preventing branches.

Then, quite unexpectedly, I came out upon the island's point and saw a dark figure outlined between the water and the sky. It was the Swede. And already he had one foot in the river! A moment more and he would have taken the plunge.

I threw myself upon him, flinging my arms about his waist and dragging him shorewards with all my strength. Of course he struggled furiously, making a noise all the time just like that cursed humming, and using the most outlandish phrases in his anger about "going *inside* to Them," and "taking the way of the water and the wind," and God only knows what more besides, that I tried in vain to recall afterwards, but which turned me sick with horror and amazement as I listened. But in the end I managed to get him into the comparative safety of the tent, and flung him breathless and cursing upon the mattress where I held him until the fit had passed.

I think the suddenness with which it all went and he grew calm, coinciding as it did with the equally abrupt cessation of the humming and pattering outside – I think this was almost the strangest part of the whole business perhaps. For he had just opened his eyes and turned his tired face up to me so that the dawn threw a pale light upon it through the doorway, and said, for all the world just like a frightened child:

"My life, old man – it's my life I owe you. But it's all over now anyhow. They've found a victim in our place!"

Then he dropped back upon his blankets and went to sleep literally under my eyes. He simply collapsed, and began to snore again as healthily as though nothing had happened and he had never tried to offer his own life as a sacrifice by drowning. And when the sunlight woke him three hours later – hours of ceaseless vigil for me – it became so clear to me that he remembered absolutely nothing of what he had attempted to do, that I deemed it wise to hold my peace and ask no dangerous questions.

He woke naturally and easily, as I have said, when the sun was already high in a windless hot sky, and he at once got up and set about the preparation of the fire for breakfast. I followed him anxiously at bathing, but he did not attempt to plunge in, merely dipping his head and making some remark about the extra coldness of the water.

"River's falling at last," he said, "and I'm glad of it."

"The humming has stopped too," I said.

He looked up at me quietly with his normal expression. Evidently he remembered everything except his own attempt at suicide.

"Everything has stopped," he said, "because—"

He hesitated. But I knew some reference to that remark he had made just before he fainted was in his mind, and I was determined to know it.

"Because 'They've found another victim'?" I said, forcing a little laugh.

"Exactly," he answered, "exactly! I feel as positive of it as though – as though – I feel quite safe again, I mean," he finished.

He began to look curiously about him. The sunlight lay in hot patches on the sand. There was no wind. The willows were motionless. He slowly rose to feet.

"Come," he said; "I think if we look, we shall find it."

He started off on a run, and I followed him. He kept to the banks, poking with a stick among the sandy bays and caves and little back-waters, myself always close on his heels.

"Ah!" he exclaimed presently, "ah!"

The tone of his voice somehow brought back to me a vivid sense of the horror of the last twenty-four hours, and I hurried up to join him. He was pointing with his stick at a large black object that lay half in the water and half on the sand. It appeared to be caught by some twisted willow roots so that the river could not sweep it away. A few hours before the spot must have been under water.

"See," he said quietly, "the victim that made our escape possible!"

And when I peered across his shoulder I saw that his stick rested on the body of a man. He turned it over. It was the corpse of a peasant, and the face was hidden in the sand. Clearly the man had been drowned, but a few hours before, and his body must have been swept down upon our island somewhere about the hour of the dawn – *at the very time the fit had passed.*

"We must give it a decent burial, you know."

"I suppose so," I replied. I shuddered a little in spite of myself, for there was something about the appearance of that poor drowned man that turned me cold.

The Swede glanced up sharply at me, an undecipherable expression on his face, and began clambering down the bank. I followed him more leisurely. The current, I noticed, had torn away much of the clothing from the body, so that the neck and part of the chest lay bare.

Halfway down the bank my companion suddenly stopped and held up his hand in warning; but either my foot slipped, or I had gained too much momentum to bring myself quickly to a halt, for I bumped into him and sent him forward with a sort of leap to save himself. We tumbled together on to the hard sand so that our feet splashed into the water. And, before anything could be done, we had collided a little heavily against the corpse.

The Swede uttered a sharp cry. And I sprang back as if I had been shot.

At the moment we touched the body there rose from its surface the loud sound of humming – the sound of several hummings – which passed with a vast commotion as of winged things in the air about us and disappeared upwards into the sky, growing fainter and fainter till they finally ceased in the distance. It was exactly as though we had disturbed some living yet invisible creatures at work.

My companion clutched me, and I think I clutched him, but before either of us had time properly to recover from the unexpected shock, we saw that a movement of the current was turning the corpse round so that it became released from the grip of the willow roots. A moment later it had turned completely over, the dead face uppermost, staring at the sky. It lay on the edge of the main stream. In another moment it would be swept away.

The Swede started to save it, shouting again something I did not catch about a "proper burial" – and then abruptly dropped upon his knees on the sand and covered his eyes with his hands. I was beside him in an instant.

I saw what he had seen.

For just as the body swung round to the current the face and the exposed chest turned full towards us, and showed plainly how the skin and flesh were indented with small hollows, beautifully formed, and exactly similar in shape and kind to the sand-funnels that we had found all over the island.

"Their mark!" I heard my companion mutter under his breath. "Their awful mark!"

And when I turned my eyes again from his ghastly face to the river, the current had done its work, and the body had been swept away into mid-stream and was already beyond our reach and almost out of sight, turning over and over on the waves like an otter.

The Secret in the Tomb

Robert Bloch

THE WIND HOWLED strangely over a midnight tomb. The moon hung like a golden bat over ancient graves, glaring through the wan mist with its baleful, nyctalopic eye. Terrors not of the flesh might lurk among cedar-shrouded sepulchers or creep unseen amid shadowed cenotaphs, for this was unhallowed ground. But tombs hold strange secrets, and there are mysteries blacker than the night, and more leprous than the moon.

It was in search of such a secret that I came, alone and unseen, to my ancestral vault at midnight. My people had been sorcerers and wizards in the olden days, so lay apart from the resting-place of other men, here in this moldering mausoleum in a forgotten spot, surrounded only by the graves of those who had been their servants. But not all the servants lay here, for there are those who do not die.

On through the mist I pressed, to where the crumbling sepulcher loomed among the brooding trees. The wind rose to torrential violence as I trod the obscure pathway to the vaulted entrance, extinguishing my lantern with malefic fury. Only the moon remained to light my way in a luminance unholy. And thus I reached the nitrous, fungus-bearded portals of the family vault. Here the moon shone upon a door that was not like other doors – a single massive slab of iron, imbedded in monumental walls of granite. Upon its outer surface was neither handle, lock nor keyhole, but the whole was covered with carvings portentous of a leering evil – cryptic symbols whose allegorical significance filled my soul with a deeper loathing than mere words can impart. There are things that are not good to look upon, and I did not care to dwell too much in thought on the possible genesis of a mind whose knowledge could create such horrors in concrete form. So in blind and trembling haste I chanted the obscure litany and performed the necessary obeisances demanded in the ritual I had learned, and at their conclusion the cyclopean portal swung open.

Within was darkness, deep, funereal, ancient; yet, somehow, uncannily *alive*. It held a pulsing adumbration, a suggestion of muted, yet purposeful rhythm, and overshadowing all, an air of black, impinging *revelation*. The simultaneous effect upon my consciousness was one of those reactions misnamed intuitions. I sensed that shadows know queer secrets, and there are some skulls that have reason to grin.

Yet I must go on into the tomb of my forebears – tonight the last of all our line would meet the first. For I was the last. Jeremy Strange had been the first – he who fled from the Orient to seek refuge in centuried Eldertown, bringing with him the loot of many tombs and a secret for ever nameless. It was he who had built his sepulcher in the twilight woods where the witch-lights gleam, and here he had interred his own remains, shunned in death as he had been in life. But buried with him was a secret, and it was this that I had come to seek. Nor was I the first in so seeking, for my father and his father before me, indeed, the eldest of each generation back to the days of Jeremy Strange himself, had likewise sought that which was so maddeningly described in the wizard's diary – the secret of eternal life after death. The musty yellowed tome had been handed down to the elder son of each successive generation, and likewise, so it seemed, the dread atavistic craving for black and accursed knowledge, the thirst for which, coupled with the damnably explicit hints set forth in the warlock's record, had sent every one of my paternal ancestors so bequeathed to a final rendezvous in the night, to seek their heritage within the tomb. What they found, none could say, for none had ever returned.

It was, of course, a family secret. The tomb was never mentioned – it had, indeed, been virtually forgotten with the passage of years that had likewise eradicated many of the old legends and fantastic accusations about the first Strange that had once been common property in the village. The family, too, had been mercifully spared all knowledge of the curse-ridden end to which so many of its men had come. Their secret delvings into black arts; the hidden library of antique lore and demonological formulae brought by Jeremy from the East; the diary and its secret – all were undreamt of save by the eldest sons. The rest of the line prospered. There had been sea captains, soldiers, merchants, statesmen. Fortunes were won. Many departed from the old mansion on the cape, so that in my father's time he had lived there alone with the servants and myself. My mother died at my birth, and it was a lonely youth I spent in the great brown house, with a father half-crazed by the tragedy of my mother's end, and shadowed by the monstrous secret of our line. It was he who initiated me into the mysteries and arcana to be found amid the shuddery speculations of such blasphemies as the *Necronomicon*, the *Book of Eibon*, the *Cabala of Saboth*, and that pinnacle of literary madness, Ludvig Prinn's *Mysteries of the Worm*. There were grim treatises on anthropomancy, necrology, lycanthropical and vampiristic spells and charms, witchcraft, and long, rambling screeds in Arabic, Sanskrit and prehistoric ideography, on which lay the dust of centuries.

All these he gave me, and more. There were times when he would whisper strange stories about voyages he had taken in his youth – of islands in the sea, and queer survivals spawning dreams beneath arctic ice. And one night he told me of the legend, and the tomb in the forest; and together we turned the worm-riddled pages of the iron-bound diary that was hidden in the panel above the chimney corner. I was very young, but not too young to know certain things, and as I swore to keep the secret as so many had sworn before me, I had a queer feeling that the time had come for Jeremy to claim his own. For in my father's somber eyes was the same light of dreadful thirst for the unknown, curiosity, and an inward urge that had glowed in the eyes of all the others before him, previous to the time they had announced their intention of "going on a trip" or "joining up" or "attending to a business matter". Most of them had waited till their children were grown, or their wives had passed on; but whenever they had left, and whatever their excuse, they had never returned.

Two days later, my father disappeared, after leaving word with the servants that he was spending the week in Boston. Before the month was out there was the usual investigation, and the usual failure. A will was discovered among my father's papers, leaving me as sole heir, but the books and the diary were secure in the secret rooms and panels known now to me alone.

Life went on. I did the usual things in the usual way – attended university, traveled, and returned at last to the house on the hill, alone. But with me I carried a mighty determination – I alone could thwart that curse; I alone could grasp the secret that had cost the lives of seven generations – and I alone must do so. The world had naught to offer one who had spent his youth in the study of the mocking truths that lie beyond the outward beauties of a purposeless existence, and I was not afraid. I dismissed the servants, ceased communication with distant relatives and a few close friends, and spent my days in the hidden chambers amid the elder lore, seeking a solution or a spell of such potency as would serve to dispel for ever the mystery of the tomb.

A hundred times I read and reread that hoary script – the diary whose fiend-penned promise had driven men to doom. I searched amid the satanic spells and cabalistic incantations of a thousand forgotten necromancers, delved into pages of impassioned prophecy, burrowed into secret legendary lore whose written thoughts writhed through me like serpents from the pit. It was in vain. All I could learn was the ceremony by which access could be obtained to the tomb in the wood. Three months of study had worn me to a wraith and filled my brain with the diabolic shadows of charnel-spawned knowledge, but that was all. And then, as if in mockery of madness, there had come the call, this very night.

I had been seated in the study, pondering upon a maggot-eaten volume of Heiriarchus' *Occultus*, when without warning, I felt a tremendous urge keening through my weary brain. It beckoned and allured with unutterable promise, like the mating-cry of the lamia of old; yet at the same time it held an inexorable power whose potence could not be defied or denied. The inevitable was at hand. I had been summoned to the tomb. I must follow the beguiling voice of inner consciousness that was the invitation and the promise, that sounded my soul like the ultra-rhythmic piping of trans-cosmic music. So I had come, alone and weaponless, to the lonely woods and to that wherein I would meet my destiny.

The moon rose redly over the manor as I left, but I did not look back. I saw its reflection in the waters of the brook that crept between the trees, and in its light the water was as blood. Then the fog rose silently from the swamp, and a yellow ghost-light rode the sky, beckoning me on from behind the black and bloated trees whose branches, swept by a dismal wind, pointed silently toward the distant tomb. Roots and creepers impeded my feet, vines and brambles restrained my body, but in my ears thundered a chorus of urgency that cannot be described and which could not be delayed, by nature or by man.

Now, as I hesitated upon the doorstep, a million idiot voices gibbered an invitation to enter that mortal mind could not withstand. Through my brain resounded the horror of my heritage – the insatiable craving to know the forbidden, to mingle and become one with it. A paean of hell-born music crescendoed in my ears, and earth was blotted out in a mad urge that engulfed all being.

I paused no longer upon the threshold. I went in, in where the smell of death filled the darkness that was like the sun over Yuggoth. The door closed, and then came – what? I do not know – I only realized that suddenly I could see and feel and hear, despite darkness, and dankness, and silence.

I was in the tomb. Its monumental walls and lofty ceiling were black and bare, lichended by the passage of centuries. In the center of the mausoleum stood a single slab of black marble. Upon it rested a gilded coffin, set with strange symbols, and covered by the dust of ages. I knew instinctively what it must contain, and the knowledge did not serve to put me at my ease. I glanced at the floor, then wished I hadn't. Upon the debris-strewn base beneath the slab lay a ghastly, disarticulated group of mortuary remains – half-fleshed cadavers and desiccated skeletons. When I thought of my father and the others, I was possessed of a sickening dismay. They too had sought, and they had failed. And now I had come, alone, to find that which had brought them to an end unholy and unknown. The secret! The secret in the tomb!

Mad eagerness filled my soul. I too would know – I must! As in a dream I swayed to the gilded coffin. A moment I tottered above it; then, with a strength born of delirium, I tore away the paneling and lifted the gilded lid, and then I knew it was no dream, for dreams cannot approach the ultimate horror that was the creature lying within the coffin – that creature with eyes like a midnight demon's, and a face of loathsome delirium that was like the death-mask of a devil. It was smiling, too, as it lay there, and my soul shrieked in the tortured realization that it was alive! Then I knew it all; the secret and the penalty paid by those who sought it, and I was ready for death, but horrors had not ceased, for even as I gazed it spoke, in a voice like the hissing of a black slug.

And there within the nighted gloom it whispered the secret, staring at me with ageless, deathless eyes, so that I should not go mad before I heard the whole of it. All was revealed – the secret crypts of blackest nightmare where the tomb-spawn dwell, and of a price whereby a man may become one with the ghouls, living after death as a devourer in darkness. Such a thing had it become, and from this shunned, accursed tomb had sent the call to the descending generations, that when they came, there might be a ghastly feast whereby it might continue a dread, eternal life. I (it breathed) would be the next to die, and in my heart I knew that it was so.

I could not avert my eyes from its accursed gaze, nor free my soul from its hypnotic bondage. The thing on the bier cackled with unholy laughter. My blood froze, for I saw two long, lean arms, like the rotted limbs of a corpse, steal slowly toward my fear-constricted throat. The monster sat up, and even in the clutches of my horror, I realized that there was a dim and awful resemblance between the creature in the coffin and a certain ancient portrait back in the Hall. But this was a transfigured reality – Jeremy the man had become Jeremy the ghoul; and I knew that it would do no good to resist. Two claws, cold as flames of icy hell, fastened around my throat, two eyes bored like maggots through my frenzied being, a laughter born of madness alone cachinnated in my ears like the thunder of doom. The bony fingers tore at my eyes and nostrils, held me helpless while yellow fangs champed nearer and nearer to my throat. The world spun, wrapped in a mist of fiery death.

Suddenly the spell broke. I wrenched my eyes away from that slavering, evil face, and instantly, like a cataclysmic flash of light, came realization. This creature's power was purely mental – by that alone were my ill-fated kinsmen drawn here, and by that alone were they overcome, but once one were free from the strength of the monster's awful eyes – good God! Was I going to be the victim of a crumbled mummy?

My right arm swung up, striking the horror between the eyes. There was a sickening crunch; then dead flesh yielded before my hand as I seized the now faceless lich in my arms and cast it into fragments upon the bone-covered floor. Streaming with perspiration and mumbling in hysteria and terrible revulsion, I saw the moldy fragments move even in a second death – a severed hand crawled across the flagging, upon musty, shredded fingers; a leg began to roll with the animation of grotesque, unholy life. With a shriek, I cast a lighted match upon that loathsome corpse, and I was still shrieking as I clawed open the portals and rushed out of the tomb and into the world of sanity, leaving behind me a smoldering fire from whose charred heart a terrible voice still faintly moaned its tortured requiem to that which had once been Jeremy Strange.

The tomb is razed now, and with it the forest graves and all the hidden chambers and manuscripts that serve as a reminder of ghoul-ridden memories that can never be forgot. For earth hides a madness and dreams a hideous reality, and monstrous things abide in the shadows of death, lurking and waiting to seize the souls of those who meddle with forbidden things.

The Place of Revelation

Ramsey Campbell

AT DINNER Colin's parents do most of the talking. His mother starts by saying "Sit down," and as soon as he does his father says "Sit up." Auntie Dot lets Colin glimpse a sympathetic grin while Uncle Lucian gives him a secret one, neither of which helps him feel less nervous. They're eating off plates as expensive as the one he broke last time they visited, when his parents acted as if he'd meant to drop it even though the relatives insisted it didn't matter and at least his uncle thought so. "Delicious as always," his mother says when Auntie Dot asks yet again if Colin's food is all right, and his father offers "I expect he's just tired, Dorothy." At least that's an excuse, which Colin might welcome except it prompts his aunt to say "If you've had enough I should scamper off to bye-byes, Colin. For a treat you can leave us the washing up."

Everyone is waiting for him to go to his room. Even though his parents keep saying how well he does in English and how the art mistress said he should take up painting at secondary school, he's expected only to mumble agreement whenever he's told to speak up for himself. For the first time he tries arguing. "I'll do it. I don't mind."

"You've heard what's wanted," his father says in a voice that seems to weigh his mouth down.

"You catch up on your sleep," his mother says more gently, "then you'll be able to enjoy yourself tomorrow."

Beyond her Uncle Lucian is nodding eagerly, but nobody else sees. Everyone watches Colin trudge into the high wide hall. It offers him a light, and there's another above the stairs that smell of their new fat brown carpet, and one more in the upstairs corridor. They only put off the dark. Colin is taking time on each stair until his father lets him hear "Is he getting ready for bed yet?" For fear of having to explain his apprehensiveness he flees to the bathroom.

With its tiles white as a blizzard it's brighter than the hall, but its floral scent makes Colin feel it's only pretending to be a room. As he brushes his teeth the mirror shows him foaming at the mouth as though his nerves have given him a fit. When he heads for his room, the doorway opposite presents him with a view across his parents' bed of the hospital he can't help thinking is a front for the graveyard down the hill. It's lit up as pale as a tombstone, whereas his window that's edged with tendrils of frost is full of nothing but darkness, which he imagines rising massively from the fields to greet the black sky. Even if the curtains shut tight they wouldn't keep out his sense of it, nor does the flimsy furniture that's yellow as the wine they're drinking downstairs. He huddles under the plump quilt and leaves the light on while he listens to the kitchen clatter. All too soon it comes to an end, and he hears someone padding upstairs so softly they might almost not be there at all.

As the door inches open with a faint creak that puts him in mind of the lifting of a lid, he grabs the edge of the quilt and hauls it over his face. "You aren't asleep yet, then," his mother says. "I thought you might have drifted off."

Colin uncovers his face and bumps his shoulders against the bars behind the pillow. "I can't get to sleep, so can I come down?"

"No need for that, Colin. I expect you're trying too hard. Just think of nice times you've had and then you'll go off. You know there's nothing really to stop you."

She's making him feel so alone that he no longer cares if he gives away his secrets. "There is."

"Colin, you're not a baby any more. You didn't act like this when you were. Try not to upset people. Will you do that for us?"

"If you want."

She frowns at his reluctance. "I'm sure it's what you want as well. Just be as thoughtful as I know you are."

Everything she says reminds him how little she knows. She leans down to kiss each of his eyes shut, and as she straightens up, the cord above the bed turns the kisses into darkness with a click. Can he hold on to the feeling long enough to fall asleep? Once he hears the door close he burrows under the quilt and strives to be aware of nothing beyond the bed. He concentrates on the faint scent of the quilt that nestles on his face, he listens to the silence that the pillow and the quilt press against his ears. The weight of the quilt is beginning to feel vague and soft as sleep when the darkness whispers his name. "I'm asleep," he tries complaining, however babyish and stupid it sounds.

"Not yet, Colin," Uncle Lucian says. "Story first. You can't have forgotten."

He hasn't, of course. He remembers every bedtime story since the first, when he didn't know it would lead to the next day's walk. "I thought we'd have finished," he protests.

"Quietly, son. We don't want anyone disturbed, do we? One last story."

Colin wants to stay where he can't see and yet he wants to know. He inches the quilt down from his face. The gap between the curtains has admitted a sliver of moonlight that turns the edges of objects a glimmering white. A sketch of his uncle's face the colour of bone hovers by the bed. His smile glints, and his eyes shine like stars so distant they remind Colin how limitless the dark is. That's one reason why he blurts "Can't we just go wherever it is tomorrow?"

"You need to get ready while you're asleep. You should know that's how it works." As Uncle Lucian leans closer, the light tinges his gaunt face except where it's hollowed out with shadows, and Colin is reminded of the moon looming from behind a cloud. "Wait now, here's an idea," his uncle murmurs. "That ought to help."

Colin realises he would rather not ask "What?"

"Tell the stories back to me. You'll find someone to tell one day, you know. You'll be like me."

The prospect fails to appeal to Colin, who pleads "I'm too tired."

"They'll wake you up. Your mother was saying how good you are at stories. That's thanks to me and mine. Go on before anyone comes up and hears."

A cork pops downstairs, and Colin knows there's little chance of being interrupted. "I don't know what to say."

"I can't tell you that, Colin. They're your stories now. They're part of you. You've got to find your own way to tell them."

As Uncle Lucian's eyes glitter like ice Colin hears himself say "Once…"

"That's the spirit. That's how it has to start."

"Once there was a boy…"

"Called Colin. Sorry. You won't hear another breath out of me."

"Once there was a boy who went walking in the country on a day like it was today. The grass in the fields looked like feathers where all the birds in the world had been fighting, and all the fallen leaves were showing their bones. The sun was so low every crumb of frost had its own shadow, and his footprints had shadows in when he looked behind him, and walking felt like breaking little bones under his feet. The day was so cold he kept thinking the clouds were bits of ice that had cracked off the sky and dropped on the edge of the earth. The wind kept scratching his face and pulling the last few leaves off the trees, only if the leaves went back he knew they were birds. It was meant to be the shortest day, but it felt as if time had died because everything was too slippery or too empty for it to get hold of. So he thought he'd done everything there was to do and seen everything there was to see when he saw a hole like a gate through a hedge."

"That's the way." Uncle Lucian's eyes have begun to shine like fragments of the moon. "Make it your story."

"He wasn't sure if there was an old gate or the hedge had grown like one. He didn't know it was one of the places where the world is twisted. All he could see was more hedge at the sides of a bendy path. So he followed it round and round, and it felt like going inside a shell. Then he got dizzy with running to find the middle, because it seemed to take hours and the bends never got any smaller. But just when he was thinking he'd stop and turn back if the spiky hedges let him, he came to where the path led all round a pond that was covered with ice. Only the pond oughtn't to have been so big, all the path he'd run round should have squeezed it little. So he was walking round the pond to see if he could find the trick when the sun showed him the flat white faces everywhere under the ice.

"There were children and parents who'd come searching for them, and old people too. They were everyone the maze had brought to the pond, and they were all calling him. Their eyes were opening as slow as holes in the ice and growing too big, and their mouths were moving like fish mouths out of water, and the wind in the hedge was their cold rattly voice telling him he had to stay for ever, because he couldn't see the path away from the pond – there was just hedge everywhere he looked. Only then he heard his uncle's voice somewhere in it, telling him he had to walk back in all his footprints like a witch dancing backwards and then he'd be able to escape."

This is the part Colin likes least, but his uncle murmurs eagerly "And was he?"

"He thought he never could till he remembered what his footprints looked like. When he turned round he could just see them with the frost creeping to swallow them up. So he started walking back in them, and he heard the ice on the pond start to crack to let all the bodies with the turned-up faces climb out. He saw thin white fingers pushing the edge of the ice up and digging their nails into the frosty path. His footprints led him back through the gap the place had tried to stop him finding in the hedge, but he could see hands flopping out of the pond like frogs. He still had to walk all the way back to the gate like that, and every step he took the hedges tried to catch him, and he heard more ice being pushed up and people crawling after him. It felt like the place had got hold of his middle and his neck and screwed them round so far he'd never be able to walk forward again. He came out of the gate at last, and then he had to walk round the fields till it was nearly dark to get back into walking in an ordinary way so his mother and father wouldn't notice there was something new about him and want to know what he'd been doing."

Colin doesn't mind if that makes his uncle feel at least a little guilty, but Uncle Lucian says "What happens next?"

Colin hears his parents and his aunt forgetting to keep their voices low downstairs. He still can't make out what they're saying, though they must think he's asleep. "The next year he went walking in the woods," he can't avoid admitting.

"What kind of a day would that have been, I wonder?"

"Sunny. Full of birds and squirrels and butterflies. So hot he felt like he was wearing the sun on his head, and the only place he could take it off was the woods, because if he went back to the house his mother and father would say he ought to be out walking. So he'd gone a long way under the trees when he felt them change."

"He could now. Most people wouldn't until it was too late, but he felt…"

"Something had crept up behind him. He was under some trees that put their branches together like hands with hundreds of fingers praying. And when he looked he saw the trees he'd already gone under were exactly the same as the ones he still had to, like he was looking in a mirror except he couldn't see himself in it. So he started to run but as soon as he moved, the half of the tunnel of trees he had to go through began to stretch itself till he couldn't see the far end, and when he looked behind him it had happened there as well."

"He knew what to do this time, didn't he? He hardly even needed to be told."

"He had to go forwards walking backwards and never look to see what was behind him. And as soon as he did he saw the way he'd come start to shrink. Only that wasn't all he saw, because leaves started running up and down the trees, except they weren't leaves. They were insects pretending to be them, or maybe they weren't insects. He could hear them scuttling about behind him, and he was afraid the way he had to go wasn't shrinking, it was growing as much longer as the way he'd come was getting shorter. Then all the scuttling things ran onto the branches over his head, and he thought they'd fall on him if he didn't stop trying to escape. But his body kept moving even though he wished it wouldn't, and he heard a great flapping as if he was in a cave and bats were flying off the roof, and then something landed on his head. It was just the sunlight, and he'd come out of the woods the same place he'd gone in. All the way back he felt he was walking away from the house, and his mother said he'd got a bit of sunstroke."

"He never told her otherwise, did he? He knew most people aren't ready to know what's behind the world."

"That's what his uncle kept telling him."

"He was proud to be chosen, wasn't he? He must have known it's the greatest privilege to be shown the old secrets."

Colin has begun to wish he could stop talking about himself as though he's someone else, but the tales won't let go of him – they've closed around him like the dark. "What was his next adventure?" it whispers with his uncle's moonlit smiling mouth.

"The next year his uncle took him walking in an older wood. Even his mother and father might have noticed there was something wrong with it and told him not to go in far." When his uncle doesn't acknowledge any criticism but only smiles wider and more whitely Colin has to add "There was nothing except sun in the sky, but as soon as you went in the woods you had to step on shadows everywhere, and that was the only way you knew there was still a sun. And the day was so still it felt like the woods were pretending they never breathed, but the shadows kept moving whenever he wasn't looking – he kept nearly seeing very tall ones hide behind the trees. So he wanted to get through the woods as fast as he could, and that's why he ran straight onto the stepping stones when he came to a stream."

Colin would like to run fast through the story too, but his uncle wants to know "How many stones were there again?"

"Ten, and they looked so close together he didn't have to stretch to walk. Only he was on the middle two when he felt them start to move. And when he looked down he saw the stream was really as deep as the sky, and lying on the bottom was a giant made out of rocks and moss that was holding up its arms to him. They were longer than he didn't know how many trees stuck together, and their hands were as big as the roots of an old tree, and he was standing on top of two of the fingers. Then the giant's eyes began to open like boulders rolling about in the mud, and its mouth opened like a cave and sent up a laugh in a bubble that spattered the boy with mud, and the stones he was on started to move apart."

"His uncle was always with him though, wasn't he?"

"The boy couldn't see him," Colin says in case this lets his uncle realise how it felt, and then he knows his uncle already did. "He heard him saying you mustn't look down, because being seen was what woke up the god of the wood. So the boy kept looking straight ahead, though he could see the shadows that weren't shadows crowding behind the trees to wait for him. He could feel how even the water underneath him wanted him to slip on the slimy stones, and how the stones were ready to swim apart so he'd fall between them if he caught the smallest glimpse of them. Then he did, and the one he was standing on sank deep into the water, but he'd jumped on the bank of the stream. The shadows that must have been the bits that were left of people who'd looked down too long let him see his uncle, and they walked to the other side of the woods. Maybe he wouldn't have got there without his uncle, because the shadows kept dancing around them to make them think there was no way between the trees."

"Brave boy, to see all that." Darkness has reclaimed the left side of Uncle Lucian's face; Colin is reminded of a moon that the night is squeezing out of shape. "Don't stop now, Colin," his uncle says. "Remember last year."

This is taking longer than his bedtime stories ever have. Colin feels as if the versions he's reciting may rob him of his whole night's sleep. Downstairs his parents and his aunt sound as if they need to talk for hours yet. "It was here in town," he says accusingly. "It was down in Lower Brichester."

He wants to communicate how betrayed he felt, by the city or his uncle or by both. He'd thought houses and people would keep away the old things, but now he knows that nobody who can't see can help. "It was where the boy's mother and father wouldn't have liked him to go," he says, but that simply makes him feel the way his uncle's stories do, frightened and excited and unable to separate the feelings. "Half the houses were shut up with boards but people were still using them, and there were men and ladies on the corners of the streets waiting for whoever wanted them or stuff they were selling. And in the middle of it all there were railway lines and passages to walk under them. Only the people who lived round there must have felt something, because there was one passage nobody walked through."

"But the boy did."

"A man sitting drinking with his legs in the road told him not to, but he did. His uncle went through another passage and said he'd meet him on the other side. Anyone could have seen something was wrong with the tunnel, because people had dropped needles all over the place except in there. But it looked like it'd just be a minute to walk through, less if you ran. So the boy started to hurry through, only he tried to be quiet because he didn't like how his feet made so much noise he kept thinking someone was following him, except it sounded more like lots of fingers tapping on the bricks behind him. When he managed to be quiet the noise didn't all go away, but he tried to think it was water dripping, because he felt it cold and wet on the top of his head. Then more of it touched the back of his neck, but he didn't want to look round, because the passage was getting darker behind him. He was in the middle of the tunnel when the cold touch landed on his face and made him look."

His uncle's face is barely outlined, but his eyes take on an extra gleam. "And when he looked…"

"He saw why the passage was so dark, with all the arms as thin as his poking out of the bricks. They could grow long enough to reach halfway down the passage and grope around till they found him with their fingers that were as wet as worms. Then he couldn't even see them, because the half of the passage he had to walk through was filling up with arms as well, so many he couldn't see out. And all he could do was what his uncle's story had said, stay absolutely still, because if he tried to run the hands would grab him and drag him through the walls into the earth, and he wouldn't even be able to die of how they did it. So he shut his eyes to be as blind as the things with the arms were, that's if there wasn't just one thing behind the walls. And after he nearly forgot how to breathe the hands stopped pawing at his head as if they were feeling how his brain showed him everything about them, maybe even brought them because he'd learned to see the old things. When he opened his eyes the arms were worming back into the walls, but he felt them all around him right to the end of the passage. And when he went outside he couldn't believe in the daylight any more. It was like a picture someone had put up to hide the dark."

"He could believe in his uncle though, couldn't he? He saw his uncle waiting for him and telling him well done. I hope he knew how much his uncle thought of him."

"Maybe."

"Well, now it's another year."

Uncle Lucian's voice is so low, and his face is so nearly invisible, that Colin isn't sure whether his words are meant to be comforting or to warn the boy that there's more. "Another story," Colin mumbles, inviting it or simply giving in.

"I don't think so any more. I think you're too old for that."

Colin doesn't know in what way he feels abandoned as he whispers "Have we finished?"

"Nothing like. Tomorrow, just go and lie down and look up."

"Where?"

"Anywhere you're by yourself."

Colin feels he is now. "Then what?" he pleads.

"You'll see. I can't begin to tell you. See for yourself."

That makes Colin more nervous than his uncle's stories ever did. He's struggling to think how to persuade his uncle to give him at least a hint when he realises he's alone in the darkness. He lies on his back and stares upwards in case that gets whatever has to happen over with, but all he sees are memories of the places his uncle has made him recall. Downstairs his parents and his aunt are still talking, and he attempts to use their voices to keep him with them, but feels as if they're dragging him down into the moonless dark. Then he's been asleep, because they're shutting their doors close to his. After that, whenever he twitches awake it's a little less dark. As soon as he's able to see he sneaks out of bed to avoid his parents and his aunt. Whatever is imminent, having to lie about where he's going would make his nerves feel even more like rusty wire about to snap.

He's as quick and as quiet in the bathroom as he can be. Once he's dressed he rolls up the quilt to lie on and slips out of the house. In the front garden he thinks moonlight has left a crust on the fallen leaves and the grass. Down the hill a train shakes itself awake while the city mutters in its sleep. He turns away and heads for the open country behind the house.

A few crows jab at the earth with their beaks and sail up as if they mean to peck the icy sky. The ground has turned into a single flattened greenish bone exactly as bright as the low vault of dull cloud. Colin walks until the fields bear the houses out of sight. That's as alone as he's likely to be. Flapping the quilt, he spreads it on the frozen ground. He throws himself on top of it and slaps his hands on it in case that starts whatever's meant to happen. He's already so cold he can't keep still.

At first he thinks that's the only reason he's shivering, and then he notices the sky isn't right. He feels as if all the stories he's had to act out have gathered in his head, or the way they've made him see has. That ability is letting him observe how thin the sky is growing, or perhaps it's leaving him unable not to. Is it also attracting whatever's looming down to peer at him from behind the sky? A shiver is drumming his heels on the ground through the quilt when the sky seems to vanish as though it has been clawed apart above him, and he glimpses as much of a face as there's room for – an eye like a sea black as space with a moon for its pupil. It seems indifferent as death and yet it's watching him. An instant of seeing is all he can take before he twists onto his front and presses his face into the quilt as though it's a magic carpet that will transport him home to bed and, better still, unconsciousness.

He digs his fingers into the quilt until he recognises he can't burrow into the earth. He stops for fear of tearing his aunt's quilt and having to explain. He straightens up in a crouch to retrieve the quilt, which he hugs as he stumbles back across the field with his head down. The sky is pretending that it never faltered, but all the way to the house he's afraid it will part to expose more of a face.

While nobody is up yet, Colin senses that his uncle isn't in the house. He tiptoes upstairs to leave the quilt on his bed, and then he sends himself out again. There's no sign of his uncle on the way downhill. Colin dodges onto the path under the trees in case his uncle prefers not to be seen. "Uncle Lucian," he pleads.

"You found me."

He doesn't seem especially pleased, but Colin demands "What did I see?"

"Not much yet. Just as much as your mind could take. It's like our stories, do you understand? Your mind had to tell you a story about what you saw, but in time you won't need it. You'll see what's really there."

"Suppose I don't want to?" Colin blurts. "What's it all for?"

"Would you rather be like my sister and only see what everyone else sees? She was no fun when she was your age, your mother."

"I never had the choice."

"Well, I wouldn't ever have said that to my grandfather. I was nothing but grateful to him."

Though his uncle sounds not merely disappointed but offended, Colin says "Can't I stop now?"

"Everything will know you can see, son. If you don't greet the old things where you find them they'll come to find you."

Colin voices a last hope. "Has it stopped for you?"

"It never will. I'm part of it now. Do you want to see?"

"No."

Presumably Colin's cry offends his uncle, because there's a spidery rustle beyond the trees that conceal the end of the path and then silence. Time passes before Colin dares to venture forward. As he steps from beneath the trees he feels as if the sky has lowered itself towards him like a mask. He's almost blind with resentment of his uncle for making him aware of so much and for leaving him alone, afraid to see even Uncle Lucian. Though it doesn't help, Colin starts kicking the stone with his uncle's name on it and the pair of years ending with this one. When he's exhausted he turns away towards the rest of his life.

Flotsam

Daniel Carpenter

THE ARRIVAL

No one could recall the storm though it is true to say that a storm had passed. The evidence was there, carried in a calm wind and the smudged grey sky like a poorly erased mistake in pencil. A curious amount of detritus had blown through the town also: a single bloodied shoe, a small doll with too many limbs to be human, a rusted bayonet (perhaps not rust, but rather ancient blood instead). Amongst the artefacts was discovered an iron helmet cleaved in two, its jagged edges cauterised and blackened.

The creature had arrived during the storm. It had erupted from the depths of the ocean, fatally wounded and had hauled itself on to the pebbled beach where it had gasped a final, inhuman breath and died, leaving behind a trail of its blood, thicker than oil, which traced its path from the ocean and spooled around in a whirlpool from where it had originated.

What the creature looked like

There was never a consensus in the town on precisely what the creature looked like. The things that most agreed on – thick black tentacles, no eyes, a ridge of spine-like hair across its back – were refuted by others who saw bright colours, scales and too many eyes. The children in the village were not scared of it, not like some of us adults. They would freely walk close by and play around it. Sometimes building it a home out of sand, or redirecting the route of the tide to create a protective moat around the thing. What did they see when they looked at it? Something friendly, or perhaps something so monstrous it could not be processed by childlike minds.

For some of us, just looking at the creature brought upon terrible headaches almost instantly. So painful that they caused bright colours to dance across your eyes. At night, those who had seen the creature dreamt dreadful things, waking up in a cold sweat, practically feverish. It would pass quickly, and after that you learned to look away.

There were a select few though, whom the creature did not appear to affect. Mrs. Bradley was the most prominent, though she was always like that at any event in the village. Mrs. Bradley made the best cakes for the school fundraiser, she won village garden of the year, and she grew the biggest cauliflowers around. Everyone knew Mrs. Bradley, or rather, everyone had to know Mrs. Bradley, and it was as though that piece of village lore had passed on subconsciously to the creature itself. When she approached it on that first day, whilst the rest of us staggered back from the pain in our heads, she was unaffected. She touched it. Stroked it. I saw an oily black residue coat her hand, dripping onto the pebbles below.

She said, "It has been brought here for a reason, and we must devour it." The way she muttered it to herself, like an affirmation.

Mrs. Bradley argues her case

There was some debate at first. Most of the village gathered in the Scout hut by the creek, squashed in to the space. It felt clandestine. As though we were hiding from this dead thing on the beach. The local councillor, Mr. Peabody, was angry that this meeting even had to be called in the first place. Why should we, on Mrs. Bradley's say-so, eat the creature that had washed up from some unknown place? There were stories, Brian Hargreaves the butcher said, about fish who were caught, cooked and eaten, who contained within them immense poisons. Did Mrs. Bradley wish to kill us all?

The thing should rot, claimed several people. It should be left there to rot and die. Maybe then the headaches and dreams would end. It should be forgotten about. We should not speak of it again. Cast it into history.

But Mrs. Bradley was adamant. 'It has come here for a reason. You all fear it and look how it treats you. I don't fear it. I admire it.'

Then, someone suggested, if Mrs. Bradley is so keen to eat the creature, would she be willing to be the first to consume it?

She would do it gladly. She would be so proud to be the first.

What did people dream when they saw the creature?

The cosmos, spiralling out and out and out, *ad infinitum*. Sparks of life exploding in interstellar clusters. A feeling of dread, of sinking into nothing. Facts and knowledge that you cannot understand and so they sit at the edge of your mind, on the tip of your tongue, waiting just out of reach for you. And then, the inhuman screams of something vast, echoing across the universe, touching signals from asteroids and moons like radar. It is a scream without emotion, but it instils a kind of fear within you which you have never felt before in your life. Louder than anything you have ever heard. How small you feel. How insignificant. How utterly pointless.

How many could touch the creature?

At first just three: Mrs. Bradley, Ms. Hobson the baker, and Mr. Stoakley the farmer. Just three to begin with, although over time, there were more.

Mrs. Bradley eats the first piece

She didn't cook it. She ate the thing raw.

After it was agreed that she would be the first to eat the creature, she retrieved a carving knife from her kitchen and made her way to the beach. Some of the villagers followed her, despite the onslaught of pain from the creature. They watched as she took the knife to the creature, slicing a small piece of one tentacle. It came away gently, slipping from the rest of the body and splattering into the bucket Mrs. Bradley had prepared for it. A little oily black blood dribbled from the wound.

Do any of the people who were present recall the creature shifting and twitching when she cut into it? No.

Mrs. Bradley took the bucket and sat on the edge of the seafront, looking out across the horizon. The trail of blood still floated on top of the water like a scar. She plunged her hand into the bucket and took out the piece of the creature. Almost immediately she tore into it with her teeth, ripping its flesh apart. The oily black substance staining her mouth and chin, dripping down onto her clothes. She smiled when she ate it. She smiled like she had never smiled before.

When did Mrs. Bradley die?

At 142. She lived the longest.

Another meeting called

No ill effects were observed of Mrs. Bradley, who continued her day to day life in the usual manner. Her vegetables grew large and impressive and she tended to her garden obsessively. However, there did appear to be a marked change in how she moved, how she carried herself. It was as if she floated, or knew some piece of impossible information. Everyone saw that change in her. Everyone wanted a part of it. It was the creature that did it. Eating a piece of it had given her a kind of revelation and why should the rest of the village not be privy to the same thing?

Mr. Peabody brought the meeting to order, but almost immediately Mr. Stoakley interrupted him. Mrs. Bradley had been permitted to eat the creature. Mrs. Bradley had seen something. Why shouldn't the rest of us get the chance?

Not all of us felt the pull of the creature. Not at this time. But after Mrs. Bradley ate the tentacle there were more who could look upon it without experiencing terrible pain. Fewer dreamers, screaming in the night.

It was decided that each man and woman would make their own choice. If they wished to eat the creature then they may do so, providing they took only a slice. If they wished to leave it be, then so be it.

The questions nobody asked

Where did the creature come from?

What kind of storm leaves a trace, but cannot be recalled?

What kind of creature wants to be consumed?

A queue forms

They brought their knives from home, scythes from the wheat fields, Stanley knives shining red in the sun from the pockets of their Scout leader uniforms. They didn't surround the creature and tear it apart. No, they formed a queue, winding its way up the beach, straggling the wall at the back, and flowing up the steps to the promenade. It snaked past the fish and chip shop on the corner, passing the B&B and up towards the high street. Mrs. Bradley paraded up and down, shaking everyone's hands. She didn't say anything, didn't have to. It was all in her eyes. Welcome, her eyes said. The first day of the mass consumption of the creature was a glorious day.

The holdouts notice a change

It was not immediately apparent. Life continued as normal. There were a few hundred or so who chose to abstain from eating the creature. Walking down the promenade, their heads throbbed and they couldn't help but turn to look at the corpse lying on the beach, slices of flesh missing, so that it resembled something even more alien that it had previously. It was not just in its fractured body that they saw a difference. There was an emptiness to the town.

In their nightmares they saw the villagers who took part in the eating. The oily blood from the creature cascading from their mouths. Not just that thick black, viscous liquid but the pieces of the creature itself, slipping from their mouths, regurgitating itself. The pieces came together in the middle of a supernova of light.

When spoken to, the villagers who ate the creature were cordial. They took part in small talk and asked questions about family members: How is Uncle John? Did little Sally get her silver in swimming? Is the kitchen going to be finished by Easter? But to the holdouts there was something missing. It felt like a performance.

It drove them away, one by one.

What of the detritus?
After the storm, the bayonet, shoe, doll and helmet were all taken to the library immediately to be photographed and retained for historical record. They remained there during the consumption. No photographs were ever taken and as with all things, no record was made. Instead, they were locked away. The relationship between these objects was never discussed or considered, and the whereabouts of the other shoe in the pair (a right) was not pondered.

They touch the creature
They stood around it one morning, all of those who had eaten a part of the creature. The remaining villagers who hadn't tasted the innards of the thing on the beach caught sight of it on their way to work, or on the school run. Hundreds of them surrounding the corpse, hand in hand. Mrs. Bradley right there and though the circle did not have a start or end point it seemed as though she was at the head of it. The day was quiet, no cars rumbling along the high street, no clinking of empty milk bottles being picked up. All that could be heard was the calm slosh of the tide, and the odd hollowness of pebbles shifting beneath feet.

Somewhere in the distance, across the horizon and far from the eyes of the villagers, a ship's horn rumbled in the air. Those watching the group encircling the creature turned to look for the source of the sound. Those with their hands clasped did not move.

It was as though they moved closer towards the creature, closing in on it. But they did not move so that couldn't be true. It was just as likely to suggest that the creature, dead as it was, expanded to fit the space created by the circle of hands. That it fattened itself. What remained of its skin rippled around it, following the ring of consumers. The people surrounding it shuddered momentarily as though being caught off guard whilst standing on a moving train, then righted themselves and offered no further movement. All save Mrs. Bradley. Her face, an assiduous look of concentration, but for the glimmer of a smile, for just a moment.

The creature expanded to touch each of the people, pushing itself against them, bulging out through the gaps between their hands, the spaces below and above their arms. One lone tentacle escaped between someone's legs, then whipped itself back into the fray just as quickly.

Those who had not consumed a part of the creature fought the vicious headaches they experienced, some practically blinded by the pain. They fought so they can watch. They felt a need to witness this that had nothing to do with its strangeness. This appeared strange to no one. No, this felt wholly expected.

What did Mrs. Bradley die of?
Unknown causes. She was cold to the touch, and stiff as a bone. No blood was discovered either outside her body nor within it. Though a tiny patch of oil close to her body was noted in the coroners report.

Inside the circle
It breathed its first in an age, taking in one or two primitive minds and expelling the scraps back out into their bodies. There they were: pieces of it, inside them all. Digested and absorbed into skin and fat and blood. There was a piece of it careening around, hidden in some minuscule vein. Another breath. The sweet taste of a soul. Memories flooded through it. Unknowable things. A party by a river, the wind picking up a tablecloth. A sudden rush indoors at the first sparks of rain. It searched within for something more filling. There: a horrible thought, an anxious woman pacing in the corridor of a hospital. The news will

be bad. She knows it will. That would do. It released what it hadn't devoured, broken and piecemeal though it was. All the while it grew, found strength that it forgot it had.

The library is opened

Mr. Peabody ran from the events on the beach. He knew each and every one of the people in that circle and he watched briefly as they shuddered and lost themselves to the creature. There were shards of glass in his head, scratching at his mind. A pain like no other he had ever felt in his life. Turning tail he abandoned them to the thing that had washed up. What had happened to his town? He thought back to the day after the storm that he could not recall, when the creature appeared. His head splintered as though a bullet had pierced it. A pain that stopped him dead in his tracks.

But he recalled the detritus that washed up in the town the same night. Recalled where it was being stored.

Mr. Peabody ran.

The streets were empty. Everyone was at the beach. Those who didn't eat, watching, those who ate participating. Mr. Peabody raced down the high street, passing open stores with no workers, dogs tied to lamp-posts, barking for owners who are far from them. From inside The Railway Arms he caught the sound of a football game being watched by no one, and heard the trickling of a tap still running. But he did not stop. He felt a burning racing across his chest, tightening his veins. Like whatever kept him running was seeping from him, being devoured piece by piece. The library could not be far.

Glass scattered on the floor when he broke the window. He found himself surprised by it. Not the act of destruction so much as the evidence left behind. Did I do that? he found himself asking as he clambered through the gap into the library.

The crowd attempts to watch

The pebbles all around the circle shifted, as though being trodden on. Pain cascaded through all of the non-eaters though they could not look away. The thing that had washed up on their shores roared in their minds. All of them. A terrible indecipherable speech that tore through them. Some were knocked to the floor, others staggered back. One or two stood their ground. No one dared get close to the events taking place at the shoreline. Those who formed the circle clutched each other's hands, but their bodies appeared limp. All except for Mrs. Bradley. Mrs. Bradley's smile was as terrible as the creature itself. She stared right at the creature. Smiling. What was the creature saying to them? What was it saying to her? Whatever it was, to those watching, it felt like the end of all things.

A bayonet, a doll, a helmet, and a shoe

They were hers once. Torn from her as she dragged the thing into the rift. The doll she had been given by her mother, so many years ago. So long that she couldn't even recall it not being in her life. It was apt then that in that moment she would lose it.

On the beach

Mr. Peabody sprinted towards the circle. The closer he got to the creature the more the pain in his head intensified. Pain unlike anything he had ever experienced. As though his brain was pouring out through his ears. But it wouldn't stop him. Brandishing the bayonet, he ran forward towards the eaters. The creature, a writhing mass, was a negative space in front of him, an absence of light. It had nearly engulfed all of the circle now, close to breaking free. Where a part of it had been eaten, it was regrown, the wounds zipped together and closed. Tentacles sneaked around the area, combing the beach, lifting pebbles. A screaming sounded in his ears and Mr. Peabody understood what it was. The creature was laughing. Laughing at his attempts to do what he was trying to do. No matter. He reached the edge of the circle and, raising the bayonet above his head, he leapt forward, toward the screaming thing.

Mr. Peabody falls

The bayonet stuck in the creature and Mr. Peabody fell. He clutched the doll in his hand, but his hand was weak and he could not hold on to it much longer. The creature screamed again and he thought, "It's in my head, and how much more of this can I take?" But it was not in his head this time. A great shockwave passed through the circle, breaking clasped hands, showering the promenade with pebbles, and washing the tide out. Mr. Peabody felt a wetness against his cheek and he touched it, bringing back a handful of blood. The doll is a curious thing, he thought. So many arms.

So many arms.

Mrs. Bradley wishes for death

At 142, don't we all? She felt a change after the creature left. A rushing of something inside of her. None of the other eaters experienced it. She understood in that moment that it was because she was the first. She was trusted and she had been gifted something. The others, they became husks. Something had been taken from all of them. Mr. Stoakley went back to running his farm, but he could never keep an animal alive for more than a couple of months. He could be seen sometimes, standing on the beach, weeping. Others who had been in that circle could be seen there sometimes too. Mr. Hobson often went there and walked across the shore, picking up pebbles and checking under them. Mrs. Bradley felt none of this, except that deep within her there was a terrible longing. She didn't go back to the beach, not for any of the many decades she remained in the village. The children who saw her named her Grandma Ankou and crossed the road to avoid her, lest she drag them to hell with her at night. It was curious as to how the stories they told about her took something from her each time she heard them. As though the children were carving little pieces of her, and eating them raw.

The Things from the Woods

Micah Castle

WONDERFUL, *she's asleep.*

Kelly left Megan, hands resting on her pregnant belly, on the couch by the blazing fireplace. She walked into the kitchen, her scrubs swishing, to fill the kettle, but found the kettle's insides caked with dirt and reeking of burnt leaves.

Never mind. .

As she set the kettle back into the sink, she peered out the small window. It was raining, and the pine woods bordering Megan's property seemed oily under the dim morning light.

She left the kitchen, checked that she was still asleep, and went into Megan's study. Although Kelly was her caretaker and home health nurse, it still felt strange walking through her home, as though she was trespassing. It was uncomfortable, but Megan's home was her home, and she wasn't forbidden anywhere.

The dusty shelves along the western wall brimmed with old books, and a deep red, cushioned chair was tucked behind the small darkwood desk in the opposite corner. A rounded bay window loomed behind the desk, letting in pale light. When Kelly learned that Megan was a librarian, she expected her personal library to be extravagant, like in the movies, but her study was nothing crazy. It was cozy, charming.

Kelly sat into the chair and leaned back, letting the cushions mold to her frame. She raised her legs to stretch her feet, but raised them too fast, too high, and kicked the desk's underside.

Something snapped, fell with a slap.

"Shit," she spat, sitting up, looking under the desk. A thin black book with a long piece of tape stuck underneath it, was on the floor. There were no words on the cover or back, and it was soft to the touch.

She stole a glance at the doorway – empty – and set the book onto the desk, and carefully flipped through the yellowed pages. Pressed pinecones, pine needles, and leaves were throughout, and the journal – for that's what it was – had the faint, ripe aroma of damp wood.

She turned to the first page.

The faded date on the top right was water stained, but she could make out the day and year.

* * *

…/20/98

I don't want to linger too much on Christopher. Although he was my husband, I rather not think of him. For my sanity's sake, I'll keep it short and sweet, like our marriage. It doesn't matter how we met or how we started dating or when we got married; all that matters is that we did and it came crumbling down when we tried for a child and failed. He supported me as I was thrown through a battery of humiliating, painful tests to determine if I was a *true* woman…

Apparently, I wasn't.

I was infertile. What parts I had didn't work as intended. Oh, Christopher said it didn't matter – we could adopt – but I saw in his big blue eyes that it did, *a lot*. And, I was right, for divorce came soon after.

He was generous, even then. He willingly gave me quite a bit of his money in the divorce – I never asked for a cent – and I assume it was out of guilt or empathy. There was enough to buy this home, bordering the sprawling evergreen woods.

That's the only thing Christopher and I truly bonded together over. The love of nature, the enriching smells and beautiful sights of forestry experienced through hikes (when we weren't stressing over our futile attempts at a child, or what the doctor would inevitably say...). If it weren't for him, I wouldn't be here, in this study, near these woods. If it weren't for him, I don't know where I'd be.

.../21/98

My morning jaunt before work was strange. Not because I decided to travel deeper into the woods than typical, wondering how far they stretched or what possible wonders I might find, but because I met someone. An old woman sat against one of the largest pine trees I've ever seen.

She wore a tattered brown cloak that looked like the tree bark. It seemed to meld into the tree itself. She looked sick – pale, hollow cheeks, black bags beneath yellow-green eyes – so I asked: "Are you all right?"

"I'm fine," she said, "just fine. Don't worry about me, dear."

"Are you lost?" I said, nearing her.

She shook her head, laughing. "No, no, never lost." She waved her gnarled hand towards the woods behind her. "I live quite close."

I wanted to ask if she owned the land, that maybe I was trespassing, but I didn't want to bother her with more questions.

"Do you live near these lovely woods, too, dear?" she said.

I nodded. "Just moved in recently, about a month or two ago."

"All alone, or is there someone waiting for your return?" She looked into my face.

"Yes, I'm alone," I said.

"By choice?"

"Not entirely, no." I wasn't sure why I answered, but the old woman had a welcoming allure; comfortable, relaxing, like speaking to my grandmother.

"Are you with child, dear?"

I bit my lower lip and felt tears coming. I shook my head. "No, I'm not."

"Oh, I'm sorry, dear – didn't mean to summon an awful memory." She leaned her head back, looking at the skeletal branches above. Her eyes widened, the yellow-green irises spreading over scleras. I hadn't noticed before but her pupils were broken apart, as though dozens of yellow-green veins spread throughout them. "You know, all women can be with child, dear. If they find the right seed, that is."

I laughed. "That's difficult, even in this day in age."

The old woman faced me, eyes still wide. "Not at all, not at all." She shoved her hand beneath her clothes, rummaged inside it, then pulled her hand out, opening it. Tiny, gray-blue berries, dried, thin twigs, shards of dark bark and crumbled leaves were in a pile in her shallow palm. She raised them towards me.

"If you consume these, dear, life anew will form within, nine months thereafter."

She was mad, certainly, but I didn't want to seem rude. She was an old woman of the woods. That might be me one day. So, I took them and put them in my jacket pocket. After I thanked her, I said, "I must be off. Nice meeting you."

"You, too, dear; you, too," she said.

Then, I made my way back home. I hadn't strayed too far, though it felt like I had when I left.

Once inside and in the kitchen, I took a mason jar from the cabinet, put the things from the woods into it, and set it sealed on the windowsill above the sink. Afterwards, I took a shower, quickly ate a sandwich, and left for work.

.../18/99

It has been a while journal, hasn't it? Six months, it seems. Not much has happened, yet things are changing. I met a man – John – two months ago at the library. He's handsome with brown hair that matches the color of his eyes, and he enjoys Blackwood and Poe. He's not too tall, but taller than me, and he's not much for nature, unfortunately. Besides that, we're doing well; we're even going to a bookstore a town over for a reading by King tomorrow night.

That's not the only change that's happened.

Recall the old woman, the things she gave me?

I hadn't until this afternoon, as I filled the kettle. It was as though they were never there on the windowsill until that moment. Dust covered the copper top, but the gray-blue berries, twigs, and so forth still looked as new as when I acquired them. As the water poured from the faucet, I became lost in thought, remembering the way the old woman appeared as though she was an extension of the giant tree, how her yellow-green eyes had dozens of pupils, how the woods smelled after rainfall, what she said: "*...life anew will form within, nine months thereafter*"—

Water flowed over the kettle's rim and soaked my sweater sleeve. I cursed and emptied the kettle a little, capped it and placed it onto the stove, turning on the burner.

I looked at the jar once more.

I didn't believe what she said could be true. It was nonsense. It wasn't reasonable or logical. Things from the woods couldn't get a woman pregnant, or help in the process, no matter what they were or how many she took. A woman requires a man in some form or another. But, I was curious, hesitant, indecisive, believing steadily I was growing as mad as the old woman. Still... My mind filled with ideas on how to prepare it: crushing it into a powder, mixing it into a drink; breaking it up and putting it in a stew or soup or oatmeal... Even though I had no intention to do so, I chose the first option: breaking it down into a fine powder.

Mad, mad, mad, I was – am.

The kettle began whistling. I made my tea, and went into the study.

.../25/99

I couldn't ignore it any longer. It had only been a week but it felt like months. I kept peering at the jar when I went into the kitchen, thinking about it when I was at the library, even had a dream about an enormous mason jar while berries and twigs rained down from above.

I gave in and bought a mortar and pestle on the way home from work. I emptied the jar into the mortar and ground them with the pestle until they were nothing more than a blue-tinged, gray and brown powder.

While the kettle boiled, I poured the powder into a mug, and added plenty of honey. I took a bag of vanilla tea out from the cabinet.

I removed the whistling kettle from the burner, poured water into the mug, stirred it until the powder and honey vanished, and slid the tea in. I let it steep for a couple extra minutes, removed the bag, and when it cooled, brought it to my lips.

I hesitated, as though I was about to drink poison. I shook my head – I was being stupid – and took a sip. Nothing but vanilla and honey. Relief washed over me. I took another sip; nothing, again, not even an aftertaste. I brought the tea with me into the study, where I reside now.

By bedtime, the cup will be empty.

…/28/99

I hadn't called in sick for years, yet on the 26th I was in the worst pain I've ever felt. Sharp, prickly burning pangs exploding in my stomach and groin. It felt like someone was prodding my insides with pine branches, twisting them deep into my muscle. Exhausted and sweaty, I remained in bed all day with an ice pack on my belly, drinking cold water and peppermint tea. I tried to eat – vomited – then tried something lighter like soup, but again; vomited. The pain was so immense I couldn't read either, for I couldn't stop crying.

The next day, the pain subsided a little. It no longer burned, but the sharp, prickly pangs remained. I still couldn't keep anything down but water and tea.

Today, oh! how amazing I feel compared to the last two days. I woke up without any pain and my hunger was ravenous, but no matter what I ate, I still puked. To help settle my stomach and mind, I took a stroll into the woods. The pinecones crunched and twigs snapped underfoot. The cool smell of dewy pine lingered in the air, tingling my nostrils. An owl hooted from somewhere; birds chirped; chipmunks scurried through damp underbrush.

The deeper I traveled, the more my mouth watered and stomach groaned. I stopped in front of a tree and… God, I find it difficult to even write… I touched the coarse, sharp bark, prodded it as though it were flesh. I snapped a piece off and rubbed it with my thumb. Saliva gathered in my mouth, and my stomach grumbled. Awkwardly, I kissed it, at first… Licked it… Waves of intense heat, of pleasure, washed over me. I couldn't resist it any longer.

I took a bite of the bark and chewed, and it was like eating the most delicious chocolate that ever existed. It tasted better than anything I've ever known. It was beyond taste. It felt *right* in my mouth. It felt *right* inside me, as though it were a piece of my body I never knew I was missing. I swallowed, tasting heaven, and my body screamed for more. I snapped pinecones in two, broke twigs in half, took handfuls of wet leaves and earth and I crunched, chomped, devoured. Lightheadedness overwhelmed me, stomach bulging, and my knees became weak. I gripped the tree I had stripped of bark, closed my eyes, and waited for the vertigo to pass.

When it did, I returned home, brushed my teeth, got my car keys, and went to the drug store.

It's impossible. It can't be. I haven't shared a bed with anyone since Christopher. Not even John. Yet, it makes sense, sitting here, the positive test before me and recalling what happened in the woods.

Strange cravings are normal for pregnant women.

I'm excited and terrified; delighted and horrified. I'm a vat of enigmatic emotions, and it's a surprise that I can even keep this pen straight with how much my hand trembles.

What am I going to do?

It's what I've always wanted, but… *alone?*

I must call John, must make sense of this all. I won't tell him what I am, but I will invite him over. We'll make love. Make it seem normal, make it *be* normal. Though I've only dated him for a little while, he seems open to help me and, perhaps, be a father.

Regardless, I still can't understand *how* I am… I just can't.

...*/31/99*

Another two months. I haven't had the chance to write. Since admitting to John about the pregnancy, he has been over nearly every day. He has leapt into fatherhood head first: borrowing parenting and baby books from the library, lotioning my feet, running me baths (though I don't take them), and spending ample time with me in and out of the bedroom. He's tried to feed me special foods and drinks that are meant to help with baby growth, but I puke them back up. I only crave a few things, which I keep in the kitchen.

They must've bothered him for quite some time... Yesterday was the breaking point, it seems. We sat at the kitchen table, and he brought up my eating habits: how strange it was for me to store jars of twigs, leaves, bark, gray-blue berries, pinecones and pine needles. It was not only the storage that bothered him, but how I ate bark and twigs like candy, how I ground the pinecones and needles and mixed them with rain water, creating a runny, brown stew; how I prepared my tea with leaves and soil boiling with the water inside the kettle; how everything, even myself, radiated the pungent, ripe stench of wilderness.

I tried to help him understand, but he couldn't. He wasn't pregnant, so how could he? And, the smell – I shower... in the runoff from the gutters, or bathe in the creeks. It sounds odd writing it, but I can't make it sound any other way. It feels *right* to me. Regular baths make my skin crawl, stomach churn, my bowels clench, and my temples pound. The cold water filtered by the earth is soothing, pleasurable, and makes me feel clean even without soap and shampoo.

Eventually, John admitted defeat after I convinced him it was only weird pregnancy cravings and tendencies, and they would end once the baby came. He assured me that he wasn't upset and he didn't want to force me to do anything, only that he was concerned for the health of me and the baby...

He didn't stay that night.

Standing nude in front of the bathroom mirror, I found my pale belly had grown quite a bit more than I expected. Faint stretch marks squirmed towards my protruding belly button. I smiled, cried. Strangely, I felt grateful to the old woman... Despite not entirely believing what she gave me caused or helped the pregnancy.

Something I hadn't considered before was that the first test could've been a false positive (those cheap tests are infamous for that), and I did make love to John that night and now, clearly, I'm pregnant... The connection's obvious. John's the father, and the old woman hadn't played a part in any of it... Still I wanted to thank her, at the very least.

I got dressed and tried my best to remember where the old woman had been. I came to a giant evergreen, and if my memory served me right, it was the same one as before. The old woman wasn't there, but she did say she lived nearby, so I searched the surrounding area for a cabin or cottage, to find only more trees.

I returned to the giant tree and discovered some of the bark had been cut away. Beneath was an impression on smooth wood and, if I tilted my head a little, it looked similar to the old woman's face. Even the tiny hollows serving as eyes looked like hers, colorless, though.

I laughed at myself. No, no, I thought, impossible. Even if the mixture in some way helped with the pregnancy, it was absurd to believe that she had actually been an extension of the tree... But, standing there, a lingering suspicion in the back of my mind slithered to the forefront... It *could* be true, and I, in some peculiar way, *wanted* it to be true, like a young girl desperately wanting fairy tales to be true.

"Thank you," I said to the tree at last, uncertain why, feeling stupid and awkward, then returned home.

...*/16/99*

John's still concerned about my and the baby's health, even with my weight gain. He mentioned how my skin has darkened, and that I'm seemingly always sweating or smelling like wet loam, despite the regular baths in the creek. He also mentioned how my teeth are browning, my gums are blackened, and my uncut nails are gray. My eyes once light brown are now tinged green. But, he hasn't complained about my breasts doubling in size or how most of the weight gain has settled into my hips and rear. So there's that.

He wants me to eat *real* food, from the grocery. I outright refused. Didn't he understand it'll make me sick? Didn't he understand that I know what's best for *my* child? He doesn't know the connection the baby and I share, but it's clear the things from the woods are working.

It became a fight soon after. One I don't want to write about or remember, boiling down to John threatening to take me to a doctor. He said if a doctor knew what I had been doing, they would force feed me real food, or, worse, they'd believe I'm mad and lock me in a padded room at the asylum until I've given birth. Then, after his tirade, he stormed off into the night.

I haven't spoken to him since.

If he wants to leave because of this, then let him. I'm certain his threats are empty. No matter what I look like, he knows deep down I'm – the baby is okay, and that if there were *real* problems with either of us, I would resolve them... Can't he see that all he has to do is be patient and wait for the baby to be born, and everything will be back to normal?

Two months, two months... and it'll all be over and we can be a family.

09/18/99

It's been a month, yet John is still hellbent on my eating habits. He hasn't visited much, hasn't helped much either. But I haven't let his absence bother me.

My stomach bulges, so much so that if I don't keep my feet placed firmly on the ground while standing, I'd tip over. The pain has returned. The sharp, bristling branches pierce my insides each time I move too fast, and it's not only in my stomach, but my lower back, too.

The stench of wet pine radiates from my pores, and my hair's clumpy and seemingly all one piece, as though caked in mud. I have to tie it back or it stains my skin and shirt brown.

One month. One month and the baby's here and this will be all over.

I fell asleep to the pitter-patter of rain outside, and I had a terrible, horrifying dream.

I walked in a dense, wildly grown forest. Damp evergreens jutted diagonally, strangely, from the earth; some dead and fallen, submerged in throngs of dewy brambles and underbrush. Fog blanketed the ground. It smelled of rain and smoke. The old woman's face took shape from bark, grinning, cackling, and melted into the tree to only appear in another. Her teeth were a mess of protruding pinecones, her tongue bristling pine needles, her broken green-yellow eyes puddles brimming with sickly rainwater, trickling down her gnarled face.

I ran, terror overwhelming me.

"Soon, I'll be here," she shouted, though it sounded like a whisper in my ear. She disappeared, reappeared. *"You carry not a babe, but something far older."*

I weaved past and leapt over fallen trees. I crashed through wet, skeletal branches, scratching and tearing clothes and flesh. The old woman appeared again and again.

"From tree to womb."

"Evergreens everlasting; bark cinders birthing a wooden phoenix."

A baby cried in the distance. Twigs and leaves snapped and crunched underfoot. It began raining. Gloom and mist suffocated the world. The infant's cries became louder, nearer. I screamed words I can't remember. I cried, too, lurching, reaching for the baby I couldn't see.

"In your belly there's a tangled forest of arms and legs," she said, vanishing.

The gloom thickened. I was a wild, wailing woman sprinting towards uncertainty. The trees gave way to an impossibly black wall. The baby's cries beyond. High-pitched, shrill. I touched the warm, oily emptiness, and the blackness peeled back, forming a slim opening, revealing a dim light. I pressed through.

The baby stopped crying, and started giggling.

I awoke in the rain, out in the woods, half-shielded by the giant pine tree. The old woman's face was more distinguished in the bark, her features harsher: eyes hollower, darker; wrinkles pronounced lines; cheeks grooved deeper into the wood. I held my journal, soaked through. Slowly I got to my feet, waited for the dizziness to pass, and stared at the impression for a moment, two, then returned home.

I undressed, toweled off, got into dry clothes and made tea. I checked my entries to find most of the ink had survived, except some parts of the dates were smudged. I was relieved. I set it open in front of the fire to dry.

10/20/99

John is no longer in my life. Surely he will return when the baby's born, unless he isn't the man I believed he was.

I hired a home nurse and caretaker until the baby arrives. She has been wonderful thus far, but there's things I can't tell her. For instance, I have black discharge that reeks of dirt, or that my urine is like muddy water, or that my stool... I rather not describe it. I can no longer walk without immense pain radiating from my pelvis and lower back, as though something's stabbing my insides with a pronged weapon.

At least the baby is due in one week.

I stood nude in front of the mirror this morning. It had been a while and I was curious. My eyes were tinged green-yellow and my tongue was dark, rough, and my hair had faded into a light-greenish blonde.

The nurse believes the changes are from malnutrition, and I'm too weak to fight with her. She makes me food, but I secretly toss them out or eat them to satisfy her before running into the bathroom to puke. Another thing she doesn't know is that I hide mason jars full of the things I truly crave in cabinets and shelves throughout the house. I feel like a child sneaking out in the middle of the night for a snack when I retrieve a handful of twigs and leaves from one of the cabinets, quickly eating them before being caught.

Soon, soon, soon.

10/26/99

Oh, God, I can't wait for this awful, terrible, hideous pain to end...

* * *

Screaming wrenched Kelly from the journal.

"It's coming! Oh, God it's coming! Kelly! Kelly!"

Kelly jumped to her feet and ran into the living room. Megan was sprawled out on the floor, her white-knuckled hands gripping the hem of her pulled-up gown. Black water spilled from her groin, pooling across the floor.

Kelly hurried to Megan.

The stench of earth and mulch sweltered in the room as the hearth blazed. She put a pillow behind Megan, propping her up.

"Breathe slowly," she said, "focus on your breathing."

The floor was wet, slippery. Kelly took towels from the nearby pile, and unfolded them under and around Megan, soaking up the dark water. She kneeled before Megan, pushing her legs apart.

"Breathe slow; steady, smooth.

"Focus, Megan, focus on the contractions – when they come, push."

Darker water spilled out, drenching the towels and Kelly's scrubs. Megan's labia was opening, stretching, peeling back.

"Keep pushing! Don't stop."

It continued to peel back, stretching further – *This isn't what's supposed to happen, this is happening too fast.* Kelly had assisted with dozens of deliveries, yet the way Megan was opening wasn't normal, wasn't *natural*... The water pouring from her thickened, became sludge, sloshing out. *Nothing I can do now. Just get the baby out.*

"Push Megan, push!"

Megan's eyes were closed, her dark teeth clenched, her chin burrowed into her chest. The stench of sweat intertwined with the ripe scent of loam.

Inside, beyond the hymen, the vagina, the uterine walls were hundreds of pine trees, as though Kelly was above an evergreen forest. The trees receded, reeling back; toppling and crashing and snapping like broken bones, giving way to an enormous pine tree surrounded by gnarled roots writhing like veins. Its rough bark jittered, and piece by piece it rattled off, revealing smooth, tan wood. The wood simmered, boiled, melted; forming a hole of throbbing pine needles and spurting branches. A dense, brown form emerged from the hole. The air trembled with a high-pitched cry. The form slid out from Megan onto the heap of solidified sludge below.

Everything within Megan reeled back, her insides retracting almost instantly, and the black water stopped.

"Is it over? Did I have my baby?" Megan gasped, out of breath, tears and sweat coating her oily face.

Kelly stared at the mold of mud before her. Her mind couldn't form the words to reply to Megan, couldn't form anything as it tried to make sense of what she had seen, making the impossible possible. The mold trembled as it began to cry, wailing like an actual baby. Her mind finally awoke. She scooped the mud form into her arms and used one of the wet towels to clear away the dirt...

A wrinkled, dark-skinned baby was inside the brown shell. Kelly cleaned it the best she could, and tore a blanket from a nearby chair and cocooned it tightly. She stood on weak knees and walked around Megan, hunkered, and carefully handed her the child.

Megan smiled, her dry lips cracked, and bobbed the baby in her shaking arms. The baby's cries quieted. Its face melted like wax, conforming to bone and contours, filling, forming its newborn face. Its eyes opened, exposing broken pupils drifting in tendrils of green-yellow irises.

"It's a girl," Megan said, smiling.

The Mask

Robert W. Chambers

Camilla: You, sir, should unmask.
Stranger: Indeed?
Camilla: Indeed it's time. We all have laid aside disguise but you.
Stranger: I wear no mask.
Camilla: (Terrified, aside to Cassilda.) No mask? No mask!
The King in Yellow: Act 1, Scene 2d

Chapter I

ALTHOUGH I knew nothing of chemistry, I listened fascinated. He picked up an Easter lily which Geneviève had brought that morning from Notre Dame and dropped it into the basin. Instantly the liquid lost its crystalline clearness. For a second the lily was enveloped in a milk-white foam, which disappeared, leaving the fluid opalescent. Changing tints of orange and crimson played over the surface, and then what seemed to be a ray of pure sunlight struck through from the bottom where the lily was resting. At the same instant he plunged his hand into the basin and drew out the flower. "There is no danger," he explained, "if you choose the right moment. That golden ray is the signal."

He held the lily toward me and I took it in my hand. It had turned to stone, to the purest marble.

"You see," he said, "it is without a flaw. What sculptor could reproduce it?"

The marble was white as snow, but in its depths the veins of the lily were tinged with palest azure, and a faint flush lingered deep in its heart.

"Don't ask me the reason of that," he smiled, noticing my wonder. 'I have no idea why the veins and heart are tinted, but they always are. Yesterday I tried one of Geneviève's goldfish – there it is."

The fish looked as if sculptured in marble. But if you held it to the light the stone was beautifully veined with a faint blue, and from somewhere within came a rosy light like the tint which slumbers in an opal. I looked into the basin. Once more it seemed filled with clearest crystal.

"If I should touch it now?" I demanded.

"I don't know," he replied, "but you had better not try."

"There is one thing I'm curious about," I said, "and that is where the ray of sunlight came from."

"It looked like a sunbeam true enough," he said. "I don't know, it always comes when I immerse any living thing, Perhaps," he continued smiling, "perhaps it is the vital spark of the creature escaping to the source from whence it came."

I saw he was mocking and threatened him with a mahl-stick, but he only laughed and changed the subject.

"Stay to lunch. Geneviève will be here directly."

"I saw her going to early mass," I said, "and she looked as fresh and sweet as that lily – before you destroyed it."

"Do you think I destroyed it?" said Boris gravely.

"Destroyed, preserved, how can we tell?"

We sat in the corner of a studio near his unfinished group of 'The Fates'. He leaned back on the sofa, twirling a sculptor's chisel and squinting at his work.

"By the way," he said, "I have finished pointing up that old academic Ariadne and I suppose it will have to go to the Salon. It's all I have ready this year, but after the success the 'Madonna', brought me I feel ashamed to send a thing like that."

The 'Madonna', an exquisite marble for which Geneviève had sat, had been the sensation of last year's Salon. I looked at the Ariadne. It was a magnificent piece of technical work, but I agreed with Boris that the world would expect something better of him than that. Still it was impossible now to think of finishing in time for the Salon, that splendid terrible group half shrouded in the marble behind me. 'The Fates' would have to wait.

We were proud of Boris Yvain. We claimed him and he claimed us on the strength of his having been born in America, although his father was French and his mother was a Russian. Everyone in the Beaux Arts called him Boris. And yet there were only two of us whom he addressed in the same familiar way; Jack Scott and myself.

Perhaps my being in love with Geneviève had something to do with his affection for me. Not that it had ever been acknowledged between us. But after all was settled, and she had told me with tears in her eyes that it was Boris whom she loved, I went over to his house and congratulated him. The perfect cordiality of that interview did not deceive either of us, I always believed, although to one at least it was a great comfort. I do not think he and Geneviève ever spoke of the matter together, but Boris knew.

Geneviève was lovely. The Madonna-like purity of her face might have been inspired by the Sanctus in Gounod's Mass. But I was always glad when she changed that mood for what we called her 'April Manœuvres'. She was often as variable as an April day. In the morning grave, dignified and sweet, at noon laughing, capricious, at evening whatever one least expected. I preferred her so rather than in that Madonna-like tranquillity which stirred the depths of my heart. I was dreaming of Geneviève when he spoke again.

"What do you think of my discovery, Alec?"

"I think it wonderful."

"I shall make no use of it, you know, beyond satisfying my own curiosity so far as may be and the secret will die with me."

"It would be rather a blow to sculpture, would it not? We painters lose more than we ever gain by photography."

Boris nodded, playing with the edge of the chisel.

"This new vicious discovery would corrupt the world of art. No, I shall never confide the secret to anyone," he said slowly.

It would be hard to find anyone less informed about such phenomena than myself; but of course I had heard of mineral springs so saturated with silica that the leaves and twigs which fell into them were turned to stone after a time. I dimly comprehended the process, how the silica replaced the vegetable matter, atom by atom, and the result was a duplicate of the object in stone. This I confess had never interested me greatly, and as for the ancient fossils thus produced, they disgusted me. Boris, it appeared, feeling curiosity instead of repugnance, had investigated the subject, and had accidentally stumbled on a solution which, attacking the immersed object with a ferocity unheard of, in a second did the work of years. This was all I could make out of the strange story he had just been telling me. He spoke again after a long silence.

"I am almost frightened when I think what I have found. Scientists would go mad over the discovery. It was so simple too; it discovered itself. When I think of that formula, and that new element precipitated in metallic scales—"

"What new element?"

"Oh, I haven't thought of naming it, and I don't believe I ever shall. There are enough precious metals now in the world to cut throats over."

I pricked up my ears. "Have you struck gold, Boris?"

"No, better – but see here, Alec!" he laughed, starting up. "You and I have all we need in this world. Ah! how sinister and covetous you look already!" I laughed too, and told him I was devoured by the desire for gold, and we had better talk of something else; so when Geneviève came in shortly after, we had turned our backs on alchemy.

Geneviève was dressed in silvery gray from head to foot. The light glinted along the soft curves of her fair hair as she turned her cheek to Boris; then she saw me and returned my greeting. She had never before failed to blow me a kiss from the tips of her white fingers, and I promptly complained of the omission. She smiled and held out her hand which dropped almost before it had touched mine; then she said, looking at Boris: "You must ask Alec to stay for luncheon." This also was something new. She had always asked me herself until today.

"I did," said Boris shortly.

"And you said yes, I hope," she turned to me with a charming conventional smile. I might have been an acquaintance of the day before yesterday. I made her a low bow. "J'avais bien l'honneur, madame," but refusing to take up our usual bantering tone she murmured a hospitable commonplace and disappeared. Boris and I looked at one another.

"I had better go home, don't you think?" I asked.

"Hanged if I know!" he replied frankly.

While we were discussing the advisability of my departure Geneviève reappeared in the doorway without her bonnet. She was wonderfully beautiful, but her color was too deep and her lovely eyes were too bright. She came straight up to me and took my arm.

"Luncheon is ready. Was I cross, Alec? I thought I had a headache but I haven't. Come here, Boris," and she slipped her other arm through his. "Alec knows that after you there is no one in the world whom I like as well as I like him, so if he sometimes feels snubbed it won't hurt him."

"À la bonheur!" I cried, "Who says there are no thunderstorms in April?"

"Are you ready?" chanted Boris. "Aye ready," and arm in arm we raced into the dining-room scandalizing the servants. After all we were not so much to blame; Geneviève was eighteen, Boris was twenty-three and I not quite twenty-one.

Chapter II

SOME WORK that I was doing about this time on the decorations for Geneviève's boudoir kept me constantly at the quaint little hotel in the rue Sainte-Cécile. Boris and I in those days labored hard but as we pleased, which was fitfully, and we all three, with Jack Scott, idled a great deal together.

One quiet afternoon I had been wandering alone over the house examining curios, prying into odd corners, bringing out sweetmeats and cigars from strange hiding-places, and at last I stopped in the bathing-room. Boris all over clay, stood there washing his hands.

The room was built of rose-colored marble excepting the floor which was tesselated in rose and gray. In the centre was a square pool sunken below the surface of the floor; steps led down into it, sculptured pillars supported a frescoed ceiling. A delicious marble Cupid appeared to have just alighted on his pedestal at the upper end of the room. The whole interior was Boris' work and mine. Boris, in his working clothes of white canvas, scraped the traces of clay and red modelling wax from his handsome hands, and coquetted over his shoulder with the Cupid.

"I see you," he insisted, "don't try to look the other way and pretend not to see me. You know who made you, little humbug!"

It was always my rôle to interpret Cupid's sentiments in these conversations, and when my turn came I responded in such a manner, that Boris seized my arm and dragged me toward the pool, declaring he would duck me. Next instant he dropped my arm and turned pale. "Good God!" he said, "I forgot the pool is full of the solution!"

I shivered a little, and drily advised him to remember better where he had stored the precious liquid.

"In Heaven's name why do you keep a small lake of that gruesome stuff here of all places!" I asked.

"I want to experiment on something large," he replied.

"On me, for instance!"

"Ah! that came too close for jesting; but I do want to watch the action of that solution on a more highly organized living body; there is that big white rabbit," he said, following me into the studio.

Jack Scott, wearing a paint-stained jacket, came wandering in, appropriated all the Oriental sweetmeats he could lay his hands on, looted the cigarette case, and finally he and Boris disappeared together to visit the Luxembourg gallery, where a new silver bronze by Rodin and a landscape of Monet's were claiming the exclusive attention of artistic France. I went back to the studio, and resumed my work. It was a Renaissance screen, which Boris wanted me to paint for Geneviève's boudoir. But the small boy who was unwillingly dawdling through a series of poses for it, today refused all bribes to be good. He never rested an instant in the same position, and inside of five minutes, I had as many different outlines of the little beggar.

"Are you posing, or are you executing a song and dance, my friend?" I inquired.

"Whichever monsieur pleases," he replied with an angelic smile.

Of course I dismissed him for the day, and of course I paid him for the full time, that being the way we spoil our models.

After the young imp had gone, I made a few perfunctory daubs at my work, but was so thoroughly out of humor, that it took me the rest of the afternoon to undo the damage I had done, so at last I scraped my palette, stuck my brushes in a bowl of black soap, and strolled into the smoking-room. I really believe that, excepting Geneviève's apartments, no room in the house was so free from the perfume of tobacco as this one. It was a queer chaos of odds and ends hung with threadbare tapestry. A sweet-toned old spinet in good repair stood by the window. There were stands of weapons, some old and dull, others bright and modern, festoons of Indian and Turkish armor over the mantel, two or three good pictures, and a pipe-rack. It was here that we used to come for new sensations in smoking. I doubt if any type of pipe ever existed which was not represented in that rack. When we had selected one, we immediately carried it somewhere else and smoked it; for the place was, on the whole, more gloomy and less inviting than any in the house. But this afternoon, the twilight was very soothing, the rugs and skins on the floor looked brown and soft and drowsy; the big couch was piled with cushions, I found my pipe and curled up there for an unaccustomed smoke in the smoking-room. I had chosen one with a long flexible stem, and lighting it fell to dreaming. After a while it went out, but I did not stir. I dreamed on and presently fell asleep.

I awoke to the saddest music I had ever heard. The room was quite dark, I had no idea what time it was. A ray of moonlight silvered one edge of the old spinet, and the polished wood seemed to exhale the sounds as perfume floats above a box of sandal wood. Someone rose in the darkness, and came away weeping quietly, and I was fool enough to cry out "Geneviève!"

She dropped at my voice, and I had time to curse myself while I made a light and tried to raise her from the floor. She shrank away with a murmur of pain. She was very quiet, and asked for Boris. I carried her to the divan, and went to look for him, but he was not in the house, and the servants were gone to bed. Perplexed and anxious, I hurried back to Geneviève. She lay where I had left her, looking very white.

"I can't find Boris nor any of the servants," I said.

"I know," she answered faintly, "Boris has gone to Ept with Mr. Scott. I did not remember when I sent you for him just now."

"But he can't get back in that case before tomorrow afternoon, and – are you hurt? Did I frighten you into falling? What an awful fool I am, but I was only half awake."

"Boris thought you had gone home before dinner. Do please excuse us for letting you stay here all this time."

"I have had a long nap," I laughed, "so sound that I did not know whether I was still asleep or not when I found myself staring at a figure that was moving toward me, and called out your name. Have you been trying the old spinet? You must have played very softly."

I would tell a thousand more lies worse than that one to see the look of relief that came into her face. She smiled adorably and said in her natural voice: "Alec, I tripped on that wolf's head, and I think my ankle is sprained. Please call Marie and then go home."

I did as she bade me and left her there when the maid came in.

Chapter III

AT NOON next day when I called, I found Boris walking restlessly about his studio.

"Geneviève is asleep just now," he told me, "the sprain is nothing, but why should she have such a high fever? The doctor can't account for it; or else he will not," he muttered.

"Geneviève has a fever?" I asked.

"I should say so, and has actually been a little light-headed at intervals all night. The idea! Gay little Geneviève, without a care in the world – and. she keeps saying her heart's broken, and she wants to die!"

My own heart stood still.

Boris leaned against the door of his studio, looking down, his hands in his pockets, his kind, keen eyes clouded, a new line of trouble drawn 'over the mouth's good mark, that made the smile.' The maid had orders to summon him the instant Geneviève opened her eyes. We waited and waited, and Boris growing restless wandered about, fussing with modelling wax and red clay. Suddenly he started for the next room. "Come and see my rose-colored bath full of death," he cried.

"Is it death?" I asked to humor his mood.

"You are not prepared to call it life, I suppose," he answered. As he spoke he plucked a solitary goldfish squirming and twisting out of its globe. "We'll send this one after the other – wherever that is," he said. There was feverish excitement in his voice. A dull weight of fever lay on my limbs and on my brain as I followed him to the fair crystal pool with its pink-tinted sides; and he dropped the creature in. Falling, its scales flashed with a hot orange gleam in its angry twistings and contortions; the moment it struck the liquid it became rigid and sank heavily to the bottom. Then came the milky foam, the splendid hues radiating on the surface and then the shaft of pure serene light broke through from seemingly infinite depths. Boris plunged in his hand and drew out an exquisite marble thing, blue-veined, rose-tinted and glistening with opalescent drops.

"Child's play," he muttered, and looked wearily, longingly at me – as if I could answer such questions! But Jack Scott came in and entered into the 'game' as he called it with ardor. Nothing would do but to try the experiment on the white rabbit then and there. I was willing that Boris should find distraction from his cares, but I hated to see the life go out of a warm, living creature and I declined to be present. Picking up a book at random I sat down in the studio to read. Alas, I had found *The King in Yellow*. After a few moments which seemed ages, I was putting it away with a nervous shudder, when Boris and Jack came in bringing their marble rabbit. At the same time the bell rang above and a cry came from the sick room. Boris was gone like a flash, and the next moment he called, "Jack, run for the doctor; bring him back with you. Alec, come here."

I went and stood at her door. A frightened maid came out in haste and ran away to fetch some remedy. Geneviève, sitting bolt upright, with crimson cheeks and glittering eyes, babbled incessantly and resisted Boris' gentle restraint. He called me to help. At my first touch she sighed and sank back, closing her eyes, and then – then – as we still bent above her, she opened them again, looked straight into Boris' face, poor fever-crazed girl, and told her secret. At the same instant, our three lives turned into new channels; the bond that had held us so long together snapped forever and a new bond was forged in its place, for she had spoken my name, and as the fever tortured her, her heart poured out its load of hidden sorrow. Amazed and dumb I bowed my head, while my face burned like a live coal, and the blood surged in my ears, stupefying me with its clamor. Incapable of movement, incapable of speech, I listened to her feverish words in an agony of shame and sorrow. I could not silence her, I could not look at Boris. Then I felt an arm upon my shoulder, and Boris turned a bloodless face to mine.

"It is not your fault, Alec, don't grieve so if she loves you—" but he could not finish; and as the doctor stepped swiftly into the room saying – "Ah, the fever!" I seized Jack Scott and hurried him to the street saying, "Boris would rather be alone." We crossed the street to our own apartments and that night, seeing I was going to be ill too, he went for the doctor again. The last thing I recollect with any distinctness was hearing Jack say, "For Heaven's sake, doctor, what ails him, to wear a face like that?" and I thought of *The King in Yellow* and the Pallid Mask.

I was very ill, for the strain of two years which I had endured since that fatal May morning when Geneviève murmured, "I love you, but I think I love Boris best" told on me at last. I had never imagined that it could become more than I could endure. Outwardly tranquil, I had deceived myself. Although the inward battle raged night after night, and I, lying alone in my room, cursed myself for rebellious thoughts unloyal to Boris and unworthy of Geneviève, the morning always brought relief, and I returned to Geneviève and to my dear Boris with a heart washed clean by the tempests of the night.

Never in word or deed or thought while with them, had I betrayed my sorrow even to myself.

The mask of self-deception was no longer a mask for me, it was a part of me. Night lifted it, laying bare the stifled truth below; but there was no one to see except myself, and when day broke the mask fell back again of its own accord. These thoughts passed through my troubled mind as I lay sick, but they were hopelessly entangled with visions of white creatures, heavy as stone, crawling about in Boris' basin – of the wolf's head on the rug, foaming and snapping at Geneviève, who lay smiling beside it. I thought, too, of The King in Yellow wrapt in the fantastic colors of his tattered mantle, and that bitter cry of Cassilda, "Not upon us, oh King, not upon us!" Feverishly I struggled to put it from me, but I saw the lake of Hali, thin and blank, without a ripple or wind to stir it, and I saw the towers of Carcosa behind the moon. Aldebaran, The Hyades, Alar, Hastur, glided through the cloud rifts which fluttered and flapped as they passed like the scolloped tatters of The King in Yellow. Among all these, one sane thought persisted. It never wavered, no matter what else was going on in my disordered mind, that my chief reason for existing was to meet some requirement of Boris and Geneviève. What this obligation was, its nature, was never clear; sometimes it seemed to be protection, sometimes support, through a great crisis. Whatever it seemed to be for the time, its weight rested only on me, and I was never so ill or so weak that I did not respond with my whole soul. There were always crowds of faces about me, mostly strange, but a few I recognized, Boris among them. Afterward they told me that this could not have been, but I know that once at least he bent over me. It was only a touch, a faint echo of his voice, then the clouds settled back on my senses, and I lost him, but he did stand there and bend over me once at least.

At last, one morning I awoke to find the sunlight falling across my bed, and Jack Scott reading beside me. I had not strength enough to speak aloud, neither could I think, much less remember, but I could smile feebly, as Jack's eye met mine, and when he jumped up and asked eagerly if I wanted anything, I could whisper, "Yes, Boris." Jack moved to the head of my bed, and leaned down to arrange my pillow: I did not see his face, but he answered heartily, "You must wait Alec, you are too weak to see even Boris."

I waited and I grew strong; in a few days I was able to see whom I would, but meanwhile I had thought and remembered. From the moment when all the past grew clear again in my mind, I never doubted what I should do when the time came, and I felt sure that Boris would have resolved upon the same course so far as he was concerned; as for what pertained to me alone, I knew he would see that also as I did. I no longer asked for anyone. I never inquired why no message came from them; why during the week I lay there, waiting and growing stronger, I never heard their name spoken. Preoccupied with my own searchings for the right way, and with my feeble but determined fight against despair, I simply acquiesced in Jack's reticence, taking for granted that he was afraid to speak of them, lest I should turn unruly and insist on seeing them. Meanwhile I said over and over to myself, how it would be when life began again for us all. We would take up our relations exactly as they were before Geneviève fell ill, Boris and I would look into each other's eyes and there would be neither rancor nor cowardice nor mistrust in that glance. I would be with them again for a little while in the dear intimacy of their home, and then, without pretext or explanation, I would disappear from their lives forever. Boris would know, Geneviève – the only comfort was that she would never know. It seemed, as I thought it over, that I had found the meaning of that sense of obligation which had persisted all through my delirium, and the only possible answer to it. So, when I was quite ready, I beckoned Jack to me one day, and said:

"Jack, I want Boris at once; and take my dearest greeting to Geneviève…"

When at last he made me understand that they were both dead, I fell into a wild rage that tore all my little convalescent strength to atoms. I raved and cursed myself into a relapse, from which I crawled forth some weeks afterward a boy of twenty-one who believed that his youth was gone forever. I seemed to be past the capability of further suffering, and one day when Jack handed me a letter and the keys to Boris' house, I took them without a tremor and asked him to tell me all. It was cruel of me to ask him, but there was no help for it, and he leaned wearily on his thin hands, to reopen the wound which could never entirely heal. He began very quietly.

"Alec, unless you have a clue that I know nothing about, you will not be able to explain any more than I, what has happened. I suspect that you would rather not hear these details, but you must learn them, else I would spare you the relation. God knows I wish I could be spared the telling. I shall use few words.

"That day when I left you in the doctor's care and came back to Boris, I found him working on the 'Fates'. Geneviève, he said, was sleeping under the influence of drugs. She had been quite out of her mind, he said. He kept on working, not talking any more, and I watched him. Before long, I saw that the third figure of the group – the one looking straight ahead, out over the world – bore his face; not as you ever saw it, but as it looked then and to the end. This is one thing for which I should like to find an explanation, but I never shall.

"Well, he worked and I watched him in silence, and we went on that way until nearly midnight. Then we heard a door open and shut sharply, and a swift rush in the next room. Boris sprang through the doorway and I followed; but we were too late. She lay at the bottom of the pool, her hands across her breast. Then Boris shot himself through the heart." Jack stopped speaking, drops of sweat stood under his eyes, and his thin cheeks twitched. "I carried Boris to his room. Then I went back and let that hellish fluid out of the pool, and turning on all the water, washed the marble clean of every drop. When at length I dared descend the steps, I found her lying there as white as snow. At last, when I had decided what was best to do, I went into the laboratory, and first emptied the solution in the basin into the waste-pipe; then I poured the contents of every jar and bottle after it. There was wood in the fireplace, so I built a fire, and breaking the locks of Boris' cabinet I burnt every paper, notebook and letter that I found there. With a mallet from the studio I smashed to pieces all the empty bottles, then loading them into a coal scuttle, I carried them to the cellar and threw them over the red-hot bed of the furnace. Six times I made the journey, and at last, not a vestige remained of anything which might again aid in seeking for the formula which Boris had found. Then at last I dared call the doctor. He is a good man, and together we struggled to keep it from the public. Without him I never could have succeeded. At last we got the servants paid and sent away into the country, where old Rosier keeps them quiet with stories of Boris' and Geneviève's travels in distant lands, from whence they will not return for years. We buried Boris in the little cemetery of Sèvres. The doctor is a good creature and knows when to pity a man who can bear no more. He gave his certificate of heart disease and asked no questions of me."

Then lifting his head from his hands, he said, "Open the letter, Alec; it is for us both."

I tore it open. It was Boris' will dated a year before. He left everything to Geneviève, and in case of her dying childless, I was to take control of the house in the Rue Sainte-Cécile, and Jack Scott, the management at Ept. On our deaths the property reverted to his mother's family in Russia, with the exception of the sculptured marbles executed by himself. These he left to me.

The page blurred under our eyes, and Jack got up and walked to the window. Presently he returned and sat down again. I dreaded to hear what he was going to say, but he spoke with the same simplicity and gentleness.

"Geneviève lies before the Madonna in the marble room. The Madonna bends tenderly above her, and Geneviève smiles back into that calm face that never would have been except for her."

His voice broke, but he grasped my hand, saying, "Courage, Alec." Next morning he left for Ept to fulfil his trust.

Chapter IV

THE SAME EVENING I took the keys and went into the house I had known so well. Everything was in order, but the silence was terrible. Though I went twice to the door of the marble room, I could not force myself to enter. It was beyond my strength. I went into the smoking-room and sat down before the spinet. A small lace handkerchief lay on the keys, and I turned away, choking. It was plain I could not stay, so I locked every door, every window, and the three front and back gates, and went away. Next morning Alcide packed my valise, and leaving him in charge of my apartments I took the Orient express for Constantinople. During the two years that I wandered through the East, at first, in our letters, we never mentioned Geneviève and Boris, but gradually their names crept in. I recollect particularly a passage in one of Jack's letters replying to one of mine.

"What you tell me of seeing Boris bending over you while you lay ill, and feeling his touch on your face, and hearing his voice of course troubles me. This that you describe must have happened a fortnight after he died. I say to myself that you were dreaming, that it was part of your delirium, but the explanation does not satisfy me, nor would it you."

Toward the end of the second year a letter came from Jack to me in India so unlike anything that I had ever known of him that I decided to return at once to Paris. He wrote, "I am well and sell all my pictures as artists do, who have no need of money. I have not a care of my own, but I am more restless than if I had. I am unable to shake off a strange anxiety about you. It is not apprehension, it is rather a breathless expectancy, of what, God knows! I can only say it is wearing me out. Nights I dream always of you and Boris. I can never recall anything afterward, but I wake in the morning with my heart beating, and all day the excitement increases until I fall asleep at night to recall the same experience. I am quite exhausted by it, and have determined to break up this morbid condition. I must see you. Shall I go to Bombay or will you come to Paris?"

I telegraphed him to expect me by the next steamer.

When we met I thought he had changed very little; I, he insisted, looked in splendid health. It was good to hear his voice again, and as we sat and chatted about what life still held for us, we felt that it was pleasant to be alive in the bright spring weather.

We stayed in Paris together a week, and then I went for a week to Ept with him, but first of all we went to the cemetery at Sèvres, where Boris lay.

"Shall we place the 'Fates' in the little grove above him?" Jack asked, and I answered:

"I think only the 'Madonna' should watch over Boris' grave." But Jack was none the better for my home-coming. The dreams of which he could not retain even the least definite outline continued, and he said that at times the sense of breathless expectancy was suffocating.

"You see I do you harm and not good," I said. "Try a change without me." So he started alone for a ramble among the Channel Islands and I went back to Paris. I had not yet entered Boris' house, now mine, since my return, but I knew it must be done. It had been kept in order by Jack; there were servants there, so I gave up my own apartment and went there to live. Instead of the agitation I had feared, I found myself able to paint there tranquilly. I visited all the rooms – all but one. I could not bring myself to enter the marble room where Geneviève lay, and yet I felt the longing growing daily to look upon her face, to kneel beside her.

One April afternoon, I lay dreaming in the smoking-room, just as I had lain two years before, and mechanically I looked among the tawny Eastern rugs for the wolf-skin. At last I distinguished the pointed ears and flat cruel head, and I thought of my dream where I saw Geneviève lying beside it. The helmets still hung against the threadbare tapestry, among them the old Spanish morion which I remembered Geneviève had once put on when we were amusing ourselves with the ancient bits of mail. I turned my eyes to the spinet; every yellow key seemed eloquent of her caressing hand, and I rose, drawn by the strength of my life's passion to the sealed door of the marble room. The heavy doors swung inward under my trembling hands. Sunlight poured through the window, tipping with gold the wings of Cupid, and lingered like a nimbus over the brows of the Madonna. Her tender face bent in compassion over a marble form so exquisitely pure that I knelt and signed myself. Geneviève lay in the shadow under the Madonna, and yet, through her white arms, I saw the pale azure vein, and beneath her softly clasped hands the folds of her dress were tinged with rose, as if from some faint warm light within her breast.

Bending with a breaking heart I touched the marble drapery with my lips, then crept back into the silent house.

A maid came and brought me a letter, and I sat down in the little conservatory to read it; but as I was about to break the seal, seeing the girl lingering, I asked her what she wanted.

She stammered something about a white rabbit that had been caught in the house and asked what should be done with it. I told her to let it loose in the walled garden behind the house and opened my letter. It was from Jack, but so incoherent that I thought he must have lost his reason. It was nothing but a series of prayers to me not to leave the house until he could get back; he could not tell me why, there were the dreams, he said – he could explain nothing, but he was sure that I must not leave the house in the Rue Sainte-Cécile.

As I finished reading I raised my eyes and saw the same maid-servant standing in the doorway holding a glass dish in which two goldfish were swimming: "Put them back into the tank and tell me what you mean by interrupting me," I said.

With a half suppressed whimper she emptied water and fish into an aquarium at the end of the conservatory, and turning to me asked my permission to leave my service. She said people were playing tricks on her, evidently with a design of getting her into trouble; the marble rabbit had been stolen and a live one had been brought into the house; the two beautiful marble fish were gone and she had just found those common live things flopping on the dining-room floor. I reassured her and sent her away saying I would look about myself. I went into the studio; there was nothing there but my canvasses and some casts, except the marble of the Easter Lily. I saw it on a table across the room. Then I strode angrily over to it. But the flower I lifted from the table was fresh and fragile and filled the air with perfume.

Then suddenly I comprehended and sprang through the hall-way to the marble room. The doors flew open, the sunlight streamed into my face and through it, in a heavenly glory, the Madonna smiled, as Geneviève lifted her flushed face from her marble couch, and opened her sleepy eyes.

The New Mother

Lucy Clifford

Chapter I

THE CHILDREN were always called Blue-Eyes and the Turkey, and they came by the names in this manner. The elder one was like her dear father who was far away at sea, and when the mother looked up she would often say, "Child, you have taken the pattern of your father's eyes," for the father had the bluest of blue eyes, and so gradually his little girl came to be called after them. The younger one had once, while she was still almost a baby, cried bitterly because a turkey that lived near to the cottage, and sometimes wandered into the forest, suddenly vanished in the middle of the winter; and to console her she had been called by its name.

Now the mother and Blue-Eyes and the Turkey and the baby all lived in a lonely cottage on the edge of the forest. The forest was so near that the garden at the back seemed a part of it, and the tall fir-trees were so close that their big black arms stretched over the little thatched roof, and when the moon shone upon them their tangled shadows were all over the white-washed walls.

It was a long way to the village, nearly a mile and a half, and the mother had to work hard and had not time to go often herself to see if there was a letter at the post-office from the dear father, and so very often in the afternoon she used to send the two children. They were very proud of being able to go alone, and often ran half the way to the post-office. When they came back tired with the long walk, there would be the mother waiting and watching for them, and the tea would be ready, and the baby crowing with delight; and if by any chance there was a letter from the sea, then they were happy indeed. The cottage room was so cosy: the walls were as white as snow inside as well as out, and against them hung the cake-tin and the baking-dish, and the lid of a large saucepan that had been worn out long before the children could remember, and the fish-slice, all polished and shining as bright as silver. On one side of the fireplace, above the bellows hung the almanac, and on the other the clock that always struck the wrong hour and was always running down too soon, but it was a good clock, with a little picture on its face and sometimes ticked away for nearly a week without stopping. The baby's high chair stood in one corner, and in another there was a cupboard hung up high against the wall, in which the mother kept all manner of little surprises. The children often wondered how the things that came out of that cupboard had got into it, for they seldom saw them put there.

"Dear children," the mother said one afternoon late in the autumn, "it is very chilly for you to go to the village, but you must walk quickly, and who knows but what you may bring back a letter saying that dear father is already on his way to England." Then Blue-Eyes and the Turkey made haste and were soon ready to go. "Don't be long," the mother said, as she always did before they started. "Go the nearest way and don't look at any strangers you meet, and be sure you do not talk with them."

"No, mother," they answered; and then she kissed them and called them dear good children, and they joyfully started on their way.

The village was gayer than usual, for there had been a fair the day before, and the people who had made merry still hung about the street as if reluctant to own that their holiday was over. "I wish we had come yesterday," Blue-Eyes said to the Turkey; "then we might have seen something."

"Look there," said the Turkey, and she pointed to a stall covered with gingerbread; but the children had no money. At the end of the street close to the Blue Lion where the coaches stopped, an old man sat on the ground with his back resting against the wall of a house, and by him, with smart collars round their necks, were two dogs. Evidently they were dancing dogs, the children thought, and longed to see them perform, but they seemed as tired as their master, and sat quite still beside him, looking as if they had not even a single wag left in their tails.

"Oh, I *do* wish we had been here yesterday," Blue-Eyes said again as they went on to the grocer's, which was also the post-office. The post-mistress was very busy weighing out half-pounds of coffee, and when she had time to attend to the children she only just said "No letter for you today," and went on with what she was doing. Then Blue-Eyes and the Turkey turned away to go home. They went back slowly down the village street, past the man with the dogs again. One dog had roused himself and sat up rather crookedly with his head a good deal on one side, looking very melancholy and rather ridiculous; but on the children went towards the bridge and the fields that led to the forest.

They had left the village and walked some way, and then, just before they reached the bridge, they noticed, resting against a pile of stones by the way-side, a strange dark figure. At first they thought it was someone asleep, then they thought it was a poor woman ill and hungry, and then they saw that it was a strange wild-looking girl, who seemed very unhappy, and they felt sure that something was the matter. So they went and looked at her, and thought they would ask her if they could do anything to help her, for they were kind children and sorry indeed for anyone in distress.

The girl seemed to be tall, and was about fifteen years old. She was dressed in very ragged clothes. Round her shoulders there was an old brown shawl, which was torn at the corner that hung down the middle of her back. She wore no bonnet, and an old yellow handkerchief which she had tied round her head had fallen backwards and was all huddled up round her neck. Her hair was coal black and hung down uncombed and unfastened, just anyhow. It was not very long, but it was very shiny, and it seemed to match her bright black eyes and dark freckled skin. On her feet were coarse grey stockings and thick shabby boots, which she had evidently forgotten to lace up. She had something hidden away under her shawl, but the children did not know what it was. At first they thought it was a baby, but when, on seeing them coming towards her, she carefully put it under her and sat upon it, they thought they must be mistaken. She sat watching the children approach, and did not move or stir till they were within a yard of her; then she wiped her eyes just as if she had been crying bitterly, and looked up.

The children stood still in front of her for a moment, staring at her and wondering what they ought to do.

"Are you crying?" they asked shyly. To their surprise she said in a most cheerful voice, "Oh dear, no! Quite the contrary. Are you?" They thought it rather rude of her to reply in this way, for anyone could see that they were not crying. They felt half in mind to walk away; but the girl looked at them so hard with her big black eyes, they did not like to do so till they had said something else. "Perhaps you have lost yourself?" they said gently. But the girl answered promptly, "Certainly not. Why, you have just found me. Besides," she added, "I live in the village."

The children were surprised at this, for they had never seen her before, and yet they thought they knew all the village folk by sight.

"We often go to the village," they said, thinking it might interest her.

"Indeed," she answered. That was all; and again they wondered what to do.

Then the Turkey, who had an inquiring mind, put a good straightforward question. "What are you sitting on?" she asked.

"On a pear drum," the girl answered, still speaking in a most cheerful voice, at which the children wondered, for she looked very cold and uncomfortable.

"What is a pear drum?" they asked.

"I am surprised at your not knowing," the girl answered. "Most people in good society have one." And then she pulled it out and showed it to them. It was a curious instrument, a good deal like a guitar in shape; it had three strings, but only two pegs by which to tune them. The third string was never tuned at all, and thus added to the singular effect produced by the village girl's music. And yet, oddly, the pear drum was not played by touching its strings, but by turning a little handle cunningly hidden on one side.

But the strange thing about the pear drum was not the music it made, or the strings, or the handle, but a little square box attached to one side. The box had a little flat lid that appeared to open by a spring. That was all the children could make out at first. They were most anxious to see inside the box, or to know what it contained, but they thought it might look curious to say so.

"It really is a most beautiful thing, is a pear drum," the girl said, looking at it, and speaking in a voice that was almost affectionate.

"Where did you get it?" the children asked.

"I bought it," the girl answered.

"Didn't it cost a great deal of money?" they asked.

"Yes," answered the girl slowly, nodding her head, "it cost a great deal of money. I am very rich," she added.

And this the children thought a really remarkable statement, for they had not supposed that rich people dressed in old clothes, or went about without bonnets. She might at least have done her hair, they thought; but they did not like to say so.

"You don't look rich," they said slowly, and in as polite a voice as possible.

"Perhaps not," the girl answered cheerfully.

At this the children gathered courage, and ventured to remark, "You look rather shabby" – they did not like to say ragged.

"Indeed?" said the girl in the voice of one who had heard a pleasant but surprising statement. "A little shabbiness is very respectable," she added in a satisfied voice. "I must really tell them this," she continued. And the children wondered what she meant. She opened the little box by the side of the pear drum, and said, just as if she were speaking to someone who could hear her, "They say I look rather shabby; it is quite lucky, isn't it?"

"Why, you are not speaking to anyone!" they said, more surprised than ever.

"Oh dear, yes! I am speaking to them both."

"Both?" they said, wondering.

"Yes. I have here a little man dressed as a peasant, and wearing a wide slouch hat with a large feather, and a little woman to match, dressed in a red petticoat, and a white handkerchief pinned across her bosom. I put them on the lid of the box, and when I play they dance most beautifully. The little man takes off his hat and waves it in the air, and the little woman holds up her petticoat a little bit on one side with one hand, and with the other sends forward a kiss."

"Oh! Let us see; do let us see!" the children cried, both at once.

Then the village girl looked at them doubtfully.

"Let you see!" she said slowly. "Well, I am not sure that I can. Tell me, are you good?"

"Yes, yes," they answered eagerly, "we are very good!"

"Then it's quite impossible," she answered, and resolutely closed the lid of the box.

They stared at her in astonishment.

"But we are good," they cried, thinking she must have misunderstood them. "We are very good. Mother always says we are."

"So you remarked before," the girl said, speaking in a tone of decision.

Still the children did not understand.

"Then can't you let us see the little man and woman?" they asked.

"Oh dear, no!" the girl answered. "I only show them to naughty children."

"To naughty children!" they exclaimed.

"Yes, to naughty children," she answered; "and the worse the children the better do the man and woman dance."

She put the pear drum carefully under her ragged cloak, and prepared to go on her way.

"I really could not have believed that you were good," she said, reproachfully, as if they had accused themselves of some great crime: "Well, good-day."

"Oh, but do show us the little man and woman," they cried.

"Certainly not. Good-day," she said again.

"Oh, but we will be naughty," they said in despair.

"I am afraid you couldn't," she answered, shaking her head. "It requires a great deal of skill, especially to be naughty well. Good-day," she said for the third time. "Perhaps I shall see you in the village tomorrow."

And swiftly she walked away, while the children felt their eyes fill with tears, and their hearts ache with disappointment.

"If we had only been naughty," they said, "we should have seen them dance; we should have seen the little woman holding her red petticoat in her hand, and the little man waving his hat. Oh, what shall we do to make her let us see them?"

"Suppose," said the Turkey, "we try to be naughty today; perhaps she would let us see them tomorrow."

"But, oh!" said Blue-Eyes, "I don't know how to be naughty; no one ever taught me."

The Turkey thought for a few minutes in silence. "I think I can be naughty if I try," she said. "I'll try tonight."

And then poor Blue-Eyes burst into tears.

"Oh, don't be naughty without me!" she cried. "It would be so unkind of you. You know I want to see the little man and woman just as much as you do. You are very, very unkind." And she sobbed bitterly.

And so, quarrelling and crying, they reached their home.

Now, when their mother saw them, she was greatly astonished, and, fearing they were hurt, ran to meet them.

"Oh, my children, oh, my dear, dear children," she said; "what is the matter?"

But they did not dare tell their mother about the village girl and the little man and woman, so they answered, "Nothing is the matter; nothing at all is the matter," and cried all the more.

"But why are you crying?" she asked in surprise.

"Surely we may cry if we like," they sobbed. "We are very fond of crying."

"Poor children!" the mother said to herself. "They are tired, and perhaps they are hungry; after tea they will be better." And she went back to the cottage, and made the fire blaze, until its reflection danced about on the tin lids upon the wall; and she put the kettle on to boil, and set the tea-things on the table, and opened the window to let in the sweet fresh air, and made all things look bright. Then she went to the little cupboard, hung up high against the wall, and took out some bread and put it on the table, and said in a loving voice, "Dear little children, come and have your tea; it is all quite ready for you. And see, there is the baby waking up from her sleep; we will put her in the high chair, and she will crow at us while we eat."

But the children made no answer to the dear mother; they only stood still by the window and said nothing.

"Come, children," the mother said again. "Come, Blue-Eyes, and come, my Turkey; here is nice sweet bread for tea."

Then Blue-Eyes and the Turkey looked round, and when they saw the tall loaf, baked crisp and brown, and the cups all in a row, and the jug of milk, all waiting for them, they went to the table and sat down and felt a little happier; and the mother did not put the baby in the high chair after all, but took it on her knee, and danced it up and down, and sang little snatches of songs to it, and laughed, and looked content, and thought of the father far away at sea, and wondered what he would say to them all when he came home again. Then suddenly she looked up and saw that the Turkey's eyes were full of tears.

"Turkey!" she exclaimed, "my dear little Turkey! What is the matter? Come to mother, my sweet; come to own mother." And putting the baby down on the rug, she held out her arms, and the Turkey, getting up from her chair, ran swiftly into them.

"Oh, mother," she sobbed, "oh, dear mother! I do so want to be naughty."

"My dear child!" the mother exclaimed.

"Yes, mother," the child sobbed, more and more bitterly. "I do so want to be very, very naughty."

And then Blue-Eyes left her chair also, and, rubbing her face against the mother's shoulder, cried sadly. "And so do I, mother. Oh, I'd give anything to be very, very naughty."

"But, my dear children," said the mother, in astonishment, "why do you want to be naughty?"

"Because we do; oh, what shall we do?" they cried together.

"I should be very angry if you were naughty. But you could not be, for you love me," the mother answered.

"Why couldn't we be naughty because we love you?" they asked.

"Because it would make me very unhappy; and if you love me you couldn't make me unhappy."

"Why couldn't we?" they asked.

Then the mother thought a while before she answered; and when she did so they hardly understood, perhaps because she seemed to be speaking rather to herself than to them.

"Because if one loves well," she said gently, "one's love is stronger than all bad feelings in one, and conquers them. And this is the test whether love be real or false, unkindness and wickedness have no power over it."

"We don't know what you mean," they cried; " and we do love you; but we want to be naughty."

"Then I should know you did not love me," the mother said.

"And what should you do?" asked Blue-Eyes.

"I cannot tell. I should try to make you better."

"But if you couldn't? If we were very, very, very naughty, and wouldn't be good, what then?"

"Then," said the mother sadly – and while she spoke her eyes filled with tears, and a sob almost choked her – "then," she said, "I should have to go away and leave you, and to send home a new mother, with glass eyes and wooden tail."

"You couldn't," they cried.

"Yes, I could," she answered in a low voice; "but it would make me very unhappy, and I will never do it unless you are very, very naughty, and I am obliged."

"We won't be naughty," they cried; " we will be good. We should hate a new mother; and she shall never come here." And they clung to their own mother, and kissed her fondly.

But when they went to bed they sobbed bitterly, for they remembered the little man and woman, and longed more than ever to see them; but how could they bear to let their own mother go away, and a new one take her place?

Chapter II

"GOOD-DAY," said the village girl, when she saw Blue-Eyes and the Turkey approach. She was again sitting by the heap of stones, and under her shawl the pear drum was hidden. She looked just as if she had not moved since the day before. "Good-day," she said, in the same cheerful voice in which she had spoken yesterday; "the weather is really charming."

"Are the little man and woman there?" the children asked, taking no notice of her remark.

"Yes; thank you for inquiring after them," the girl answered; "they are both here and quite well. The little man is learning how to rattle the money in his pocket, and the little woman has heard a secret – she tells it while she dances."

"Oh, do let us see," they entreated.

"Quite impossible, I assure you," the girl answered promptly. "You see, you are good."

"Oh!" said Blue-Eyes, sadly; "but mother says if we are naughty she will go away and send home a new mother, with glass eyes and a wooden tail."

"Indeed," said the girl, still speaking in the same unconcerned voice, "that is what they all say."

"What do you mean?" asked the Turkey.

"They all threaten that kind of thing. Of course really there are no mothers with glass eyes and wooden tails; they would be much too expensive to make." And the common sense of this remark the children, especially the Turkey, saw at once, but they merely said, half crying:

"We think you might let us see the little man and woman dance."

"The kind of thing you would think," remarked the village girl.

"But will you if we are naughty?" they asked in despair.

"I fear you could not be naughty – that is, really – even if you tried," she said scornfully.

"Oh, but we will try; we will indeed," they cried; "so do show them to us."

"Certainly not beforehand," answered the girl, getting up and preparing to walk away.

"But if we are very naughty tonight, will you let us see them tomorrow?"

"Questions asked today are always best answered tomorrow," the girl said, and turned round as if to walk on. "Good-day," she said blithely; "I must really go and play a little to myself; good-day," she repeated, and then suddenly she began to sing:

> *"Oh, sweet and fair's the ladybird,*
> *And so's the bumble-bee.*
> *But I myself have long preferred*
> *The gentle chimpanzee,*
> *The gentle chimpanzee-e-e,*
> *The gentle chim—"*

"I beg your pardon," she said, stopping, and looking over her shoulder; "it's very rude to sing without leave before company. I won't do it again."

"Oh, do go on," the children said.

"I'm going," she said, and walked away.

"No, we meant go on singing," they explained, "and do let us just hear you play," they entreated, remembering that as yet they had not heard a single sound from the pear drum.

"Quite impossible," she called out as she went along. "You are good, as I remarked before. The pleasure of goodness centres in itself; the pleasures of naughtiness are many and varied. Good-day," she shouted, for she was almost out of hearing.

For a few minutes the children stood still looking after her, then they broke down and cried.

"She might have let us see them," they sobbed.

The Turkey was the first to wipe away her tears.

"Let us go home and be very naughty," she said; "then perhaps she will let us see them tomorrow."

"But what shall we do?" asked Blue-Eyes, looking up. Then together all the way home they planned how to begin being naughty. And that afternoon the dear mother was sorely distressed, for, instead of sitting at their tea as usual with smiling happy faces, and then helping her to clear away and doing all she told them, they broke their mugs and threw their bread and butter on the floor, and when the mother told them to do one thing they carefully went and did another, and as for helping her to put away, they left her to do it all by herself, and only stamped their feet with rage when she told them to go upstairs until they were good.

"We won't be good," they cried. "We hate being good, and we always mean to be naughty. We like being naughty very much."

"Do you remember what I told you I should do if you were very very naughty?" she asked sadly.

"Yes, we know, but it isn't true," they cried. "There is no mother with a wooden tail and glass eyes, and if there were we should just stick pins into her and send her away; but there is none."

Then the mother became really angry at last, and sent them off to bed, but instead of crying and being sorry at her anger they laughed for joy, and when they were in bed they sat up and sang merry songs at the top of their voices.

* * *

The next morning quite early, without asking leave from the mother, the children got up and ran off as fast as they could over the fields towards the bridge to look for the village girl. She was sitting as usual by the heap of stones with the pear drum under her shawl.

"Now please show us the little man and woman," they cried, "and let us hear the pear drum. We were very naughty last night." But the girl kept the pear drum carefully hidden. "We were very naughty," the children cried again.

"Indeed," she said in precisely the same tone in which she had spoken yesterday.

"But we were," they repeated; "we were indeed."

"So you say," she answered. "You were not half naughty enough."

"Why, we were sent to bed!"

"Just so," said the girl, putting the other corner of the shawl over the pear drum. "If you had been really naughty you wouldn't have gone; but you can't help it, you see. As I remarked before, it requires a great deal of skill to be naughty well."

"But we broke our mugs, we threw our bread and butter on the floor, we did everything we could to be tiresome."

"Mere trifles," answered the village girl scornfully. "Did you throw cold water on the fire, did you break the clock, did you pull all the tins down from the walls, and throw them on the floor?"

"No!" exclaimed the children, aghast, "we did not do that."

"I thought not," the girl answered. "So many people mistake a little noise and foolishness for real naughtiness; but, as I remarked before, it wants skill to do the thing properly. Well, good-day," and before they could say another word she had vanished.

"We'll be much worse," the children cried, in despair. "We'll go and do all the things she says," and then they went home and did all these things. They threw water on the fire; they pulled down the baking-dish and the cake-tin, the fish-slice and the lid of the saucepan they had never seen, and banged them on the floor; they broke the clock and danced on the butter; they turned everything upside down; and then they sat still and wondered if they were naughty enough. And when the mother saw all that they had done she did not scold them as she had the day before or send them to bed, but she just broke down and cried, and then she looked at the children and said sadly:

"Unless you are good tomorrow, my poor Blue-Eyes and Turkey, I shall indeed have to go away and come back no more, and the new mother I told you of will come to you."

They did not believe her; yet their hearts ached when they saw how unhappy she looked, and they thought within themselves that when they once had seen the little man and woman dance, they would be good to the dear mother forever afterwards; but they could not be good now till they had heard the sound of the pear drum, seen the little man and woman dance, and heard the secret told – then they would be satisfied.

The next morning, before the birds were stirring, before the sun had climbed high enough to look in at their bedroom window, or the flowers had wiped their eyes ready for the day, the children got up and crept out of the cottage and ran across the fields. They did not think the village girl would be up so very early, but their hearts had ached so much at the sight of the mother's sad face that they had not been able to sleep, and they longed to know if they had been naughty enough, and if they might just once hear the pear drum and see the little man and woman, and then go home and be good for ever.

To their surprise they found the village girl sitting by the heap of stones, just as if it were her natural home. They ran fast when they saw her, and they noticed that the box containing the little man and woman was open, but she closed it quickly when she saw them, and they heard the clicking of the spring that kept it fast.

"We have been very naughty," they cried. "We have done all the things you told us; now will you show us the little man and woman?" The girl looked at them curiously, then drew the yellow silk handkerchief she sometimes wore round her head out of her pocket, and began to smooth out the creases in it with her hands.

"You really seem quite excited," she said in her usual voice. "You should be calm; calmness gathers in and hides things like a big cloak, or like my shawl does here, for instance," and she looked down at the ragged covering that hid the pear drum.

"We have done all the things you told us," the children cried again, "and we do so long to hear the secret," but the girl only went on smoothing out her handkerchief.

"I am so very particular about my dress," she said. They could hardly listen to her in their excitement.

"But do tell if we may see the little man and woman," they entreated again. "We have been so very naughty, and mother says she will go away today and send home a new mother if we are not good."

"Indeed," said the girl, beginning to be interested and amused. "The things that people say are most singular and amusing. There is an endless variety in language." But the children did not understand, only entreated once more to see the little man and woman.

"Well, let me see,"" the girl said at last, just as if she were relenting. "When did your mother say she would go?"

"But if she goes what shall we do?" they cried in despair. "We don't want her to go; we love her very much. Oh! what shall we do if she goes?"

"People go and people come; first they go and then they come. Perhaps she will go before she comes; she couldn't come before she goes. You had better go back and be good," the girl added suddenly; "you are really not clever enough to be anything else; and the little woman's secret is very important; she never tells it for make-believe naughtiness."

"But we did do all the things you told us," the children cried, despairingly.

"You didn't throw the looking-glass out of window, or stand the baby on its head."

"No, we didn't do that," the children gasped.

"I thought not," the girl said triumphantly. "Well, good-day. I shall not be here tomorrow. Good-day."

"Oh, but don't go away," they cried. "We are so unhappy; do let us see them just once."

"Well, I shall go past your cottage at eleven o'clock this morning," the girl said. "Perhaps I shall play the pear drum as I go by."

"And will you show us the man and woman?" they asked.

"Quite impossible, unless you have really deserved it; make-believe naughtiness is only spoilt goodness. Now if you break the looking-glass and do the things that are desired—"

"Oh, we will," they cried. "We will be very naughty till we hear you coming."

"It's waste of time, I fear," the girl said politely; "but of course I should not like to interfere with you. You see the little man and woman, being used to the best society, are very particular. Good-day," she said, just as she always said, and then quickly turned away, but she looked back and called out, "Eleven o'clock, I shall be quite punctual; I am very particular about my engagements."

Then again the children went home, and were naughty, oh, so very very naughty that the dear mother's heart ached, and her eyes filled with tears, and at last she went upstairs and slowly put on her best gown and her new sun-bonnet, and she dressed the baby all in its Sunday clothes, and then she came down and stood before Blue-Eyes and the Turkey, and just as she did so the Turkey threw the looking-glass out of window, and it fell with a loud crash upon the ground.

"Good-bye, my children," the mother said sadly, kissing them. "Good-bye, my Blue-Eyes; good-bye, my Turkey; the new mother will be home presently. Oh, my poor children!" and then weeping bitterly the mother took the baby in her arms and turned to leave the house.

"But, mother," the children cried, "we are—" and then suddenly the broken clock struck half-past ten, and they knew that in half an hour the village girl would come by playing on the pear drum. "But, mother, we will be good at half-past eleven, come back at half-past eleven," they cried, "and we'll both be good, we will indeed; we must be naughty till eleven o'clock." But the mother only picked up the little bundle in which she had tied up her cotton apron and a pair of old shoes, and went slowly out at the door. It seemed as if the children were spellbound, and they could not follow her. They opened the window wide, and called after her:

"Mother! Mother! Oh, dear mother, come back again! We will be good, we will be good now, we will be good for evermore if you will come back."

But the mother only looked round and shook her head, and they could see the tears falling down her cheeks.

"Come back, dear mother!" cried Blue-Eyes; but still the mother went on across the fields.

"Come back, come back!" cried the Turkey; but still the mother went on. Just by the corner of the field she stopped and turned, and waved her handkerchief, all wet with tears, to the children at the window; she made the baby kiss its hand; and in a moment mother and baby had vanished from their sight.

Then the children felt their hearts ache with sorrow, and they cried bitterly just as the mother had done, and yet they could not believe that she had gone. Surely she would come back, they thought; she would not leave them altogether; but, oh, if she did – if she did – if she did. And then the broken clock struck eleven, and suddenly there was a sound – a quick, clanging, jangling sound, with a strange discordant one at intervals; and they looked at each other, while their hearts stood still, for they knew it was the pear drum. They rushed to the open window, and there they saw the village girl coming towards them from the fields, dancing along and playing as she did so. Behind her, walking slowly, and yet ever keeping the same distance from her, was the man with the dogs whom they had seen asleep by the Blue lion, on the day they first saw the girl with the pear drum. He was playing on a flute that had a strange shrill sound; they could hear it plainly above the jangling of the pear drum. After the man followed the two dogs, slowly waltzing round and round on their hind legs.

"We have done all you told us," the children called, when they had recovered from their astonishment. "Come and see; and now show us the little man and woman."

The girl did not cease her playing or her dancing, but she called out in a voice that was half speaking half singing, and seemed to keep time to the strange music of the pear drum.

"You did it all badly. You threw the water on the wrong side of the fire, the tin things were not quite in the middle of the room, the clock was not broken enough, you did not stand the baby on its head."

Then the children, still standing spellbound by the window, cried out, entreating and wringing their hands, "Oh, but we have done everything you told us, and mother has gone away. Show us the little man and woman now, and let us hear the secret."

As they said this the girl was just in front of the cottage, but she did not stop playing. The sound of the strings seemed to go through their hearts. She did not stop dancing; she was already passing the cottage by. She did not stop singing, and all she said sounded like part of a terrible song. And still the man followed her, always at the same distance, playing shrilly on his flute; and still the two dogs waltzed round and round after him – their tails motionless, their legs straight, their collars clear and white and stiff. On they went, all of them together.

"Oh, stop!" the children cried, "and show us the little man and woman now."

But the girl sang out loud and clear, while the string that was out of tune twanged above her voice.

"The little man and woman are far away. See, their box is empty."

And then for the first time the children saw that the lid of the box was raised and hanging back, and that no little man and woman were in it.

"I am going to my own land," the girl sang, "to the land where I was born." And she went on towards the long straight road that led to the city many many miles away.

"But our mother is gone," the children cried; "our dear mother, will she ever come back?"

"No," sang the girl; "she'll never come back, she'll never come back. I saw her by the bridge: she took a boat upon the river; she is sailing to the sea; she will meet your father once again, and they will go sailing on, sailing on to the countries far away."

And when they heard this, the children cried out, but could say no more, for their hearts seemed to be breaking.

Then the girl, her voice getting fainter and fainter in the distance, called out once more to them. But for the dread that sharpened their ears they would hardly have heard her, so far was she away, and so discordant was the music.

"Your new mother is coming. She is already on her way; but she only walks slowly, for her tail is rather long, and her spectacles are left behind; but she is coming, she is coming – coming – coming."

The last word died away; it was the last one they ever heard the village girl utter. On she went, dancing on; and on followed the man, they could see that he was still playing, but they could no longer hear the sound of his flute; and on went the dogs round and round and round. On they all went, farther and farther away, till they were separate things no more, till they were just a confused mass of faded colour, till they were a dark misty object that nothing could define, till they had vanished altogether – altogether and forever.

Then the children turned, and looked at each other and at the little cottage home, that only a week before had been so bright and happy, so cosy and so spotless. The fire was out, and the water was still among the cinders; the baking-dish and cake-tin, the fish-slice and the saucepan lid, which the dear mother used to spend so much time in rubbing, were all pulled down from the nails on which they had hung so long, and were lying on the floor. And there was the clock all broken and spoilt, the little picture upon its face could be seen no more; and though it sometimes struck a stray hour, it was with the tone of a clock whose hours are numbered. And there was the baby's high chair, but no little baby to sit in it; there was the cupboard on the wall, and never a sweet loaf on its shelf; and there were the broken mugs, and the bits of bread tossed about, and the greasy boards which the mother had knelt down to scrub until they were white as snow. In the midst of all stood the children, looking at the wreck they had made, their hearts aching, their eyes blinded with tears, and their poor little hands clasped together in their misery.

"Oh, what shall we do?" cried Blue-Eyes. "I wish we had never seen the village girl and the nasty, nasty pear drum."

"Surely mother will come back," sobbed the Turkey. "I am sure we shall die if she doesn't come back."

"I don't know what we shall do if the new mother comes," cried Blue-Eyes. "I shall never, never like any other mother. I don't know what we shall do if that dreadful mother comes."

"We won't let her in," said the Turkey.

"But perhaps she'll walk in," sobbed Blue-Eyes.

Then Turkey stopped crying for a minute, to think what should be done.

"We will bolt the door," she said, "and shut the window; and we won't take any notice when she knocks."

So they bolted the door, and shut the window, and fastened it And then, in spite of all they had said, they felt naughty again, and longed after the little man and woman they had never seen, far more than after the mother who had loved them all their lives. But then they did not really believe that their own mother would not come back, or that any new mother would take her place.

When it was dinner-time, they were very hungry, but they could only find some stale bread, and they had to be content with it.

"Oh, I wish we had heard the little woman's secret," cried the Turkey; "I wouldn't have cared then."

All through the afternoon they sat watching and listening for fear of the new mother; but they saw and heard nothing of her, and gradually they became less and less afraid lest she should come. Then they thought that perhaps when it was dark their own dear mother would come home; and perhaps if they asked her to forgive them she would. And then Blue-Eyes thought that if their mother did come she would be very cold, so. they crept out at the back door and gathered in some wood, and at last, for the grate was wet, and it was a great deal of trouble to manage it, they made a fire. When they saw the bright fire burning, and the little flames leaping and playing among the wood and coal, they began to be happy again, and to feel certain that their own mother would return; and the sight of the pleasant fire reminded them of all the times she had waited for them to come from the post-office, and of how she had welcomed them, and comforted them, and given them nice warm tea and sweet bread, and talked to them. Oh, how sorry they were they had been naughty, and all for that nasty village girl! They did not care a bit about the little man and woman now, or want to hear the secret.

They fetched a pail of water and washed the floor; they found some rag, and rubbed the tins till they looked bright again, and, putting a footstool on a chair, they got up on it very carefully and hung up the things in their places; and then they picked up the broken mugs and made the room as neat as they could, till it looked more and more as if the dear mother's hands had been busy about it. They felt more and more certain she would return, she and the dear little baby together, and they thought they would set the tea-things for her, just as she had so often set them for her naughty children. They took down the tea-tray, and got out the cups, and put the kettle on the fire to boil, and made everything look as home-like as they could. There was no sweet loaf to put on the table, but perhaps the mother would bring something from the village, they thought. At last all was ready, and Blue-Eyes and the Turkey washed their faces and their hands, and then sat and waited, for of course they did not believe what the village girl had said about their mother sailing away.

Suddenly, while they were sitting by the fire, they heard a sound as of something heavy being dragged along the ground outside, and then there was a loud and terrible knocking at the door. The children felt their hearts stand still. They knew it could not be their own mother, for she would have turned the handle and tried to come in without any knocking at all.

"Oh, Turkey!" whispered Blue-Eyes, "if it should be the new mother, what shall we do?"

"We won't let her in," whispered the Turkey, for she was afraid to speak aloud, and again there came a long and loud and terrible knocking at the door.

"What shall we do? Oh, what shall we do?" cried the children, in despair. "Oh, go away!" they called out. "Go away; we won't let you in; we will never be naughty anymore; go away, go away!"

But again there came a loud and terrible knocking.

"She'll break the door if she knocks so hard," cried Blue-Eyes.

"Go and put your back to it," whispered the Turkey, "and I'll peep out of the window and try to see if it is really the new mother."

So in fear and trembling Blue-Eyes put her back against the door, and the Turkey went to the window, and, pressing her face against one side of the frame, peeped out. She could just see a black satin poke bonnet with a frill round the edge, and a long bony arm carrying a black leather bag. From beneath the bonnet there flashed a strange bright light, and Turkey's heart sank and her cheeks turned pale, for she knew it was the flashing of two glass eyes. She crept up to Blue-Eyes. "It is – it is – it is!" she whispered, her voice shaking with fear, "it is the new mother! She has come, and brought her luggage in a black leather bag that is hanging on her arm!"

"Oh, what shall we do?" wept Blue-Eyes; and again there was the terrible knocking.

"Come and put your back against the door too, Turkey," cried Blue-Eyes; "I am afraid it will break."

So together they stood with their two little backs against the door. There was a long pause. They thought perhaps the new mother had made up her mind that there was no one at home to let her in, and would go away, but presently the two children heard through the thin wooden door the new mother move a little, and then say to herself – "I must break open the door with my tail."

For one terrible moment all was still, but in it the children could almost hear her lift up her tail, and then, with a fearful blow, the little painted door was cracked and splintered.

With a shriek the children darted from the spot and fled through the cottage, and out at the back door into the forest beyond. All night long they stayed in the darkness and the cold, and all the next day and the next, and all through the cold, dreary days and the long dark nights that followed.

They are there still, my children. All through the long weeks and months have they been there, with only green rushes for their pillows and only the brown dead leaves to cover them, feeding on the wild strawberries in the summer, or on the nuts when they hang green; on the blackberries when they are no longer sour in the autumn, and in the winter on the little red berries that ripen in the snow. They wander about among the tall dark firs or beneath the great trees beyond. Sometimes they stay to rest beside the little pool near the copse where the ferns grow thickest, and they long and long, with a longing that is greater than words can say, to see their own dear mother again, just once again, to tell her that they'll be good for evermore – just once again.

And still the new mother stays in the little cottage, but the windows are closed and the doors are shut, and no one knows what the inside looks like. Now and then, when the darkness has fallen and the night is still, hand in hand Blue-Eyes and the Turkey creep up near to the home in which they once were so happy, and with beating hearts they watch and listen; sometimes a blinding flash comes through the window, and they know it is the light from the new mother's glass eyes, or they hear a strange muffled noise, and they know it is the sound of her wooden tail as she drags it along the floor.

The Terror of Blue John Gap

Arthur Conan Doyle

THE FOLLOWING NARRATIVE was found among the papers of Dr. James Hardcastle, who died of phthisis on February 4th, 1908, at 36, Upper Coventry Flats, South Kensington. Those who knew him best, while refusing to express an opinion upon this particular statement, are unanimous in asserting that he was a man of a sober and scientific turn of mind, absolutely devoid of imagination, and most unlikely to invent any abnormal series of events. The paper was contained in an envelope, which was docketed, *A Short Account of the Circumstances which occurred near Miss Allerton's Farm in North-West Derbyshire in the Spring of Last Year.* The envelope was sealed, and on the other side was written in pencil:

> *DEAR SEATON—*
> *It may interest, and perhaps pain you, to know that the incredulity with which you met my story has prevented me from ever opening my mouth upon the subject again. I leave this record after my death, and perhaps strangers may be found to have more confidence in me than my friend.*

Inquiry has failed to elicit who this Seaton may have been. I may add that the visit of the deceased to Allerton's Farm, and the general nature of the alarm there, apart from his particular explanation, have been absolutely established. With this foreword I append his account exactly as he left it. It is in the form of a diary, some entries in which have been expanded, while a few have been erased.

* * *

April 17.—Already I feel the benefit of this wonderful upland air. The farm of the Allertons lies fourteen hundred and twenty feet above sea-level, so it may well be a bracing climate. Beyond the usual morning cough I have very little discomfort, and, what with the fresh milk and the home-grown mutton, I have every chance of putting on weight. I think Saunderson will be pleased.

The two Miss Allertons are charmingly quaint and kind, two dear little hard-working old maids, who are ready to lavish all the heart which might have gone out to husband and to children upon an invalid stranger. Truly, the old maid is a most useful person, one of the reserve forces of the community. They talk of the superfluous woman, but what would the poor superfluous man do without her kindly presence? By the way, in their simplicity they very quickly let out the reason why Saunderson recommended their farm. The Professor rose from the ranks himself, and I believe that in his youth he was not above scaring crows in these very fields.

It is a most lonely spot, and the walks are picturesque in the extreme. The farm consists of grazing land lying at the bottom of an irregular valley. On each side are the fantastic limestone hills, formed of rock so soft that you can break it away with your hands. All this country is hollow. Could you strike it with some gigantic hammer it would boom like a drum, or possibly cave in altogether and expose some huge subterranean sea. A great sea there must surely be, for on all sides the streams run into the mountain itself, never to reappear. There are gaps everywhere amid the rocks, and when you pass through them you find yourself in great caverns, which wind down into the bowels of the earth. I have a small bicycle lamp, and it is a perpetual joy to me to carry it into these weird solitudes, and to see the wonderful silver and black effect when I throw its light upon the stalactites which drape the lofty roofs. Shut off the lamp, and you are in the blackest darkness. Turn it on, and it is a scene from the Arabian Nights.

But there is one of these strange openings in the earth which has a special interest, for it is the handiwork, not of nature, but of man. I had never heard of Blue John when I came to these parts. It is the name given to a peculiar mineral of a beautiful purple shade, which is only found at one or two places in the world. It is so rare that an ordinary vase of Blue John would be valued at a great price. The Romans, with that extraordinary instinct of theirs, discovered that it was to be found in this valley, and sank a horizontal shaft deep into the mountain side. The opening of their mine has been called Blue John Gap, a clean-cut arch in the rock, the mouth all overgrown with bushes. It is a goodly passage which the Roman miners have cut, and it intersects some of the great water-worn caves, so that if you enter Blue John Gap you would do well to mark your steps and to have a good store of candles, or you may never make your way back to the daylight again. I have not yet gone deeply into it, but this very day I stood at the mouth of the arched tunnel, and peering down into the black recesses beyond, I vowed that when my health returned I would devote some holiday to exploring those mysterious depths and finding out for myself how far the Roman had penetrated into the Derbyshire hills.

Strange how superstitious these countrymen are! I should have thought better of young Armitage, for he is a man of some education and character, and a very fine fellow for his station in life. I was standing at the Blue John Gap when he came across the field to me.

"Well, doctor," said he, "you're not afraid, anyhow."

"Afraid!" I answered. "Afraid of what?"

"Of it," said he, with a jerk of his thumb towards the black vault, "of the Terror that lives in the Blue John Cave."

How absurdly easy it is for a legend to arise in a lonely countryside! I examined him as to the reasons for his weird belief. It seems that from time to time sheep have been missing from the fields, carried bodily away, according to Armitage. That they could have wandered away of their own accord and disappeared among the mountains was an explanation to which he would not listen. On one occasion a pool of blood had been found, and some tufts of wool. That also, I pointed out, could be explained in a perfectly natural way. Further, the nights upon which sheep disappeared were invariably very dark; cloudy nights with no moon. This I met with the obvious retort that those were the nights which a commonplace sheep-stealer would naturally choose for his work. On one occasion a gap had been made in a wall, and some of the stones scattered for a considerable distance. Human agency again, in my opinion. Finally, Armitage clinched all his arguments by telling me that he had actually heard the Creature – indeed, that anyone could hear it who remained long enough at the Gap. It was a distant roaring of an immense volume. I could not but smile at this, knowing, as I do, the strange reverberations which come out of an underground water system running amid the chasms of a limestone formation. My incredulity annoyed Armitage so that he turned and left me with some abruptness.

And now comes the queer point about the whole business. I was still standing near the mouth of the cave turning over in my mind the various statements of Armitage, and reflecting how readily they could be explained away, when suddenly, from the depth of the tunnel beside me, there issued a most extraordinary sound. How shall I describe it? First of all, it seemed to be a great distance away, far down in the bowels of the earth. Secondly, in spite of this suggestion of distance, it was very loud. Lastly, it was not a boom, nor a crash, such as one would associate with falling water or tumbling rock, but it was a high whine, tremulous and vibrating, almost like the whinnying of a horse. It was certainly a most remarkable experience, and one which for a moment, I must admit, gave a new significance to Armitage's words. I waited by the Blue John Gap for half an hour or more, but there was no return of the sound, so at last I wandered back to the farmhouse, rather mystified by what had occurred. Decidedly I shall explore that cavern when my strength is restored. Of course, Armitage's explanation is too absurd for discussion, and yet that sound was certainly very strange. It still rings in my ears as I write.

April 20.—In the last three days I have made several expeditions to the Blue John Gap, and have even penetrated some short distance, but my bicycle lantern is so small and weak that I dare not trust myself very far. I shall do the thing more systematically. I have heard no sound at all, and could almost believe that I had been the victim of some hallucination suggested, perhaps, by Armitage's conversation. Of course, the whole idea is absurd, and yet I must confess that those bushes at the entrance of the cave do present an appearance as if some heavy creature had forced its way through them. I begin to be keenly interested. I have said nothing to the Miss Allertons, for they are quite superstitious enough already, but I have bought some candles, and mean to investigate for myself.

I observed this morning that among the numerous tufts of sheep's wool which lay among the bushes near the cavern there was one which was smeared with blood. Of course, my reason tells me that if sheep wander into such rocky places they are likely to injure themselves, and yet somehow that splash of crimson gave me a sudden shock, and for a moment I found myself shrinking back in horror from the old Roman arch. A fetid breath seemed to ooze from the black depths into which I peered. Could it indeed be possible that some nameless thing, some dreadful presence, was lurking down yonder? I should have been incapable of such feelings in the days of my strength, but one grows more nervous and fanciful when one's health is shaken.

For the moment I weakened in my resolution, and was ready to leave the secret of the old mine, if one exists, for ever unsolved. But tonight my interest has returned and my nerves grown more steady. Tomorrow I trust that I shall have gone more deeply into this matter.

April 22.—Let me try and set down as accurately as I can my extraordinary experience of yesterday. I started in the afternoon, and made my way to the Blue John Gap. I confess that my misgivings returned as I gazed into its depths, and I wished that I had brought a companion to share my exploration. Finally, with a return of resolution, I lit my candle, pushed my way through the briars, and descended into the rocky shaft.

It went down at an acute angle for some fifty feet, the floor being covered with broken stone. Thence there extended a long, straight passage cut in the solid rock. I am no geologist, but the lining of this corridor was certainly of some harder material than limestone, for there were points where I could actually see the tool-marks which the old miners had left in their excavation, as fresh as if they had been done yesterday. Down this strange, old-world corridor I stumbled, my feeble flame throwing a dim circle of light around me, which made the shadows beyond the more threatening and obscure. Finally, I came to a spot where the Roman tunnel opened into a water-worn cavern – a huge hall, hung with long white icicles of lime deposit. From this central chamber I could dimly perceive that a number of passages worn by the subterranean streams wound away into the depths of the earth. I was standing there wondering whether I had better return, or whether I dare venture farther into this dangerous labyrinth, when my eyes fell upon something at my feet which strongly arrested my attention.

The greater part of the floor of the cavern was covered with boulders of rock or with hard incrustations of lime, but at this particular point there had been a drip from the distant roof, which had left a patch of soft mud. In the very centre of this there was a huge mark – an ill-defined blotch, deep, broad and irregular, as if a great boulder had fallen upon it. No loose stone lay near, however, nor was there anything to account for the impression. It was far too large to be caused by any possible animal, and besides, there was only the one, and the patch of mud was of such a size that no reasonable stride could have covered it. As I rose from the examination of that singular mark and then looked round into the black shadows which hemmed me in, I must confess that I felt for a moment a most unpleasant sinking of my heart, and that, do what I could, the candle trembled in my outstretched hand.

I soon recovered my nerve, however, when I reflected how absurd it was to associate so huge and shapeless a mark with the track of any known animal. Even an elephant could not have produced it. I determined, therefore, that I would not be scared by vague and senseless fears from carrying out my exploration. Before proceeding, I took good note of a curious rock formation in the wall by which I could recognise the entrance of the Roman tunnel. The precaution was very necessary, for the great cave, so far as I could see it, was intersected by passages. Having made sure of my position, and reassured myself by examining my spare candles and my matches, I advanced slowly over the rocky and uneven surface of the cavern.

And now I come to the point where I met with such sudden and desperate disaster. A stream, some twenty feet broad, ran across my path, and I walked for some little distance along the bank to find a spot where I could cross dry-shod. Finally, I came to a place where a single flat boulder lay near the centre, which I could reach in a stride. As it chanced, however, the rock had been cut away and made top-heavy by the rush of the stream, so that it tilted over as I landed on it and shot me into the ice-cold water. My candle went out, and I found myself floundering about in utter and absolute darkness.

I staggered to my feet again, more amused than alarmed by my adventure. The candle had fallen from my hand, and was lost in the stream, but I had two others in my pocket, so that it was of no importance. I got one of them ready, and drew out my box of matches to light it. Only then did I realise my position. The box had been soaked in my fall into the river. It was impossible to strike the matches.

A cold hand seemed to close round my heart as I realised my position. The darkness was opaque and horrible. It was so utter one put one's hand up to one's face as if to press off something solid. I stood still, and by an effort I steadied myself. I tried to reconstruct in my mind a map of the floor of the cavern as I had last seen it. Alas! the bearings which had impressed themselves upon my mind were high on the wall, and not to be found by touch. Still, I remembered in a general way how the sides were situated, and I hoped that by groping my way along them I should at last come to the opening of the Roman tunnel. Moving very slowly, and continually striking against the rocks, I set out on this desperate quest.

But I very soon realised how impossible it was. In that black, velvety darkness one lost all one's bearings in an instant. Before I had made a dozen paces, I was utterly bewildered as to my whereabouts. The rippling of the stream, which was the one sound audible, showed me where it lay, but the moment that I left its bank I was utterly lost. The idea of finding my way back in absolute darkness through that limestone labyrinth was clearly an impossible one.

I sat down upon a boulder and reflected upon my unfortunate plight. I had not told anyone that I proposed to come to the Blue John mine, and it was unlikely that a search party would come after me. Therefore I must trust to my own resources to get clear of the danger. There was only one hope, and that was that the matches might dry. When I fell into the river, only half of me had got thoroughly wet. My left shoulder had remained above the water. I took the box of matches, therefore, and put it into my left armpit. The moist air of the cavern might possibly be counteracted by the heat of my body, but even so, I knew that I could not hope to get a light for many hours. Meanwhile there was nothing for it but to wait.

By good luck I had slipped several biscuits into my pocket before I left the farm-house. These I now devoured, and washed them down with a draught from that wretched stream which had been the cause of all my misfortunes. Then I felt about for a comfortable seat among the rocks, and, having discovered a place where I could get a support for my back, I stretched out my legs and settled myself down to wait. I was wretchedly damp and cold, but I tried to cheer myself with the reflection that modern science prescribed open windows and walks in all weather for my disease. Gradually, lulled by the monotonous gurgle of the stream, and by the absolute darkness, I sank into an uneasy slumber.

How long this lasted I cannot say. It may have been for an hour, it may have been for several. Suddenly I sat up on my rock couch, with every nerve thrilling and every sense acutely on the alert. Beyond all doubt I had heard a sound – some sound very distinct from the gurgling of the waters. It had passed, but the reverberation of it still lingered in my ear. Was it a search party? They would most certainly have shouted, and vague as this sound was which had wakened me, it was very distinct from the human voice. I sat palpitating and hardly daring to breathe. There it was again! And again! Now it had become continuous. It was a tread – yes, surely it was the tread of some living creature. But what a tread it was! It gave one the impression of enormous weight carried upon sponge-like feet, which gave forth a muffled but ear-filling sound. The darkness was as complete as ever, but the tread was regular and decisive. And it was coming beyond all question in my direction.

My skin grew cold, and my hair stood on end as I listened to that steady and ponderous footfall. There was some creature there, and surely by the speed of its advance, it was one which could see in the dark. I crouched low on my rock and tried to blend myself into it. The steps grew nearer still, then stopped, and presently I was aware of a loud lapping and gurgling. The creature was drinking at the stream. Then again there was silence, broken by a succession of long sniffs and snorts of tremendous volume and energy. Had it caught the scent of me? My own nostrils were filled by a low fetid odour, mephitic and abominable. Then I heard the steps again. They were on my side of the stream now. The stones rattled within a few yards of where I lay. Hardly daring to breathe, I crouched upon my rock. Then the steps drew away. I heard the splash as it returned across the river, and the sound died away into the distance in the direction from which it had come.

For a long time I lay upon the rock, too much horrified to move. I thought of the sound which I had heard coming from the depths of the cave, of Armitage's fears, of the strange impression in the mud, and now came this final and absolute proof that there was indeed some inconceivable monster, something utterly unearthly and dreadful, which lurked in the hollow of the mountain. Of its nature or form I could frame no conception, save that it was both light-footed and gigantic. The combat between my reason, which told me that such things could not be, and my senses, which told me that they were, raged within me as I lay. Finally, I was almost ready to persuade myself that this experience had been part of some evil dream, and that my abnormal condition might have conjured up an hallucination. But there remained one final experience which removed the last possibility of doubt from my mind.

I had taken my matches from my armpit and felt them. They seemed perfectly hard and dry. Stooping down into a crevice of the rocks, I tried one of them. To my delight it took fire at once.

I lit the candle, and, with a terrified backward glance into the obscure depths of the cavern, I hurried in the direction of the Roman passage. As I did so I passed the patch of mud on which I had seen the huge imprint. Now I stood astonished before it, for there were three similar imprints upon its surface, enormous in size, irregular in outline, of a depth which indicated the ponderous weight which had left them. Then a great terror surged over me. Stooping and shading my candle with my hand, I ran in a frenzy of fear to the rocky archway, hastened up it, and never stopped until, with weary feet and panting lungs, I rushed up the final slope of stones, broke through the tangle of briars, and flung myself exhausted upon the soft grass under the peaceful light of the stars. It was three in the morning when I reached the farm-house, and today I am all unstrung and quivering after my terrific adventure. As yet I have told no one. I must move warily in the matter. What would the poor lonely women, or the uneducated yokels here think of it if I were to tell them my experience? Let me go to someone who can understand and advise.

April 25.—I was laid up in bed for two days after my incredible adventure in the cavern. I use the adjective with a very definite meaning, for I have had an experience since which has shocked me almost as much as the other. I have said that I was looking round for someone who could advise me. There is a Dr. Mark Johnson who practices some few miles away, to whom I had a note of recommendation from Professor Saunderson. To him I drove, when I was strong enough to get about, and I recounted to him my whole strange experience. He listened intently, and then carefully examined me, paying special attention to my reflexes and to the pupils of my eyes. When he had finished, he refused to discuss my adventure, saying that it was entirely beyond him, but he gave me the card of a Mr. Picton at Castleton, with the advice that I should instantly go to him and tell him the story exactly as I had done to himself. He was, according to my adviser, the very man who was pre-eminently suited to help me. I went on to the station, therefore, and made my way to the little town, which is some ten miles away. Mr. Picton appeared to be a man of importance, as his brass plate was displayed upon the door of a considerable building on the outskirts of the town. I was about to ring his bell, when some misgiving came into my mind, and, crossing to a neighbouring shop, I asked the man behind the counter if he could tell me anything of Mr. Picton. "Why," said he, "he is the best mad doctor in Derbyshire, and yonder is his asylum." You can imagine that it was not long before I had shaken the dust of Castleton from my feet and returned to the farm, cursing all unimaginative pedants who cannot conceive that there may be things in creation which have never yet chanced to come across their mole's vision. After all, now that I am cooler, I can afford to admit that I have been no more sympathetic to Armitage than Dr. Johnson has been to me.

April 27.—When I was a student I had the reputation of being a man of courage and enterprise. I remember that when there was a ghost-hunt at Coltbridge it was I who sat up in the haunted house. Is it advancing years (after all, I am only thirty-five), or is it this physical malady which has caused degeneration? Certainly my heart quails when I think of that horrible cavern in the hill, and the certainty that it has some monstrous occupant. What shall I do? There is not an hour in the day that I do not debate the question. If I say nothing, then the mystery remains unsolved. If I do say anything, then I have the alternative of mad alarm over the whole countryside, or of absolute incredulity which may end in consigning me to an asylum. On the whole, I think that my best course is to wait, and to prepare for some expedition which shall be more deliberate and better thought out than the last. As a first step I have been to Castleton and obtained a few essentials – a large acetylene lantern for one thing, and a good double-barrelled sporting rifle for another. The latter I have hired, but I have bought a dozen heavy game cartridges, which would bring down a rhinoceros. Now I am ready for my troglodyte friend. Give me better health and a little spate of energy, and I shall try conclusions with him yet. But who and what is he? Ah! there is the question which stands between me and my sleep. How many theories do I form, only to discard each in turn! It is all so utterly unthinkable. And yet the cry, the footmark, the tread in the cavern – no reasoning can get past these I think of the old-world legends of dragons and of other monsters. Were they, perhaps, not such fairy-tales as we have thought? Can it be that there is some fact which underlies them, and am I, of all mortals, the one who is chosen to expose it?

May 3.—For several days I have been laid up by the vagaries of an English spring, and during those days there have been developments, the true and sinister meaning of which no one can appreciate save myself. I may say that we have had cloudy and moonless nights of late, which according to my information were the seasons upon which sheep disappeared. Well, sheep have disappeared. Two of Miss Allerton's, one of old Pearson's of the Cat Walk, and one of Mrs. Moulton's. Four in all during three nights. No trace is left of them at all, and the countryside is buzzing with rumours of gipsies and of sheep-stealers.

But there is something more serious than that. Young Armitage has disappeared also. He left his moorland cottage early on Wednesday night and has never been heard of since. He was an unattached man, so there is less sensation than would otherwise be the case. The popular explanation is that he owes money, and has found a situation in some other part of the country, whence he will presently write for his belongings. But I have grave misgivings. Is it not much more likely that the recent tragedy of the sheep has caused him to take some steps which may have ended in his own destruction? He may, for example, have lain in wait for the creature and been carried off by it into the recesses of the mountains. What an inconceivable fate for a civilised Englishman of the twentieth century! And yet I feel that it is possible and even probable. But in that case, how far am I answerable both for his death and for any other mishap which may occur? Surely with the knowledge I already possess it must be my duty to see that something is done, or if necessary to do it myself. It must be the latter, for this morning I went down to the local police-station and told my story. The inspector entered it all in a large book and bowed me out with commendable gravity, but I heard a burst of laughter before I had got down his garden path. No doubt he was recounting my adventure to his family.

June 10.—I am writing this, propped up in bed, six weeks after my last entry in this journal. I have gone through a terrible shock both to mind and body, arising from such an experience as has seldom befallen a human being before. But I have attained my end. The danger from the Terror which dwells in the Blue John Gap has passed never to return. Thus much at least I, a broken invalid, have done for the common good. Let me now recount what occurred as clearly as I may.

The night of Friday, May 3rd, was dark and cloudy – the very night for the monster to walk. About eleven o'clock I went from the farm-house with my lantern and my rifle, having first left a note upon the table of my bedroom in which I said that, if I were missing, search should be made for me in the direction of the Gap. I made my way to the mouth of the Roman shaft, and, having perched myself among the rocks close to the opening, I shut off my lantern and waited patiently with my loaded rifle ready to my hand.

It was a melancholy vigil. All down the winding valley I could see the scattered lights of the farm-houses, and the church clock of Chapel-le-Dale tolling the hours came faintly to my ears. These tokens of my fellow-men served only to make my own position seem the more lonely, and to call for a greater effort to overcome the terror which tempted me continually to get back to the farm, and abandon for ever this dangerous quest. And yet there lies deep in every man a rooted self-respect which makes it hard for him to turn back from that which he has once undertaken. This feeling of personal pride was my salvation now, and it was that alone which held me fast when every instinct of my nature was dragging me away. I am glad now that I had the strength. In spite of all that is has cost me, my manhood is at least above reproach.

Twelve o'clock struck in the distant church, then one, then two. It was the darkest hour of the night. The clouds were drifting low, and there was not a star in the sky. An owl was hooting somewhere among the rocks, but no other sound, save the gentle sough of the wind, came to my ears. And then suddenly I heard it! From far away down the tunnel came those muffled steps, so soft and yet so ponderous. I heard also the rattle of stones as they gave way under that giant tread. They drew nearer. They were close upon me. I heard the crashing of the bushes round the entrance, and then dimly through the darkness I was conscious of the loom of some enormous shape, some monstrous inchoate creature, passing swiftly and very silently out from the tunnel. I was paralysed with fear and amazement. Long as I had waited, now that it had actually come I was unprepared for the shock. I lay motionless and breathless, whilst the great dark mass whisked by me and was swallowed up in the night.

But now I nerved myself for its return. No sound came from the sleeping countryside to tell of the horror which was loose. In no way could I judge how far off it was, what it was doing, or when it might be back. But not a second time should my nerve fail me, not a second time should it pass unchallenged. I swore it between my clenched teeth as I laid my cocked rifle across the rock.

And yet it nearly happened. There was no warning of approach now as the creature passed over the grass. Suddenly, like a dark, drifting shadow, the huge bulk loomed up once more before me, making for the entrance of the cave. Again came that paralysis of volition which held my crooked forefinger impotent upon the trigger. But with a desperate effort I shook it off. Even as the brushwood rustled, and the monstrous beast blended with the shadow of the Gap, I fired at the retreating form. In the blaze of the gun I caught a glimpse of a great shaggy mass, something with rough and bristling hair of a withered grey colour, fading away to white in its lower parts, the huge body supported upon short, thick, curving legs. I had just that glance, and then I heard the rattle of the stones as the creature tore down into its burrow. In an instant, with a triumphant revulsion of feeling, I had cast my fears to the wind, and uncovering my powerful lantern, with my rifle in my hand, I sprang down from my rock and rushed after the monster down the old Roman shaft.

My splendid lamp cast a brilliant flood of vivid light in front of me, very different from the yellow glimmer which had aided me down the same passage only twelve days before. As I ran, I saw the great beast lurching along before me, its huge bulk filling up the whole space from wall to wall. Its hair looked like coarse faded oakum, and hung down in long, dense masses which swayed as it moved. It was like an enormous unclipped sheep in its fleece, but in size it was far larger than the largest elephant, and its breadth seemed to be nearly as great as its height. It fills me with amazement now to think that I should have dared to follow such a horror into the bowels of the earth, but when one's blood is up, and when one's quarry seems to be flying, the old primeval hunting-spirit awakes and prudence is cast to the wind. Rifle in hand, I ran at the top of my speed upon the trail of the monster.

I had seen that the creature was swift. Now I was to find out to my cost that it was also very cunning. I had imagined that it was in panic flight, and that I had only to pursue it. The idea that it might turn upon me never entered my excited brain. I have already explained that the passage down which I was racing opened into a great central cave. Into this I rushed, fearful lest I should lose all trace of the beast. But he had turned upon his own traces, and in a moment we were face to face.

That picture, seen in the brilliant white light of the lantern, is etched for ever upon my brain. He had reared up on his hind legs as a bear would do, and stood above me, enormous, menacing – such a creature as no nightmare had ever brought to my imagination. I have said that he reared like a bear, and there was something bear-like – if one could conceive a bear which was ten-fold the bulk of any bear seen upon earth – in his whole pose and attitude, in his great crooked forelegs with their ivory-white claws, in his rugged skin, and in his red, gaping mouth, fringed with monstrous fangs. Only in one point did he differ from the bear, or from any other creature which walks the earth, and even at that supreme moment a shudder of horror passed over me as I observed that the eyes which glistened in the glow of my lantern were huge, projecting bulbs, white and sightless. For a moment his great paws swung over my head. The next he fell forward upon me, I and my broken lantern crashed to the earth, and I remember no more.

When I came to myself I was back in the farm-house of the Allertons. Two days had passed since my terrible adventure in the Blue John Gap. It seems that I had lain all night in the cave insensible from concussion of the brain, with my left arm and two ribs badly fractured. In the morning my note had been found, a search party of a dozen farmers assembled, and I had been tracked down and carried back to my bedroom, where I had lain in high delirium ever since. There was, it seems, no sign of the creature, and no bloodstain which would show that my bullet had found him as he passed. Save for my own plight and the marks upon the mud, there was nothing to prove that what I said was true.

Six weeks have now elapsed, and I am able to sit out once more in the sunshine. Just opposite me is the steep hillside, grey with shaly rock, and yonder on its flank is the dark cleft which marks the opening of the Blue John Gap. But it is no longer a source of terror. Never again through that ill-omened tunnel shall any strange shape flit out into the world of men. The educated and the scientific, the Dr. Johnsons and the like, may smile at my narrative, but the poorer folk of the countryside had never a doubt as to its truth. On the day after my recovering consciousness they assembled in their hundreds round the Blue John Gap. As the Castleton Courier said:

> It was useless for our correspondent, or for any of the adventurous gentlemen who had come from Matlock, Buxton, and other parts, to offer to descend, to explore the cave to the end, and to finally test the extraordinary narrative of Dr. James Hardcastle. The country people had taken the matter into their own hands, and from an early hour of the morning they had worked hard in stopping up the entrance of the tunnel. There is a sharp slope where the shaft begins, and great boulders, rolled along by many willing hands, were thrust down it until the Gap was absolutely sealed. So ends the episode which has caused such excitement throughout the country. Local opinion is fiercely divided upon the subject. On the one hand are those who point to Dr. Hardcastle's impaired health, and to the possibility of cerebral lesions of tubercular origin giving rise to strange hallucinations. Some idée fixe, according to these gentlemen, caused the doctor to wander down the tunnel, and a fall among the rocks was sufficient to account for his injuries. On the other hand, a legend of a strange creature in the Gap has existed for some months back, and the farmers look upon Dr. Hardcastle's narrative and his personal injuries as a final corroboration. So the matter stands, and so the matter will continue to stand, for no definite solution seems to us to be now possible. It transcends human wit to give any scientific explanation which could cover the alleged facts.

Perhaps before the Courier published these words they would have been wise to send their representative to me. I have thought the matter out, as no one else has occasion to do, and it is possible that I might have removed some of the more obvious difficulties of the narrative and brought it one degree nearer to scientific acceptance. Let me then write down the only explanation which seems to me to elucidate what I know to my cost to have been a series of facts. My theory may seem to be wildly improbable, but at least no one can venture to say that it is impossible.

My view is – and it was formed, as is shown by my diary, before my personal adventure – that in this part of England there is a vast subterranean lake or sea, which is fed by the great number of streams which pass down through the limestone. Where there is a large collection of water there must also be some evaporation, mists or rain, and a possibility of vegetation. This in turn suggests that there may be animal life, arising, as the vegetable life would also do, from those seeds and types which had been introduced at an early period of the world's history, when communication with the outer air was more easy. This place had then developed a fauna and flora of its own, including such monsters as the one which I had seen, which may well have been the old cave-bear, enormously enlarged and modified by its new environment. For countless aeons the internal and the external creation had kept apart, growing steadily away from each other. Then there had come some rift in the depths of the mountain which had enabled one creature to wander up and, by means of the Roman tunnel, to reach the open air. Like all subterranean life, it had lost the power of sight, but this had no doubt been compensated for by nature in other directions. Certainly it had some means of finding its way about, and of hunting down the sheep upon the hillside. As to its choice of dark nights, it is part of my theory that light was painful to those great white eyeballs, and that it was only a pitch-black world which it could tolerate. Perhaps, indeed, it was the glare of my lantern which saved my life at that awful moment when we were face to face. So I read the riddle. I leave these facts behind me, and if you can explain them, do so; or if you choose to doubt them, do so. Neither your belief nor your incredulity can alter them, nor affect one whose task is nearly over.

* * *

So ended the strange narrative of Dr. James Hardcastle.

The Next Heir

H.D. Everett

Chapter I

FRYER AND FRYER, solicitors, of Lincoln's Inn, the original firm and their successors, have for the past hundred years acted as guardians of the interests of the landed gentry, buying and selling portions of estates, proving wills, drawing up marriage settlements and the like. And a glance at the japanned deed-boxes in their somewhat shabby office would discover among the inscriptions sundry names of note.

The original Fryers have long been dead and gone, but there is still a Fryer at the head of the firm. And on a certain day of spring, this ruling Fryer was alone in his private office-room, when his clerk brought in a message.

"Mr. Richard Quinton to see you, sir. He has no card to send up, but he says you will know his name and his business, as he has called to answer an advertisement."

Without doubt Mr. Fryer did know the name of Quinton, as it was legibly painted on a deed-box full in view, but something in his countenance expressed surprise. He signified his willingness to see Mr. Richard Quinton, and presently the visitor entered, a pleasant-faced youngish man, brown of attire, and indeed altogether a brown man, except for the whitish patch where his forehead had been screened from the sun. Bronzed of skin, brown of short cut hair, and opening on the world a frank pair of hazel eyes, which looked as if they had been used to regard the wide spaces of waste lands, and were not fully used to the pressure and hurry and strenuousness of our over-civilised older world.

"I have called, sir, about an advertisement inserted by Fryer and Fryer in a Montreal paper. I have it here to show you. It was posted to me at the London hospital, where I have been since my wound, I see that the representative of Richard Morley Quinton, who emigrated to Canada in 1827, will hear on applying to you of something to his advantage."

"*May* hear of something," corrected the man of law. "Are you the representative in this generation?"

"I am, sir. Richard Morley Quinton was my grandfather."

"Great-grandfather, surely? You are under thirty, and he was twenty-six years old when he left England."

"No: grandfather. He had a hard struggle in his first years on the other side. His English brother was not the sort to help him, and he never asked for help: he would not. He did not marry until late in life, and my old dad was the only son who survived infancy. There was a daughter who married and had children. But I don't suppose you want to know about her."

"We want the male heir. Or at least to know where he might be found."

"My dad married earlier, but he had no children by his first wife. He was well over fifty when he married my mother, and I am their only child. I can put you in the way of getting all the certificates you want, and vouchers from responsible people who have known the family. And now, tell me. Why am I advertised for? Is it an inheritance?"

"Not at the present moment, but it may be."

"Of Quinton and Quinton Verney – is that so? My dad would have been pleased. He thought much of Quinton, hearing about it from his father, who was born at the Court."

"If the present Mr. Quinton, your second cousin, makes no will, the Quinton property goes to the heir-male of your mutual great-grandfather. But he has the power of willing the whole where he pleases – to a hospital, or to a beggar in the street. You can count on no certain inheritance. You understand?"

"Then why?"

"We advertised because Mr. Quinton wished to ascertain who represented the Canadian branch of the family, and also to make your personal acquaintance. We can give you no certainty, but I gather from what he has written, that, if your cousin likes you, and if you agree to certain stipulations respecting the property, he intends to make you his heir. When the particulars you give me are verified, you will have to go down to Quinton, but he will reimburse any expense you may be put to, through loss of time and detention in England. You can hold yourself at our disposal?"

"If military orders do not interfere – yes, gladly, for the sake of a look at old Quinton Court, even with nothing to come after. But perhaps Mr. Quinton may prefer to meet me in London."

"You will have to go down there. Mr. Quinton is a complete invalid, and keeps a resident doctor: he is still under sixty, but most unlikely, I should say, to marry. His father was killed in the hunting-field; he had not been long married, but his wife, who was one of the Pengwyns, gave birth to twin sons, posthumous children. This Clement was the younger of the two, but his elder brother died at nineteen, also from an accident. There you have the family history in a nutshell. Give me an address, where a letter will certainly find you when I have looked into this."

* * *

Richard had not long to wait for the expected letter. Mr. Clement Quinton seemed disposed to take his young kinsman on trust, without holding aloof till his story was verified. Mr. Fryer was still in correspondence with Canada when the summons came for Richard to present himself at Quinton Verney. The young Canadian was prompt in obeying, and on the day following he took train for the nearest railway point. No day or time had been named for arrival, so, after changing at the junction and alighting at a small wayside station, no conveyance was there to meet him. Nor, on enquiry, was any trap to be hired. His portmanteau could be sent by a returning cart in the course of a couple of hours, but for himself there was no alternative. He would have to walk the four miles, or rather more, which separated the station from Mount Verney.

Mount Verney, these people styled Mr. Quinton's dwelling, and not Quinton Court as he expected; the Quinton Court his old father used to talk of, told by the grandfather reminiscent of his youth. Why had the original name been changed – that should be a first question when the time for putting questions came. Meanwhile he was not ill-pleased to be approaching Quinton on foot and alone, and a walk of four miles and over was but a light matter.

Four miles of lovely country verdant with the early green of spring, hill and dale unfolding wooded glimpses here and there, and the ancient Roman road stretching its white line before him, enduring still after all these centuries. He could hardly mistake the way, but after a while he thought it better to ask direction. There were iron gates and an avenue leading to Mount Verney, so he was told, and when he came to the iron gates he must turn in.

Gates and an avenue! His father had spoken of no such appendage to Quinton Court, but no doubt they were additions of a later time. He had his father much in mind during that walk, and the interest he would have felt in this possible – nay, probable – inheritance for his son. His grandfather too; the grandfather who died before his birth: it was as if the two old men went beside him along the green-fenced way, made fair by the sunshine of late April. And he had another person in mind, one who up to now has not been named. Nan, his girl, who waited for him far off across the Atlantic, full of love and faith. If this succession truly came to pass, if it were even an assured future to him and to his heirs, marriage would be no longer an imprudence, it might be entered into at once on his return, released from war-service. That hope was enough to gild the sunshine, and spread the pastures with a brighter green. And then he came to the gates, and they stood open.

Mount Verney did not boast a lodge, though the drive was a long one. The avenue had been closely planted with ilex and pine, too closely for the good of the trees, and it was consequently dark in shadow: as he turned in he was conscious of a certain chill.

The open gates were hung on stone pillars, and the ornamentation of these uprights caught his eye. On either side, inwards and outwards, a face was carved in relief, but a face that was not human: the mask of a satyr, with pricked animal ears and sprouting horns, and an evil leering grin. Richard had seen nothing of this sort in his backwoods experience, though possibly other things that were starker and grimmer. The leering faces filled him with repugnance; they should not remain there, he thought, to watch over the comings and goings of the house, did ever that house become his own.

The dark avenue had a bend in it; he could not see to the end, but he thought he knew well what he would find there, the old Quinton homestead had been so often described to him. The grey stone house, with its gables and mullioned windows, diamond-paned; the steep roof, up and down which the pigeons strutted and plumed themselves; the paved courtyard with its breast-high wall and mounted urns. He had a clear picture of it in his mind, and this was what at the turn of the avenue he expected to see. But when the turn was reached, his joyful anticipations fell dead. This was quite another place. Had he been misdirected after all?

What lay before him was a white stuccoed villa, spreading over much ground, but so pierced with big window-spaces that it presented to the beholder scant solidity of wall. This was the entrance side; towards the valley the walls rounded themselves into two semi-circles with a flat central division, and here again were the big sash windows of plate-glass, overlooking the view. But there was no mistake. This was Mount Verney.

A grave-looking elderly manservant answered the bell, and it became evident the Canadian visitor had arrived too soon. Mr. Richard Quinton was expected, yes certainly, but the day had not been named, and Mr. Quinton was at present out in the car, and Dr. Lindsay with him. If Mr. Richard would step into the library, tea should be brought to him – unless he preferred sherry. His room had been so far prepared that it could be quickly made ready; he, Peters, would tell the housekeeper. And would Mr. Richard come this way?

So tea was served to Richard in the library, and his first meal under the Mount Verney roof was taken in solitude, as the master of the house did not return. The library possessed one of the wide bows overlooking the valley, but in spite of the tall sash windows the room was a dark one. They were, it is true, heavily draped with crimson curtains, and the furniture was also heavy, and of an inartistic period. He tried to picture Nan in these surroundings, sitting in the opposite big chair (it would have swallowed her up entirely unless she perched on the arm) and pouring out for him from the huge old teapot, but the effort was in vain. The fancy portrait of his little love would not fit into this frame, but doubtless the frame could be altered: like the grinning masks on the gates, there was much it would be possible to change. Meanwhile hurrying footsteps were heard on the floor overhead, housemaids were busy there; and presently Peters came again to ask if he should conduct the guest to his room.

Richard left the dull library with a sensation of relief. The chamber immediately above had been prepared for him, of equal size, and with windows commanding the view. Richard made some appreciative comment, which seemed to please the old servant.

"Yes, sir," he said, "this is the best bedroom, it has the finest look-out. Mr. Quinton himself gave orders for it to be yours. It used to be Lady Anna Quinton's."

"Lady Anna Quinton!" Richard repeated the name in surprise. "I did not know Mr. Quinton had ever been married."

"No, sir, and he never was. Her ladyship was his mother. She went away to France and died there; it is getting on for thirty years ago, but Mr. Quinton couldn't bear to take the room to be his, though it is the best in the house. I'll send up your portmanteau, sir, directly it arrives." And with that, Peters withdrew.

Here Richard was certainly well lodged. He stood at the middle window which had been set open, and looked out over a wide prospect. The sun was now beginning to decline, and the first flush of rosy cloud was reflected in the chain of pools which filled the valley to the right, widened out almost to the dimensions of a lake – no doubt artificially formed by damning up the natural stream, which rushed over a weir out of sight. In the middle distance, between the house and the water, was a grove of young oaks, not thickly set like the planting of the avenue, but high-trimmed and rising tall and bare-stemmed out of evergreen undergrowth. The shimmer of water was visible through them in the background, not wholly concealed though it might be when leafage was full.

The name of Quinton Verney was familiar, cherished among those legends of the importance of the family which the Canadian branch had preserved and handed down; but the lake was to Richard another innovation and surprise. Was it good fishing water, he wondered, and would rainbow trout flourish and breed there? As he stood looking, a boat shot out from the headland to the right, and, crossing the field of view, was lost behind the grove: it was only after it had disappeared that Richard began to wonder what had been the motive power. He could not recall any flash of oars or figures of rowers, or indeed any occupier of the boat.

This might have puzzled him still more, but his attention was diverted by the sound of an arrival below. A car had drawn up at the entrance, voices were now heard in the hall, footsteps on the stairs. After a brief interval, a sharp, rather authoritative knock came at his door and a man entered, a man still on the younger side of middle-age, reddish-haired and short of stature, with a close-trimmed bristly moustache.

"Mr. Quinton!" Richard exclaimed, coming forward. If this was his host, he was quite unlike the fancy picture he had formed. But then at Mount Verney everything was unlike and unexpected.

"No – my name's Lindsay – I'm the doctor. Mr. Quinton is sorry you were not met, but he had not understood you were arriving today."

"I hope my coming has not been inconvenient?"

"Not at all – not at all, unless to yourself. But I do not suppose you minded the walk from the station; it is pretty country, and you came here especially to acquaint yourself with the place and its surroundings. One thing more. I have to ask you to excuse Mr. Quinton for this evening, and put up with my company only. Mr. Quinton is, as you know, an invalid, and I have been with him today to his dentist for some extractions under an anaesthetic. He is a wreck in consequence" – here the little reddish man shrugged his shoulders – "and will not leave his own rooms again tonight. You are comfortable here, I hope?" – this after Richard had expressed concern at his host's condition. Now it was necessary he should praise his quarters, which he did without stint.

"Mr. Quinton would have it that Lady Anna's room should be made ready for the heir, and we were all surprised, as it has been long out of use. Well, adieu for the present: come down as soon as you are ready. Dinner is at seven: we keep early hours here in the country. What!

your portmanteau not come? Then nevermind about dressing; we will not stand on ceremony for tonight."

With that, Lindsay the doctor took himself off. But, after he had closed the door, some of his last words kept repeating in Richard's mind. *Made ready for the heir!* That was taking intention for granted in a way for which he was not prepared; and, suddenly, he felt strangely doubtful of his own wish in the matter. Did he really desire to be the owner of the Quinton property, and, if not, from what hidden root did disinclination spring?

Presently a gong sounded from below, and he went down to find the dining room lighted up, though it was scarcely more than dusk without, and the window-screens were still undrawn. The table was set out with some fine old silver and an abundance of flowers, the service of the meal was faultless, and Lindsay made an excellent deputy host. Good food has a cheering influence, and the causeless depression which had threatened to engulf Richard's spirit was lifted, at least for the time.

"I hope you will like Quinton Verney," Lindsay was saying with apparent heartiness. "Mr. Quinton is particularly anxious that you should like the place, and take an interest in his hobbies. He will explain better than I can what they are. But be prepared to hear a great deal about Roman remains in Britain, and to be cross-questioned about your knowledge."

"Then I can only avow ignorance. It is a study that has not come in my way, but I am at least ready to be interested."

"Ah, well, interest won't be difficult in what has been discovered on your own land, for that is his especial pride. A fine tessellated pavement down there by the pools, and an altar in what is now the grove. I am a duffer myself in these matters, but Mr. Quinton is a downright enthusiast about the old pagans and their times. It was he who replanted the grove where it is supposed that a sacred one existed, and set up in the midst of it a statue of Pan copied from the antique. I chaff him sometimes about it, and tell him I believe there is nothing he would like better than to revive the Lupercalia, and convert the entire neighbourhood. That's an exaggeration, of course, but the element of mystery appeals to him. As you will discover."

Following this touch of personal revelation, Richard remarked:

"You know Mr. Quinton very well. I suppose you have been with him a long time?"

"Eighteen months – no less, no more. But you can get to know a man pretty well in that time, especially when you happen to be his doctor as well as his house-mate. He has been an invalid for many years – since boyhood in fact: a sad case; you'll know more about it after a while. I was at the war before that: got knocked out, and when free of hospital could only take on a soft job, and fate or luck sent me here. Quinton and I have got on well together. Indeed I may tell you in confidence that he offered to leave me all he possessed, provided I would bind myself by his conditions."

So the Quinton inheritance had been offered and refused elsewhere. Here was a matter that might well give Richard food for thought.

"And why did you not—?" he began impulsively.

"Why didn't I grasp at such a chance? Well, I allow it was tempting enough, to a man who is a damaged article – a damage that will be lifelong. But I couldn't consent to bind myself as he would have me bound; and there was another reason. I would have been suspected of using my position here to exercise undue influence, and that I couldn't stomach. It was I who suggested to Mr. Quinton that he should seek out his next of kin – eh, what; what is the matter?"

The query was to Peters, who was whispering at his elbow.

"Pray excuse me. I am sorry, but my patient is not so well." And the little doctor hurried away. Peters brought in the next course.

"Dr. Lindsay hopes you will go on with the dinner, sir, and not wait for him. He may be detained some time."

For the rest of the meal Richard was solitary. He declined after-dinner wine and dessert, so Peters, who felt himself responsible towards the guest, suggested that he might like to smoke in the library, and coffee would be brought to him there. Richard rose from the table, and, as he did so, turned towards the unscreened window behind his chair, and experienced the shock of a surprise. There stood a strange-looking figure, gazing in at him and at the room, with face pressed against the glass. His exclamation recalled Peters, who was in the act of carrying out a tray; but by the time the old butler returned, the figure had disappeared. Who, or what was it? But Peters could not tell.

"I'll have it inquired into, sir. No one had any call to be there. These windows look into the enclosed garden, that is always kept private. A man, did you say, sir? Like a tramp?"

"A man," Richard assented, but he did not add in what likeness. Surely it must have been some freak of fancy that suggested those lineaments, the white leering face which resembled the bestial masks at the gate of the avenue, with their pricked ears and budding horns; and suggested also the naked torso, of which a glimpse was afforded by the light.

Peters brought word with the coffee that no one was found in the garden, but he meant to be extra careful in locking up, "lest it should be somebody after the plate." And indeed, were ill characters about, the unscreened window was likely to bring danger, as the display of silver on sideboard and table might well excite the cupidity of a looker-in.

Dr. Lindsay came down an hour later, but it was only to ask whether Richard had all he wanted for comfort and for the night.

"I shall be sitting up with Mr. Quinton," he explained. "Unluckily, haemorrhage has followed these extractions, and he is morbidly affected by the sight and taste of blood. No, not a sufficient loss to be alarming: it will be subdued by tomorrow I don't doubt; it is serious only as it affects his special case. You'll give Peters your orders, will you not, and tell him when you wish to be called, and all that. I understand your portmanteau has arrived."

So Richard found himself back again in the best bedroom at an early hour, with the night before him, and his luggage unpacked, and despatch-case set on the writing-table. Now was the time for the letter he had promised Nan, with his first impressions of Quinton Verney, about which she was naturally curious; the old homestead he had described to her, which might someday be his home and hers. But when he spread paper before him, he felt an overmastering reluctance to write that letter. What could he say if he told her the truth – and surely nothing less than the truth and the whole truth was due to Nan, however much it might disappoint and puzzle her. Could he tell her, with no reason to allege, of the distaste he felt for this place, for the house and all that it contained? – a distaste which began with the first sight of those leering masks at the avenue gate: how tell her of that other living face which resembled them, seen peering into the lighted dining room, pressed against the glass of the shut window a couple of hours ago? Better delay, than that he should fill a letter with maunderings such as these, when another day's experience, or a personal interview with the invisible cousin, might bring about an altered mind.

He was tired and out of spirits, and though he rejected with scorn the suggestion that a walk of less than five miles could have fatigued him, he was only lately out of hospital, and it was long since so much pedestrian exercise had come his way. And there had been throughout a certain excitement of highly strung expectation, from which no doubt reaction played its part. No, he would not attempt to write to Nan; the letter should be postponed until the morrow. And he would betake himself at once to bed.

Chapter II

IT HAS BEEN SAID that the chamber allotted to him was spacious and well-appointed, a private bathroom opened from it, and with one notable exception, it fulfilled every modern requirement. The rest of the house had been wired, and electric light installed, but here there were no means of illumination but candles, and, though these had been abundantly supplied on toilet and mantelpiece, and also at the bedside, the result was curiously dull. It was as if the walls and hangings of the apartment absorbed and did not reflect the light; a room of ordinary size would have been as well illuminated by a farthing dip. One of the windows was opened down a hand's breadth behind the curtains, and they stirred faintly in the air. Richard drew them apart to push up the lower sash, and then was struck by the beauty of the scene below. The valley had put on a veil of silvery mist, so delicate as hardly to obscure, and away to the left the moon was rising, a full yellow moon, magnified by its nearness to the horizon.

How still it all was. He had been used of late to the roar of a great city, audible even through hospital walls; before that to the thudding of great guns, and the scream of shell. How silent, and how peaceful: but presently not completely silent, for music broke into the stillness.

Somebody down below was playing on the flute, long-drawn notes and a simple air, but of enthralling sweetness. The music was difficult to locate; sometimes it seemed to come from near the house, sometimes from the grove of trees, and now to be a mere echo from a greater distance still. Could some rustic lover be serenading a housemaid? but no, that seemed impossible. Richard was himself no musician, but he knew enough to appreciate the rare quality of the performer. And then the final notes died away, and silence reigned under the rising moon.

He dropped the curtain over the window, leaving it open, and now applied himself quickly to prepare for bed. Tired as he was, he expected to sleep as soon as his head touched the pillow: such was his custom in high health, and the habit had served him in good stead when recruiting strength. But on this first night at Mount Verney sleep and he were to be strangers. No doubt there was some excitement of nerve or brain, the cause of which might be looked for entirely in himself. This at first; but by-and-by there was something external, something more, though it was nameless and undefined.

A change had set in: this was no restlessness of his own that he was suffering, it was the misery and torture of another; a misery all the greater that it could not be expressed. It seemed to him that he was divided; he recognised that he was lying on the bed, but he was also walking the room from wall to wall, with tossed arms, with hands clenched and threatening, and then spread open; gestures foreign to his nature under any extreme of passion. He, or the entity which absorbed him, did not weep: no tears came to the relief of this distress, and his own voice was dumb in his throat; there could be no cry of appeal. Whether the passion which tore him was fury solely, or grief solely, he could not tell; or whether in its extreme anguish it combined the two.

For a while he was completely paralysed by this strange experience: he was walking the room with the sufferer; he *was* the sufferer: and then again he knew the personality and the agony were not his own; that his real self was stretched upon the bed, though he could neither lift a finger nor move a limb. How long did this endure in its alternations?

Keen as was his after memory, he could not tell: moments count as hours when under torture, and in an experience so abnormal time does not exist, even as we are told it will be effaced for us hereafter. One fragment of knowledge informed his brain; how he knew cannot be told, for no voice spoke. The entity was a woman. It was no man's agony into the vortex of which he had been drawn; this was a woman who knew both love and hate, a mother who had possessed and also lost.

Then, in a moment, the strain upon him snapped: he could move again, he had the government of his limbs, he was in his own body and not that other, if the other was a body indeed. Candles – the means of striking a light – were at his hand; in less time than it takes to write, both flames were kindled: the whole room was plain to see, and there was nothing, nothing but empty air. And yet he knew, he knew that the woman was still there – that she was pacing up and down from wall to wall – that she was still torn with fury, from the vortex of which his own spirit was scarcely yet set free, as consciousness of it remained.

This would have been a staggering experience, even to one versed in psychic marvels, but of such matters Richard Quinton was completely ignorant. To him the ordeal he had passed through was as unique as it was unaccountable – a horror to have so penetrated another's being, and also in a way a thing of shame, to be covered up shuddering from the light of day. He leapt out of bed; he must seek the window, the free air, if he would not choke and die. In his rush forward it seemed as if he encountered and passed through the frantic figure that yet was invisible and disembodied; but the collision, if it was collision, affected neither: roused as he was, the grip of individuality was too strong. He tore the curtains apart, and there at last was the cool night, the serene moon, the wafting of free air, in which, behind him in the room, the lighted candles flared.

The moon was now high in heaven, the scene was bathed in white light, the shadows, where shadows fell, were black and sharply defined. The silvery mist of the earlier evening had disappeared, the light veil of it withdrawn, rolled up and swept away before that stirring of air. There was a path of reflected light across the quiet water of the pool, the headland stood out dark. And, strange to relate, from behind it again shot out the mysterious boat, the boat he had seen before, but now there were two men on board. He saw, or thought he saw, one man attack the other; for a dozen seconds they were locked together struggling. Then the rocking boat capsized and sank, and the men also disappeared.

Richard saw this, and yet in some dim way he realised that he had witnessed no actual disaster for which he need give the alarm: it was a scene projected into his mind from the mind of another. It did not even occur to him that there, within a bowshot of the house, were men drowning who might be saved. The moon-path on the water was smooth again now, undisturbed by even a ripple, the night utterly still. But a moment later the silence was broken by the same flute music which had discoursed so sweetly earlier in the night. It was, however, tuned to a livelier measure this second time, one that might accompany dancing feet. It sounded from the grove, and underneath the clear light Richard could distinguish moving figures, leaping among the trees.

There were five or six of them apparently, men or boys, and the figures looked as if naked above the waist. And the dance was not solely a dance, for they seemed to be chasing, or driving before them, some large animal which fled with leaps through the undergrowth, a goat possibly, or a sheep. The animal and the pursuing figures disappeared among the trees, and then appeared again as if they had made a circuit of the grove; the goat (if it was a goat) leaping in front, and the others pursuing. This was the end; a cloud drifted over the moon, and when it passed there was no more sign of movement in the grove, and the jocund fluting had ceased.

Richard turned back into the room, and now his perception of that fury and distress, if not wholly effaced, was dulled as if here, too, was the shadowing of a merciful cloud. But stretch himself on that bed he could not, nor address himself to sleep, lest it should be renewed with all the former horror. He would keep the lights burning, if only he had a book he would occupy himself with reading, but literature had formed no part of his light luggage.

He might seek one in the library below, treading softly in stocking-soles so as not to disturb the sleeping house.

But as he issued forth, candle in hand, he found a burner switched on on the landing, and the dressing-gowned small doctor crossing over from an opposite door. Lindsay at once accosted him.

"Can I do anything: what is the matter? – oh, can't sleep, and want a book: is that it? I can find you one close at hand, and mine are livelier than the fossils in the library. Come this way."

Lindsay's room opened over the entrance, next to Mr. Quinton's bedchamber. A set of bookshelves filled a recess.

"Help yourself. The yellow-backs on the top shelf are French – I daresay you read French. But you'll find English ones below, and perhaps they are more likely to put you asleep." He snapped on an extra light, and then turned for a fuller scrutiny of his companion. "You look pretty bad," was his remark. "Does a sleepless night always knock you up like this? I'm doctor to the establishment you know, and I prescribe a peg. Whisky or brandy will you have? Both of them are here, and so is a syphon. Sit down while I get it ready. Three fingers – two – one? Good: you do well to be moderate. Get outside that, and you'll feel better. And then you can pick your book."

Lindsay did not question further as to the cause of disturbance, though he looked inquisitive, as if suspicions were aroused. Richard for his part remained tongue-tied, time was needed to digest and try to understand his experience: he might speak of it later on, but not now, while still his nerves were vibrating from the strain. The human companionship was, however, reassuring, and by the time the prescribed dose was swallowed, he felt altogether more normal. He inquired for Mr. Quinton, sat for a while conversing on indifferent subjects, and then departed with a book.

He did not venture again to lie down, but installed himself in a deep chair, the candles burning at his elbow. The effect of the novel may have been soporific, though he was an inattentive reader. After a long interval he fell asleep, and waked to find morning already brightening in the east.

The night was over, its perplexities and distresses had sunk into the past, and a new day had begun. It was refreshing to spirit as well as body to wash and re-clothe, to undo the bolts and chains which guarded the front door, and find himself in the free air. Though it was still the air which breathed over Mount Verney, he was delivered from the evil shadow of that roof. He retraced his steps of the day before, down the dark curving drive, out through the satyr-headed gates, to the highroad which was free to all, the road traversed by Roman legions in centuries that were past. He turned to the right, with the eastern sky behind him, and walked on, without object, but steeping himself in the freshness of the newly awakened world.

At first he appeared to be the only person astir and observant, but presently an old man of the labouring class pushed open a gate some way ahead and came towards him, a shepherd accompanied by his dog. Richard would have liked to exchange ideas with an English working man, but felt too suddenly shy to venture on more than a good-morning as they drew abreast. The man, however, stopped and accosted him.

"Beg pardon, master, but as you came along, did you mebbe happen on a straying sheep? A ewe she is, and has taken her lamb with her, one getting on in size, as it was dropped early. Me and the dog have been after her since first it was light."

Richard had no information to give; he had not seen the ewe and her lamb. And then he bethought him.

"I stayed last night at Mount Verney, and, looking out in the moonlight, I saw a sheep leaping about in the grove, the coppice of oaks by the water. Would that be the one you have lost?"

The man shook his head.

"No, sir, that would be Mr. Quinton's sheep. I drove it down myself, a prime wether, only a day ago; and my heart was sore for the poor thing. It seemed as if the dog here was sorry too, for he didna like the job. Mr. Quinton he buys one at the spring full moon, and again at harvest, of my master or one of the other breeders, always to be driven into the coppice and left there, and I doubt if ever the creatures live as much as two days. What he wants them for 'tis beyond me to say. Seems a waste of good meat and good wool, for it is just a hole in the field and dig them under, so I am told, and not a soul the better. Some folks will eat braxy mutton, meat being dear as it is; but not one of them would touch a sheep that had died up there in the wood, poisoned as like as not. 'Tis just a mystery to all of us. But I've no call to be passing remarks, seeing you know Mr. Quinton, and are staying at Mount Verney.

Richard might have replied with truth that he did not know Mr. Quinton, their acquaintance was still to make. But he asked instead for direction, and was told to cross a stile to the right into a certain field-path, which would bring him out opposite the house, by the bridge over the water.

The bridge was a rustic affair of planks and a hand-rail, and beyond it the way diverged to right and left, the path on the left entering the grove, barred only by a light iron turnstile. Was it curiosity, or another sort of attraction which drew Richard thither, to see by daylight the spot on which he had looked down under the moon the night before? Now it seemed ordinary enough; the paths cut through it were grassed over and green, but here and there, where the turf was soft, he noticed they were trampled by divided hoofs, larger than those of sheep. The trees, young and slender, shorn of their lower branches, were now faintly green with unexpanded leafage; the undergrowth, which was chiefly rhododendron, was here and there breaking into purple and pinkish flower.

While still some way from it, he could distinguish among the trees the statue of which Lindsay had spoken. It was mounted on a pedestal, and was, as he said, a modern copy of the antique. Pan with his pipes in bronze, an abhorrent half-animal figure; the brooding face less repulsive perhaps than those of the satyrs at the gate, but the regard it appeared to bend on the observer who approached had a keener expression of intelligence and evil power. Richard as he drew near, his attention riveted on that face and crouching figure, almost stumbled over an object lying at the foot of the column.

It was the dead sheep. Had it been dragged thither with a purpose, or hunted till it fell exhausted where it lay? There was no mark upon it that he could see, of the knife of the executioner, but the swollen tongue protruded from the half-open jaws, and thick blood had flowed from both nostrils, staining the ground.

Truly Mount Verney was a spot where there were strange happenings. The shudder of the night again passed over Richard, and he had now no least desire to linger in the grove, or to make further discoveries. Passing through another gate he gained a steep slope of lawn, leading up to the gravelled terrace on which the windows of the library opened. His approach had been observed, and here was Lindsay waving him a cheerful greeting, with the intelligence of waiting breakfast.

Chapter III

"BEEN FOR an early ramble? – that was well done. Mr. Quinton wants you to see as much as possible of the place before he speaks to you of the future. A lovely morning. And this house stands well, does it not, above the valley? Gives you a first-rate view."

Richard assented. And then put the question he had been meditating.

"Was this house built on the site of another, do you know? The house my father used to speak about was called Quinton Court. It was built long before his father's time, and was of stone; it had a walled courtyard and mullioned windows. I don't suppose it was ever a grand mansion. But that was what I expected to find in coming down here."

"Quinton Court is still in existence; the man lives there who has the farm. It is a fine-looking old place, but I expect it has gone a long way downhill since it was given up as the family residence. You will find it about a mile from here, on the other side of the hill."

"I should like to see it. I should greatly like to see it—!"

"Make it the object of your next walk. Go the length of the lake to the head water, and through the field beyond, and you will come upon a cart-road. I would show you the way, but I may have difficulty in leaving. And perhaps you would rather go alone."

That he would prefer to make the visit alone was so true that Richard left the suggestion uncontested. Lindsay passed lightly to another subject; one on which he was not improbably curious.

"I hope the novel and the 'peg' helped on to sleep? I hate to lie awake myself, but sometimes a strange bed—! There is fish, I think, under that cover. Or do you prefer bacon?"

"I am a good sleeper usually, in any sort of bed, strange or familiar. Dr. Lindsay, I am sorry to be a troublesome guest, but can I change my room? And, if you will allow me, I will do so before tonight."

"You can, without doubt. There are other guest-rooms, though with fewer advantages than the bow-room, as we call it. I will see about the exchange. But – may I be so indiscreet as to ask why? Because Mr. Quinton will put the question to me, and I had better be prepared to answer him."

"Then perhaps I may put a question on my side. I understand that bedroom has been long out of use. I know nothing about ghosts, and have never believed in them, but – it is not like other rooms. Is it supposed to be haunted? And, if so, why was it chosen for me?"

"I can't tell you much about it; remember I only came here eighteen months ago. As for why it was chosen, you must ask Mr. Quinton: it was his doing, not mine. I never heard of any ghost being seen there. The only queer thing said about the room sounds like illusion, and could not disturb a sleeper. Nor would it, I suppose, be visible at night. But perhaps you, as a Quinton, would be more sensitive than a stranger."

"What is the queer thing?"

"Why it seems absurd, but they say whoever looks through that window sees a boat on the lake. I saw something like it myself on one occasion, but I expect it is a flaw in the glass. Was there a ghost last night?"

"No ghost in the sense you mean, but such an impression of misery – and not misery only, anger – that I found sleep impossible. That is all I have to tell. If Mr. Quinton is affronted by my wish to change, I must find quarters elsewhere till he is ready to speak to me."

"Nonsense: he won't be affronted, it would be absurd. I doubt if you will see him today, but he is decidedly better, and I shall not need to sit up another night. You'll like him, I think. He has his eccentricities, that must be allowed. But you would be sorry for him from your heart if you knew all."

"He is eccentric? I heard a strange story about him this morning, from an old shepherd I met in the road. Is it true that he purchases a sheep twice a year, and that it is driven into the grove to die? There is one lying dead there now, at the foot of the statue of Pan."

Lindsay shrugged his shoulders.

"I told you he was half a pagan, and I don't defend the sheep business. That sacrifice is one of the things he wants continued, and makes a condition; but I told him straight out that no successor would pledge himself to a thing so out of reason, and you had better be firm about it when he speaks. Of course it is natural he should wish Mount Verney kept up as the residence of the owner; there one can be in sympathy. His grandfather built it, and his father planned the grounds, and the ornamental water and all that. Odd about the lake, seeing what happened after.

Why, don't you know? The elder son was drowned there. Mr. Quinton's twin brother. Archibald, his name was. He was the Quinton heir."

Richard saw again, in a flash of memory, the two figures struggling in the boat and disappearing under water; but where was the good of taking Lindsay into confidence? He had said enough, and made it plain he would occupy the room no more, nor look from it over the lake: he did not care to what sort of apartment he was transferred; it would serve him for the time, however mean.

The doctor hurried away as soon as they had breakfasted, apologising for his enforced absence, but Richard was well content to be alone. He wanted to think out the warning again given about conditions. That which concerned the sheep was unthinkable, and could hardly be pressed; but evidently there were others, by reason of which Lindsay had refused the offered heirship. If he was required to live at Mount Verney in the future, and make it his home and his wife's home – what then? In one way the prospect of the inheritance was tempting enough to him, and would be to any man – an inheritance that would at once convert him into a person of importance, with a stake in the country as the saying is; a good position to offer his wife, ample means, provision for the children that might be born to them. But if what he began dimly to suspect was fact; if the place had somehow fallen under a curse, in pagan times or now – such a curse as affected inanimate building, and tainted the very ground – it would be no fit home for her. And Nan was not covetous of riches – she would not mind struggling on with him and being poor; she would approve, so he justly thought, of a refusal made for the sake of right.

There was nothing to detain him indoors, so with these cogitations in mind, he set out in the direction Lindsay had indicated, following the north shore of the artificial lake, and crossing the headland which, viewed from above, had been the departure point of the mysterious boat. On the western side of the headland, furthest from the house and half hidden by the bank, were the remains of what certainly had been a boathouse; but in these days no boat sheltered there, and the timbers of the roof had rotted and fallen in decay. He passed through the gate by the head-water, a clear and fast running stream; found and followed the cart-road, which after a while was merged in a superior approach, now well-nigh as worn and deeply rutted as the other.

He came upon the old Court suddenly, round a fold of the hill, and there he stood for a while, his heart moved by a mysterious feeling of kinship – if not utterly fantastic to suppose flesh and blood can feel itself akin to walls of stone. The old homestead had fallen from its first estate, but there was a dignity about it still, the dignity of fine proportion and high quality, differing widely from the jerry building of today. The grey gables were there as of old, the roof of slabbed stone, the panes of diamond lattice; there the flagged courtyard with its breast-high boundary wall, and five of the six urns mounted in place; the sixth had fallen, and lay broken at the foot.

The front door was fast shut, an oak door studded with iron, but Richard drew near and knocked, treading the very stones the footsteps of the dead had worn. Why, why had the later degenerates forsaken this dear place, and fixed their abode at Mount Verney?

A neatly-dressed young woman opened to him, and looked inquiringly at the stranger.

"I'm sorry, sir, my father is not in, if so be as you come seeking him."

No, Richard said, that was not his errand; but might he be allowed to see inside the house, if only a couple of the rooms?

"Why certainly, if you are thinking of taking the place. I didn't know as it had got about that we are leaving, but news do fly apace. But we shall not be out until September."

"My name is Quinton, and I am from Canada. My great-grandfather lived here, and it was here that my grandfather was born. I am anxious to see the Court now I am in England. If you would be so good as to allow—"

"Come in, sir, and look where you like; you are kindly welcome. My father would make you so I know, for he is the oldest tenant on the estate. We have no fault to find with the place, but the farm is too big for father now he has no son with him, and the house too large for us too. I am the only one at home, and mother is laid by with the rheumatics. These long stone passages take a lot of cleaning, to say nothing of the many rooms, though more than half of them we shut away."

So upon this invitation Richard had his wish, and saw over the house upstairs and down. In some of the rooms put out of use there were still pieces of old furniture, Quinton property, his guide told him: an oak chest or two, corner cupboards with carven doors, a worm-eaten dresser, chairs in the last stage of decrepitude. They were let with the house, having been thought unworthy of removal to Mount Verney. In the best parlour sacks of grain were stored, and on the threshold of two of the empty bedrooms he was warned to step warily, as the floors were thought to be unsafe.

Quinton Court had fallen from its first estate, but it was still lovely in the eyes of this late descended son. It had been cleanly kept, however roughly, and there was an air of purity about its homeliness, of open casements and scents of lavender and apples. He could picture his Nan here, a happy house-mistress under the ancient roof of his forefathers; but not as the chatelaine of Mount Verney with all its wealth: never at Mount Verney. Ah, if only Mr. Quinton would make this place his bequest to the next heir, the old Court and the surrounding farm which he might work for a living; and leave Quinton Verney and his accumulated thousands, where else and to whom else he pleased!

Chapter IV

SUCH WERE Richard's thoughts as he walked back along the green shores of the lake, and under the midday sun. He and the doctor were again tête-à-tête at luncheon; but he was told Mr. Quinton desired to see him that afternoon in his private room above stairs; also that he intended to dine with them, being greatly better than the day before. So the first interview with his host came about earlier than he had been led to expect.

The appearance of his elderly cousin took him by surprise. Mr. Clement Quinton was strikingly handsome, though older-looking than his two and fifty years. He might have been taken for a man advanced in the seventies, though his tall thin figure was still upright. He owned a thick thatch of grey hair, a close-cut white beard, and bushy grey eyebrows above eyes of steely blue, rather unnaturally wide open. He welcomed Richard cordially, shaking him by the hand: a cold hand, his was, and yet the younger man felt uncomfortably, the instant they were palm to palm, that he touched something sticky and moist. Mr. Quinton's left hand was gloved, and Richard remembered after that he held a dark silk handkerchief in the other while they talked together.

There was nothing embarrassing or noteworthy about the earlier conversation. Mr. Quinton appeared kindly interested in Richard's past history, asking about his father and home, how he had been educated and where, and also the details of his military service. They had been talking together for half an hour, before any reference was made to the future.

"I want you to be interested in this place," he said with emphasis. "I want you to be particularly interested. For there are various things I am bound to leave to the doing of others, and much will depend on their punctual carrying on. It will smooth my pillow – as the saying is – if I may be assured of the co-operation of my successor."

This was not very easy to answer, as Richard could not assume successorship on a hint so vague. So he struck out into an account of his visit to Quinton Court, and pleasure over the discovery that the old house of which his grandfather had spoken with affection, was still solidly existent.

"I was afraid it had been pulled down, and Mount Verney built on its site."

"No, we destroyed nothing. My respect for antiquity is too great. As I will show you later, it has been my great desire to – call back into life, I may say – associations from the dead past of an earlier period still. Traces of what had been, were thick on the ground hereabouts: you shall have the complete history of how, and why, and what. You will find it remarkable indeed. I will tell you frankly, my young cousin, it is here and on Mount Verney I want your interest focussed. This place dates back to the Roman occupation of Britain, and in comparison with the relics here, Quinton Court is but a thing of yesterday."

"Dr. Lindsay told me Roman remains had been unearthed. I think he said some portions of a pavement."

"There was a villa here, on this very spot; baths in the valley, with the water running through them; and an altar where you see the grove, which was once a dense thicket of wood. I have other means of knowing, besides conclusions drawn from the fragments that remain, and these communications the excavations have strikingly confirmed. I was directed where to dig. There was a special cult connected with this place. The worship of Pan."

"I observed the statue in the grove."

"It marks the site of the old altar. Pan is a deity about whom little has been known and much mistaken. From the sources of information at my command, I have compiled a treatise. And that is one thing I require of my successor. If unpublished at the time of my decease, I wish it given to the world."

The posthumous publication of a treatise! It would be well if other conditions were no more formidable than this.

"Some writers have made the mistake of confounding Pan with Faunus; surely an extraordinary error. My theory is entirely different. Cain was his prototype. Cain."

Here the recluse seemed to be stirred by some inward excitement, and he got up to pace the room.

"Cain!" he repeated. "Of course you know the scriptural narrative, and probably little else about that founder of an early race. There are mistakes in that account – it is libellous, the fabrication of an enemy. Eve put about unworthy slanders. If Cain did truly kill his brother, it was in self-defence, or in a fury of panic anger: I say if, for I do not allow it to be – the truth. Abel, the favourite, was a sneak and a coward, and he knew whatever lie he set up, so long as it was against the other, would stand as unassailable truth. He was better blotted out, than left to be the father of a degenerate race. Cain was at least a man—. And it is said the Lord put a mark on him. What did that mean, think you?"

"I have not the least idea. Does anybody know?"

"I know this much, that it was the curse of the partly animal form. Cain was crippled into that likeness, and some of his sons took after him. Not the daughters, for they were in the likeness of Eve. And it is on record that they were beautiful. The sons of God saw the daughters of men that they were fair. But that does not come into the argument, nor concern us now. It was because of the mark set on him that Pan loved solitary places, the cool depths of caves and the shadow of woods. It was he in the beginning, and not Abel, who was the keeper of flocks. Abel did nothing but laze in the sun and watch the fruits ripen, and then gather them for an offering. I told you that the record lied. Do you wonder how I know all this?"

Richard could do nothing but assent.

"I will tell you – show you. I wish to instruct you in my methods, that they may be yours hereafter. It is not all who have the gift of sight. Lindsay is psychically blind. But something tells me you have it, or will have it. Come here with me."

He opened a door and showed an inner, smaller room, probably intended as a dressing-closet in the original design of the house. There was a writing-table and chair in the sole window, but the only other furniture was a high stand, on which was some object covered over with black velvet drapery. Mr. Quinton turned back part of the covering, and directed Richard to seat himself before it. The lifted flap revealed the smooth and shining surface of a large crystal, or ball of glass, set into a frame.

"You know what this is, and what its use? I want to test whether I can make a scryer of you. The black cloth is used only to prevent confusing lights. Now look steadily into the crystal, and tell me what you see."

Richard looked, in some amusement and complete incredulity.

"I see the reflection of my own face," he said presently. "Nothing more. Except – yes – something which looks like smoke."

"Go on looking, and be patient. There will be more."

As Richard gazed, his own reflection disappeared, the smoke cleared away, and there were the gates of the avenue with the leering faces, exactly as he saw them the day before. Then the cloud of smoke returned, blotting them out; cleared again, and showed the spy of the evening, peering in at the window of the dining room. Succeeding this, came the scene of the grove by moonlight, with the figures leaping among the trees, and driving the doomed sheep.

"I am seeing a procession of scenes," he replied to a further question. "But only what are in my mind and memory. Nothing new."

"Go on looking," was again the command. "What is new will come."

The next scene was, as Richard half expected, the grove as he entered it that morning, with the statue of Pan on its pedestal, and the sheep before it lying dead. This persisted, not small as dwarfed within the limits of the ball, but now as if a window opened before him on the actual scene. But a change was taking place in the figure of the god. The bronze seemed to soften and warm into flesh, the terrible, wise face was no longer serene and meditative, the eyes looked into his, and now there was mockery in them, revelling in his surprise. The thing was alive, moving, surely about to descend.

But no. The figure, without leaving its pedestal, stretched out one hairy ape-like arm, and clutched the body of the sheep, drawing it up to rest on his crossed hocks, while the mocking face bent closer, as if to sniff or lick the blood. Was the monstrous creature about to tear the victim open, ready to devour? The action of the hands looked like it.

Richard could look no longer. A sweat of horror broke out over him, and stood in beads on his forehead; he started up gasping for air.

"Let me go," he cried out wildly: "let me go!"

Mr. Quinton replaced the velvet covering.

"That is enough for today," he said. "I am sufficiently answered. You can see."

Richard hardly knew how he got out of the room, whether it was by Mr. Quinton's dismissal or his own will. Or how long a time elapsed before, finding himself alone, he happened to look at the palm of his right hand, which had felt curiously sticky after contact with Mr. Quinton's. The smear on it was dry and easily effaced by washing, but without doubt what he had touched was blood.

Mr. Quinton seemed to have been in no way affronted by Richard's abrupt withdrawal. He was in a genial mood when he joined the two younger men at dinner, now with his loose wrapping gown put off, and faultlessly attired in evening dress. A handsome man; and Richard noticed that his hands were beautifully shaped and white. But, to the guest's vision, there was one striking peculiarity about his appearance, a peculiarity which seemed to increase as the meal went forward. Perhaps the opening of Richard's clairvoyance, artificially induced some hours before, had not wholly closed. For doubtless what he now perceived, would not have been visible to ordinary sight.

Most of us in these later days have heard of the existence of auras, a species of halo which is supposed to emanate from every mortal, indicative of spiritual values and degrees of power; but it is doubtful whether our backwoodsman was aware. What he saw, however, was an aura, though formed of shadow and not light. It encompassed the seated figure of his host with a surrounding of grey haze, spreading to a yard or more from either shoulder, and equally above the head; not obstructing the view of the room behind him, but dimming it, as might a stretched veil of grey crape. It was curious to see Peters waiting on him and passing through this, evidently unaware; his hand and the bottle advancing into the full light as he filled Mr. Quinton's glass, and then withdrawing to leave the veil as perfect as before. Mr. Quinton made an excellent dinner, and chaffed Richard on his want of appetite; he also drank freely of the wines Peters was handing round, and pressed them on his guests. The glasses were particularly elegant, of Venetian pattern, slender stemmed and fragile. Peters had just replenished his master's glass, when Mr. Quinton in the course of argument, lifted and brought it down sharply on the table with the result of breakage. The accident attracted little notice; Peters cleared away the fragments and mopped up the spilt wine, and another glass was set in its place and filled. But as Mr. Quinton raised the fresh glass to his lips, Richard noticed that blood was dripping from his right hand in heavy spots, staining his shirt-cuff and the cloth.

"I am afraid, sir, you have cut yourself," he exclaimed impulsively; and almost at the same instant Peters appeared at his master's elbow offering a dark silk handkerchief.

Mr. Quinton did not answer, but uttered an exclamation of annoyance, and abruptly rose from the table and left the room. Lindsay followed him, but presently returned, looking unusually grave. Richard inquired if the cut was serious.

"Mr. Quinton did not cut his hand," Lindsay answered. "I am charged to tell you what is the matter. Though it is as far as possible kept secret, he thinks it better you should know."

The gravity of Lindsay's countenance did not relax . He poured out half a glass of wine and drank it, as if to nerve himself for the telling of the tale.

"When I came here as resident doctor eighteen months ago, I heard the story: it was, of course, necessary I should be informed as I had to treat his case. I shall have to go a long way back to make you understand. Lady Anna, Quinton's mother, had twin sons, born shortly after her husband's death. She must have been a strange woman. They were her only children, but almost from infancy she made a difference between them, setting all her affection on Archibald, the elder, and treating the other, Clement, with coldness and every evidence of dislike. Quinton says he can never remember his mother caressing him, or even speaking kindly. He was always the one held to blame for any childish fault or mischief, and pushed into the background, while everything was for Archibald the heir. We cannot wonder that this folly of hers led to bad feeling between the lads. It was active in their school days, though they were educated at different schools, and met only in the holidays. Whenever they met they fought. What the last quarrel was about I cannot say, but Archibald was entering an expensive regiment, and the army could not be afforded for Clement, though it was his great desire: he owns to having been very sore. They were in a boat on the lake, and they fought there, and the boat capsized.

"It was said that Archibald hadn't a chance; he had been stunned by a blow on the head, or else had struck his head in falling. They both could swim a little, but he went down like a stone, and Clement reached the shore: the distance could not have been great, nor could one have expected such an accident to result in anything worse than a ducking. The horrible part of it was that Lady Anna saw what happened from her window in the bow-room."

"Ah—!"

"Yes, the room you had, and where you were disturbed last night. She saw the fight and the struggle, and was convinced of Clement's guilt: that he had plotted the occasion and killed Archibald, so that he might take his place. She wanted to have the boy tried for murder; ay, and would have had her way, had it not been for her brother, Lord Pengwyn, who was guardian to both the lads. He got the thing passed over as an accident, as no doubt it was. But the point I am coming to, though I've been long about it, is this. When Clement was drawn from the water, and brought in, sick and dazed. Lady Anna met him in a fury of passion. He was Cain over again, the first murderer who slew his brother: I wonder, did Eve do the like! 'Your brother's blood,' she said, 'will be upon your hands for ever.' Quinton says he would not have cared, after that, if they had hung him then and there. He had an illness, and the palms of his hands began to bleed – from the pores as it were, without a wound – and they have continued to bleed at intervals from that day to this. You saw what happened tonight."

"It sounds like a miracle. Is there no cure?"

"Everything has been tried – styptics, hypnotism even. Sometimes the symptom remits for two or three weeks, and the bleeding is generally early in the day; he thought himself safe this evening. Miracle? no, unless the power of the mind over the body is held to be miraculous. You have read of the stigmatists – women, ay and men too – on whom the wounds of Christ have broken out, to bleed always on Fridays?"

"I have heard of them – certainly. But I set it down as a fraud – a monkish trick."

"It is as well vouched for as any other physical phenomenon. And this case of Quinton's is nearly allied, though horror created it in his case, and not saintly adoration. It has spoiled his life; for over thirty years he has been an invalid, and will so continue to the end. His aberration of mind has all arisen from this root: his queer fancies about Cain and Pan, blood-sacrifices to Pagan gods – satyrs and fauns and hobgoblins, and I know not what!"

"You speak of aberration, and yet assert that he is sane?"

"He is sane enough for all practical purposes – a good man of business even, with a sharp eye to the main chance. Take him apart from these cranks of his, I like him – I can't help liking him. You'll like him too, when you know him better. You have seen the least attractive side of him, coming down like this, with the misgiving he is driving you into a corner. I'd have you stand up to him and speak your mind about what you will and will not do. And I believe he will hear reason in the end."

* * *

Next morning's post brought Richard a letter, forwarded on from London: a notice requiring his appearance before a certain Medical Board, and obliging his return to town. He sent a message to Mr. Quinton by Lindsay, explaining his abrupt departure, but saying he was willing to return if desired. The reply message requested an interview, in the same upstairs room as before.

It proved to be a long one. Lindsay, waiting in the hall for the car to come round, wondered what was the delay, and what was passing between the two. At last a door in the upper regions opened and shut, and Richard came down the stairs. He was white as chalk, staggering like a man dizzy or blind, and a cold sweat stood in beads on his forehead, as happened after the scrying of the day before. Lindsay sprang forward to meet him, and propped him with a hand under his arm. He leaned against the wall, and gasped out:

"It's all over – I've refused – you were right to refuse too. The thing he asks is impossible. This house is full of devils – of devils, I tell you – and they come out of Quinton's crystal. He made me look again – against my will, and I saw – what I can't speak of – what I never can forget—!"

"Come into the dining room with me, and I'll give you a dram. You have been upset; you may think differently when you are calm."

"No – no. Never this place for me. He is beyond reason: he is given over to the fiend. I told him I would thank him for ever for just Quinton Court and a farm, but he would not part the property. It had to be all or nothing. And not even to gain Quinton Court would I be owner here. No, I'll have no dram. I want to get away."

The car was now heard coming round, and drawing up at the door.

"Goodbye, Lindsay, and thank you for your kindness. We may never meet again, but I shall not forget."

These were last words, and the next moment he was shut in and speeding away, the open gates with their watchful faces left behind.

Chapter V

RICHARD reached London only to fall ill. The doctor diagnosed influenza, but seemed to think his system had received a shock: as to this he was not communicative. He had a week in bed, and another of tardy convalescence, a prey to depression and all the ills resulting from exhaustion. A fortnight had gone by since he left Mount Verney, when he received a communication from Fryer and Fryer asking for an interview. Mr. Fryer wished to see Mr. Richard Quinton on a matter of business, and would be obliged if he could make it convenient to call.

"I ought to have written to the old bird, to tell him I am out of the running," was Richard's comment, spoken to himself. "But, as I have been remiss, I had better go and hear what he has to say. I shall have to take a taxi."

He had no strength left for the walking distance, and even the office stairs were something of a trial. He was shown in at once to Mr. Fryer, and began with an apology.

"I have only just ascertained your address," said the man of law. "Are you aware, Mr. Quinton, that your cousin and late host is dead?"

"Indeed no, sir, I was not aware." And that Richard was shocked by the intelligence was plain to see.

"He died suddenly of heart-failure the night after you left. And, so far as Dr. Lindsay and I can ascertain after a careful search through all his papers, he has left no will."

This communicatory did not seem to inform Richard; he was still too dazed by what he had just heard.

Mr. Fryer tapped the blotting-pad before him, which was a way he had when irritated.

"You don't realise what that means? The whole property goes to you, both real estate and personal. Mount Verney, and all that it contains."

Richard gave a cry, which sounded more like horror than elation.

"You are telling me – that I am the owner of Mount Verney?"

"If no will is discovered later, certainly you are the owner."

"And does this bind me to live there? Because I cannot – I will not. I told Mr. Quinton so before leaving, and, as he made it a condition, I refused the inheritance."

"So I understand from Dr. Lindsay. No, you are bound to nothing. You can live where you please. And, as soon as the legal processes of succession are gone through, you can sell the property, should you prefer investment abroad."

Richard still sat half-stunned, slowly taking it in. He could rid himself of Mount Verney and all that it contained, and Quinton Court, the home of his desire, would be his own.

"You would have wished, of course, to attend your cousin's funeral, but you had quitted the address left with me, and we were unable to let you know in time. He was cremated, according to his own often-expressed desire. There is one thing, Mr. Quinton, I would like to say to you – to suggest, though you may think I am exceeding my province. Your cousin's intestacy benefits you, but there are others who suffer by it. Old Peters, a servant who had been with him from boyhood: he would have been provided for without doubt. Probably there would have been gratuities to the other domestics, according to their length of service; and his resident doctor, Lindsay, would have come in for a legacy. Of course it is quite at your option what."

"I will thank you, sir, to put down what you would have advised Mr. Quinton in all these cases, had you prepared his will, and I will make it good."

It was not always easy to divine Mr. Fryer's sentiments, but he seemed to receive the instruction with pleasure. Lawyer and client shook hands, and then Richard was on the street again, hurrying away. O, what a letter – what a letter he would have to write to Nan!

* * *

Legal processes take time, and summer was waning into autumn before Richard was fully established as owner of the Quinton property. Up to now he had sedulously avoided Mount Verney, though he had been in the near neighbourhood, and had several times visited Quinton Court. He knew only by the agent's report that his orders were carried out, the heads removed from the gate-pillars and the statue from the grove, which was a grove no longer, as the young oaks had been felled and carted away. The Roman relics had been presented to a local museum, and the house was now shut up, and emptied of most of its furniture. Lindsay, at Richard's desire, had chosen such of the plenishings as he cared for and could make useful, receiving these in addition to the money gift advised by Mr. Fryer.

All this was accomplished, the last load removed, and now the big white villa was shut up and vacant, and Clement Quinton's heir was about to enter for the first time as its possessor. But, strange to say, he had elected to make the visit late at night and in secret, so planning his approach across country that his coming and going might be unnoticed and unknown. A thief's visit, one would have said, rather than that of the lawful owner, who could have commanded all.

The latter part of the journey was made on foot, and throughout he carried with him, under his own eye and hand, a large and heavy gladstone-bag. He had studied incendiary methods when serving in France, and materials for swift destruction were contained within.

It was a wild evening; a gale, forestalling the equinox, hurtled overhead, tearing the clouds into shreds as they flew before it, and making clear spaces for some shining of stars. Rain was not yet, though doubtless it would fall presently. The wind would help Richard's purpose, rain would not, though he thought it could hardly defeat it. That intermittent shining of the stars gave little light. The night was very nearly 'as dark as hell's mouth', and Richard had much the feeling that he was venturing into the mouth of hell.

It had needed the mustering of a desperate courage, this expedition on which he was bent, but he could entrust his purpose to no other hand. Purification by fire: there could be, it seemed to him, no other cleansing. He intended no oblation to the infernal gods, that was far from his thought: what he dimly designed was a final breaking of their power.

With this purpose in mind he turned into the dark avenue, the shut gates yielding to his hand, between the pillars from which the satyrs' heads were gone. Did faces pry on him from between the close-ranked trees? He would not think of it: and for this night at least he would shut the eyes of his soul, the eyes with which he had perceived before, or he might happen upon something which would make him altogether a coward. In the darkness he left the road more than once, and blundered into the plantation, needing to have recourse to the electric torch in his pocket before he could find the way. But at last he came upon the open sweep of drive, and there was the villa before him, stark and white, eyeless and shuttered, the corpse of a house from which the soul had gone out.

This new owner had been careful to carry with him the keys which admitted. He unlocked a side door and entered, and now the torch was a necessity in the pitch darkness which prevailed within. His first act was to go through the lower rooms, unshuttering and opening everywhere, so as to let in a free draught of air. Here a certain amount of the heavier furniture still remained: Lindsay had been moderate in his selection, though he might, with Richard's approval, have grasped at all. Then he mounted to the attics, opening as he went, and here the incendiary work started. The flames were beginning to creep over the floors and about the back staircase, when he turned his attention to the better apartments on the first floor, entering and igniting one after another. He left Mr. Quinton's private rooms until the last; the rooms where those momentous interviews had taken place, and where the devils had issued from the glass.

The private den had been wholly stripped, both of furniture and books; no doubt Lindsay, who was free to take what he pleased, had valued these mementoes of a patient who was also a friend. Richard was glad to find the apartment empty; there was less to recall the past. But as he moved the illuminating torch from left to right in his survey, it seemed to him for an instant that a tall figure stood before him – long enough to realise its presence, though gone in the space of a couple of agitated heartbeats. He never doubted that it was Quinton, present to reproach him, to arrest the course of destruction if that were possible. But in spite of what he had seen – if indeed he did see – he gritted his teeth and went on.

The inner cabinet was next to enter. Here nothing had been removed or changed; the writing-table in the window still had its equipment of inkpot and blotting-pad, and on the latter, Richard noticed, a sheet of blank paper was spread out. The velvet cover thrown over the high stand no doubt concealed the uncanny crystal into which he had been forced to look. No one would look into it again after the destruction of this night! And then somehow, he knew not how, his attention was drawn to the white paper on the table.

Most of us have seen the development of a photographic plate, and how magically the image starts into view on a surface which before was blank. That was what appeared to happen under his eyes upon the paper, and the image was the imprint of a large hand, a man's hand, red as if dipped in blood.

The same awful sensation of sick faintness experienced before with the crystal, overcame him once again. It was a marvel to him afterwards that he did not fall unconscious, to perish in the burning house. He saved himself by a desperate effort of will, flinging what was left of his incendiary material behind him on the floor. As he gained the staircase, a rush of air met him from below, and this was perhaps his salvation. But the house was now filling with smoke, and from the upper regions came already the crackle of spreading flame.

The crackle of flame, and something more. Something which sounded like the clatter of hoofs over bare floors, and a cackle of hellish laughter; unless his senses were by this time wholly dazed and confused, hearing bewitched as well as sight. He found the door by which he entered, locked it behind him and fled into the night, now no longer bewilderingly dark, but faintly illuminated by the rising moon.

He did not take the direction of the avenue and the road, but climbed fences and made his way up the hill behind; and when on the wind-swept summit he turned to look back. He had done his work effectually; the white villa was alight in all its windows, fiercely ablaze within, and, as he still lingered and watched, a portion of the roof fell in, and flame and smoke shot up into the sky.

* * *

From the local paper of the following Saturday:

> We regret to state that the mansion of Mount Verney, recently the residence of the late Clement Quinton, Esquire, and now the property of Mr. Richard Quinton, was destroyed by fire on Tuesday night. The origin of the fire is wrapped in mystery, as the house was unoccupied and shut up, and the electric light disconnected, so there could have been no fusion of wires. Much valuable property is destroyed, and part of the building is completely gutted. The blaze was first noticed between twelve and one o'clock, by a man driving home late from market. He gave notice to the police, but by the time the fire-engines arrived, the conflagration had taken such hold that it could not be checked, though abundant water was at hand in the Mount Verney lake. The loss to Mr. Richard Quinton will be very considerable, as we understand no part of it is covered by insurance.

From the same paper in the following December:

> We understand that a gift has been made to our hospital fund, of the shell of the Mount Verney house with the grounds that surround it, to be converted into a sanatorium for the treatment of tuberculosis, and Mr. Richard Quinton also adds to the subscription list the. sum of £1,000. This munificent donation of money and a site, will enable the work to be put in hand at once; and it is believed that what is left of the original mansion can be incorporated in the scheme.
>
> The Mount Verney house, which, as will be remembered, was destroyed by a disastrous fire about three months ago, was not insured, and Mr. Richard Quinton had no wish to rebuild for his own occupation. He will, we understand, make his future residence at Quinton Court, the ancestral home of his family, so soon as he returns from Canada with his bride.

The Distortion out of Space

Francis Flagg

BACK OF Bear Mountain the meteor fell that night. Jim Blake and I saw it falling through the sky. As large as a small balloon it was and trailed a fiery tail. We knew it struck earth within a few miles of our camp, and later we saw the glare of a fire dully lighting the heavens. Timber is sparse on the farther slope of Bear Mountain, and what little there is of it is stunted and grows in patches, with wide intervals of barren and rocky ground. The fire did not spread to any extent and soon burned itself out.

Seated by our campfire we talked of meteoroids, those casual visitants from outer space which are usually small and consumed by heat on entering earth's atmosphere. Jim spoke of the huge one that had fallen in northern Arizona before the coming of the white man; and of another, more recent, which fell in Siberia.

"Fortunately," he said, "meteors do little damage; but if a large one were to strike a densely populated area, I shudder to think of the destruction to life and property. Ancient cities may have been blotted out in some such catastrophe. I don't believe that this one we just saw fell anywhere near Simpson's ranch."

"No," I said, "it hit too far north. Had it landed in the valley we couldn't have seen the reflection of the fire it started. We're lucky it struck no handier to us."

The next morning, full of curiosity, we climbed to the crest of the mountain, a distance of perhaps two miles. Bear Mountain is really a distinctive hog's-back of some height, with more rugged and higher mountain peaks around and beyond it. No timber grows on the summit, which, save for tufts of bear-grass and yucca, is rocky and bare. Looking down the farther side from the eminence attained, we saw that an area of hillside was blasted and still smoking. The meteor, however, had buried itself out of sight in earth and rock, leaving a deep crater some yards in extent.

About three miles away, in the small valley below, lay Henry Simpson's ranch, seemingly undamaged. Henry was a licensed guide, and when he went into the mountains after deer, we made his place our headquarters. Henry was not visible as we approached, nor his wife; and a certain uneasiness hastened our steps when we perceived that a portion of the house-roof – the house was built of adobe two stories high and had a slightly pitched roof made of rafters across which corrugated iron strips were nailed – was twisted and rent.

"Good heavens!" said Jim; "I hope a fragment of that meteorite hasn't done any damage here."

Leaving the burros to shift for themselves, we rushed into the house. "Hey, Henry!" I shouted. "Henry! Henry!"

Never shall I forget the sight of Henry Simpson's face as he came tottering down the broad stairs. Though it was eight o'clock in the morning, he still wore pajamas. His gray hair was tousled, his eyes staring.

"Am I mad, dreaming?" he cried hoarsely.

He was a big man, all of six feet tall, not the ordinary mountaineer, and though over sixty years of age possessed of great physical strength. But now his shoulders sagged, he shook as if with palsy.

"For heaven's sake, what's the matter?" demanded Jim. "Where's your wife?"

Henry Simpson straightened himself with an effort.

"Give me a drink." Then he said strangely: "I'm in my right mind – of course I must be in my right mind – but how can that thing upstairs be possible?"

"What thing? What do you mean?"

"I don't know. I was sleeping soundly when the bright light wakened me. That was last night, hours and hours ago. Something crashed into the house."

"A piece of the meteorite," said Jim, looking at me.

"Meteorite?"

"One fell last night on Bear Mountain, We saw it fall."

Henry Simpson lifted a gray face. "It may have been that."

"You wakened, you say?"

"Yes, with a cry of fear. I thought the place had been struck by lightning, 'Lydia!' I screamed, thinking of my wife. But Lydia never answered. The bright light had blinded me. At first I could see nothing. Then my vision cleared. Still I could see nothing – though the room wasn't dark."

"What!"

"Nothing, I tell you. No room, no walls, no furniture; only whichever way I looked, emptiness. I had leapt from bed in my first waking moments and couldn't find it again. I walked and walked, I tell you, and ran and ran; but the bed had disappeared, the room had disappeared. It was like a nightmare. I tried to wake up. I was on my hands and knees, crawling, when someone shouted my name. I crawled toward the sound of that voice, and suddenly I was in the hallway above, outside my room door. I dared not look back. I was afraid, I tell you, afraid. I came down the steps."

He paused, wavered. We caught him and eased his body down on a sofa.

"For God's sake," he whispered, "go find my wife."

Jim said soothingly: "There, there, sir, your wife is all right." He motioned me imperatively with his hand. "Go out to our cabin. Bill, and bring me my bag."

I did as he bade. Jim was a practising physician and never travelled without his professional kit. He dissolved a morphine tablet, filled a hypodermic, and shot its contents into Simpson's arm. In a few minutes, the old man sighed, relaxed, and fell into heavy slumber. "Look," said Jim, pointing.

The soles of Simpson's feet were bruised, bleeding, the pajamas shredded at the knees, the knees lacerated.

"He didn't dream it," muttered Jim at length. "He's been walking and crawling, all right."

We stared at each other. "But, good Lord, man!" I exclaimed.

"I know," said Jim. He straightened up. "There's something strange here. I'm going upstairs. Are you coming?"

Together we mounted to the hall above. I didn't know what we expected to find. I remember wondering if Simpson had done away with his wife and was trying to act crazy. Then I recollected that both Jim and I had observed the damage to the roof. Something had struck the house. Perhaps that something had killed Mrs. Simpson. She was an energetic woman, a few years younger than her husband, and not the sort to be lying quietly abed at such an hour.

Filled with misgivings, we reached the landing above and stared down the corridor. The corridor was well lighted by means of a large window at its extreme end. Two rooms opened off this corridor, one on each side. The doors to both were ajar.

The first room into which we glanced was a kind of writing-room and library. I have said that Simpson was no ordinary mountaineer. As a matter of fact, he was a man who read widely and kept abreast of the better publications in current literature.

The second room was the bedchamber. Its prosaic door – made of smoothed planks – swung outward. It swung toward us, half open, and in the narrow corridor we had to draw it still further open to pass. Then:

"My God!" said Jim.

Rooted to the floor, we both stared. Never shall I forget the sheer astonishment of that moment. For beyond the door, where a bedroom should have been, there was—

"Oh, it's impossible!" I muttered.

I looked away. Yes, I was in a narrow corridor, a house. Then I glanced back, and the effect was that of gazing into the emptiness of illimitable space. My trembling fingers gripped Jim's arm. I am not easily terrified. Men of my calling – aviation – have to possess steady nerves. Yet there was something so strange, so weird about the sight that I confess to a wave of fear. The space stretched away on all sides beyond that door, as space stretches away from one who, lying on his back on a clear day, stares at the sky. But this space was not bright with sunlight. It was a gloomy space, gray, intimidating; a space in which no stars or moon or sun were discernible. And it was a space that had – aside from its gloom – a quality of indirectness…

"Jim," I whispered hoarsely, "do you see it too?"

"Yes, Bill, yes."

"What does it mean?"

"I don't know. An optical illusion, perhaps. Something has upset the perspective in that room."

"Upset?"

"I'm trying to think."

He brooded a moment. Though a practising physician, Jim is interested in physics and higher mathematics. His papers on the relativity theory have appeared in many scientific journals.

"Space," he said, "has no existence aside from matter. You know that. Nor aside from time." He gestured quickly. "There's Einstein's concept of matter being a kink in space, of a universe at once finite and yet infinite. It's all abstruse and hard to grasp." He shook his head. "But in outer space, far beyond the reach of our most powerful telescopes, things may not function exactly as they do on earth. Laws may vary, phenomena the direct opposite of what we are accustomed to may exist."

His voice sank. I stared at him, fascinated.

"And that meteoroid from God knows where!" He paused a moment. "I am positive that this phenomenon we witness is connected with it. Something came to earth in that meteor and has lodged in this room, something possessing alien properties, that is able to distort, warp—" His voice died away.

I stared fearfully through the open door. "Good heavens," I said, "what can it be? What would have the power to create such an illusion?"

"If it *is* an illusion," muttered Jim.

"Perhaps it is no more an illusion than the environment in which we have our being and which we scarcely question. Don't forget that Simpson wandered through it for hours. Oh, it sounds fantastic, impossible, I know, and at first I believed he was raving; but now…now…"

He straightened abruptly. "Mrs. Simpson is somewhere in that room, in that incredible space, perhaps wandering about, lost, frightened. I'm going in."

I pleaded with him to wait, to reconsider. "If you go. I'll go too," I said.

He loosened my grip. "No, you must stay by the door to guide me with your voice."

Despite my further protestations, he stepped through the doorway. In doing so it seemed that he must fall into an eternity of nothing.

"Jim!" I called fearfully. He glanced back, but whether he heard my voice I could not say. Afterward he said he hadn't.

It was weird to watch him walking – a lone figure in the midst of infinity. I tell you it was the weirdest and most incredible sight the eye of man has ever seen. "I must be asleep, dreaming," I thought; "this can't be real."

I had to glance away, to assure myself by a sight of the hall that I was actually awake. The room at most was only thirty feet from door to wall; yet Jim went on and on, down an everlasting vista of gray distance, until his figure began to shorten, dwindle. Again I screamed, "Jim! Jim! Come back, Jim!" But in the very moment of my screaming, his figure flickered, went out, and in all the vast lonely reaches of that gloomy void, nowhere was he to be seen – nowhere!

I wonder if anyone can imagine a tithe of the emotions which swept over me at that moment. I crouched by the doorway to that incredible room, a prey to the most horrible fears and surmises. Anon I called out, "Jim! Jim!" but no voice ever replied, no familiar figure loomed on my sight.

The sun was high overhead when I went heavily down the stairs and out into the open. Simpson was still sleeping on the couch, the sleep of exhaustion. I remembered that he had spoken of hearing our voices calling him as he wandered through gray space, and it came over me as ominous and suggestive of disaster that my voice had, apparently, never reached Jim's ears, that no sound had come to my own ears out of the weird depths.

After the long hours of watching in the narrow corridor, of staring into alien space, it was with an inexpressible feeling of relief, of having escaped something horrible and abnormal, that I greeted the sun-drenched day. The burros were standing with drooping heads in the shade of a live-oak tree. Quite methodically I relieved them of their packs; then I filled and lit my pipe, doing everything slowly, carefully, as if aware of the need for restraint, calmness. On such little things does a man's sanity often depend. And all the time I stared at the house, at the upper portion of it where the uncanny room lay. Certain cracks showed in its walls and the roof above was twisted and torn. I asked myself, how was this thing possible? How, within the narrow confines of a single room, could the phenomenon of infinite space exist? Einstein, Eddington, Jeans – I had read their theories, and Jim might be correct, but the strangeness of it, the horror! You're mad, Bill, I said to myself, mad, mad! But there were the burros, there was the house. A scarlet tanager soared by, a hawk wheeled overhead, a covey of ring-necked mountain quail scuttled through tangled brush. No, I wasn't mad, I couldn't be dreaming, and Jim – Jim was somewhere in that accursed room, that distortion out of space, lost, wandering!

It was the most courageous thing I ever did in my life – to re-enter that house, climb those stairs. I had to force myself to do it, for I was desperately afraid and my feet dragged. But Simpson's ranch was in a lonely place, the nearest town or neighbor miles distant. It would take hours to fetch help, and of what use would it be when it did arrive? Besides, Bill needed aid, now, at once.

Though every nerve and fiber of my body rebelled at the thought, I fastened the end of a rope to a nail driven in the hall floor and stepped through the doorway. Instantly I was engulfed by endless space. It was a terrifying sensation. So far as I could see, my feet rested on nothing. Endless distance was below me as well as above. Sick and giddy, I paused and looked back, but the doorway had vanished. Only the coil of rope in my hands, and the heavy pistol in my belt, saved me from giving way to utter panic.

Slowly I paid out the rope as I advanced. At first it stretched into infinity like a sinuous serpent. Then suddenly all but a few yards of it disappeared. Fearfully I tugged at the end in my hands. It resisted the tug. The rope was still there, even if invisible to my eyes, every inch of it paid out; yet I was no nearer the confines of that room. Standing there with emptiness above, around, below me. I knew the meaning of utter desolation, of fear and loneliness. This way and that I groped, at the end of my tether. Somewhere Jim must be searching and groping too. "Jim!" I shouted; and miraculously enough, in my very ear it seemed, Jim's voice bellowed, "Bill! Bill! Is that you. Bill?"

"Yes," I almost sobbed. "Where are you, Jim?"

"I don't know. This place has me bewildered. I've been wandering around for hours. Listen, Bill; everything is out of focus here, matter warped, light curved. Can you hear me. Bill?"

"Yes, yes. I'm here too, clinging to the end of a rope that leads to the door. If you could follow the sound of my voice—"

"I'm trying to do that. We must be very close to each other. Bill—" His voice grew faint, distant.

"Here!" I shouted, "Here!"

Far off I heard his voice calling, receding.

"For God's sake, Jim, this way, this way!"

Suddenly the uncanny space appeared to shift, to eddy – I can describe what occurred in no other fashion – and for a moment in remote distance I saw Jim's figure. It was toiling up an endless hill, away from me; up, up; a black dot against an immensity of nothing. Then the dot flickered, went out, and he was gone. Sick with nightmarish horror, I sank to my knees, and even as I did so the realization of another disaster made my heart leap suffocatingly to my throat. In the excitement of trying to attract Jim's attention, I had dropped hold of the rope!

Panic leapt at me, sought to overwhelm me, but I fought it back. Keep calm, I told myself; don't move, don't lose your head; the rope must be lying at your feet. But though I felt carefully on all sides, I could not locate it. I tried to recollect if I had moved from my original position. Probably I had taken a step or two away from it, but in what direction? Hopeless to ask. In that infernal distortion of space and matter, there was nothing by which to determine direction. Yet I did not, I could not, abandon hope. The rope was my only guide to the outer world, the world of normal phenomena and life.

This way and that I searched, wildly, frantically, but to no purpose. At last I forced myself to stand quite still, closing my eyes to shut out the weird void. My brain functioned chaotically. Lost in a thirty-foot room, Jim, myself, and a woman, unable to locate one another – the thing was impossible, incredible. With trembling fingers I took out my pipe, pressed tobacco in the charred bowl and applied a match. Thank God for nicotine! My thoughts flowed more clearly. Incredible or not, here I was, neither mad. nor dreaming. Some quirk of circumstance had permitted Simpson to stagger from the web of illusion, but that quirk had evidently been one in a thousand. Jim and I might go wandering through alien depths until we died of hunger and exhaustion.

I opened my eyes. The gray clarity of space – a clarity of subtle indirection – still hemmed me in. Somewhere within a few feet of where I stood – as distance is computed in a three-dimensional world – Jim must be walking or standing. But this space was not three-dimensional. It was a weird dimension from outside the solar system which the mind of man could never hope to understand or grasp. And it was terrifying to reflect that within its depths Jim and I might be separated by thousands of miles and yet be cheek by jowl. I walked on. I could not stand still forever. God, I thought, there must be a way out of this horrible place, there must be! Ever and anon I called Jim's name. After a while I glanced at my watch, but it had ceased to run. Every muscle in my body began to ache, and thirst was adding its tortures to those of the mind. "Jim!" I cried hoarsely, again and again, but silence pressed in on me until I felt like screaming.

Conceive of it if you can. Though I walked on matter firm enough to the feet, seemingly space stretched below as well as above. Sometimes I had the illusion of being inverted, of walking head-downward. There was an uncanny sensation of being translated from spot to spot without the need of intermediate action. God! I prayed inwardly, God! I sank to my knees, pressing my hands over my eyes. But of what use was that? Of what use was anything? I staggered to my feet, fighting the deadly fear gnawing at my heart, and forced myself to walk slowly, without haste, counting the steps, one, two, three...

When it was I first noticed the shimmering radiation, I cannot say. Like heat radiation it was, only more subtle, like waves of heat rising from an open furnace. I rubbed my eyes, I stared tensely. Yes, waves of energy were being diffused from some invisible source. Far off in the illimitable depths of space I saw them pulsing; but I soon perceived that I was fated – like a satellite fixed in its groove – to travel in a vast circle of which they were the center.

And perhaps in that direction lay the door!

Filled with despair I again sank to my knees, and kneeling I thought drearily, "This is the end, there is no way out," and calmer than I had been for hours – there *is* a calmness of despair, a fatalistic giving over of struggle – I raised my head and looked apathetically around.

Strange, strange; weird and strange. Could this be real, was I myself? Could an immensity of nothing lie within a thirty-foot radius, be caused by something out of space, something brought by the meteor, something able to distort, warp?

Distort, warp!

With an oath of dawning comprehension I leapt to my feet and glared at the shimmering radiation. Why couldn't I approach it? What strange and invisible force forbade? Was it because the source of this incredible space lay lurking there? Oh, I was mad, I tell you, a little insane, yet withal possessed of a certain coolness and clarity of thought. I drew the heavy pistol from its holster. A phrase of Jim's kept running through my head: Vibration, vibration, everything is varying rates of vibration. Yet for a moment I hesitated. Besides myself, in this incredible space two others were lost, and what if I were to shoot either of them? Better that, I told myself, than to perish without a struggle.

I raised the pistol. The shimmering radiation was something deadly, inimical, the diffusing waves of energy were loathsome tentacles reaching out to slay.

"Damn you," I muttered, "take that – and that!"

I pulled the trigger.

Of what followed I possess but a kaleidoscopic and chaotic memory. The gray void seemed to breathe in and out. Alternately I saw space and room, room and space; and leering at me through the interstices of this bewildering change something indescribably loathsome, something that lurked at the center of a crystal ball my shots had perforated. Through the bullet-holes in this crystal a slow vapor oozed, and as it oozed, the creature inside of the ball struggled and writhed; and as it struggled I had the illusion of being lifted in and out, in and out; into the room, out into empty space. Then suddenly the crystal ball shivered and broke; I heard it break with a tinkling as of glass; the luminous vapor escaped in a swirl, the gray void vanished, and sick and giddy I found myself definitely encompassed by the walls of a room and within a yard of the writhing monstrosity.

As I stood with rooted feet, too dazed to move, the monstrosity reared. I saw it now in all its hideousness. A spidery thing it was, and yet not a spider. Up it reared, up, four feet in the air, its saucer-like eyes goggling out at me, its hairy paws reaching. Sick with terror, I was swept forward into the embrace of the loathsome creature. Then happened that which I can never forget till my dying day, so strange it was, so weird. Imagination, you say, the fantastic thoughts of a temporarily disordered mind. Perhaps, perhaps; but suddenly I seemed to know – know beyond a doubt – that this spider-like visitant from outer space was an intelligent, reasoning being. Those eyes – they seemed to bore into the innermost recesses of my brain, seemed to establish a species of communication between myself and the intelligence back of them. It was not a malignant intelligence – I realized that – but in comparison to myself something god-like, remote. And yet it was a mortal intelligence. My bullets had shattered its protective covering, had reached to its vulnerable body, and as it held me to itself, it was in the very throes of dissolution. All this I sensed, all this it told me; not through language, but through some subtle process of picture transference which it is hopeless for me to attempt to explain. I seemed to see a gray, weird place where delicate traceries were spun and silver devices shimmered and shone – the habitat of the strange visitant from outer space. Perhaps the receiving-cells of my brain were not developed enough to receive all the impressions it tried to convey.

Nothing was clear, distinct, nothing definite. I had the agonizing consciousness that much was slipping through my brain, uncorrelated, unregistered. But a meteoroid was hurtling through the blackness of space – and I saw that meteoroid. I saw it falling to earth. I saw a portion of it swing clear, crash through the roof of Simpson's house and lodge in the bedroom. And I saw the strange visitant from outside our universe utilize the incredible power he possessed to distort space, iron out the kinks of matter in it, veil himself in immensity while studying his alien surroundings.

And then all his expiring emotions seemed to rush over me in a flood and I felt – *felt* – what he was thinking. He had made a journey from one star system to another, he had landed safely on earth, a trillion, trillion light-years distant, but never would he return to his own planet to tell of his success – never, never! All this I seemed to understand, to grasp, in a split second or so, his loneliness and pain, his terrible nostalgia; then the hairy paws relaxed their grip, the hideous body collapsed in on itself, and as I stared at it sprawling on the floor, I was suddenly conscious of Mrs. Simpson crouching, unharmed, in one corner of the room, of Jim standing beside me, clutching my arm.

"Bill," he said hoarsely, "are you hurt?" And then in a whisper, "What is it? What is it?"

"I don't know," I returned chokingly, "I don't know. But whatever it is, it is dead now – the Distortion out of Space."

And unaccountably I buried my face in my hands and began to weep.

White Noise

Kevin M. Folliard

THEY COME when it's quiet, Doc. They're why I surround my bed with old TVs. Why I keep the radio on low. White noise keeps my senses occupied. Keeps those things at bay.

Even a steady drone, like a fan, stops the silence from capturing my thoughts. Once everything is still, there's a void – a path to my mind – that they cross.

I know professionally you think it's all in my head. But if they were in your head, you'd understand.

They've been visiting since I was about three. I'd lay awake, and they would creep into my bedroom. I was too terrified to scream, or move, or…

Well that's just it, I sort of *am* awake when it happens. Awake enough.

And I know what night terrors are. I know about sleep paralysis. You're not my first shrink. But maybe science doesn't totally understand what the mind opens up to in this weird half-awake state.

If you searched my apartment, of course, you wouldn't find evidence. That doesn't mean they're not real on some level.

They look like…stencils. This is hard to explain. We see objects in three-dimensional space, right? These things are *shaped* like beings, anthropomorphic, maybe ten feet tall with lanky arms and legs, spherical heads. But they're not flesh and blood; there's no substance, just form.

It's like they're carved out of reality, a recess of space moving about. Sometimes on two legs. Sometimes all fours.

They don't have faces. They don't really even have features except the shape and what's inside. Remember TV snow, that frantic static when the cable went out, before everything went digital? Inside their forms is a mess of white and gray light particles, as if their bodies are portals into some dimension of static.

And there's something else – this pure fucking evil that you feel in your guts. It's a sickness inducing…unnaturalness. Look, if there truly is a God that's good, then I swear, he had nothing to do with *these*.

Sorry.

You know, I like talking to someone like you. It helps *me* feel better.

But it doesn't stop them.

* * *

Why do you people always ask about parents?

Parents aren't the root of every problem. Definitely not this problem.

Of course, my mom and dad didn't believe me growing up. Why would they? It bothered me at the time, but I understand now. My mom, like everyone, like you, reasonably thought I was dreaming about things creeping into my room.

Most kids have nightmares, Doc. But this is a whole other world of unpleasant.

I'll never forget lying in my bedroom in our house on Ash Street. The brown carpet, the gold striped wallpaper. They'd crawl on those long arms and legs and duck in from the hallway.

And within a few strides, they're right in my face. It feels like my eyes are popping out of my head, like my mind is being sucked into that fuzzy gray static. And it hurts. Physically hurts. Like a muscle cramp over my whole body.

They came almost every night until I was about thirteen. That year, my parents let me have the old TV for my bedroom. That's when I figured out that if I fell asleep with the TV on, they didn't come. The white noise kept them away, kept my mind occupied as I drifted to sleep. I don't know for sure the psychological or scientific reason, but it worked. It still…sort of works.

Anyway, as a teenager, I got in the habit of sleeping with the TV on. My mom used to scream at me for wasting electricity, "Colin!" she'd say. "You're gonna drive us to the welfare office!" Which I still don't understand because how much does it cost to keep a TV on overnight?

Anyway, things got better in high school. Even a faint crackle of radio static, I learned, canceled them out somehow. But they knew I was thwarting them.

You know bed bugs, Doc? They hide in the bed frame, or wherever, and wait until their human host falls asleep. The bugs depend on that human every night, sleeping in that same spot, so they can suck their blood.

That's like my problem. So imagine you're one of these beings, and you know every night this kid with these tasty brainwaves or whatever – this fear or pain they feed on, my aura, I don't know – is in that bed in that room. And suddenly he figures out how to shut the door.

Well these things are like bed bugs with a vendetta, because when I figured out how to block them, they took it personally.

A few of these encounters stand out, and summer before high school, that's burned in my memory. It was a scorcher of a night, and we had all these window unit air conditioners – so did everyone on the block – so of course: *ZAP!* Power goes out, around 9 p.m. Pitch black. Dead silent.

At that point, it had been a while since my last encounter, so I'd grown cocky. I thought I'd put the whole thing behind me. That's when I learned just how cruel they were.

At first, I thought they were my parents. But they started screaming, accusing me of…doing things an adolescent might do at night…you know. And for a long while, I thought my mom and dad were truly there, in a rage, calling their kid a pervert. But then, Doc, you eventually notice their faces are missing. Not the TV static, but this time a human face with the elements – the eyes, nose, and mouth – replaced by a film of fleshy…blankness.

It was still my parents' voices though. And I tell you, Doc, maybe technically I was 'asleep' or in a trance for ten, fifteen minutes. But it felt like hours.

When the power came back, it was 10:15 p.m. Just imagine a kid, trapped in this time warp with his parents tearing his most embarrassing secrets out of him.

…Sorry. I'm done for today.

* * *

It got worse in college.

Until then, they'd only ever visited my parents' house. If I had a sleepover or we went to a motel or something, I somehow knew they couldn't find me.

My college roommate Ted was a great guy. By then, I thought I'd outgrown the whole thing. And I didn't want to ask my roommate if I could sleep with a TV on or the radio crackling. He'd wonder why, and I wasn't going to tell him the real reason.

So in that little dorm room, every night, it was quiet, it was still, and it was dark.

And within a month, they found me again.

After years of keeping them away with my white noise trick, there was hell to pay.

I distinctly remember the first time they entered my dorm. Ted slept on the top bunk. We had the window open. And this is weird, because I know they aren't physical creatures, but they crawled through the window, one-by-one, three of them. Their negative-forms just sprang in. And they stalked up to my bottom bunk. One of them touched my forehead with an electric finger.

I had never experienced pain like that. It was like a white-hot sword stabbed my brain. Its finger twisted, like it was drilling into my soul.

I screamed for – I don't know how long. And this is the worst part. My roommate, nice eighteen-year-old kid from Iowa, shakes me, wakes me, and all the beings vanish. Ted thinks I'm having a medical emergency.

And tears are running down my face. I tell him it was a nightmare.

But it doesn't end there. Ted starts shouting. Starts calling me a crybaby, shaming me. Acting totally out of character. His face is meaner than he ever was in real life. He's calling me a pants-wetter, a pansy, a million other things I hadn't heard since I was a little kid.

And then his features blur into that fleshy nothing.

And I realize, I'm still trapped.

This isn't Ted; it's those things twisting my perceptions, even more than normal. The fake Ted berates me. All night long.

The next morning, the real Ted slept through it. He never noticed, which on the one hand was good, because I'd have been embarrassed. But after a while, when it kept happening, it started to feel... I don't know, lonely. I wanted Ted to care that it was happening. And somehow, every time, they'd trick me for a moment into thinking he did.

It messed with me to the point where, even in broad daylight, I'd be talking to Ted, unsure if he was real or not.

I tried sleeping with headphones. But I still ended up seeing the evil Ted. I just couldn't stand being in that room with him...even though I knew that wasn't really him.

Ever since college, the encounters have been more like that, torment that escalates. It's why I never finished my degree; why I ended up back home. I could never face Ted without being afraid that, any second, I'd find myself stuck in some agonizing warp.

My parents were livid. I attended community college, but it was a setback. Even so, I was happy. I had my TV in my room that I controlled.

Except eventually even that stopped working. They were adapting. That year at college helped them figure me out a little more, figure out a way around my white noise trick. Now just one TV didn't keep them away. Just having the radio on low didn't work either.

And the things they say, Doc, things you have to lay frozen and hear all night...

Sorry. It's just...

...Sometimes when you talk about it, when you tell someone, it happens. Because it's on your mind, because you externalized it...

They're coming tonight. I know it.

* * *

They've come several times since we started talking. After last week's session, I had a bad episode, like I knew I would...

It was not a self-fulfilling prophecy. Don't start with that, okay?

I was lying there, exhausted. I had all the TVs on. I have eight bedroom TVs on a power switch. I just – CLICK – pop them on, volumes on low. They're like a night light, I guess. But I've explained this before. If one TV works, then two must work better, and so on.

I know it's crazy for an adult to live like this.

Anyway. I look up, and it's you, Doc. And at first, I'm thrown, but for some reason, your mind just rolls with it. Eventually, you realize: Hey it's crazy unprofessional for the Doc to visit me in my home!

As soon as I figure it out, you drop into demon-mode. You've got dirt on me, Doc, and you're using it to wound me every way you know how. You're calling me a pansy, a pussy, a crybaby, bed-wetter, queer, faggot, a pathetic little wanker. You go on and on…

Of course you wouldn't say that here – not out loud – but hey, I still had to listen to it, and even though I know it's not *really* you, it *feels* real, like…

Sometimes I wonder if those things are hurtful because they're lying or because they *know* what people really think, but never say…

Of course you'd say that. But what are you *thinking*?

It's enough to drive you crazy.

* * *

Don't really date much. Who wants to date a 37-year-old copy-shop clerk buried in debt? And what do I do, bring them home to my TV chamber? Besides anytime I get close to someone, they get… inducted into those things' repertoire of faces.

I'll admit it: I had a little crush on Ted. That's what you've been thinking about me all this time isn't it, like I'm so repressed and it's making me hallucinate because I can't be myself.

Try again. I'm cool with it. I mostly go in for women though.

I dated this barista named Trudy in my early thirties. She was a sweetheart. She even knew about the stuff I experience. I think it kind of endeared me to her. She was a little wacky, but good cook. Good listener.

She wanted kids and a house and… We both knew I didn't have that up my sleeves.

I loved her, but it's strange. I wonder how important she could have been. They've never worn her face.

* * *

I tried, Doc, like you suggested, I tried a night without TVs. And I… I can't do that again. It's too dangerous.

It was like they'd broken my mind, like I was staring into nothingness forever.

It started with one of them, upside down on the ceiling. Its staticky neck stretched to my face. That painful eye-socket-bulging feeling sucked me deep into the gray-white mess of its head. Only the particles grew bigger and bigger, like pixels in an old videogame, big white-gray squares, until I fell into one of the white squares.

And then it was white, white nothing. Like I was dead. Stuck forever on my final thought.

And my last thought was terror.

It felt like days, weeks, I couldn't say. Eventually, the physical pain faded, because I had no body. I was just a…detached perspective. They struck this final discordant note of fear inside me that echoed nonstop.

Eventually, I woke up.

It was 2 a.m. Only a couple hours passed in real time. But it was an eternity. And I was not meant to escape. They must have slipped their grip or something.

Doc, you have to believe me, I cannot mess around with this anymore. This nothingness is where they want me; this is what it's all been building to, a final moment where they trap me forever.

And I don't know what happens on your end when I'm there for good. Does my brain just echo in that nothing, and paramedics find me, comatose or dead?

Does it look like my heart gave out? Like a stroke? An aneurysm?

What good are a bunch of expensive medical tests? These things don't operate on any plane – in any way – we can measure. They're here to fuck with me and only me, I guess.

And I know how that sounds! I know what you're scribbling on your fucking pad! I'm not going to calm down or humor you or make nice. I know you think I'm crazy. So let's drop the bullshit.

If I listen to you, I will end up dead, or worse.

…God, I'm sorry. I didn't mean to shout or swear or…

You know what's so scary about it? When you're stuck in a state of total fear and defeat, a part of you starts to slowly accept it. Your mind decides, "I have no choice, so I guess this could be worse."

That's waiting for me. A gradual humiliating acceptance that I must deserve this.

Because sooner or later, there will be a power outage. Or I'll nod off somewhere, somehow, in a place where they can find me.

And you know what? I'm glad you all think I'm fucking nuts, because you have no frame of reference for what this is like for me. And hopefully it means that you, and everyone else, doesn't have that waiting for them.

Because I know I do.

* * *

Colin is not dead. He will never die, Doctor Taylor. Though his body rots, the final part of him sinks forever inside us. If you go there, you will never meet him. You will each float forever and never cross paths.

To Colin, you were a dichotomy of stress and support. You and every person he wanted to confide in.

He loved you and he hated you, and in his fading moments, he wished he had never met you.

Your words cut through the hum of Colin's lonely world. You sliced his pain open, and we swam to him.

We've worn your form, as we now wear Colin's.

And Colin was right. When we speak for another, it is more than a lie.

It is a dark truth, sharpened into a surgical tool.

You hide a molten core of judgement beneath a veil of compassion.

We used that to dig at him.

To carve him away and cherish his eternal pain like a precious jewel.

And because you wish so desperately to understand Colin, we have come to teach you.

And you will know.

Dark Skies

Anastasia Garcia

US Air Force Base
San Antonio, Texas
March 1943

MY NAME is Margaret Raskova of the 588th Night Bomber Regiment of the US Air Force. I am writing to you, the brother of the deceased Rosalinda 'Rosie' Gutierrez, because I am a close friend of your sister, and because I was there the day she went missing.

I know you received official communication that her plane crashed in the Gulf of Mexico during a routine training exercise. No doubt they mentioned her machinery was faulty and that she was overtired from a previous evening of raids on enemy ships. But that is an outright lie perpetrated by commanding officers to cover up what really happened.

* * *

Once America joined the war, women were left to crowd around scratchy radios listening to reports from the front lines, but the news only got worse. And soon that waiting turned to longing, turned to aching to do more than sit at home and wait for the men to return from war. So we did the only thing left in our power, we enlisted.

I was sent to training camp in San Antonio where I befriended your sister, Rosie, as I would come to call her. We met on my very first day. That day the new recruits were a motley crew of women hailing from all corners of the United States, selected to join the Air Force because our skills could be useful on an airbase, even if some of us could only type.

We gathered on the base, everyone wearing the standard issue ill-fitting men's uniform of tall boots and wide-shoulder jackets. Most donned lipstick, some wore their black flight caps at a jaunty angle, others tucked their long hair into buns hidden under the brim. We carried ourselves with a nervous sort of formality, because the uniforms made us stiff and rigid, like dancing in someone else's skin.

The new recruits were allowed to sit down to a meal in the mess hall to become acquainted. As the only all-women squadron, there was some sort of assumption that maybe we would all prefer to meet over coffee and crackers. Perhaps this charade of tea time would ease our homesickness, or draw it into stark relief. Soon the mess hall filled with the rising din of women swapping stories of the life they left behind and the men they loved shipped to distant lands, some never coming home. But beneath the pleasantries, there was a growing realization that after our training we, too, might never return home.

Watching these strong and capable women smile and laugh, I felt alien among them. I squirmed on the hard bench, shoulders pressed on either side, uncomfortable in my own uniform and jittery from the coffee. I was just little Margie from Kansas, what could I possibly contribute to the great world war? But just as darkening doubt was inching its fingers across my mind, Rosie stood to address the group.

A giddy girl beside me whispered behind cupped hands, "It's her, the Night Witch!"

Whispers of *night witch* hissed through the mess hall like a draft from an opened window.

"Why do they call her that?" someone asked.

"The Nazis call her that. Well, the ones that survive. Because she glides low over enemy lines," the girl demonstrated with a flying hand. "She does it with the engine off to drop bombs, silent and deadly."

I peered a little closer at the woman standing before us. She wore a sergeant's uniform that displayed her rank proudly on her chest. Her dark hair was tucked into her flight cap and her tanned skin was now bronzed from days in the cockpit.

Rosie returned our gaze, eyes sweeping all corners of the tent, settling on me. I burned hot under the collar with her fleeting attention. With the most flying experience she was to be our flight instructor. She laid out the facts as she saw them, harsh truths many in the tent were not ready to hear. "You will be held to unreasonable standards because we are both women and pilots – and from now on, we will never be taken seriously as either." Murmurs of vexation permeated the crowd. "But given the war shows no sign of slowing and our country needs us, I expect you to prove your mettle." She lifted her mug of coffee and closed with a toast, "To finding our sense of direction."

There was an eruption of cheers and Rosie smiled to the room. She caught my gaze again, only this time my eyes sparkled with tears. I was quick to wipe them away, but she noticed all the same. My heart began to pound as she strode over to join my table. After addressing the table's questions and praise, she finally turned to me, silent through it all, to say. "Tell me about home." Her brown eyes meet mine.

I looked away, cheeks burning. I managed to stammer out my experience flying crop dusters on my family's farm. Of helping my father with the harvest, helping my mother with the chores, of not feeling fulfilled with either. I told her I was running away from my parents and all the other things required of me – teaching school children, Sunday dresses, marriage. By signing my name on the dotted line in the enlistment office, maybe now I could run straight towards something, even if it was a war.

Somehow she seemed to understand, and replied, "With your flight experience, I want you on my first squadron." She stood to leave. "If you stay close to me, I'll teach you how to cast some spells of your own." She said with a wink and her knockout smile. My breath caught in my throat.

But what I didn't tell her was that she was the reason for my courage. That I read about her latest raid on the front lines in the papers. It was only after hearing that a woman from South Texas was striking fear into the hearts of Nazis that I finally believed that any of us could do something meaningful. I also didn't tell her that I still carried that newspaper clipping in my front pocket.

* * *

During training Rosie and I are inseparable. With our last names near in the alphabet we are stationed together for training, meal times, and sleeping. Most days are long and grueling as we fly hundreds of miles a day to almost exhaustion just to prove we can and that we deserve the chance to hold the controls. Often when I am weary enough to feel the ache in my bones, I think back to that first day when I was just a girl running away from home and how we clinked tin cups of black coffee.

In training, Rosie watches over me. She critiques my performance, she praises my risks, and she ignites my smoldering ambition. Now I am a girl turned woman turned soldier and I thrive under Rosie's direction. In the sky, I enjoy the push of the wind beneath my metal wings and the raw strength coiled in my newfound muscles as I expertly operate the cyclic stick. I like the sound of my voice over the radio, confident without a hint of hesitation. In the sky I am no longer a woman, but a machine performing at optimum potential.

Rosie and I grow closer and I begin to recognize the depth of her gaze, the warmth in her smile, and the comfort of her touch. With a silky shiver, I realize our friendship is blossoming in ways I never felt before. If I am a new machine, Rosie is the skilled operator deep within maneuvering the toggles and switches. I think she begins to feel it, too.

One day before we go up, as we wait for routine maintenance on the fighters, Rosie pulls off her goggles. She stares at me as if seeing me clearly for the very first time. She reaches across to gently push a stray strand of hair over my ear causing a spray of goosebumps down my neck. She says in a voice barely above a whisper, "Margie, is it sinful to be grateful for a war?" I begin to tremble, because I've had the same guilty thought while alone in the barracks. In that fleeting moment of warmth, she holds my cheek in her rough palm and our paths entwine and I vow to follow her to the end of the earth.

Before our next flight, using my navigational pencil, I draw flowers near her cockpit access, so she will think of me every time she climbs in. I hope this would make her less daring, less cavalier in the face of the enemy. But I will soon find out that nothing can stop Rosie from going any direction she pleases.

* * *

It is the day of my first real mission when it all begins to unravel. At the morning briefing, I notice unfamiliar officers sitting in the back of our briefing room. Their faces are impassive and their rank denotes a high security clearance. The officers consult a manila folder of material that even I can see is mostly redacted. They eye us brazenly and whisper to each other, careful not to move their lips. Rosie and I lock eyes, a silent signal that she is reading the room as well. I can often guess what men say to each other when seeing us for the first time, but this feels different.

The instructions are clear: one of us will fly out over the ocean, activate stealth mode when approaching the coordinates, and report back anything we see. It's a simple mission, perfect for a new recruit like me, a perfect opportunity. When the commanding officer calls my name and asks for my experience, I stand out of my seat at attention. I clench my jaw to remain stoic as my spinning thoughts coalesce – *my first solo mission!* – while taking deep breaths to keep the shake out of my voice. But before I can state my qualifications, Rosie rises beside me. "As Margaret's training instructor, I do not believe she is qualified to make this trip alone. I will do it."

The rejection stings, smarts deep like a flesh wound. I can barely hide the grimace from my face. At first the officers protest, a small argument ensues but Rosie is determined. She will fly this mission, she will report back her findings, I will be left behind. The mysterious officers leave with barely a nod in our direction, tucking the folders into their jackets.

Once we are dismissed and out of earshot, I pull Rosie into the bathroom and ask in a hurried breath, "Why would you say that in there?" I want to sound fierce, but there's a hitch in my voice, evidence of how betrayed I feel. "How can you say I'm not ready? I've flown hundreds of these simulations already. This is my chance!"

"No!" She shouts, looking into my eyes. "Something is wrong. There's something they aren't telling us."

"What do you mean? They never tell us anything." I ask, confusion paints my face.

"Those officers are not Air Force." Her brow knits and she paces, the first time I've seen her nervous. She turns back to me to say, "While I'm up there, I need you down here, to find out what you can."

* * *

Rosie is escorted to the tarmac for the mission, flanked on either side by high-ranking officers. I watch her suit up and climb into the cockpit before I slink back to the command room where all radio communications will take place. I position myself near the backup aircraft communicator in the corner of the room, a clear line of sight to the unfamiliar officers stationed in the front of the room, and within earshot of the radio.

At first all is quiet, only the soft hiss of static on the radio. As Rosie gains altitude and speed she signals *all clear* into the radio, and I let out a shaky breath. As Rosie nears the coordinates of the mission, the ground team frets at their instruments, shouting questions, sharing readouts. A storm begins to build in her flight path, a strange occurrence since no weather patterns predicted a storm of this magnitude now swelling across the sea – towards Rosie. The unfamiliar officers, unsettlingly calm, jot notes in their folder. The ground team requests an immediate return to base, but the officers void the call. The ground team continues to insist, they gesture wildly at their instruments. My palms begin to sweat, eyes darting between the ground team lobbying for Rosie's return and the officers outright refusal – until the sound of Rosie's voice fills the room.

"There's something out there!" Her once rational voice now sounds feverish, yelling over the thunder and the rain pelting her windscreen. "It's too big – huge!" Machines in the control room begin to whistle and beep, men jump to action consulting their figures, making adjustments. "My instruments are not functioning, I can't get an accurate reading."

The ground control team attempts to ask her questions to discern her location and altitude. But, strangely, Rosie's voice lilts and it begins to slur, as if she's talking in her sleep. "I hear it… speaking." The machines slow their beeping and all ears are tuned to Rosie's voice. My heart is pounding, my fists are painfully clenched at my sides, as I hold my breath.

A sound like a thousand screams erupts from the radio. Everyone in the control room yells and covers their ears, the cacophony almost drowns out thought.

Until… silence. All radio communication blips off and the machines power down.

Everyone in the room freezes waiting in the darkness. The silence lasts only a brief pregnant moment until the power returns with a rising hum. And in an instant, Rosie is shouting over the radio, she's taken some sort of enemy fire! She's making a hasty return to base, requesting a medic. There's a frenzy of movement as everyone rushes to the exits to see her landing with their own eyes.

All tactical units and medical personnel converge on the tarmac to watch her bumpy return to earth with the sickening sound of scraping metal. Sparks alight her tires as the motor putters off, the plane slowing to a stop at an angle. The sides of her P-51 Mustang are scorched black and riddled with scratches, as if she piloted through Hell itself.

Rosie is pulled nearly unconscious from the still-smoking cockpit and hurried to the medical ward. Gripped by concern and curiosity, I sneak a seat behind the nurses desk and listen in on the uniformed men as they confer outside of Rosie's hospital room. I catch snippets of *too dangerous, the anomaly, a greater threat* pass their lips.

When the officers change their shift, I take this chance to soundlessly enter Rosie's room, closing the door behind me. In the darkened room, Rosie is staring out of the window at the blackened night sky. "Rosie?" I ask, uncertain if she is responsive or in pain. She turns to look at me, her eyes clouded with a sedative. I rush to her side to hold her hand, "Rosie, are you alright? What happened up there? All I could hear on the comms were…screams." I shake the memory of the sound from my mind.

"Margie, I saw something up there. Not human things." The words pull her from the sedative stupor and her eyes shine bright and focused, searching for something beyond her field of vision. "They're coming." She hisses between clenched teeth. Her lip trembles with terror and she squeezes my hand in a vice grip, "The war, the death, and all the death that will come, it calls to them!" Her voice rising, she begins to shake as a bone-clattering shiver racks her body, "Make it stop! Make it stop!" She begins to flail just as nurses and officers rush back into the room. My eyes are wide, staring at Rosie fighting the hands pinning her down, the frenzied look in her red-rimmed eyes and the spittle flying from her lips. In the chaos, I slip out as Rosie begins to scream.

* * *

Weeks pass with Rosie imprisoned in the medical ward, while I am left going through the motions of training, like a dutiful soldier. I pretend to see nothing, hear nothing, and know nothing. Until one day, I am surprised to find Rosie resuming her position as the lead pilot of our training squadron, her disposition markedly changed. She wears a mask of duty and acquiescence in the presence of her superiors, but I can see something haunting in her eyes, a darkness lingering.

On her first day back, our unit embarks on a reconnaissance mission (that part is true).

In a stolen moment, Rosie pulls me aside. "Margie. Something is coming." She is sweating, her cheeks flushed. "It's bigger than any human war and a thousand times more powerful than any A-bomb!" she hisses. Her eyes are wide, she grips my wrist with a fearsome strength. "Margie, please believe me. I hear it even now, still speaking to me in the dark."

"You aren't making sense, Rosie." I search for the Rosie I know in her face, I touch her cheek with my fingertips, but she recoils from my touch as if burned. All I find is fear in those unseeing eyes.

"Come with me, when we're up there." She turns her rolling eyes skyward, pointing with a gloved hand, "I'll show you." I tear my wrist free from her grasp, hurrying to my plane. As we suit up, I watch her over my shoulder, wary that this mission might be too soon for Rosie, she's not well.

As soon as we take flight, I know something is wrong.

I gaze out into the ocean, noticing that the fog setting in is unseasonal and unanticipated. Once we are over the ocean, the sky deepens to a troublesome shade of plum with billowing clouds bursting with a static charge. My instinct says to turn back, but Rosie yells over the radio that she knows a way through the encroaching storm. We remain in formation against our better judgment and follow her lead.

As the strange clouds envelop us, I see a peculiar sight: a hole in this world like a picture laid over another. Through the hole I see a brilliant black night sky and with no time to course-correct, we fly directly into it. All radio sound winks out, filling our ears with a deafening silence, and ground communication is lost.

The sensation is like unzipping our bodies from this world to become weightless, suspended like floating berries in a tin of homemade jello. We are awash in the glow of a million glittering stars close enough to reach out and touch. A pressure in my chest begins to build – I'm not breathing.

I attempt to intake breath, my mouth agape with only a hollow suction. Panic rushes blood to my face and a darkness seeps into the edge of my vision, pulsing with my slowing heart. I swing my arms wildly to break the cockpit window, but my gloved fists lose inertia. I reach for Rosie, who is just out of my left window. I can see her in the cockpit, she slumps in her seat, her helmeted head lolling propped up only by her restraints. Her plane drifts higher and away towards the zenith, somewhere I could not follow.

My vision blackens and pops of light dance across my eyes. Each burst of lighting, like fireworks on a hot July night, begins to expand into flashing visions. Visions of tumbling bricks, hollow-cheeked living skeletons with bulging eyes, blood and viscera splashed across a floor, the gnashing teeth of screaming people, naked children running from a burning jungle, incinerating skin against the glare of an impossibly bright light, bodies hanging from trees, death, death, death. The visions dissipate, leaving behind only a vast emptiness within, a gaping pit of sucking despair that drains the color and warmth from existence.

There is something out there in the dark, watching me, lapping up my fading hope. It watches me with a hundred inky black eyeballs boring deep into my mind, it crawls across my skin like a million wriggling legs. It tugs on the threads of time like a spider twitching across its web. I want to run, back to my parents farm, back to the mind-numbing dullness of a sunny afternoon, back to feeling and desire and… love.

I think of Rosie and how every minute spent with her felt like eons squeezed into narrow slips of time. She would never resign herself to a hopeless life, not when she could crank the propellers, look out over the horizon, and route her own flight path.

When my vision returns my hands drift near my face. With my last adrenaline-fueled spasm I seize the *ratatattat* gun and blast away into the darkness beyond the light, where I know the thing to be. I bare my teeth in a silent scream.

The nose of my plane begins to dip down, down, down. With a sickening *blip, gurgle, pop* a heaviness returns to my limbs, as does the blinding afternoon sun. The pull of gravity sucks me towards the sea. My ears fill with the roar of rushing wind as I grab wildly for the controls. Using my whole body, I strain against the joystick to pull up at the last moment just skimming the water's reflecting surface.

My breathing returns heavy and panicked just as I hear an ear-splitting radio squeal and a crackling voice. The ground team sounds aggressive, confused, asking for my coordinates, regiment, and name. With my reply I hear them yell, "Sir, it's her. She's back!"

Upon landing, I am so weak they are forced to pull me from the cockpit. An unfamiliar sergeant leans over me with his clinking medals screaming questions I barely understand: *what happened to your aircraft, where did you go, where are the others?*

Through medical tests, cognitive tests, and more, I demand to see Rosie. They draw enough blood to fill vials, while I am poked and prodded in all unspeakable ways. I scream and upset a tray, until a sinister squadron of commanding officers crowd into my hospital room to deliver the news.

Two weeks. We were lost in flight for two weeks.

Of the six of us to disappear, I am the only one to come back.

* * *

Now I know what I wrote might sound crazy, downright insane. Maybe I should be locked up for speaking my mind and I'm sure I will be. If you try to investigate this there will be no answers, all communication transcripts from our flight are now classified. The official report is *there is no report.*

Enclosed are Rosie's personal effects which I promised to return to you in the event of her death. Included is a picture of us taken just before that fateful flight: Rosie stands next to her plane staring into the sun with that famous smile while I shade my eyes at her side. Take this as proof that I am who I say I am, that my unit was real, that we existed.

I am honest when I write to you that I have no conceivable notion as to what happened to us that night. But I am going to look for her. Right where the clouds meet the sky in that zipper of space and time. I know she's up there and I intend to find her.

Margaret Raskova
588th Night Bomber Regiment

The Crimson Weaver

R. Murray Gilchrist

MY MASTER and I had wandered from our track and lost ourselves on the side of a great 'edge'. It was a two-days journey from the Valley of the Willow Brakes, and we had roamed aimlessly; eating at hollow-echoing inns where grey-haired hostesses ministered, and sleeping side by side through the dewless midsummer nights on beds of fresh-gathered heather.

Beyond a single-arched wall-less bridge that crossed a brown stream whose waters leaped straight from the upland, we reached the Domain of the Crimson Weaver. No sooner had we reached the keystone when a beldam, wrinkled as a walnut and bald as an egg, crept from a cabin of turf and osier and held out her hands in warning.

"Enter not the Domain of the Crimson Weaver!" she shrieked. "One I loved entered – I am here to warn men. Behold, I was beautiful once!"

She tore her ragged smock apart and discovered the foulness of her bosom, where the heart pulsed behind a curtain of livid skin. My Master drew money from his wallet and scattered it on the ground.

"She is mad," he said. "The evil she hints cannot exist. There is no fiend."

So we passed on, but the bridge-keeper took no heed of the coins. For a while we heard her bellowed sighs issuing from the openings of her den.

Strangely enough, the tenour of our talk changed from the moment that we left the bridge. He had been telling me of the Platonists, but when our feet pressed the sun-dried grass I was impelled to question him of love. It was the first time I had thought of the matter.

"How does passion first touch a man's life?" I asked, laying my hand on his arm.

His ruddy colour faded, he smiled wryly.

"You divine what passes in my brain," he replied. "I also had begun to meditate… But I may not tell you… In my boyhood – I was scarce older than you at the time – I loved the true paragon. 'Twere sacrilege to speak of the birth of passion. Let it suffice that ere I tasted of wedlock the woman died, and her death sealed for ever the door of that chamber of my heart… Yet, if one might see therein, there is an altar crowned with ever-burning tapers and with wreaths of unwithering asphodels."

By this time we had reached the skirt of a yew-forest, traversed in every direction by narrow paths. The air was moist and heavy, but ever and anon a light wind touched the tree-tops and bowed them, so that the pollen sank in golden veils to the ground.

Everywhere we saw half-ruined fountains, satyrs vomiting senilely, nymphs emptying wine upon the lambent flames of dying phoenixes, creatures that were neither satyrs nor nymphs, nor gryphins, but grotesque adminglings of all, slain by one another, with water gushing from wounds in belly and thigh.

At length the path we had chosen terminated beside an oval mere that was surrounded by a colonnade of moss-grown arches. Huge pike quivered on the muddy bed, crayfish moved sluggishly amongst the weeds.

There was an island in the middle, where a leaden Diana, more compassionate than a crocodile, caressed Actaeon's horns ere delivering him to his hounds. The huntress's head and shoulders were white with the excrement of a crowd of culvers that moved as if entangled in a snare.

Northwards an avenue rose for the space of a mile, to fall abruptly before an azure sky. For many years the yew-mast on the pathway had been undisturbed by human foot; it was covered with a crust of greenish lichen.

My Master pressed my fingers. "There is some evil in the air of this place," he said. "I am strong, but you – you may not endure. We will return."

"'Tis an enchanted country," I made answer, feverishly. "At the end of yonder avenue stands the palace of the sleeping maiden who awaits the kiss. Nay, since we have pierced the country thus far, let us not draw back. You are strong, Master – no evil can touch us." ·

So we fared to the place where the avenue sank, and then our eyes fell on the wondrous sight of a palace, lying in a concave pleasaunce, all treeless, but so bestarred with fainting flowers, that neither blade of grass nor grain of earth was visible.

Then came a rustling of wings above our heads, and looking skywards I saw flying towards the house a flock of culvers like unto those that had drawn themselves over Diana s head. The hindmost bird dropped its neck, and behold it gazed upon us with the face of a mannikin!

"They are charmed birds, made thus by the whim of the Princess," I said.

As the birds passed through the portals of a columbary that crowned a western tower, their white wings beat against a silver bell that glistened there, and the whole valley was filled with music.

My Master trembled and crossed himself. "In the name of our Mother," he exclaimed, "let us return. I dare not trust your life here."

But a great door in front of the palace swung open, and a woman with a swaying walk came out to the terrace. She wore a robe of crimson worn into tatters at skirt-hem and shoulders. She had been forewarned of our presence, for her face turned instantly in our direction. She smiled subtly, and her smile died away into a most tempting sadness.

She caught up such remnants of her skirt as trailed behind, and strutted about with the gait of a peacock. As the sun touched the glossy fabric I saw eyes inwrought in deeper hue.

My Master still trembled, but he did not move, for the gaze of the woman was fixed upon him. His brows twisted and his white hair rose and stood erect, as if he viewed some unspeakable horror.

Stooping, with sidelong motions of the head, she approached; bringing with her the smell of such an incense as when amidst Eastern herbs burns the corse… She was perfect of feature as the Diana, but her skin was deathly white and her lips fretted with pain.

She took no heed of me, but knelt at my Master's feet – a Magdalene before an impregnable priest.

"Prince and Lord, Tower of Chastity, hear!" she murmured. "For lack of love I perish. See my robe in tatters!"

He strove to avert his face, but his eyes still dwelt upon her. She half rose and shook nut-brown tresses over his knees.

Youth came back in a flood to my Master. His shrivelled skin filled out; the dying sunlight turned to gold the whiteness of his hair. He would have raised her had I not caught his hands. The anguish of foreboding made me cry:

"One forces roughly the door of your heart's chamber. The wreaths wither, the tapers bend and fall."

He grew old again. The Crimson Weaver turned to me.

"O marplot!" she said laughingly, "think not to vanquish me with folly. I am too powerful. Once that a man enter my domain he is mine."

But I drew my Master away.

"'Tis I who am strong," I whispered. "We will go hence at once. Surely we may find our way back to the bridge. The journey is easy."

The woman, seeing that the remembrance of an old love was strong within him, sighed heavily, and returned to the palace. As she reached the doorway the valves opened, and I saw in a distant chamber beyond the hall an ivory loom with a golden stool.

My Master and I walked again on the track we had made in the yew-mast. But twilight was falling, and ere we could reach the pool of Diana all was in utter darkness; so at the foot of a tree, where no anthill rose, we lay down and slept.

Dreams came to me – gorgeous visions from the romances of eld. Everywhere I sought vainly for a beloved. There was the Castle of the Ebony Dwarf, where a young queen reposed in the innermost casket of the seventh crystal cabinet; there was the Chamber of Gloom, where Lenore danced, and where I groped for ages around columns of living flesh; there was the White Minaret, where twenty-one princesses poised themselves on balls of burnished bronze; there was Melisandra's arbour, where the sacred toads crawled over the enchanted cloak.

Unrest fretted me: I woke in spiritual pain. Dawn was breaking – a bright yellow dawn, and the glades were full of vapours.

I turned to the place where my Master had lain. He was not there. I felt with my hands over his bed: it was key-cold. Terror of my loneliness overcame me, and I sat with covered face.

On the ground near my feet lay a broken riband, whereon was strung a heart of chrysolite. It enclosed a knot of ash-coloured hair – hair of the girl my Master had loved.

The mists gathered together and passed sunwards in one long many-cornered veil. When the last shred had been drawn into the great light, I gazed along the avenue, and saw the topmost bartizan of the Crimson Weaver's palace.

It was midday ere I dared start on my search. The culvers beat about my head. I walked in pain, as though giant spiders had woven about my body.

On the terrace strange beasts – dogs and pigs with human limbs – tore ravenously at something that lay beside the balustrade. At sight of me they paused and lifted their snouts and bayed. Awhile afterwards the culvers rang the silver bell, and the monsters dispersed hurriedly amongst the drooping blossoms of the pleasaunce, and where they had swarmed I saw naught but a steaming sanguine pool.

I approached the house and the door fell open, admitting me to a chamber adorned with embellishments beyond the witchery of art. There I lifted my voice and cried eagerly: "My Master, my Master, where is my Master?" The alcoves sent out a babble of echoes, blended together like a harp-cord on a dulcimer: "My Master, my Master, where is my Master? For the love of Christ, where is my Master?" The echo replied only, "Where is my Master?"

Above, swung a globe of topaz, where a hundred suns gambolled. From its centre a convoluted horn, held by a crimson cord, sank lower and lower. It stayed before my lips and I blew therein, and heard the sweet voices of youth chant with one accord.

"Fall open, oh doors: fall open and show the way to the princess!"

Ere the last of the echoes had died a vista opened, and at the end of an alabaster gallery I saw the Crimson Weaver at her loom. She had doffed her tattered robe for one new and lustrous as freshly drawn blood. And marvellous as her beauty had seemed before, its wonder was now increased a hundredfold.

She came towards me with the same stately walk, but there was now a lightness in her demeanour that suggested the growth of wings.

Within arm's length she curtseyed, and curtseying showed me the firmness of her shoulders, the fulness of her breast. The sight brought no pleasure: my cracking tongue appealed in agony:

"My Master, where is my Master?"

She smiled happily. "Nay, do not trouble. He is not here. His soul talks with the culvers in the cote. He has forgotten you. In the night we supped, and I gave him of Nepenthe."

"Where is my Master? Yesterday he told me of the shrine in his heart – of ever-fresh flowers – of a love dead yet living."

Her eyebrows curved mirthfully.

"'Tis foolish boys talk," she said. "If you sought till the end of time you would never find him – unless I chose. Yet – if you buy of me – myself to name the price."

I looked around hopelessly at the unimaginable riches of her home. All that I have is this Manor of the Willow Brakes – a moorish park, an ancient house where the thatch gapes and the casements swing loose.

"My possessions are pitiable," I said, "but they are all yours. I give all to save him."

"Fool, fool!" she cried. "I have no need of gear. If I but raise my hand, all the riches of the world fall to me. 'Tis not what I wish for."

Into her eyes came such a glitter as the moon makes on the moist skin of a sleeping snake. The firmness of her lips relaxed; they grew child-like in their softness. The atmosphere became almost tangible: I could scarce breathe.

"What is it? All that I can do, if it be no sin."

"Come with me to my loom," she said, "and if you do the thing I desire you shall see him. There is no evil in't – in past times kings have sighed for the same."

So I followed slowly to the loom, before which she had seated herself, and watched her deftly passing crimson thread over crimson thread.

She was silent for a space, and in that space her beauty fascinated me, so that I was no longer master of myself.

"What you wish for I will give, even if it be life."

The loom ceased. "A kiss of the mouth, and you shall see him who passed in the night."

She clasped her arms about my neck and pressed my lips. For one moment heaven and earth ceased to be; but there was one paradise, where we were sole governors…

Then she moved back and drew aside the web and shoved me the head of my Master, and the bleeding heart whence a crimson cord unravelled into many threads.

"I wear men's lives," the woman said. "Life is necessary to me, or even I – who have existed from the beginning – must die. But yesterday I feared the end, and he came. His soul is not dead – 'tis truth that it plays with my culvers."

I fell back.

"Another kiss," she said. "Unless I wish, there is no escape for you. Yet you may return to your home, though my power over you shall never wane. Once more – lip to lip."

I crouched against the wall like a terrified dog. She grew angry; her eyes darted fire.

"A kiss," she cried, "for the penalty!"

My poor Master's head, ugly and cadaverous, glared from the loom. I could not move.

The Crimson Weaver lifted her skirt, uncovering feet shapen as those of a vulture. I fell prostrate. With her claws she fumbled about the flesh of my breast. Moving away she bade me pass from her sight…

So, half-dead, I lie here at the Manor of the Willow Brakes, watching hour by hour the bloody clew ever unwinding from my heart and passing over the western hills to the Palace of the Siren.

The Animal King

Timothy Granville

THE TWINS discovered it in one of the derelict outbuildings, huddled into a corner behind tins of creosote and garden tools with blades so rusted they resembled archaeological finds. The window of the outbuilding had been boarded up and at first in the gloom they took it simply for a dead or injured bird, before noticing the pointed snout and small furry body emerging from the dark plumage. Both sets of eyes were shut.

Max thought that they'd found a place where a predator kept its food. But Ollie said no, the shrew was coming out of the chest of the jackdaw, they were attached – though neither of them could bring themselves to touch the ruff of feathery fur around the shrew's abdomen to make sure.

The twins knew about the chimera and the cockatrice and Pegasus. But they were made up, their pictures were just funny. This wasn't the same at all.

When they got back to the house, Mummy was preparing lunch while trying to keep an eye on Freddie clambering into his high-chair.

"Mummy? Mummy?"

"Yes, boys?"

"We wanted to ask you something."

"Mmm…? Don't stand there, please."

The twins fumbled for words: the outbuildings were unsafe and they had promised not to play in them. They started trying to explain about the shrew and the jackdaw as though it had happened to some children in their class, but Mummy interrupted them.

"I don't think it's very nice of your friends to go around telling stories. That's fibbing."

"But they weren't…"

"Nat a fibbin!" parroted Freddie, holding out a chubby palm. "No!"

"That's right, pickle," said Mummy, blowing on the first spoonful of his mush. "Big boys tell the truth, don't they?"

The twins had a lot to do that summer and several days passed before they thought to return to the outbuilding. In their absence, the shadow in the corner had grown. A rat was now embracing the jackdaw's back and flank, fastened by membranous cords that crisscrossed its body. This webbing looked faintly iridescent, like the glow-in-the-dark sea creatures the twins had seen on an Attenborough documentary. It was strange, hard to take your eyes off. They thought it must be eating the animals, but when Ollie tried prodding them with a stick, the cluster of bodies seemed to flinch. So they weren't dead, only sleeping.

The twins left the outbuilding, worming between grimy garden furniture back into the glare of the sun. Halfway to the house, they sat down on an abandoned iron roller nearly swamped by weeds. They felt different somehow, good but also bad. It was like when they'd found the pictures of naked people on their parents' tablet, the same awareness of having seen something exciting that was also something that perhaps they shouldn't have seen.

After a minute, Max said, "I thought there'd be a rat."

Ollie carried on picking scabs of corroded metal off the drum of the roller. "Why?"

Max reminded him about the book that Daddy had eventually let them have from the box outside the charity shop. It was called *Stranger Than Fiction* and had UFOs and snake charmers and a giant squid on the cover. In the book there was a page about rat kings, bizarre groups of rats bound together at the tail. It bore a single black-and-white picture: a wheel of mummified snarls radiating from a knot of skin and bone.

"But ours isn't only rats."

"It must be an animal king then."

They were both relieved to have named it.

The twins revisited the animal king several times, seeing the iridescent webbing vanish as the rat merged with the other bodies and then reappear to swaddle a large copper-eyed toad. But by this point Mummy was getting suspicious, asking them where they'd been playing, commenting on the streamers of cobweb hanging from their T-shirts, so they were forced to keep away from the outbuilding for a while.

One sweltering afternoon, they had a fight over a computer game. Ollie kept using the same special move to win again and again, crowing in Max's face. It ended with Max throwing his controller across the living room and running out of the house. He found himself storming through the tear-blurred garden, trampling brushwood and nettles in the overgrown orchard. When he finally dried his eyes, he was approaching the outbuilding. The thought came to him that he could go and look at the animal king without Ollie. He wasn't a baby, he could do it on his own. That way they would be even.

Max ducked past the twisted door fallen off its hinges. Before he'd crept halfway down the length of the outbuilding, he realized something had changed. It smelt funny and there was a shimmering light coming from the animal king's corner. He went towards it, ignoring the part of him saying to turn back, no one would know. The animal king was now covered in thin, many-branched antlers of membrane. They were alive with iridescence, a play of colours crawling back and forth along their tines. Max came to a standstill, watching them flicker. He felt calmer, glad of the dusty coolness in the outbuilding after the heat outside. His ears began to ring.

"Hi. I'm sorry."

Max looked round, blinking away a daze. Ollie was standing there by a littered workbench. He shrugged at him, surprised to find he wasn't angry.

"You can choose the next game. Come on, Mummy's looking for you."

"Why?"

"We couldn't find you anywhere. It's nearly five."

Max held his head, trying to think how it had got so late. He noticed that the light from the animal king had faded. The antlers had withdrawn, but the shadow in the corner was larger still, more straggling. And its outline was somehow familiar.

"Hey, is that…?"

"Missy?"

The twins saw the latest addition to the animal king was their young tabby cat. She was lashed to its side by webbing, still visibly breathing, her paws dangling free. But though it was unmistakably Missy, the rest of the mass was no longer so easy to pick apart. The several bodies were fused into grotesque shapes. A raw protuberance like a vulture's head studded with teeth had erupted from the commingled pelt. Another bird must have been lured in to form a moulting fan of wings. Whatever the animal king was becoming, the twins understood all at once that it wouldn't be healthy. They both started to feel sick.

"Are we going to tell them?"

"I don't know. It's not our fault."

"We have to help her."

There was desperation in Ollie's voice. "I know," he said. "We'll take her somewhere else. Into the house."

"We can't… What about Mummy?"

"We'll come back tomorrow."

Max had given Mummy a scare though, and the next day she hovered round the twins until both of them were tetchy and on edge. But that night Freddie didn't sleep through. Mummy appeared with bloodshot eyes at breakfast next morning and when it was time for his nap she announced she would have a lie down too. The twins listened to her climb the stairs. They waited as long as they could bear, then ran all the way to the outbuilding.

Max had thought about refusing to help, but he knew that meant having to put into words exactly why the animal king worried him. It was easier to go along with Ollie, rooting through the junk until they found a stray plastic milk crate and a pair of gauntlets which he helped him put on. He watched as Ollie approached the animal king, puffing out his cheeks. He couldn't help feeling that they were too late: Missy's body had already begun to warp and bloat. Though Ollie lowered her gently into the crate, he shut his eyes while he did it.

They hurried back through the orchard and across the garden. The ground was bumpy in places and once Ollie tripped on a root, but Missy slept on with the rest of the animal king. Max went into the house first to make sure Mummy was still sleeping too. They'd decided to leave the animal king behind the sofa where it would be sure to be found, so he beckoned Ollie through the kitchen and into the living room. Stepping round the sofa, he set down the crate and tipped it up. The sprawling body flopped out onto the carpet with a string of soft thuds.

They hesitated, staring at it. At Missy. At it. Here among the flower vases and family photos.

Ollie swallowed and said that she'd be all right now. Max looked away, embarrassed. He could tell he was close to tears.

The twins had expected Mummy to discover the animal king almost immediately. The sofa stood at an angle to the walls, and to reach the doors of the conservatory or the bookcase she would have to walk right past it. But once she'd got up, she kept coming and going only feet away without ever straying into that corner of the room. Before they knew it, Daddy was home from the nearby compound where he worked and then it was dinner time and then nearly time for bed. They pretended to play their console, glancing sidelong at the sofa where Daddy was lost in his phone, still wearing his security pass on a lanyard. Any minute, he would remember to send them upstairs.

It was Max who broke first, getting to his feet and wandering over to the bookcase. As he passed the sofa, Ollie saw him look down, his eyes widening. He came back across the room without saying anything to Daddy.

"It's gone," he whispered.

"What?"

"It must've woken up."

They tried to make a cautious search of the living room, but Daddy told them they should go and play outside if they wanted to fidget. Instead, Ollie went and got *Stranger Than Fiction* and the two of them sat on the floor with the rat king page open until Daddy asked what they were doing.

"Reading about rat kings."

"Oh yes, I know. Bit macabre."

"They're very interesting."

"Daddy, what should you do if you find a rat king?"

Daddy started polishing his glasses. "Hmm? Offer it to a museum, probably."

"But what if you find one that's still alive? Are they dangerous?"

"I don't think you need to worry about that. There's almost no hard evidence of them occurring naturally."

The twins stared at him. "Then how do they happen?"

"People make them."

"Why?"

Daddy held up his glasses to the light. Satisfied, he replaced them. "Because they can. Now, it's about time for bed…"

The twins went up to their room stunned, not understanding. It was hours before either of them slept, thinking about the animal king loose in the house, trailing useless limbs of plaited tails and claws, its many eyes open.

Still, Ollie must have dropped off at some point, because he woke on the landing in the dark. He'd never sleepwalked before, but through his confusion he was aware of a sound just dying away in the house below. He strained his ears, unable to make it out. Though the sound – if there had really been one – wasn't repeated, he now detected a faint smell, something he didn't recognize, both heady and oddly metallic.

Turning, he saw Max slumped half-asleep against the doorway to their room. As he went to shake him, Mummy came out onto the landing.

"What's going on?" she hissed. "You'll wake your brother."

They tried to explain, but she sent them straight back to bed. Before the door to Mummy and Daddy's room closed again, Ollie heard her sniff twice.

The next day was a Saturday and the twins got up yawning and gritty-eyed to watch cartoons. They waited for Mummy and Freddie to come downstairs in front of episode after episode, nervous because they'd agreed to confess. Eventually, they got hungry and helped themselves to the special cereal that Mummy usually doled out to them at weekends. As they filled their bowls, they were half-conscious of the sunshine flooding the kitchen, the busy drone of the distant main road. They returned to the TV, eating as they went, bolting the sugary lumps to bury the feeling in their stomachs.

Shortly afterwards, there were raised voices overhead and footsteps came running down the stairs. Mummy entered the living room wearing her dressing gown.

"Boys, boys, where's Freddie?"

They looked at her blankly. Daddy was calling Freddie's name, his voice muffled by the ceiling.

"Freddie!" she snapped. "Have you seen him?!"

"No," they said. "No."

"He must have climbed out of his cot. I can't believe…"

Mummy tailed off as she carried on into the kitchen. By now Daddy had come down too and was hurrying after her. "Everything's fine," he said, his glance skating past the twins as though they were pieces of furniture. Above the gabbling of the TV, they heard him and Mummy beginning to argue. Then she screamed.

The twins met each other's eyes, fear echoing between them like something caught in a pair of mirrors. They stood up and followed the voices into the dining room.

As they came through the doorway, Mummy told them not to look, but Daddy was holding on to her and she had no way to stop them. They saw Freddie asleep under the dining table, curled up in the foetal position. The animal king was clinging to his back, with what had once been Missy's head resting on his shoulder, joined to his own head by a lustrous skein of webbing which covered half his face. Outgrowths of membrane had sprouted all over the animal king and were feeling for his body.

"This isn't possible," said Daddy.

"Chris, let go of me!" moaned Mummy. "Help him!"

"Just everyone stay back. There's nothing to be frightened of, boys."

The twins carried on gazing at Freddie. They felt cold and funny, their lips twitching with smiles that didn't seem to belong to them. They were only dimly aware of Mummy begging Daddy to call an ambulance and him telling her he needed to call work first, he just had to, and Mummy saying, "What is that? What is that on him?"

And then the animal king stirred. One of Freddie's eyes and one of Missy's blinked open.

"Freddie," the twins said together.

Mummy started another scream, choked off almost instantly by the back of her hand. "Pickle? Can you hear me?"

The two eyes – human and cat – drifted in her direction. The free part of Freddie's mouth worked. His arm trembled and a faint riffle passed through the fan of wings along the side of the animal king. The twins didn't like it at all and tried to look away.

"My god," said Daddy.

The next moment, Freddie began to sing. His lips parted and he drew in a breath and let out a long, semi-musical shriek. All the deformed mouths of the animal king opened and added their own notes: sustained hisses and chirpings and screeches. The sound was shrill enough to set objects in the room buzzing in sympathy. Daddy tried to say something, but his words were drowned out.

A dizzying smell like perfume that was also like the taste of handlebars filled the air. The twins stared at the luminous rainbow pulses which were running through the animal king's antlers and webbing. They became brighter and brighter, faster and faster, a multicoloured strobe.

All the other light in the room faded, until the twins could only see the animal king at the end of a long tunnel, until they were walking down a long ringing tunnel, heading for the only light.

As one, the family started towards the dining table.

Isle of the Dead

Steve Hanson

"PAPA?" Ada's voice broke through a shallow and dreamless sleep. Mattias opened his eyes to a room no less dark than the space behind his eyelids. He reached for either the bedside lamp or for Miriam, before remembering he was sleeping on the couch.

"Papa?" his daughter asked again.

"Yes, *Liebling*?" he choked out in a dry throat.

A pause cut through the living room of their flat, sharper than Mattias would have thought possible. He heard only his eight-year-old daughter, already so bold for her age, breathing haltingly as her soft footsteps approached his couch.

"I saw the face in the painting again."

Mattias's lips clenched, and the unkempt hair on his mustache tickled his nose. He sat up. Ada's small frame was barely visible as a silhouette set in dark obsidian by the few lights streaming in from the Berlin streets outside their third-story window. Going by shape alone, Mattias could see that she still wore her nightgown, and clutched in both hands the raggedy stuffed rabbit she had christened with the Hebrew letter Aleph for reasons that neither Mattias nor his wife were certain of.

"Ah, my love," Mattias attempted. In the dark of both the room and his mind, he needed to fumble around for a tone that was paternal and reassuring. "A bad dream then? Such an imagination my girl was cursed with. But still a sign of a strong mind."

"I wasn't dreaming," Ada said. Her voice conveyed the same matter-of-fact certainty as a mathematician reciting a proof, or a Rabbi speaking the Torah.

"You are certain, my love?" He knew this question was useless, but was not far enough removed from sleep – however restless and troubled – to come up with something better.

In the darkness, the silhouette of his daughter shook her head. "I had to get up," she said. "I needed to make water."

"Ah," Mattias attempted. He pulled his creaky limbs and stiff torso out of bed, grunting in his ever-increasing age. "Well then," he said. "Let us take a look." He reached for his glasses and portable lamp on the table opposite the couch, more out of reflex than the hope of them doing anything in the dark. "Fortunately, God made few faces homelier than your father's, so one glare from me should frighten away this interloper."

That, at least, elicited a brief giggle.

And is that why you came to me instead of your mother? he thought. *God knows she's comfortable enough in her warm bed, best not disturb her.* He extended his right hand into the darkness and waited until he felt Ada's soft fingertips.

"Onward then, my brave girl," he said in a pantomime of happier days. "Show your father where this face dared disturb his daughter's peace."

Of course, he already knew which painting it was. But Ada gave an ephemeral pull on his hand, so light and graceful that Mattias felt he may have been drawn forth by something more elemental in the air itself. Dutifully he followed and, as he had predicted, was led to the small corridor in the far back corner of their flat, lying between the storage closet, the washroom, and Ada's room. There, hung just behind a small flower vase, and flanked on either side by fading daguerreotypes of Ada's grandparents, was the painting, a medium-sized print of Arnold Böcklin's *Isle of the Dead*, captured in a simple wooden frame and contrasted with the fading and peeling wallpaper behind.

"This one again, eh?" he said. Though he couldn't see by the meager light from his small lamp, he could tell that Ada nodded. "You've seen this…face here three times now?"

"Four," she said. "I wasn't sure the first time I saw it. So I didn't say anything. But now I'm sure."

By lamplight and memory, Mattias could decipher the contents of the painting well enough. A dark, ominous sea against a gray, cloud-addled sky. Skeletal rocks jutting forth from the water, piercing into the air around them. Dark cypress trees, indicative of funeral laments, stuck as drying bones between the rocks of the small island. Below, a single boat approached, its oarsman guiding the vessel towards the small dock awaiting between two white columns. Its single passenger obscured from the viewer, with their back turned, facing the island they approached, head bowed before it, dressed in a ghostly white cloak that hung from their head to its feet. Below the figure, at the bow of the boat, lay a coffin-shaped box, adorned in the same white cloak as was borne on the figure, and festooned in a simple but striking funeral wreath of crimson flowers.

Facing the single figure was the painting's epicenter, a vanishing point between the columns and cypress trees, where the already-darkened colors descended into a bleak and dense cluster of malignant blackness, its contents unseen but omnipresent in the atmosphere.

"It was right there," Ada said. Mattias didn't need to look down to know where she pointed.

"What did it look like?" he asked.

Ada said nothing, but he could hear her breath draw inside her body in a waxing terror. She squeezed his hand tighter, and he could feel her pulse picking up even in her fingertips.

"Was it a man? Woman?" he asked. "Did it have hair? Was it making a funny face?"

"It wasn't made by God," Ada said. The straightforward nature of this assertion was so abrupt that Mattias was rendered silent for a few seconds, his still-sleepy brain needing a brief interlude to analyze what it had just heard for any better meaning.

"What's that you say?" he managed.

"Mama told me how God created man and woman, there in the Garden of Eden, right?"

"Yes…well…" Mattias crinkled his lips once again. Despite reflexive appearances at the temple, theirs had always been a more or less secular household. Even before outward devotion as a Jew had grown as dangerous as it had. "That is what the Torah says. Of course, many of our wisest Rabbis would have us regard these writings not as literal histories, but rather more like fables that can teach us a greater…"

"I know, I know," Ada said impatiently. Mattias found himself both annoyed and somewhat proud at the same time. If nothing else, his daughter had never suffered from a lack of self-assertion. For good or ill. "What I meant was, it was like if something that wasn't God, something from a dark, scary place that God didn't make or never went, came here and tried to make a human face like God did. But couldn't get it right."

Mattias swallowed more dry air than saliva. "Like the story of the blind men and the elephant?"

In the lamplight his daughter nodded.

Mattias stared into the black hole at the center of the painting. He watched the phantasmagoria behind his eyes twist and mold the darkness in and around it. Watched the patterns form and evolve. Almost into twisted bodies.

Or faces.

He gave Ada's hand a squeeze. "So, Satan then?"

Ada shook her head. "Satan was created by God." Mattias never heard a Rabbi speak so confidently on theological matters.

The black water around the boat began to dance, and in the otherwise silence Mattias thought he could hear the caustic lapping of the waves against Böcklin's island of the dead. Feel its coldness pierce his flesh, stab into his bones. Twist the air from his lungs.

Suddenly, his sense of balance seemed to be undone. He felt his stomach drop and ascend, as if their small tenement building had been lifted from its foundation and cast adrift on a merciless, infinite black sea, in whose depths one could sink impossible distances before reaching the bottom, and where lurked gargantuan beasts, outcasts of the Creation of God, the Leviathan born of the blackness but ascending, ever-ascending, to his tiny, helpless boat with open maw and bared fangs...

He shook his head. "Well then," he said. In one determined motion, he ripped the painting from the wall with his one free hand. "This problem has an easy enough solution." Really, he had bought the print only the previous year, at an exhibition at Baumgartner's gallery in Nollendorfplatz, which he hadn't even wanted to go to. Böcklin's works had become quite popular on the walls of the more sophisticated flats all around Germany beginning a few years back, and Mattias had thought that the Schwartzberg family could perhaps blend in a bit with their gentile peers by joining the fun.

Of course, he had never even liked the painting that much anyway.

"What will you do with it?" Ada asked.

"We'll store it in the closet for tonight," Mattias said. "Then, after work tomorrow, I'll see if I can sell it to some art-loving Goyim. Let them worry about this face for a change."

He could feel Ada smile, and his anxiety eased somewhat. Still, the cold of Berlin's winter night seeped into his flesh, and the darkness still sat in front of his eyes. At that undead hour he could not read a difference between those two and the icy clutches of a black sea under a stormy sky, or the darkening abyss waiting with a primordial hunger between dark cypress trees on a small, stony island.

* * *

He awoke the next morning from a still-dreamless sleep filled with no fewer troubles. Rising from the couch, he saw Miriam already sitting, gargoyle-like, at the kitchen table. She sipped a cup of coffee and read a newspaper, not looking up as her nominal husband stumbled in.

"Von Schleicher's resigning," she said. Mattias collapsed his weary bones into the chair opposite her.

"Good morning to you too," he said.

"Do you know what that means?" Her tone conveyed neither warmth nor terror, but rather a dim and unsurprised resignation.

"Good morning?"

She finally looked up from the paper with the most tired of eyes.

"It means Hitler's going to be Chancellor," she said.

Mattias rubbed his mustache. "Have they announced that yet? We ought not worry too much until something official..."

"Who else would it be?" This was more of a statement than a question. Mattias tried to relax his back into the chair, but only found its hardwood cutting into his spine.

"Well," he managed. "What's he going to do? We have rights."

"Did you read this?" Miriam said.

"We have rights…wait, a minute…" Mattias just then noticed the name emblazoned above the front-page headline of Miriam's newspaper. "Are you reading *Der Stürmer*?"

"It was free on the train last night."

"Miriam, what in God's name…"

"Listen to this: 'The Jewish menace does not end in our banks, in our armies, or in our great cultural centers. Rather, the Jew has turned his insidious gaze to the most precious and innocent of our Aryan lifeblood: our school children. Jewish indoctrination…'"

"Miriam…"

"'…Jewish indoctrination, brother to communist indoctrination, is slithering into the classrooms of even the youngest of our children, infecting their minds, infesting their…'"

"Miriam!"

Mattias grabbed the paper and pulled it from his wife's hands, tearing it in two in the process. Miriam merely turned her blunt and fatigued eyes towards the man sharing a kitchen table with her.

"Do you know what your daughter asked me the other day?" she said.

"I don't want to hear it…"

"She asked me if she's a bad person because she's a Jew. Now where do you think she got that from?"

"I don't…"

"How many parents of her precious school friends enjoy reading that very same paper you just ripped from my hands, and are well past eager to share such views with their children…"

"Gah!" Mattias shouted. He launched himself from the table as best as his aging frame would allow. "Should we change our name then to something more Aryan? Is *Schwartzberg* not working for you?"

Miriam lit a cigarette instead of replying. Mattias stormed towards the washroom to empty the bladder that he just then noticed was full to the point of aching. But as he turned the corner, he stopped, his eyes suddenly fuzzy, and his brain suddenly thrown into a chaos of confusion and dim recollection.

On the wall leading to the bathroom, above the flowers, between the daguerreotypes, where it had been since last year, was the family's print of *Isle of the Dead*. Mattias stared, rendered mute. He *had*, he thought he remembered, torn it from the wall and buried it in the closet the previous night. But here it was, its darkened sea as tempestuous and threatening as ever. Its cypress trees looming with their quiet intensity. Its epicenter still a bottomless pool of violent darkness, which now seemed to sap the light from the room and, despite the morning, once again render it the darkest hour of the night.

Mattias shook his head. *Miriam must have dug it out and placed it back there*, he thought. *Probably for no reason other than to spite me.*

His bladder sent a wave of pain through his groin, which tore him from his reverie and sent him waddling once more to the toilet at the end of the hall. But before he took his eyes away he caught sight of something that would have registered greater significance if he was in a better mood or a clearer state of mind. As it happened, he dismissed it as a child's carelessness, something for Miriam to deal with when Ada got home from school.

What he saw was *Aleph*, the stuffed rabbit so beloved by his daughter, lying on its back, in a corpse-like pose, on the floor just below the painting.

* * *

Working late, out of as much preference as necessity, Mattias left for home just as the sun was setting. Outside, threats of violence had poisoned the air of the streets of Berlin. On every corner, it seemed, brown-shirted Nazis had gathered to shout their slogans and make their salutes in some frenzy of victory at the ascent of their *Führer*, sneering at their enemies and making threatening shouts of *Juden!* or *Kommunistische!* at passersby. Mattias pulled his hat down his head as he passed them, hoping they wouldn't notice the size of his nose, shape of his lips, or whatever idiot phrenology they had taken as gospel.

As it so happened, the Nazis had also congregated on the already-crowded *U-Bahn* train that would have taken Mattias home. One look at the clusters of brown shirts and short, blond hair packed into the train convinced Mattias that it would perhaps be a better idea to walk home. It was, after all, only about a dozen blocks. In the German winter.

Thus, Mattias did not get home until well after dark, when the streets had grown quiet and the stars were blinded by the nighttime lights of the city. Tired as he was, and rattled by everything, Mattias needed a few moments after entering his flat to realize that it was just as dark inside as it was outside.

"Hello?" he spoke to the empty room. The silence that responded was louder, somehow, than any human voice. He lit the nearest lamp, but, though he could see the light, it seemed to have no effect on the darkness of their flat. Indeed, if anything the darkness seemed to *grow*, conjuring itself into something thicker and more threatening in response to sudden provocation by the light. The simple furniture of their flat maintained their shadowed silhouette, morphing in the darkness into strange, deformed figures of what seemed to be an unearthly (*ungodly*) geometry.

Then, across the room, he saw something else. A light? No, a spark. The small, red glow of a barely-burning ember. He walked towards it, and as he approached, he smelled the lingering odor of cigarette smoke.

"...Miriam?" he called out. The ember, he eventually saw, was from a half-smoked cigarette lying crumpled on the floor just by the wall. Its fire was fading, but it still burned enough to suggest it had been lit (and dropped) a short while ago. Next to it was a larger, softer shape, almost a human figure.

No.

A rabbit. A stuffed rabbit.

"*Aleph*..." Mattias gasped.

Even as he turned his eyes up the wall, he already knew what he would see there. Miriam's cigarette and Ada's stuffed rabbit lay – no, were placed – just below the *Isle of the Dead* painting that still hung, inexplicably, in its place on the wall.

But the picture had changed. In a sudden, horrified moment, Mattias saw something else in the scene depicted. Something new. The boat was still there, its grim ferryman manning the oars, its figure cloaked in white approaching the central blackness with its offering. But now, at the bow of the boat, the coffin that once lay there had been replaced by two human bodies. An adult and a child. Both female. Both lying bound and prostrate, lashed to the front of the boat. Their faces were turned upward, staring into the blackness. Though he couldn't see their faces, he knew they were screaming.

It wasn't created by God.

Two hands, impossibly cold, fell upon his shoulders. He didn't need to look to know they were cloaked in white cloth. The floor shuddered as it was lifted on a black tide. The cold winter air turned into the frigid winds of a dead, black, infinite sea.

"...we have rights," he sputtered. The figure pushed him forward. In the blackness of the isle of the dead, a face began to form. The barest of human features. And, behind it, Mattias could see its true inhuman nature. Chaos personified. Malevolence incarnate. Something wholly alien, born out of space and time, brushed into his world through the random pulses of cosmic tides too immeasurably vast for him to comprehend.

Not created by God.

The face opened its mouth. Mattias's scream was drowned by the hollow roar of the black waves as his boat reached the dock.

The Brightest Lights of Heaven

Maria Haskins

I HAVEN'T SEEN Moira for fourteen years, but I dream about her all the time. The dream is always the same. We're six years old and we're dragons again – jumping off the roof together – but this time we don't hit the ground and we don't end up in the hospital and we don't need any stitches. Instead we just spread our wings and fly.

Last time I saw Moira in the flesh she was eleven – gap-toothed and nearsighted. I was eleven, too – all gangly energy, frizzy hair, and braces. It was the same night our last game began, and it was also Moira's last night in Canada. Her parents had divorced the year before; now her dad was gone and her mom had decided to move back to Australia, taking Moira with her. I didn't want her to go, didn't even want to think about what my life would be like without her, but Moira said we had time for one last game, and I wouldn't have missed that for the world.

She always made up the best games: zombie tag, cops and aliens, wolves and hunters, vampires and slayers. Ever since preschool, she'd been turning yards and playgrounds into battlefields of fear and glory; turning us into something other than what we seemed to be: generic girls – awkward, studious, shy.

We already knew we were different than people thought we were, knew enough to hide it, too. We knew that beneath the surface we were something else entirely – something hungry, something jagged, something crooked and impatient.

That night we met in an empty storage locker in the basement of the rickety old apartment building she lived in with her mom in Burnaby. We'd sneak down there as often as we could, a fickle flashlight our only protection from pervs and ghosts. That night I brought my incense sticks and a box of matches. Moira brought a book on witchcraft and her penknife.

The book was from the library, dog-eared, severely overdue, its plastic slipcover torn. We took turns reading spells and stories from it, looking at the pictures while the incense made the small space smell like Friday nights at my Aunt Jackie's house.

"Mom says I'll forget you," Moira said, holding onto a lit match so long the flame singed her fingertips. "She says you'll forget me too. Everyone forgets, she says. When they get older. It's better that way. Easier."

I watched the match burn between us, my eyes stinging.

"That's stupid." The words hitched in my throat. "You won't, will you?"

She shook her head. Another match – lit, burning, singeing, extinguished.

"One last game, right?" she said, and I nodded. "But you have to promise you won't chicken out on me. It won't work if you chicken out."

"I won't. I promise." And I meant it.

When we were six, we played knights and dragons for a whole day in the backyard, taking turns wielding swords and claws, shields and fangs. Right before Moira had to go home for dinner, she changed the game. She told me we were both dragons and made me jump off the roof with her, saying we could fly. I knew we'd probably die, but I jumped anyway. Ten stitches and a fractured ankle was a small price to pay for that one dizzying moment when we were airborne, when we were dragons – scaled and fanged, hands entwined – together.

Our parents must have figured we'd grow out of playing those kinds of games but we just got better at hiding what we did. At age eleven, sitting in that patchouli-scented basement, all I knew about myself for sure was that I never wanted to stop playing with Moira, and that I would never be what my parents expected me to be. Moira knew it too, of course. She knew me better than anyone ever has, before or since.

"Hold out your hand," Moira said after sitting quietly with her eyes closed and the book open on her lap for a long time. She brought out the penknife, wiping the blade on her shirt, and I felt the darkness quicken around us, tickling my face and limbs with ghost breaths and spirit sighs.

She grabbed my wrist, harder than I thought necessary, and cut my palm with the knife. It took her a while to work up enough determination to penetrate the skin with that small, dull blade, but I kept still the whole time. Next, she cut her own palm – quicker then – and we clasped hands in the coiling tendrils of scented smoke, blood dripping on the floor between us.

Moira leaned in close – face lit by the flashlight, thick glasses framed by yellow plastic distorting her blue eyes.

"I had a vision, Rae." Her voice was an unfamiliar, hoarse whisper, skittering up my spine. As if she'd found another voice in the dark. As if another voice had found her. "You are a daemon escaped from the deepest depths of the void. And I am a daemon hunter blessed by the brightest lights of heaven. We are enemies henceforth. Before we both turn twenty-five, one of us must kill the other."

My palm stung and I felt dizzy. I already knew it was more than pretend, more than imagination. Moira had always made our games seem real, but that night was different. I felt the blood and smoke twitch together between our palms, as if we had stirred up something sleeping, something dormant – whether within or without, I couldn't tell. I felt it shudder and twine, snaking around my flesh and bones. Words and smoke and blood binding me, changing me. Changing Moira, too.

"We did it," she said and laughed out loud, her voice her own again, though it scared me still.

* * *

The next day, Moira was gone.

"She'll probably write, once they've settled in," Mom said, but I knew better. I knew the game was on. I knew something had wriggled its way into this world, that Moira and I had made it real, and that she would stick to the game no matter what I did or didn't do.

Don't chicken out, Moira had said, and I knew she never would.

* * *

After Moira left, nothing much happened for a few years, though there were flickers and murmurs of something stirring. An open window Mom said she'd closed before she went to bed. A dead crow in the yard with its eyes gouged out. Our cat, gutted in the street. Run over by a car, people said. They didn't see the runes drawn in blood on a wall nearby. I'd seen those runes in the book – the book that was still in Moira's possession, as far as I knew.

* * *

The first murder didn't happen until I was twenty. I was at university, and one Friday my roommate asked if she could have our apartment to herself over the weekend. On the Monday, police tape was strung across the door, blood was soaked into the mattress, and her mutilated body was removed from my bed. Everyone always said the two of us looked alike, even though I could never see it. The room smelled of cheap incense and there was a pile of fragrant ash on the floor but, in the end, the police pinned it on her boyfriend, who was nowhere to be found.

I tried harder to find Moira after that, searched for her online and elsewhere, but turned up nothing. It was as if she'd been extinguished and erased, or maybe her mom had just changed their last name. Either way, I couldn't find her. All I had left to prove that she had ever existed were my old class photos where she stared at me through those thick glasses: awkward and forgettable, just like me.

Then Aunt Jackie died: diabetic coma. That familiar smell of incense wafted off her corpse when she lay in the coffin, but it didn't mean anything to anyone but me. Jackie's place always smelled of smudge sticks and incense and vegetarian chili – all the better to cover up the pot she smoked.

Mom cried and so did I, my hands clutched in prayer as I sat in church between her and Dad. I prayed to find Moira, but I didn't.

* * *

A year after we buried Aunt Jackie, one of our old teachers was killed in a hiking accident. I'd called her to see if she might know where Moira had ended up. She didn't, but said she'd ask around. A week later that same teacher made the evening news: she'd fallen into a ravine on a North Shore hiking trail. Fractures, broken neck, contusions. Convenient.

"For fuck's sake, stop it with this black magic shit," my boyfriend at the time told me after we got drunk one night and I spilled my guts about Moira. "You were kids and played a stupid game. You're so fucked up sometimes."

But he was not a daemon, nor a daemon hunter, so what did he know? He certainly didn't know what it was like that first time you wake up in the middle of the night and feel your teeth suddenly too sharp beneath your tongue, your vision too clear in the dark, your skin scaly and feverish, your flesh crawling like maggots and beetles, and you ran into the bathroom to see, to see what a daemon really looks like, finding only your own face in the mirror.

That boyfriend is dead too. Pickup truck. Highway. Ice. Pole. Goodbye.

I never did manage to track Moira down.

Maybe my parents could have helped me find her but Mom died in hospital two years ago, that year the flu was so bad. They thought she'd be OK but overnight, she slipped away. Her hospital room might have smelled like incense, but what difference did it make? No one cared. She was dead. Dad died shortly after. A ferry sank when he was on holidays in Thailand. Lots of people died. He was a lousy swimmer.

That was a long summer.

* * *

I'm turning twenty-five tomorrow. It's Moira's birthday in a week. Suck on that: all the birthdays we've almost shared. And here I am, outside a club in downtown Vancouver saying goodbye to all my almost-friends from work, turning down the offer of a ride home. An icy tendril slithers up my spine and I know Moira is close. I feel her presence as I walk up Granville Street, as I ride the

SkyTrain home. The words she said so long ago twitch and squirm beneath my skin, through my veins: worms and leeches bred in darkness.

Last year someone plowed into the car I was sitting in on a side street in New Westminster. A hit and run. The doctors couldn't believe I got away with only scrapes and bruises. I was in hospital for a few days afterward, for observation, waiting every minute for Moira to come and finish what she started. She didn't. There were flowers though. No note. I felt Moira's presence real close that time.

"You don't know what it's like," I told Mom once, "to have to wait for Moira to hunt me down, for the game to play out to the end."

"Who is Moira?" She didn't even remember.

"My best friend, the one with the glasses."

But Mom didn't remember until I showed her the class photo.

"Oh, that girl. I thought they moved to Australia."

Right.

"Moira said I was a daemon," I told Dad just before he died. "I'd never felt like one until she said the words. But for a moment in that storage locker, it was like I forgot who I was. Or maybe I remembered. I mean, everybody has a wriggling bit of darkness inside them, right? A worm in the flesh, hatched in the warmth of your pulse. Fed by hate and anger and depravity, growing fat and lush through the years, like a leech. But I know I never even dreamed of being a daemon until Moira told me I was one."

That was the same day Dad told me I wasn't his. That Mom had already been pregnant when he met her. She was dead now, so he could tell me, he figured. He cried about how hard that had been for him, and how sad he was that they never had any kids together.

Thanks, Dad.

I'm walking down the street from the station. We're really playing the game out to the very end. No surprise, really. I knew she wouldn't chicken out, and neither will I.

"You're a daemon," she'd said as the incense burned.

Why did I have to be the daemon this whole time? Being a daemon is hard work, and I should at least have had a say. But she just stuck me there, in the deepest depths of the void, and for almost fifteen years I've had to make the best of it.

I open the door to my apartment.

Even though I know Moira is there, I close the door, locking it behind me, securing the chain and deadbolt. I can feel the shift in the air, the smell. It's not incense, just her skin, just her breath. She's been here for a while, waiting for me to come home. Rifling through my belongings, no doubt. Looking for daemon spawn and daemon spells and daemon food: Tupperware containers filled with blood in the fridge; Ziploc bags of human flesh in the freezer. I don't know what she might have found.

Most nights, this daemon prefers sushi or Mexican.

"Hi, Rae."

She's sitting on my couch. No lights. Just us.

"Hi, Moira."

I feel my palm pulsing where she cut me all those years ago. I feel the words and blood twitching in me, livelier than they've been for a long time – since Dad died, really – twirling tighter around veins and marrow.

"Where've you been, Rae?"

"Oh, you know. Around."

"Yeah, I know. So busy playing."

"You've been busy, too."

"Not as busy as I should have been. Took me too long to get back here from Australia, but airfare is so goddamn expensive. You had time to kill a lot of people. Just like a good little daemon should."

"Me? Kill people?" I give her the wide eyes, the meek smile: the mask of skin and pretense I've used to hide my true features all these years.

Moira laughs, ever so softly.

"Oh, Rae." Her tone is one of admiration. "You've got guts and flair. Always did. That's why I love playing with you."

It feels good, even now, even here, to finally get the credit I deserve.

I lick my lips and feel the sharpness of my suddenly razor-edged teeth. My tongue feels rough and long as it flicks in and out, tasting her on the air. My nails are claws now, scratching my skirt, my thighs beneath, my scarred palm so hot that I can feel the flesh burning, sizzling, steaming.

"Well, what could I do? You turned me into this."

"We turned us into this." Her eyes shine a luminescent blue, reflecting the light from the street outside. "All I wanted was a good game, something so good we couldn't forget each other. And what a game it's been. The best, right?"

"The best," I whisper and then I run at her, trying to slash her throat with my claws, but she evades, a silver blade etched with runes cutting into my arm. That hurts. Silver is bad for daemons. Just like it said in that library book.

And Moira has more. She's remembered it all: spell-wound spikes of ivory, holy water, an amulet of malachite and black onyx around her neck to sap my strength.

We fight: parry-strike-parry-slash. Things around us crash and break: TV, vase, glass-topped table. My arm breaks too and I heal it up as best I can. Good stuff, these daemon powers. They're the bee's knees after single-car accidents on icy roads. (Come on. I just tugged the wheel a tiny bit.) They can even help you crawl out of the wreckage and get away scot-free while your fucked-up boyfriend's innards spill over the seat.

Moira's got some moves too and, in the end, I'm bleeding everywhere and so is she. She ties me to the bed, my scaly arms twitching helplessly as she binds me with a rope soaked in holy water. It sears and burns my wrists, but I don't hold that against her. It's all part of the game, after all.

"You should have made me the hunter, you the daemon," I tell Moira. "You'd be good at it. Even better than I was."

In the red and blue light from the neon sign across the street I finally see her face clearly, and she's smiling. Such a wicked good girl.

"What are you waiting for?" I growl. "Game's over. You made me. Now unmake me."

My life flashes before my eyes while I wait for Moira to get on with it. That roommate at uni, she might have looked like me, but her blood tasted ever so much sweeter. Mom's machine unplugged in that hospital room, just for a little while. Her soul slipping out at last, tender and quavering. Bye bye. Dad on that ferry as it went down, and me, beside him in the water, watching him sink. His soul took its time to leave: a cold sliver of life, bitter and stale when I devoured it. An acquired taste, I guess. That father-daughter trip to Thailand was so expensive, and I didn't much like swimming with all those corpses until the rescue boats came, but whatever.

There are others too – the cat, the crow, Aunt Jackie, that nosy teacher (I barely touched her, just gave her a little nudge) – but you can't expect a daemon to keep an accurate body count.

Moira's silvery blade shivers at my neck.

"I missed you," she whispers, leaning close, words and breath tickling my skin.

"I missed you too," I whisper back, and I mean it.

"At least you didn't forget about me."

I watch the light change colour between us – red, blue, red – my eyes stinging.

"You didn't forget either," I mutter, words hitching in my throat.

Next, I smell incense. The same kind I use before a kill – patchouli, the cheapest stuff – and for a moment I think the game is over. For a moment I wonder what will be left of me once it's done, and who I would have been without this game, without Moira.

Awkward, studious, shy.

Bored. Generic. Alone.

"Moira…" I whisper, doubting everything, past and present, future imperfect.

Moira rips my skin with the knife, but the cut is shallow and reluctant. She cuts me again, but not my belly, or my chest, or my throat. Just my palm – the other one – slicing deep and true.

"I had a vision, Rae." The voice is a familiar hoarse whisper in the dark, the face a mask of shadows slipped over Moira's features. "I am a daemon escaped from the deepest depths of the void. And you are a daemon hunter blessed by the brightest lights of heaven. We are enemies, henceforth. Before we both turn forty, one of us must kill the other."

Our bleeding hands clasp and hold fast, the darkness around us quickening with ghost breaths and spirit sighs and oh, oh, there it is again: that jagged and impatient hunger, words and blood and smoke twitching together between our palms, shuddering and twining around my flesh and bones. Unmaking. Remaking.

"Don't chicken out on me," I whisper, relishing the pain, relishing the feeling of her hand in mine.

"I won't."

I see the glint of fangs where none were before when she smiles, the flick of that cloven tongue between her lips. She likes the feeling of it: the strength and daring, I can tell. I liked it too. Now I'm kind of relieved to be rid of it. Being the daemon can be a hard slog, as she'll find out soon enough.

Then Moira laughs and so do I because, for one dizzying moment before the new game begins, before the words and blood take hold, we are the same. We are twins, airborne, suspended between the void and heaven – cursed and fanged, blessed and brightest – hands entwined. Together.

Rappaccini's Daughter
From the Writings of Aubépine

Nathaniel Hawthorne

WE DO NOT remember to have seen any translated specimens of the productions of M. de l'Aubépine – a fact the less to be wondered at, as his very name is unknown to many of his own countrymen as well as to the student of foreign literature. As a writer, he seems to occupy an unfortunate position between the Transcendentalists (who, under one name or another, have their share in all the current literature of the world) and the great body of pen-and-ink men who address the intellect and sympathies of the multitude. If not too refined, at all events too remote, too shadowy, and unsubstantial in his modes of development to suit the taste of the latter class, and yet too popular to satisfy the spiritual or metaphysical requisitions of the former, he must necessarily find himself without an audience, except here and there an individual or possibly an isolated clique. His writings, to do them justice, are not altogether destitute of fancy and originality; they might have won him greater reputation but for an inveterate love of allegory, which is apt to invest his plots and characters with the aspect of scenery and people in the clouds, and to steal away the human warmth out of his conceptions. His fictions are sometimes historical, sometimes of the present day, and sometimes, so far as can be discovered, have little or no reference either to time or space. In any case, he generally contents himself with a very slight embroidery of outward manners – the faintest possible counterfeit of real life – and endeavors to create an interest by some less obvious peculiarity of the subject. Occasionally a breath of Nature, a raindrop of pathos and tenderness, or a gleam of humor, will find its way into the midst of his fantastic imagery, and make us feel as if, after all, we were yet within the limits of our native earth. We will only add to this very cursory notice that M. de l'Aubépine's productions, if the reader chance to take them in precisely the proper point of view, may amuse a leisure hour as well as those of a brighter man; if otherwise, they can hardly fail to look excessively like nonsense.

Our author is voluminous; he continues to write and publish with as much praiseworthy and indefatigable prolixity as if his efforts were crowned with the brilliant success that so justly attends those of Eugene Sue. His first appearance was by a collection of stories in a long series of volumes entitled *Contes deux fois racontees*. The titles of some of his more recent works (we quote from memory) are as follows: *Le Voyage Celeste a Chemin de Fer*, 3 tom., 1838; *Le nouveau Pere Adam et la nouvelle Mere Eve*, 2 tom., 1839; *Roderic; ou le Serpent a l'estomac*, 2 tom., 1840; *Le Culte du Feu*, a folio volume of ponderous research into the religion and ritual of the old Persian Ghebers, published in 1841; *La Soiree du Chateau en Espagne*, 1 tom., 8vo, 1842; and *L'Artiste du Beau; ou le Papillon Mecanique*, 5 tom., 4to, 1843. Our somewhat wearisome perusal of this startling catalogue of volumes has left behind it a certain personal affection and sympathy, though by no means admiration, for M. de l'Aubépine; and we would fain do the little in our power towards introducing him favorably to the American public. The ensuing tale is a translation of his *Beatrice; ou la Belle Empoisonneuse*, recently published in *La Revue Anti-Aristocratique*. This journal, edited by the Comte de Bearhaven, has for some years past led the defence of liberal principles and popular rights with a faithfulness and ability worthy of all praise.

* * *

A young man, named Giovanni Guasconti, came, very long ago, from the more southern region of Italy, to pursue his studies at the University of Padua. Giovanni, who had but a scanty supply of gold ducats in his pocket, took lodgings in a high and gloomy chamber of an old edifice which looked not unworthy to have been the palace of a Paduan noble, and which, in fact, exhibited over its entrance the armorial bearings of a family long since extinct. The young stranger, who was not unstudied in the great poem of his country, recollected that one of the ancestors of this family, and perhaps an occupant of this very mansion, had been pictured by Dante as a partaker of the immortal agonies of his Inferno. These reminiscences and associations, together with the tendency to heartbreak natural to a young man for the first time out of his native sphere, caused Giovanni to sigh heavily as he looked around the desolate and ill-furnished apartment.

"Holy Virgin, signor!" cried old Dame Lisabetta, who, won by the youth's remarkable beauty of person, was kindly endeavoring to give the chamber a habitable air, "what a sigh was that to come out of a young man's heart! Do you find this old mansion gloomy? For the love of Heaven, then, put your head out of the window, and you will see as bright sunshine as you have left in Naples."

Guasconti mechanically did as the old woman advised, but could not quite agree with her that the Paduan sunshine was as cheerful as that of southern Italy. Such as it was, however, it fell upon a garden beneath the window and expended its fostering influences on a variety of plants, which seemed to have been cultivated with exceeding care.

"Does this garden belong to the house?" asked Giovanni.

"Heaven forbid, signor, unless it were fruitful of better pot herbs than any that grow there now," answered old Lisabetta. "No; that garden is cultivated by the own hands of Signor Giacomo Rappaccini, the famous doctor, who, I warrant him, has been heard of as far as Naples. It is said that he distils these plants into medicines that are as potent as a charm. Oftentimes you may see the signor doctor at work, and perchance the signora, his daughter, too, gathering the strange flowers that grow in the garden."

The old woman had now done what she could for the aspect of the chamber; and, commending the young man to the protection of the saints, took her departure.

Giovanni still found no better occupation than to look down into the garden beneath his window. From its appearance, he judged it to be one of those botanic gardens which were of earlier date in Padua than elsewhere in Italy or in the world. Or, not improbably, it might once have been the pleasure-place of an opulent family; for there was the ruin of a marble fountain in the centre, sculptured with rare art, but so woefully shattered that it was impossible to trace the original design from the chaos of remaining fragments. The water, however, continued to gush and sparkle into the sunbeams as cheerfully as ever. A little gurgling sound ascended to the young man's window, and made him feel as if the fountain were an immortal spirit that sung its song unceasingly and without heeding the vicissitudes around it, while one century imbodied it in marble and another scattered the perishable garniture on the soil. All about the pool into which the water subsided grew various plants, that seemed to require a plentiful supply of moisture for the nourishment of gigantic leaves, and in some instances, flowers gorgeously magnificent. There was one shrub in particular, set in a marble vase in the midst of the pool, that bore a profusion of purple blossoms, each of which had the lustre and richness of a gem; and the whole together made a show so resplendent that it seemed enough to illuminate the garden, even had there been no sunshine. Every portion of the soil was peopled with plants and herbs, which, if less beautiful, still bore tokens of assiduous care, as if all had their individual virtues, known to the scientific mind that fostered them. Some were placed in urns, rich with old carving, and others in common garden pots; some crept serpent-like along the ground or climbed on high, using whatever means of ascent was offered them. One plant had wreathed itself round a statue of Vertumnus, which was thus quite veiled and shrouded in a drapery of hanging foliage, so happily arranged that it might have served a sculptor for a study.

While Giovanni stood at the window he heard a rustling behind a screen of leaves, and became aware that a person was at work in the garden. His figure soon emerged into view, and showed itself to be that of no common laborer, but a tall, emaciated, sallow, and sickly-looking man, dressed in a scholar's garb of black. He was beyond the middle term of life, with gray hair, a thin, gray beard, and a face singularly marked with intellect and cultivation, but which could never, even in his more youthful days, have expressed much warmth of heart.

Nothing could exceed the intentness with which this scientific gardener examined every shrub which grew in his path: it seemed as if he was looking into their inmost nature, making observations in regard to their creative essence, and discovering why one leaf grew in this shape and another in that, and wherefore such and such flowers differed among themselves in hue and perfume. Nevertheless, in spite of this deep intelligence on his part, there was no approach to intimacy between himself and these vegetable existences. On the contrary, he avoided their actual touch or the direct inhaling of their odors with a caution that impressed Giovanni most disagreeably; for the man's demeanor was that of one walking among malignant influences, such as savage beasts, or deadly snakes, or evil spirits, which, should he allow them one moment of license, would wreak upon him some terrible fatality. It was strangely frightful to the young man's imagination to see this air of insecurity in a person cultivating a garden, that most simple and innocent of human toils, and which had been alike the joy and labor of the unfallen parents of the race. Was this garden, then, the Eden of the present world? And this man, with such a perception of harm in what his own hands caused to grow – was he the Adam?

The distrustful gardener, while plucking away the dead leaves or pruning the too luxuriant growth of the shrubs, defended his hands with a pair of thick gloves. Nor were these his only armor. When, in his walk through the garden, he came to the magnificent plant that hung its purple gems beside the marble fountain, he placed a kind of mask over his mouth and nostrils, as if all this beauty did but conceal a deadlier malice; but, finding his task still too dangerous, he drew back, removed the mask, and called loudly, but in the infirm voice of a person affected with inward disease, "Beatrice! Beatrice!"

"Here am I, my father. What would you?" cried a rich and youthful voice from the window of the opposite house – a voice as rich as a tropical sunset, and which made Giovanni, though he knew not why, think of deep hues of purple or crimson and of perfumes heavily delectable. "Are you in the garden?"

"Yes, Beatrice," answered the gardener, "and I need your help."

Soon there emerged from under a sculptured portal the figure of a young girl, arrayed with as much richness of taste as the most splendid of the flowers, beautiful as the day, and with a bloom so deep and vivid that one shade more would have been too much. She looked redundant with life, health, and energy; all of which attributes were bound down and compressed, as it were and girdled tensely, in their luxuriance, by her virgin zone. Yet Giovanni's fancy must have grown morbid while he looked down into the garden; for the impression which the fair stranger made upon him was as if here were another flower, the human sister of those vegetable ones, as beautiful as they, more beautiful than the richest of them, but still to be touched only with a glove, nor to be approached without a mask. As Beatrice came down the garden path, it was observable that she handled and inhaled the odor of several of the plants which her father had most sedulously avoided.

"Here, Beatrice," said the latter, "see how many needful offices require to be done to our chief treasure. Yet, shattered as I am, my life might pay the penalty of approaching it so closely as circumstances demand. Henceforth, I fear, this plant must be consigned to your sole charge."

"And gladly will I undertake it," cried again the rich tones of the young lady, as she bent towards the magnificent plant and opened her arms as if to embrace it. "Yes, my sister, my splendour, it shall be Beatrice's task to nurse and serve thee; and thou shalt reward her with thy kisses and perfumed breath, which to her is as the breath of life."

Then, with all the tenderness in her manner that was so strikingly expressed in her words, she busied herself with such attentions as the plant seemed to require; and Giovanni, at his lofty window, rubbed his eyes and almost doubted whether it were a girl tending her favorite flower, or one sister performing the duties of affection to another. The scene soon terminated. Whether Dr. Rappaccini had finished his labors in the garden, or that his watchful eye had caught the stranger's face, he now took his daughter's arm and retired. Night was already closing in; oppressive exhalations seemed to proceed from the plants and steal upward past the open window; and Giovanni, closing the lattice, went to his couch and dreamed of a rich flower and beautiful girl. Flower and maiden were different, and yet the same, and fraught with some strange peril in either shape.

But there is an influence in the light of morning that tends to rectify whatever errors of fancy, or even of judgment, we may have incurred during the sun's decline, or among the shadows of the night, or in the less wholesome glow of moonshine. Giovanni's first movement, on starting from sleep, was to throw open the window and gaze down into the garden which his dreams had made so fertile of mysteries. He was surprised and a little ashamed to find how real and matter-of-fact an affair it proved to be, in the first rays of the sun which gilded the dew-drops that hung upon leaf and blossom, and, while giving a brighter beauty to each rare flower, brought everything within the limits of ordinary experience. The young man rejoiced that, in the heart of the barren city, he had the privilege of overlooking this spot of lovely and luxuriant vegetation. It would serve, he said to himself, as a symbolic language to keep him in communion with Nature. Neither the sickly and thought-worn Dr. Giacomo Rappaccini, it is true, nor his brilliant daughter, were now visible; so that Giovanni could not determine how much of the singularity which he attributed to both was due to their own qualities and how much to his wonder-working fancy; but he was inclined to take a most rational view of the whole matter.

In the course of the day he paid his respects to Signor Pietro Baglioni, professor of medicine in the university, a physician of eminent repute to whom Giovanni had brought a letter of introduction. The professor was an elderly personage, apparently of genial nature, and habits that might almost be called jovial. He kept the young man to dinner, and made himself very agreeable by the freedom and liveliness of his conversation, especially when warmed by a flask or two of Tuscan wine. Giovanni, conceiving that men of science, inhabitants of the same city, must needs be on familiar terms with one another, took an opportunity to mention the name of Dr. Rappaccini. But the professor did not respond with so much cordiality as he had anticipated.

"Ill would it become a teacher of the divine art of medicine," said Professor Pietro Baglioni, in answer to a question of Giovanni, "to withhold due and well-considered praise of a physician so eminently skilled as Rappaccini; but, on the other hand, I should answer it but scantily to my conscience were I to permit a worthy youth like yourself, Signor Giovanni, the son of an ancient friend, to imbibe erroneous ideas respecting a man who might hereafter chance to hold your life and death in his hands. The truth is, our worshipful Dr. Rappaccini has as much science as any member of the faculty – with perhaps one single exception – in Padua, or all Italy; but there are certain grave objections to his professional character."

"And what are they?" asked the young man.

"Has my friend Giovanni any disease of body or heart, that he is so inquisitive about physicians?" said the professor, with a smile. "But as for Rappaccini, it is said of him – and I, who know the man well, can answer for its truth – that he cares infinitely more for science than for mankind. His patients are interesting to him only as subjects for some new experiment. He would sacrifice human life, his own among the rest, or whatever else was dearest to him, for the sake of adding so much as a grain of mustard seed to the great heap of his accumulated knowledge."

"Methinks he is an awful man indeed," remarked Guasconti, mentally recalling the cold and purely intellectual aspect of Rappaccini. "And yet, worshipful professor, is it not a noble spirit? Are there many men capable of so spiritual a love of science?"

"God forbid," answered the professor, somewhat testily; "at least, unless they take sounder views of the healing art than those adopted by Rappaccini. It is his theory that all medicinal virtues are comprised within those substances which we term vegetable poisons. These he cultivates with his own hands, and is said even to have produced new varieties of poison, more horribly deleterious than Nature, without the assistance of this learned person, would ever have plagued the world withal. That the signor doctor does less mischief than might be expected with such dangerous substances is undeniable. Now and then, it must be owned, he has effected, or seemed to effect, a marvellous cure; but, to tell you my private mind, Signor Giovanni, he should receive little credit for such instances of success – they being probably the work of chance – but should be held strictly accountable for his failures, which may justly be considered his own work."

The youth might have taken Baglioni's opinions with many grains of allowance had he known that there was a professional warfare of long continuance between him and Dr. Rappaccini, in which the latter was generally thought to have gained the advantage. If the reader be inclined to judge for himself, we refer him to certain black-letter tracts on both sides, preserved in the medical department of the University of Padua.

"I know not, most learned professor," returned Giovanni, after musing on what had been said of Rappaccini's exclusive zeal for science – "I know not how dearly this physician may love his art; but surely there is one object more dear to him. He has a daughter."

"Aha!" cried the professor, with a laugh. "So now our friend Giovanni's secret is out. You have heard of this daughter, whom all the young men in Padua are wild about, though not half a dozen have ever had the good hap to see her face. I know little of the Signora Beatrice save that Rappaccini is said to have instructed her deeply in his science, and that, young and beautiful as fame reports her, she is already qualified to fill a professor's chair. Perchance her father destines her for mine! Other absurd rumors there be, not worth talking about or listening to. So now, Signor Giovanni, drink off your glass of lachryma."

Guasconti returned to his lodgings somewhat heated with the wine he had quaffed, and which caused his brain to swim with strange fantasies in reference to Dr. Rappaccini and the beautiful Beatrice. On his way, happening to pass by a florist's, he bought a fresh bouquet of flowers.

Ascending to his chamber, he seated himself near the window, but within the shadow thrown by the depth of the wall, so that he could look down into the garden with little risk of being discovered. All beneath his eye was a solitude. The strange plants were basking in the sunshine, and now and then nodding gently to one another, as if in acknowledgment of sympathy and kindred. In the midst, by the shattered fountain, grew the magnificent shrub, with its purple gems clustering all over it; they glowed in the air, and gleamed back again out of the depths of the pool, which thus seemed to overflow with colored radiance from the rich reflection that was steeped in it. At first, as we have said, the garden was a solitude. Soon, however – as Giovanni had half hoped, half feared, would be the case – a figure appeared beneath the antique sculptured portal, and came down between the rows of plants, inhaling their various perfumes as if she were one of those beings of old classic fable that lived upon sweet odors. On again beholding Beatrice, the young man was even startled to perceive how much her beauty exceeded his recollection of it; so brilliant, so vivid, was its character, that she glowed amid the sunlight, and, as Giovanni whispered to himself, positively illuminated the more shadowy intervals of the garden path. Her face being now more revealed than on the former occasion, he was struck by its expression of simplicity and sweetness – qualities that had not entered into his idea of her character, and which made him ask anew what manner of mortal she might be. Nor did he fail again to observe, or imagine, an analogy between the beautiful girl and the gorgeous shrub that hung its gemlike flowers over the fountain – a resemblance which Beatrice seemed to have indulged a fantastic humor in heightening, both by the arrangement of her dress and the selection of its hues.

Approaching the shrub, she threw open her arms, as with a passionate ardor, and drew its branches into an intimate embrace – so intimate that her features were hidden in its leafy bosom and her glistening ringlets all intermingled with the flowers.

"Give me thy breath, my sister," exclaimed Beatrice; "for I am faint with common air. And give me this flower of thine, which I separate with gentlest fingers from the stem and place it close beside my heart."

With these words the beautiful daughter of Rappaccini plucked one of the richest blossoms of the shrub, and was about to fasten it in her bosom. But now, unless Giovanni's draughts of wine had bewildered his senses, a singular incident occurred. A small orange-colored reptile, of the lizard or chameleon species, chanced to be creeping along the path, just at the feet of Beatrice. It appeared to Giovanni – but, at the distance from which he gazed, he could scarcely have seen anything so minute – it appeared to him, however, that a drop or two of moisture from the broken stem of the flower descended upon the lizard's head. For an instant the reptile contorted itself violently, and then lay motionless in the sunshine. Beatrice observed this remarkable phenomenon and crossed herself, sadly, but without surprise; nor did she therefore hesitate to arrange the fatal flower in her bosom. There it blushed, and almost glimmered with the dazzling effect of a precious stone, adding to her dress and aspect the one appropriate charm which nothing else in the world could have supplied. But Giovanni, out of the shadow of his window, bent forward and shrank back, and murmured and trembled.

"Am I awake? Have I my senses?" said he to himself. "What is this being? Beautiful shall I call her, or inexpressibly terrible?"

Beatrice now strayed carelessly through the garden, approaching closer beneath Giovanni's window, so that he was compelled to thrust his head quite out of its concealment in order to gratify the intense and painful curiosity which she excited. At this moment there came a beautiful insect over the garden wall; it had, perhaps, wandered through the city, and found no flowers or verdure among those antique haunts of men until the heavy perfumes of Dr. Rappaccini's shrubs had lured it from afar. Without alighting on the flowers, this winged brightness seemed to be attracted by Beatrice, and lingered in the air and fluttered about her head. Now, here it could not be but that Giovanni Guasconti's eyes deceived him. Be that as it might, he fancied that, while Beatrice was gazing at the insect with childish delight, it grew faint and fell at her feet; its bright wings shivered; it was dead – from no cause that he could discern, unless it were the atmosphere of her breath. Again Beatrice crossed herself and sighed heavily as she bent over the dead insect.

An impulsive movement of Giovanni drew her eyes to the window. There she beheld the beautiful head of the young man – rather a Grecian than an Italian head, with fair, regular features, and a glistening of gold among his ringlets – gazing down upon her like a being that hovered in mid-air. Scarcely knowing what he did, Giovanni threw down the bouquet which he had hitherto held in his hand.

"Signora," said he, "there are pure and healthful flowers. Wear them for the sake of Giovanni Guasconti."

"Thanks, signor," replied Beatrice, with her rich voice, that came forth as it were like a gush of music, and with a mirthful expression half childish and half woman-like. "I accept your gift, and would fain recompense it with this precious purple flower; but if I toss it into the air it will not reach you. So Signor Guasconti must even content himself with my thanks."

She lifted the bouquet from the ground, and then, as if inwardly ashamed at having stepped aside from her maidenly reserve to respond to a stranger's greeting, passed swiftly homeward through the garden. But few as the moments were, it seemed to Giovanni, when she was on the point of vanishing beneath the sculptured portal, that his beautiful bouquet was already beginning to wither in her grasp. It was an idle thought; there could be no possibility of distinguishing a faded flower from a fresh one at so great a distance.

For many days after this incident the young man avoided the window that looked into Dr. Rappaccini's garden, as if something ugly and monstrous would have blasted his eyesight had he been betrayed into a glance. He felt conscious of having put himself, to a certain extent, within the influence of an unintelligible power by the communication which he had opened with Beatrice. The wisest course would have been, if his heart were in any real danger, to quit his lodgings and Padua itself at once; the next wiser, to have accustomed himself, as far as possible, to the familiar and daylight view of Beatrice – thus bringing her rigidly and systematically within the limits of ordinary experience. Least of all, while avoiding her sight, ought Giovanni to have remained so near this extraordinary being that the proximity and possibility even of intercourse should give a kind of substance and reality to the wild vagaries which his imagination ran riot continually in producing. Guasconti had not a deep heart – or, at all events, its depths were not sounded now; but he had a quick fancy, and an ardent southern temperament, which rose every instant to a higher fever pitch. Whether or no Beatrice possessed those terrible attributes, that fatal breath, the affinity with those so beautiful and deadly flowers which were indicated by what Giovanni had witnessed, she had at least instilled a fierce and subtle poison into his system. It was not love, although her rich beauty was a madness to him; nor horror, even while he fancied her spirit to be imbued with the same baneful essence that seemed to pervade her physical frame; but a wild offspring of both love and horror that had each parent in it, and burned like one and shivered like the other. Giovanni knew not what to dread; still less did he know what to hope; yet hope and dread kept a continual warfare in his breast, alternately vanquishing one another and starting up afresh to renew the contest. Blessed are all simple emotions, be they dark or bright! It is the lurid intermixture of the two that produces the illuminating blaze of the infernal regions.

Sometimes he endeavored to assuage the fever of his spirit by a rapid walk through the streets of Padua or beyond its gates: his footsteps kept time with the throbbings of his brain, so that the walk was apt to accelerate itself to a race. One day he found himself arrested; his arm was seized by a portly personage, who had turned back on recognizing the young man and expended much breath in overtaking him.

"Signor Giovanni! Stay, my young friend!" cried he. "Have you forgotten me? That might well be the case if I were as much altered as yourself."

It was Baglioni, whom Giovanni had avoided ever since their first meeting, from a doubt that the professor's sagacity would look too deeply into his secrets. Endeavoring to recover himself, he stared forth wildly from his inner world into the outer one and spoke like a man in a dream.

"Yes; I am Giovanni Guasconti. You are Professor Pietro Baglioni. Now let me pass!"

"Not yet, not yet, Signor Giovanni Guasconti," said the professor, smiling, but at the same time scrutinizing the youth with an earnest glance. "What! did I grow up side by side with your father? and shall his son pass me like a stranger in these old streets of Padua? Stand still, Signor Giovanni; for we must have a word or two before we part."

"Speedily, then, most worshipful professor, speedily," said Giovanni, with feverish impatience. "Does not your worship see that I am in haste?"

Now, while he was speaking there came a man in black along the street, stooping and moving feebly like a person in inferior health. His face was all overspread with a most sickly and sallow hue, but yet so pervaded with an expression of piercing and active intellect that an observer might easily have overlooked the merely physical attributes and have seen only this wonderful energy. As he passed, this person exchanged a cold and distant salutation with Baglioni, but fixed his eyes upon Giovanni with an intentness that seemed to bring out whatever was within him worthy of notice. Nevertheless, there was a peculiar quietness in the look, as if taking merely a speculative, not a human interest, in the young man.

"It is Dr. Rappaccini!" whispered the professor when the stranger had passed. "Has he ever seen your face before?"

"Not that I know," answered Giovanni, starting at the name.

"He *has* seen you! he must have seen you!" said Baglioni, hastily. "For some purpose or other, this man of science is making a study of you. I know that look of his! It is the same that coldly illuminates his face as he bends over a bird, a mouse, or a butterfly, which, in pursuance of some experiment, he has killed by the perfume of a flower; a look as deep as Nature itself, but without Nature's warmth of love. Signor Giovanni, I will stake my life upon it, you are the subject of one of Rappaccini's experiments!"

"Will you make a fool of me?" cried Giovanni, passionately. "*That*, signor professor, were an untoward experiment."

"Patience! patience!" replied the imperturbable professor. "I tell thee, my poor Giovanni, that Rappaccini has a scientific interest in thee. Thou hast fallen into fearful hands! And the Signora Beatrice – what part does she act in this mystery?"

But Guasconti, finding Baglioni's pertinacity intolerable, here broke away, and was gone before the professor could again seize his arm. He looked after the young man intently and shook his head.

"This must not be," said Baglioni to himself. "The youth is the son of my old friend, and shall not come to any harm from which the arcana of medical science can preserve him. Besides, it is too insufferable an impertinence in Rappaccini, thus to snatch the lad out of my own hands, as I may say, and make use of him for his infernal experiments. This daughter of his! It shall be looked to. Perchance, most learned Rappaccini, I may foil you where you little dream of it!"

Meanwhile Giovanni had pursued a circuitous route, and at length found himself at the door of his lodgings. As he crossed the threshold he was met by old Lisabetta, who smirked and smiled, and was evidently desirous to attract his attention; vainly, however, as the ebullition of his feelings had momentarily subsided into a cold and dull vacuity. He turned his eyes full upon the withered face that was puckering itself into a smile, but seemed to behold it not. The old dame, therefore, laid her grasp upon his cloak.

"Signor! signor!" whispered she, still with a smile over the whole breadth of her visage, so that it looked not unlike a grotesque carving in wood, darkened by centuries. "Listen, signor! There is a private entrance into the garden!"

"What do you say?" exclaimed Giovanni, turning quickly about, as if an inanimate thing should start into feverish life. "A private entrance into Dr. Rappaccini's garden?"

"Hush! hush! not so loud!" whispered Lisabetta, putting her hand over his mouth. "Yes; into the worshipful doctor's garden, where you may see all his fine shrubbery. Many a young man in Padua would give gold to be admitted among those flowers."

Giovanni put a piece of gold into her hand.

"Show me the way," said he.

A surmise, probably excited by his conversation with Baglioni, crossed his mind, that this interposition of old Lisabetta might perchance be connected with the intrigue, whatever were its nature, in which the professor seemed to suppose that Dr. Rappaccini was involving him. But such a suspicion, though it disturbed Giovanni, was inadequate to restrain him. The instant that he was aware of the possibility of approaching Beatrice, it seemed an absolute necessity of his existence to do so. It mattered not whether she were angel or demon; he was irrevocably within her sphere, and must obey the law that whirled him onward, in ever-lessening circles, towards a result which he did not attempt to foreshadow; and yet, strange to say, there came across him a sudden doubt whether this intense interest on his part were not delusory; whether it were really of so deep and positive a nature as to justify him in now thrusting himself into an incalculable position; whether it were not merely the fantasy of a young man's brain, only slightly or not at all connected with his heart.

He paused, hesitated, turned half about, but again went on. His withered guide led him along several obscure passages, and finally undid a door, through which, as it was opened, there came the sight and sound of rustling leaves, with the broken sunshine glimmering among them. Giovanni stepped forth, and, forcing himself through the entanglement of a shrub that wreathed its tendrils over the hidden entrance, stood beneath his own window in the open area of Dr. Rappaccini's garden.

How often is it the case that, when impossibilities have come to pass and dreams have condensed their misty substance into tangible realities, we find ourselves calm, and even coldly self-possessed, amid circumstances which it would have been a delirium of joy or agony to anticipate! Fate delights to thwart us thus. Passion will choose his own time to rush upon the scene, and lingers sluggishly behind when an appropriate adjustment of events would seem to summon his appearance. So was it now with Giovanni. Day after day his pulses had throbbed with feverish blood at the improbable idea of an interview with Beatrice, and of standing with her, face to face, in this very garden, basking in the Oriental sunshine of her beauty, and snatching from her full gaze the mystery which he deemed the riddle of his own existence. But now there was a singular and untimely equanimity within his breast. He threw a glance around the garden to discover if Beatrice or her father were present, and, perceiving that he was alone, began a critical observation of the plants.

The aspect of one and all of them dissatisfied him; their gorgeousness seemed fierce, passionate, and even unnatural. There was hardly an individual shrub which a wanderer, straying by himself through a forest, would not have been startled to find growing wild, as if an unearthly face had glared at him out of the thicket. Several also would have shocked a delicate instinct by an appearance of artificialness indicating that there had been such commixture, and, as it were, adultery, of various vegetable species, that the production was no longer of God's making, but the monstrous offspring of man's depraved fancy, glowing with only an evil mockery of beauty. They were probably the result of experiment, which in one or two cases had succeeded in mingling plants individually lovely into a compound possessing the questionable and ominous character that distinguished the whole growth of the garden. In fine, Giovanni recognized but two or three plants in the collection, and those of a kind that he well knew to be poisonous. While busy with these contemplations he heard the rustling of a silken garment, and, turning, beheld Beatrice emerging from beneath the sculptured portal.

Giovanni had not considered with himself what should be his deportment; whether he should apologize for his intrusion into the garden, or assume that he was there with the privity at least, if not by the desire, of Dr. Rappaccini or his daughter; but Beatrice's manner placed him at his ease, though leaving him still in doubt by what agency he had gained admittance. She came lightly along the path and met him near the broken fountain. There was surprise in her face, but brightened by a simple and kind expression of pleasure.

"You are a connoisseur in flowers, signor," said Beatrice, with a smile, alluding to the bouquet which he had flung her from the window. "It is no marvel, therefore, if the sight of my father's rare collection has tempted you to take a nearer view. If he were here, he could tell you many strange and interesting facts as to the nature and habits of these shrubs; for he has spent a lifetime in such studies, and this garden is his world."

"And yourself, lady," observed Giovanni, "if fame says true – you likewise are deeply skilled in the virtues indicated by these rich blossoms and these spicy perfumes. Would you deign to be my instructress, I should prove an apter scholar than if taught by Signor Rappaccini himself."

"Are there such idle rumors?" asked Beatrice, with the music of a pleasant laugh. "Do people say that I am skilled in my father's science of plants? What a jest is there! No; though I have grown up among these flowers, I know no more of them than their hues and perfume; and sometimes methinks I would fain rid myself of even that small knowledge. There are many flowers here, and those not the least brilliant, that shock and offend me when they meet my eye. But pray, signor, do not believe these stories about my science. Believe nothing of me save what you see with your own eyes."

"And must I believe all that I have seen with my own eyes?" asked Giovanni, pointedly, while the recollection of former scenes made him shrink. "No, signora; you demand too little of me. Bid me believe nothing save what comes from your own lips." ·

It would appear that Beatrice understood him. There came a deep flush to her cheek; but she looked full into Giovanni's eyes, and responded to his gaze of uneasy suspicion with a queenlike haughtiness.

"I do so bid you, signor," she replied. "Forget whatever you may have fancied in regard to me. If true to the outward senses, still it may be false in its essence; but the words of Beatrice Rappaccini's lips are true from the depths of the heart outward. Those you may believe."

A fervor glowed in her whole aspect and beamed upon Giovanni's consciousness like the light of truth itself; but while she spoke there was a fragrance in the atmosphere around her, rich and delightful, though evanescent, yet which the young man, from an indefinable reluctance, scarcely dared to draw into his lungs. It might be the odor of the flowers. Could it be Beatrice's breath which thus embalmed her words with a strange richness, as if by steeping them in her heart? A faintness passed like a shadow over Giovanni and flitted away; he seemed to gaze through the beautiful girl's eyes into her transparent soul, and felt no more doubt or fear.

The tinge of passion that had colored Beatrice's manner vanished; she became gay, and appeared to derive a pure delight from her communion with the youth not unlike what the maiden of a lonely island might have felt conversing with a voyager from the civilized world.

Evidently her experience of life had been confined within the limits of that garden. She talked now about matters as simple as the daylight or summer clouds, and now asked questions in reference to the city, or Giovanni's distant home, his friends, his mother, and his sisters – questions indicating such seclusion, and such lack of familiarity with modes and forms, that Giovanni responded as if to an infant. Her spirit gushed out before him like a fresh rill that was just catching its first glimpse of the sunlight and wondering at the reflections of earth and sky which were flung into its bosom. There came thoughts, too, from a deep source, and fantasies of a gemlike brilliancy, as if diamonds and rubies sparkled upward among the bubbles of the fountain. Ever and anon there gleamed across the young man's mind a sense of wonder that he should be walking side by side with the being who had so wrought upon his imagination, whom he had idealized in such hues of terror, in whom he had positively witnessed such manifestations of dreadful attributes – that he should be conversing with Beatrice like a brother, and should find her so human and so maidenlike. But such reflections were only momentary; the effect of her character was too real not to make itself familiar at once.

In this free intercourse they had strayed through the garden, and now, after many turns among its avenues, were come to the shattered fountain, beside which grew the magnificent shrub, with its treasury of glowing blossoms. A fragrance was diffused from it which Giovanni recognized as identical with that which he had attributed to Beatrice's breath, but incomparably more powerful. As her eyes fell upon it, Giovanni beheld her press her hand to her bosom as if her heart were throbbing suddenly and painfully.

"For the first time in my life," murmured she, addressing the shrub, "I had forgotten thee."

"I remember, signora," said Giovanni, "that you once promised to reward me with one of these living gems for the bouquet which I had the happy boldness to fling to your feet. Permit me now to pluck it as a memorial of this interview."

He made a step towards the shrub with extended hand; but Beatrice darted forward, uttering a shriek that went through his heart like a dagger. She caught his hand and drew it back with the whole force of her slender figure. Giovanni felt her touch thrilling through his fibres.

"Touch it not!" exclaimed she, in a voice of agony. "Not for thy life! It is fatal!"

Then, hiding her face, she fled from him and vanished beneath the sculptured portal. As Giovanni followed her with his eyes, he beheld the emaciated figure and pale intelligence of Dr. Rappaccini, who had been watching the scene, he knew not how long, within the shadow of the entrance.

No sooner was Guasconti alone in his chamber than the image of Beatrice came back to his passionate musings, invested with all the witchery that had been gathering around it ever since his first glimpse of her, and now likewise imbued with a tender warmth of girlish womanhood. She was human; her nature was endowed with all gentle and feminine qualities; she was worthiest to be worshipped; she was capable, surely, on her part, of the height and heroism of love. Those tokens which he had hitherto considered as proofs of a frightful peculiarity in her physical and moral system were now either forgotten, or, by the subtle sophistry of passion transmitted into a golden crown of enchantment, rendering Beatrice the more admirable by so much as she was the more unique. Whatever had looked ugly was now beautiful; or, if incapable of such a change, it stole away and hid itself among those shapeless half ideas which throng the dim region beyond the daylight of our perfect consciousness. Thus did he spend the night, nor fell asleep until the dawn had begun to awake the slumbering flowers in Dr. Rappaccini's garden, whither Giovanni's dreams doubtless led him. Up rose the sun in his due season, and, flinging his beams upon the young man's eyelids, awoke him to a sense of pain. When thoroughly aroused, he became sensible of a burning and tingling agony in his hand – in his right hand – the very hand which Beatrice had grasped in her own when he was on the point of plucking one of the gemlike flowers. On the back of that hand there was now a purple print like that of four small fingers, and the likeness of a slender thumb upon his wrist.

Oh, how stubbornly does love – or even that cunning semblance of love which flourishes in the imagination, but strikes no depth of root into the heart – how stubbornly does it hold its faith until the moment comes when it is doomed to vanish into thin mist! Giovanni wrapped a handkerchief about his hand and wondered what evil thing had stung him, and soon forgot his pain in a reverie of Beatrice.

After the first interview, a second was in the inevitable course of what we call fate. A third; a fourth; and a meeting with Beatrice in the garden was no longer an incident in Giovanni's daily life, but the whole space in which he might be said to live; for the anticipation and memory of that ecstatic hour made up the remainder. Nor was it otherwise with the daughter of Rappaccini. She watched for the youth's appearance, and flew to his side with confidence as unreserved as if they had been playmates from early infancy – as if they were such playmates still. If, by any unwonted chance, he failed to come at the appointed moment, she stood beneath the window and sent up the rich sweetness of her tones to float around him in his chamber and echo and reverberate throughout his heart: "Giovanni! Giovanni! Why tarriest thou? Come down!" And down he hastened into that Eden of poisonous flowers.

But, with all this intimate familiarity, there was still a reserve in Beatrice's demeanor, so rigidly and invariably sustained that the idea of infringing it scarcely occurred to his imagination. By all appreciable signs, they loved; they had looked love with eyes that conveyed the holy secret from the depths of one soul into the depths of the other, as if it were too sacred to be whispered by the way; they had even spoken love in those gushes of passion when their spirits darted forth in articulated breath like tongues of long-hidden flame; and yet there had been no seal of lips, no clasp of hands, nor any slightest caress such as love claims and hallows. He had never touched one of the gleaming ringlets of her hair; her garment – so marked was the physical barrier between them – had never been waved against him by a breeze. On the few occasions when Giovanni had seemed tempted to overstep the limit, Beatrice grew so sad, so stern, and withal wore such a look of desolate separation, shuddering at itself, that not a spoken word was requisite to repel him. At such times he was startled at the horrible suspicions that rose, monster-like, out of the caverns of his heart and stared him in the face; his love grew thin and faint as the morning mist, his doubts alone had substance. But, when Beatrice's face brightened again after the momentary shadow, she was transformed at once from the mysterious, questionable being whom he had watched with so much awe and horror; she was now the beautiful and unsophisticated girl whom he felt that his spirit knew with a certainty beyond all other knowledge.

A considerable time had now passed since Giovanni's last meeting with Baglioni. One morning, however, he was disagreeably surprised by a visit from the professor, whom he had scarcely thought of for whole weeks, and would willingly have forgotten still longer. Given up as he had long been to a pervading excitement, he could tolerate no companions except upon condition of their perfect sympathy with his present state of feeling. Such sympathy was not to be expected from Professor Baglioni.

The visitor chatted carelessly for a few moments about the gossip of the city and the university, and then took up another topic.

"I have been reading an old classic author lately," said he, "and met with a story that strangely interested me. Possibly you may remember it. It is of an Indian prince, who sent a beautiful woman as a present to Alexander the Great. She was as lovely as the dawn and gorgeous as the sunset; but what especially distinguished her was a certain rich perfume in her breath – richer than a garden of Persian roses. Alexander, as was natural to a youthful conqueror, fell in love at first sight with this magnificent stranger; but a certain sage physician, happening to be present, discovered a terrible secret in regard to her."

"And what was that?" asked Giovanni, turning his eyes downward to avoid those of the professor.

"That this lovely woman," continued Baglioni, with emphasis, "had been nourished with poisons from her birth upward, until her whole nature was so imbued with them that she herself had become the deadliest poison in existence. Poison was her element of life. With that rich perfume of her breath she blasted the very air. Her love would have been poison – her embrace death. Is not this a marvellous tale?"

"A childish fable," answered Giovanni, nervously starting from his chair. "I marvel how your worship finds time to read such nonsense among your graver studies."

"By the by," said the professor, looking uneasily about him, "what singular fragrance is this in your apartment? Is it the perfume of your gloves? It is faint, but delicious; and yet, after all, by no means agreeable. Were I to breathe it long, methinks it would make me ill. It is like the breath of a flower; but I see no flowers in the chamber."

"Nor are there any," replied Giovanni, who had turned pale as the professor spoke; "nor, I think, is there any fragrance except in your worship's imagination. Odors, being a sort of element combined of the sensual and the spiritual, are apt to deceive us in this manner. The recollection of a perfume, the bare idea of it, may easily be mistaken for a present reality."

"Ay; but my sober imagination does not often play such tricks," said Baglioni; "and, were I to fancy any kind of odor, it would be that of some vile apothecary drug, wherewith my fingers are likely enough to be imbued. Our worshipful friend Rappaccini, as I have heard, tinctures his medicaments with odors richer than those of Araby. Doubtless, likewise, the fair and learned Signora Beatrice would minister to her patients with draughts as sweet as a maiden's breath; but woe to him that sips them!"

Giovanni's face evinced many contending emotions. The tone in which the professor alluded to the pure and lovely daughter of Rappaccini was a torture to his soul; and yet the intimation of a view of her character opposite to his own, gave instantaneous distinctness to a thousand dim suspicions, which now grinned at him like so many demons. But he strove hard to quell them and to respond to Baglioni with a true lover's perfect faith.

"Signor professor," said he, "you were my father's friend; perchance, too, it is your purpose to act a friendly part towards his son. I would fain feel nothing towards you save respect and deference; but I pray you to observe, signor, that there is one subject on which we must not speak. You know not the Signora Beatrice. You cannot, therefore, estimate the wrong – the blasphemy, I may even say – that is offered to her character by a light or injurious word."

"Giovanni! My poor Giovanni!" answered the professor, with a calm expression of pity, "I know this wretched girl far better than yourself. You shall hear the truth in respect to the poisoner Rappaccini and his poisonous daughter; yes, poisonous as she is beautiful. Listen; for, even should you do violence to my gray hairs, it shall not silence me. That old fable of the Indian woman has become a truth by the deep and deadly science of Rappaccini and in the person of the lovely Beatrice."

Giovanni groaned and hid his face

"Her father," continued Baglioni, "was not restrained by natural affection from offering up his child in this horrible manner as the victim of his insane zeal for science; for, let us do him justice, he is as true a man of science as ever distilled his own heart in an alembic. What, then, will be your fate? Beyond a doubt you are selected as the material of some new experiment.

Perhaps the result is to be death; perhaps a fate more awful still. Rappaccini, with what he calls the interest of science before his eyes, will hesitate at nothing."

"It is a dream," muttered Giovanni to himself; "surely it is a dream."

"But," resumed the professor, "be of good cheer, son of my friend. It is not yet too late for the rescue. Possibly we may even succeed in bringing back this miserable child within the limits of ordinary nature, from which her father's madness has estranged her. Behold this little silver vase! It was wrought by the hands of the renowned Benvenuto Cellini, and is well worthy to be a love gift to the fairest dame in Italy. But its contents are invaluable. One little sip of this antidote would have rendered the most virulent poisons of the Borgias innocuous. Doubt not that it will be as efficacious against those of Rappaccini. Bestow the vase, and the precious liquid within it, on your Beatrice, and hopefully await the result."

Baglioni laid a small, exquisitely wrought silver vial on the table and withdrew, leaving what he had said to produce its effect upon the young man's mind.

"We will thwart Rappaccini yet," thought he, chuckling to himself, as he descended the stairs; "but, let us confess the truth of him, he is a wonderful man – a wonderful man indeed; a vile empiric, however, in his practice, and therefore not to be tolerated by those who respect the good old rules of the medical profession."

Throughout Giovanni's whole acquaintance with Beatrice, he had occasionally, as we have said, been haunted by dark surmises as to her character; yet so thoroughly had she made herself felt by him as a simple, natural, most affectionate, and guileless creature, that the image now held up by Professor Baglioni looked as strange and incredible as if it were not in accordance with his own original conception. True, there were ugly recollections connected with his first glimpses of the beautiful girl; he could not quite forget the bouquet that withered in her grasp, and the insect that perished amid the sunny air, by no ostensible agency save the fragrance of her breath. These incidents, however, dissolving in the pure light of her character, had no longer the efficacy of facts, but were acknowledged as mistaken fantasies, by whatever testimony of the senses they might appear to be substantiated. There is something truer and more real than what we can see with the eyes and touch with the finger. On such better evidence had Giovanni founded his confidence in Beatrice, though rather by the necessary force of her high attributes than by any deep and generous faith on his part. But now his spirit was incapable of sustaining itself at the height to which the early enthusiasm of passion had exalted it; he fell down, grovelling among earthly doubts, and defiled therewith the pure whiteness of Beatrice's image. Not that he gave her up; he did but distrust. He resolved to institute some decisive test that should satisfy him, once for all, whether there were those dreadful peculiarities in her physical nature which could not be supposed to exist without some corresponding monstrosity of soul. His eyes, gazing down afar, might have deceived him as to the lizard, the insect, and the flowers; but if he could witness, at the distance of a few paces, the sudden blight of one fresh and healthful flower in Beatrice's hand, there would be room for no further question. With this idea he hastened to the florist's and purchased a bouquet that was still gemmed with the morning dew-drops.

It was now the customary hour of his daily interview with Beatrice. Before descending into the garden, Giovanni failed not to look at his figure in the mirror – a vanity to be expected in a beautiful young man, yet, as displaying itself at that troubled and feverish moment, the token of a certain shallowness of feeling and insincerity of character. He did gaze, however, and said to himself that his features had never before possessed so rich a grace, nor his eyes such vivacity, nor his cheeks so warm a hue of superabundant life.

"At least," thought he, "her poison has not yet insinuated itself into my system. I am no flower to perish in her grasp."

With that thought he turned his eyes on the bouquet, which he had never once laid aside from his hand. A thrill of indefinable horror shot through his frame on perceiving that those dewy flowers were already beginning to droop; they wore the aspect of things that had been fresh and lovely yesterday. Giovanni grew white as marble, and stood motionless before the mirror, staring at his own reflection there as at the likeness of something frightful. He remembered Baglioni's remark about the fragrance that seemed to pervade the chamber. It must have been the poison in his breath! Then he shuddered – shuddered at himself. Recovering from his stupor, he began to watch with curious eye a spider that was busily at work hanging its web from the antique cornice of the apartment, crossing and recrossing the artful system of interwoven lines – as vigorous and active a spider as ever dangled from an old ceiling. Giovanni bent towards the insect, and emitted a deep, long breath. The spider suddenly ceased its toil; the web vibrated with a tremor originating in the body of the small artisan. Again Giovanni sent forth a breath, deeper, longer, and imbued with a venomous feeling out of his heart: he knew not whether he were wicked, or only desperate. The spider made a convulsive gripe with his limbs and hung dead across the window.

"Accursed! Accursed!" muttered Giovanni, addressing himself. "Hast thou grown so poisonous that this deadly insect perishes by thy breath?"

At that moment a rich, sweet voice came floating up from the garden.

"Giovanni! Giovanni! It is past the hour! Why tarriest thou? Come down!"

"Yes," muttered Giovanni again. "She is the only being whom my breath may not slay! Would that it might!"

He rushed down, and in an instant was standing before the bright and loving eyes of Beatrice. A moment ago his wrath and despair had been so fierce that he could have desired nothing so much as to wither her by a glance; but with her actual presence there came influences which had too real an existence to be at once shaken off: recollections of the delicate and benign power of her feminine nature, which had so often enveloped him in a religious calm; recollections of many a holy and passionate outgush of her heart, when the pure fountain had been unsealed from its depths and made visible in its transparency to his mental eye; recollections which, had Giovanni known how to estimate them, would have assured him that all this ugly mystery was but an earthly illusion, and that, whatever mist of evil might seem to have gathered over her, the real Beatrice was a heavenly angel. Incapable as he was of such high faith, still her presence had not utterly lost its magic. Giovanni's rage was quelled into an aspect of sullen insensibility. Beatrice, with a quick spiritual sense, immediately felt that there was a gulf of blackness between them which neither he nor she could pass. They walked on together, sad and silent, and came thus to the marble fountain and to its pool of water on the ground, in the midst of which grew the shrub that bore gem-like blossoms. Giovanni was affrighted at the eager enjoyment – the appetite, as it were – with which he found himself inhaling the fragrance of the flowers.

"Beatrice," asked he, abruptly, "whence came this shrub?"

"My father created it," answered she, with simplicity.

"Created it! Created it!" repeated Giovanni. "What mean you, Beatrice?"

"He is a man fearfully acquainted with the secrets of Nature," replied Beatrice; "and, at the hour when I first drew breath, this plant sprang from the soil, the offspring of his science, of his intellect, while I was but his earthly child. Approach it not!" continued she, observing with terror that Giovanni was drawing nearer to the shrub. "It has qualities that you little dream of. But I, dearest Giovanni – I grew up and blossomed with the plant and was nourished with its breath. It was my sister, and I loved it with a human affection; for, alas! – hast thou not suspected it? – there was an awful doom."

Here Giovanni frowned so darkly upon her that Beatrice paused and trembled. But her faith in his tenderness reassured her, and made her blush that she had doubted for an instant.

"There was an awful doom," she continued, "the effect of my father's fatal love of science, which estranged me from all society of my kind. Until Heaven sent thee, dearest Giovanni, oh, how lonely was thy poor Beatrice!"

"Was it a hard doom?" asked Giovanni, fixing his eyes upon her.

"Only of late have I known how hard it was," answered she, tenderly. "Oh, yes; but my heart was torpid, and therefore quiet."

Giovanni's rage broke forth from his sullen gloom like a lightning flash out of a dark cloud.

"Accursed one!" cried he, with venomous scorn and anger. "And, finding thy solitude wearisome, thou hast severed me likewise from all the warmth of life and enticed me into thy region of unspeakable horror!"

"Giovanni!" exclaimed Beatrice, turning her large bright eyes upon his face. The force of his words had not found its way into her mind; she was merely thunderstruck.

"Yes, poisonous thing!" repeated Giovanni, beside himself with passion. "Thou hast done it! Thou hast blasted me! Thou hast filled my veins with poison! Thou hast made me as hateful, as ugly, as loathsome and deadly a creature as thyself – a world's wonder of hideous monstrosity! Now, if our breath be happily as fatal to ourselves as to all others, let us join our lips in one kiss of unutterable hatred, and so die!"

"What has befallen me?" murmured Beatrice, with a low moan out of her heart. "Holy Virgin, pity me, a poor heart-broken child!"

"Thou – dost thou pray?" cried Giovanni, still with the same fiendish scorn. "Thy very prayers, as they come from thy lips, taint the atmosphere with death. Yes, yes; let us pray! Let us to church and dip our fingers in the holy water at the portal! They that come after us will perish as by a pestilence! Let us sign crosses in the air! It will be scattering curses abroad in the likeness of holy symbols!"

"Giovanni," said Beatrice, calmly, for her grief was beyond passion, "why dost thou join thyself with me thus in those terrible words? I, it is true, am the horrible thing thou namest me. But thou – what hast thou to do, save with one other shudder at my hideous misery to go forth out of the garden and mingle with thy race, and forget there ever crawled on earth such a monster as poor Beatrice?"

"Dost thou pretend ignorance?" asked Giovanni, scowling upon her. "Behold! this power have I gained from the pure daughter of Rappaccini."

There was a swarm of summer insects flitting through the air in search of the food promised by the flower odors of the fatal garden. They circled round Giovanni's head, and were evidently attracted towards him by the same influence which had drawn them for an instant within the sphere of several of the shrubs. He sent forth a breath among them, and smiled bitterly at Beatrice as at least a score of the insects fell dead upon the ground.

"I see it! I see it!" shrieked Beatrice. "It is my father's fatal science! No, no, Giovanni; it was not I! Never! never! I dreamed only to love thee and be with thee a little time, and so to let thee pass away, leaving but thine image in mine heart; for, Giovanni, believe it, though my body be nourished with poison, my spirit is God's creature, and craves love as its daily food. But my father – he has united us in this fearful sympathy. Yes; spurn me, tread upon me, kill me! Oh, what is death after such words as thine? But it was not I. Not for a world of bliss would I have done it."

Giovanni's passion had exhausted itself in its outburst from his lips. There now came across him a sense, mournful, and not without tenderness, of the intimate and peculiar relationship between Beatrice and himself. They stood, as it were, in an utter solitude, which would be made none the less solitary by the densest throng of human life. Ought not, then, the desert of humanity around them to press this insulated pair closer together? If they should be cruel to one another, who was there to be kind to them? Besides, thought Giovanni, might there not still be a hope of his returning within the limits of ordinary nature, and leading Beatrice, the redeemed Beatrice, by the hand? O, weak, and selfish, and unworthy spirit, that could dream of an earthly union and earthly happiness as possible, after such deep love had been so bitterly wronged as was Beatrice's love by Giovanni's blighting words! No, no; there could be no such hope. She must pass heavily, with that broken heart, across the borders of Time – she must bathe her hurts in some fount of paradise, and forget her grief in the light of immortality, and *there* be well.

But Giovanni did not know it.

"Dear Beatrice," said he, approaching her, while she shrank away as always at his approach, but now with a different impulse, "dearest Beatrice, our fate is not yet so desperate. Behold! there is a medicine, potent, as a wise physician has assured me, and almost divine in its efficacy. It is composed of ingredients the most opposite to those by which thy awful father has brought this calamity upon thee and me. It is distilled of blessed herbs. Shall we not quaff it together, and thus be purified from evil?"

"Give it me!" said Beatrice, extending her hand to receive the little silver vial which Giovanni took from his bosom. She added, with a peculiar emphasis, "I will drink; but do thou await the result."

She put Baglioni's antidote to her lips; and, at the same moment, the figure of Rappaccini emerged from the portal and came slowly towards the marble fountain. As he drew near, the pale man of science seemed to gaze with a triumphant expression at the beautiful youth and maiden, as might an artist who should spend his life in achieving a picture or a group of statuary and finally be satisfied with his success. He paused; his bent form grew erect with conscious power; he spread out his hands over them in the attitude of a father imploring a blessing upon his children; but those were the same hands that had thrown poison into the stream of their lives. Giovanni trembled. Beatrice shuddered nervously, and pressed her hand upon her heart.

"My daughter," said Rappaccini, "thou art no longer lonely in the world. Pluck one of those precious gems from thy sister shrub and bid thy bridegroom wear it in his bosom. It will not harm him now. My science and the sympathy between thee and him have so wrought within his system that he now stands apart from common men, as thou dost, daughter of my pride and triumph, from ordinary women. Pass on, then, through the world, most dear to one another and dreadful to all besides!"

"My father," said Beatrice, feebly – and still as she spoke she kept her hand upon her heart – "wherefore didst thou inflict this miserable doom upon thy child?"

"Miserable!" exclaimed Rappaccini. "What mean you, foolish girl? Dost thou deem it misery to be endowed with marvellous gifts against which no power nor strength could avail an enemy – misery, to be able to quell the mightiest with a breath – misery, to be as terrible as thou art beautiful? Wouldst thou, then, have preferred the condition of a weak woman, exposed to all evil and capable of none?"

"I would fain have been loved, not feared," murmured Beatrice, sinking down upon the ground. "But now it matters not. I am going, father, where the evil which thou hast striven to mingle with my being will pass away like a dream-like the fragrance of these poisonous flowers, which will no longer taint my breath among the flowers of Eden. Farewell, Giovanni! Thy words of hatred are like lead within my heart; but they, too, will fall away as I ascend. Oh, was there not, from the first, more poison in thy nature than in mine?"

To Beatrice – so radically had her earthly part been wrought upon by Rappaccini's skill – as poison had been life, so the powerful antidote was death; and thus the poor victim of man's ingenuity and of thwarted nature, and of the fatality that attends all such efforts of perverted wisdom, perished there, at the feet of her father and Giovanni. Just at that moment Professor Pietro Baglioni looked forth from the window, and called loudly, in a tone of triumph mixed with horror, to the thunderstricken man of science, "Rappaccini! Rappaccini! And is *this* the upshot of your experiment!"

The Hog

William Hope Hodgson

Chapter I

WE HAD FINISHED dinner and Carnacki had drawn his big chair up to the fire, and started his pipe.

Jessop, Arkright, Taylor and I had each of us taken up our favourite positions, and waited for Carnacki to begin.

"What I'm going to tell you about happened in the next room," he said, after drawing at his pipe for a while. "It has been a terrible experience. Doctor Witton first brought the case to my notice. We'd been chatting over a pipe at the Club one night about an article in the Lancet, and Witton mentioned having just such a similar case in a man called Bains. I was interested at once. It was one of those cases of a gap or flaw in a man's protection barrier, I call it. A failure to be what I might term efficiently insulated – spiritually – from the outer monstrosities.

"From what I knew of Witton, I knew he'd be no use. You all know Witton. A decent sort, hard-headed, practical, stand-no-kind-of-nonsense sort of man, all right at his own job when that job's a fractured leg or a broken collarbone; but he'd never have made anything of the Bains case."

For a space Carnacki puffed meditatively at his pipe, and we waited for him to go on with his tale.

"I told Witton to send Bains to me," he resumed, "and the following Saturday he came up. A little sensitive man. I liked him as soon as I set eyes on him. After a bit, I got him to explain what was troubling him, and questioned him about what Doctor Witton had called his 'dreams'.

"'They're more than dreams,' he said, 'they're so real that they're actual experiences to me. They're simply horrible. And yet there's nothing very definite in them to tell you about. They generally come just as I am going off to sleep. I'm hardly over before suddenly I seem to have got down into some deep, vague place with some inexplicable and frightful horror all about me. I can never understand what it is, for I never see anything, only I always get a sudden knowledge like a warning that I have got down into some terrible place – a sort of hellplace I might call it, where I've no business ever to have wandered; and the warning is always insistent – even imperative – that I must get out, get out, or some enormous horror will come at me.'

"'Can't you pull yourself back?' I asked him. 'Can't you wake up?'

"'No,' he told me. 'That's just what I can't do, try as I will. I can't stop going along this labyrinth-of-hell as I call it to myself, towards some dreadful unknown Horror. The warning is repeated, ever so strongly – almost as if the live me of my waking moments was awake and aware. Something seems to warn me to wake up, that whatever I do I must wake, wake, and then my consciousness comes suddenly alive and I know that my body is there in the bed, but my essence or spirit is still down there in that hell, wherever it is, in a danger that is both unknown and inexpressible; but so overwhelming that my whole spirit seems sick with terror.'

"'I keep saying to myself all the time that I must wake up,' he continued, 'but it is as if my spirit is still down there, and as if my consciousness knows that some tremendous invisible Power is fighting against me. I know that if I do not wake then, I shall never wake up again, but go down deeper and deeper into some stupendous horror of soul destruction. So then I fight. My body lies in the bed there, and pulls. And the power down there in that labyrinth exerts itself too so that a feeling of despair, greater than any I have ever known on this earth, comes on me. I know that if I give way and cease to fight, and do not wake, then I shall pass out – out to that monstrous Horror which seems to be silently calling my soul to destruction.'

"'Then I make a final stupendous effort,' he continued, 'and my brain seems to fill my body like the ghost of my soul. I can even open my eyes and see with my brain, or consciousness, out of my own eyes. I can see the bedclothes, and I know just how I am lying in the bed; yet the real me is down in that hell in terrible danger. Can you get me?' he asked."

"'Perfectly,' I replied."

"'Well, you know,' he went on, 'I fight and fight. Down there in that great pit my very soul seems to shrink back from the call of some brooding horror that impels it silently a little further, always a little further round a visible corner, which if I once pass I know I shall never return again to this world. Desperately I fight brain and consciousness fighting together to help it. The agony is so great that I could scream were it not that I am rigid and frozen in the bed with fear.

"'Then, just when my strength seems almost gone, soul and body win, and blend slowly. And I lie there worn out with this terrible extraordinary fight. I have still a sense of a dreadful horror all about me, as if out of that horrible place some brooding monstrosity had followed me up, and hangs still and silent and invisible over me, threatening me there in my bed. Do I make it clear to you?' he asked. 'It's like some monstrous Presence.'

"'Yes,' I said. 'I follow you.'"

"The man's forehead was actually covered with sweat, so keenly did he live again through the horrors he had experienced.

"After a while he continued:

"'Now comes the most curious part of the dream or whatever it is,' he said. 'There's always a sound I hear as I lie there exhausted in the bed. It comes while the bedroom is still full of the sort of atmosphere of monstrosity that seems to come up with me when I get out of that place. I hear the sound coming up out of that enormous depth, and it is always the noise of pigs – pigs grunting, you know. It's just simply dreadful. The dream is always the same. Sometimes I've had it every single night for a week, until I fight not to go to sleep; but, of course, I have to sleep sometimes. I think that's how a person might go mad, don't you?' he finished."

"I nodded, and looked at his sensitive face. Poor beggar! He had been through it, and no mistake.

"'Tell me some more,' I said. 'The grunting – what does it sound like exactly?'

"'It's just like pigs grunting,' he told me again. 'Only much more awful. There are grunts, and squeals and pighowls, like you hear when their food is being brought to them at a pig farm. You know those large pig farms where they keep hundreds of pigs. All the grunts, squeals and howls blend into one brutal chaos of sound – only it isn't a chaos. It all blends in a queer horrible way. I've heard it. A sort of swinish clamouring melody that grunts and roars and shrieks in chunks of grunting sounds, all tied together with squealings and shot through with pig howls. I've sometimes thought there was a definite beat in it; for every now and again there comes a gargantuan GRUNT, breaking through the million pig-voiced roaring – a stupendous GRUNT that comes in with a beat. Can you understand me? It seems to shake everything... It's like a spiritual earthquake. The howling, squealing, grunting, rolling clamour of swinish noise coming up out of that place, and then the monstrous GRUNT rising up through it all, an ever-recurring beat out of the depth – the voice of the swine-mother of monstrosity beating up from below through that chorus of mad swine-hunger... It's no use! I can't explain it. No one ever could. It's just terrible! And I'm afraid you're saying to yourself that I'm in a bad way; that I want a change or a tonic; that I must buck up or I'll land myself in a madhouse. If only you could understand! Doctor Witton seemed to half understand, I thought; but I know he's only sent me to you as a sort of last hope. He thinks I'm booked for the asylum. I could tell it.'

"'Nonsense!' I said. 'Don't talk such rubbish. You're as sane as I am. Your ability to think clearly what you want to tell me, and then to transmit it to me so well that you compel my mental retina to see something of what you have seen, stands sponsor for your mental balance.'

"'I am going to investigate your case, and if it is what I suspect, one of those rare instances of a 'flaw' or 'gap' in your protective barrier (what I might call your spiritual insulation from the Outer Monstrosities) I've no doubt we can end the trouble. But we've got to go properly into the matter first, and there will certainly be danger in doing so.'

"'I'll risk it,' replied Bains. 'I can't go on like this any longer.'

"'Very well,' I told him. 'Go out now, and come back at five o'clock. I shall be ready for you then. And don't worry about your sanity. You're all right, and we'll soon make things safe for you again. Just keep cheerful and don't brood about it.'"

Chapter II

"**I PUT** in the whole afternoon preparing my experimenting room, across the landing there, for his case. When he returned at five o'clock I was ready for him and took him straight into the room.

"It gets dark now about six-thirty, as you know, and I had just nice time before it grew dusk to finish my arrangements. I prefer always to be ready before the dark comes.

"Bains touched my elbow as we walked into the room.

"'There's something I ought to have told you,' he said, looking rather sheepish. 'I've somehow felt a bit ashamed of it.'"

"'Out with it,' I replied.

"He hesitated a moment, then it came out with a jerk.

"'I told you about the grunting of the pigs,' he said. 'Well, I grunt too. I know it's horrible. When I lie there in bed and hear those sounds after I've come up, I just grunt back as if in reply. I can't stop myself. I just do it. Something makes me. I never told Doctor Witton that. I couldn't. I'm sure now you think me mad,' he concluded.

"He looked into my face, anxious and queerly ashamed.

"'It's only the natural sequence of the abnormal events, and I'm glad you told me,' I said, slapping him on the back. 'It follows logically on what you had already told me. I have had two cases that in some way resembled yours.'

"'What happened?' he asked me. 'Did they get better?'

"'One of them is alive and well today, Mr. Bains,' I replied. 'The other man lost his nerve, and fortunately for all concerned, he is dead.'

"I shut the door and locked it as I spoke, and Bains stared round, rather alarmed, I fancy, at my apparatus.

"'What are you going to do?' he asked. 'Will it be a dangerous experiment?'

"'Dangerous enough,' I answered, 'if you fail to follow my instructions absolutely in everything. We both run the risk of never leaving this room alive. Have I your word that I can depend on you to obey me whatever happens?'

"He stared round the room and then back at me.

"'Yes,' he replied. And, you know, I felt he would prove the right kind of stuff when the moment came.

"I began now to get things finally in train for the night's work. I told Bains to take off his coat and his boots. Then I dressed him entirely from head to foot in a single thick rubber combination-overall, with rubber gloves, and a helmet with ear-flaps of the same material attached.

"I dressed myself in a similar suit. Then I began on the next stage of the night's preparations.

"First I must tell you that the room measures thirty-nine feet by thirty-seven, and has a plain board floor over which is fitted a heavy, half-inch rubber covering.

"I had cleared the floor entirely, all but the exact centre where I had placed a glass-legged, upholstered table, a pile of vacuum tubes and batteries, and three pieces of special apparatus which my experiment required.

"'Now Bains,' I called, 'come and stand over here by this table. Don't move about. I've got to erect a protective 'barrier' round us, and on no account must either of us cross over it by even so much as a hand or foot, once it is built.'

"We went over to the middle of the room, and he stood by the glass-legged table while I began to fit the vacuum tubing together round us.

"I intended to use the new spectrum 'defense' which I have been perfecting lately. This, I must tell you, consists of seven glass vacuum circles with the red on the outside, and the colour circles lying inside it, in the order of orange, yellow, green, blue, indigo and violet.

"The room was still fairly light, but a slight quantity of dusk seemed to be already in the atmosphere, and I worked quickly.

"Suddenly, as I fitted the glass tubes together I was aware of some vague sense of nerve-strain, and glancing round at Bains who was standing there by the table I noticed him staring fixedly before him. He looked absolutely drowned in uncomfortable memories.

"'For goodness' sake stop thinking of those horrors,' I called out to him. 'I shall want you to think hard enough about them later; but in this specially constructed room it is better not to dwell on things of that kind till the barriers are up. Keep your mind on anything normal or superficial – the theatre will do – think about that last piece you saw at the Gaiety. I'll talk to you in a moment.'

"Twenty minutes later the 'barrier' was completed all round us, and I connected up the batteries. The room by this time was greying with the coming dusk, and the seven differently coloured circles shone out with extraordinary effect, sending out a cold glare.

"'By Jove!' cried Bains, 'that's very wonderful – very wonderful!'

"My other apparatus which I now began to arrange consisted of a specially made camera, a modified form of phonograph with ear-pieces instead of a horn, and a glass disk composed of many fathoms of glass vacuum tubes arranged in a special way. It had two wires leading to an electrode constructed to fit round the head.

"By the time I had looked over and fixed up these three things, night had practically come, and the darkened room shone most strangely in the curious upward glare of the seven vacuum tubes.

"'Now, Bains,' I said, 'I want you to lie on this table. Now put your hands down by your sides and lie quiet and think. You've just got two things to do,' I told him. 'One is to lie there and concentrate your thoughts on the details of the dream you are always having, and the other is not to move off this table whatever you see or hear, or whatever happens, unless I tell you. You understand, don't you?'

"'Yes,' he answered, 'I think you may rely on me not to make a fool of myself. I feel curiously safe with you somehow.'

"'I'm glad of that,' I replied. 'But I don't want you to minimise the possible danger too much. There may be horrible danger. Now, just let me fix this band on your head,' I added, as I adjusted the electrode. I gave him a few more instructions, telling him to concentrate his thoughts particularly upon the noises he heard just as he was waking, and I warned him again not to let himself fall asleep. 'Don't talk,' I said, 'and don't take any notice of me. If you find I disturb your concentration keep your eyes closed.'

"He lay back and I walked over to the glass disk, arranging the camera in front of it on its stand in such a way that the lens was opposite the centre of the disk.

"I had scarcely done this when a ripple of greenish light ran across the vacuum tubes of the disk. This vanished, and for maybe a minute there was complete darkness. Then the green light rippled once more across it – rippled and swung round, and began to dance in varying shades from a deep heavy green to a rank ugly shade; back and forward, back and forward.

"Every half second or so there shot across the varying greens a flicker of yellow, an ugly, heavy repulsive yellow, and then abruptly there came sweeping across the disk a great beat of muddy red. This died as quickly as it came, and gave place to the changing greens shot through by the unpleasant and ugly yellow hues. About every seventh second the disk was submerged, and the other colours momentarily blotted out by the great beat of heavy, muddy red which swept over everything.

"'He's concentrating on those sounds,' I said to myself, and I felt queerly excited as I hurried on with my operations. I threw a word over my shoulder to Bains.

"'Don't get scared, whatever happens,' I said. 'You're all right!'

"I proceeded now to operate my camera. It had a long roll of specially prepared paper ribbon in place of a film or plates. By turning the handle the roll passed through the machine exposing the ribbon.

"It took about five minutes to finish the roll, and during all that time the green lights predominated; but the dull heavy beat of muddy red never ceased to flow across the vacuum tubes of the disk at every seventh second. It was like a recurrent beat in some unheard and somehow displeasing melody.

"Lifting the exposed spool of paper ribbon out of the camera I laid it horizontally in the two 'rests' that I had arranged for it on my modified gramaphone. Where the paper had been acted upon by the varying coloured lights which had appeared on the disk, the prepared surface had risen in curious, irregular little waves.

"I unrolled about a foot of the ribbon and attached the loose end to an empty spool-roller (on the opposite side of the machine) which I had geared to the driving clockwork mechanism of the gramophone. Then I took the diaphragm and lowered it gently into place above the ribbon. Instead of the usual needle the diaphragm was fitted with a beautifully made metal-filament brush, about an inch broad, which just covered the whole breadth of the ribbon. This fine and fragile brush rested lightly on the prepared surface of the paper, and when I started the machine the ribbon began to pass under the brush, and as it passed, the delicate metal-filament 'bristles' followed every minute inequality of those tiny, irregular wave-like excrescences on the surface.

"I put the ear-pieces to my ears, and instantly I knew that I had succeeded in actually recording what Bains had heard in his sleep. In fact, I was even then hearing 'mentally' by means of his effort of memory. I was listening to what appeared to be the faint, far-off squealing and grunting of countless swine. It was extraordinary, and at the same time exquisitely horrible and vile. It frightened me, with a sense of my having come suddenly and unexpectedly too near to something foul and most abominably dangerous.

"So strong and imperative was this feeling that I twitched the ear-pieces out of my ears, and sat a while staring round the room trying to steady my sensations back to normality.

"The room looked strange and vague in the dull glow of light from the circles, and I had a feeling that a taint of monstrosity was all about me in the air. I remembered what Bains had told me of the feeling he'd always had after coming up out of 'that place' – as if some horrible atmosphere had followed him up and filled his bedroom. I understood him perfectly now – so much so that I had mentally used almost his exact phrase in explaining to myself what I felt.

"Turning round to speak to him I saw there was something curious about the centre of the 'defense'.

"Now, before I tell you fellows any more I must explain that there are certain, what I call 'focussing', qualities about this new 'defense' I've been trying.

"The Sigsand manuscript puts it something like this: 'Avoid diversities of colour; nor stand ye within the barrier of the colour lights; for in colour hath Satan a delight. Nor can he abide in the Deep if ye adventure against him armed with red purple. So be warned. Neither forget that in blue, which is God's colour in the Heavens, ye have safety.'

"You see, from that statement in the Sigsand manuscript I got my first notion for this new 'defense' of mine. I have aimed to make it a 'defense' and yet have 'focussing' or 'drawing' qualities such as the Sigsand hints at. I have experimented enormously, and I've proved that reds and purples – the two extreme colours of the spectrum – are fairly dangerous; so much so that I suspect they actually 'draw' or 'focus' the outside forces. Any action or 'meddling' on the part of the experimentalist is tremendously enhanced in its effect if the action is taken within barriers composed of these colours, in certain proportions and tints.

"In the same way blue is distinctly a 'general defense'. Yellow appears to be neutral, and green a wonderful protection within limits. Orange, as far as I can tell, is slightly attractive and indigo is dangerous by itself in a limited way, but in certain combinations with the other colours it becomes a very powerful 'defense'. I've not yet discovered a tenth of the possibilities of these circles of mine. It's a kind of colour organ upon which I seem to play a tune of colour combinations that can be either safe or infernal in its effects. You know I have a keyboard with a separate switch to each of the colour circles.

"Well, you fellows will understand now what I felt when I saw the curious appearance of the floor in the middle of the 'defense'. It looked exactly as if a circular shadow lay, not just on the floor, but a few inches above it. The shadow seemed to deepen and blacken at the centre even while I watched it. It appeared to be spreading from the centre outwardly, and all the time it grew darker.

"I was watchful, and not a little puzzled; for the combination of lights that I had switched on approximated a moderately safe 'general defense'. Understand, I had no intention of making a focus until I had learnt more. In fact, I meant that first investigation not to go beyond a tentative inquiry into the kind of thing I had got to deal with.

"I knelt down quickly and felt the floor with the palm of my hand, but it was quite normal to the feel, and that reassured me that there was no Saaaiti mischief abroad; for that is a form of danger which can involve, and make use of, the very material of the 'defense' itself. It can materialise out of everything except fire.

"As I knelt there I realised all at once that the legs of the table on which Bains lay were partly hidden in the ever blackening shadow, and my hands seemed to grow vague as I felt at the floor.

"I got up and stood away a couple of feet so as to see the phenomenon from a little distance. It struck me then that there was something different about the table itself. It seemed unaccountably lower.

"'It's the shadow hiding the legs,' I thought to myself. 'This promises to be interesting; but I'd better not let things go too far.'

"I called out to Bains to stop thinking so hard. 'Stop concentrating for a bit,' I said; but he never answered, and it occurred to me suddenly that the table appeared to be still lower.

"'Bains,' I shouted, 'stop thinking a moment.' Then in a flash I realised it. 'Wake up, man! Wake up!' I cried.

"He had fallen over asleep – the very last thing he should have done; for it increased the danger twofold. No wonder I had been getting such good results! The poor beggar was worn out with his sleepless nights. He neither moved nor spoke as I strode across to him.

"'Wake up!' I shouted again, shaking him by the shoulder.

"My voice echoed uncomfortably round the big empty room; and Bains lay like a dead man.

"As I shook him again I noticed that I appeared to be standing up to my knees in the circular shadow. It looked like the mouth of a pit. My legs, from the knees downwards, were vague. The floor under my feet felt solid and firm when I stamped on it; but all the same I had a feeling that things were going a bit too far, so striding across to the switchboard I switched on the 'full defense'.

"Stepping back quickly to the table I had a horrible and sickening shock. The table had sunk quite unmistakably. Its top was within a couple of feet of the floor, and the legs had that fore-shortened appearance that one sees when a stick is thrust into water. They looked vague and shadowy in the peculiar circle of dark shadows which had such an extraordinary resemblance to the black mouth of a pit. I could see only the top of the table plainly with Bains lying motionless on it; and the whole thing was going down, as I stared, into that black circle."

Chapter III

"**THERE WAS NOT** a moment to lose, and like a flash I caught Bains round his neck and body and lifted him clean up into my arms off the table. And as I lifted him he grunted like a great swine in my ear.

"The sound sent a thrill of horrible funk through me. It was just as though I held a hog in my arms instead of a human. I nearly dropped him. Then I held his face to the light and stared down at him. His eyes were half opened, and he was looking at me apparently as if he saw me perfectly.

"Then he grunted again. I could feel his small body quiver with the sound.

"I called out to him. 'Bains,' I said, 'can you hear me?'

"His eyes still gazed at me; and then, as we looked at each other, he grunted like a swine again.

"I let go one hand, and hit him across the cheek, a stinging slap.

"'Wake up, Bains!' I shouted. 'Wake up!' But I might have hit a corpse. He just stared up at me. And, suddenly I bent lower and looked into his eyes more closely. I never saw such a fixed, intelligent, mad horror as I saw there. It knocked out all my sudden disgust. Can you understand?

"I glanced round quickly at the table. It stood there at its normal height; and, indeed, it was in every way normal. The curious shadow that had somehow suggested to me the black mouth of the pit had vanished. I felt relieved; for it seemed to me that I had entirely broken up any possibility of a partial 'focus' by means of the full 'defense' which I had switched on.

"I laid Bains on the floor, and stood up to look round and consider what was best to do. I dared not step outside of the barriers, until any 'dangerous tensions' there might be in the room had been dissipated. Nor was it wise, even inside the full 'defense', to have him sleeping the kind of sleep he was in; not without certain preparations having been made first, which I had not made.

"I can tell you, I felt beastly anxious. I glanced down at Bains, and had a sudden fresh shock; for the peculiar circular shadow was forming all round him again, where he lay on the floor. His hands and face showed curiously vague, and distorted, as they might have looked through a few inches of faintly stained water. But his eyes were somehow clear to see. They were staring up, mute and terrible, at me, through that horrible darkening shadow.

"I stopped, and with one quick lift, tore him up off the floor into my arms, and for the third time he grunted like a swine, there in my arms. It was damnable.

"I stood up, in the barrier, holding Bains, and looked about the room again; then back at the floor. The shadow was still thick round about my feet, and I stepped quickly across to the other side of the table. I stared at the shadow, and saw that it had vanished; then I glanced down again at my feet, and had another shock; for the shadow was showing faintly again, all round where I stood.

"I moved a pace, and watched the shadow become invisible; and then, once more, like a slow stain, it began to grow about my feet.

"I moved again, a pace, and stared round the room, meditating a break for the door. And then, in that instant, I saw that this would be certainly impossible; for there was something indefinite in the atmosphere of the room – something that moved, circling slowly about the barrier.

"I glanced down at my feet, and saw that the shadow had grown thick about them. I stepped a pace to the right, and as it disappeared, I stared again round the big room and somehow it seemed tremendously big and unfamiliar. I wonder whether you can understand.

"As I stared I saw again the indefinite something that floated in the air of the room. I watched it steadily for maybe a minute. It went twice completely round the barrier in that time. And, suddenly, I saw it more distinctly. It looked like a small puff of black smoke.

"And then I had something else to think about; for all at once I was aware of an extraordinary feeling of vertigo, and in the same moment, a sense of sinking – I was sinking bodily. I literally sickened as I glanced down, for I saw in that moment that I had gone down, almost up to my thighs into what appeared to be actually the shadowy, but quite unmistakable, mouth of a pit. Do you understand? I was sinking down into this thing, with Bains in my arms.

"A feeling of furious anger came over me, and I swung my right boot forward with a fierce kick. I kicked nothing tangible, for I went clean through the side of the shadowy thing, and fetched up against the table, with a crash. I had come through something that made all my skin creep and tingle – an invisible, vague something which resembled an electric tension. I felt that if it had been stronger, I might not have been able to charge through as I had. I wonder if I make it clear to you?

"I whirled round, but the beastly thing had gone; yet even as I stood there by the table, the slow greying of a circular shadow began to form again about my feet.

"I stepped to the other side of the table, and leaned against it for a moment: for I was shaking from head to foot with a feeling of extraordinary horror upon me, that was in some way, different from any kind of horror I have ever felt. It was as if I had in that one moment been near something no human has any right to be near, for his soul's sake. And abruptly, I wondered whether I had not felt just one brief touch of the horror that the rigid Bains was even then enduring as I held him in my arms.

"Outside of the barrier there were now several of the curious little clouds. Each one looked exactly like a little puff of black smoke. They increased as I watched them, which I did for several minutes; but all the time as I watched, I kept moving from one part to another of the 'defense', so as to prevent the shadow forming round my feet again.

"Presently, I found that my constant changing of position had resolved into a slow monotonous walk round and round, inside the 'defense'; and all the time I had to carry the unnaturally rigid body of poor Bains.

"It began to tire me; for though he was small, his rigidity made him dreadfully awkward and tiring to hold, as you can understand; yet I could not think what else to do; for I had stopped shaking him, or trying to wake him, for the simple reason that he was as wide awake as I was mentally; though but physically inanimate, through one of those partial spiritual disassociations which he had tried to explain to me.

"Now I had previously switched out the red, orange, yellow and green circles, and had on the full defense of the blue end of the spectrum – I knew that one of the repelling vibrations of each of the three colours: blue, indigo and violet were beating out protectingly into space; yet they were proving insufficient, and I was in the position of having either to take some desperate action to stimulate Bains to an even greater effort of will than I judged him to be making, or else to risk experimenting with fresh combinations of the defensive colours.

"You see, as things were at that moment, the danger was increasing steadily; for plainly, from the appearance of the air of the room outside the barrier, there were some mighty dangerous tensions generating. While inside the danger was also increasing; the steady recurrence of the shadow proving that the 'defense' was insufficient.

"In short, I feared that Bains in his peculiar condition was literally a 'doorway' into the 'defense'; and unless I could wake him or find out the correct combinations of circles necessary to set up stronger repelling vibrations against that particular danger, there were very ugly possibilities ahead. I felt I had been incredibly rash not to have foreseen the possibility of Bains falling asleep under the hypnotic effect of deliberately paralleling the associations of sleep.

"Unless I could increase the repulsion of the barriers or wake him there was every likelihood of having to choose between a rush for the door – which the condition of the atmosphere outside the barrier showed to be practically impossible – or of throwing him outside the barrier, which, of course, was equally not possible.

"All this time I was walking round and round inside the barrier, when suddenly I saw a new development of the danger which threatened us. Right in the centre of the 'defense' the shadow had formed into an intensely black circle, about a foot wide.

"This increased as I looked at it. It was horrible to see it grow. It crept out in an ever widening circle till it was quite a yard across.

"Quickly I put Bains on the floor. A tremendous attempt was evidently going to be made by some outside force to enter the 'defense', and it was up to me to make a final effort to help Bains to 'wake up'. I took out my lancet, and pushed up his left coat sleeve.

"What I was going to do was a terrible risk, I knew, for there is no doubt that in some extraordinary fashion blood attracts.

"The Sigsand mentions it particularly in one passage which runs something like this: 'In blood there is the Voice which calleth through all space. Ye Monsters in ye Deep hear, and hearing, they lust. Likewise hath it a greater power to reclaim backward ye soul that doth wander foolish adrift from ye body in which it doth have natural abiding. But woe unto him that doth spill ye blood in ye deadly hour; for there will be surely Monsters that shall hear ye Blood Cry.'

"That risk I had to run. I knew that the blood would call to the outer forces; but equally I knew that it should call even more loudly to that portion of Bains' 'Essence' that was adrift from him, down in those depths.

"Before lancing him, I glanced at the shadow. It had spread out until the nearest edge was not more than two feet away from Bains' right shoulder; and the edge was creeping nearer, like the blackening edge of burning paper, even while I stared. The whole thing had a less shadowy, less ghostly appearance than at any time before. And it looked simply and literally like the black mouth of a pit.

"'Now, Bains,' I said, 'pull yourself together, man. Wake up!' And at the same time as I spoke to him, I used my lancet quickly but superficially.

"I watched the little red spot of blood well up, then trickle round his wrist and fall to the floor of the 'defense'. And in the moment that it fell the thing that I had feared happened. There was a sound like a low peal of thunder in the room, and curious deadly-looking flashes of light rippled here and there along the floor outside the barrier.

"Once more I called to him, trying to speak firmly and steadily as I saw that the horrible shadowy circle had spread across every inch of the floor space of the centre of the 'defense', making it appear as if both Bains and I were suspended above an unutterable black void – the black void that stared up at me out of the throat of that shadowy pit. And yet, all the time I could feel the floor solid under my knees as I knelt beside Bains holding his wrist.

"'Bains!' I called once more, trying not to shout madly at him. 'Bains, wake up! Wake up, man! Wake up!"

"But he never moved, only stared up at me with eyes of quiet horror that seemed to be looking at me out of some dreadful eternity.'"

Chapter IV

"BY THIS TIME the shadow had blackened all around us, and I felt that strangely terrible vertigo coming over me again. Jumping to my feet I caught up Bains in my arms and stepped over the first of the protective circles – the violet, and stood between it and the indigo circle, holding Bains as close to me as possible so as to prevent any portion of his helpless body from protruding outside the indigo and blue circles.

"From the black shadowy mouth which now filled the whole of the centre of the 'defense' there came a faint sound – not near but seeming to come up at me out of unknown abysses. Very, very faint and lost it sounded, but I recognised it as unmistakably the infinitely remote murmur of countless swine.

"And that same moment Bains, as if answering the sound, grunted like a swine in my arms.

"There I stood between the glass vacuum tubes of the circles, gazing dizzily into that black shadowy pit-mouth, which seemed to drop sheer into hell from below my left elbow.

"Things had gone so utterly beyond all that I had thought of, and it had all somehow come about so gradually and yet so suddenly, that I was really a bit below my natural self. I felt mentally paralysed, and could think of nothing except that not twenty feet away was the door and the outer natural world; and here was I face to face with some unthought-of danger, and all adrift, what to do to avoid it.

"You fellows will understand this better when I tell you that the bluish glare from the three circles showed me that there were now hundreds and hundreds of those small smoke-like puffs of black cloud circling round and round outside the barrier in an unvarying, unending procession.

"And all the time I was holding the rigid body of Bains in my arms, trying not to give way to the loathing that got me each time he grunted. Every twenty or thirty seconds he grunted, as if in answer to the sounds which were almost too faint for my normal hearing. I can tell you, it was like holding something worse than a corpse in my arms, standing there balanced between physical death on the one side and soul destruction on the other.

"Abruptly, from out of the deep that lay so close that my elbow and shoulder overhung it, there came again a hint, marvellously faint murmur of swine, so utterly far away that the sound was as remote as a lost echo.

"Bains answered it with a pig-like squeal that set every fibre in me protesting in sheer human revolt, and I sweated coldly from head to foot. Pulling myself together I tried to pierce down into the mouth of the great shadow when, for the second time, a low peel of thunder sounded in the room, and every joint in my body seemed to jolt and burn.

"In turning to look down the pit I had allowed one of Bains' heels to protrude for a moment slightly beyond the blue circle, and a fraction of the 'tension' outside the barrier had evidently discharged through Bains and me. Had I been standing directly inside the 'defense' instead of being 'insulated' from it by the violet circle, then no doubt things might have been much more serious. As it was, I had, psychically, that dreadful soiled feeling which the healthy human always experiences when he comes too closely in contact with certain Outer Monstrosities. Do you fellows remember how I had just the same feeling when the Hand came too near me in the 'Gateway' case?

"The physical effects were sufficiently interesting to mention; for Bains' left boot had been ripped open, and the leg of his trousers was charred to the knee, while all around the leg were numbers of bluish marks in the form of irregular spirals.

"I stood there holding Bains, and shaking from head to foot. My head ached and each joint had a queer numbish feeling; but my physical pains were nothing compared with my mental distress. I felt that we were done! I had no room to turn or move for the space between the violet circle which was the innermost, and the blue circle which was the outermost of those in use was thirty-one inches, including the one inch of the indigo circle. So you see I was forced to stand there like an image, fearing each moment lest I should get another shock, and quite unable to think what to do.

"I daresay five minutes passed in this fashion. Bains had not grunted once since the 'tension' caught him, and for this I was just simply thankful; though at first I must confess I had feared for a moment that he was dead.

"No further sounds had come up out of the black mouth to my left, and I grew steady enough again to begin to look about me, and think a bit. I leant again so as to look directly down into the shadowy pit. The edge of the circular mouth was now quite defined, and had a curious solid look, as if it were formed out of some substance like black glass.

"Below the edge, I could trace the appearance of solidity for a considerable distance, though in a vague sort of way. The centre of this extraordinary phenomenon was simple and unmitigated blackness – an utter velvety blackness that seemed to soak the very light out of the room down into it. I could see nothing else, and if anything else came out of it except a complete silence, it was the atmosphere of frightening suggestion that was affecting me more and more every minute.

"I turned away slowly and carefully, so as not to run any risks of allowing either Bains or myself to expose any part of us over the blue circle. Then I saw that things outside of the blue circle had developed considerably; for the odd, black puffs of smoke-like cloud had increased enormously and blent into a great, gloomy, circular wall of tufted cloud, going round and round and round eternally, and hiding the rest of the room entirely from me.

"Perhaps a minute passed, while I stared at this thing; and then, you know, the room was shaken slightly. This shaking lasted for three or four seconds, and then passed; but it came again in about half a minute, and was repeated from time to time. There was a queer oscillating quality in the shaking, that made me think suddenly of that Jarvee Haunting case. You remember it?

"There came again the shaking, and a ripple of deadly light seemed to play round the outside of the barrier; and then, abruptly, the room was full of a strange roaring – a brutish enormous yelling, grunting storm of swine-sounds.

"They fell away into a complete silence, and the rigid Bains grunted twice in my arms, as if answering. Then the storm of swine noise came again, beating up in a gigantic riot of brute sound that roared through the room, piping, squealing, grunting, and howling. And as it sank with a steady declination, there came a single gargantuan grunt out of some dreadful throat of monstrousness, and in one beat, the crashing chorus of unknown millions of swine came thundering and raging through the room again.

"There was more in that sound than mere chaos – there was a mighty devilish rhythm in it. Suddenly, it swept down again into a multitudinous swinish whispering and minor gruntings of unthinkable millions; and then with a rolling deafening bellow of sound came the single vast grunt. And, as if lifted upon it the swine roar of the millions of the beasts beat up through the room again; and at every seventh second, as I knew well enough without the need of the watch on my wrist, came the single storm beat of the great grunt out of the throat of unknowable monstrosity – and in my arms, Bains, the human, grunted in time to the swine melody – a rigid grunting monster there in my two arms.

"I tell you from head to foot I shook and sweated. I believe I prayed; but if I did I don't know what I prayed. I have never before felt or endured just what I felt, standing there in that thirty-one-inch space, with that grunting thing in my arms, and the hell melody beating up out of the great Deeps: and to my right, 'tensions' that would have torn me into a bundle of blazing tattered flesh, if I had jumped out over the barriers.

"And then, with an effect like a clap of unexpected thunder, the vast storm of sound ceased; and the room was full of silence and an unimaginable horror.

"This silence continued. I want to say something which may sound a bit silly; but the silence seemed to trickle round the room. I don't know why I felt it like that; but my words give you just what I seemed to feel, as I stood there holding the softly grunting body of Bains.

"The circular, gloomy wall of dense black cloud enclosed the barrier as completely as ever, and moved round and round and round, with a slow, 'eternal' movement. And at the back of that black wall of circling cloud, a dead silence went trickling round the room, out of my sight. Do you understand at all…?

"It seemed to me to show very clearly the state of almost insane mental and psychic tension I was enduring… The way in which my brain insisted that the silence was trickling round the room, interests me enormously; for I was either in a state approximating a phase of madness, or else I was, psychically, tuned to some abnormal pitch of awareness and sensitiveness in which silence had ceased to be an abstract quality, and had become to me a definite concrete element, much as (to use a stupidly crude illustration), the invisible moisture of the atmosphere becomes a visible and concrete element when it becomes deposited as water. I wonder whether this thought attracts you as it does me?

"And then, you know, a slow awareness grew in me of some further horror to come. This sensation or knowledge or whatever it should be named, was so strong that I had a sudden feeling of suffocation… I felt that I could bear no more; and that if anything else happened, I should just pull out my revolver and shoot Bains through the head, and then myself, and so end the whole dreadful business.

"This feeling, however, soon passed; and I felt stronger and more ready to face things again. Also, I had the first, though still indefinite, idea of a way in which to make things a bit safer; but I was too dazed to see how to 'shape' to help myself efficiently.

"And then a low, far-off whining stole up into the room, and I knew that the danger was coming. I leant slowly to my left, taking care not to let Bains' feet stick over the blue circle, and stared down into the blackness of the pit that dropped sheer into some Unknown, from under my left elbow.

"The whining died; but far down in the blackness, there was something – just a remote luminous spot. I stood in a grim silence for maybe ten long minutes, and looked down at the thing. It was increasing in size all the time, and had become much plainer to see; yet it was still lost in the far, tremendous Deep.

"Then, as I stood and looked, the low whining sound crept up to me again, and Bains, who had lain like a log in my arms all the time, answered it with a long animallike whine, that was somehow newly abominable.

"A very curious thing happened then; for all around the edge of the pit, that looked so peculiarly like black glass, there came a sudden, luminous glowing. It came and went oddly, smouldering queerly round and round the edge in an opposite direction to the circling of the wall of black, tufted cloud on the outside of the barrier.

"This peculiar glowing finally disappeared, and, abruptly, out of the tremendous Deep, I was conscious of a dreadful quality or 'atmosphere' of monstrousness that was coming up out of the pit. If I said there had been a sudden waft of it, this would very well describe the actuality of it; but the spiritual sickness of distress that it caused me to feel, I am simply stumped to explain to you. It was something that made me feel I should be soiled to the very core of me, if I did not beat it off from me with my will.

"I leant sharply away from the pit towards the outer of the burning circles. I meant to see that no part of my body should overhang the pit whilst that disgusting power was beating up out of the unknown depths.

"And thus it was, facing so rigidly away from the centre of the 'defense', I saw presently a fresh thing; for there was something, many things, I began to think, on the other side of the gloomy wall that moved everlastingly around the outside of the barrier.

"The first thing I noticed was a queer disturbance of the ever circling cloud-wall. This disturbance was within eighteen inches of the floor, and directly before me. There was a curious, 'puddling' action in the misty wall; as if something were meddling with it. The area of this peculiar little disturbance could not have been more than a foot across, and it did not remain opposite to me; but was taken round by the circling of the wall.

"When it came past me again, I noticed that it was bulging slightly inwards towards me: and as it moved away from me once more, I saw another similar disturbance, and then a third and a fourth, all in different parts of the slowly whirling black wall; and all of them were no more than about eighteen inches from the floor.

"When the first one came opposite me again, I saw that the slight bulge had grown into a very distinct protuberance towards me.

"All around the moving wall, there had now come these curious swellings. They continued to reach inwards, and to elongate; and all the time they kept in a constant movement.

"Suddenly, one of them broke, or opened, at the apex, and there protruded through, for an instant, the tip of a pallid, but unmistakable snout. It was gone at once, but I had seen the thing distinctly; and within a minute, I saw another one poke suddenly through the wall, to my right, and withdraw as quickly. I could not look at the base of the strange, black, moving circle about the barrier without seeing a swinish snout peep through momentarily, in this place or that.

"I stared at these things in a very peculiar state of mind. There was so great a weight of the abnormal about me, before and behind and every way, that to a certain extent it bred in me a sort of antidote to fear. Can you understand? It produced in me a temporary dazedness in which things and the horror of things became less real. I stared at them, as a child stares out from a fast train at a quickly passing night-landscape, oddly hit by the furnaces of unknown industries. I want you to try to understand.

"In my arms Bains lay quiet and rigid; and my arms and back ached until I was one dull ache in all my body; but I was only partly conscious of this when I roused momentarily from my psychic to my physical awareness, to shift him to another position, less intolerable temporarily to my tired arms and back.

"There was suddenly a fresh thing – a low but enormous, solitary grunt came rolling, vast and brutal into the room. It made the still body of Bains quiver against me, and he grunted thrice in return, with the voice of a young pig.

"High up in the moving wall of the barrier, I saw a fluffing out of the black tufted clouds; and a pig's hoof and leg, as far as the knuckle, came through and pawed a moment. This was about nine or ten feet above the floor. As it gradually disappeared I heard a low grunting from the other side of the veil of clouds which broke out suddenly into a diafaeon of brute-sound, grunting, squealing and swine-howling; all formed into a sound that was the essential melody of the brute – a grunting, squealing howling roar that rose, roar by roar, howl by howl and squeal by squeal to a crescendo of horrors – the bestial growths, longings, zests and acts of some grotto of hell… It is no use, I can't give it to you. I get dumb with the failure of my command over speech to tell you what that grunting, howling, roaring melody conveyed to me. It had in it something so inexplicably below the horizons of the soul in its monstrousness and fearfulness that the ordinary simple fear of death itself, with all its attendant agonies and terrors and sorrows, seemed like a thought of something peaceful and infinitely holy compared with the fear of those unknown elements in that dreadful roaring melody. And the sound was with me inside the room – there right in the room with me. Yet I seemed not to be aware of confining walls, but of echoing spaces of gargantuan corridors. Curious! I had in my mind those two words – gargantuan corridors.

"As the rolling chaos of swine melody beat itself away on every side, there came booming through it a single grunt, the single recurring grunt of the Hog; for I knew now that I was actually and without any doubt hearing the beat of monstrosity, the Hog.

"In the Sigsand the thing is described something like this: 'Ye Hogge which ye Almighty alone hath power upon. If in sleep or in ye hour of danger ye hear the voice of ye Hogge, cease ye to meddle. For ye Hogge doth be of ye outer Monstrous Ones, nor shall any human come nigh him nor continue meddling when ye hear his voice, for in ye earlier life upon the world did the Hogge have power, and shall again in ye end. And in that ye Hogge had once a power upon ye earth, so doth he crave sore to come again. And dreadful shall be ye harm to ye soul if ye continue to meddle, and to let ye beast come nigh. And I say unto all, if ye have brought this dire danger upon ye, have memory of ye cross, for of all sign hath ye Hogge a horror.'

"There's a lot more, but I can't remember it all and that is about the substance of it.

"There was I holding Bains who was all the time howling that dreadful grunt out with the voice of a swine. I wonder I didn't go mad. It was, I believe, the antidote of dazedness produced by the strain which helped me through each moment.

"A minute later, or perhaps five minutes, I had a sudden new sensation, like a warning cutting through my dulled feelings. I turned my head; but there was nothing behind me, and bending over to my left I seemed to be looking down into that black depth which fell away sheer under my left elbow. At that moment the roaring bellow of swine-noise ceased and I seemed to be staring down into miles of black aether at something that hung there – a pallid face floating far down and remote – a great swine face.

"And as I gazed I saw it grow bigger. A seemingly motionless, pallid swine-face rising upward out of the depth. And suddenly I realised that I was actually looking at the Hog."

Chapter V

"FOR PERHAPS a full minute I stared down through the darkness at that thing swimming like some far-off, deadwhite planet in the stupendous void. And then I simply woke up bang, as you might say, to the possession of my faculties. For just a certain over-degree of strain had brought about the dumbly helpful anaesthesia of dazedness, so this sudden overwhelming supreme fact of horror produced, in turn, its reaction from inertness to action. I passed in one moment from listlessness to a fierce efficiency.

"I knew that I had, through some accident, penetrated beyond all previous 'bounds', and that I stood where no human soul had any right to be, and that in but a few of the puny minutes of earth's time I might be dead.

"Whether Bains had passed beyond the 'lines of retraction' or not, I could not tell. I put him down carefully but quickly on his side, between the inner circles – that is, the violet circle and the indigo circle – where he lay grunting slowly. Feeling that the dreadful moment had come I drew out my automatic. It seemed best to make sure of our end before that thing in the depth came any nearer: for once Bains in his present condition came within what I might term the 'inductive forces' of the monster, he would cease to be human. There would happen, as in that case of Aster who stayed outside the pentacles in the Black Veil Case, what can only be described as a pathological, spiritual change – literally in other words, soul destruction.

"And then something seemed to be telling me not to shoot. This sounds perhaps a bit superstitious; but I meant to kill Bains in that moment, and what stopped me was a distinct message from the outside.

"I tell you, it sent a great thrill of hope through me, for I knew that the forces which govern the spinning of the outer circle were intervening. But the very fact of the intervention proved to me afresh the enormous spiritual peril into which we had stumbled; for that inscrutable Protective Force only intervenes between the human soul and the Outer Monstrosities.

"The moment I received that message I stood up like a flash and turned towards the pit, stepping over the violet circle slap into the mouth of darkness. I had to take the risk in order to get at the switch board which lay on the glass shelf under the table top in the centre. I could not shake free from the horror of the idea that I might fall down through that awful blackness. The floor felt solid enough under me; but I seemed to be walking on nothing above a black void, like an inverted starless night, with the face of the approaching Hog rising up from far down under my feet – a silent, incredible thing out of the abyss – a pallid, floating swine-face, framed in enormous blackness.

"Two quick, nervous strides took me to the table standing there in the centre with its glass legs apparently resting on nothing. I grabbed out the switch board, sliding out the vulcanite plate which carried the switch-control of the blue circle. The battery which fed this circle was the right-hand one of the row of seven, and each battery was marked with the letter of its circle painted on it, so that in an emergency I could select any particular battery in a moment.

"As I snatched up the B switch I had a grim enough warning of the unknown dangers that I was risking in that short journey of two steps; for that dreadful sense of vertigo returned suddenly and for one horrible moment I saw everything through a blurred medium as if I were trying to look through water.

"Below me, far away down between my feet I could see the Hog which, in some peculiar way, looked different – clearer and much nearer, and enormous. I felt it had got nearer to me all in a moment. And suddenly I had the impression I was descending bodily.

"I had a sense of a tremendous force being used to push me over the side of that pit, but with every shred of will power I had in me I hurled myself into the smoky appearance that hid everything and reached the violet circle where Bains lay in front of me.

"Here I crouched down on my heels, and with my two arms out before me I slipped the nails of each forefinger under the vulcanite base of the blue circle, which I lifted very gently so that when the base was far enough from the floor I could push the tips of my fingers underneath. I took care to keep from reaching farther under than the inner edge of the glowing tube which rested on the two-inch-broad foundation of vulcanite.

"Very slowly I stood upright, lifting the side of the blue circle with me. My feet were between the indigo and the violet circles, and only the blue circle between me and sudden death; for if it had snapped with the unusual strain I was putting upon it by lifting it like that, I knew that I should in all probability go west pretty quickly.

"So you fellows can imagine what I felt like. I was conscious of a disagreeable faint prickling that was strongest in the tips of my fingers and wrists, and the blue circle seemed to vibrate strangely as if minute particles of something were impinging upon it in countless millions. Along the shining glass tubes for a couple of feet on each side of my hands a queer haze of tiny sparks boiled and whirled in the form of an extraordinary halo.

"Stepping forward over the indigo circle I pushed the blue circle out against the slowly moving wall of black cloud causing a ripple of tiny pale flashes to curl in over the circle. These flashes ran along the vacuum tube until they came to the place where the blue circle crossed the indigo, and there they flicked off into space with sharp cracks of sound.

"As I advanced slowly and carefully with the blue circle a most extraordinary thing happened, for the moving wall of cloud gave from it in a great belly of shadow, and appeared to thin away from before it. Lowering my edge of the circle to the floor I stepped over Bains and right into the mouth of the pit, lifting the other side of the circle over the table. It creaked as if it were about to break in half as I lifted it, but eventually it came over safely.

"When I looked again into the depth of that shadow I saw below me the dreadful pallid head of the Hog floating in a circle of night. It struck me that it glowed very slightly – just a vague luminosity. And quite near – comparatively. No one could have judged distances in that black void.

"Picking up the edge of the blue circle again as I had done before, I took it out further till it was half clear of the indigo circle. Then I picked up Bains and carried him to that portion of the floor guarded by the part of the blue circle which was clear of the 'defense'. Then I lifted the circle and started to move it forward as quickly as I dared, shivering each time the joints squeaked as the whole fabric of it groaned with the strain I was putting upon it. And all the time the moving wall of tufted clouds gave from the edge of the blue circle, bellying away from it in a marvellous fashion as if blown by an unheard wind.

"From time to time little flashes of light had begun to flick in over the blue circle, and I began to wonder whether it would be able to hold out the 'tension' until I had dragged it clear of the defense.

"Once it was clear I hoped the abnormal stress would cease from about us, and concentrate chiefly around the 'defense' again, and the attractions of the negative 'tension'.

"Just then I heard a sharp tap behind me, and the blue circle jarred somewhat, having now ridden completely over the violet and indigo circles, and dropped clear on to the floor. The same instant there came a low rolling noise as of thunder, and a curious roaring. The black circling wall had thinned away from around us and the room showed clearly once more, yet nothing was to be seen except that now and then a peculiar bluish flicker of light would ripple across the floor.

"Turning to look at the 'defense' I noticed it was surrounded by the circling wall of black cloud, and looked strangely extraordinary seen from the outside. It resembled a slightly swaying squat funnel of whirling black mist reaching from the floor to the ceiling, and through it I could see glowing, sometimes vague and sometimes plain, the indigo and violet circles. And then as I watched, the whole room seemed suddenly filled with an awful presence which pressed upon me with a weight of horror that was the very essence of spiritual deathliness.

"Kneeling there in the blue circle by Bains, my initiative faculties stupefied and temporarily paralysed, I could form no further plan of escape, and indeed I seemed to care for nothing at the moment. I felt I had already escaped from immediate destruction and I was strung up to an amazing pitch of indifference to any minor horrors.

"Bains all this while had been quietly lying on his side. I rolled him over and looked closely at his eyes, taking care on account of his condition not to gaze into them; for if he had passed beyond the 'line of retraction' he would be dangerous. I mean, if the 'wandering' part of his essence had been assimilated by the Hog, then Bains would be spiritually accessible and might be even then no more than the outer form of the man, charged with radiation of the monstrous ego of the Hog, and therefore capable of what I might term for want of a more exact phrase, a psychically infective force; such force being more readily transmitted through the eyes than any other way, and capable of producing a brain storm of an extremely dangerous character.

"I found Bains, however, with both eyes with an extraordinary distressed interned quality; not the eyeballs, remember, but a reflex action transmitted from the 'mental eye' to the physical eye, and giving to the physical eye an expression of thought instead of sight. I wonder whether I make this clear to you?

"Abruptly, from every part of the room there broke out the noise of those hoofs again, making the place echo with the sound as if a thousand swine had started suddenly from an absolute immobility into a mad charge. The whole riot of animal sound seemed to heave itself in one wave towards the oddly swaying and circling funnel of black cloud which rose from floor to ceiling around the violet and indigo circles.

"As the sounds ceased I saw something was rising up through the middle of the 'defense'. It rose with a slow steady movement. I saw it pale and huge through the swaying, whirling funnel of cloud – a monstrous pallid snout rising out of that unknowable abyss... It rose higher like a huge pale mound. Through a thinning of the cloud curtain I saw one small eye... I shall never see a pig's eye again without feeling something of what I felt then. A pig's eye with a sort of hell-light of vile understanding shining at the back of it."

Chapter VI

AND THEN suddenly a dreadful terror came over me, for I saw the beginning of the end that I had been dreading all along – I saw through the slow whirl of the cloud curtains that the violet circle had begun to leave the floor. It was being taken up on the spread of the vast snout.

"Straining my eyes to see through the swaying funnel of clouds I saw that the violet circle had melted and was running down the pale sides of the snout in streams of violet-coloured fire. And as it melted there came a change in the atmosphere of the room. The black funnel shone with a dull gloomy red, and a heavy red glow filled the room.

"The change was such as one might experience if one had been looking through a protective glass at some light and the glass had been suddenly removed. But there was a further change that I realised directly through my feelings. It was as if the horrible presence in the room had come closer to my own soul. I wonder if I am making it at all clear to you. Before, it had oppressed me somewhat as a death on a very gloomy and dreary day beats down upon one's spirit. But now there was a savage menace, and the actual feeling of a foul thing close up against me. It was horrible, simply horrible.

"And then Bains moved. For the first time since he went to sleep the rigidity went out of him, and rolling suddenly over on to his stomach he fumbled up in a curious animallike fashion, on to his hands and feet. Then he charged straight across the blue circle towards the thing in the 'defense'.

"With a shriek I jumped to pull him back; but it was not my voice that stopped him. It was the blue circle. It made him give back from it as though some invisible hand had jerked him backwards. He threw up his head like a hog, squealing with the voice of a swine, and started off round the inside of the blue circle. Round and round it he went, twice attempting to bolt across it to the horror in that swaying funnel of cloud. Each time he was thrown back, and each time he squealed like a great swine, the sounds echoing round the room in a horrible fashion as though they came from somewhere a long way off.

"By this time I was fairly sure that Bains had indeed passed the 'line of retraction', and the knowledge brought a fresh and more hopeless horror and pity to me, and a grimmer fear for myself. I knew that if it were so, it was not Bains I had with me in the circle but a monster, and that for my own last chance of safety I should have to get him outside of the circle.

"He had ceased his tireless running round and round, and now lay on his side grunting continually and softly in a dismal kind of way. As the slowly whirling clouds thinned a little I saw again that pallid face with some clearness. It was still rising, but slowly, very slowly, and again a hope grew in me that it might be checked by the 'defense'. Quite plainly I saw that the horror was looking at Bains, and at that moment I saved my own life and soul by looking down. There, close to me on the floor was the thing that looked like Bains, its hands stretched out to grip my ankles. Another second, and I should have been tripped outwards. Do you realise what that would have meant?

"It was no time to hesitate. I simply jumped and came down crash with my knees on top of Bains. He lay quiet enough after a short struggle; but I took off my braces and lashed his hands up behind him. And I shivered with the very touch of him, as though I was touching something monstrous.

"By the time I had finished I noticed that the reddish glow in the room had deepened quite considerably, and the whole room was darker. The destruction of the violet circle had reduced the light perceptibly; but the darkness that I am speaking of was something more than that. It seemed as if something now had come into the atmosphere of the room – a sort of gloom, and in spite of the shining of the blue circle and the indigo circle inside the funnel of cloud, there was now more red light than anything else.

"Opposite me the huge, cloud-shrouded monster in the indigo circle appeared to be motionless. I could see its outline vaguely all the time, and only when the cloud funnel thinned could I see it plainly – a vast, snouted mound, faintly and whitely luminous, one gargantuan side turned towards me, and near the base of the slope a minute slit out of which shone one whitish eye.

"Presently through the thin gloomy red vapour I saw something that killed the hope in me, and gave me a horrible despair; for the indigo circle, the final barrier of the defense, was being slowly lifted into the air – the Hog had begun to rise higher. I could see its dreadful snout rising upwards out of the cloud. Slowly, very slowly, the snout rose up, and the indigo circle went up with it.

"In the dead stillness of that room I got a strange sense that all eternity was tense and utterly still as if certain powers knew of this horror I had brought into the world... And then I had an awareness of something coming... something from far, far away. It was as if some hidden unknown part of my brain knew it. Can you understand? There was somewhere in the heights of space a light that was coming near. I seemed to hear it coming. I could just see the body of Bains on the floor, huddled and shapeless and inert. Within the swaying veil of cloud the monster showed as a vast pale, faintly luminous mound, hugely snouted – an infernal hillock of monstrosity, pallid and deadly amid the redness that hung in the atmosphere of the room.

"Something told me that it was making a final effort against the help that was coming. I saw the indigo circle was now some inches from the floor, and every moment I expected to see it flash into streams of indigo fire running down the pale slopes of the snout. I could see the circle beginning to move upward at a perceptible speed. The monster was triumphing.

"Out in some realm of space a low continuous thunder sounded. The thing in the great heights was coming fast, but it could never come in time. The thunder grew from a low, far mutter into a deep steady rolling of sound... It grew louder and louder, and as it grew I saw the indigo circle, now shining through the red gloom of the room, was a whole foot off the floor. I thought I saw a faint splutter of indigo light... The final circle of the barrier was beginning to melt.

"That instant the thunder of the thing in flight which my brain heard so plainly, rose into a crashing, a worldshaking bellow of speed, making the room rock and vibrate to an immensity of sound. A strange flash of blue flame ripped open the funnel of cloud momentarily from top to base, and I saw for one brief instant the pallid monstrosity of the Hog, stark and pale and dreadful.

"Then the sides of the funnel joined again hiding the thing from me as the funnel became submerged quickly into a dome of silent blue light – God's own colour! All at once it seemed the cloud had gone, and from floor to ceiling of the room, in awful majesty, like a living Presence, there appeared that dome of blue fire banded with three rings of green light at equal distances. There was no sound or movement, not even a flicker, nor could I see anything in the light: for looking into it was like looking into the cold blue of the skies. But I felt sure that there had come to our aid one of those inscrutable forces which govern the spinning of the outer circle, for the dome of blue light, banded with three green bands of silent fire, was the outward or visible sign of an enormous force, undoubtedly of a defensive nature.

"Through ten minutes of absolute silence I stood there in the blue circle watching the phenomenon. Minute by minute I saw the heavy repellent red driven out of the room as the place lightened quite noticeably. And as it lightened, the body of Bains began to resolve out of a shapeless length of shadow, detail by detail, until I could see the braces with which I had lashed his wrists together.

"And as I looked at him his body moved slightly, and in a weak but perfectly sane voice he said:

"'I've had it again! My God! I've had it again!'

"I knelt down quickly by his side and loosened the braces from his wrists, helping him to turn over and sit up. He gripped my arm a little crazily with both hands.

"'I went to sleep after all,' he said. 'And I've been down there again. My God! It nearly had me. I was down in that awful place and it seemed to be just round a great corner, and I was stopped from coming back. I seemed to have been fighting for ages and ages. I felt I was going mad. Mad! I've been nearly down into a hell. I could hear you calling down to me from some awful height. I could hear your voice echoing along yellow passages. They were yellow. I know they were. And I tried to come and I couldn't.'

"'Did you see me?' I asked him when he stopped, gasping.

"'No,' he answered, leaning his head against my shoulder. 'I tell you it nearly got me that time. I shall never dare go to sleep again as long as I live. Why didn't you wake me?'

"'I did,' I told him. 'I had you in my arms most of the time. You kept looking up into my eyes as if you knew I was there.'

"'I know,' he said. 'I remember now; but you seemed to be up at the top of a frightful hole, miles and miles up from me, and those horrors were grunting and squealing and howling, and trying to catch me and keep me down there. But I couldn't see anything – only the yellow walls of those passages. And all the time there was something round the corner.'

"'Anyway, you're safe enough now,' I told him. 'And I'll guarantee you shall be safe in the future.'

"The room had grown dark save for the light from the blue circle. The dome had disappeared, the whirling funnel of black cloud had gone, the Hog had gone, and the light had died out of the indigo circle. And the atmosphere of the room was safe and normal again as I proved by moving the switch, which was near me, so as to lessen the defensive power of the blue circle and enable me to 'feel' the outside tension. Then I turned to Bains.

"'Come along,' I said. 'We'll go and get something to eat, and have a rest.'

"But Bains was already sleeping like a tired child, his head pillowed on his hand. 'Poor little devil!' I said as I picked him up in my arms. 'Poor little devil!'

"I walked across to the main switchboard and threw over the current so as to throw the 'V' protective pulse out of the four walls and the door; then I carried Bains out into the sweet wholesome normality of everything. It seemed wonderful, coming out of that chamber of horrors, and it seemed wonderful still to see my bedroom door opposite, wide open, with the bed looking so soft and white as usual – so ordinary and human. Can you chaps understand?

"I carried Bains into the room and put him on the couch; and then it was I realised how much I'd been up against, for when I was getting myself a drink I dropped the bottle and had to get another.

"After I had made Bains drink a glass I laid him on the bed.

"'Now,' I said, 'look into my eyes fixedly. Do you hear me? You are going off to sleep safely and soundly, and if anything troubles you, obey me and wake up. Now, sleep – sleep – sleep!'

"I swept my hands down over his eyes half a dozen times, and he fell over like a child. I knew that if the danger came again he would obey my will and wake up. I intend to cure him, partly by hypnotic suggestion, partly by a certain electrical treatment which I am getting Doctor Witton to give him.

"That night I slept on the couch, and when I went to look at Bains in the morning I found him still sleeping, so leaving him there I went into the test room to examine results. I found them very surprising.

"Inside the room I had a queer feeling, as you can imagine. It was extraordinary to stand there in that curious bluish light from the 'treated' windows, and see the blue circle lying, still glowing, where I had left it; and further on, the 'defense', lying circle within circle, all 'out'; and in the centre the glass-legged table standing where a few hours before it had been submerged in the horrible monstrosity of the Hog. I tell you, it all seemed like a wild and horrible dream as I stood there and looked. I have carried out some curious tests in there before now, as you know, but I've never come nearer to a catastrophe.

"I left the door open so as not to feel shut in, and then I walked over to the 'defense'. I was intensely curious to see what had happened physically under the action of such a force as the Hog. I found unmistakable signs that proved the thing had been indeed a Saaitii manifestation, for there had been no psychic or physical illusion about the melting of the violet circle. There remained nothing of it except a ring of patches of melted glass. The gutta base had been fused entirely, but the floor and everything was intact. You see, the Saaitii forms can often attack and destroy, or even make use of, the very defensive material used against them.

"Stepping over the outer circle and looking closely at the indigo circle I saw that it was melted clean through in several places. Another fraction of time and the Hog would have been free to expand as an invisible mist of horror and destruction into the atmosphere of the world. And then, in that very moment of time, salvation had come. I wonder if you can get my feelings as I stood there staring down at the destroyed barrier."

Carnacki began to knock out his pipe which is always a sign that he has ended his tale, and is ready to answer any questions we may want to ask.

Taylor was first in. "Why didn't you use the Electric Pentacle as well as your new spectrum circles?" he asked.

"Because," replied Carnacki, "the pentacle is simply 'defensive' and I wished to have the power to make a 'focus' during the early part of the experiment, and then, at the critical moment, to change the combination of the colours so as to have a 'defense' against the results of the 'focus'. You follow me.

"You see," he went on, seeing we hadn't grasped his meaning, "there can be no 'focus' within a pentacle. It is just of a 'defensive' nature. Even if I had switched the current out of the electric pentacle I should still have had to contend with the peculiar and undoubtedly 'defensive' power that its form seems to exert, and this would have been sufficient to 'blur' the focus.

"In this new research work I'm doing, I'm bound to use a 'focus' and so the pentacle is barred. But I'm not sure it matters. I'm convinced this new spectrum 'defense' of mine will prove absolutely invulnerable when I've learnt how to use it; but it will take me some time. This last case has taught me something new. I had never thought of combining green with blue; but the three bands of green in the blue of that dome has set me thinking. If only I knew the right combinations! It's the combinations I've got to learn. You'll understand better the importance of these combinations when I remind you that green by itself is, in a very limited way, more deadly than red itself – and red is the danger colour of all."

"Tell us, Carnacki," I said, "what is the Hog? Can you? I mean what kind of monstrosity is it? Did you really see it, or was it all some horrible, dangerous kind of dream? How do you know it was one of the outer monsters? And what is the difference between that sort of danger and the sort of thing you saw in the Gateway of the Monster case? And what...?"

"Steady!" laughed Carnacki. "One at a time! I'll answer all your questions; but I don't think I'll take them quite in your order. For instance, speaking about actually seeing the Hog, I might say that, speaking generally, things seen of a 'ghostly' nature are not seen with the eyes; they are seen with the mental eye which has this psychic quality, not always developed to a useable state, in addition to its 'normal' duty of revealing to the brain what our physical eyes record.

"You will understand that when we see 'ghostly' things it is often the 'mental' eye performing simultaneously the duty of revealing to the brain what the physical eye sees as well as what it sees itself. The two sights blending their functions in such a fashion gives us the impression that we are actually seeing through our physical eyes the whole of the 'sight' that is being revealed to the brain.

"In this way we get an impression of seeing with our physical eyes both the material and the immaterial parts of an 'abnormal' scene; for each part being received and revealed to the brain by machinery suitable to the particular purpose appears to have equal value of reality that is, it appears to be equally material. Do you follow me?"

We nodded our assent, and Carnacki continued:

"In the same way, were anything to threaten our psychic body we should have the impression, generally speaking, that it was our physical body that had been threatened, because our psychic sensations and impressions would be super-imposed upon our physical, in the same way that our psychic and our physical sight are super-imposed.

"Our sensations would blend in such a way that it would be impossible to differentiate between what we felt physically and what we felt psychically. To explain better what I mean. A man may seem to himself, in a 'ghostly' adventure, to fall actually. That is, to be falling in a physical sense; but all the while it may be his psychic entity, or being – call it what you will – that is falling. But to his brain there is presented the sensation of falling all together. Do you get me?

"At the same time, please remember that the danger is none the less because it is his psychic body that falls. I am referring to the sensation I had of falling during the time of stepping across the mouth of that pit. My physical body could walk over it easily and feel the floor solid under me; but my psychic body was in very real danger of falling. Indeed, I may be said to have literally carried my psychic body over, held within me by the pull of my lifeforce. You see, to my psychic body the pit was as real and as actual as a coal pit would have been to my physical body. It was merely the pull of my life-force which prevented my psychic body from falling out of me, rather like a plummet, down through the everlasting depths in obedience to the giant pull of the monster.

"As you will remember, the pull of the Hog was too great for my life-force to withstand, and, psychically, I began to fall. Immediately on my brain was recorded a sensation identical with that which would have been recorded on it had my actual physical body been falling. It was a mad risk I took, but as you know, I had to take it to get to the switch and the battery. When I had that physical sense of falling and seemed to see the black misty sides of the pit all around me, it was my mental eye recording upon the brain what it was seeing. My psychic body had actually begun to fall and was really below the edge of the pit but still in contact with me. In other words my physical magnetic and psychic 'haloes' were still mingled. My physical body was still standing firmly upon the floor of the room, but if I had not each time by effort or will forced my physical body across to the side, my psychic body would have fallen completely out of 'contact' with me, and gone like some ghostly meteorite, obedient to the pull of the Hog.

"The curious sensation I had of forcing myself through an obstructing medium was not a physical sensation at all, as we understand that word, but rather the psychic sensation of forcing my entity to re-cross the 'gap' that had already formed between my falling psychic body now below the edge of the pit and my physical body standing on the floor of the room. And that 'gap' was full of a force that strove to prevent my body and soul from rejoining. It was a terrible experience. Do you remember how I could still see with my brain through the eyes of my psychic body, though it had already fallen some distance out of me? That is an extraordinary thing to remember.

"However, to get ahead, all 'ghostly' phenomena are extremely diffuse in a normal state. They become actively physically dangerous in all cases where they are concentrated. The best off-hand illustration I can think of is the all-familiar electricity – a force which, by the way, we are too prone to imagine we understand because we've named and harnessed it, to use a popular phrase. But we don't understand it at all! It is still a complete fundamental mystery. Well, electricity when diffused is an 'imagined and unpictured something', but when concentrated it is sudden death. Have you got me in that?

"Take, for instance, that explanation, as a very, very crude sort of illustration of what the Hog is. The Hog is one of those million-mile-long clouds of 'nebulosity' lying in the Outer Circle. It is because of this that I term those clouds of force the Outer Monsters.

"What they are exactly is a tremendous question to answer. I sometimes wonder whether Dodgson there realises just how impossible it is to answer some of his questions," and Carnacki laughed.

"But to make a brief attempt at it. There is around this planet, and presumably others, of course, circles of what I might call 'emanation'. This is an extremely light gas, or shall I say ether. Poor ether, it's been hard worked in its time!

"Go back one moment to your school-days, and bear in mind that at one time the earth was just a sphere of extremely hot gases. These gases condensed in the form of materials and other 'solid' matters; but there are some that are not yet solidified – air, for instance. Well, we have an earth-sphere of solid matter on which to stamp as solidly as we like; and round about that sphere there lies a ring of gases the constituents of which enter largely into all life, as we understand life – that is, air.

"But this is not the only circle of gas which is floating round us. There are, as I have been forced to conclude, larger and more attenuated 'gas' belts lying, zone on zone, far up and around us. These compose what I have called the inner circles. They are surrounded in turn by a circle or belt of what I have called, for want of a better word, 'emanations'.

"This circle which I have named the Outer Circle cannot lie less than a hundred thousand miles off the earth, and has a thickness which I have presumed to be anything between five and ten million miles. I believe, but I cannot prove, that it does not spin with the earth but in the opposite direction, for which a plausible cause might be found in the study of the theory upon which a certain electrical machine is constructed.

"I have reason to believe that the spinning of this, the Outer Circle, is disturbed from time to time through causes which are quite unknown to me, but which I believe are based in physical phenomena. Now, the Outer Circle is the psychic circle, yet it is also physical. To illustrate what I mean I must again instance electricity, and say that just as electricity discovered itself to us as something quite different from any of our previous conceptions of matter, so is the Psychic or Outer Circle different from any of our previous conceptions of matter. Yet it is none the less physical in its origin, and in the sense that electricity is physical, the Outer or Psychic Circle is physical in its constituents. Speaking pictorially it is, physically, to the Inner Circle what the Inner Circle is to the upper strata of the air, and what the air – as we know that intimate gas – is to the waters and the waters to the solid world. You get my line of suggestion?"

We all nodded, and Carnacki resumed.

"Well, now let me apply all this to what I am leading up to. I suggest that these million-mile-long clouds of monstrosity which float in the Psychic or Outer Circle, are bred of the elements of that circle. They are tremendous psychic forces, bred out of its elements just as an octopus or shark is bred out of the sea, or a tiger or any other physical force is bred out of the elements of its earth-and-air surroundings.

"To go further, a physical man is composed entirely from the constituents of earth and air, by which terms I include sunlight and water and 'condiments'! In other words without earth and air he could not *be*! Or to put it another way, earth and air breed within themselves the materials of the body and the brain, and therefore, presumably, the machine of intelligence.

"Now apply this line of thought to the Psychic or Outer Circle which though so attenuated that I may crudely presume it to be approximate to our conception of aether, yet contains all the elements for the production of certain phases of force and intelligence. But these elements are in a form as little like matter as the emanations of scent are like the scent itself. Equally, the force-and-intelligence-producing capacity of the Outer Circle no more approximates to the life-and-intelligence – producing capacity of the earth and air than the results of the Outer Circle constituents resemble the results of earth and air. I wonder whether I make it clear.

"And so it seems to me we have the conception of a huge psychic world, bred out of the physical, lying far outside of this world and completely encompassing it, except for the doorways about which I hope to tell you some other evening. This enormous psychic world of the Outer Circle 'breeds' – if I may use the term, its own psychic forces and intelligences, monstrous and otherwise, just as this world produces its own physical forces and intelligences – beings, animals, insects, etc., monstrous and otherwise.

"The monstrosities of the Outer Circle are malignant towards all that we consider most desirable, just in the same way a shark or a tiger may be considered malignant, in a physical way, to all that we consider desirable. They are predatory – as all positive force is predatory. They have desires regarding us which are incredibly more dreadful to our minds when comprehended than an intelligent sheep would consider our desires towards its own carcass. They plunder and destroy to satisfy lusts and hungers exactly as other forms of existence plunder and destroy to satisfy their lusts and hungers. And the desire of these monsters is chiefly, if not always, for the psychic entity of the human.

"But that's as much as I can tell you tonight. Some evening I want to tell you about the tremendous mystery of the Psychic Doorways. In the meantime, have I made things a bit clearer to you, Dodgson?"

"Yes, and no," I answered. "You've been a brick to make the attempt, but there are still about ten thousand other things I want to know."

Carnacki stood up. "Out you go!" he said using the recognised formula in friendly fashion. "Out you go! I want a sleep."

And shaking him by the hand we strolled out on to the quiet Embankment.

Mive

Carl Jacobi

CARLING'S MARSH, some called it, but more often it was known by the name of Mive. Strange name that – Mive. And it was a strange place. Five wild, desolate miles of thick water, green masses of some kind of kelp, and violent vegetable growth. To the east the cypress trees swelled more into prominence, and this district was vaguely designated by the villagers as the Flan. Again a strange name, and again I offer no explanation. A sense of depression, of isolation perhaps, which threatened to crush any buoyancy of feeling possessed by the most hardened traveler, seemed to emanate from this lonely wasteland. Was it any wonder that its observers always told of seeing it at night, before a storm, or in the spent afternoon of a dark and frowning day? And even if they had wandered upon it, say on a bright morning in June, the impression probably would have been the same, for the sun glittering upon the surface of the olive water would have lost its exuberant brilliance and become absorbed in the roily depths below. However, the presence of this huge marsh would have interested no one, had not the east road skirted for a dismal quarter-mile its melancholy shore.

The east road, avoided, being frequently impassable because of high water, was a roundabout connection between the little towns of Twellen and Lamarr. The road seemed to have been irresistibly drawn toward the Mive, for it cut a huge half-moon across the country for seemingly no reason at all. But this arc led through a wilderness of an entirely different aspect from the land surrounding the other trails. Like the rest it started among the hills, climbed the hills, and rambled down the hills, but after passing Echo Lake, that lowering tarn locked in a deep ravine, it straggled up a last hillock and swept down upon a large flat. And as one proceeded, the flat steadily sank lower; it forgot the hills, and the ground, already damp, became sodden and quivering under the feet.

And then looming up almost suddenly – Mive! …a morass at first, a mere bog, then a jungle of growth repulsive in its over-luxuriance, and finally a sea of kelp, an inland Sargasso.

Just why I had chosen the east road for a long walk into the country I don't really know. In fact, my reason for taking such a hike at all was rather vague. The day was certainly anything but ideal; a raw wind whipping in from the south, and a leaden sky typical of early September lent anything but an inviting aspect to those rolling Rentharpian hills. But walk I did, starting out briskly as the inexperienced all do, and gradually slowing down until four o'clock found me plodding almost mechanically along the flat. I dare say every passer-by, no matter how many times he frequented the road, always stopped at exactly the same spot I did and suffered the same feeling of awe and depression that came upon me as my eyes fell upon that wild marsh. But instead of hurrying on, instead of quickening my steps in search of the hills again, I for some unaccountable reason which I have always laid to curiosity, left the trail and plunged through oozing fungi to the water's very edge.

A wave of warm humid air, heavy with the odor of growth, swept over me as though I had suddenly opened the door of some monstrous hothouse. Great masses of vines with fat creeping tendrils hung from the cypress trees. Razor-edged reeds, marsh grass, long waving cat-tails, swamp vegetation of a thousand kinds flourished here with luxuriant abundance. I went on along the shore; the water lapped steadily the sodden earth at my feet, oily-looking water, grim-looking, reflecting a sullen and overcast sky.

There was something fascinating in it all, and while I am not one of those adventurous souls who revel in the unusual, I gave no thought of turning back to the road, but plodded through the soggy, clinging soil, and over rotting logs as though hurrying toward some destination. The very contrast, the voluptuousness of all the growth seemed some mighty lure, and I came to a halt only when gasping for breath from exertion.

For perhaps half an hour I stumbled forward at intervals, and then from the increasing number of cypress trees I saw that I was approaching that district known as the Flan. A large lagoon lay here, stagnant, dark, and entangled among the rip-grass and reeds, reeds that rasped against each other in a dry, unpleasant manner like some sleeper constantly clearing his throat.

All the while I had been wondering over the absolute absence of all animate life. With its dank air, its dark appeal, and its wildness, the Eden recesses of the Mive presented a glorious place for all forms of swamp life. And yet not a snake, not a toad, nor an insect had I seen. It was rather strange, and I looked curiously about me as I walked.

And then…and then as if in contradiction to my thoughts it fluttered before me.

With a gasp of amazement I found myself staring at an enormous, a gigantic ebony-black butterfly. Its jet coloring was magnificent, its proportions startling, for from wing tip to wing tip it measured fully fifteen inches. It approached me slowly, and as it did I saw that I was wrong in my classification. It was not a butterfly; neither was it a moth; nor did it seem to belong to the order of the *Lepidoptera* at all. As large as a bird, its great body came into prominence over the wings, disclosing a huge proboscis, ugly and repulsive.

I suppose it was instinctively that I stretched out my hand to catch the thing as it suddenly drew nearer. My fingers closed over it, but with a frightened whir it tore away, darted high in the air, and fluttered proudly into the undergrowth. An exclamation of disappointment burst from me, and I glanced ruefully at my hand where the prize should have been.

It was then that I became aware that the first two fingers and a part of my palm were lightly coated with a powdery substance that had rubbed off the delicate membrane of the insect's wings. The perspiration of my hand was fast changing this powder into a sticky bluish substance, and I noticed that this gave off a delightfully sweet odor. The odor grew heavier; it changed to a perfume, an incense, luring, exotic, fascinating. It seemed to fill the air, to crowd my lungs, to create an irresistible desire to taste it. I sat down on a log; I tried to fight it off, but like a blanket it enveloped me, tearing down my resistance in a great attraction as magnet to steel. Like a sword it seared its way into my nostrils, and the desire became maddening, irresistible.

At length I could stand it no longer, and I slowly brought my fingers to my lips. A horribly bitter taste which momentarily paralyzed my entire mouth and throat was the result. It ended in a long coughing spell.

Disgusted at my lack of will-power and at this rather foolish episode, I turned and began to retrace my steps toward the road. A feeling of nausea and of sluggishness began to seep into me, and I quickened my pace to get away from the stifling air. But at the same time I kept watch for a reappearance of that strange butterfly. No sound now save the washing of the heavy water against the reeds and the sucking noise of my steps.

I had gone farther than I realized, and I cursed the foolish whim that had sent me here. As for the butterfly – whom could I make believe the truth of its size or even of its existence? I had nothing for proof, and… I stopped suddenly!

A peculiar formation of vines had attracted my attention – and yet not vines either. The thing was oval, about five feet in length, and appeared to be many weavings or coils of some kind of hemp. It lay fastened securely in a lower crotch of a cypress. One end was open, and the whole thing was a grayish color like a cocoon… a cocoon! An instinctive shudder of horror swept over me as the meaning of my thoughts struck me with full force.

With a cocoon as large as this, the size of the butterfly would be enormous. In a flash I saw the reason for the absence of all other life in the Mive. These butterflies, developed as they were to such proportions, had evolved into some strange order and become carnivorous. The fifteen-inch butterfly which had so startled me before faded into insignificance in the presence of this cocoon.

I seized a huge stick for defense and hurried on toward the road. A low muttering of thunder from somewhere off to the west added to my discomfort. Black threatening clouds, harbingers of an oncoming storm, were racing in from the horizon, and my spirits fell even lower with the deepening gloom. The gloom blurred into a darkness, and I picked my way forward along the shore with more and more difficulty. Suddenly the mutterings stopped, and there came that expectant, sultry silence that precedes the breaking of a storm.

But no storm came. The clouds all moved slowly, lava-like toward a central formation directly above me, and there they stopped, became utterly motionless, engraved upon the sky. There was something ominous about that monstrous cloud bank, and in spite of the growing feeling of nausea, I watched it pass through a series of strange color metamorphoses, from a black to a greenish black, and from a decided green to a yellow, and from a yellow to a blinding, glaring red.

And then as I looked those clouds gradually opened; a ray of peculiar colorless light pierced through as the aperture enlarged disclosing an enormous vault-shaped cavern cut through the stratus. The whole vision seemed to move nearer, to change from an indistinguishable blur as though magnified a thousand times. And then towers, domes, streets, and walls took form, and these coagulated into a city painted stereoscopically in the sky. I forgot everything and lost myself in a weird panorama of impossible happenings above me.

Crowds, mobs, millions of men clothed in mediaeval armor of chain mail with high helmets were hurrying on, racing past in an endless procession of confusion. Regiment upon regiment, men and more men, a turbulent sea of marching humanity were fleeing, retreating as if from some horrible enemy!

And then it came, a swarm, a horde of butterflies…enormous, ebony-black, carnivorous butterflies, approaching a doomed city. They met – the men and that strange form of life. But the defensive army and the gilded city seemed to be swallowed up, to be dissolved under this terrible force of incalculable power. The entire scene began to disintegrate into a mass, a river of molten gray, swirling and revolving like a wheel – a wheel with a hub, a flaming, fantastic, colossal ball of effulgence.

I was mad! My eyes were mad! I screamed in horror, but like Cyprola turned to stone, stood staring at this blasphemy in the heavens.

Again it began to coalesce; again a picture took form, but this time a design, gigantic, magnificent. And there under tremendous proportions with its black wings outspread was the butterfly I had sought to catch. The whole sky was covered by its massive form, a mighty repulsive tapestry.

It disappeared! The thunder mutterings, which had become silenced before, now burst forth without warning in unrestrained simultaneous fury. The clouds suddenly raced back again, erasing outline and detail, devouring the sight, and there was only the blackness, the gloom of a brooding, overcast sky.

With a wild cry, I turned and ran, plunged through the underbrush, my sole thought being to escape from this insane marsh. Vines and creepers lashed at my face as I tore on; knife reeds and swamp grass penetrated my clothing, leaving stinging burns of pain. Streak lightning of blinding brilliance, thunderations like some volcanic upheaval belched forth from the sky. A wind sprang up, and the reeds and long grasses undulated before it like a thousand writhing serpents. The sullen water of the Mive was black now and racing in toward the shore in huge waves, and the thunder above swelled into one stupendous crescendo.

Suddenly I threw myself flat upon the oozing ground and with wild fear wormed my way deep into the undergrowth. It was coming!

A moment later with a loud flapping the giant butterfly raced out of the storm toward me. Scarcely ten feet away I could see its enormous, sword-like proboscis, its repulsive, disgusting body, and I could hear its sucking inhalations of breath. A wave of horror seared its way through my very brain; the pulsations of my heart throbbed at my temples and at my throat, and I continued to stare helplessly at it. *A thing of evil it was, transnormal, bred in a leprous, feverish swamp, a hybrid growth from a paludinous place of rot and over-luxuriant vegetation.*

But I was well hidden in the reeds. The monstrosity passed on unseeing. In a flash I was up and lunging on again. The crashing reverberations of the storm seemed to pound against me as if trying to hold me back. A hundred times I thought I heard that terrible flapping of wings behind me, only to discover with a prayer of thanks that I was mistaken. But at last the road! Without stopping, without slackening speed, I tore on, away from the Mive, across the quivering flat, and on and on to the hills. I climbed; I stumbled; I ran; my sole thought was to go as far as possible. At length exhaustion swept over me, and I fell gasping to the ground.

It seemed hours that I lay there, motionless, unheeding the driving rain on my back, and yet fully conscious. My brain was wild now. It pawed over the terrible events that had crowded themselves into the past few hours, re-pictured them, and strove for an answer.

What had happened to me? What had happened to me? And then suddenly I gave an exclamation. I remembered now, fool that I was. The fifteen-inch butterfly which had so startled me near the district of the Flan…I had tried to catch the thing, and it had escaped, leaving in my hand only a powderish substance that I had vainly fought off and at last brought to my lips. That was it. What had happened after that? A feeling of nausea had set in, a great inward sickness like the immediate effects of a powerful drug. A strange insect of an unknown order, a thing resembling and yet differing from all forms of the *Lepidoptera*, a butterfly and yet not a butterfly… Who knows what internal effect that powder would have on one? Had I been wandering in a delirium, a delirium caused by the tasting of that powder from the insect's wings? And if so, where did the delirium fade into reality? The vision in the sky…a vagary of a poisoned brain perhaps, but the monstrosity which had pursued me and the telltale cocoon…again the delirium? No, and again no! That was too real, too horrible, and yet everything was all so strange and fantastic.

But what master insect was this that could play with a man's brain at will? What drug, what unknown opiate existed in the membrane of its ebony-black wings?

And I looked back, confused, bewildered, expecting perhaps an answer. There it lay, far below me, vague and indistinct in the deepening gloom, the black outlines of the cypress trees writhing in the night wind, silent, brooding, mysterious – the Mive.

The Diary of Mr. Poynter

M.R. James

THE SALE-ROOM of an old and famous firm of book auctioneers in London is, of course, a great meeting-place for collectors, librarians, dealers: not only when an auction is in progress, but perhaps even more notably when books that are coming on for sale are upon view. It was in such a sale-room that the remarkable series of events began which were detailed to me not many months ago by the person whom they principally affected, namely, Mr. James Denton, M.A., F.S.A., etc., etc., some time of Trinity Hall, now, or lately, of Rendcomb Manor in the county of Warwick.

He, on a certain spring day not many years since, was in London for a few days upon business connected principally with the furnishing of the house which he had just finished building at Rendcomb. It may be a disappointment to you to learn that Rendcomb Manor was new; that I cannot help. There had, no doubt, been an old house; but it was not remarkable for beauty or interest. Even had it been, neither beauty nor interest would have enabled it to resist the disastrous fire which about a couple of years before the date of my story had razed it to the ground. I am glad to say that all that was most valuable in it had been saved, and that it was fully insured. So that it was with a comparatively light heart that Mr. Denton was able to face the task of building a new and considerably more convenient dwelling for himself and his aunt who constituted his whole *ménage*.

Being in London, with time on his hands, and not far from the sale-room at which I have obscurely hinted, Mr. Denton thought that he would spend an hour there upon the chance of finding, among that portion of the famous Thomas collection of MSS., which he knew to be then on view, something bearing upon the history or topography of his part of Warwickshire.

He turned in accordingly, purchased a catalogue and ascended to the sale-room, where, as usual, the books were disposed in cases and some laid out upon the long tables. At the shelves, or sitting about at the tables, were figures, many of whom were familiar to him. He exchanged nods and greetings with several, and then settled down to examine his catalogue and note likely items. He had made good progress through about two hundred of the five hundred lots – every now and then rising to take a volume from the shelf and give it a cursory glance – when a hand was laid on his shoulder, and he looked up. His interrupter was one of those intelligent men with a pointed beard and a flannel shirt, of whom the last quarter of the nineteenth century was, it seems to me, very prolific.

It is no part of my plan to repeat the whole conversation which ensued between the two. I must content myself with stating that it largely referred to common acquaintances, e.g., to the nephew of Mr. Denton's friend who had recently married and settled in Chelsea, to the sister-in-law of Mr. Denton's friend who had been seriously indisposed, but was now better, and to a piece of china which Mr. Denton's friend had purchased some months before at a price much below its true value. From which you will rightly infer that the conversation was rather in the nature of a monologue. In due time, however, the friend bethought himself that Mr. Denton was there for a purpose, and said he, "What are you looking out for in particular? I don't think there's much in this lot." "Why, I thought there might be some Warwickshire collections, but I don't see anything under Warwick in the catalogue." "No, apparently not," said the friend. "All the same, I believe I noticed something like a Warwickshire diary. What was the name again? Drayton? Potter? Painter – either a P or a D, I feel sure." He turned over the leaves quickly. "Yes, here it is. Poynter. Lot 486. That might interest you. There are the books, I think: out on the table. Someone has been looking at them. Well, I must be getting on. Goodbye, you'll look us up, won't you? Couldn't you come this afternoon? we've got a little music about four. Well, then, when you're next in town." He went off. Mr. Denton looked at his watch and found to his confusion that he could spare no more than a moment before retrieving his luggage and going for the train. The moment was just enough to show him that there were four largish volumes of the diary – that it concerned the years about 1710, and that there seemed to be a good many insertions in it of various kinds. It seemed quite worth while to leave a commission of five and twenty pounds for it, and this he was able to do, for his usual agent entered the room as he was on the point of leaving it.

That evening he rejoined his aunt at their temporary abode, which was a small dower-house not many hundred yards from the Manor. On the following morning the two resumed a discussion that had now lasted for some weeks as to the equipment of the new house. Mr. Denton laid before his relative a statement of the results of his visit to town – particulars of carpets, of chairs, of wardrobes, and of bedroom china. "Yes, dear," said his aunt, "but I don't see any chintzes here. Did you go to—?"Mr. Denton stamped on the floor (where else, indeed, could he have stamped?). "Oh dear, oh dear," he said, "the one thing I missed. I *am* sorry. The fact is I was on my way there and I happened to be passing Robins's." His aunt threw up her hands. "Robins's! Then the next thing will be another parcel of horrible old books at some outrageous price. I do think, James, when I am taking all this trouble for you, you might contrive to remember the one or two things which I specially begged you to see after. It's not as if I was asking it for myself. I don't know whether you think I get any pleasure out of it, but if so I can assure you it's very much the reverse. The thought and worry and trouble I have over it you have no idea of, and *you* have simply to go to the shops and order the things." Mr. Denton interposed a moan of penitence. "Oh, aunt—" "Yes, that's all very well, dear, and I don't want to speak sharply, but you *must* know how very annoying it is: particularly as it delays the whole of our business for I can't tell how long: here is Wednesday – the Simpsons come tomorrow, and you can't leave them. Then on Saturday we have friends, as you know, coming for tennis. Yes, indeed, you spoke of asking them yourself, but, of course, I had to write the notes, and it is ridiculous, James, to look like that. We must occasionally be civil to our neighbours: you wouldn't like to have it said we were perfect bears. What was I saying? Well, anyhow it comes to this, that it must be Thursday in next week at least, before you can go to town again, and until we have decided upon the chintzes it is impossible to settle upon one single other thing."

Mr. Denton ventured to suggest that as the paint and wallpapers had been dealt with, this was too severe a view: but this his aunt was not prepared to admit at the moment. Nor, indeed, was there any proposition he could have advanced which she would have found herself able to accept. However, as the day went on, she receded a little from this position: examined with lessening disfavour the samples and price lists submitted by her nephew, and even in some cases gave a qualified approval to his choice.

As for him, he was naturally somewhat dashed by the consciousness of duty unfulfilled, but more so by the prospect of a lawn-tennis party, which, though an inevitable evil in August, he had thought there was no occasion to fear in May. But he was to some extent cheered by the arrival on the Friday morning of an intimation that he had secured at the price of £12 10s. the four volumes of Poynter's manuscript diary, and still more by the arrival on the next morning of the diary itself.

The necessity of taking Mr. and Mrs. Simpson for a drive in the car on Saturday morning and of attending to his neighbours and guests that afternoon prevented him from doing more than open the parcel until the party had retired to bed on the Saturday night. It was then that he made certain of the fact, which he had before only suspected, that he had indeed acquired the diary of Mr. William Poynter, Squire of Acrington (about four miles from his own parish) – that same Poynter who was for a time a member of the circle of Oxford antiquaries, the centre of which was Thomas Hearne, and with whom Hearne seems ultimately to have quarrelled – a not uncommon episode in the career of that excellent man. As is the case with Hearne's own collections, the diary of Poynter contained a good many notes from printed books, descriptions of coins and other antiquities that had been brought to his notice, and drafts of letters on these subjects, besides the chronicle of everyday events. The description in the sale-catalogue had given Mr. Denton no idea of the amount of interest which seemed to lie in the book, and he sat up reading in the first of the four volumes until a reprehensibly late hour.

On the Sunday morning, after church, his aunt came into the study and was diverted from what she had been going to say to him by the sight of the four brown leather quartos on the table. "What are these?" she said suspiciously. "New, aren't they? Oh! Are these the things that made you forget my chintzes? I thought so. Disgusting. What did you give for them, I should like to know? Over Ten Pounds? James, it is really sinful. Well, if you have money to throw away on this kind of thing, there *can* be no reason why you should not subscribe – and subscribe handsomely – to my anti-Vivisection League. There is not, indeed, James, and I shall be very seriously annoyed if—. Who did you say wrote them? Old Mr. Poynter, of Acrington? Well, of course, there is some interest in getting together old papers about this neighbourhood. But Ten Pounds!" She picked up one of the volumes – not that which her nephew had been reading – and opened it at random, dashing it to the floor the next instant with a cry of disgust as a earwig fell from between the pages. Mr. Denton picked it up with a smothered expletive and said, "Poor book! I think you're rather hard on Mr. Poynter." "Was I, my dear? I beg his pardon, but you know I cannot abide those horrid creatures. Let me see if I've done any mischief." "No, I think all's well: but look here what you've opened him on." "Dear me, yes, to be sure! how very interesting. Do unpin it, James, and let me look at it."

It was a piece of patterned stuff about the size of the quarto page, to which it was fastened by an old-fashioned pin. James detached it and handed it to his aunt, carefully replacing the pin in the paper.

Now, I do not know exactly what the fabric was; but it had a design printed upon it, which completely fascinated Miss Denton. She went into raptures over it, held it against the wall, made James do the same, that she might retire to contemplate it from a distance: then pored over it at close quarters, and ended her examination by expressing in the warmest terms her appreciation of the taste of the ancient Mr. Poynter who had had the happy idea of preserving this sample in his diary. "It is a most charming pattern," she said, "and remarkable too. Look, James, how delightfully the lines ripple. It reminds one of hair, very much, doesn't it. And then these knots of ribbon at intervals. They give just the relief of colour that is wanted. I wonder—" "I was going to say," said James with deference, "I wonder if it would cost much to have it copied for our curtains." "Copied? how could you have it copied, James?" "Well, I don't know the details, but I suppose that is a printed pattern, and that you could have a block cut from it in wood or metal." "Now, really, that is a capital idea, James. I am almost inclined to be glad that you were so – that you forgot the chintzes on Monday. At any rate, I'll promise to forgive and forget if you get this lovely old thing copied. No one will have anything in the least like it, and mind, James, we won't allow it to be sold. Now I must go, and I've totally forgotten what it was I came in to say: never mind, it'll keep."

After his aunt had gone James Denton devoted a few minutes to examining the pattern more closely than he had yet had a chance of doing. He was puzzled to think why it should have struck Miss Denton so forcibly. It seemed to him not specially remarkable or pretty. No doubt it was suitable enough for a curtain pattern: it ran in vertical bands, and there was some indication that these were intended to converge at the top. She was right, too, in thinking that these main bands resembled rippling – almost curling – tresses of hair. Well, the main thing was to find out by means of trade directories, or otherwise, what firm would undertake the reproduction of an old pattern of this kind. Not to delay the reader over this portion of the story, a list of likely names was made out, and Mr. Denton fixed a day for calling on them, or some of them, with his sample.

The first two visits which he paid were unsuccessful: but there is luck in odd numbers. The firm in Bermondsey which was third on his list was accustomed to handling this line. The evidence they were able to produce justified their being entrusted with the job. "Our Mr. Cattell" took a fervent personal interest in it. "It's 'eartrending, isn't it, sir," he said, "to picture the quantity of reelly lovely medeevial stuff of this kind that lays well-nigh unnoticed in many of our residential country 'ouses: much of it in peril, I take it, of being cast aside as so much rubbish. What is it Shakespeare says – unconsidered trifles. Ah, I often say he 'as a word for us all, sir. I say Shakespeare, but I'm well aware all don't 'old with me there – I 'ad something of an upset the other day when a gentleman came in – a titled man, too, he was, and I think he told me he'd wrote on the topic, and I 'appened to cite out something about 'Ercules and the painted cloth. Dear me, you never see such a pother. But as to this, what you've kindly confided to us, it's a piece of work we shall take a reel enthusiasm in achieving it out to the very best of our ability. What man 'as done, as I was observing only a few weeks back to another esteemed client, man can do, and in three to four weeks' time, all being well, we shall 'ope to lay before you evidence to that effect, sir. Take the address, Mr. 'Iggins, if you please."

Such was the general drift of Mr. Cattell's observations on the occasion of his first interview with Mr. Denton. About a month later, being advised that some samples were ready for his inspection, Mr. Denton met him again, and had, it seems, reason to be satisfied with the faithfulness of the reproduction of the design. It had been finished off at the top in accordance with the indication I mentioned, so that the vertical bands joined. But something still needed to be done in the way of matching the colour of the original. Mr. Cattell had suggestions of a technical kind to offer, with which I need not trouble you. He had also views as to the general desirability of the pattern which were vaguely adverse. "You say you don't wish this to be supplied excepting to personal friends equipped with a authorisation from yourself, sir. It shall be done. I quite understand your wish to keep it exclusive: lends a catchit, does it not, to the suite? What's every man's, it's been said, is no man's."

"Do you think it would be popular if it were generally obtainable?" asked Mr. Denton.

"I 'ardly think it, sir," said Cattell, pensively clasping his beard. "I 'ardly think it. Not popular: it wasn't popular with the man that cut the block, was it, Mr. 'Iggins?"

"Did he find it a difficult job?"

"He'd no call to do so, sir; but the fact is that the artistic temperament – and our men are artists, sir, every man of them – true artists as much as many that the world styles by that term – it's apt to take some strange 'ardly accountable likes or dislikes, and here was an example. The twice or thrice that I went to inspect his progress: language I could understand, for that's 'abitual to him, but reel distaste for what I should call a dainty enough thing, I did not, nor am I now able to fathom. It seemed," said Mr. Cattell, looking narrowly upon Mr. Denton, "as if the man scented something almost Hevil in the design."

"Indeed? did he tell you so? I can't say I see anything sinister in it myself."

"Neether can I, sir. In fact I said as much. 'Come, Gatwick,' I said, 'what's to do here? What's the reason of your prejudice – for I can call it no more than that?' But, no! no explanation was forthcoming. And I was merely reduced, as I am now, to a shrug of the shoulders, and a *cui bono*. However, here it is," and with that the technical side of the question came to the front again.

The matching of the colours for the background, the hem, and the knots of ribbon was by far the longest part of the business, and necessitated many sendings to and fro of the original pattern and of new samples. During part of August and September, too, the Dentons were away from the Manor. So that it was not until October was well in that a sufficient quantity of the stuff had been manufactured to furnish curtains for the three or four bedrooms which were to be fitted up with it.

On the feast of Simon and Jude the aunt and nephew returned from a short visit to find all completed, and their satisfaction at the general effect was great. The new curtains, in particular, agreed to admiration with their surroundings. When Mr. Denton was dressing for dinner, and took stock of his room, in which there was a large amount of the chintz displayed, he congratulated himself over and over again on the luck which had first made him forget his aunt's commission and had then put into his hands this extremely effective means of remedying his mistake. The pattern was, as he said at dinner, so restful and yet so far from being dull. And Miss Denton – who, by the way, had none of the stuff in her own room – was much disposed to agree with him.

At breakfast next morning he was induced to qualify his satisfaction to some extent – but very slightly. "There is one thing I rather regret," he said, "that we allowed them to join up the vertical bands of the pattern at the top. I think it would have been better to leave that alone."

"Oh?" said his aunt interrogatively.

"Yes: as I was reading in bed last night they kept catching my eye rather. That is, I found myself looking across at them every now and then. There was an effect as if someone kept peeping out between the curtains in one place or another, where there was no edge, and I think that was due to the joining up of the bands at the top. The only other thing that troubled me was the wind."

"Why, I thought it was a perfectly still night."

"Perhaps it was only on my side of the house, but there was enough to sway my curtains and rustle them more than I wanted."

That night a bachelor friend of James Denton's came to stay, and was lodged in a room on the same floor as his host, but at the end of a long passage, halfway down which was a red baize door, put there to cut off the draught and intercept noise.

The party of three had separated. Miss Denton a good first, the two men at about eleven. James Denton, not yet inclined for bed, sat him down in an arm-chair and read for a time. Then he dozed, and then he woke, and bethought himself that his brown spaniel, which ordinarily slept in his room, had not come upstairs with him. Then he thought he was mistaken: for happening to move his hand which hung down over the arm of the chair within a few inches of the floor, he felt on the back of it just the slightest touch of a surface of hair, and stretching it out in that direction he stroked and patted a rounded something. But the feel of it, and still more the fact that instead of a responsive movement, absolute stillness greeted his touch, made him look over the arm. What he had been touching rose to meet him. It was in the attitude of one that had crept along the floor on its belly, and it was, so far as could be collected, a human figure. But of the face which was now rising to within a few inches of his own no feature was discernible, only hair. Shapeless as it was, there was about it so horrible an air of menace that as he bounded from his chair and rushed from the room he heard himself moaning with fear: and doubtless he did right to fly. As he dashed into the baize door that cut the passage in two, and – forgetting that it opened towards him – beat against it with all the force in him, he felt a soft ineffectual tearing at his back which, all the same, seemed to be growing in power, as if the hand, or whatever worse than a hand was there, were becoming more material as the pursuer's rage was more concentrated. Then he remembered the trick of the door – he got it open – he shut it behind him – he gained his friend's room, and that is all we need know.

It seems curious that, during all the time that had elapsed since the purchase of Poynter's diary, James Denton should not have sought an explanation of the presence of the pattern that had been pinned into it. Well, he had read the diary through without finding it mentioned, and had concluded that there was nothing to be said. But, on leaving Rendcomb Manor (he did not know whether for good), as he naturally insisted upon doing on the day after experiencing the horror I have tried to put into words, he took the diary with him. And at his seaside lodgings he examined more narrowly the portion whence the pattern had been taken. What he remembered having suspected about it turned out to be correct. Two or three leaves were pasted together, but written upon, as was patent when they were held up to the light. They yielded easily to steaming, for the paste had lost much of its strength, and they contained something relevant to the pattern.

The entry was made in 1707.

Old Mr. Casbury, of Acrington, told me this day much of young Sir Everard Charlett, whom he remember'd Commoner of University College, and thought was of the same Family as Dr. Arthur Charlett, now master of ye Coll. This Charlett was a personable young gent., but a loose atheistical companion, and a great Lifter, as they then call'd the hard drinkers, and for what I know do so now. He was noted, and subject to severall censures at different times for his extravagancies: and if the full history of his debaucheries had bin known, no doubt would have been expell'd ye Coll., supposing that no interest had been imploy'd on his behalf, of which Mr. Casbury had some suspicion. He was a very beautiful person, and constantly wore his own Hair, which was very abundant, from which, and his loose way of living, the cant name for him was Absalom, and he was accustom'd to say that indeed he believ'd he had shortened old David's days, meaning his father, Sir Job Charlett, an old worthy cavalier.

Note that Mr. Casbury said that he remembers not the year of Sir Everard Charlett's death, but it was 1692 or 3. He died suddenly in October. [Several lines describing his unpleasant habits and reputed delinquencies are omitted.] Having seen him in such topping spirits the night before, Mr. Casbury was amaz'd when he learn'd the death. He was found in the town ditch, the hair as was said pluck'd clean off his head. Most bells in Oxford rung out for him, being a nobleman, and he was buried next night in St. Peter's in the East. But two years after, being to be moved to his country estate by his successor, it was said the coffin, breaking by mischance, proved quite full of Hair: which sounds fabulous, but yet I believe precedents are upon record, as in Dr. Plot's History of Staffordshire.

His chambers being afterwards stripp'd, Mr. Casbury came by part of the hangings of it, which 'twas said this Charlett had design'd expressly for a memoriall of his Hair, giving the Fellow that drew it a lock to work by, and the piece which I have fasten'd in here was parcel of the same, which Mr. Casbury gave to me. He said he believ'd there was a subtlety in the drawing, but had never discover'd it himself, nor much liked to pore upon it.

* * *

The money spent upon the curtains might as well have been thrown into the fire, as they were. Mr. Cattell's comment upon what he heard of the story took the form of a quotation from Shakespeare. You may guess it without difficulty. It began with the words 'There are more things'.

He Led

Nyx Kain

I WISH I had followed him.

Sometimes, even now. When life starts to feel stale around the edges, and I realize how easily it could go on this way. I could live for another fifty years without ever making another decision that important, then die as a dull surprise. I remember how alive I felt, walking at his heels.

How real, running through the forest. We were young then, and always together. Not quite in the way of childhood anymore, when we had shared all our time as naturally as our dreams, but the way of feeling a change in the wind. Our parents had started looking at us with puzzlement, almost disappointment, when we said we had no productive plans for the day. Dreams were becoming something we were supposed to take courses to achieve.

The world was tightening around us, trying to force us into its own shapes. Neither of us had said it, but we both knew that summer was our last refuge.

Neither of us had admitted we were afraid. Though, looking back, I think we were always trying to tell each other. The way we looked at the stars, and he wondered aloud how many could be seen from the city.

The way he ran, and I followed. Barefoot down the paths we'd made, not as if running towards something anymore, but as if being chased. Branches whipped my arms, reaching out, as if recognizing the path as something they'd have a right to reclaim soon. Birds scattered in wind-chime clamours, flocks to the sky.

He had always been the faster one between us. It was only his patience that let me keep up, and even then, I was always blown, bent gasping over my knees by the time we reached the cliff. Catching my breath in its shadow, until I could straighten to find him staring at me.

Was it pity in his face that day? Hope? I want to look back and be sure. To know what it was, exactly, that I pretended not to see.

My cheeks burned with more than August that day. Whatever I saw in his face, it made me feel like something he was trying to leave behind. He would have the easier time of it. There was no question of that.

He had always been the stronger one between us. Lifting the ladder from where it lay, half-hidden in dense, shiny undergrowth. I hurried to take hold of one side of it, as if he still needed me to, and together, we leaned it into place against the cliff.

It settled against a springy cushion of roots, and he started climbing almost before it had. He seemed called that day, somehow. Or perhaps that's just me trying to make sense of it again, looking back. His eyes were sharp everywhere but when he looked at me.

I watched him climb. The ladder bowing and swaying, his hands flashing up into the hazy light that crowned the cliff and day. I loved him then, in a way so much like trying to be left behind.

He leapt from the top of the ladder. Almost two metres to the root-thick top of the cliff, and caught hold. He kicked his feet, soles black with dirt, and pulled and wriggled himself up and out of sight.

The idea of actually being left behind was still a sharp tug of panic in my chest. I hurried after him, hauling myself up the ladder with a speed that shook dust from the roots above. The dry sage-smell of trees' secrets disturbed, trickling between my fingers and settling fine in my hair.

I didn't hesitate as I always had at the top of the ladder. I leapt, and my body's weight seemed to drop through me, tied by parachute cords to my stomach. That awful second, always, when I was sure I would fall short.

My hand slapped onto the thicker, winding roots atop the cliff, and his was there. An instant later, wrapped rough, warm around my wrist. He heaved me up so quickly I could only kick at the face of the cliff, making the motions of climbing without any control over how I rose or whether I fell.

He pulled me to my feet, to face him. In that moment, it seemed ridiculous to think anything could ever separate us. He smiled, his eyes the pale, canny green of running wild in summer.

"Come on," he said. I remember. The urgency in his voice. The turn of my stomach I should have recognized as something wrong. He turned to continue on, and I thought of not following him.

It would have surprised me as much as him if I'd been the one to leave him behind. Or it could have been mutual, in that moment. He didn't look back as the shadows' tree-cast hands hurried him down the path. I could have used the roots to lower myself back onto the ladder. How long would it have taken him to even notice I was gone?

Would he have come looking for me? That question was what started me after him. I didn't want to know the answer. Not any sooner than life forced it on me.

The shadows took me in. The roots that grew across the path were smooth where we'd stepped up and over them so many times before. The forest seemed to welcome us, at least up to a certain point.

Silence fell where we weren't wanted. Vines grew spindling white across the path, between the trees, biting into them with thorns that rattled no rhythm in the rare wind. Even in the summer storms that sometimes chased us home, they had always hung perfectly still.

We both still bore the scars of the only time we'd tried to pry through them. I could see the largest of his, a scalpel-neat white curve around his elbow, stretching pearlish and elastic as he reached out to take hold of the vines.

Between the thorns, as if they'd grown for his fingers to fit there. Scythe-curved white bristled between his knuckles, making still no sound but snapping, settling as he pulled the thicket open.

Like a set of heavy curtains, while I stood and watched. If I'd done anything else that day, anything other than watching and following...

It doesn't matter now. Or, it can't be changed now. I can't pretend it doesn't still matter.

He stooped through the hole he'd torn in the thicket, and I followed, stepping carefully over bone-dry, fallen thorns. He didn't; blood spotted his footprints, and wetted the end of the thorn he kicked loose from his heel as he walked.

I followed. What else could I do? So many times, I've asked myself—what else could I have done? I could have stopped. If I'd loved him, instead of just being afraid of losing him.

I could have called his name. I should have planted myself like an anchor, pulled taut whatever connection was left between us. Forced him to explain himself before I would agree to go on.

But I didn't. I followed, even as the silence grew tauter around us. I tried to tell myself it was just the heat.

But even then, there should have been sound. Breezes skimming the canopy. Dozy birdsong dropping from the trees. I shouldn't have been able to hear my heart flinching with every step, or the focused hum of the sun's rays through every gap in the branches.

Higher, brighter light than it had been before. I was almost sure of that. It pinned the stillness and the shadows' hands in place; I squinted, but couldn't see past it to the sky.

There was no undergrowth on that side of the thorns. The trees rose from a thin, uniform carpet of fallen leaves, rain-soft and autumn-orange. None had fallen on the path where we walked.

A straight line of grey dust, leading through the trees. I didn't realize it had become something more until I scraped my foot against a stone, and saw the dust sinking between others ahead.

White stones surfacing through the forest's forgetfulness, skimmed clean by his steps. They rose in a broken arch over the path ahead, scabbed with dirt and the faint impression of words. Letters I didn't know, traced, near the ground, by roots like blind fingers. The forest trying to make sense of what it remembered.

I'd never seen a map that showed the forest as more than a dark smudge. We'd made most of its paths ourselves. Who had lived there, once? Who had built in a way it would remember all those years later?

I would have asked him, if I'd been able to catch my breath. He must have heard of it somewhere. He must have brought me out there, past our usual bounds, to surprise me with those ruins that hushed the world like a cemetery around them.

It put everything right in my mind. Everything but the hush, the air pinned by sunlight and suffocating on the forest floor. But I'd have ignored that gladly if it meant the rest of the world could make sense again.

"Where did you find out about this?" I managed a breath, at last, deep enough to ask.

He didn't turn to me. I couldn't see whether he smiled the way I'd hoped.

The rush to reach the surprise was over. There should have been nothing left to do but enjoy it, but still, he didn't stop. Didn't slow, striding through the archway, one step in its broken shadow.

Framed in its scabbed, healing letters. The path curved sharply ahead. The trees crowded too thickly around it to stand straight, jostling each other to rotten angles for pride of place.

As if the path had cupped itself around them and shoved them all roughly aside. He didn't seem to notice anything strange about them. He didn't seem to notice anything at all, rounding that bend like an automaton, with swinging arms and eyes set forward. Two long strides, and out of sight behind the trees.

The same fear that had pulled me up the ladder reeled in taut between us again. I ran after him, the slap of my bare feet echoing from the stone and breaking a thousand ways between the trees.

The shadow of the archway slipped cold over me. The trees strangling each other to form that blind corner bluntly refused every echo I threw off, groaning with their own private pains and secrets.

I sprinted past them. Around the corner at speed, and stopped.

Unravelling the last of my momentum and fear in a few stumbling steps. I don't know what I expected to see there.

More of the forest? That stone path running straight through pillared, shadowed silence, rare breaks of sunlight pinning the hidden sky to the ground and humming as if to warn they would be dangerous to touch?

The sunlight blinded me instead. In full, humming force; I blinked against it, midday bloom in a sky it had bleached almost white. The world swayed naked and green beneath it, a luxurious blur my eyes refined only slowly into grass.

Sleek, tossing kilometres of grass, like the lakes you see only in aerial photos. The sort with no strand of beach, nothing to suggest they've ever known anything but the sky peering down into them, loon calls, and the close company of the trees.

It shouldn't have been possible for that clearing to feel so forsaken. The path ran, bare white stone, straight through the centre of it. Someone had been there. Someone must have built what the path led to, at the centre of the clearing.

The stories I'd read as a child – I was realizing, or admitting, I suppose, at that moment, that I no longer was one – had promised me I would be amazed when that moment came. Excited and curious and brave when the world finally, inevitably cracked along one of the lines I had trusted.

When a portal opened, or a magical bird opened its beak to tell me my destiny, or – as there – a low, impossible building of white stone stood in an empty field.

In a silence so large, I could feel it from the forest's edge. If I'd called after him then, I doubt he would have been able to hear me.

Or maybe that's just what I want to believe. Can't I be at least that kind to myself? Don't I deserve at least one excuse?

He must not have stopped. The sun must not have stunned him; the strange building must not have given him pause. He was already halfway to it, arms swinging out with the urgency of each stride.

I thought of not following him. Not to be the one who turned away first, but because it felt too late for that. He felt untouchable in that moment, like a figure in a painting. Flat and distant, romantic and almost certainly already dead.

Would he have come back for me? I wish I'd done something, anything to answer that question that day. I wish I'd been that kind to myself; I wish I'd had that much trust in him.

But I ran after him instead. I could see myself – I can see myself, the way I would have looked in a painting. Arms pumping, hair beaten gold by the sun, floating through a waist-deep undertow of summer grass.

Towards the building's wrecking coastline. The pillars upholding its façade fanned shadows between them at snapped angles. I wanted to say I had seen their kind in history books before, but that felt like trying to identify bones too long, subtly too thick, as human.

The stairs descending from them narrowed to the end of the path. A trick of perspective that made the building – the temple? – seem much farther away than it was, and funnelled the sunlight down to an accusatory point.

Even there, he didn't slow. He stepped up onto those stairs like a prodigal prince, straight-backed, fists swung once more and then locked in a stiff rest at his sides. His shadow poured down behind him, struck out from the sun's landing site at the centre of the temple.

It had no ceiling. Limping closer, losing breath, I could see no rubble to suggest that one had ever collapsed. Only the pillars, cracked at broken-tooth angles, at the top, hinted that anything was missing.

Sound. The swaying of the grass. The closer I came to the temple, the more of the world seemed to still itself to watch me.

I stumbled over the first step as he reached the top. The sun resounded from the stone, glaring its dense, single electric note into my eyes.

I followed him. Those three words alone could tell all of my story, except the end.

I stopped at the top of the stairs. Trying to catch my breath, a tug-of-war with the thick, sun-humming air. He stood, slumped shoulders now, in front of the only other thing the temple held.

A pedestal, chest-high, scabbed with the same carvings that covered the pillars and the arch in the forest. Its top curved into a shallow bowl, and I told myself – as many times as I've woken gasping in the night, I've told myself that what shone in the bowl had to be rainwater. Never mind the scorching week since it had last rained, or how directly the sun stared down into that dead temple, or that, beneath its sheen, what shone in the bowl had colour.

What colour, I don't know. I couldn't see; I stayed where I had stopped, at the top of the stairs.

I could feel it from there. His focus on whatever filled the bowl, and its, perhaps, on him. As strange as that sounds. From where I stood, it felt like a gravity, a slope in something more real than the floor trying to urge me forward.

To follow him. As always. But I stood, and could barely hear his voice when he spoke.

"It's here," he said. I remember. The wonder in his voice, in what little I could see of his face. "I knew it would be. Look. Come here, look."

I remember. All of it so clearly, it cuts at the edges. I wanted to. We had always shared our secrets before; I wanted to be standing there next to him, seeing whatever he saw beneath the sun's sheen, in the bowl.

But my feet wouldn't move to take me there. They knew better than I did.

He looked at me then, finally. Smiling, but not the way I had wanted him to.

"It's all right," he tried to tell me, while his smile and wild green eyes said otherwise. "It's just a sip. That's what it told me – just a sip. You can't tell me you haven't been feeling it, too."

I shook my head. The silence I'd tried to ignore in the forest was stronger there. So much stronger, as if everything but us that could have broken it had forgotten that place even existed. Wind and birdsong, and time. As if that temple had stood untouched by any of them since it had first been built. It should have felt miraculous. Maybe it did. Maybe miracles, concentrated, are just something a human being can't breathe.

Something I couldn't breathe. He didn't seem to have any trouble; he tilted his head towards me, still smiling, sweet, knowing, chiding.

"Yes, you have," he said. "I've felt it all summer. You know what's going to happen after this. I'll go to uni in the city. You'll stay here. We'll promise to see each other on the holidays, and then we won't."

His gaze fell away from me, back into that strange gravity. The light that skinned the surface of the bowl swam in viscous ripples – had it been moving before? – against his face.

Pulling predictive shadows from the corners of his lips, eyes. Every eventual line where time would show. I had felt it as well.

Of course I had. I had watched all summer as the bones had sharpened, reshaped his face like white stones surfacing from the forest. As his body had stretched itself to fit the shape the world would insist on soon.

I had felt the changes in myself. The future wasn't something we could run from. It was already happening in us, with permission from the parts of us we couldn't speak for.

"But it doesn't have to be that way." As if he'd been listening to my thoughts. My fears, sharing them, even when neither of us had dared to name them aloud. "This can stop it. It told me. Just a sip, and we can stay here, together. Forever."

Together. Forever. I can't describe how it felt to hear those words from him. All the fears I'd thought I'd had alone, about being left behind, forgotten, and he stood there in the pinning sunlight and said no. He would never leave me behind, as long as I would always follow him.

I almost did. That's what still frightens me, and amazes me, after all these years. All that summer, he'd seemed to be pulling away from me. Listening more to the voices of impatience and disapproval, and to mine less and less. For him to look at me and smile, and say he had heard every word…

I was pathetic for him. If he'd asked me to follow him into almost any other life, I wouldn't have hesitated a second.

But I could still feel that silence like a plunge in front of me. Like a pit the air had been trying to fill for as long as that temple had stood, and had failed.

I couldn't feel anything else there. The wind that had quickened the grass outside. The flush of the sun on my skin turning to sore heat. The working parts of myself I couldn't control, the ones that said I ought to be taller, broader, because time said so, and my body belonged more to it than it ever would to me.

I could have given it to something else there. Perhaps something that cared for it more. But I couldn't make myself step forward into that silence. Not even for him; it wasn't a choice. I was too afraid, in that moment, even to choose.

He smiled at me. Not as a scold or a poorly-hidden hunger this time. The smile I knew from him, the one I had followed for so long. The confidence I had tried to emulate. The dare he knew I couldn't turn down. The trust that said it was, would always be, all right. He would go first.

The way he always had, and I would follow. He believed that to the end. I'm sure he did. He dipped his hand into the bowl.

Could I have stopped him, even then? Speaking would have felt like giving up the only real air in that place, but if I'd forced myself to do it, to call his name, would he have hesitated?

If I'd run for him, could I have grabbed his hand before he tipped it to his mouth?

The sunlight masked a colour I couldn't name. A drop slid down his jaw, his throat, to his collarbone; when I try to remember its colour there, shaded from the sun, my memory chokes on rain and forest soil thick with rot, and the flash of sympathetic pain I felt watching him walk barefoot over fallen thorns, as if his body were something he wouldn't have to bother with for long.

I didn't stay to watch what happened next. I caught only the first moment of it from the corner of my eye, the awful crack, the sunlight breaking across his back. He bent beneath it, gripping the edges of the pedestal, clinging to his own height and shape even as his spine fractured and squirmed to escape them.

The colour I couldn't name dripped from his widening mouth. I ran.

With every step, the question chased me – what would belong there? What could, where all the workings of a human being came to a halt?

All but love. I stumbled down the steps. Sprinted back through the sea of grass. The forest caught me into its shadows, but I didn't stop even there, barefoot, hair streaming. I went around the arch, running off the path, and, as I did, far behind me, I heard him scream.

In pain? Anger? In grief, for losing me? I don't think he ever thought I could be the one to break stride. To him, I was a promise of love. Someone who would always accept him, always be close behind whenever he wanted me.

Forever, he said. It was a promise I would have made almost any other way.

I stumbled out of the forest alone that day. I went straight home, before anyone could see me, and washed off all the evidence of where I'd been. I sat pretending to read in my room, and when his father finally came looking, I said I hadn't seen him all day.

I left him there, alone. I was the one who went away to school – I surprised everyone, including myself, by making grades good enough. I scared off three roommates with nightmares that left me moaning and thrashing in the dark.

I lied and said I didn't remember what my dreams were about. I lied and said my childhood had been lonely. When the roommate who stayed asked me about the first person I'd ever loved, I made someone up.

I left him there in every way I could. So why, after all these years and lies, have I come back?

I told myself I didn't have a destination in mind when I climbed into the car. Then I told myself I wanted to see the old homestead again, the red-brick house where I lived for as long as I knew him.

Where my parents lived for as long as they lived. When I ran from that temple, I accepted everything time would someday take from me. I said it was better to lose and grieve and be ordinary.

Now? I don't know. Now I'm standing with the red-brick house at my back and a funeral invitation in my pocket. I'm facing the overgrown lane that leads from it through the fields, to the forest.

I'm walking in my own footsteps. There have been so many funerals lately. Time has been less leading me than pulling me along; when I ask where we're going, it only shakes its head.

The path we beat through the forest with bare feet is gone. Only the familiar runic shape of the trees tells me it was ever here. I step into the weeds, wearing denim down to my ankles, and sturdy shoes.

The brambles catch on them, tangling burrs into their laces. Summer is almost over again, and the forest's silence is cold to me. I can't talk myself out of the sense that it remembers.

Everything. My bare feet beating scars into it, and the way I left it last time. Is that the tree I caught myself on when my legs buckled, weak and bloody, under me? Thorn scars still rip and curve across them, my chest, my arms like senseless orbit maps. Is that the mound of grass where I looked back and saw my footprints spotted red behind me, and thought, frantic, *it's got me?*

It's got me. It'll never let me go now. I didn't understand what I meant by it then. I think I do now.

I pry my way through the undergrowth where once I ran free. Every step fought for tells me I'm a stranger here now, but I still know my way to the cliff.

Straight ahead, towards the setting sun. Nothing pins its light or the forest in place here. Time runs freely, and I don't know how I feel about that anymore.

My parents are dead. My friends are messages on an answering machine, *sorry I missed you,* or, more and more often, funeral invitations.

When I was young, I thought shaping myself to the world was the choice that wouldn't hurt. Now I'm in pain every day, in ways I'm supposed to be grateful for. Because the world is still changing shape, and pain means it hasn't closed in enough to crush me yet.

The forest is changing shape. The cliff is smaller than I remember, worn down between the roots by years of rain. The trees that couldn't keep its shape slouch forward, baring their branches out over the edge as if reaching to catch themselves when they inevitably fall.

Their leaves shiver a mildewed, premature yellow. Most have already fallen, smothering the grass where the ladder should have lain.

Where I threw it after I slipped and tumbled down that day. I felt him chasing me even then, in the sunset's real light and spreading shadows. I don't know whether he actually was, breathing down my neck, his shadow stretching to catch me against the sun, but I felt him. I have, ever since.

The ladder is lying in the shadow of the cliff. Neatly, the way we always left it. I look up at the cliff again, cold, and see roots torn in a straight line down its face.

And dirt gouged deep, not by rain, but fresh, ragged-edged lacerations raked through mud to clay. My lungs swell. I don't know whether it's fear filling them, or hope. I don't know whether I'll scream, or ask if he can ever forgive me.

I hear him. So close, and the sound cuts through fear, hope, paralysis, to something buried deep, soft and primal along my spinal cord. It's the sound I didn't want to hear in the wake of his scream. The chuffing sound of breath being dragged through the maze of a body remade, and it turns me to run.

I can't stop myself. I'm nothing in this moment but nerves and ordinary, the need to live, to keep being exactly as I am. Sturdy shoes and stagnant dreams and messages on an answering machine. I see him as a blur from the corner of my eye, and he is none of those things, and he is chasing me.

He is chasing me, and I am running. I am leading, and he is following. The smell of him is in my lungs, rain-soaked stone and animal, and I am sobbing, and I still don't know whether it's out of fear or grief or love.

He's been waiting for me. All this time, he's been waiting where I left him. I don't know whether it's relief, hope or fear or laughter, but I know I'm too slow for him now. My shoes tangle in the weeds. My bones have worn down to blunt, lucky pain at the edges. My vision is hemmed in by small, smart glasses, and I don't see the root until it's already hooked over my foot, sprawling me into the weeds.

All those years, griefs, rotten dreams fall with me. All the weight of them on top of me, and I know I won't be able to push myself up quickly enough. His shadow is already over me. His breath beats warm against me, stone and animal, and the scent deeper, lonely, lost, of a boy left behind in the forest.

Of rain and sympathetic pain. Searching, scratched deep in dirt, sweat, screaming at the sunlight that pins time through its heart.

The scent, in all parts, of not wanting to go alone. I wish—

More than anything, I wish I had followed him. Not so I would never have had to grieve, but just so I'd never have had to see—

I'm turning my head to see—

—what all these years alone, forsaken by time and I, have done to him.

The Call of El Tunche

Shona Kinsella

NATHAN STEPPED OUT of the jeep, the heat hitting him like a physical force, despite the day being overcast. The call of a howler monkey accompanied the slamming of the car doors. The village was still, the locals watching the newcomers, wary and curious all at once. He took off his hat, pushing blond hair out of his eyes.

"We need guides," Nathan called, nodding towards the rainforest, which loomed over the village. 'We'll pay good money."

"*Mucho dinero*," James said, slowly and loudly, as if speaking to someone who was hard of hearing. Sweat streamed down his ruddy, boxer's face.

"I'll handle this," Nathan said, glaring at James. The big man had been nothing but a pain in Nathan's backside since they had arrived in Peru. Honest to God, he was the type of guy who gave Americans a bad name.

Lisbeth, the other member of their team, was leaning against the side of the jeep, watching it all with a bored expression, hands shoved into the pockets of her tight-fitting jeans.

A young man stepped forward and spoke to them in English. 'What do you want? Why go in the jungle?"

Nathan shot James a look, warning him not to open his mouth. 'We're working for a conservation group. We're here to log rare species of plants and animals, so they can use the information to protect the rainforest."

"You don't look like charity workers," the young man said, eyeing them suspiciously.

"We're freelancers," Nathan answered, which was true. They just weren't freelancing for a charity – but multiple guides back in the city had turned them down. That seemed to happen as soon as they admitted they were working for a pharmaceutical company.

A tiny old woman in a colourful wrap stepped forward and spoke to the young man rapidly in a language Nathan didn't recognise. The team leader let his gaze wander around the village. Small huts, half-naked kids, women sitting on stools weaving, or preparing food, few men around. From somewhere nearby Nathan could hear the clanking of cow bells, most likely attached to goats. A simple place. Hopefully simple enough to believe his lie.

He caught the phrase "El Tunche" being spoken repeatedly by both the old woman and the young man, but he had no idea what it meant. It seemed to be the source of some disagreement between the two, and the woman crossed herself every time she said it. The young man said something emphatic, and the old woman flapped a hand at him and walked away.

"I will take you," he said. "My name is Ernesto."

Nathan and the team waited by the jeep while Ernesto and his cousin Renzo packed their bags and got ready to go. The younger kids ran around near them, getting close to the jeep and then dancing away, laughing. They reminded Nathan of his own boy; he must be what, eight? Nine? It had been a couple of years since he had seen the kid, so it was hard to keep track. Maybe he'd stop by for a visit after this trip.

Lisbeth wandered over and offered him her hip flask, but he shook his head. 'Not while I'm on duty."

She shrugged. "Suit yourself." She put it to her own lips and took a deep swallow.

"Any of that for me?" James asked, sidling up next to her and looming over her smaller frame, his eyes crawling over the front of her T-shirt.

"Sorry, just finished it." She gave him a tight smile before wandering off to check on their equipment.

Ernesto and Renzo appeared side-by-side, matching backpacks slung over their shoulders. "Let's go," Ernesto said grimly.

* * *

Nathan lay in his hammock, trying to sleep, the sounds of the jungle washing over him. He had a tarp strung above his hammock, but the air was so damp that water managed to collect on the underside and drip down on top of him. He had no idea how Lisbeth was able to keep the camera equipment dry; it seemed a miracle. He carefully adjusted his position, trying not to rock so much he fell out. James had done that on the first night and the guides had laughed mockingly. For a minute it had looked like things were going to get ugly, but he had grabbed James and pulled him away, saying, "Just think of all the cash you're gonna earn when we take those plants back to the pharmaceutical companies. We'll get thousands, and these guys'll have their homes invaded by diggers and businessmen. Who'll be laughing then?"

Since then, James kept looking at him and tapping the side of his nose with a stupid, sneering grin on his face. When they got back home Nathan would make damn sure that he never worked with the oaf again.

Something big moved through the canopy far above them, causing branches to shake and birds to take off, calling loudly in the dark. An insect whined near his ear and Nathan idly swatted at it, glancing over to where Ernesto and Renzo sat huddled together on the jungle floor, beneath a tarp. Wrapped in brightly coloured shawls, they were easy to see, even in the gloom of the jungle at night.

A loud snore came from the direction of James's hammock. Nathan glanced over to where Lisbeth sat, leaning against a tree, sipping from her hip flask. He was pretty sure it held straight scotch. That girl could really drink. She met his gaze and rolled her eyes, nodding towards James. Nathan snorted a laugh. James had been hitting on Lisbeth since the day they met; he had no idea Nathan was already fucking her. Strictly speaking, as team leader, he shouldn't be fraternising with the employees but out here, who cared? Breaking the rules was only a problem if you got caught, after all.

A piercing whistle cut through the night, silencing the bird calls and animal shrieks that were the permanent soundtrack to the jungle. The two guides leapt to their feet, colour draining from their face.

"You must be silent," one hissed.

Nathan slid out of the hammock, responding to the fear the guides displayed, almost without thought. Lisbeth, too, got to her feet, frowning, while James continued to snore. The whistle sounded again, and Nathan felt compelled to respond, his lips forming into a pucker without his command. Renzo leapt across the space between them and clamped a hand over his mouth. Nathan instinctively struggled but Renzo only clamped down harder, the sour tang of fear rolling off his skin, settling over Nathan like a shroud. His heart pounded in the base of his throat. They stood like that, in a silent, anxious tableau, for minutes that felt like hours. Eventually, the birds and animals resumed their chatter and Renzo let go, stepping back, muttering, and crossing himself.

Nathan whirled on him. "What the fuck, man?"

"The danger has passed," Renzo said, walking away. "Get some sleep."

The part of Nathan that was embarrassed and angered by his fear wanted to take it out on Renzo, to use his fists to convince himself he was still in charge. He took a step towards the retreating guide but then he spotted Lisbeth watching him, eyes wide, knuckles white as she gripped the hip flask. He turned back to his hammock.

* * *

The next day, Lisbeth and Nathan were able to laugh over what had happened, teasing James for sleeping through all the drama, but the guides were subdued. Nathan overhead Renzo muttering about El Tunche but Ernesto hissed at him to shut up. Nathan felt almost buoyed by the whole thing; the adrenaline shot had made him feel alive. He pushed through the undergrowth with renewed vigour and almost whooped for joy when he found a patch of Cat's Claw, one of the plants they were sent to look for. He tucked a sample into his pack and marked the location on his map, making sure Lisbeth got photos of everything.

When they made camp that night, Nathan and Lisbeth snuck off for a quick fumble under the guise of collecting water. The excitement of doing something forbidden added heat to their encounters, which Nathan suspected would not be there at home. He didn't see the affair lasting, but he was determined to get as much out of it as he could while they were in Peru.

They were heading back when they heard shouting. Nathan picked up his pace and burst through hanging vines to the place where they had started stringing the hammocks. James and Ernesto stood toe-to-toe, while Renzo was shoving things into his backpack, blood streaming from his nose and mouth.

"What's going on here?" Nathan snapped.

"You lied to us." Ernesto spun on his heel to glare at Nathan. "You do not come here to protect."

Nathan glared at James and then held his hands up in a conciliatory gesture. "There's obviously been some misunderstanding here. What happened while I was gone?"

"'Who will be laughing when the diggers come and we're making millions while their home is destroyed?' Your friend here cannot keep a secret." Ernesto accepted a backpack from his bleeding cousin and slipped his arms through the straps.

"Look, we work for a large organisation. We're here to do research, we have no control over what they do with the information we give them, okay? It's not up to us," Nathan said.

"We would not have agreed to bring you here, had we known this thing. We are going."

"Be serious, mate." Nathan gave an indignant laugh. "You can't just leave us out here in the middle of nowhere. You've been paid to do a job."

Ernesto placed a wad of notes on the ground between them. 'We do not want your money. We are going now. Do not follow." He turned and followed Renzo.

"You can't just fucking leave us. At least take us back to the village." Nathan was furious. He wasn't sure who he wanted to hit more, Ernesto or James. He fought to keep his temper in check – they needed the guides; he couldn't afford to do anything to make things worse.

"I'm sorry. I hope El Tunche does not find you."

Before he could stop them, the two guides melted away into the jungle, disappearing so quickly it was as if they had never been there.

Nathan pinched the bridge of his nose and tried really hard to think of all the reasons he shouldn't just beat the shit out of James right now. What were they going to do?

"James, would you care to explain why you saw fit to tell them what we're really doing here?" he said through gritted teeth, not yet looking at the other man.

"They laughed at me again and it just slipped out, boss," James answered, looking at his feet.

A scream of rage and frustration fought to burst free from Nathan's throat, but he forced it back, using everything he had to control his temper. He was the boss out here, and if he wanted to try and salvage this trip, he would have to stay calm and think clearly. The other two stood looking at him anxiously.

"It's getting dark. We can't do anything tonight, so we'll camp here as planned. Tomorrow, we'll follow the stream Lisbeth and I got the water from. Sooner or later, it'll join the Ucayali or Marañón and we'll be able to follow it out. We'll take pictures and samples as we go and hope to find something that makes all of this worthwhile." He looked between Lisbeth and James. "Any questions?"

"No, boss," James said.

Lisbeth just shook her head and turned away.

* * *

Nathan jerked awake, unsure of what had woken him. The jungle was silent. Was that it? The absence of the sounds that had become the backdrop of every moment was unsettling all on its own. He lay still, eyelids sagging despite the shot of adrenaline still making itself known in his body.

Then it came again, that weird whistle from last night. Without being able to stop himself, Nathan whistled back, imitating the sound.

"Don't!" Lisbeth hissed urgently from her hammock.

The whistle sounded again. It was louder, closer. Nathan slid to the ground, fighting the urge to make the same sound again, but his body overrode his will and he whistled. He clamped his hands over his mouth.

"What's going on?" James asked, tumbling out of his hammock. 'Why are you making so much noise?"

Again, the whistle pierced the darkness, and it was definitely closer. Nothing else moved; the jungle lay silent and tense, waiting for the next whistle. This time it was James who answered. Nathan looked around. James stood about six feet away, beside his hammock, looking confused. To Nathan's other side, Lisbeth stood beside her own hammock, hands pressed hard across her lower face, eyes wide and staring.

The hair on the back of Nathan's neck stood up and he had a moment to think about how odd it felt, before a dark shape drifted from between the trees behind James. It was tall, at least seven feet, and wore a hooded, ragged cloak. Beneath the hood was a face that looked like a skull with a thin layer of grey skin stretched over it, lips pulled back from teeth that resembled the fangs of a large primate. The eyes were just gaping sockets, filled with a flickering, cold blue light.

"What the…" Nathan croaked, his mouth suddenly dry.

James started to turn, but before he made it all the way around, the creature lifted a clawed hand and sliced open James's throat.

Everything seemed to slow down. Blood sprayed from James's neck. The big man clamped his hands to the tattered wound and then sank to the ground. The creature looked down at him, the light in its eye sockets flaring bright white. Gurgling, James reached a hand towards his comrades. Nathan was rooted to the spot. He felt like there was something he should do but his thoughts were sluggish and his body unresponsive.

Lisbeth shrieked and the sound broke Nathan's paralysis. He stepped back, putting more distance between himself and James, who was lying on his side now, the blood coming out in rhythmic spurts between his fingers. It looked black in the moonlight, and Nathan could almost believe that James was covered in paint or ink, something far less threatening than the reality.

Lisbeth rushed to James's side and knelt to cradle his head. She looked up at Nathan, face white, eyes wide.

"Do something. Help him." Tears glistened on her cheeks. For a split-second Nathan almost rushed to her side.

But then the creature stepped towards Lisbeth and Nathan turned and fled.

He heard a strangled scream, cut off with a spluttering sound. He didn't look back. Part of him hoped Lisbeth would be okay, that she would somehow make it out of this, but another part of him just hoped she died slowly enough to give him some time to get away.

He crashed through the jungle, his ragged breathing the only sound. He should have been able to hear animals and birds; his frantic flight should be sending them flapping with indignant calls into the air. Instead, the jungle held its breath, waiting for the confrontation to reach its conclusion.

Nathan had no sense of where he was going, only that he had to get away. He stumbled over roots and pushed his way through dense vegetation, heedless of the danger. The mundane threat of snakes and spiders and other venomous creatures paled in comparison to what he ran from. Eventually he slowed, chest heaving, sweat stinging his eyes. He didn't hear anything pursuing him, but then he also didn't hear normal jungle sounds so the danger couldn't have passed. He couldn't run all night with no sense of direction. He had to find somewhere to hide. Then he could wait out the night and start moving again in daylight.

He stumbled on until he found a large patch of giant ferns. Cautiously, he crawled in amongst them, praying he wasn't disturbing the home of anything dangerous. He sat between the plants, his knees pulled up to his chest, his forehead resting on them. Slowly, his breathing and heart rate returned to normal. He had no idea what time it was or how long he would have to wait until daylight.

A whistle broke the silence and Nathan fought back a scream. He shoved his hands against his mouth and moaned. Should he run again or stay here, hidden?

The whistle was louder this time. Closer. More insistent.

The urge to respond was almost overpowering. Nathan bit down hard on his hand, the fleshy bit below his thumb. The pain sparked his mind and kept him from doing anything stupid. He huddled down more, pulling in his limbs and squeezing his eyes shut, like a child believing they can't be seen if they can't see.

The whistle came three times, each one closer than the last. Nathan bit his hand so hard he tasted blood. Everything in him fought to whistle back. The power it had over him was incredible, making him feel out of control and utterly violated. The heat pressed down on top of him, the taste of salt and iron filled his mouth, his jaw cramped from being clenched so tight.

The next whistle was like a shriek, loud and insistent and unbearable.

Nathan whistled back.

The Hill and the Hole

Fritz Leiber

TOM DIGBY swabbed his face against the rolled-up sleeve of his drill shirt, and good-naturedly damned the whole practice of measuring altitudes by barometric instruments. Now that he was back at the bench mark, which was five hundred eleven feet above sea level, he could see that his reading for the height of the hill was ridiculously off. It figured out to about four hundred forty-seven feet, whereas the hill, in plain view hardly a quarter of a mile away, was obviously somewhere around five hundred seventy or even five hundred eighty. The discrepancy made it a pit instead of a hill. Evidently either he or the altimeter had been cock-eyed when he'd taken the reading at the hilltop. And since the altimeter was working well enough now, it looked as if he had been the one.

He would have liked to get away early for lunch with Ben Shelley at Beltonville, but he needed this reading to finish off the State oil survey for this Midwestern region. He hadn't been able to spot the sandstone-limestone contact he was looking for anywhere but near the top of this particular hill. So he picked up the altimeter, stepped out of the cool shadow of the barn behind which the bench mark happened to be located, and trudged off. He figured he would be able to finish this little job properly and still be in time for Ben. A grin came to his big, square, youthful face as he thought of how they would chew the fat and josh each other. Ben, like himself, was on the State Geologic Survey.

Fields of shoulder-high corn, dazzlingly green under the broiling sun, stretched away from the hill to the flat horizon. The noonday hush was beginning. Blue-bottle flies droned momentarily around him as he skirted a manure heap and slid between the weather-gray rails of an old fence. There was no movement, save for a vague breeze rippling the corn a couple of fields away and a farmer's car raising a lazy trail of dust far off in the opposite direction. The chunky competent-looking figure of Tom Digby was the only thing with purpose in the whole landscape.

When he had pushed through the fringe of tall, dry-stalked weeds at the base of the hill, he glanced back at the shabby one-horse farm where the bench mark was located. It looked deserted. Then he made out a little tow-headed girl watching him around the corner of the barn, and he remembered having noticed her earlier. He waved, and chuckled when she dodged back out of sight. Sometimes these farmers' kids were mighty shy. Then he started up the hill at a brisker pace, toward where the bit of strata was so invitingly exposed.

When he reached the top, he didn't get the breeze he expected. It seemed, if anything, more stiflingly hot than it had been down below, and there was a feeling of dustiness. He swabbed at his face again, set down the altimeter on a level spot, carefully twisted the dial until the needle stood directly over the mid line of the scale, and started to take the reading from the pointer below. Then his face clouded. He felt compelled to joggle the instrument, although he knew it was no use. Forcing himself to work very slowly and methodically, he took a second reading. The result was the same as the first. Then he stood up and relieved his feelings with a fancy bit of swearing, more vigorous, but just as good-natured as the blast he had let off at the bench mark.

Allowing for any possible change in barometric pressure during the short period of his walk up from the bench mark, it still gave the height of the hill as under four hundred fifty. Even a tornado of fantastic proportions couldn't account for such a difference in pressure.

It wouldn't have been so bad, he told himself disgustedly, if he'd been using an old-fashioned aneroid. But a five-hundred-dollar altimeter of the latest design isn't supposed to be temperamental. However, there was nothing to do about it now. It had evidently given its last accurate gasp at the bench mark and gone blooey for good. It would have to be shipped back East to be fixed. And he would have to get along without this particular reading.

He flopped down for a breather, before starting back. As he looked out over the checkerboard of fields and the larger checkerboard of dirt roads, it occurred to him how little most people knew about the actual dimensions and boundaries of the world they lived in. They looked at straight lines on a map, and innocently supposed they were straight in reality. They might live all their lives believing their homes were in one county, when accurate surveying would show them to be in another. They were genuinely startled if you explained that the Mason-Dixon line had more jags in it than one of those rail fences down there, or if you told them that it was next to impossible to find an accurate and up-to-date detail map of any given district. They didn't know how rivers jumped back and forth, putting bits of land first in one State and then in another. They went along believing that they lived in a world as neat as a geometry-book diagram, while chaps like himself and Ben went around patching the edges together and seeing to it that one mile plus one mile equaled at least something like two miles. Or proving that hills were really hills and not pits in disguise.

It suddenly seemed devilishly hot and close and the bare ground unpleasantly gritty. He tugged at his collar, and unbuttoned it further. Time to be getting on to Beltonville. Couple glasses of iced coffee would go very good. He hitched himself up, and noticed that the little girl had come out from behind the barn again. She seemed to be waving at him now, with a queer, jerky, beckoning movement; but that was probably just the effect of the heat-shimmer rising from the fields. He waved, too, and the movement brought on an abrupt spell of dizziness. A shadow seemed to surge menacingly across the landscape, and he had difficulty in breathing. Then he started down the hill, and pretty soon he was feeling all right again.

"I was a fool to come this far without a hat," he told himself. "This sun will get you, even if you're healthy as a horse. Well, I'm through with this job, anyway."

Something was nagging at his mind, however, as he realized when he got down in the corn again. It was that he didn't like the idea of letting the hill lick him. It occurred to him that he might persuade Ben to come over this afternoon, if he hadn't anything else to do, and get a precise measurement, with alidade and plane table.

When he neared the farm, he saw that the little girl had retreated again to the corner of the barn.

He gave her a friendly, "Hello." She didn't answer but she didn't run away, either. He became aware that she was staring at him in an intent, appraising way.

"You live here?" he asked, to start a conversation.

She didn't answer the question. After a while, she said in a strangely hungry voice, "What did you want to go down there for?"

"The State hires me to measure land," he replied. He had reached the bench mark and was automatically starting to take a reading, before he remembered that the altimeter was useless. "This your father's farm?" he asked.

Again she didn't answer. She was barefooted, and wore a cotton dress of washed-out blue. The sun had bleached her hair and eyebrows several degrees lighter than her skin, vaguely giving the effect of a photographic negative. Her mouth hung open. Her whole face had a vacuous, yet not exactly stupid expression.

Finally she shook her head solemnly, and said, "You shouldn't 'a' gone down there. You might not have been able to get out again."

"Say, just what are you talking about?" he inquired, humorously puzzled, but keeping his voice gentle so she wouldn't run away.

"The hole," she answered, almost dreamily. "I mean the hole."

Tom Digby felt a shiver run over him. "Sun must have hit me harder than I thought," he told himself.

"You mean there's some sort of pit down that way?" he asked quickly. "Maybe an old well or cesspool hidden in the weeds? Well, I didn't fall in anyway. Is it on this side of the hill?" He was still on his knees beside the bench mark.

A look of understanding, mixed with a slight disappointment, came over her face. She nodded wisely, and observed, "You're just like papa. He's always telling me there's a hill there, so I won't be scared of the hole. But he doesn't need to. I know all about it, and I wouldn't go near it again for anything."

"Say, what the dickens are you talking about?" His voice got out of control, and he rather boomed the question at her. But she didn't dart away, only continued to stare at him thoughtfully.

"Maybe I've been wrong," she observed finally, as if talking to herself. "Maybe papa and you and other people really do see a hill there. Maybe *They* make you see a hill there, so you won't know about them being there. *They* don't like to be bothered. I know. There was a man come up here about two years ago, trying to find out about them. He had a kind of spyglass on sticks. *They* made him dead. That was why I didn't want you to go down there. I was afraid *They* would do the same thing to you."

He disregarded the shiver that was creeping persistently along his spine, just as he had disregarded from the very beginning, with automatic, scientific distaste for eeriness, the odd coincidence between the girl's fancy and the inaccurate altimeter readings.

He looked at her closely. He had run across mental cases once or twice before in the course of his work, but he also knew that many children like to fabricate nonsense with great seriousness.

"Who are *They*?" he asked cheerfully.

The little girl's blank, watery blue eyes stared past him, as if she were looking at nothing – or everything.

"*They* are dead. Bones: Just Bones. But They move around. They live at the bottom of the hole, and They do things there."

"Yes?" he prompted, feeling a trifle guilty at encouraging her. From the corner of his eye he could see that an old Model-T was chugging up the rutted drive, raising clouds of dust.

"When I was little," she continued in a low trancelike voice, so he had to listen hard to catch the words, "I used to go right up to the edge and look down at them. There's a way to climb down in, but I never did. Then one day *They* looked up and caught me spying. Just white bone faces; everything else black. I knew They were thinking of making me dead. So I ran away and never went back."

The Model-T rattled to a stop beside the garage, and a tall hulk of a man in old blue overalls swung out and strode swiftly toward them.

"School Board sent you over?" he shot brusquely at Tom. It was more an accusation than a question. "You from the County Hospital?"

He clamped his big paw around the girl's hand. He had the same bleached hair and eyebrows, but his face was burnt to a brick red. There was a strong facial resemblance.

"I want to tell you something," he immediately went on, his voice heavy with anger but under control. "My little girl's all right in the head. It's up to me to judge, isn't it? What if she don't always give the answers the teachers expect. She's got a mind of her own, hasn't she? And I'm perfectly fit to take care of her. I don't like the idea of your sneaking around to put a lot of questions to her while I'm gone."

Then his eye fell on the altimeter, and he stopped his tirade. He glanced at Tom sharply, especially at the riding breeches and high, laced boots.

"I guess I went and made a damn fool of myself," he said swiftly. "You an oil man?"

Tom got to his feet. "I'm on the State Geologic Survey," he said guardedly.

The farmer's manner changed completely. He stepped forward, his voice was confidential. "But you saw signs of oil here, didn't you?"

Tom shrugged his shoulders and grinned pleasantly. He had heard a hundred farmers ask that same question in the same way. "I couldn't say anything about that. I'd have to finish my mapping before I could make any guesses."

The farmer smiled back, knowingly but not unfriendly. "I know what you mean," he said. "I know you fellows got orders not to talk. So long, mister."

Tom said, "So long," nodded goodbye to the little girl, who was still gazing at him steadily, and walked around the barn to his own car. As he plumped the altimeter down on the front seat beside him, he yielded to the impulse to take another reading. Once more he swore, this time under his breath.

The altimeter seemed to be working properly again.

"Well," he told himself, "that settles it. I'll come back and get a reliable alidade reading, if not with Ben, then with somebody else. I'll nail that hill down before I do anything."

* * *

Ben Shelley slupped down the last drops of coffee, pushed back from the table, and thumbed tobacco into his battered brier, as Tom explained his proposition for that afternoon.

A wooden-bladed fan was wheezing ponderously overhead, causing pendant strips of fly paper to sway and tremble.

"Hold on a minute," he interrupted near the end. "That reminds me of something I was bringing over for you. May save the trouble." And he fished in his briefcase.

"You don't mean to tell me there's some map for this region I didn't know about?" The tragic disgust in Tom's voice was only half jocular. "They swore up and down to me at the office there wasn't."

"Yeah, I'm afraid I mean just that," Ben confirmed, nodding. "Here she is. A special topographic job. Only issued yesterday." Tom snatched the folded sheet.

"You're right," he proclaimed, a few moments later. "This might have been of some help to me." His voice became sarcastic. "I wonder what they wanted to keep it a mystery for?"

"Oh, you know how it is," said Ben easily. "They take a long time getting maps out. The work for this was done two years ago, before you were on the Survey. It's rather an unusual map, and the person you talked to at the office probably didn't connect it up with your structural job. And there's a yarn about it, which might explain why there was some confusion."

Tom had pushed the dishes away from in front of him and was studying the map intently. Now he gave a muffled exclamation which made Ben look up. Then he hurriedly reinspected the whole map and the printed material in the corner, as though he couldn't believe his eyes. Then he stared at one spot for so long that Ben chuckled and said, "What have you found? A gold mine?"

Tom turned a serious face on him. "Look, Ben," he said slowly. "This map is no good. I've found a terrible mistake in it." Then he added, "It looks as if they did some of the readings by sighting through a rolled-up newspaper as a yardstick." It didn't sound funny, because his face was still serious.

"I knew you wouldn't be happy until you found something wrong with it," said Ben, good-naturedly. "Can't say I blame you. What is it?"

Tom slid the map across to him, indicating one spot with his thumbnail. "Just read that off to me," he directed. "What do you see there?"

Ben paused while he lit his pipe, eying the map. Then he answered promptly, "An elevation of four hundred forty-one feet. And it's got a name lettered in – 'The Hole'. Poetic, aren't we? Well, what is it? A stone quarry?"

"Ben, I was out at that very spot this morning," said Tom unsmiling, "and there isn't any depression there at all, but a hill. This reading is merely off some trifle of a hundred and forty feet!"

"Go on," countered Ben. "You were somewhere else this morning. Got mixed up. I've done it myself."

"Impossible," Tom shook his head. "There's a five-hundred-eleven-foot bench mark right next door to it."

"Then you got an old bench mark." Ben was still amusedly skeptical. "You know, one of the pre-Columbus ones."

"Oh, rot. Look, Ben, how about coming out with me this afternoon, and we'll shoot it with your alidade? I've got to do it some time or other, anyway, now that my altimeter's out of whack. And I'll prove to you this map is chock-full of errors. How about it?"

Ben applied another match to his pipe. He nodded. "All right, I'm game. But don't be angry when you find you turned in at the wrong farm."

* * *

It wasn't until they were rolling along the highway, with Ben's equipment in the back seat, that Tom remembered something. "Say, Ben, didn't you start to tell me about a yarn connected with this map?"

"It doesn't amount to much really. Just that the surveyor – an old chap named Wolcraftson – died of heart failure while he was still in the field. At first they thought someone would have to re-do the job, but then they found that he had practically completed it. Maybe that explains why some of the people at the office were in doubt as to whether there was such a map."

Tom was concentrating on the road ahead. They were getting near the turn-off. "That would have been about two years ago?" he asked. "I mean, when he died."

"Uh-huh. Or two and a half. It happened somewhere around here. Oh, there was some kind of a mess about it. I seem to remember that some fool country coroner – a local Sherlock Holmes – said there were signs of strangulation, or suffocation, or some other awful nonsense, and wanted to hold Wolcraftson's rodman. Of course, we put a stop to that."

Tom didn't answer. Certain words he had heard a couple of hours earlier were coming back to him, just as if a phonograph had been turned on: "Two years ago there was a man come up here, trying to find out about them. He had a kind of spyglass on sticks. *They* made him dead. That's why I didn't want you to go down there. I was afraid They would do the same thing to you."

He angrily shut his ears to those words. If there was anything he detested, it was admitting the possibility of supernatural agencies, even in jest. Anyway what difference did her words make? After all, a man had really died, and it was only natural that her defective imagination should cook up some wild fancy.

Of course, as he had to admit, the screwy entry on the map made one more coincidence, counting the girl's story and the cockeyed altimeter readings as the first. But it was so much of a coincidence. Perhaps Wolcraftson had listened to the girl's prattling and noted down 'The Hole' and an approximate reading for it as a kind of private joke, intending to erase it later. Besides, what difference did it make if there *had* been two genuine coincidences? The Universe was full of them. Every molecular collision was a coincidence. You could pile a thousand coincidences on top of another, he averred, and not get Tom Digby one step nearer to believing in the supernatural. Oh, he knew intelligent people enough, all right, who coddled such beliefs. Some of his best friends liked to relate 'yarns' and toy with eerie possibilities for the sake of a thrill. But the only emotion Tom ever got out of such stuff was a nauseating disgust. It cut too deep for joking. It was a reversion to that primitive, fear-bound ignorance from which science had slowly lifted man, inch by inch, against the most bitter opposition. Take this silly matter about the hill. Once admit that the dimensions of a thing might not be real, down to the last fraction of an inch, and you cut the foundations from under the world.

He'd be damned, he told himself, if he ever told anyone about the altimeter readings. It was just the silly sort of 'yarn' that Ben, for instance, would like to play around with. Well, he'd had to do without it.

With a feeling of relief he turned off for the farm. He had worked himself up into quite an angry state of mind, and part of the anger was at himself, for even bothering to think about such matters. Now they'd finish it off neatly, as scientists should, without leaving any loose ends around for morbid imaginations to knit together.

He led Ben around back of the barn, and indicated the bench mark and the hill. Ben got his bearings, studied the map, inspected the bench mark closely, then studied the map again.

Finally he turned with an apologetic grin. "I've got to admit you're absolutely right. This map is as screwy as a surrealist painting, at least as far as that hill is concerned. I'll go around to the car and get my stuff. We can shoot its altitude from right off the bench mark." He paused, frowning. "Gosh, though, I can't understand how Wolcraftson ever got it so screwed up."

"Probably they misinterpreted something on his original manuscript map."

"I suppose that must have been it."

After they had set up the plane table and telescopelike alidade directly over the bench mark, Tom shouldered the rod, with its inset level and conspicuous markings.

"I'll go up there and be rodman for you," he said. "I'd like you to shoot this yourself. Then they won't have any comeback when you walk into the office and blow them up for issuing such a map."

"OK," answered Ben, laughing. "I'll look forward to doing that."

This far they had been alone. Now, as Tom started out, he noticed the farmer coming toward them from the field ahead. He was relieved to see that the little girl wasn't with him, although he wouldn't have admitted that even to himself. As they passed one another, the farmer winked triumphantly at him. "Found something worth coming back for, eh?" Tom didn't answer. But the farmer's manner tickled his sense of humor, and he found himself feeling pretty good, all irritation gone, as he stepped along toward the hill.

The farmer introduced himself to Ben by saying, "Found signs of a pretty big gusher, eh?" His pretense at being matter-of-fact wasn't very convincing.

"I don't know anything about it," Ben answered cheerfully. "He just roped me in to help him take a reading."

The farmer cocked his big head and looked sidewise at Ben. "My, you State fellows are pretty close-mouthed, aren't you? Well, you needn't worry, because I *know* there's oil under here. Five years ago a fellow took a drilling lease on all my land at a dollar a year. But then he never showed up again. Course, I know what happened. The big companies bought him out. They know there's oil under here, but they won't drill. Want to keep the price of gasoline up."

Ben made a vaguely affirmative sound, and busied himself loading his pipe. Then he sighted through the alidade at Tom's back, for no particular reason. The farmer's gaze swung out in the same direction. When he spoke again it was in a different voice, reminiscent, reflective.

"Well, that's a funny thing now, come to think of it. Right out where he's going, is where that other chap keeled over a couple of years ago."

Ben's interest quickened. "A surveyor named Wolcraftson?" he inquired.

"Something like that. It happened right on top of that hill. They'd been fooling around here all day – something gone wrong with the instruments, the other chap said. Course I knew they'd found signs of oil and didn't want to let on. Along toward evening the same old chap – Wolcraftson, like you said – took the pole out there himself – the other chap had done it twice before – and stood atop the hill. It was right then he keeled over. We run out there, but it was too late. Heart got him. He must have thrashed around a lot before he died, though, because he was all covered with dust."

Ben grunted appreciatively. "Wasn't there some question about it afterward?"

"Oh, our coroner made a fool of himself, as he generally does. But I stepped in and told exactly what happened, and that settled it. Say, mister, why don't you break down and tell me what you know about the oil under there?"

Ben's protestations of total ignorance on the subject were cut short by the sudden appearance of a little tow-headed girl from the direction of the road. She seemed to be out of breath as if she had been running. She gasped "Papa!" and grabbed the farmer's hand. Ben walked over toward the alidade. He could see the figure of Tom emerging from the tall weeds and starting up the hill. Then his attention was caught by what the girl was saying.

"You've got to stop him, papa!" She was dragging at her father's wrist. "You can't let him go down in the hole. *They* got it fixed to make him dead, this time."

"Shut your mouth, Sue!" the farmer shouted down at her, but his voice was more anxious than angry. "You'll get me into trouble with the school board, the queer things you say. That man's just going out there to find out how high the hill is."

"But, papa, can't you see?" She twisted away and pointed at Tom's steadily mounting figure. "He's already started down in. *They're* set to trap him. Squattin' down there in the dark, all quiet so he won't hear their bones scrapin' together – stop him, papa!"

With an apprehensive look at Ben, the farmer got down on his knees beside the little girl and put his arms around her. "Look, Sue, you're a big girl now," he argued in a gruff, coaxing voice. "It don't do for you to talk that way. I know you're just playing, but other people don't know you so well. They might get to thinking things. You wouldn't want them to take you away from me, would you?"

And all the while she was twisting from side to side in his arms, trying to catch a glimpse of Tom over his shoulder. Suddenly, with an unexpected backward lunge, she jerked loose and ran off toward the hill. The farmer got to his feet and lumbered after her, calling, "Stop, Sue! Stop!"

Crazy as a couple of hoot owls, Ben decided, watching them go. Both of them think there's something under the ground. One says oil, the other says ghosts. You pay your money and you take your choice.

Then he noticed that during the excitement Tom had gotten to the top of the hill and had the rod up. He hurriedly sighted through the alidade, which was in the general direction of the hilltop. For some reason he couldn't see anything through it – just blackness. He felt forward to make sure the lens cover was off. He swung it around a little, hoping something hadn't dropped out of place inside the tube. Then abruptly, through it, he caught sight of Tom, and involuntarily he uttered a short, frightened cry and jumped away.

Ben's face was pale as death. He was trembling. On the hilltop, Tom was no longer in sight. Ben stood still for a moment, frozen. Then he raced off for it, running at top speed.

He found the farmer looking around perplexedly near the far fence. "Come on," Ben gasped out. "There's trouble," and vaulted over.

When they reached the hilltop, Ben stooped to the sprawling body, then recoiled with a convulsive movement and for a second time uttered a smothered cry and stood motionless. For every square inch of skin and clothes was smeared with a fine, dark-gray dust, totally different from the light-brown soil of the hilltop. And close beside Tom's lifeless hand was a tiny white bone.

Because a certain hideous vision still dominated his memory, Ben needed no one to tell him that it was a bone from a human finger. He buried his face in his hands, fighting that vision.

For what he had seen, or thought he had seen, through the alidade, had been a tiny struggling figure of Tom, buried in darkness, with dim skeletal figures clutching him all around and dragging him down into a thicker blackness.

The farmer kneeled by the body. "Dead as dead," he muttered in a hushed voice. "Just like the other. He's got the stuff fairly rubbed into him. It's even in his mouth and nose. Like he'd been buried in ashes and then dug up again."

From between the rails of the fence, the little girl stared up at them, terrified, but avid.

The Whisperer in Darkness

H.P. Lovecraft

Chapter I

BEAR IN MIND closely that I did not see any actual visual horror at the end. To say that a mental shock was the cause of what I inferred – that last straw which sent me racing out of the lonely Akeley farmhouse and through the wild domed hills of Vermont in a commandeered motor at night – is to ignore the plainest facts of my final experience. Notwithstanding the deep things I saw and heard, and the admitted vividness the impression produced on me by these things, I cannot prove even now whether I was right or wrong in my hideous inference. For after all Akeley's disappearance establishes nothing. People found nothing amiss in his house despite the bullet-marks on the outside and inside. It was just as though he had walked out casually for a ramble in the hills and failed to return. There was not even a sign that a guest had been there, or that those horrible cylinders and machines had been stored in the study. That he had mortally feared the crowded green hills and endless trickle of brooks among which he had been born and reared, means nothing at all, either; for thousands are subject to just such morbid fears. Eccentricity, moreover, could easily account for his strange acts and apprehensions toward the last.

The whole matter began, so far as I am concerned, with the historic and unprecedented Vermont floods of November 3, 1927. I was then, as now, an instructor of literature at Miskatonic University in Arkham, Massachusetts, and an enthusiastic amateur student of New England folklore. Shortly after the flood, amidst the varied reports of hardship, suffering, and organized relief which filled the press, there appeared certain odd stories of things found floating in some of the swollen rivers; so that many of my friends embarked on curious discussions and appealed to me to shed what light I could on the subject. I felt flattered at having my folklore study taken so seriously, and did what I could to belittle the wild, vague tales which seemed so clearly an outgrowth of old rustic superstitions. It amused me to find several persons of education who insisted that some stratum of obscure, distorted fact might underlie the rumors.

The tales thus brought to my notice came mostly through newspaper cuttings; though one yarn had an oral source and was repeated to a friend of mine in a letter from his mother in Hardwick, Vermont. The type of thing described was essentially the same in all cases, though there seemed to be three separate instances involved – one connected with the Winooski River near Montpelier, another attached to the West River in Windham County beyond Newfane, and a third centering in the Passumpsic in Caledonia County above Lyndonville. Of course many of the stray items mentioned other instances, but on analysis they all seemed to boil down to these three. In each case country folk reported seeing one or more very bizarre and disturbing objects in the surging waters that poured down from the unfrequented hills, and there was a widespread tendency to connect these sights with a primitive, half-forgotten cycle of whispered legend which old people resurrected for the occasion.

What people thought they saw were organic shapes not quite like any they had ever seen before. Naturally, there were many human bodies washed along by the streams in that tragic period; but those who described these strange shapes felt quite sure that they were not human, despite some superficial resemblances in size and general outline. Nor, said the witnesses, could they have been any kind of animal known to Vermont. They were pinkish things about five feet long; with crustaceous bodies bearing vast pairs of dorsal fins or membranous wings and several sets of articulated limbs, and with a sort of convoluted ellipsoid, covered with multitudes of very short antennae, where a head would ordinarily be. It was really remarkable how closely the reports from different sources tended to coincide; though the wonder was lessened by the fact that the old legends, shared at one time throughout the hill country, furnished a morbidly vivid picture which might well have colored the imaginations of all the witnesses concerned. It was my conclusion that such witnesses – in every case naive and simple backwoods folk – had glimpsed the battered and bloated bodies of human beings or farm animals in the whirling currents; and had allowed the half-remembered folklore to invest these pitiful objects with fantastic attributes.

The ancient folklore, while cloudy, evasive, and largely forgotten by the present generation, was of a highly singular character, and obviously reflected the influence of still earlier Indian tales. I knew it well, though I had never been in Vermont, through the exceedingly rare monograph of Eli Davenport, which embraces material orally obtained prior to 1839 among the oldest people of the state. This material, moreover, closely coincided with tales which I had personally heard from elderly rustics in the mountains of New Hampshire. Briefly summarized, it hinted at a hidden race of monstrous beings which lurked somewhere among the remoter hills – in the deep woods of the highest peaks, and the dark valleys where streams trickle from unknown sources. These beings were seldom glimpsed, but evidences of their presence were reported by those who had ventured farther than usual up the slopes of certain mountains or into certain deep, steep-sided gorges that even the wolves shunned.

There were queer footprints or claw-prints in the mud of brook-margins and barren patches, and curious circles of stones, with the grass around them worn away, which did not seem to have been placed or entirely shaped by Nature. There were, too, certain caves of problematical depth in the sides of the hills; with mouths closed by boulders in a manner scarcely accidental, and with more than an average quota of the queer prints leading both toward and away from them – if indeed the direction of these prints could be justly estimated. And worst of all, there were the things which adventurous people had seen very rarely in the twilight of the remotest valleys and the dense perpendicular woods above the limits of normal hill-climbing.

It would have been less uncomfortable if the stray accounts of these things had not agreed so well. As it was, nearly all the rumors had several points in common; averring that the creatures were a sort of huge, light-red crab with many pairs of legs and with two great batlike wings in the middle of the back. They sometimes walked on all their legs, and sometimes on the hindmost pair only, using the others to convey large objects of indeterminate nature. On one occasion they were spied in considerable numbers, a detachment of them wading along a shallow woodland watercourse three abreast in evidently disciplined formation. Once a specimen was seen flying – launching itself from the top of a bald, lonely hill at night and vanishing in the sky after its great flapping wings had been silhouetted an instant against the full moon.

These things seemed content, on the whole, to let mankind alone; though they were at times held responsible for the disappearance of venturesome individuals – especially persons who built houses too close to certain valleys or too high up on certain mountains. Many localities came to be known as inadvisable to settle in, the feeling persisting long after the cause was forgotten. People would look up at some of the neighboring mountain-precipices with a shudder, even when not recalling how many settlers had been lost, and how many farmhouses burnt to ashes, on the lower slopes of those grim, green sentinels.

But while according to the earliest legends the creatures would appear to have harmed only those trespassing on their privacy; there were later accounts of their curiosity respecting men, and of their attempts to establish secret outposts in the human world. There were tales of the queer claw-prints seen around farmhouse windows in the morning, and of occasional disappearances in regions outside the obviously haunted areas. Tales, besides, of buzzing voices in imitation of human speech which made surprising offers to lone travelers on roads and cart-paths in the deep woods, and of children frightened out of their wits by things seen or heard where the primal forest pressed close upon their door-yards. In the final layer of legends – the layer just preceding the decline of superstition and the abandonment of close contact with the dreaded places – there are shocked references to hermits and remote farmers who at some period of life appeared to have undergone a repellent mental change, and who were shunned and whispered about as mortals who had sold themselves to the strange beings. In one of the northeastern counties it seemed to be a fashion about 1800 to accuse eccentric and unpopular recluses of being allies or representatives of the abhorred things.

As to what the things were – explanations naturally varied. The common name applied to them was 'those ones', or 'the old ones', though other terms had a local and transient use. Perhaps the bulk of the Puritan settlers set them down bluntly as familiars of the devil, and made them a basis of awed theological speculation. Those with Celtic legendry in their heritage – mainly the Scotch-Irish element of New Hampshire, and their kindred who had settled in Vermont on Governor Wentworth's colonial grants – linked them vaguely with the malign fairies and 'little people' of the bogs and raths, and protected themselves with scraps of incantation handed down through many generations. But the Indians had the most fantastic theories of all. While different tribal legends differed, there was a marked consensus of belief in certain vital particulars; it being unanimously agreed that the creatures were not native to this earth.

The Pennacook myths, which were the most consistent and picturesque, taught that the Winged Ones came from the Great Bear in the sky, and had mines in our earthly hills whence they took a kind of stone they could not get on any other world. They did not live here, said the myths, but merely maintained outposts and flew back with vast cargoes of stone to their own stars in the north. They harmed only those earth-people who got too near them or spied upon them. Animals shunned them through instinctive hatred, not because of being hunted. They could not eat the things and animals of earth, but brought their own food from the stars. It was bad to get near them, and sometimes young hunters who went into their hills never came back. It was not good, either, to listen to what they whispered at night in the forest with voices like a bee's that tried to be like the voices of men. They knew the speech of all kinds of men – Pennacooks, Hurons, men of the Five Nations – but did not seem to have or need any speech of their own. They talked with their heads, which changed color in different ways to mean different things.

All the legendry, of course, white and Indian alike, died down during the nineteenth century, except for occasional atavistical flareups. The ways of the Vermonters became settled; and once their habitual paths and dwellings were established according to a certain fixed plan, they remembered less and less what fears and avoidances had determined that plan, and even that there had been any fears or avoidances. Most people simply knew that certain hilly regions were considered as highly unhealthy, unprofitable, and generally unlucky to live in, and that the farther one kept from them the better off one usually was. In time the ruts of custom and economic interest became so deeply cut in approved places that there was no longer any reason for going outside them, and the haunted hills were left deserted by accident rather than by design. Save during infrequent local scares, only wonder-loving grandmothers and retrospective nonagenarians ever whispered of beings dwelling in those hills; and even such whispers admitted that there was not much to fear from those things now that they were used to the presence of houses and settlements, and now that human beings let their chosen territory severely alone.

All this I had long known from my reading, and from certain folk tales picked up in New Hampshire; hence when the flood-time rumors began to appear, I could easily guess what imaginative background had evolved them. I took great pains to explain this to my friends, and was correspondingly amused when several contentious souls continued to insist on a possible element of truth in the reports. Such persons tried to point out that the early legends had a significant persistence and uniformity, and that the virtually unexplored nature of the Vermont hills made it unwise to be dogmatic about what might or might not dwell among them; nor could they be silenced by my assurance that all the myths were of a well-known pattern common to most of mankind and determined by early phases of imaginative experience which always produced the same type of delusion.

It was of no use to demonstrate to such opponents that the Vermont myths differed but little in essence from those universal legends of natural personification which filled the ancient world with fauns and dryads and satyrs, suggested the kallikanzarai of modern Greece, and gave to wild Wales and Ireland their dark hints of strange, small, and terrible hidden races of troglodytes and burrowers. No use, either, to point out the even more startlingly similar belief of the Nepalese hill tribes in the dreaded Mi-Go or 'Abominable Snow-Men' who lurk hideously amidst the ice and rock pinnacles of the Himalayan summits. When I brought up this evidence, my opponents turned it against me by claiming that it must imply some actual historicity for the ancient tales; that it must argue the real existence of some queer elder earth-race, driven to hiding after the advent and dominance of mankind, which might very conceivably have survived in reduced numbers to relatively recent times – or even to the present.

The more I laughed at such theories, the more these stubborn friends asseverated them; adding that even without the heritage of legend the recent reports were too clear, consistent, detailed, and sanely prosaic in manner of telling, to be completely ignored. Two or three fanatical extremists went so far as to hint at possible meanings in the ancient Indian tales which gave the hidden beings a nonterrestrial origin; citing the extravagant books of Charles Fort with their claims that voyagers from other worlds and outer space have often visited the earth. Most of my foes, however, were merely romanticists who insisted on trying to transfer to real life the fantastic lore of lurking 'little people' made popular by the magnificent horror-fiction of Arthur Machen.

Chapter II

AS WAS ONLY NATURAL under the circumstances, this piquant debating finally got into print in the form of letters to the *Arkham Advertiser*; some of which were copied in the press of those Vermont regions whence the flood-stories came. The *Rutland Herald* gave half a page of extracts from the letters on both sides, while the *Brattleboro Reformer* reprinted one of my long historical and mythological summaries in full, with some accompanying comments in 'The

Pendrifter's' thoughtful column which supported and applauded my skeptical conclusions. By the spring of 1928 I was almost a well-known figure in Vermont, notwithstanding the fact that I had never set foot in the state. Then came the challenging letters from Henry Akeley which impressed me so profoundly, and which took me for the first and last time to that fascinating realm of crowded green precipices and muttering forest streams.

Most of what I know of Henry Wentworth Akeley was gathered by correspondence with his neighbors, and with his only son in California, after my experience in his lonely farmhouse. He was, I discovered, the last representative on his home soil of a long, locally distinguished line of jurists, administrators, and gentlemen-agriculturists. In him, however, the family mentally had veered away from practical affairs to pure scholarship; so that he had been a notable student of mathematics, astronomy, biology, anthropology, and folklore at the University of Vermont. I had never previously heard of him, and he did not give many autobiographical details in his communications; but from the first I saw he was a man of character, education, and intelligence, albeit a recluse with very little worldly sophistication.

Despite the incredible nature of what he claimed, I could not help at once taking Akeley more seriously than I had taken any of the other challengers of my views. For one thing, he was really close to the actual phenomena – visible and tangible – that he speculated so grotesquely about; and for another thing, he was amazingly willing to leave his conclusions in a tentative state like a true man of science. He had no personal preferences to advance, and was always guided by what he took to be solid evidence. Of course I began by considering him mistaken, but gave him credit for being intelligently mistaken; and at no time did I emulate some of his friends in attributing his ideas, and his fear of the lonely green hills, to insanity. I could see that there was a great deal to the man, and knew that what he reported must surely come from strange circumstance deserving investigation, however little it might have to do with the fantastic causes he assigned. Later on I received from him certain material proofs which placed the matter on a somewhat different and bewilderingly bizarre basis.

I cannot do better than transcribe in full, so far as is possible, the long letter in which Akeley introduced himself, and which formed such an important landmark in my own intellectual history. It is no longer in my possession, but my memory holds almost every word of its portentous message; and again I affirm my confidence in the sanity of the man who wrote it. Here is the text – a text which reached me in the cramped, archaic-looking scrawl of one who had obviously not mingled much with the world during his sedate, scholarly life.

R.F.D. #2,
Townshend, Windham Co., Vermont.
May 5, 1928

Albert N. Wilmarth, Esq.,
118 Saltonstall St.,
Arkham, Mass.

My Dear Sir:
I have read with great interest the Brattleboro Reformer's reprint (Apr. 23, '28) of your letter on the recent stories of strange bodies seen floating in our flooded streams last fall, and on the curious folklore they so well agree with. It is easy to see why an outlander would take the position you take, and even why 'Pendrifter' agrees with you. That is the attitude generally taken by educated persons both in and out of Vermont, and was

my own attitude as a young man (I am now 57) before my studies, both general and in Davenport's book, led me to do some exploring in parts of the hills hereabouts not usually visited.

I was directed toward such studies by the queer old tales I used to hear from elderly farmers of the more ignorant sort, but now I wish I had let the whole matter alone. I might say, with all proper modesty, that the subject of anthropology and folklore is by no means strange to me. I took a good deal of it at college, and am familiar with most of the standard authorities such as Tylor, Lubbock, Frazer, Quatrefages, Murray, Osborn, Keith, Boule, G. Elliott Smith, and so on. It is no news to me that tales of hidden races are as old as all mankind. I have seen the reprints of letters from you, and those agreeing with you, in the Rutland Herald, and guess I know about where your controversy stands at the present time.

What I desire to say now is, that I am afraid your adversaries are nearer right than yourself, even though all reason seems to be on your side. They are nearer right than they realize themselves – for of course they go only by theory, and cannot know what I know. If I knew as little of the matter as they, I would feel justified in believing as they do. I would be wholly on your side.

You can see that I am having a hard time getting to the point, probably because I really dread getting to the point; but the upshot of the matter is that I have certain evidence that monstrous things do indeed live in the woods on the high hills which nobody visits. I have not seen any of the things floating in the rivers, as reported, but I have seen things like them under circumstances I dread to repeat. I have seen footprints, and of late have seen them nearer my own home (I live in the old Akeley place south of Townshend Village, on the side of Dark Mountain) than I dare tell you now. And I have overheard voices in the woods at certain points that I will not even begin to describe on paper.

At one place I heard them so much that I took a phonograph therewith a dictaphone attachment and wax blank – and I shall try to arrange to have you hear the record I got. I have run it on the machine for some of the old people up here, and one of the voices had nearly scared them paralyzed by reason of its likeness to a certain voice (that buzzing voice in the woods which Davenport mentions) that their grandmothers have told about and mimicked for them. I know what most people think of a man who tells about 'hearing voices' – but before you draw conclusions just listen to this record and ask some of the older backwoods people what they think of it. If you can account for it normally, very well; but there must be something behind it. 'Ex nihilo nihil fit', you know.

Now my object in writing you is not to start an argument but to give you information which I think a man of your tastes will find deeply interesting. This is private. Publicly I am on your side, for certain things show me that it does not do for people to know too much about these matters. My own studies are now wholly private, and I would not think of saying anything to attract people's attention and cause them to visit the places I have explored. It is true – terribly true – that there are non-human creatures watching us all the time; with spies among us gathering information. It is from a wretched man who, if he was sane (as I think he was) was one of those spies, that I got a large part of my clues to the matter. He later killed himself, but I have reason to think there are others now.

The things come from another planet, being able to live in interstellar space and fly through it on clumsy, powerful wings which have a way of resisting the aether but which are too poor at steering to be of much use in helping them about on earth. I will tell you about this later if you do not dismiss me at once as a madman. They come here to get metals from mines that go deep under the hills, and I think I know where they come from. They will not hurt us if we let them alone, but no one can say what will happen if we get too curious about them. Of course a good army of men could wipe out their mining colony. That is what they are afraid of. But if that happened, more would come from outside – any number of them. They could easily conquer the earth, but have not tried so far because they have not needed to. They would rather leave things as they are to save bother.

I think they mean to get rid of me because of what I have discovered. There is a great black stone with unknown hieroglyphics half worn away which I found in the woods on Round Hill, east of here; and after I took it home everything became different. If they think I suspect too much they will either kill me or take me off the earth to where they come from. They like to take away men of learning once in a while, to keep informed on the state of things in the human world.

This leads me to my secondary purpose in addressing you – namely, to urge you to hush up the present debate rather than give it more publicity. People must be kept away from these hills, and in order to effect this, their curiosity ought not to be aroused any further. Heaven knows there is peril enough anyway, with promoters and real estate men flooding Vermont with herds of summer people to overrun the wild places and cover the hills with cheap bungalows.

I shall welcome further communication with you, and shall try to send you that phonograph record and black stone (which is so worn that photographs don't show much) by express if you are willing. I say 'try' because I think those creatures have a way of tampering with things around here. There is a sullen furtive fellow named Brown, on a farm near the village, who I think is their spy. Little by little they are trying to cut me off from our world because I know too much about their world.

They have the most amazing way of finding out what I do. You may not even get this letter. I think I shall have to leave this part of the country and go live with my son in San Diego, Cal., if things get any worse, but it is not easy to give up the place you were born in, and where your family has lived for six generations. Also, I would hardly dare sell this house to anybody now that the creatures have taken notice of it. They seem to be trying to get the black stone back and destroy the phonograph record, but I shall not let them if I can help it. My great police dogs always hold them back, for there are very few here as yet, and they are clumsy in getting about. As I have said, their wings are not much use for short flights on earth. I am on the very brink of deciphering that stone – in a very terrible way – and with your knowledge of folklore you may be able to supply the missing links enough to help me. I suppose you know all about the fearful myths antedating the coming of man to the earth – the Yog-Sothoth and Cthulhu cycles – which are hinted at in the Necronomicon. I had access to a copy of that once, and hear that you have one in your college library under lock and key.

To conclude, Mr. Wilmarth, I think that with our respective studies we can be very useful to each other. I don't wish to put you in any peril, and suppose I ought to warn you that possession of the stone and the record won't be very safe; but I think you will find any risks worth running for the sake of knowledge. I will drive down to Newfane or Brattleboro to send whatever you authorize me to send, for the express offices there are more to be trusted. I might say that I live quite alone now, since I can't keep hired help any more. They won't stay because of the things that try to get near the house at night, and that keep the dogs barking continually. I am glad I didn't get as deep as this into the business while my wife was alive, for it would have driven her mad.

Hoping that I am not bothering you unduly, and that you will decide to get in touch with me rather than throw this letter into the waste basket as a madman's raving, I am
Yrs. very truly,
Henry W. Akeley
P.S. I am making some extra prints of certain photographs taken by me, which I think will help to prove a number of the points I have touched on. The old people think they are monstrously true. I shall send you these very soon if you are interested.
H.W.A.

It would be difficult to describe my sentiments upon reading this strange document for the first time. By all ordinary rules, I ought to have laughed more loudly at these extravagances than at the far milder theories which had previously moved me to mirth; yet something in the tone of the letter made me take it with paradoxical seriousness. Not that I believed for a moment in the hidden race from the stars which my correspondent spoke of; but that, after some grave preliminary doubts, I grew to feel oddly sure of his sanity and sincerity, and of his confrontation by some genuine though singular and abnormal phenomenon which he could not explain except in this imaginative way. It could not be as he thought it, I reflected, yet on the other hand, it could not be otherwise than worthy of investigation. The man seemed unduly excited and alarmed about something, but it was hard to think that all cause was lacking. He was so specific and logical in certain ways – and after all, his yarn did fit in so perplexingly well with some of the old myths – even the wildest Indian legends.

That he had really overheard disturbing voices in the hills, and had really found the black stone he spoke about, was wholly possible despite the crazy inferences he had made – inferences probably suggested by the man who had claimed to be a spy of the outer beings and had later killed himself. It was easy to deduce that this man must have been wholly insane, but that he probably had a streak of perverse outward logic which made the naive Akeley – already prepared for such things by his folklore studies – believe his tale. As for the latest developments – it appeared from his inability to keep hired help that Akeley's humbler rustic neighbors were as convinced as he that his house was besieged by uncanny things at night. The dogs really barked, too.

And then the matter of that phonograph record, which I could not but believe he had obtained in the way he said. It must mean something; whether animal noises deceptively like human speech, or the speech of some hidden, night-haunting human being decayed to a state not much above that of lower animals. From this my thoughts went back to the black hieroglyphed stone, and to speculations upon what it might mean. Then, too, what of the photographs which Akeley said he was about to send, and which the old people had found so convincingly terrible?

As I re-read the cramped handwriting I felt as never before that my credulous opponents might have more on their side than I had conceded. After all, there might be some queer and perhaps hereditarily misshapen outcasts in those shunned hills, even though no such race of star-born monsters as folklore claimed. And if there were, then the presence of strange bodies in the flooded streams would not be wholly beyond belief. Was it too presumptuous to suppose that both the old legends and the recent reports had this much of reality behind them? But even as I harbored these doubts I felt ashamed that so fantastic a piece of bizarrerie as Henry Akeley's wild letter had brought them up.

In the end I answered Akeley's letter, adopting a tone of friendly interest and soliciting further particulars. His reply came almost by return mail; and contained, true to promise, a number of Kodak views of scenes and objects illustrating what he had to tell. Glancing at these pictures as I took them from the envelope, I felt a curious sense of fright and nearness to forbidden things; for in spite of the vagueness of most of them, they had a damnably suggestive power which was intensified by the fact of their being genuine photographs – actual optical links with what they portrayed, and the product of an impersonal transmitting process without prejudice, fallibility, or mendacity.

The more I looked at them, the more I saw that my serious estimate of Akeley and his story had not been unjustified. Certainly, these pictures carried conclusive evidence of something in the Vermont hills which was at least vastly outside the radius of our common knowledge and belief. The worst thing of all was the footprint – a view taken where the sun shone on a mud patch somewhere in a deserted upland. This was no cheaply counterfeited thing, I could see at a glance; for the sharply defined pebbles and grassblades in the field of vision gave a clear index of scale and left no possibility of a tricky double exposure. I have called the thing a 'footprint', but 'claw-print' would be a better term. Even now I can scarcely describe it save to say that it was hideously crablike, and that there seemed to be some ambiguity about its direction. It was not a very deep or fresh print, but seemed to be about the size of an average man's foot. From a central pad, pairs of saw-toothed nippers projected in opposite directions – quite baffling as to function, if indeed the whole object were exclusively an organ of locomotion.

Another photograph – evidently a time-exposure taken in deep shadow – was of the mouth of a woodland cave, with a boulder of rounded regularity choking the aperture. On the bare ground in front of it, one could just discern a dense network of curious tracks, and when I studied the picture with a magnifier I felt uneasily sure that the tracks were like the one in the other view. A third picture showed a druid-like circle of standing stones on the summit of a wild hill. Around the cryptic circle the grass was very much beaten down and worn away, though I could not detect any footprints even with the glass. The extreme remoteness of the place was apparent from the veritable sea of tenantless mountains which formed the background and stretched away toward a misty horizon.

But if the most disturbing of all the views was that of the footprint, the most curiously suggestive was that of the great black stone found in the Round Hill woods. Akeley had photographed it on what was evidently his study table, for I could see rows of books and a bust of Milton in the background. The thing, as nearly as one might guess, had faced the camera vertically with a somewhat irregularly curved surface of one by two feet; but to say anything definite about that surface, or about the general shape of the whole mass, almost defies the power of language. What outlandish geometrical principles had guided its cutting – for artificially cut it surely was – I could not even begin to guess; and never before had I seen anything which struck me as so strangely and unmistakably alien to this world. Of the hieroglyphics on the surface I could discern very few, but one or two that I did see gave rather a shock. Of course they might be fraudulent, for others besides myself had read the monstrous and abhorred *Necronomicon* of the mad Arab Abdul Alhazred; but it nevertheless made me shiver to recognize certain ideographs which study had taught me to link with the most blood-curdling and blasphemous whispers of things that had had a kind of mad half-existence before the earth and the other inner worlds of the solar system were made.

Of the five remaining pictures, three were of swamp and hill scenes which seemed to bear traces of hidden and unwholesome tenancy. Another was of a queer mark in the ground very near Akeley's house, which he said he had photographed the morning after a night on which the dogs had barked more violently than usual. It was very blurred, and one could really draw no certain conclusions from it; but it did seem fiendishly like that other mark or claw-print photographed on

THE WHISPERER IN DARKNESS

the deserted upland. The final picture was of the Akeley place itself: a trim white house of two stories and attic, about a century and a quarter old, and with a well-kept lawn and stone-bordered path leading up to a tastefully carved Georgian doorway. There were several huge police dogs on the lawn, squatting near a pleasant-faced man with a close-cropped gray beard whom I took to be Akeley himself – his own photographer, one might infer from the tube-connected bulb in his right hand.

From the pictures I turned to the bulky, closely-written letter itself; and for the next three hours was immersed in a gulf of unutterable horror. Where Akeley had given only outlines before, he now entered into minute details; presenting long transcripts of words overheard in the woods at night, long accounts of monstrous pinkish forms spied in thickets at twilight on the hills, and a terrible cosmic narrative derived from the application of profound and varied scholarship to the endless bygone discourses of the mad self-styled spy who had killed himself. I found myself faced by names and terms that I had heard elsewhere in the most hideous of connections – Yuggoth, Great Cthulhu, Tsathoggua, YogSothoth, R'lyeh, Nyarlathotep, Azathoth, Hastur, Yian, Leng, the Lake of Hali, Bethmoora, the Yellow Sign, L'mur-Kathulos, Bran, and the Magnum Innominandum – and was drawn back through nameless aeons and inconceivable dimensions to worlds of elder, outer entity at which the crazed author of the *Necronomicon* had only guessed in the vaguest way. I was told of the pits of primal life, and of the streams that had trickled down therefrom; and finally, of the tiny rivulets from one of those streams which had become entangled with the destinies of our own earth.

My brain whirled; and where before I had attempted to explain things away, I now began to believe in the most abnormal and incredible wonders. The array of vital evidence was damnably vast and overwhelming; and the cool, scientific attitude of Akeley – an attitude removed as far as imaginable from the demented, the fanatical, the hysterical, or even the extravagantly speculative – had a tremendous effect on my thought and judgment. By the time I laid the frightful letter aside I could understand the fears he had come to entertain, and was ready to do anything in my power to keep people away from those wild, haunted hills. Even now, when time has dulled the impression and made me half-question my own experience and horrible doubts, there are things in that letter of Akeley's which I would not quote, or even form into words on paper. I am almost glad that the letter and record and photographs are gone now – and I wish, for reasons I shall soon make clear, that the new planet beyond Neptune had not been discovered.

With the reading of that letter my public debating about the Vermont horror permanently ended. Arguments from opponents remained unanswered or put off with promises, and eventually the controversy petered out into oblivion. During late May and June I was in constant correspondence with Akeley; though once in a while a letter would be lost, so that we would have to retrace our ground and perform considerable laborious copying. What we were trying to do, as a whole, was to compare notes in matters of obscure mythological scholarship and arrive at a clearer correlation of the Vermont horrors with the general body of primitive world legend.

For one thing, we virtually decided that these morbidities and the hellish Himalayan Mi-Go were one and the same order of incarnated nightmare. There was also absorbing zoological conjectures, which I would have referred to Professor Dexter in my own college but for Akeley's imperative command to tell no one of the matter before us. If I seem to disobey that command now, it is only because I think that at this stage a warning about those farther Vermont hills – and about those Himalayan peaks which bold explorers are more and more determined to ascend – is more conducive to public safety than silence would be. One specific thing we were leading up to was a deciphering of the hieroglyphics on that infamous black stone – a deciphering which might well place us in possession of secrets deeper and more dizzying than any formerly known to man.

Chapter III

TOWARD THE END of June the phonograph record came – shipped from Brattleboro, since Akeley was unwilling to trust conditions on the branch line north of there. He had begun to feel an increased sense of espionage, aggravated by the loss of some of our letters; and said much about the insidious deeds of certain men whom he considered tools and agents of the hidden beings. Most of all he suspected the surly farmer Walter Brown, who lived alone on a run-down hillside place near the deep woods, and who was often seen loafing around corners in Brattleboro, Bellows Falls, Newfane, and South Londonderry in the most inexplicable and seemingly unmotivated way. Brown's voice, he felt convinced, was one of those he had overheard on a certain occasion in a very terrible conversation; and he had once found a footprint or claw-print near Brown's house which might possess the most ominous significance. It had been curiously near some of Brown's own footprints – footprints that faced toward it.

So the record was shipped from Brattleboro, whither Akeley drove in his Ford car along the lonely Vermont back roads. He confessed in an accompanying note that he was beginning to be afraid of those roads, and that he would not even go into Townshend for supplies now except in broad daylight. It did not pay, he repeated again and again, to know too much unless one were very remote from those silent and problematical hills. He would be going to California pretty soon to live with his son, though it was hard to leave a place where all one's memories and ancestral feelings centred.

Before trying the record on the commercial machine which I borrowed from the college administration building I carefully went over all the explanatory matter in Akeley's various letters. This record, he had said, was obtained about 1 a.m. on the 1st of May, 1915, near the closed mouth of a cave where the wooded west slope of Dark Mountain rises out of Lee's swamp. The place had always been unusually plagued with strange voices, this being the reason he had brought the phonograph, dictaphone, and blank in expectation of results. Former experience had told him that May Eve – the hideous Sabbat-night of underground European legend – would probably be more fruitful than any other date, and he was not disappointed. It was noteworthy, though, that he never again heard voices at that particular spot.

Unlike most of the overheard forest voices, the substance of the record was quasi-ritualistic, and included one palpably human voice which Akeley had never been able to place. It was not Brown's, but seemed to be that of a man of greater cultivation. The second voice, however, was the real crux of the thing – for this was the accursed buzzing which had no likeness to humanity despite the human words which it uttered in good English grammar and a scholarly accent.

The recording phonograph and dictaphone had not worked uniformly well, and had of course been at a great disadvantage because of the remote and muffled nature of the overheard ritual; so that the actual speech secured was very fragmentary. Akeley had given me a transcript of what he believed the spoken words to be, and I glanced through this again as I prepared the machine for action. The text was darkly mysterious rather than openly horrible, though a knowledge of its origin and manner of gathering gave it all the associative horror which any words could well possess. I will present it here in full as I remember it – and I am fairly confident that I know it correctly by heart, not only from reading the transcript, but from playing the record itself over and over again. It is not a thing which one might readily forget!

(Indistinguishable Sounds)

(A Cultivated Male Human Voice)
... is the Lord of the Wood, even to ...and the gifts of the men of Leng ...so from the wells of night to the gulfs of space, and from the gulfs of space to the wells of night, ever the praises of Great Cthulhu, of Tsathoggua, and of Him Who is not to be Named. Ever Their praises, and abundance to the Black Goat of the Woods. Ia! Shub-Niggurath! The Goat with a Thousand Young!

(A Buzzing Imitation of Human Speech)
Iä! Shub-Niggurath! The Black Goat of the Woods with a Thousand Young!

(Human Voice)
And it has come to pass that the Lord of the Woods, being ...seven and nine, down the onyx steps ...(tri)butes to Him in the Gulf, Azathoth, He of Whom Thou has taught us marv(els) ...on the wings of night out beyond space, out beyond th ...to That whereof Yuggoth is the youngest child, rolling alone in black aether at the rim ...

(Buzzing Voice)
... go out among men and find the ways thereof, that He in the Gulf may know. To Nyarlathotep, Mighty Messenger, must all things be told. And He shall put on the semblance of men, the waxen mask and the robe that hides, and come down from the world of Seven Suns to mock ...

(Human Voice)
(Nyarl)athotep, Great Messenger, bringer of strange joy to Yuggoth through the void, Father of the Million Favored Ones, Stalker among ...

(Speech Cut Off by End of Record)

Such were the words for which I was to listen when I started the phonograph. It was with a trace of genuine dread and reluctance that I pressed the lever and heard the preliminary scratching of the sapphire point, and I was glad that the first faint, fragmentary words were in a human voice – a mellow, educated voice which seemed vaguely Bostonian in accent, and which was certainly not that of any native of the Vermont hills. As I listened to the tantalizingly feeble rendering, I seemed to find the speech identical with Akeley's carefully prepared transcript. On it chanted, in that mellow Bostonian voice ..."*Ia! Shub-Niggurath! The Goat with a Thousand Young! ...*"

And then I heard *the other voice*. To this hour I shudder retrospectively when I think of how it struck me, prepared though I was by Akeley's accounts. Those to whom I have since described the record profess to find nothing but cheap imposture or madness in it; but *could they have the accursed thing itself*, or read the bulk of Akeley's correspondence, (especially that terrible and encyclopaedic second letter), I know they would think differently. It is, after all, a tremendous pity that I did not disobey Akeley and play the record for others – a tremendous pity, too, that all of his letters were lost. To me, with my first-hand impression of the actual sounds, and with my knowledge of the background and surrounding circumstances, the voice was a monstrous thing. It swiftly followed the human voice in ritualistic response, but in my imagination it was a morbid echo winging its way across unimaginable abysses from unimaginable outer hells. It is more than two years now since I last ran off that blasphemous waxen cylinder; but at this moment, and at all other moments, I can still hear that feeble, fiendish buzzing as it reached me for the first time.

"*Iä! Shub-Niggurath!* The Black Goat of the Woods with a Thousand Young!"

But though the voice is always in my ears, I have not even yet been able to analyze it well enough for a graphic description. It was like the drone of some loathsome, gigantic insect ponderously shaped into the articulate speech of an alien species, and I am perfectly certain that the organs producing it can have no resemblance to the vocal organs of man, or indeed to those of any of the mammalia. There were singularities in timbre, range, and overtones which placed this phenomenon wholly outside the sphere of humanity and earth-life. Its sudden advent that first time almost stunned me, and I heard the rest of the record through in a sort of abstracted daze. When the longer passage of buzzing came, there was a sharp intensification of that feeling of blasphemous infinity which had struck me during the shorter and earlier passage. At last the record ended abruptly, during an unusually clear speech of the human and Bostonian voice; but I sat stupidly staring long after the machine had automatically stopped.

I hardly need say that I gave that shocking record many another playing, and that I made exhaustive attempts at analysis and comment in comparing notes with Akeley. It would be both useless and disturbing to repeat here all that we concluded; but I may hint that we agreed in believing we had secured a clue to the source of some of the most repulsive primordial customs in the cryptic elder religions of mankind. It seemed plain to us, also, that there were ancient and elaborate alliance; between the hidden outer creatures and certain members of the human race. How extensive these alliances were, and how their state today might compare with their state in earlier ages, we had no means of guessing; yet at best there was room for a limitless amount of horrified speculation. There seemed to be an awful, immemorial linkage in several definite stages betwixt man and nameless infinity. The blasphemies which appeared on earth, it was hinted, came from the dark planet Yuggoth, at the rim of the solar system; but this was itself merely the populous outpost of a frightful interstellar race whose ultimate source must lie far outside even the Einsteinian space-time continuum or greatest known cosmos.

Meanwhile we continued to discuss the black stone and the best way of getting it to Arkham – Akeley deeming it inadvisable to have me visit him at the scene of his nightmare studies. For some reason or other, Akeley was afraid to trust the thing to any ordinary or expected transportation route. His final idea was to take it across country to Bellows Falls and ship it on the Boston and Maine system through Keene and Winchendon and Fitchburg, even though this would necessitate his driving along somewhat lonelier and more forest-traversing hill roads than the main highway to Brattleboro. He said he had noticed a man around the express office at Brattleboro when he had sent the phonograph record, whose actions and expression had been far from reassuring. This man had seemed too anxious to talk with the clerks, and had taken the train on which the record was shipped. Akeley confessed that he had not felt strictly at ease about that record until he heard from me of its safe receipt.

About this time – the second week in July – another letter of mine went astray, as I learned through an anxious communication from Akeley. After that he told me to address him no more at Townshend, but to send all mail in care of the General Delivery at Brattleboro; whither he would make frequent trips either in his car or on the motor-coach line which had lately replaced passenger service on the lagging branch railway. I could see that he was getting more and more anxious, for he went into much detail about the increased barking of the dogs on moonless nights, and about the fresh claw-prints he sometimes found in the road and in the mud at the back of his farmyard when morning came. Once he told about a veritable army of prints drawn up in a line facing an equally thick and resolute line of dog-tracks, and sent a loathsomely disturbing Kodak picture to prove it. That was after a night on which the dogs had outdone themselves in barking and howling.

On the morning of Wednesday, July 18, I received a telegram from Bellows Falls, in which Akeley said he was expressing the black stone over the B. & M. on Train No. 5508, leaving Bellows Falls at 12:15 p.m., standard time, and due at the North Station in Boston at 4:12 p.m. It ought, I calculated, to get up to Arkham at least by the next noon; and accordingly I stayed in all Thursday morning to receive it. But noon came and went without its advent, and when I telephoned down to the express office I was informed that no shipment for me had arrived. My next act, performed amidst a growing alarm, was to give a long-distance call to the express agent at the Boston North Station; and I was scarcely surprised to learn that my consignment had not appeared. Train No. 5508 had pulled in only 35 minutes late on the day before, but had contained no box addressed to me. The agent promised, however, to institute a searching inquiry; and I ended the day by sending Akeley a night-letter outlining the situation.

With commendable promptness a report came from the Boston office on the following afternoon, the agent telephoning as soon as he learned the facts. It seemed that the railway express clerk on No. 5508 had been able to recall an incident which might have much bearing on my loss – an argument with a very curious-voiced man, lean, sandy, and rustic-looking, when the train was waiting at Keene, N.H., shortly after one o'clock standard time. The man, he said, was greatly excited about a heavy box which he claimed to expect, but which was neither on the train nor entered on the company's books. He had given the name of Stanley Adams, and had had such a queerly thick droning voice, that it made the clerk abnormally dizzy and sleepy to listen to him. The clerk could not remember quite how the conversation had ended, but recalled starting into a fuller awakeness when the train began to move. The Boston agent added that this clerk was a young man of wholly unquestioned veracity and reliability, of known antecedents and long with the company.

That evening I went to Boston to interview the clerk in person, having obtained his name and address from the office. He was a frank, prepossessing fellow, but I saw that he could add nothing to his original account. Oddly, he was scarcely sure that he could even recognize the strange inquirer again. Realizing that he had no more to tell, I returned to Arkham and sat up till morning writing letters to Akeley, to the express company and to the police department and station agent in Keene. I felt that the strange-voiced man who had so queerly affected the clerk must have a pivotal place in the ominous business, and hoped that Keene station employees and telegraph-office records might tell something about him and about how he happened to make his inquiry when and where he did.

I must admit, however, that all my investigations came to nothing. The queer-voiced man had indeed been noticed around the Keene station in the early afternoon of July 18, and one lounger seemed to couple him vaguely with a heavy box; but he was altogether unknown, and had not been seen before or since. He had not visited the telegraph office or received any message so far as could be learned, nor had any message which might justly be considered a notice of the black stone's presence on No. 5508 come through the office for anyone. Naturally Akeley joined with me in conducting these inquiries, and even made a personal trip to Keene to question the people around the station; but his attitude toward the matter was more fatalistic than mine. He seemed to find the loss of the box a portentous and menacing fulfillment of inevitable tendencies, and had no real hope at all of its recovery. He spoke of the undoubted telepathic and hypnotic powers of the hill creatures and their agents, and in one letter hinted that he did not believe the stone was on this earth any longer. For my part, I was duly enraged, for I had felt there was at least a chance of learning profound and astonishing things from the old, blurred hieroglyphs. The matter would have rankled bitterly in my mind had not Akeley's immediately subsequent letters brought up a new phase of the whole horrible hill problem which at once seized all my attention.

Chapter IV

THE UNKNOWN THINGS, Akeley wrote in a script grown pitifully tremulous, had begun to close in on him with a wholly new degree of determination. The nocturnal barking of the dogs whenever the moon was dim or absent was hideous now, and there had been attempts to molest him on the lonely roads he had to traverse by day. On the second of August, while bound for the village in his car, he had found a tree-trunk laid in his path at a point where the highway ran through a deep patch of woods; while the savage barking of the two great dogs he had with him told all too well of the things which must have been lurking near. What would have happened had the dogs not been there, he did not dare guess – but he never went out now without at least two of his faithful and powerful pack. Other road experiences had occurred on August fifth and sixth; a shot grazing his car on one occasion, and the barking of the dogs telling of unholy woodland presences on the other.

On August fifteenth I received a frantic letter which disturbed me greatly, and which made me wish Akeley could put aside his lonely reticence and call in the aid of the law. There had been frightful happening on the night of the 12–13th, bullets flying outside the farmhouse, and three of the twelve great dogs being found shot dead in the morning. There were myriads of claw-prints in the road, with the human prints of Walter Brown among them. Akeley had started to telephone to Brattleboro for more dogs, but the wire had gone dead before he had a chance to say much. Later he went to Brattleboro in his car, and learned there that linemen had found the main cable neatly cut at a point where it ran through the deserted hills north of Newfane. But he was about to start home with four fine new dogs, and several cases of ammunition for his big-game repeating rifle. The letter was written at the post office in Brattleboro, and came through to me without delay.

My attitude toward the matter was by this time quickly slipping from a scientific to an alarmedly personal one. I was afraid for Akeley in his remote, lonely farmhouse, and half afraid for myself because of my now definite connection with the strange hill problem. The thing was reaching out so. Would it suck me in and engulf me? In replying to his letter I urged him to seek help, and hinted that I might take action myself if he did not. I spoke of visiting Vermont in person in spite of his wishes, and of helping him explain the situation to the proper authorities. In return, however, I received only a telegram from Bellows Falls which read thus:

> *APPRECIATE YOUR POSITION BUT CAN DO NOTHING TAKE NO ACTION YOURSELF FOR IT COULD ONLY HARM BOTH WAIT FOR EXPLANATION*
> *HENRY AKELY*

But the affair was steadily deepening. Upon my replying to the telegram I received a shaky note from Akeley with the astonishing news that he had not only never sent the wire, but had not received the letter from me to which it was an obvious reply. Hasty inquiries by him at Bellows Falls had brought out that the message was deposited by a strange sandy-haired man with a curiously thick, droning voice, though more than this he could not learn. The clerk showed him the original text as scrawled in pencil by the sender, but the handwriting was wholly unfamiliar. It was noticeable that the signature was misspelled – A-K-E-L-Y, without the second 'E'. Certain conjectures were inevitable, but amidst the obvious crisis he did not stop to elaborate upon them.

He spoke of the death of more dogs and the purchase of still others, and of the exchange of gunfire which had become a settled feature each moonless night. Brown's prints, and the prints of at least one or two more shod human figures, were now found regularly among the claw-prints in the road, and at the back of the farmyard. It was, Akeley admitted, a pretty bad business; and before long he would probably have to go to live with his California son whether or not he could sell the old place. But it was not easy to leave the only spot one could really think of as home. He must try to hang on a little longer; perhaps he could scare off the intruders – especially if he openly gave up all further attempts to penetrate their secrets.

Writing Akeley at once, I renewed my offers of aid, and spoke again of visiting him and helping him convince the authorities of his dire peril. In his reply he seemed less set against that plan than his past attitude would have led one to predict, but said he would like to hold off a little while longer – long enough to get his things in order and reconcile himself to the idea of leaving an almost morbidly cherished birthplace. People looked askance at his studies and speculations and it would be better to get quietly off without setting the countryside in a turmoil and creating widespread doubts of his own sanity. He had had enough, he admitted, but he wanted to make a dignified exit if he could.

This letter reached me on the 28th of August, and I prepared and mailed as encouraging a reply as I could. Apparently the encouragement had effect, for Akeley had fewer terrors to report when he acknowledged my note. He was not very optimistic, though, and expressed the belief that it was only the full moon season which was holding the creatures off. He hoped there would not be many densely cloudy nights, and talked vaguely of boarding in Brattleboro when the moon waned. Again I wrote him encouragingly but on September 5th there came a fresh communication which had obviously crossed my letter in the mails; and to this I could not give any such hopeful response. In view of its importance I believe I had better give it in full – as best I can do from memory of the shaky script. It ran substantially as follows:

Monday

Dear Wilmarth

A rather discouraging P.S. to my last. Last night was thickly cloudy – though no rain – and not a bit of moonlight got through. Things were pretty bad, and I think the end is getting near, in spite of all we have hoped. After midnight something landed on the roof of the house, and the dogs all rushed up to see what it was. I could hear them snapping and tearing around, and then one managed to get on the roof by jumping from the low ell. There was a terrible fight up there, and I heard a frightful buzzing which I'll never forget. And then there was a shocking smell. About the same time bullets came through the window and nearly grazed me. I think the main line of the hill creatures had got close to the house when the dogs divided because of the roof business. What was up there I don't know yet, but I'm afraid the creatures are learning to steer better with their space wings. I put out the light and used the windows for loopholes, and raked all around the house with rifle fire aimed just high enough not to hit the dogs. That seemed to end the business, but in the morning I found great pools of blood in the yard, besides pools of a green sticky stuff that had the worst odor I have ever smelled. I climbed up on the roof and found more of the sticky stuff there. Five of the dogs were killed – I'm afraid I hit one myself by aiming too low, for he was shot in the back. Now I am setting the panes the shots broke, and am going to Brattleboro for more dogs. I guess the men at the kennels think I am crazy. Will drop another note later. Suppose I'll be ready for moving in a week or two, though it nearly kills me to think of it.

Hastily – Akeley

But this was not the only letter from Akeley to cross mine. On the next morning – September 6th – still another came; this time a frantic scrawl which utterly unnerved me and put me at a loss what to say or do next. Again I cannot do better than quote the text as faithfully as memory will let me.

Tuesday

Clouds didn't break, so no moon again – and going into the wane anyhow. I'd have the house wired for electricity and put in a searchlight if I didn't know they'd cut the cables as fast as they could be mended.

I think I am going crazy. It may be that all I have ever written you is a dream or madness. It was bad enough before, but this time it is too much. They talked to me last night – talked in that cursed buzzing voice and told me things that I dare not repeat to you. I heard them plainly above the barking of the dogs, and once when they were drowned out a human voice helped them. Keep out of this, Wilmarth – it is worse than either you or I ever suspected. They don't mean to let me get to California now – they want to take me off alive, or what theoretically and mentally amounts to alive – not only to Yuggoth, but beyond that – away outside the galaxy and possibly beyond the last curved rim of space. I told them I wouldn't go where they wish, or in the terrible way they propose to take me, but I'm afraid it will be no use. My place is so far out that they may come by day as well as by night before long. Six more dogs killed, and I felt presences all along the wooded parts of the road when I drove to Brattleboro today. It was a mistake for me to try to send you that phonograph record and black stone. Better smash the record before it's too late. Will drop you another line tomorrow if I'm still here. Wish I could arrange to get my books and things to Brattleboro and board there. I would run off without anything if I could but something inside my mind holds me back. I can slip out to Brattleboro, where I ought to be safe, but I feel just as much a prisoner there as at the house. And I seem to know that I couldn't get much farther even if I dropped everything and tried. It is horrible – don't get mixed up in this.

Yrs – Akeley

I did not sleep at all the night after receiving this terrible thing, and was utterly baffled as to Akeley's remaining degree of sanity. The substance of the note was wholly insane, yet the manner of expression – in view of all that had gone before – had a grimly potent quality of convincingness. I made no attempt to answer it, thinking it better to wait until Akeley might have time to reply to my latest communication. Such a reply indeed came on the following day, though the fresh material in it quite overshadowed any of the points brought up by the letter nominally answered. Here is what I recall of the text, scrawled and blotted as it was in the course of a plainly frantic and hurried composition.

Wednesday

W–

Your letter came, but it's no use to discuss anything any more. I am fully resigned. Wonder that I have even enough will power left to fight them off. Can't escape even if I were willing to give up everything and run. They'll get me.

Had a letter from them yesterday – R.F.D. man brought it while I was at Brattleboro. Typed and postmarked Bellows Falls. Tells what they want to do with me – I can't repeat it. Look out for yourself, too! Smash that record. Cloudy nights keep up, and moon waning all the time. Wish I dared to get help – it might brace up my will power – but everyone who would dare to come at all would call me crazy unless there happened to be some proof. Couldn't ask people to come for no reason at all – am all out of touch with everybody and have been for years.

But I haven't told you the worst, Wilmarth. Brace up to read this, for it will give you a shock. I am telling the truth, though. It is this – I have seen and touched one of the things, or part of one of the things. God, man, but it's awful! It was dead, of course. One of the dogs had it, and I found it near the kennel this morning. I tried to save it in the woodshed to convince people of the whole thing, but it all evaporated in a few hours. Nothing left. You know, all those things in the rivers were seen only on the first morning after the flood. And here's the worst. I tried to photograph it for you, but when I developed the film there wasn't anything visible except the woodshed. What can the thing have been made of? I saw it and felt it, and they all leave footprints. It was surely made of matter – but what kind of matter? The shape can't be described. It was a great crab with a lot of pyramided fleshy rings or knots of thick, ropy stuff covered with feelers where a man's head would be. That green sticky stuff is its blood or juice. And there are more of them due on earth any minute.

Walter Brown is missing – hasn't been seen loafing around any of his usual corners in the villages hereabouts. I must have got him with one of my shots, though the creatures always seem to try to take their dead and wounded away.

Got into town this afternoon without any trouble, but am afraid they're beginning to hold off because they're sure of me. Am writing this in Brattleboro P.O. This may be goodbye – if it is, write my son George Goodenough Akeley, 176 Pleasant St., San Diego, Cal., but don't come up here. Write the boy if you don't hear from me in a week, and watch the papers for news.

I'm going to play my last two cards now – if I have the will power left. First to try poison gas on the things (I've got the right chemicals and have fixed up masks for myself and the dogs) and then if that doesn't work, tell the sheriff. They can lock me in a madhouse if they want to – it'll be better than what the other creatures would do. Perhaps I can get them to pay attention to the prints around the house – they are faint, but I can find them every morning. Suppose, though, police would say I faked them somehow; for they all think I'm a queer character.

Must try to have a state policeman spend a night here and see for himself – though it would be just like the creatures to learn about it and hold off that night. They cut my wires whenever I try to telephone in the night – the linemen think it is very queer, and may testify for me if they don't go and imagine I cut them myself. I haven't tried to keep them repaired for over a week now.

I could get some of the ignorant people to testify for me about the reality of the horrors, but everybody laughs at what they say, and anyway, they have shunned my place for so long that they don't know any of the new events. You couldn't get one of those rundown farmers to come within a mile of my house for love or money. The mail-carrier hears what they say and jokes me about it – God! If I only dared tell him how real it is! I think I'll try to get him to notice the prints, but he comes in the afternoon and they're usually about gone by that time. If I kept one by setting a box or pan over it, he'd think surely it was a fake or joke.

Wish I hadn't gotten to be such a hermit, so folks don't drop around as they used to. I've never dared show the black stone or the Kodak pictures, or play that record, to anybody but the ignorant people. The others would say I faked the whole business and do nothing but laugh. But I may yet try showing the pictures. They give those claw-prints *clearly, even if the things that made them can't be photographed. What a shame nobody else saw that thing this morning before it went to nothing!*

But I don't know as I care. After what I've been through, a madhouse is as good a place as any. The doctors can help me make up my mind to get away from this house, and that is all that will save me.

Write my son George if you don't hear soon. Goodbye, smash that record, and don't mix up in this.

Yrs – Akeley

This letter frankly plunged me into the blackest of terror. I did not know what to say in answer, but scratched off some incoherent words of advice and encouragement and sent them by registered mail. I recall urging Akeley to move to Brattleboro at once, and place himself under the protection of the authorities; adding that I would come to that town with the phonograph record and help convince the courts of his sanity. It was time, too, I think I wrote, to alarm the people generally against this thing in their midst. It will be observed that at this moment of stress my own belief in all Akeley had told and claimed was virtually complete, though I did think his failure to get a picture of the dead monster was due not to any freak of Nature but to some excited slip of his own.

Chapter V

THEN, apparently crossing my incoherent note and reaching me Saturday afternoon, September 8th, came that curiously different and calming letter neatly typed on a new machine; that strange letter of reassurance and invitation which must have marked so prodigious a transition in the whole nightmare drama of the lonely hills. Again I will quote from memory – seeking for special reasons to preserve as much of the flavor of the style as I can. It was postmarked Bellows Falls, and the signature as well as the body of the letter was typed – as is frequent with beginners in typing. The text, though, was marvellously accurate for a tyro's work; and I concluded that Akeley must have used a machine at some previous period – perhaps in college. To say that the letter relieved me would be only fair, yet beneath my relief lay a substratum of uneasiness. If Akeley had been sane in his terror, was he now sane in his deliverance? And the sort of 'improved rapport' mentioned ... what was it? The entire thing implied such a diametrical reversal of Akeley's previous attitude! But here is the substance of the text, carefully transcribed from a memory in which I take some pride.

Townshend, Vermont,
Thursday, Sept. 6, 1928.

TO ALBERT N. WILMARTH, ESQ.,
MISKATONIC UNIVERSITY,
ARKHAM, MASS.

My dear Wilmarth:
It gives me great pleasure to be able to set you at rest regarding all the silly things I've been writing you. I say 'silly,' although by that I mean my frightened attitude rather than my descriptions of certain phenomena. Those phenomena are real and important enough; my mistake had been in establishing an anomalous attitude toward them.

I think I mentioned that my strange visitors were beginning to communicate with me, and to attempt such communication. Last night this exchange of speech became actual. In response to certain signals I admitted to the house a messenger from those outside – a fellow-human, let me hasten to say. He told me much that neither you nor I had even begun to guess, and showed clearly how totally we had misjudged and misinterpreted the purpose of the Outer Ones in maintaining their secret colony on this planet.

It seems that the evil legends about what they have offered to men, and what they wish in connection with the earth, are wholly the result of an ignorant misconception of allegorical speech – speech, of course, moulded by cultural backgrounds and thought-habits vastly different from anything we dream of. My own conjectures, I freely own, shot as widely past the mark as any of the guesses of illiterate farmers and savage Indians. What I had thought morbid and shameful and ignominious is in reality awesome and mind-expanding and even glorious – my previous estimate being merely a phase of man's eternal tendency to hate and fear and shrink from the utterly different.

Now I regret the harm I have inflicted upon these alien and incredible beings in the course of our nightly skirmishes. If only I had consented to talk peacefully and reasonably with them in the first place! But they bear me no grudge, their emotions being organized very differently from ours. It is their misfortune to have had as their human agents in Vermont some very inferior specimens – the late Walter Brown, for example. He prejudiced me vastly against them. Actually, they have never knowingly harmed men, but have often been cruelly wronged and spied upon by our species. There is a whole secret cult of evil men (a man of your mystical erudition will understand me when I link them with Hastur and the Yellow Sign) devoted to the purpose of tracking them down and injuring them on behalf of monstrous powers from other dimensions. It is against these aggressors – not against normal humanity – that the drastic precautions of the Outer Ones are directed. Incidentally, I learned that many of our lost letters were stolen not by the Outer Ones but by the emissaries of this malign cult.

All that the Outer Ones wish of man is peace and non-molestation and an increasing intellectual rapport. This latter is absolutely necessary now that our inventions and devices are expanding our knowledge and motions, and making it more and more impossible for the Outer Ones' necessary outposts to exist secretly on this planet. The alien beings desire to know mankind more fully, and to have a few of mankind's philosophic and scientific leaders know more about them. With such an exchange of knowledge all perils will pass, and a satisfactory modus vivendi be established. The very idea of any attempt to enslave or degrade mankind is ridiculous.

As a beginning of this improved rapport, the Outer Ones have naturally chosen me – whose knowledge of them is already so considerable – as their primary interpreter on earth. Much was told me last night – facts of the most stupendous and vista-opening nature – and more will be subsequently communicated to me both orally and in writing. I shall not be called upon to make any trip outside just yet, though I shall probably wish to do so later on – employing special means and transcending everything which we have hitherto been accustomed to regard as human experience. My house will be besieged no longer. Everything has reverted to normal, and the dogs will have no further occupation. In place of terror I have been given a rich boon of knowledge and intellectual adventure which few other mortals have ever shared.

The Outer Beings are perhaps the most marvellous organic things in or beyond all space and time-members of a cosmos-wide race of which all other life-forms are merely degenerate variants. They are more vegetable than animal, if these terms can be applied to the sort of matter composing them, and have a somewhat fungoid structure; though the presence of a chlorophyll-like substance and a very singular nutritive system differentiate them altogether from true cormophytic fungi. Indeed, the type is composed of a form of matter totally alien to our part of space – with electrons having a wholly different vibration-rate. That is why the beings cannot be photographed on the ordinary camera films and plates of our known universe, even though our eyes can see them. With proper knowledge, however, any good chemist could make a photographic emulsion which would record their images.

The genus is unique in its ability to traverse the heatless and airless interstellar void in full corporeal form, and some of its variants cannot do this without mechanical aid or curious surgical transpositions. Only a few species have the ether-resisting wings characteristic of the Vermont variety. Those inhabiting certain remote peaks in the Old World were brought in other ways. Their external resemblance to animal life, and to the sort of structure we understand as material, is a matter of parallel evolution rather than of close kinship. Their brain-capacity exceeds that of any other surviving life-form, although the winged types of our hill country are by no means the most highly developed. Telepathy is their usual means of discourse, though we have rudimentary vocal organs which, after a slight operation (for surgery is an incredibly expert and everyday thing among them), can roughly duplicate the speech of such types of organism as still use speech.

Their main immediate abode is a still undiscovered and almost lightless planet at the very edge of our solar system – beyond Neptune, and the ninth in distance from the sun. It is, as we have inferred, the object mystically hinted at as 'Yuggoth' in certain ancient and forbidden writings; and it will soon be the scene of a strange focussing of thought upon our world in an effort to facilitate mental rapport. I would not be surprised if astronomers become sufficiently sensitive to these thought-currents to discover Yuggoth when the Outer Ones wish them to do so. But Yuggoth, of course, is only the stepping-stone. The main body of the beings inhabits strangely organized abysses wholly beyond the utmost reach of any human imagination. The space-time globule which we recognize as the totality of all cosmic entity is only an atom in the genuine infinity which is theirs. And as much of this infinity as any human brain can hold is eventually to be opened up to me, as it has been to not more than fifty other men since the human race has existed. .

You will probably call this raving at first, Wilmarth, but in time you will appreciate the titanic opportunity I have stumbled upon. I want you to share as much of it as is possible, and to that end must tell you thousands of things that won't go on paper. In the past I have warned you not to come to see me. Now that all is safe, I take pleasure in rescinding that warning and inviting you.

Can't you make a trip up here before your college term opens? It would be marvelously delightful if you could. Bring along the phonograph record and all my letters to you as consultative data – we shall need them in piecing together the whole tremendous story. You might bring the Kodak prints, too, since I seem to have mislaid the negatives and my own prints in all this recent excitement. But what a wealth of facts I have to add to all this groping and tentative material – and what a stupendous device I have to supplement my additions!

Don't hesitate – I am free from espionage now, and you will not meet anything unnatural or disturbing. Just come along and let my car meet you at the Brattleboro *station – prepare to stay as long as you can, and expect many an evening of discussion of things beyond all human conjecture. Don't tell anyone about it, of course – for this matter must not get to the promiscuous public.*

The train service to Brattleboro is not bad – you can get a timetable in Boston. Take the B. & M. to Greenfield, and then change for the brief remainder of the way. I suggest your taking the convenient 4:10 p.m. – standard – from Boston. This gets into Greenfield at 7:35, and at 9:19 a train leaves there which reaches Brattleboro at 10:01. That is weekdays. Let me know the date and I'll have my car on hand at the station.

Pardon this typed letter, but my handwriting has grown shaky of late, as you know, and I don't feel equal to long stretches of script. I got this new Corona in Brattleboro yesterday – it seems to work very well.

Awaiting word, and hoping to see you shortly with the phonograph record and all my letters – and the Kodak prints –

I am

Yours in anticipation,

Henry W. Akeley

The complexity of my emotions upon reading, re-reading, and pondering over this strange and unlooked-for letter is past adequate description. I have said that I was at once relieved and made uneasy, but this expresses only crudely the overtones of diverse and largely subconscious feelings which comprised both the relief and the uneasiness. To begin with, the thing was so antipodally at variance with the whole chain of horrors preceding it – the change of mood from stark terror to cool complacency and even exultation was so unheralded, lightning-like, and complete! I could scarcely believe that a single day could so alter the psychological perspective of one who had written that final frenzied bulletin of Wednesday, no matter what relieving disclosures that day might have brought. At certain moments a sense of conflicting unrealities made me wonder whether this whole distantly reported drama of fantastic forces were not a kind of half-illusory dream created largely within my own mind. Then I thought of the phonograph record and gave way to still greater bewilderment.

The letter seemed so unlike anything which could have been expected! As I analyzed my impression, I saw that it consisted of two distinct phases. First, granting that Akeley had been sane before and was still sane, the indicated change in the situation itself was so swift and unthinkable. And secondly, the change in Akeley's own manner, attitude, and language was so vastly beyond the normal or the predictable. The man's whole personality seemed to have undergone an insidious mutation – a mutation so deep that one could scarcely reconcile his two aspects with the supposition that both represented equal sanity. Word-choice, spelling – all were subtly different. And with my academic sensitiveness to prose style, I could trace profound divergences in his commonest reactions and rhythm-responses. Certainly, the emotional cataclysm or revelation which could produce so radical an overturn must be an extreme one indeed! Yet in another way the letter seemed quite characteristic of Akeley. The same old passion for infinity – the same old scholarly inquisitiveness. I could not a moment – or more than a moment – credit the idea of spuriousness or malign substitution. Did not the invitation – the willingness to have me test the truth of the letter in person – prove its genuineness?

I did not retire Saturday night, but sat up thinking of the shadows and marvels behind the letter I had received. My mind, aching from the quick succession of monstrous conceptions it had been forced to confront during the last four months, worked upon this startling new material in a cycle of doubt and acceptance which repeated most of the steps experienced in facing the earlier wonders; till long before dawn a burning interest and curiosity had begun to replace the original storm of perplexity and uneasiness. Mad or sane, metamorphosed or merely relieved, the chances were that Akeley had actually encountered some stupendous change of perspective in his hazardous research; some change at once diminishing his danger – real or fancied – and opening dizzy new vistas of cosmic and superhuman knowledge. My own zeal for the unknown flared up to meet his, and I felt myself touched by the contagion of the morbid barrier-breaking. To shake off the maddening and wearying limitations of time and space and natural law – to be linked with the vast outside – to come close to the nighted and abysmal secrets of the infinite and the ultimate – surely such a thing was worth the risk of one's life, soul, and sanity! And Akeley had said there was no longer any peril – he had invited me to visit him instead of warning me away as before. I tingled at the thought of what he might now have to tell me – there was an almost paralyzing fascination in the thought of sitting in that lonely and lately-beleaguered farmhouse with a man who had talked with actual emissaries from outer space; sitting there with the terrible record and the pile of letters in which Akeley had summarized his earlier conclusions.

So late Sunday morning I telegraphed Akeley that I would meet him in Brattleboro on the following Wednesday – September 12th – if that date were convenient for him. In only one respect did I depart from his suggestions, and that concerned the choice of a train. Frankly, I did not feel like arriving in that haunted Vermont region late at night; so instead of accepting the train he chose I telephoned the station and devised another arrangement. By rising early and taking the 8:07 a.m. (standard) into Boston, I could catch the 9:25 for Greenfield; arriving there at 12:22 noon. This connected exactly with a train reaching Brattleboro at 1:08 p.m. – a much more comfortable hour than 10:01 for meeting Akeley and riding with him into the close-packed, secret-guarding hills.

I mentioned this choice in my telegram, and was glad to learn in the reply which came toward evening that it had met with my prospective host's endorsement. His wire ran thus:

ARRANGEMENT SATISFACTORY WILL MEET ONE EIGHT TRAIN WEDNESDAY DONT FORGET RECORD AND LETTERS AND PRINTS KEEP DESTINATION QUIET EXPECT GREAT REVELATIONS
AKELEY

Receipt of this message in direct response to one sent to Akeley – and necessarily delivered to his house from the Townshend station either by official messenger or by a restored telephone service – removed any lingering subconscious doubts I may have had about the authorship of the perplexing letter. My relief was marked – indeed, it was greater than I could account for at the time; since all such doubts had been rather deeply buried. But I slept soundly and long that night, and was eagerly busy with preparations during the ensuing two days.

Chapter VI

ON WEDNESDAY I started as agreed, taking with me a valise full of simple necessities and scientific data, including the hideous phonograph record, the Kodak prints, and the entire file of Akeley's correspondence. As requested, I had told no one where I was going; for I could see that the matter demanded utmost privacy, even allowing for its most favorable turns. The thought of actual mental contact with alien, outside entities was stupefying enough to my trained and somewhat prepared mind; and this being so, what might one think of its effect on the vast masses of uninformed laymen? I do not know whether dread or adventurous expectancy was uppermost in me as I changed trains at Boston and began the long westward run out of familiar regions into those I knew less thoroughly. Waltham – Concord – Ayer – Fitchburg – Gardner – Athol –

My train reached Greenfield seven minutes late, but the northbound connecting express had been held. Transferring in haste, I felt a curious breathlessness as the cars rumbled on through the early afternoon sunlight into territories I had always read of but had never before visited. I knew I was entering an altogether older-fashioned and more primitive New England than the mechanized, urbanized coastal and southern areas where all my life had been spent; an unspoiled, ancestral New England without the foreigners and factory-smoke, bill-boards and concrete roads, of the sections which modernity has touched. There would be odd survivals of that continuous native life whose deep roots make it the one authentic outgrowth of the landscape – the continuous native life which keeps alive strange ancient memories, and fertilizes the soil for shadowy, marvellous, and seldom-mentioned beliefs.

Now and then I saw the blue Connecticut River gleaming in the sun, and after leaving Northfield we crossed it. Ahead loomed green and cryptical hills, and when the conductor came around I learned that I was at last in Vermont. He told me to set my watch back an hour, since the northern hill country will have no dealings with new-fangled daylight time schemes. As I did so it seemed to me that I was likewise turning the calendar back a century.

The train kept close to the river, and across in New Hampshire I could see the approaching slope of steep Wantastiquet, about which singular old legends cluster. Then streets appeared on my left, and a green island showed in the stream on my right. People rose and filed to the door, and I followed them. The car stopped, and I alighted beneath the long train-shed of the Brattleboro station.

Looking over the line of waiting motors I hesitated a moment to see which one might turn out to be the Akeley Ford, but my identity was divined before I could take the initiative. And yet it was clearly not Akeley himself who advanced to meet me with an outstretched hand and a mellowly phrased query as to whether I was indeed Mr. Albert N. Wilmarth of Arkham. This man bore no resemblance to the bearded, grizzled Akeley of the snapshot; but was a younger and more urbane person, fashionably dressed, and wearing only a small, dark moustache. His cultivated voice held an odd and almost disturbing hint of vague familiarity, though I could not definitely place it in my memory.

As I surveyed him I heard him explaining that he was a friend of my prospective host's who had come down from Townshend in his stead. Akeley, he declared, had suffered a sudden attack of some asthmatic trouble, and did not feel equal to making a trip in the outdoor air. It was not serious, however, and there was to be no change in plans regarding my visit. I could not make out just how much this Mr. Noyes – as he announced himself – knew of Akeley's researches and discoveries, though it seemed to me that his casual manner stamped him as a comparative outsider. Remembering what a hermit Akeley had been, I was a trifle surprised at the ready availability of such a friend; but did not let my puzzlement deter me from entering the motor to which he gestured me. It was not the small ancient car I had expected from Akeley's descriptions, but a large and immaculate specimen of recent pattern – apparently Noyes's own, and bearing Massachusetts license plates with the amusing 'sacred codfish' device of that year. My guide, I concluded, must be a summer transient in the Townshend region.

Noyes climbed into the car beside me and started it at once. I was glad that he did not overflow with conversation, for some peculiar atmospheric tensity made me feel disinclined to talk. The town seemed very attractive in the afternoon sunlight as we swept up an incline and turned to the right into the main street. It drowsed like the older New England cities which one remembers from boyhood, and something in the collocation of roofs and steeples and chimneys and brick walls formed contours touching deep viol-strings of ancestral emotion. I could tell that I was at the gateway of a region half-bewitched through the piling-up of unbroken time-accumulations; a region where old, strange things have had a chance to grow and linger because they have never been stirred up.

As we passed out of Brattleboro my sense of constraint and foreboding increased, for a vague quality in the hill-crowded countryside with its towering, threatening, close-pressing green and granite slopes hinted at obscure secrets and immemorial survivals which might or might not be hostile to mankind. For a time our course followed a broad, shallow river which flowed down from unknown hills in the north, and I shivered when my companion told me it was the West River. It was in this stream, I recalled from newspaper items, that one of the morbid crablike beings had been seen floating after the floods.

Gradually the country around us grew wilder and more deserted. Archaic covered bridges lingered fearsomely out of the past in pockets of the hills, and the half-abandoned railway track paralleling the river seemed to exhale a nebulously visible air of desolation. There were awesome sweeps of vivid valley where great cliffs rose, New England's virgin granite showing gray and austere through the verdure that scaled the crests. There were gorges where untamed streams leaped, bearing down toward the river the unimagined secrets of a thousand pathless peaks. Branching away now and then were narrow, half-concealed roads that bored their way through solid, luxuriant masses of forest among whose primal trees whole armies of elemental spirits might well lurk. As I saw these I thought of how Akeley had been molested by unseen agencies on his drives along this very route, and did not wonder that such things could be.

The quaint, sightly village of Newfane, reached in less than an hour, was our last link with that world which man can definitely call his own by virtue of conquest and complete occupancy. After that we cast off all allegiance to immediate, tangible, and time-touched things, and entered a fantastic world of hushed unreality in which the narrow, ribbon-like road rose and fell and curved with an almost sentient and purposeful caprice amidst the tenantless green peaks and half-deserted valleys. Except for the sound of the motor, and the faint stir of the few lonely farms we passed at infrequent intervals, the only thing that reached my ears was the gurgling, insidious trickle of strange waters from numberless hidden fountains in the shadowy woods.

The nearness and intimacy of the dwarfed, domed hills now became veritably breath-taking. Their steepness and abruptness were even greater than I had imagined from hearsay, and suggested nothing in common with the prosaic objective world we know. The dense, unvisited woods on those inaccessible slopes seemed to harbor alien and incredible things, and I felt that the very outline of the hills themselves held some strange and aeon-forgotten meaning, as if they were vast hieroglyphs left by a rumored titan race whose glories live only in rare, deep dreams. All the legends of the past, and all the stupefying imputations of Henry Akeley's letters and exhibits, welled up in my memory to heighten the atmosphere of tension and growing menace. The purpose of my visit, and the frightful abnormalities it postulated struck at me all at once with a chill sensation that nearly over-balanced my ardor for strange delvings.

My guide must have noticed my disturbed attitude; for as the road grew wilder and more irregular, and our motion slower and more jolting, his occasional pleasant comments expanded into a steadier flow of discourse. He spoke of the beauty and weirdness of the country, and revealed some acquaintance with the folklore studies of my prospective host. From his polite questions it was obvious that he knew I had come for a scientific purpose, and that I was bringing data of some importance; but he gave no sign of appreciating the depth and awfulness of the knowledge which Akeley had finally reached.

His manner was so cheerful, normal, and urbane that his remarks ought to have calmed and reassured me; but oddly enough. I felt only the more disturbed as we bumped and veered onward into the unknown wilderness of hills and woods. At times it seemed as if he were pumping me to see what I knew of the monstrous secrets of the place, and with every fresh utterance that vague, teasing, baffling familiarity in his voice increased. It was not an ordinary or healthy familiarity despite the thoroughly wholesome and cultivated nature of the voice. I somehow linked it with forgotten nightmares, and felt that I might go mad if I recognized it. If any good excuse had existed, I think I would have turned back from my visit. As it was, I could not well do so – and it occurred to me that a cool, scientific conversation with Akeley himself after my arrival would help greatly to pull me together.

Besides, there was a strangely calming element of cosmic beauty in the hypnotic landscape through which we climbed and plunged fantastically. Time had lost itself in the labyrinths behind, and around us stretched only the flowering waves of faery and the recaptured loveliness of vanished centuries – the hoary groves, the untainted pastures edged with gay autumnal blossoms, and at vast intervals the small brown farmsteads nestling amidst huge trees beneath vertical precipices of fragrant brier and meadow-grass. Even the sunlight assumed a supernal glamor, as if some special atmosphere or exhalation mantled the whole region. I had seen nothing like it before save in the magic vistas that sometimes form the backgrounds of Italian primitives. Sodoma and Leonardo conceived such expanses, but only in the distance, and through the vaultings of Renaissance arcades. We were now burrowing bodily through the midst of the picture, and I seemed to find in its necromancy a thing I had innately known or inherited and for which I had always been vainly searching.

Suddenly, after rounding an obtuse angle at the top of a sharp ascent, the car came to a standstill. On my left, across a well-kept lawn which stretched to the road and flaunted a border of whitewashed stones, rose a white, two-and-a-half-story house of unusual size and elegance for the region, with a congenes of contiguous or arcade-linked barns, sheds, and windmill behind and to the right. I recognized it at once from the snapshot I had received, and was not surprised to see the name of Henry Akeley on the galvanized-iron mailbox near the road. For some distance back of the house a level stretch of marshy and sparsely-wooded land extended, beyond which soared a steep, thickly-forested hillside ending in a jagged leafy crest. This latter, I knew, was the summit of Dark Mountain, half way up which we must have climbed already.

Alighting from the car and taking my valise, Noyes asked me to wait while he went in and notified Akeley of my advent. He himself, he added, had important business elsewhere, and could not stop for more than a moment. As he briskly walked up the path to the house I climbed out of the car myself, wishing to stretch my legs a little before settling down to a sedentary conversation. My feeling of nervousness and tension had risen to a maximum again now that I was on the actual scene of the morbid beleaguering described so hauntingly in Akeley's letters, and I honestly dreaded the coming discussions which were to link me with such alien and forbidden worlds.

Close contact with the utterly bizarre is often more terrifying than inspiring, and it did not cheer me to think that this very bit of dusty road was the place where those monstrous tracks and that foetid green ichor had been found after moonless nights of fear and death. Idly I noticed that none of Akeley's dogs seemed to be about. Had he sold them all as soon as the Outer Ones made peace with him? Try as I might, I could not have the same confidence in the depth and sincerity of that peace which appeared in Akeley's final and queerly different letter. After all, he was a man of much simplicity and with little worldly experience. Was there not, perhaps, some deep and sinister undercurrent beneath the surface of the new alliance?

Led by my thoughts, my eyes turned downward to the powdery road surface which had held such hideous testimonies. The last few days had been dry, and tracks of all sorts cluttered the rutted, irregular highway despite the unfrequented nature of the district. With a vague curiosity I began to trace the outline of some of the heterogeneous impressions, trying meanwhile to curb the flights of macabre fancy which the place and its memories suggested. There was something menacing and uncomfortable in the funereal stillness, in the muffled, subtle trickle of distant brooks, and in the crowding green peaks and black-wooded precipices that choked the narrow horizon.

And then an image shot into my consciousness which made those vague menaces and flights of fancy seem mild and insignificant indeed. I have said that I was scanning the miscellaneous prints in the road with a kind of idle curiosity – but all at once that curiosity was shockingly snuffed out by a sudden and paralyzing gust of active terror. For though the dust tracks were in general confused and overlapping, and unlikely to arrest any casual gaze, my restless vision had caught certain details near the spot where the path to the house joined the highway; and had recognized beyond doubt or hope the frightful significance of those details. It was not for nothing, alas, that I had pored for hours over the Kodak views of the Outer Ones' claw-prints which Akeley had sent. Too well did I know the marks of those loathsome nippers, and that hint of ambiguous direction which stamped the horrors as no creatures of this planet. No chance had been left me for merciful mistake. Here, indeed, in objective form before my own eyes, and surely made not many hours ago, were at least three marks which stood out blasphemously among the surprising plethora of blurred footprints leading to and from the Akeley farmhouse. They were the hellish tracks of the living fungi from Yuggoth.

I pulled myself together in time to stifle a scream. After all, what more was there than I might have expected, assuming that I had really believed Akeley's letters? He had spoken of making peace with the things. Why, then, was it strange that some of them had visited his house? But the terror was stronger than the reassurance. Could any man be expected to look unmoved for the first time upon the claw-marks of animate beings from outer depths of space? Just then I saw Noyes emerge from the door and approach with a brisk step. I must, I reflected, keep command of myself, for the chances were that this genial friend knew nothing of Akeley's profoundest and most stupendous probings into the forbidden.

Akeley, Noyes hastened to inform me, was glad and ready to see me; although his sudden attack of asthma would prevent him from being a very competent host for a day or two. These spells hit him hard when they came, and were always accompanied by a debilitating fever and general weakness. He never was good for much while they lasted – had to talk in a whisper, and was very clumsy and feeble in getting about. His feet and ankles swelled, too, so that he had to bandage them like a gouty old beef-eater. Today he was in rather bad shape, so that I would have to attend very largely to my own needs; but he was none the less eager for conversation. I would find him in the study at the left of the front hall – the room where the blinds were shut. He had to keep the sunlight out when he was ill, for his eyes were very sensitive.

As Noyes bade me adieu and rode off northward in his car I began to walk slowly toward the house. The door had been left ajar for me; but before approaching and entering I cast a searching glance around the whole place, trying to decide what had struck me as so intangibly queer about it. The barns and sheds looked trimly prosaic enough, and I noticed Akeley's battered Ford in its capacious, unguarded shelter. Then the secret of the queerness reached me. It was the total silence. Ordinarily a farm is at least moderately murmurous from its various kinds of livestock, but here all signs of life were missing. What of the hens and the dogs? The cows, of which Akeley had said he possessed several, might conceivably be out to pasture, and the dogs might possibly have been sold; but the absence of any trace of cackling or grunting was truly singular.

I did not pause long on the path, but resolutely entered the open house door and closed it behind me. It had cost me a distinct psychological effort to do so, and now that I was shut inside I had a momentary longing for precipitate retreat. Not that the place was in the least sinister in visual suggestion; on the contrary, I thought the graceful late-colonial hallway very tasteful and wholesome, and admired the evident breeding of the man who had furnished it. What made me wish to flee was something very attenuated and indefinable. Perhaps it was a certain odd odor which I thought I noticed – though I well knew how common musty odors are in even the best of ancient farmhouses.

Chapter VII

REFUSING TO LET these cloudy qualms overmaster me, I recalled Noyes's instructions and pushed open the six-paneled, brass-latched white door on my left. The room beyond was darkened as I had known before; and as I entered it I noticed that the queer odor was stronger there. There likewise appeared to be some faint, half-imaginary rhythm or vibration in the air. For a moment the closed blinds allowed me to see very little, but then a kind of apologetic hacking or whispering sound drew my attention to a great easy-chair in the farther, darker corner of the room. Within its shadowy depths I saw the white blur of a man's face and hands; and in a moment I had crossed to greet the figure who had tried to speak. Dim though the light was, I perceived that this was indeed my host. I had studied the Kodak picture repeatedly, and there could be no mistake about this firm, weather-beaten face with the cropped, grizzled beard.

But as I looked again my recognition was mixed with sadness and anxiety; for certainly, his face was that of a very sick man. I felt that there must be something more than asthma behind that strained, rigid, immobile expression and unwinking glassy stare; and realized how terribly the strain of his frightful experiences must have told on him. Was it not enough to break any human being – even a younger man than this intrepid delver into the forbidden? The strange and sudden relief, I feared, had come too late to save him from something like a general breakdown. There was a touch of the pitiful in the limp, lifeless way his lean hands rested in his lap. He had on a loose dressing gown, and was swathed around the head and high around the neck with a vivid yellow scarf or hood.

And then I saw that he was trying to talk in the same hacking whisper with which he had greeted me. It was a hard whisper to catch at first, since the gray moustache concealed all movements of the lips, and something in its timbre disturbed me greatly; but by concentrating my attention I could soon make out its purport surprisingly well. The accent was by no means a rustic one, and the language was even more polished than correspondence had led me to expect.

"Mr. Wilmarth, I presume? You must pardon my not rising. I am quite ill, as Mr. Noyes must have told you; but I could not resist having you come just the same. You know what I wrote in my last letter – there is so much to tell you tomorrow when I shall feel better. I can't say how glad I am to see you in person after all our many letters. You have the file with you, of course? And the Kodak prints and records? Noyes put your valise in the hall – I suppose you saw it. For tonight I fear you'll have to wait on yourself to a great extent. Your room is upstairs – the one over this – and you'll see the bathroom door open at the head of the staircase. There's a meal spread for you in the dining-room – right through this door at your right – which you can take whenever you feel like it. I'll be a better host tomorrow – but just now weakness leaves me helpless.

"Make yourself at home – you might take out the letters and pictures and records and put them on the table here before you go upstairs with your bag. It is here that we shall discuss them – you can see my phonograph on that corner stand.

"No, thanks – there's nothing you can do for me. I know these spells of old. Just come back for a little quiet visiting before night, and then go to bed when you please. I'll rest right here – perhaps sleep here all night as I often do. In the morning I'll be far better able to go into the things we must go into. You realize, of course, the utterly stupendous nature of the matter before us. To us, as to only a few men on this earth, there will be opened up gulfs of time and space and knowledge beyond anything within the conception of human science or philosophy.

"Do you know that Einstein is wrong, and that certain objects and forces can move with a velocity greater than that of light? With proper aid I expect to go backward and forward in time, and actually see and feel the earth of remote past and future epochs. You can't imagine the degree to which those beings have carried science. There is nothing they can't do with the mind and body of living organisms. I expect to visit other planets, and even other stars and galaxies. The first trip will be to Yuggoth, the nearest world fully peopled by the beings. It is a strange dark orb at the very rim of our solar system – unknown to earthly astronomers as yet. But I must have written you about this. At the proper time, you know, the beings there will direct thought-currents toward us and cause it to be discovered – or perhaps let one of their human allies give the scientists a hint.

"There are mighty cities on Yuggoth – great tiers of terraced towers built of black stone like the specimen I tried to send you. That came from Yuggoth. The sun shines there no brighter than a star, but the beings need no light. They have other subtler senses, and put no windows in their great houses and temples. Light even hurts and hampers and confuses them, for it does not exist at all in the black cosmos outside time and space where they came from originally. To visit Yuggoth would drive any weak man mad – yet I am going there. The black rivers of pitch that flow under those mysterious cyclopean bridges – things built by some elder race extinct and forgotten before the beings came to Yuggoth from the ultimate voids – ought to be enough to make any man a Dante or Poe if he can keep sane long enough to tell what he has seen.

"But remember – that dark world of fungoid gardens and windowless cities isn't really terrible. It is only to us that it would seem so. Probably this world seemed just as terrible to the beings when they first explored it in the primal age. You know they were here long before the fabulous epoch of Cthulhu was over, and remember all about sunken R'lyeh when it was above the waters. They've been inside the earth, too – there are openings which human beings know nothing of – some of them in these very Vermont hills – and great worlds of unknown life down there; blue-litten K'n-yan, red-litten Yoth, and black, lightless N'kai. It's from N'kai that frightful Tsathoggua came – you know, the amorphous, toad-like god-creature mentioned in the Pnakotic Manuscripts and the *Necronomicon* and the Commoriom myth-cycle preserved by the Atlantean high-priest Klarkash-Ton.

"But we will talk of all this later on. It must be four or five o'clock by this time. Better bring the stuff from your bag, take a bite, and then come back for a comfortable chat."

Very slowly I turned and began to obey my host; fetching my valise, extracting and depositing the desired articles, and finally ascending to the room designated as mine. With the memory of that roadside claw-print fresh in my mind, Akeley's whispered paragraphs had affected me queerly; and the hints of familiarity with this unknown world of fungous life – forbidden Yuggoth – made my flesh creep more than I cared to own. I was tremendously sorry about Akeley's illness, but had to confess that his hoarse whisper had a hateful as well as pitiful quality. If only he wouldn't gloat so about Yuggoth and its black secrets!

My room proved a very pleasant and well-furnished one, devoid alike of the musty odor and disturbing sense of vibration; and after leaving my valise there I descended again to greet Akeley and take the lunch he had set out for me. The dining-room was just beyond the study, and I saw that a kitchen elI extended still farther in the same direction. On the dining-table an ample array of sandwiches, cake, and cheese awaited me, and a Thermos-bottle beside a cup and saucer testified that hot coffee had not been forgotten. After a well-relished meal I poured myself a liberal cup of coffee, but found that the culinary standard had suffered a lapse in this one detail. My first spoonful revealed a faintly unpleasant acrid taste, so that I did not take more. Throughout the lunch I thought of Akeley sitting silently in the great chair in the darkened next room.

Once I went in to beg him to share the repast, but he whispered that he could eat nothing as yet. Later on, just before he slept, he would take some malted milk – all he ought to have that day.

After lunch I insisted on clearing the dishes away and washing them in the kitchen sink – incidentally emptying the coffee which I had not been able to appreciate. Then returning to the darkened study I drew up a chair near my host's corner and prepared for such conversation as he might feel inclined to conduct. The letters, pictures, and record were still on the large centre-table, but for the nonce we did not have to draw upon them. Before long I forgot even the bizarre odor and curious suggestions of vibration.

I have said that there were things in some of Akeley's letters – especially the second and most voluminous one – which I would not dare to quote or even form into words on paper. This hesitancy applies with still greater force to the things I heard whispered that evening in the darkened room among the lonely hills. Of the extent of the cosmic horrors unfolded by that raucous voice I cannot even hint. He had known hideous things before, but what he had learned since making his pact with the Outside Things was almost too much for sanity to bear. Even now I absolutely refused to believe what he implied about the constitution of ultimate infinity, the juxtaposition of dimensions, and the frightful position of our known cosmos of space and time in the unending chain of linked cosmos-atoms which makes up the immediate super-cosmos of curves, angles, and material and semi-material electronic organization.

Never was a sane man more dangerously close to the arcana of basic entity – never was an organic brain nearer to utter annihilation in the chaos that transcends form and force and symmetry. I learned whence Cthulhu first came, and why half the great temporary stars of history had flared forth. I guessed – from hints which made even my informant pause timidly – the secret behind the Magellanic Clouds and globular nebulae, and the black truth veiled by the immemorial allegory of Tao. The nature of the Doels was plainly revealed, and I was told the essence (though not the source) of the Hounds of Tindalos. The legend of Yig, Father of Serpents, remained figurative no longer, and I started with loathing when told of the monstrous nuclear chaos beyond angled space which the *Necronomicon* had mercifully cloaked under the name of Azathoth. It was shocking to have the foulest nightmares of secret myth cleared up in concrete terms whose stark, morbid hatefulness exceeded the boldest hints of ancient and mediaeval mystics. Ineluctably I was led to believe that the first whisperers of these accursed tales must have had discourse with Akeley's Outer Ones, and perhaps have visited outer cosmic realms as Akeley now proposed visiting them.

I was told of the Black Stone and what it implied, and was glad that it had not reached me. My guesses about those hieroglyphics had been all too correct! And yet Akeley now seemed reconciled to the whole fiendish system he had stumbled upon; reconciled and eager to probe farther into the monstrous abyss. I wondered what beings he had talked with since his last letter to me, and whether many of them had been as human as that first emissary he had mentioned. The tension in my head grew insufferable, and I built up all sorts of wild theories about that queer, persistent odor and those insidious hints of vibration in the darkened room.

Night was falling now, and as I recalled what Akeley had written me about those earlier nights I shuddered to think there would be no moon. Nor did I like the way the farmhouse nestled in the lee of that colossal forested slope leading up to Dark Mountain's unvisited crest. With Akeley's permission I lighted a small oil lamp, turned it low, and set it on a distant bookcase beside the ghostly bust of Milton; but afterward I was sorry I had done so, for it made my host's strained, immobile face and listless hands look damnably abnormal and corpselike. He seemed half-incapable of motion, though I saw him nod stiffly once in awhile.

After what he had told, I could scarcely imagine what profounder secrets he was saving for the morrow; but at last it developed that his trip to Yuggoth and beyond – and my own possible participation in it – was to be the next day's topic. He must have been amused by the start of horror I gave at hearing a cosmic voyage on my part proposed, for his head wabbled violently when I showed my fear. Subsequently he spoke very gently of how human beings might accomplish – and several times had accomplished – the seemingly impossible flight across the interstellar void. It seemed that complete human bodies did not indeed make the trip, but that the prodigious surgical, biological, chemical, and mechanical skill of the Outer Ones had found a way to convey human brains without their concomitant physical structure.

There was a harmless way to extract a brain, and a way to keep the organic residue alive during its absence. The bare, compact cerebral matter was then immersed in an occasionally replenished fluid within an ether-tight cylinder of a metal mined in Yuggoth, certain electrodes reaching through and connecting at will with elaborate instruments capable of duplicating the three vital faculties of sight, hearing, and speech. For the winged fungus-beings to carry the brain-cylinders intact through space was an easy matter. Then, on every planet covered by their civilization, they would find plenty of adjustable faculty-instruments capable of being connected with the encased brains; so that after a little fitting these traveling intelligences could be given a full sensory and articulate life – albeit a bodiless and mechanical one – at each stage of their journeying through and beyond the space-time continuum. It was as simple as carrying a phonograph record about and playing it wherever a phonograph of corresponding make exists. Of its success there could be no question. Akeley was not afraid. Had it not been brilliantly accomplished again and again?

For the first time one of the inert, wasted hands raised itself and pointed stiffly to a high shelf on the farther side of the room. There, in a neat row, stood more than a dozen cylinders of a metal I had never seen before – cylinders about a foot high and somewhat less in diameter, with three curious sockets set in an isosceles triangle over the front convex surface of each. One of them was linked at two of the sockets to a pair of singular-looking machines that stood in the background. Of their purport I did not need to be told, and I shivered as with ague. Then I saw the hand point to a much nearer corner where some intricate instruments with attached cords and plugs, several of them much like the two devices on the shelf behind the cylinders, were huddled together.

"There are four kinds of instruments here, Wilmarth," whispered the voice. "Four kinds – three faculties each – makes twelve pieces in all. You see there are four different sorts of beings represented in those cylinders up there. Three humans, six fungoid beings who can't navigate space corporeally, two beings from Neptune (God! if you could see the body this type has on its own planet!), and the rest entities from the central caverns of an especially interesting dark star beyond the galaxy. In the principal outpost inside Round Hill you'll now and then find more cylinders and machines – cylinders of extra-cosmic brains with different senses from any we know – allies and explorers from the uttermost Outside – and special machines for giving them impressions and expression in the several ways suited at once to them and to the comprehensions of different types of listeners. Round Hill, like most of the beings' main outposts all through the various universes, is a very cosmopolitan place. Of course, only the more common types have been lent to me for experiment.

"Here – take the three machines I point to and set them on the table. That tall one with the two glass lenses in front – then the box with the vacuum tubes and sounding-board – and now the one with the metal disc on top. Now for the cylinder with the label 'B-67' pasted on it. Just stand in that Windsor chair to reach the shelf. Heavy? Never mind! Be sure of the number – B-67. Don't bother that fresh, shiny cylinder joined to the two testing instruments – the one with my name on it. Set B-67 on the table near where you've put the machines – and see that the dial switch on all three machines is jammed over to the extreme left.

"Now connect the cord of the lens machine with the upper socket on the cylinder – there! Join the tube machine to the lower left-hand socket, and the disc apparatus to the outer socket. Now move all the dial switches on the machine over to the extreme right – first the lens one, then the disc one, and then the tube one. That's right. I might as well tell you that this is a human being – just like any of us. I'll give you a taste of some of the others tomorrow."

To this day I do not know why I obeyed those whispers so slavishly, or whether I thought Akeley was mad or sane. After what had gone before, I ought to have been prepared for anything; but this mechanical mummery seemed so like the typical vagaries of crazed inventors and scientists that it struck a chord of doubt which even the preceding discourse had not excited. What the whisperer implied was beyond all human belief – yet were not the other things still farther beyond, and less preposterous only because of their remoteness from tangible concrete proof?

As my mind reeled amidst this chaos, I became conscious of a mixed grating and whirring from all three of the machines lately linked to the cylinder – a grating and whirring which soon subsided into a virtual noiselessness. What was about to happen? Was I to hear a voice? And if so, what proof would I have that it was not some cleverly concocted radio device talked into by a concealed but closely watched speaker? Even now I am unwilling to swear just what I heard, or just what phenomenon really took place before me. But something certainly seemed to take place.

To be brief and plain, the machine with the tubes and sound-box began to speak, and with a point and intelligence which left no doubt that the speaker was actually present and observing us. The voice was loud, metallic, lifeless, and plainly mechanical in every detail of its production. It was incapable of inflection or expressiveness, but scraped and rattled on with a deadly precision and deliberation.

"Mr. Wilmarth," it said, "I hope I do not startle you. I am a human being like yourself, though my body is now resting safely under proper vitalising treatment inside Round Hill, about a mile and a half east of here. I myself am here with you – my brain is in that cylinder and I see, hear, and speak through these electronic vibrators. In a week I am going across the void as I have been many times before, and I expect to have the pleasure of Mr. Akeley's company. I wish I might have yours as well; for I know you by sight and reputation, and have kept close track of your correspondence with our friend. I am, of course, one of the men who have become allied with the outside beings visiting our planet. I met them first in the Himalayas, and have helped them in various ways. In return they have given me experiences such as few men have ever had.

"Do you realize what it means when I say I have been on thirty-seven different celestial bodies – planets, dark stars, and less definable objects – including eight outside our galaxy and two outside the curved cosmos of space and time? All this has not harmed me in the least. My brain has been removed from my body by fissions so adroit that it would be crude to call the operation surgery. The visiting beings have methods which make these extractions easy and almost normal – and one's body never ages when the brain is out of it. The brain, I may add, is virtually immortal with its mechanical faculties and a limited nourishment supplied by occasional changes of the preserving fluid.

"Altogether, I hope most heartily that you will decide to come with Mr. Akeley and me. The visitors are eager to know men of knowledge like yourself, and to show them the great abysses that most of us have had to dream about in fanciful ignorance. It may seem strange at first to meet them, but I know you will be above minding that. I think Mr. Noyes will go along, too – the man who doubtless brought you up here in his car. He has been one of us for years – I suppose you recognized his voice as one of those on the record Mr. Akeley sent you."

At my violent start the speaker paused a moment before concluding. "So Mr. Wilmarth, I will leave the matter to you; merely adding that a man with your love of strangeness and folklore ought never to miss such a chance as this. There is nothing to fear. All transitions are painless; and there is much to enjoy in a wholly mechanized state of sensation. When the electrodes are disconnected, one merely drops off into a sleep of especially vivid and fantastic dreams.

"And now, if you don't mind, we might adjourn our session till tomorrow. Good night – just turn all the switches back to the left; never mind the exact order, though you might let the lens machine be last. Good night, Mr. Akeley – treat our guest well! Ready now with those switches?"

That was all. I obeyed mechanically and shut off all three switches, though dazed with doubt of everything that had occurred. My head was still reeling as I heard Akeley's whispering voice telling me that I might leave all the apparatus on the table just as it was. He did not essay any comment on what had happened, and indeed no comment could have conveyed much to my burdened faculties. I heard him telling me I could take the lamp to use in my room, and deduced that he wished to rest alone in the dark. It was surely time he rested, for his discourse of the afternoon and evening had been such as to exhaust even a vigorous man. Still dazed, I bade my host good night and went upstairs with the lamp, although I had an excellent pocket flashlight with me.

I was glad to be out of that downstairs study with the queer odor and vague suggestions of vibration, yet could not of course escape a hideous sense of dread and peril and cosmic abnormality as I thought of the place I was in and the forces I was meeting. The wild, lonely region, the black, mysteriously forested slope towering so close behind the house; the footprint in the road, the sick, motionless whisperer in the dark, the hellish cylinders and machines, and above all the invitations to strange surgery and stranger voyagings – these things, all so new and in such sudden succession, rushed in on me with a cumulative force which sapped my will and almost undermined my physical strength.

To discover that my guide Noyes was the human celebrant in that monstrous bygone Sabbat-ritual on the phonograph record was a particular shock, though I had previously sensed a dim, repellent familiarity in his voice. Another special shock came from my own attitude toward my host whenever I paused to analyze it; for much as I had instinctively liked Akeley as revealed in his correspondence, I now found that he filled me with a distinct repulsion. His illness ought to have excited my pity; but instead, it gave me a kind of shudder. He was so rigid and inert and corpselike – and that incessant whispering was so hateful and unhuman!

It occurred to me that this whispering was different from anything else of the kind I had ever heard; that, despite the curious motionlessness of the speaker's moustache-screened lips, it had a latent strength and carrying-power remarkable for the wheezing of an asthmatic. I had been able to understand the speaker when wholly across the room, and once or twice it had seemed to me that the faint but penetrant sounds represented not so much weakness as deliberate repression – for what reason I could not guess. From the first I had felt a disturbing quality in their timbre. Now, when I tried to weigh the matter, I thought I could trace this impression to a kind of subconscious familiarity like that which had made Noyes's voice so hazily ominous. But when or where I had encountered the thing it hinted at, was more than I could tell.

One thing was certain – I would not spend another night here. My scientific zeal had vanished amidst fear and loathing, and I felt nothing now but a wish to escape from this net of morbidity and unnatural revelation. I knew enough now. It must indeed be true that strange cosmic linkages do exist – but such things are surely not meant for normal human beings to meddle with.

Blasphemous influences seemed to surround me and press chokingly upon my senses. Sleep, I decided, would be out of the question; so I merely extinguished the lamp and threw myself on the bed fully dressed. No doubt it was absurd, but I kept ready for some unknown emergency; gripping in my right hand the revolver I had brought along, and holding the pocket flashlight in my left. Not a sound came from below, and I could imagine how my host was sitting there with cadaverous stiffness in the dark.

Somewhere I heard a clock ticking, and was vaguely grateful for the normality of the sound. It reminded me, though, of another thing about the region which disturbed me – the total absence of animal life. There were certainly no farm beasts about, and now I realized that even the accustomed night-noises of wild living things were absent. Except for the sinister trickle of distant unseen waters, that stillness was anomalous – interplanetary – and I wondered what star-spawned, intangible blight could be hanging over the region. I recalled from old legends that dogs and other beasts had always hated the Outer Ones, and thought of what those tracks in the road might mean.

Chapter VIII

DO NOT ASK ME how long my unexpected lapse into slumber lasted, or how much of what ensued was sheer dream. If I tell you that I awakened at a certain time, and heard and saw certain things, you will merely answer that I did not wake then; and that everything was a dream until the moment when I rushed out of the house, stumbled to the shed where I had seen the old Ford, and seized that ancient vehicle for a mad, aimless race over the haunted hills which at last landed me – after hours of jolting and winding through forest-threatened labyrinths – in a village which turned out to be Townshend.

You will also, of course, discount everything else in my report; and declare that all the pictures, record-sounds, cylinder-and-machine sounds, and kindred evidences were bits of pure deception practiced on me by the missing Henry Akeley. You will even hint that he conspired with other eccentrics to carry out a silly and elaborate hoax – that he had the express shipment removed at Keene, and that he had Noyes make that terrifying wax record. It is odd, though, that Noyes has not ever yet been identified; that he was unknown at any of the villages near Akeley's place, though he must have been frequently in the region. I wish I had stopped to memorize the license-number of his car – or perhaps it is better after all that I did not. For I, despite all you can say, and despite all I sometimes try to say to myself, know that loathsome outside influences must be lurking there in the half-unknown hills – and that, those influences have spies and emissaries in the world of men. To keep as far as possible from such influences and such emissaries is all that I ask of life in future.

When my frantic story sent a sheriff's posse out to the farmhouse, Akeley was gone without leaving a trace. His loose dressing gown, yellow scarf, and foot-bandages lay on the study floor near his corner easy-chair, and it could not be decided whether any of his other apparel had vanished with him. The dogs and livestock were indeed missing, and there were some curious bullet-holes both on the house's exterior and on some of the walls within; but beyond this nothing unusual could be detected. No cylinders or machines, none of the evidences I had brought in my valise, no queer odor or vibration-sense, no foot-prints in the road, and none of the problematical things I glimpsed at the very last.

I stayed a week in Brattleboro after my escape, making inquiries among people of every kind who had known Akeley; and the results convince me that the matter is no figment of dream or delusion. Akeley's queer purchase of dogs and ammunition and chemicals, and the cutting of his telephone wires, are matters of record; while all who knew him – including his son in California – concede that his occasional remarks on strange studies had a certain consistency. Solid citizens believe he was mad, and unhesitatingly pronounce all reported evidences mere hoaxes devised with insane cunning and perhaps abetted by eccentric associates; but the lowlier country folk sustain his statements in every detail. He had showed some of these rustics his photographs and black stone, and had played the hideous record for them; and they all said the footprints and buzzing voice were like those described in ancestral legends.

They said, too, that suspicious sights and sounds had been noticed increasingly around Akeley's house after he found the black stone, and that the place was now avoided by everybody except the mail man and other casual, tough-minded people. Dark Mountain and Round Hill were both notoriously haunted spots, and I could find no one who had ever closely explored either. Occasional disappearances of natives throughout the district's history were well attested, and these now included the semi-vagabond Walter Brown, whom Akeley's letters had mentioned. I even came upon one farmer who thought he had personally glimpsed one of the queer bodies at flood-time in the swollen West River, but his tale was too confused to be really valuable.

When I left Brattleboro I resolved never to go back to Vermont, and I feel quite certain I shall keep my resolution. Those wild hills are surely the outpost of a frightful cosmic race – as I doubt all the less since reading that a new ninth planet has been glimpsed beyond Neptune, just as those influences had said it would be glimpsed. Astronomers, with a hideous appropriateness they little suspect, have named this thing 'Pluto'. I feel, beyond question, that it is nothing less than nighted Yuggoth – and I shiver when I try to figure out the real reason why its monstrous denizens wish it to be known in this way at this especial time. I vainly try to assure myself that these daemoniac creatures are not gradually leading up to some new policy hurtful to the earth and its normal inhabitants.

But I have still to tell of the ending of that terrible night in the farmhouse. As I have said, I did finally drop into a troubled doze; a doze filled with bits of dream which involved monstrous landscape-glimpses. Just what awaked me I cannot yet say, but that I did indeed awake at this given point I feel very certain. My first confused impression was of stealthily creaking floor-boards in the hall outside my door, and of a clumsy, muffled fumbling at the latch. This, however, ceased almost at once; so that my really clear impressions begin with the voices heard from the study below. There seemed to be several speakers, and I judged that they were controversially engaged.

By the time I had listened a few seconds I was broad awake, for the nature of the voices was such as to make all thought of sleep ridiculous. The tones were curiously varied, and no one who had listened to that accursed phonograph record could harbor any doubts about the nature of at least two of them. Hideous though the idea was, I knew that I was under the same roof with nameless things from abysmal space; for those two voices were unmistakably the blasphemous buzzings which the Outside Beings used in their communication with men. The two were individually different – different in pitch, accent, and tempo – but they were both of the same damnable general kind.

A third voice was indubitably that of a mechanical utterance-machine connected with one of the detached brains in the cylinders. There was as little doubt about that as about the buzzings; for the loud, metallic, lifeless voice of the previous evening, with its inflectionless, expressionless scraping and rattling, and its impersonal precision and deliberation, had been utterly unforgettable. For a time I did not pause to question whether the intelligence behind the scraping was the identical one which had formerly talked to me; but shortly afterward I reflected that any brain would emit vocal sounds of the same quality if linked to the same mechanical speech-producer; the only possible differences being in language, rhythm, speed, and pronunciation. To complete the eldritch colloquy there were two actually human voices – one the crude speech of an unknown and evidently rustic man, and the other the suave Bostonian tones of my erstwhile guide Noyes.

As I tried to catch the words which the stoutly-fashioned floor so bafflingly intercepted, I was also conscious of a great deal of stirring and scratching and shuffling in the room below; so that I could not escape the impression that it was full of living beings – many more than the few whose speech I could single out. The exact nature of this stirring is extremely hard to describe, for very few good bases of comparison exist. Objects seemed now and then to move across the room like conscious entities; the sound of their footfalls having something about it like a loose, hard-surfaced clattering – as of the contact of ill-coordinated surfaces of horn or hard rubber. It was, to use a more concrete but less accurate comparison, as if people with loose, splintery wooden shoes were shambling and rattling about on the polished board floor. Of the nature and appearance of those responsible for the sounds, I did not care to speculate.

Before long I saw that it would be impossible to distinguish any connected discourse. Isolated words – including the names of Akeley and myself – now and then floated up, especially when uttered by the mechanical speech-producer; but their true significance was lost for want of continuous context. Today I refuse to form any definite deductions from them, and even their frightful effect on me was one of suggestion rather than of revelation. A terrible and abnormal conclave, I felt certain, was assembled below me; but for what shocking deliberations I could not tell. It was curious how this unquestioned sense of the malign and the blasphemous pervaded me despite Akeley's assurances of the Outsider's friendliness.

With patient listening I began to distinguish clearly between voices, even though I could not grasp much of what any of the voices said. I seemed to catch certain typical emotions behind some of the speakers. One of the buzzing voices, for example, held an unmistakable note of authority; whilst the mechanical voice, notwithstanding its artificial loudness and regularity, seemed to be in a position of subordination and pleading. Noyes's tones exuded a kind of conciliatory atmosphere. The others I could make no attempt to interpret. I did not hear the familiar whisper of Akeley, but well knew that such a sound could never penetrate the solid flooring of my room.

I will try to set down some of the few disjointed words and other sounds I caught, labeling the speakers of the words as best I know how. It was from the speech-machine that I first picked up a few recognizable phrases.

(The Speech-Machine)

"... *brought it on myself ...sent back the letters and the record ...end on it ...taken in ...seeing and hearing ...damn you ...impersonal force, after all ...fresh, shiny cylinder ...great God ...*"

(First Buzzing Voice)

"... *time we stopped ...small and human ...Akeley ...brain ...saying ...*"

(Second Buzzing Voice)

"... *Nyarlathotep ...Wilmarth ...records and letters ...cheap imposture ...*"

(Noyes)

"... *(an unpronounceable word or name, possibly N'gah-Kthun) harmless ...peace ...couple of weeks ...theatrical ...told you that before ...*"

(First Buzzing Voice)

"... *no reason ...original plan ...effects ...Noyes can watch Round Hill ...fresh cylinder ...Noyes's car ...*"

(Noyes)

"... *well ...all yours ...down here ...rest ...place ...*"

(Several Voices at Once in Indistinguishable Speech)

(Many Footsteps, Including the Peculiar Loose Stirring or Clattering)

(A Curious Sort of Flapping Sound)

(The Sound of an Automobile Starting and Receding)

(Silence)

That is the substance of what my ears brought me as I lay rigid upon that strange upstairs bed in the haunted farmhouse among the daemoniac hills – lay there fully dressed, with a revolver clenched in my right hand and a pocket flashlight gripped in my left. I became, as I have said, broad awake; but a kind of obscure paralysis nevertheless kept me inert till long after the last echoes of the sounds had died away. I heard the wooden, deliberate ticking of the ancient Connecticut clock somewhere far below, and at last made out the irregular snoring of a sleeper. Akeley must have dozed off after the strange session, and I could well believe that he needed to do so.

Just what to think or what to do was more than I could decide After all, what had I heard beyond things which previous information might have led me to expect? Had I not known that the nameless Outsiders were now freely admitted to the farmhouse? No doubt Akeley had been surprised by an unexpected visit from them. Yet something in that fragmentary discourse had chilled me immeasurably, raised the most grotesque and horrible doubts, and made me wish fervently that I might wake up and prove everything a dream. I think my subconscious mind must have caught something which my consciousness has not yet recognized. But what of Akeley? Was he not my friend, and would he not have protested if any harm were meant me? The peaceful snoring below seemed to cast ridicule on all my suddenly intensified fears.

Was it possible that Akeley had been imposed upon and used as a lure to draw me into the hills with the letters and pictures and phonograph record? Did those beings mean to engulf us both in a common destruction because we had come to know too much? Again I thought of the abruptness and unnaturalness of that change in the situation which must have occurred between Akeley's penultimate and final letters. Something, my instinct told me, was terribly wrong. All was not as it seemed. That acrid coffee which I refused – had there not been an attempt by some hidden, unknown entity to drug it? I must talk to Akeley at once, and restore his sense of proportion. They had hypnotized him with their promises of cosmic revelations, but now he must listen to reason. We must get out of this before it would be too late. If he lacked the will power to make the break for liberty. I would supply it. Or if I could not persuade him to go, I could at least go myself. Surely he would let me take his Ford and leave it in a garage in Brattleboro. I had noticed it in the shed – the door being left unlocked and open now that peril was deemed past – and I believed there was a good chance of its being ready for instant use. That momentary dislike of Akeley which I had felt during and after the evening's conversation was all gone now. He was in a position much like my own, and we must stick together. Knowing his indisposed condition, I hated to wake him at this juncture, but I knew that I must. I could not stay in this place till morning as matters stood.

At last I felt able to act, and stretched myself vigorously to regain command of my muscles. Arising with a caution more impulsive than deliberate, I found and donned my hat, took my valise, and started downstairs with the flashlight's aid. In my nervousness I kept the revolver clutched in my right hand, being able to take care of both valise and flashlight with my left. Why I exerted these precautions I do not really know, since I was even then on my way to awaken the only other occupant of the house.

As I half-tiptoed down the creaking stairs to the lower hall I could hear the sleeper more plainly, and noticed that he must be in the room on my left – the living-room I had not entered. On my right was the gaping blackness of the study in which I had heard the voices. Pushing open the unlatched door of the living-room I traced a path with the flashlight toward the source of the snoring, and finally turned the beams on the sleeper's face. But in the next second I hastily turned them away and commenced a catlike retreat to the hall, my caution this time springing from reason as well as from instinct. For the sleeper on the couch was not Akeley at all, but my quondam guide Noyes.

Just what the real situation was, I could not guess; but common sense told me that the safest thing was to find out as much as possible before arousing anybody. Regaining the hall, I silently closed and latched the living-room door after me; thereby lessening the chances of awakening Noyes. I now cautiously entered the dark study, where I expected to find Akeley, whether asleep or awake, in the great corner chair which was evidently his favorite resting-place. As I advanced, the beams of my flashlight caught the great centre-table, revealing one of the hellish cylinders with sight and hearing machines attached, and with a speech machine standing close by, ready to be connected at any moment. This, I reflected, must be the encased brain I had heard talking during the frightful conference; and for a second I had a perverse impulse to attach the speech machine and see what it would say.

It must, I thought, be conscious of my presence even now; since the sight and hearing attachments could not fail to disclose the rays of my flashlight and the faint creaking of the floor beneath my feet. But in the end I did not dare meddle with the thing. I idly saw that it was the fresh shiny cylinder with Akeley's name on it, which I had noticed on the shelf earlier in the evening and which my host had told me not to bother. Looking back at that moment, I can only regret my timidity and wish that I had boldly caused the apparatus to speak. God knows what mysteries and horrible doubts and questions of identity it might have cleared up! But then, it may be merciful that I let it alone.

From the table I turned my flashlight to the corner where I thought Akeley was, but found to my perplexity that the great easy-chair was empty of any human occupant asleep or awake. From the seat to the floor there trailed voluminously the familiar old dressing gown, and near it on the floor lay the yellow scarf and the huge foot-bandages I had thought so odd. As I hesitated, striving to conjecture where Akeley might be, and why he had so suddenly discarded his necessary sick-room garments, I observed that the queer odor and sense of vibration were no longer in the room. What had been their cause? Curiously it occurred to me that I had noticed them only in Akeley's vicinity. They had been strongest where he sat, and wholly absent except in the room with him or just outside the doors of that room. I paused, letting the flashlight wander about the dark study and racking my brain for explanations of the turn affairs had taken.

Would to Heaven I had quietly left the place before allowing that light to rest again on the vacant chair. As it turned out, I did not leave quietly; but with a muffled shriek which must have disturbed, though it did not quite awake, the sleeping sentinel across the hall. That shriek, and Noyes's still-unbroken snore, are the last sounds I ever heard in that morbidity-choked farmhouse beneath the black-wooded crest of haunted mountain – that focus of transcosmic horror amidst the lonely green hills and curse-muttering brooks of a spectral rustic land.

It is a wonder that I did not drop flashlight, valise, and revolver in my wild scramble, but somehow I failed to lose any of these. I actually managed to get out of that room and that house without making any further noise, to drag myself and my belongings safely into the old Ford in the shed, and to set that archaic vehicle in motion toward some unknown point of safety in the black, moonless night. The ride that followed was a piece of delirium out of Poe or Rimbaud or the drawings of Doré, but finally I reached Townshend. That is all. If my sanity is still unshaken, I am lucky. Sometimes I fear what the years will bring, especially since that new planet Pluto has been so curiously discovered.

As I have implied, I let my flashlight return to the vacant easy-chair after its circuit of the room; then noticing for the first time the presence of certain objects in the seat, made inconspicuous by the adjacent loose folds of the empty dressing gown. These are the objects, three in number, which the investigators did not find when they came later on. As I said at the outset, there was nothing of actual visual horror about them. The trouble was in what they led one to infer. Even now I have my moments of half-doubt – moments in which I half-accept the scepticism of those who attribute my whole experience to dream and nerves and delusion.

The three things were damnably clever constructions of their kind, and were furnished with ingenious metallic clamps to attach them to organic developments of which I dare not form any conjecture. I hope – devoutly hope – that they were the waxen products of a master artist, despite what my inmost fears tell me. Great God! That whisperer in darkness with its morbid odor and vibrations! Sorcerer, emissary, changeling, outsider …that hideous repressed buzzing …and all the time in that fresh, shiny cylinder on the shelf …poor devil … "Prodigious surgical, biological, chemical, and mechanical skill…"

For the things in the chair, perfect to the last, subtle detail of microscopic resemblance – or identity – were the face and hands of Henry Wentworth Akeley.

Novel of the White Powder

Arthur Machen

MY NAME is Leicester; my father. Major General Wyn Leicester, a distinguished officer of artillery, succumbed five years ago to a complicated liver complaint acquired in the deadly climate of India. A year later my only brother, Francis, came home after an exceptionally brilliant career at the University, and settled down with the resolution of a hermit to master what has been well called the great legend of the law. He was a man who seemed to live in utter indifference to everything that is called pleasure; and though he was handsomer than most men, and could talk as merrily and wittily as if he were a mere vagabond, he avoided society, and shut himself up in a large room at the top of the house to make himself a lawyer. Ten hours a day of hard reading was at first his allotted portion; from the first light in the east to the late afternoon he remained shut up with his books, taking a hasty half-hour's lunch with me as if he grudged the wasting of the moments, and going out for a short walk when it began to grow dusk. I thought that such relentless application must be injurious, and tried to cajole him from the crabbed text-books; but his ardor seemed to grow rather than diminish, and his daily tale of hours increased. I spoke to him seriously, suggesting some occasional relaxation, if it were but an idle afternoon with a harmless novel; but he laughed, and said that he read about feudal tenures when he felt in need of amusement, and scoffed at the notion of theatres, or a month's fresh confessed that he looked well, and seemed not to suffer from his labors; but I knew that such unnatural toil would take revenge at last, and I was not mistaken. A look of anxiety began to lurk about his eyes, and he seemed languid, and at last he avowed that he was no longer in perfect health; he was troubled, he said, with a sensation of dizziness, and awoke now and then of nights from fearful dreams, terrified and cold with icy sweats. "I am taking care of myself," he said; "so you must not trouble. I passed the whole of yesterday afternoon in idleness, leaning back in that comfortable chair you gave me, and scribbling nonsense on a sheet of paper. No, no; I will not overdo my work. I shall be well enough in a week or two, depend upon it."

Yet, in spite of his assurances, I could see that he grew no better, but rather worse; he would enter the drawing-room with a face all miserably wrinkled and despondent, and endeavor to look gayly when my eyes fell on him, and I thought such symptoms of evil omen, and was frightened sometimes at the nervous irritation of his movements, and at glances which I could not decipher. Much against his will, I prevailed on him to have medical advice, and with an ill grace he called in our old doctor.

Dr. Haberden cheered me after his examination of his patient.

"There is nothing really much amiss," he said to me. "No doubt he reads too hard, and eats hastily, and then goes back again to his books in too great a hurry; and the natural consequence is some digestive trouble, and a little mischief in the nervous system. But I think – I do, indeed, Miss Leicester – that we shall be able to set this all right. I have written him a prescription which ought to do great things. So you have no cause for anxiety."

My brother insisted on having the prescription made up by a chemist in the neighborhood; it was an odd old-fashioned shop, devoid of the studied coquetry and calculated glitter that make so gay a show on the counters and shelves of the modern apothecary; but Francis liked the old chemist, and believed in the scrupulous purity of his drugs. The medicine was sent in due course, and I saw that my brother took it regularly after lunch and dinner. It was an innocent-looking white powder, of which a little was dissolved, in a glass of cold water. I stirred it in, and it seemed to disappear, leaving the water clear and colorless. At first Francis seemed to benefit greatly; the weariness vanished from his face, and he became more cheerful than he had ever been since the time when he left school; he talked gayly of reforming himself, and avowed to me that he had wasted his time.

"I have given too many hours to law," he said, laughing; "I think you have saved me in the nick of time. Come, I shall be Lord Chancellor yet, but I must not forget life. You and I will have a holiday together before long; we will go to Paris and enjoy ourselves, and keep away from the Bibliothèque Nationale."

I confessed myself delighted with the prospect.

"When shall we go?" I said. "I can start the day after tomorrow, if you like."

"Ah, that is perhaps a little too soon; after all, I do not know London yet, and I suppose a man ought to give the pleasures of his own country the first choice. But we will go off together in a week or two, so try and furbish up your French. I only know law French myself, and I am afraid that wouldn't do."

We were just finishing dinner, and he quaffed off his medicine with a parade of carousal as if it had been wine from some choicest bin.

"Has it any particular taste?" I said.

"No; I should not know I was not drinking water," and he got up from his chair, and began to pace up and down the room as if he were undecided as to what he should do next.

"Shall we have coffee in the drawing-room," I said, "or would you like to smoke?"

"No; I think I will take a turn, it seems a pleasant evening. Look at the afterglow; why, it is as if a great city were burning in flames, and down there between the dark houses it is raining blood fast, fast. Yes, I will go out. I may be in soon, but I shall take my key, so goodnight, dear, if I don't see you again."

The door slammed behind him, and I saw him walk lightly down the street, swinging his malacca cane, and I felt grateful to Dr. Haberden for such an improvement.

I believe my brother came home very late that night; but he was in a merry mood the next morning.

"I walked on without thinking where I was going," he said, "enjoying the freshness of the air, and livened by the crowds as I reached more frequented quarters. And then I met an old college friend, Orford, in the press of the pavement, and then – well, we enjoyed ourselves. I have felt what it is to be young and a man, I find I have blood in my veins, as other men have. I made an appointment with Orford for tonight; there will be a little party of us at the restaurant. Yes, I shall enjoy myself for a week or two, and hear the chimes at midnight, and then we will go for our little trip together."

Such was the transmutation of my brother's character that in a few days he became a lover of pleasure, a careless and merry idler of western pavements, a hunter-out of snug restaurants, and a fine critic of fantastic dancing; he grew fat before my eyes, and said no more of Paris, for he had clearly found his Paradise in London. I rejoiced, and yet wondered a little, for there was, I thought, something in his gayety that indefinitely displeased me, though I could not have defined my feeling. But by degrees there came a change; he returned still in the cold, hours of the morning, but I heard no more about his pleasures, and one morning as we sat at breakfast together, I looked suddenly into his eyes and saw a stranger before me.

"Oh, Francis!" I cried; "Oh, Francis, Francis, what have you done?" and rending sobs cut the words short, and I went weeping out of the room, for though I knew nothing, yet I knew all, and by some odd play of thought I remembered the evening when he first went abroad to prove his manhood, and the picture of the sunset sky glowed before me; the clouds like a city in burning flames, and the rain of blood. Yet I did battle with such thoughts, resolving that perhaps, after all, no great harm had been done, and in the evening at dinner I resolved to press him to fix a day for our holiday in Paris. We had talked easily enough, and my brother had just taken his medicine, which he had continued all the while. I was about to begin my topic, when the words forming in my mind vanished, and I wondered for a second what icy and intolerable weight oppressed my heart and suffocated me as with the unutterable horror of the coffin-lid nailed down on the living.

We had dined without candles, and the room had slowly grown from twilight to gloom, and the walls and corners were indistinct in the shadow. But from where I sat I looked out into the street; and as I thought of what I would say to Francis, the sky began to flush and shine, as it had done on a well-remembered evening, and in the gap between two dark masses that were houses an awful pageantry of flame appeared. Lurid whorls of writhed cloud, and utter depths burning, and grey masses like the fume blown from a smoking city, and an evil glory blazing far above shot with tongues of more ardent fire, and below as if there were a deep pool of blood. I looked down to where my brother sat facing me, and the words were shaped on my lips, when I saw his hand resting on the table. Between the thumb and forefinger of the closed hand, there was a mark, a small patch about the size of a sixpence, and somewhat of the colour of a bad bruise. Yet, by some sense I cannot define, I knew that what I saw was no bruise at all. Oh, if human flesh could burn with flame, and if flame could be black as pitch, such was that before me! Without thought or fashioning of words, grey horror shaped within me at the sight, and in an inner cell it was known to be a brand. For a moment the stained sky became dark as midnight, and when the light returned to me, I was alone in the silent room, and soon after I heard my brother go out.

Late as it was, I put on my bonnet and went to Dr. Haberden, and in his great consulting-room, ill-lighted by a candle which the doctor brought in with him, with stammering lips, and a voice that would break in spite of my resolve, I told him all; from the day on which my brother began to take the medicine down to the dreadful thing I had seen scarcely half an hour before.

When I had done, the doctor looked at me for a minute with an expression of great pity on his face.

"My dear Miss Leicester," he said, "you have evidently been anxious about your brother; you have been worrying over him, I am sure. Come, now, is it not so?"

"I have certainly been anxious," I said. "For the last week or two I have not felt at ease."

"Quite so; you know, of course, what a queer thing the brain is?"

"I understand what you mean; but I was not deceived. I saw what I have told you with my own eyes."

"Yes, yes, of course. But your eyes had been staring at that very curious sunset we had tonight. That is the only explanation. You will see it in the proper light tomorrow, I am sure. But, remember, I am always ready to give any help that is in my power; do not scruple to come to me, or to send for me if you are in any distress."

I went away but little comforted, all confusion and terror and sorrow, not knowing where to turn. When my brother and I met the next day, I looked quickly at him, and noticed, with a sickening at heart, that the right hand, the hand on which I had clearly seen the patch as of a black fire, was wrapped up with a handkerchief.

"What is the matter with your hand, Francis?" I said in a steady voice.

"Nothing of consequence. I cut a finger last night, and it bled rather awkwardly, so I did it up roughly to the best of my ability."

"I will do it neatly for you, if you like."

"No, thank you, dear, this will answer very well. Suppose we have breakfast; I am quite hungry."

We sat down, and I watched him. He scarcely ate or drank at all, but tossed his meat to the dog when he thought my eyes were turned away; and there was a look in his eyes that I had never yet seen, and the thought fled across my mind that it was a look that was scarcely human. I was firmly convinced that awful and incredible as was the thing I had seen the night before, yet it was no illusion, no glamour of bewildered sense, and in the course of the morning I went again to the doctor's house.

He shook his head with an air puzzled and incredulous, and seemed to reflect for a few minutes.

"And you say he still keeps up the medicine? But why? As I understand, all the symptoms he complained of have disappeared long ago; why should he go on taking the stuff when he is quite well? And by the by where did he get it made up? At Sayce's? I never send anyone there; the old man is getting careless. Suppose you come with me to the chemist's; I should like to have some talk with him."

We walked together to the shop. Old Sayce knew Dr. Haberden, and was quite ready to give any information.

"You have been sending that in to Mr. Leicester for some weeks, I think, on my prescription," said the doctor, giving the old man a pencilled scrap of paper.

The chemist put on his great spectacles with trembling uncertainty, and held up the paper with a shaking hand.

"Oh, yes," he said, "I have very little of it left; it is rather an uncommon drug, and I have had it in stock some time. I must get in some more, if Mr. Leicester goes on with it."

"Kindly let me have a look at the stuff," said Haberden; and the chemist gave him a glass bottle. He took out the stopper and smelt the contents, and looked strangely at the old man.

"Where did you get this?" he said, "and what is it? For one thing, Mr. Sayce, it is not what I prescribed. Yes, yes, I see the label is right enough, but I tell you this is not the drug."

"I have had it a long time," said the old man, in feeble terror. "I got it from Burbage's in the usual way. It is not prescribed often, and I have had it on the shelf for some years. You see there is very little left."

"You had better give it to me," said Haberden. "I am afraid something wrong has happened."

We went out of the shop in silence, the doctor carrying the bottle neatly wrapped in paper under his arm.

"Dr. Haberden," I said when we had walked a little way – "Dr. Haberden."

"Yes," he said, looking at me gloomily enough.

"I should like you to tell me what my brother has been taking twice a day for the last month or so."

"Frankly, Miss Leicester, I don't know. We will speak of this when we get to my house."

We walked on quickly without another word till we reached Dr. Haberden's. He asked me to sit down, and began pacing up and down the room, his face clouded over, as I could see, with no common fears.

"Well," he said at length, "this is all very strange; it is only natural that you should feel alarmed, and I must confess that my mind is far from easy. We will put aside, if you please, what you told me last night and this morning, but the fact remains that for the last few weeks Mr. Leicester has been impregnating his system with a drug which is completely unknown to me. I tell you, it is not what I ordered; and what that stuff in the bottle really is remains to be seen."

He undid the wrapper, and cautiously tilted a few grains of the white powder on to a piece of paper, and peered curiously at it.

"Yes," he said, "it is like the sulphate of quinine, as you say; it is flaky. But smell it."

He held the bottle to me, and I bent over it. It was a strange sickly smell, vaporous and overpowering, like some strong anaesthetic.

"I shall have it analyzed," said Haberden. "I have a friend who has devoted his whole life to chemistry as a science. Then we shall have something to go upon. No, no, say no more about that other matter; I cannot listen to that, and take my advice and think no more about it yourself."

That evening my brother did not go out as usual after dinner.

"I have had my fling," he said with a queer laugh; "and I must go back to my old ways. A little law will be quite a relaxation after so sharp a dose of pleasure," and he grinned to himself, and soon after went up to his room. His hand was still all bandaged.

Dr. Haberden called a few days later.

"I have no special news to give you," he said. "Chambers is out of town, so I know no more about that stuff than you do. But I should like to see Mr. Leicester if he is in."

"He is in his room," I said; "I will tell him you are here."

"No, no, I will go up to him; we will have a little quiet talk together. I dare say that we have made a good deal of fuss about very little; for, after all, whatever the white powder may be, it seems to have done him good."

The doctor went upstairs, and standing in the hall I heard his knock, and the opening and shutting of the door; and then I waited in the silent house for an hour, and the stillness grew more and more intense as the hands of the clock crept round. Then there sounded from above the noise of a door shut sharply, and the doctor was coming down the stairs. His footsteps crossed the hall, and there was a pause at the door. I drew a long sick breath with difficulty, and saw my face white in a little mirror, and he came in and stood at the door. There was an unutterable horror shining in his eyes; he steadied himself by holding the back of a chair with one hand, and his lower lip trembled like a horse's, and he gulped and stammered unintelligible sounds before he spoke.

"I have seen that man," he began in a dry whisper. "I have been sitting in his presence for the last hour. My God! and I am alive and in my senses! I, who have dealt with death all my life, and have dabbled with the melting ruins of the earthly tabernacle. But not this! Oh, not this," and he covered his face with his hands as if to shut out the sight of something before him.

"Do not send for me again, Miss Leicester," he said with more composure. "I can do nothing in this house. Goodbye."

As I watched him totter down the steps and along the pavement towards his house, it seemed to me that he had aged by ten years since the morning.

My brother remained in his room. He called out to me in a voice I hardly recognized, that he was very busy, and would like his meals brought to his door and left there, and I gave the order to the servants. From that day it seemed as if the arbitrary conception we call time had been annihilated for me. I lived in an ever-present sense of horror, going through the routine of the house mechanically, and only speaking a few necessary words to the servants. Now and then I went out and paced the streets for an hour or two and came home again; but whether I were without or within, my spirit delayed before the closed door of the upper room, and, shuddering, waited for it to open. I have said that I scarcely reckoned time, but I suppose it must have been a fortnight after Dr. Haberden's visit that I came home from my stroll a little refreshed and lightened. The air was sweet and pleasant, and the hazy form of green leaves, floating cloud-like in the square, and the smell of blossoms, had charmed my senses, and I felt happier and walked more briskly. As I delayed a moment at the verge of the pavement, waiting for a van to pass by before crossing over to the house, I happened to look up at the windows, and instantly there was the rush and swirl of deep cold waters in my ears, and my heart leapt up, and fell down, down as into a deep hollow, and I was amazed with a dread and terror without form or shape. I stretched out a hand blindly through folds of thick darkness, from the black and shadowy valley, and held myself from falling, while the stones beneath my feet rocked and swayed and tilted, and the sense of solid things seemed to sink away from under me. I had glanced up at the window of my brother's study, and at that moment the blind was drawn aside, and something that had life stared out into the world. Nay, I cannot say I saw a face or any human likeness; a living thing, two eyes of burning flame glared at me, and they were in the midst of something as formless as my fear, the symbol and presence of all evil and all hideous corruption. I stood shuddering and quaking as with the grip of ague, sick with unspeakable agonies of fear and loathing, and for five minutes I could not summon force or motion to my limbs. When I was within the door, I ran up the stairs to my brother's room, and knocked.

"Francis, Francis," I cried, "for heaven's sake answer me. What is the horrible thing in your room? Cast it out, Francis, cast it from you!"

I heard a noise as of feet shuffling slowly and awkwardly, and a choking, gurgling sound, as if someone was struggling to find utterance, and then the noise of a voice, broken and stifled, and words that I could scarcely understand.

"There is nothing here," the voice said, "Pray do not disturb me. I am not very well today."

I turned away, horrified and yet helpless. I could do nothing, and I wondered why Francis had lied to me, for I had seen the appearance beyond the glass too plainly to be deceived, though it was but the sight of a moment. And I sat still, conscious that there had been something else, something I had seen in the first flash of terror before those burning eyes had looked at me. Suddenly I remembered; as I lifted my face the blind was being drawn back, and I had had an instant's glance of the thing that was moving it, and in my recollection I knew that a hideous image was engraved forever on my brain. It was not a hand: there were no fingers that held the blind, but a black stump pushed it aside; the mouldering outline and the clumsy movement as of a beast's paw had glowed into my senses before the darkling waves of terror had overwhelmed me as I went down quick into the pit. My mind was aghast at the thought of this, and of the awful presence that dwelt with my brother in his room; I went to his door and cried to him again, but no answer came. That night one of the servants came up to me and told me in a whisper that for three days food had been regularly placed at the door and left untouched; the maid had knocked, but had received no answer; she had heard the noise of shuffling feet that I had noticed. Day after day went by, and still my brother's meals were brought to his door and left untouched; and though I knocked and called again and again, I could get no answer. The servants began to talk to me; it appeared they were as alarmed as I. The cook said that when my brother first shut himself up in his room, she used to hear him come out at night and go about the house; and once, she said, the hall door had opened and closed again, but for several nights she had heard no sound. The climax came at last. It was in the dusk of the evening, and I was sitting in the darkening dreary room when a terrible shriek jarred and rang harshly out of the silence, and I heard a frightened scurry of feet dashing down the stairs. I waited, and the servant maid staggered into the room and faced me, white and trembling.

"O Miss Helen," she whispered. "Oh, for the Lord's sake, Miss Helen, what has happened? Look at my hand, miss; look at that hand!" I drew her to the window, and saw there was a black wet stain upon her hand.

"I do not understand you," I said. "Will you explain to me?"

"I was doing your room just now," she began. "I was turning down the bedclothes, and all of a sudden there was something fell upon my hand wet, and I looked up, and the ceiling was black and dripping on me."

I looked hard at her, and bit my lip. "Come with me," I said. "Bring your candle with you."

The room I slept in was beneath my brother's, and as I went in I felt I was trembling. I looked up at the ceiling, and saw a patch, all black and wet and a dew of black drops upon it, and a pool of horrible liquor soaking into the white bedclothes.

I ran upstairs and knocked loudly.

"O Francis, Francis, my dear brother," I cried, "what has happened to you?"

And I listened. There was a sound of choking, and a noise like water bubbling and regurgitating, but nothing else, and I called louder, but no answer came.

In spite of what Dr. Haberden had said, I went to him, and with tears streaming down my cheeks, I told him of all that had happened, and he listened to me with a face set hard and grim.

"For your father's sake," he said at last, "I will go with you, though I can do nothing."

We went out together; the streets were dark and silent, and heavy with heat and a drought of many weeks. I saw the doctor's face white under the gas-lamps, and when we reached the house his hand was shaking. We did not hesitate, but went upstairs directly. I held the lamp, and he called out in a loud, determined voice:

"Mr. Leicester, do you hear me? I insist on seeing you. Answer me at once."

There was no answer, but we both heard that choking noise I have mentioned.

"Mr. Leicester, I am waiting for you. Open the door this instant, or I shall break it down." And he called a third time in a voice that rang and echoed from the walls.

"Mr. Leicester! For the last time I order you to open the door."

"Ah!" he said, after a pause of heavy silence, "we are wasting time here. Will you be so kind as to get me a poker, or something of the kind?"

I ran into a little room at the back where odd articles were kept, and found a heavy adze-like tool that I thought might serve the doctor's purpose.

"Very good," he said, "that will do, I dare say. I give you notice, Mr. Leicester," he cried loudly at the keyhole, "that I am now about to break into your room."

Then I heard the wrench of the adze, and the woodwork split and cracked under it, and with a loud crash the door suddenly burst open; and for a moment we started back aghast at a fearful screaming cry, no human voice, but as the roar of a monster, that burst forth inarticulate and struck at us out of the darkness.

"Hold the lamp," said the doctor, and we went in and glanced quickly round the room. "There it is," said Dr. Haberden, drawing a quick breath; "look, in that corner."

I looked, and a pang of horror seized my heart as with a white-hot iron. There upon the floor was a dark and putrid mass, seething with corruption and hideous rottenness, neither liquid nor solid, but melting and changing before our eyes, and bubbling with unctuous oily bubbles like boiling pitch. And out of the midst of it shone two burning points like eyes, and I saw a writhing and stirring as of limbs, and something moved and lifted up that might have been an arm. The doctor took a step forward, and raised the iron bar and struck at the burning points, and drove in the weapon, and struck again and again in a fury of loathing. At last the thing was quiet.

* * *

A week or two later, when I had to some extent recovered from the terrible shock, Dr. Haberden came to see me.

"I have sold my practice," he began, "and tomorrow I am sailing on a long voyage. I do not know whether I shall ever return to England; in all probability I shall buy a little land in California, and settle there for the remainder of my life. I have brought you this packet, which you may open and read when you feel able to do so. It contains the report of Dr. Chambers on what I submitted to him. Goodbye, Miss Leicester, goodbye."

When he was gone, I opened the envelope; I could not wait, and proceeded to read the papers within. Here is the manuscript; and if you will allow me, I will read you the astounding story it contains.

"My dear Haberden," the letter began, "I have delayed inexcusably in answering your questions as to the white substance you sent me. To tell you the truth, I have hesitated for some time as to what course I should adopt, for there is a bigotry and an orthodox standard in physical science as in theology, and I knew that if I told you the truth I should offend rooted prejudices which I once held dear myself. However, I have determined to be plain with you, and first I must enter into a short personal explanation.

"You have known me, Haberden, for many years as a scientific man; you and I have often talked of our profession together, and discussed the hopeless gulf that opens before the feet of those who think to attain to truth by any means whatsoever, except the beaten way of experiment and observation, in the sphere of material things. I remember the scorn with which you have spoken to me of men of science who have dabbled a little in the unseen, and have timidly hinted that perhaps the senses are not, after all, the eternal, impenetrable bounds of all knowledge, the everlasting walls beyond which no human being has ever passed. We have laughed together heartily, and I think justly, at the 'occult' follies of the day, disguised under various names – the mesmerisms, spiritualisms, materializations, theosophies, all the rabble rant of imposture, with their machinery of poor tricks and feeble conjuring, the true back-parlor magic of shabby London streets. Yet, in spite of what I have said, I must confess to you that I am no materialist, taking the word of course in its usual signification. It is now many years since I have convinced myself, convinced myself a sceptic remember, that the old iron-bound theory is utterly and entirely false. Perhaps this confession will not wound you so sharply as it would have done twenty years ago; for I think you cannot have failed to notice that for some time hypotheses have been advanced by men of pure science which are nothing less than transcendental, and I suspect that most modern chemists and biologists of repute would not hesitate to subscribe the dictum of the old Schoolman, *Omnia exeunt in mysterium*, which means, I take it, that every branch of human knowledge if traced up to its source and final principles vanishes into mystery. I need not trouble you now with a detailed account of the painful steps which led me to my conclusions; a few simple experiments suggested a doubt as to my then standpoint, and a train of thought that rose from circumstances comparatively trifling brought me far. My old conception of the universe has been swept away, and I stand in a world that seems as strange and awful to me as the endless waves of the ocean seen for the first time, shining, from a Peak in Darien. Now I know that the walls of sense that seemed so impenetrable, that seemed to loom up above the heavens and to be founded below the depths, and to shut us in forevermore, are no such everlasting impassable barriers as we fancied, but thinnest and most airy veils that melt away before the seeker, and dissolve as the early mist of the morning about the brooks. I know that you never adopted the extreme materialistic position: you did not go about trying to prove a universal negative, for your logical sense withheld you from that crowning absurdity; yet I am sure that you will find all that I am saying strange and repellent to your habits of thought. Yet, Haberden, what I tell you is the truth, nay, to adopt our common language, the sole and scientific truth, verified by experience; and the universe is verily more splendid and more awful than we used to dream. The whole universe, my friend, is a tremendous sacrament; a mystic, ineffable force and energy, veiled by an outward form of matter; and man, and the sun and the other stars, and the flower of the grass, and the crystal in the test-tube, are each and every one as spiritual, as material, and subject to an inner working.

"You will perhaps wonder, Haberden, whence all this tends; but I think a little thought will make it clear. You will understand that from such a standpoint the whole view of things is changed, and what we thought incredible and absurd may be possible enough. In short, we must look at legend and belief with other eyes, and be prepared to accept tales that had become mere fables. Indeed, this is no such great demand. After all, modern science will concede as much, in a hypocritical manner. You must not, it is true, believe in witchcraft, but you may credit hypnotism; ghosts are out of date, but there is a good deal to be said for the theory of telepathy. Give a superstition a Greek name, and believe in it, should almost be a proverb.

"So much for my personal explanation. You sent me, Haberden, a phial, stoppered and sealed, containing a small quantity of a flaky white powder, obtained from a chemist who has been dispensing it to one of your patients. I am not surprised to hear that this powder refused to yield any results to your analysis. It is a substance which was known to a few many hundred years ago, but which I never expected to have submitted to me from the shop of a modern apothecary. There seems no reason to doubt the truth of the man's tale; he no doubt got, as he says, the rather uncommon salt you prescribed from the wholesale chemist's; and it has probably remained on his shelf for twenty years, or perhaps longer. Here what we call chance and coincidence begins to work; during all these years the salt in the bottle was exposed to certain recurring variations of temperature, variations probably ranging from 40° to 80°. And, as it happens, such changes, recurring year after year at irregular intervals, and with varying degrees of intensity and duration, have constituted a process, and a process so complicated and so delicate, that I question whether modern scientific apparatus directed with the utmost precision could produce the same result. The white powder you sent me is something very different from the drug you prescribed; it is the powder from which the wine of the Sabbath, the Vinum Sabbati was prepared. No doubt you have read of the Witches' Sabbath, and have laughed at the tales which terrified our ancestors; the black cats, and the broomsticks, and dooms pronounced against some old woman's cow. Since I have known the truth I have often reflected that it is on the whole a happy thing that such burlesque as this is believed, for it serves to conceal much that is better should not be known generally. However, if you care to read the appendix to Payne Knight's monograph, you will find that the true Sabbath was something very different, though the writer has very nicely refrained from printing all he knew. The secrets of the true Sabbath were the secrets of remote times surviving into the Middle Ages, secrets of an evil science which existed long before Aryan man entered Europe. Men and women, seduced from their homes on specious pretences, were met by beings well qualified to assume, as they did assume, the part of devils, and taken by their guides to some, desolate and lonely place, known to the initiate by long tradition and unknown to all else. Perhaps it was a cave in some bare and wind-swept hill; perhaps some inmost recess of a great forest, and there the Sabbath was held. There, in the blackest hour of night, the Vinum Sabbati was prepared, and this evil graal was poured forth and offered to the neophytes, and they partook of an infernal sacrament; *sumentes calicem principis inferorum*, as an old author well expresses it. And suddenly, each one that had drunk found himself attended by a companion, a shape of glamour and unearthly allurement, beckoning him apart to share in joys more exquisite, more piercing than the thrill of any dream, to the consummation of the marriage of the Sabbath. It is hard to write of such things as these, and chiefly because that shape that allured with loveliness was no hallucination, but, awful as it is to express, the man himself. By the power of that Sabbath wine, a few grains of white powder thrown into a glass of water, the house of life was riven asunder, and the human trinity dissolved, and the worm which never dies, that which lies sleeping within us all, was made tangible and an external thing, and clothed with a garment of flesh. And then in the hour of midnight, the primal fall was repeated and represented, and the awful thing veiled in the mythos of the Tree in the Garden was done anew. Such was the nuptiae Sabbati.

"I prefer to say no more; you, Haberden, know as well as I do that the most trivial laws of life are not to be broken with impunity; and for so terrible an act as this, in which the very inmost place of the temple was broken open and defiled, a terrible vengeance followed. What began with corruption ended also with corruption."

* * *

Underneath is the following in Dr. Haberden's writing:

> *The whole of the above is unfortunately strictly and entirely true. Your brother confessed all to me on that morning when I saw him in his room. My attention was first attracted to the bandaged hand, and I forced him to show it me. What I saw made me, a medical man of many years standing, grow sick with loathing; and the story I was forced to listen to was infinitely more frightful than I could have believed possible. It has tempted me to doubt the Eternal Goodness which can permit nature to offer such hideous possibilities; and if you had not with your own eyes seen the end, I should have said to you – disbelieve it all. I have not, I think, many more weeks to live, but you are young, and may forget all this.*
> *JOSEPH HABERDEN, M.D.*

In the course of two or three months I heard that Dr. Haberden had died at sea, shortly after the ship left England.

Miss Leicester ceased speaking, and looked pathetically at Dyson, who could not refrain from exhibiting some symptoms of uneasiness.

He stuttered out some broken phrases expressive of his deep interest in her extraordinary history, and then said with a better grace:

"But, pardon me, Miss Leicester, I understood you were in some difficulty. You were kind enough to ask me to assist you in some way."

"Ah," she said, "I had forgotten that. My own present trouble seems of such little consequence in comparison with what I have told you. But as you are so good to me, I will go on. You will scarcely believe it, but I found that certain persons suspected, or rather pretended to suspect that I had murdered my brother. These persons were relatives of mine, and their motives were extremely sordid ones; but I actually found myself subject to the shameful indignity of being watched. Yes, sir, my steps were dogged when I went abroad, and at home I found myself exposed to constant if artful observation. With my high spirit this was more than I could brook, and I resolved to set my wits to work and elude the persons who were shadowing me. I was so fortunate as to succeed. I assumed this disguise, and for some time have lain snug and unsuspected. But of late I have reason to believe that the pursuer is on my track; unless I am greatly deceived, I saw yesterday the detective who is charged with the odious duty of observing my movements. You, sir, are watchful and keen-sighted; tell me, did you see anyone lurking about this evening?"

"I hardly think so," said Dyson, "but perhaps you would give me some description of the detective in question."

"Certainly; he is a youngish man, dark, with dark whiskers. He has adopted spectacles of large size in the hope of disguising himself effectually, but he cannot disguise his uneasy manner, and the quick, nervous glances he casts to right and left."

This piece of description was the last straw for the unhappy Dyson, who was foaming with impatience to get out of the house, and would gladly have sworn eighteenth-century oaths if propriety had not frowned on such a course.

"Excuse me, Miss Leicester," he said with cold politeness, "I cannot assist you."

"Ah!" she said sadly, "I have offended you in some way. Tell me what I have done, and I will ask you to forgive me."

"You are mistaken," said Dyson, grabbing his hat, but speaking with some difficulty; "you have done nothing. But, as I say, I cannot help you. Perhaps," he added, with some tinge of sarcasm, "my friend Russell might be of service."

"Thank you," she replied; "I will try him," and the lady went off into a shriek of laughter, which filled up Mr. Dyson's cup of scandal and confusion.

He left the house shortly afterwards, and had the peculiar delight of a five-mile walk, through streets which slowly changed from black to grey, and from grey to shining passages of glory for the sun to brighten. Here and there he met or overtook strayed revellers, but he reflected that no one could have spent the night in a more futile fashion than himself; and when he reached his home he had made resolves for reformation. He decided that he would abjure all Milesian and Arabian methods of entertainment, and subscribe to Mudie's for a regular supply of mild and innocuous romance.

Lola

Lena Ng

IT RESEMBLED a puppy. I found it one day as I went for my walk. I usually travelled clockwise around Rose Hill Park, observing the birds and nodding to fellow *flâneurs*, but as today was an exploring type of day, I let my feet take the helm and I ended up at some far, over-grown, unexplored corner of the park.

As I craned my neck to catch a glimpse of a yellow-breasted finch, I heard a whimpering in the bushes. It sounded like a cross between a gurgling baby and a kitten mewling. The sound was so insistent and pitiful, I left my bird-watching, and eased closer to the bushes. The leaves quivered.

With its black paw-like limbs, it oozed its way from under the bushes, moving in the way of a fat, engorged slug, if a slug evolved to have short, fleshy nubs that helped it to transport. Now, bear with me, I know it sounds horrific, but it had these big, shining black eyes, like a newborn babe, and it made such a woeful, mewling noise, it played a hidden, dormant maternal chord in my middle-aged man's body, and instead of drawing back, I peered closer to it.

It gave a shiver that travelled from the front of its plump flesh down to its end tip. "Are you cold?" I asked, my voice in the register you talk to babies with.

It made a movement with its mouth that made it looked like it was pouting. I put my hand out, and after a second where it didn't bite me, I slid it under its squelchy body. The cold slime didn't bother me, but no wonder it was shivering.

I wrapped it in the rolled-up ends of my coat and made my way home. It snuggled against the warmth of my belly. I could feel the limb-nubs kneading my torso like a kitten kneads its mother as it suckles. I cradled it in the nest of my coat for the rest of the way home.

* * *

After I got home to my pre-war apartment, slightly out of breath after climbing three flights of stairs, I gently set my new pet on the kitchen counter and then searched for a box. I heard its squelching as it oozed along the counter. I lined the shoe box with newspaper and a soft chamois for it to snuggle against. It took to it very well, at first burying itself under the cloth, then sucking on it with its toothless mouth. It looked at me with its marble-shiny eyes.

All the while, I tried to come up with a name. Martha? No, too strait-laced. *Carol*? That didn't seem right either. But as I kept looking at my new pet, a name arose unbidden in my mind. Lola. That was its name. "Lola," I whispered. It mewled in reply. I stared into its galaxy-deep, liquid eyes, and after a while, the noise sounded like my name, 'Sydney', like it read my thoughts and pulled my name out of my mind. After this acquaintance, I ran my fingertips over its glistening head and it gave a trilling purr.

* * *

Later that day, as it was our Wednesday habit, I met up with my old friend Gloriana for afternoon tea at the Waterland Hotel. We had been friends from our college days, when I was the assistant editor of *The Varsity Tribune* and she was the gossip columnist, under a nom-de-plume of course.

"Darling," she said as she arose from the table, air kissing both of my cheeks. "How lovely it is to see you. And what a charmingly coloured bow-tie." I had picked a deep magenta silk to go with my large, round, plastic spectacles. The tie's bright colour was a statement piece against my white, three-piece suit. We were a fashion-conscious people, straddling the line between trendy and ridiculous. She wore a draping, bat-winged, dark purple caftan, and looked chic as always.

"New perfume?" I asked as I pulled up a chair, removing my matching white Panama hat and placing it on the side of the tea table.

"Astute as always," she replied. The waiter came with the tiered cake and sandwich tray and I with my old-fashioned manners served Gloriana her choice of cucumber and cream cheese finger sandwiches and scones using the accompanying pair of silver tongs.

"Now," she said as she buttered her scone, her diamond pavé bracelet glittering under the lights, "have you heard anything from Nadine?" Although her gossip-columnist days were long behind her, Gloriana was still a magpie for any information, no matter how small.

The miniature berry tarts were delicious and I finished the last morsel. "What's there to hear?" I replied, and after patting the linen napkin to my lips, I refreshed both our cups. "She just got back from—"

Time to feed Lola.

"From where?" asked Gloriana, her powdered brow creased as she leaned closer to me.

I blinked twice and realized I sat frozen with teapot in hand. "Sorry, I must have been distracted for a moment. Anyway, she just got back from her trip to Bora Bora and was too jet-lagged to really get into things when the doorbell rang and—"

Time to feed Lola.

I looked again at Gloriana's expectant face. "I'll have to tell you another time." I signalled the waiter for the bill. "Well, it's been lovely to see you, but I must be off. It's time to feed Lola."

"Oh," she said in astonishment, moving her napkin from her lap to the table. "You have a pet? What is it? A budgie?" she asked, knowing my love for birds.

"Ummm, no," I replied. I didn't know exactly what it was so I quickly said, "It's a dog. A little poodle mix I couldn't resist when I passed by the pet shop window," before she could ask any more questions. "She's expecting me." Instead of waiting for the bill, I headed to the counter to settle up and with a last wave, hurried out of the restaurant.

* * *

I could hear the poor thing crying as I unlocked the apartment door. I rushed over to the cardboard box. The bowl of water and the fruit and vegetable mix I had left for her had remained untouched.

"My little dear," I said, voice trembling as I ran my fingertips over her clammy ridge, "I'm so sorry. I didn't know what you wanted to eat."

Those limpid eyes looked up at me from the box and I got up to see what I could tempt her with from the fridge. I took out four small porcelain plates from the kitchen cabinet and filled them with this and that: thin slices of beef tongue, slivers of Parmigiano-Reggiano, a spoonful of chicken and duck liver pâté, half of a hard-boiled egg seasoned with paprika. She turned up her nose at all of these tidbits. I was starting to think she was a bit of a snob.

She kept crying and I couldn't think of what to do to console her. I held her against me, not minding the brown slime across my once-pristine suit. Finally, I stuck my thumb in her mouth, in imitation of how a baby would stop crying with a soother. Her black eyes grew larger and she slurped as she sucked on my thumb. Her gurgling noise sounded content, and after a while, she fell asleep, giving a soft, grumbling snore.

* * *

I didn't leave my apartment for days. She wouldn't eat, all she wanted to do was cuddle and sleep. She began teething, and I would feel the milk teeth gnawing gently on my thumb, not hard enough to hurt. Between pacing, I would try to read the paper, the headlines about this or that corrupt politician and the country going to pot all a big blur.

Her glistening body seemed to dry, despite my wiping it with a damp face cloth and misting it with plant spray. She slept more and more. Was she going into hibernation? There was only a hint of an autumn breeze outside but what did I know of Lola's life cycle?

Time to pray for Lola.

I wasn't religious and thus didn't know any prayers so I offered my prayer to the big cosmic entity in the sky. I tilted my head toward the fireplace. Please save Lola. Please save Lola. Please save Lola.

Time to pray for Lola.

I cried and wept, and cried and wept again, in between incoherent prayers. Her breathing became slower and slower until it stopped altogether and only her desiccated body remained.

I couldn't send her out in a shoebox that would end up in the trash, so I yanked the pothos by the roots, and buried Lola in the planter instead. I lit some candles and incense, and the corner of the apartment became a proper shrine. I dried my tears and took myself to bed.

* * *

The next morning, when I headed into the living room, I was greeted by a miraculous sight. A plant, glorious, had sprouted its green tendrils. Overnight, it developed a thick trunk with three braiding branches that stretched and grew up the corner wall, its vines like pulsing green veins creeping along the ceiling. The ends of the tendrils curled and waved like seaweed in the ocean. It seemed like a sentient vegetation. As I was admiring this turn of events—

Time to pray to Lola.

My legs moved of their own volition. I dropped to my knees in front of the massive plant. I prostrated myself before it. I kissed the green base where it emerged from the soil. I rubbed the nubs that ran along the sides of her trunk, felt their movement beneath the green skin.

Time to pray to Lola.

I stayed there the entire day. I didn't want for food or sleep. I was nourished by her. She was all that I required. I hugged the planter until I knew that she slept before I attended to any of my body's needs.

* * *

I didn't want to go, but it was Gloriana's fiftieth birthday (again). I had missed the two previous weekly teas and I didn't want her sending out the search party. Lola wasn't yet ready to accept newcomers. The time wasn't right. Gloriana opened the door with a coral-lipped smile and waved me in with a red-nailed hand. She had just had her hair set by the looks of things, and it curled in a light brown perm at the top of her head. We made our way into her opulent living room which bordered on tacky, all gilt mirrors and Louis XIV style furniture. Nothing like excess, she always said.

It was the usual bunch of rag tags, hovering about in their finery. Bunty, her imperial gaze barely acknowledging me, with her new third husband, Cliff – or was it Biff? It really doesn't matter – stood by the fireplace, sipping their cocktails.

I engaged in the vapid conversational chit-chat though my mind was directed elsewhere. At eight o'clock, the caterers started to bring out the food and the dozen of us seated ourselves by our placeholders at the table.

The meal was splendid since Gloriana's tastes were quite discerning, but it all tasted like chalk. The courses could not come out quickly enough. The soup, salad, amuse-bouche … it was all too much. I was eating as fast as I could, dizzy, and before the cake arrived and before I could stop myself, I blurted out, "Time to go home to feed Mother."

The room stopped and all eyes turned in my direction. Gloriana looked at me strangely. "But Sydney, your mother is dead."

I put my hand over my mouth and gave a small laugh to cover my slip of the tongue. "Lola's new nickname."

"You call your dog Mother?"

A flash of rage stunned me silent. The sound of my heartbeat drummed in my ears. When I found my voice again, I said, "Don't call her that. She would be offended to be called a dog."

Gloriana tilted her head quizzically to look at me with heavily made-up eyes. "Isn't that your new pet? If it's not a dog, then what is it?"

"You wouldn't understand." The party remained silent as I pushed back the chair, grabbed my coat, and took my leave. I didn't care if this was the last time I saw the lot of them again.

I got home and ranted to Mother. She rustled her branches in her infinite patience, her presence looming over me like a giant, green umbrella. "She called you a dog. I can't believe the disrespect." Mother looked at me with her understanding and peace washed over me as I saw her projected visions. I sensed what the future held.

* * *

Time to visit Mother.

I knew there would be a knock before I heard the rap on the door. Gloriana stood at the door, draped in cashmere and wool slacks. It still wasn't quite the right time, but since she was here already and at Mother's urging, I opened the door and let her inside.

She gaped at Mother's magnificence. The ends of her tendrils had fledged brown, slug-like masses and the nubs on the trunk had developed into eyes. Gloriana, in her shock, had for the first time lost her words.

"Isn't she amazing?" I asked in a hushed, awestruck voice. "I wouldn't have believed it."

"Is this Lola?" asked Gloriana, crouching at the pot's base and running her manicured, bejewelled hand along her trunk.

I nodded, both of us pleased at Gloriana's reaction. "You can call her Mother."

I excused myself to go to the powder room. Mother wanted to spend some alone time with Gloriana and I didn't want to see what would happen next. I don't have a strong stomach, I'm afraid.

After what I had thought a suitable time had passed, I returned to the living room. Gloriana had disappeared. Not even her clothes remained nor one drop of blood was spilled at the scene. Some of the trunk eyes glittered with the colours of jewels.

Mother purred. One of her leaves unfurled, and in her gratitude, she presented me with a gift. I took the round fruit with both hands, bowing my head in appreciation.

I took a bite of the apple-like meat. When its skin broke, a burst of powdery spores flooded my mouth and throat. I held back my coughing. I wouldn't want any of Mother's seed to go to waste.

I could feel myself emptying out, making room for spores and galaxies and entities and green alien-like vegetation growing all over the world. All-encompassing Mother. Despite my clothes, I could feel my legs fusing together, like a giant root. Beneath my skin, the tendrils unfurled.

I could hear all her thoughts. She could hear all of mine.

Lola is my mother. I am Lola's mother.

I am Lola.

Lola is me.

The Black Ship

Reggie Oliver

> *Far out at sea was a retreating sail*
> *White as hard years of ancient winds could bleach*
> *But evil with some portent beyond speech*
> *So that I did not wave my hand or hail.*
> 'The Port' by H. P. Lovecraft

Some papers and notes collected by the late George Vilier, Consulting Professor of Ontography, Miskatonic University, Massachusetts.

"MAGOTIE HEADED" was how Anthony à Wood described his friend John Aubrey (1626–1697), and with some justification; all the same, we owe him a great deal. Aubrey was a collector of esoteric learning, and his Brief Lives is a treasure house of anecdotal detail about figures from the 16th and 17th century. He hardly published anything in his lifetime, and at his death in 1697 Aubrey's papers were found to be in a fantastic state of confusion – hence "magotie headed," I suppose. Manuscripts of his are still being rediscovered, and I was the lucky – or unlucky? – discoverer of one such cache.

In 1957, the National Trust took over an ancient 16th-century manor house called Old Pierce Hall in the English county of Morsetshire. Aubrey had inherited the Hall in the 1650s and lived there for a while before he was forced to sell it, being no man of business and constantly short of money.

It was bought by Aubrey's brother-in-law, one Trismegistus Moreby, in whose family the house remained until the Moreby line apparently died out sometime after the last war, since when the property was maintained by a private management company. However, by that time, the place was in a state of near-ruin – there were great holes in the roof, it was overrun with rats, and a thick layer of dust carpeted most of the rooms.

The last Moreby inhabitant had been a recluse of strange and unpleasant habits, and when the National Trust was unexpectedly offered the Hall in lieu of unpaid taxes, they were at first reluctant to take it on. Various experts were summoned to look at furniture, fabrics, pictures, and so on, to see if the place was worth rescuing. I was called in to examine the documents and papers, which were gathered in boxes in a "muniment room." My academic specialization is in personal manuscript records (diaries, letters, and the like) from the 17th and 18th centuries.

The papers were mostly routine stuff that you find in nearly all old country houses – account ledgers, legal documents, game books, letters, interesting enough in their way; but the contents of one box made my time at Old Pierce Hall worthwhile, or memorable at least. The box itself is rather a handsome thing: wooden, studded with round-headed brass nails, and covered in what had once been scarlet velvet, now faded to a sort of mildewed greenish pink. On the top of the box had been pasted a vellum label on which in sepia ink, faded almost to illegibility, was inscribed the words:

Olde Fellowes

I had no idea what this could possibly mean, but I was excited because I thought I recognized on that label the strange, crabbed hand of John Aubrey himself.

The box was locked, with the key nowhere to be found, and it took some time to get the Trust's permission to force it open by means of a chisel and a hacksaw. I, and my assistant Helen – a girl from the United States, and the brightest of my graduate research students – took some trouble in our efforts to break open the box without damaging it too much.

When we eventually succeeded, we found it filled with documents neatly tied with ribbon into packages. They were written in a number of hands, one of which was Aubrey's, and it was his handwriting that inscribed a sheet of paper on top of all the others. It read:

> *Concerning the Olde Fellowes, their wayes, darke customes and origins: some remarkes and testimonies, together with a narrative of the Black Ship.*
> *Johannes Aubrey, anno 1696.*

And then a verse quatrain:

> *Lette no one read that doth not knowe,*
> *And those who knowe, lette them be ware*
> *For shadowed Feare doth stalke in woe*
> *And meets you sudden on the staire.*

I had no idea what this might mean. Helen gazed at the inscription and then shook her head.

"Well," she said with a show of cheeriness. "Sooner you than me. I'll leave you to it." And she did. It was odd, because I had put Helen down as one of life's enthusiasts, but not this time. Is it some kind of retrospective imagination which makes me recall that, as she left the muniment room, a sudden breath of damp, cold air invaded it?

The neat packaging of the manuscripts was misleading. It took me some time before I was able to make any sense of them, and now I am not at all sure that I should have done.

It begins with a packet of notes which seem to be a supplement to Aubrey's life of Dr. John Dee, the famous Elizabethan occultist and astrologer to Queen Elizabeth I. It consists in a detailed record of a conversation in the 1650s with an old lady called Goodwife Faldo, who knew Dee in his last years in Mortlake. As Aubrey's spelling is erratic and Faldo's narration, though comprehensive, is rambling and repetitive, I will summarize, quoting directly where necessary.

* * *

By 1608, Dee's glory days were long over and he was living in an impoverished state, at his house in Mortlake, then a village outside London on the south bank of the River Thames. He was just about subsisting by drawing up horoscopes for money, and occasionally accepting handouts from rich aristocratic friends. His young wife, Jane, had died of the plague two years previously and Dee himself, now aged eighty, was not long for this world.

The one thing that remained to him was his great library, consisting of some 700 volumes, many of them in manuscript, an extraordinary number for those days. But, with creditors pressing, even that was under threat. Goodwife Faldo, who kept house for him after a fashion, would often see him slip out of the building at night with several books under his arm, only to return much later without them. She could not think what he was doing, but later it was discovered that he had buried them in a field next to his home.

Faldo, being a shrewd and observant woman, though illiterate, noticed that there were certain volumes that Dee kept close by him, and he would often move them from room to room in his house, "as if they were his verie companious." There was one in particular – "about the size of the greate churche Bible at Mortlak and all bounde in black with a claspe and a lock on it" – with which he was inseparable. It was such a weight that she would often offer to carry it for him, but he would never allow her to do so.

One night in October, a great storm blew up and battered Dee's house at Mortlake. Goodwife Faldo insisted on laying a fire in the parlor, and though Dee at first opposed it on the grounds of expense, he finally agreed. Fuel was costly, and the old man had little money to spare. As soon as it was lit, Faldo saw Dee seat himself near the fire and stare into it, crouched and withered, but his eyes blazing with some inscrutable flame of their own.

Beside him on a stool was the great book, whose smooth binding of black leather he occasionally stroked but did not open. "For it was locked with a claspe," said Faldo, "and he had the key to it ever about his neck upon a silver chaine."

Suddenly there was a knocking at the door. "Such a knocking as never I heard," said Faldo, "and never hope to againe, as Christe is my Saviour." Before Dee had time to prevent her, Faldo had unbarred the door and let in a stranger, in a black cloak and steepled Puritan hat, who stood wet and dripping from the rain.

He was, according to Faldo, "an exceeding tall black man," (by which I think she means dark-complexioned, not actually of African descent) "and verie gaunt withal."

When Dee turned and saw the stranger, he seemed fearful. There then ensued a conversation which Faldo only partly heard because she was very soon dismissed from the room. The dark man gave her such a threatening look that she was glad to go, but she listened behind the door.

From this she gathered that the man had come from Edward Kelley. At this Dee expressed both astonishment and dismay. Kelley had been his one-time assistant and medium in a series of séances, during which Kelley would stare at a stone of polished black obsidian called a "scrying stone" and then announce what he heard or saw while Dee wrote it down. These were the famous "angelic conversations" later published by Meric Casaubon, though some of the words spoken were far from angelic.

Kelley and Dee moved to Prague where, after the famous wife-swapping incident (apparently encouraged by the "angels"), Dee abandoned his medium and returned to England. Kelley prospered for a while in Prague and then, apparently, died in mysterious circumstances. Accounts of his death had been vague and conflicting, but, according to the dark man, Kelley was not dead at all, but was now a powerful figure in a society calling itself the "Odd Fellowes" or the "Olde Fellowes," Faldo could not say which. At this, her old master Dr. Dee was "much affrighted."

The man, who introduced himself as "Master Moreby," seemed to be demanding the return of a book from Dr. Dee, a book called "The Necropicon" according to Faldo, though she could not be sure. Apparently, while they were in Prague in the 1590s, Kelley and Dee had discovered and acquired this volume which contained "much curious and very ancient knowledge." Kelley was now claiming it as his because it had been his "scrying" (i.e. Mediumistic clairvoyance) that had pointed Dee to where the book could be found.

Dee refused emphatically to release the volume, at which voices were raised and the dark man began snarling "like unto a wilde beaste." At this point Faldo felt it her duty to intervene and, grasping her "good besom" (a broom), she entered the room. At which point Master Moreby glared at the two with malignant eyes and strode out of the house.

Dr. Dee seemed utterly cowed by the encounter. "He prayed me barre the door and permit no one in until I was sure they were no enemy." For about a week after this encounter, Dee rarely left the house and became more secretive than ever.

Then there came a night when Faldo had to be away to tend to a sick relative in the village. Dee had begged her to stay, but Faldo insisted. She told him that if he barred and locked all the windows he could come to no harm. Reluctantly, Dee let her go.

When she returned the next morning she found the door still barred, but her knocking would not rouse the Doctor. Then she saw that one of the windows at the front had been smashed in. Being at the time an active young woman, Faldo climbed in through the shattered casement. The house was in disarray. She found Dee lying on the floor of the parlor incapable of moving, but still alive and moaning slightly.

When she had got him into a chair and made him a posset, Dee was able to tell her what had happened. Thieves had broken in during the night and had terrorized Dee. They had not stolen much, but what they had taken had greatly distressed him. They had taken, said Faldo, "his black polish'd stone for scrying and 'the booke,' and when I asked what booke he would not say, but asked for pen and paper and on it he wrote a worde which I, being unlettered, could not tell, but I have the paper still."

Then, writes Aubrey, *this good old woman did fetch the paper and did give it me and on it was written but one word which I here sett down:*

NEKRONOMIKON

But yet I cannot tell what this may signifye, yet others who come after might.

Dee went on to tell that the thieves had set on him brutally, and threatened him. He showed her the scars on his neck where the key on the silver chain had been brutally wrenched from his ancient body. After that, Faldo told Aubrey, Dee had entered into a decline and died "of a seizure" a few months later.

"He spoke but once thereafter of that night," said Faldo "and that was to say that if they had but let him to finish the translation of the booke, he would have died content, but it was not to be. And woe be to them, sayd hee, who look into the book without understanding, for they would see forms and portents which they cannot containe and which will bring destructioun."

Aubrey writes that: *On hearing this most marvellous relation from Goodwife Faldo, I took much paines to discover who were these "olde fellowes" and what this Nekronomikon was, for I had heard tell of these "olde fellowes" from another source.* [His own family connection with the Morebys?] *And though I found little concerning the latter, yet what I found of the former, is here contained. Yet let them be ware who read.*

The other relevant documents come mainly from two sources: the journal of one Martha Edwards, and the log of Captain Reynolds, Master of the ship *Speedwell*, which was intended to accompany the *Mayflower* on its voyage to the New World.

How Aubrey acquired these records is a mystery I have yet to uncover. Again, I will paraphrase and summarize somewhat.

* * *

In the cold upper room of a house in the Dutch city of Leiden, on an evening in July 1620, the curtains are drawn. One candle lights the scene. The emaciated figure of Hopewell Edwards lies in bed, while his wife Martha and daughter Mercy look on. Hopewell stretches out a hand to Martha. It is like a skeleton, with a thin covering of pale skin and veins.

"You must go," he says. "Your passage is paid for. There is nothing for you here, and I am not long for this world."

"I cannot leave you."

"You must. It is the Promised Land. I am sick unto death and cannot join you, but I shall be with you in spirit. Promise me you will go."

Martha did so and made her oath, at her husband's urging, on the Bible. A few days later she and her daughter Mercy took their berth on the *Speedwell*, which left the port of Delfshaven on July 22nd. Her account of the voyage to Southampton and then on to Plymouth in the company of fellow Pilgrims is perfunctory, but she makes one remark: "My fellow voyagers did ask why I went alone with my daughter. I told them that my husband was lately deceased, and it was he who had enjoined me to seek out a new life in the Promised Land, if he did not live, for he was sick unto death. But methinks few did believe me, wherefore I was contemned most unjustly by these good people."

When the ship reached Plymouth, most of the families aboard the *Speedwell* transferred to the *Mayflower*, a larger ship and more suited to the voyage across the Atlantic. It was made clear to Martha that she and her daughter would not be welcome aboard the *Mayflower*, "on account of some malicious and wagging tongues which sayd that I had deserted my husband, or even that I had made away with him by some wicked device, and nothing could persuade them to the contrary. Wherefore I did despaire and thought to return to Leiden with my daughter, but for the sacred promise I gave to my husband on his deathbed. But Captain Reynolds, the master of the *Speedwell*, took pity on me and sayd that his vessell was to followe the *Mayflower*, taking aboard more company, and that I might stay aboard and fulfil my vow. He sayd, moreover, that though his vessell was smaller than *Mayflower*, yet it was handier and a well-found craft and might yet touch the shores of the New World before the greater ship.

"With this I was mightily consoled, but I asked him who might be my companions on this voyage, for the far greater part of my fellow colonists from Leiden were gone into the *Mayflower*. To which Master Reynolds replyed that he did not know, but was assured of a goodly company."

This account is confirmed by Captain Reynolds's briefer account in the ship's log. However, his version is more circumstantial about later events. On September 4th, 1620, two days before *Mayflower* set sail for the New World after two aborted attempts to begin the voyage, *Speedwell* was at anchor alongside it in Plymouth harbor. Reynolds was in the aft cabin at six in the evening when the ship's boy announced the arrival of a man on board carrying documents from the ship's sponsor. Reynolds writes:

> I commanded him to be brought to me, and when he came in to my quarters I beheld a dark man so tall that he stooped beneath the roof beams of the cabin. This indignity seemed to put him in an ill-humour, so I requested him to be seated and to tell me his business. When he had sat, he told me that he was now the true holder of this vessell and showed me letters patent establishing this title. At this I was much dismayed, for I had not been informed of such a change, but he paid no heed to my distress, saying that I must bustle about and prepare with all speed for our voyage to the New World. When I asked him who was to be the passengers on this voyage, for now all but two of those who had come from Leiden were gone into Mayflower, he sayd he would attend to that, and he asked to see those two that remained aboard.

Martha's narrative now takes up the story:

> *Having little money to pay for an inn at Plymouth, my daughter Mercy and I had remained aboard, and shifted as best we might in the 'tween decks. It was a most noisome and damp situation, even in port, and the old beams did creak. Moreover we were much plagued with rats who contrived to come aboard in harbour. I had arranged our effects and some curtains so that we had some solace of privacy. At that time no one was aboard but us and some sailors, coarse, idle fellows to my eyes, and much given to strong drink and bawdry.*
>
> *But two days after our coming into harbour and at about ten in the forenoon, there was some commotion, and Captain Reynolds did come down to the 'tween decks accompanied by a man, a certain Master Moreby. He was of middling age and very tall and thin. Though soberly dressed with all neatness, I and my daughter Mercy thought him most ill-favoured. He spoke to us insolently, as if we had no right to be there. I showed him my documents, which ensured my passage to the New World, either in* Speedwell *or* Mayflower. *But he sayd he had bought the vessell at auction, and he was the Master of* Speedwell *now and I had no rights. Yet, sayd he, with a strange kind of a smile which I did not like, he would suffer me to remain, and he assured me that there would be company for me on the voyage. When I asked him the nature of that company, whether like myself and Mercy, they were Pilgrims in quest of the Promised Land, he smiled again but made no answer.*

Over the next two days the ship was fitted out for its long voyage. Speedwell had been a leaky vessel, and Moreby had ordered its sides to be painted with pitch, "So that," remarked Captain Reynolds, "the ship became very black in its outward aspect, and some sayd they would not know it to be in very truth the Speedwell, but called it 'The Black Ship.'" Martha complained much of the smell while this procedure was going forward, but even more of the company that was coming aboard to take up residence with them in the 'tween decks.

She wrote: "They seem a most ill-assorted and ungodly crowd, for when I asked them if there was a Pastor or Elder among them who might conduct prayers or read to us from Holy Scripture, they did look upon us with amazement. Then one, a toothless old crone who went by the name of Mother Demdyke, let out such a cackle of hideous mirth, I thought the very Devill Himself had come to mock us in our travail." Finally, on September 8th, Moreby came aboard and they slipped out of Plymouth on the tide the following morning.

The first few weeks of the voyage would appear to be relatively uneventful, but one can gather that the journey was not an easy or a comfortable one from the start, even in relatively fine weather. In spite of its coating of pitch, the *Speedwell* was still very leaky and conditions on the 'tween decks were (as they had been on *Mayflower*) extremely damp and uncomfortable. Martha and her daughter Mercy kept themselves aloof from the other passengers, whom they did not like. There was in their attitude no doubt a certain element of puritan self-righteousness, but one can also sympathize when Martha writes:

> *They were forever restless and unquiet, and did utter strange cries or chaunts at all hours of day and night. Oft times they did seem to talk in a strange tongue that I knew not of, and I heard certain words repeated which filled me with great uncertainty and dread, such as "Ctholhoo fertagen" [sic] and other such strange locutions. When I did ask them what language it was they spoke, they did say naught; but one, Mother Demdyke, did*

say it was the tongue of the "Olde Ones." Then several of the others did look upon her very sharply at this and she spoke no more.

Though we subsisted on the ship's food and drink as we were entitled – and very ill it was – we had brought some supplies of our own for the journey, such as some barrels of dried fruit and pease, the which one night we offered to share with the other passengers, but they did refuse, eying us with much suspicion.

That same evening as we were preparing to settle to our sleep, behind the curtain we had erected, of a sudden the curtains parted and we beheld a face grinning at us. It was only one of the boys – a strange lad of a familie called Curwen, as we discovered – but so filthy and malignant was his aspect that we were much affrighted. He drew the curtains round him so that we saw naught but his head, which continued to grin and leer until my Mercy took her besom and knocked him o'er the mazard with it.

This is to be a most black and lonely voyage in the midst of this ungodly rabble, but we put our trust in the Lord that by His Good Grace, we shall make landfall and find rest and companionship once more in His Saints.

Four weeks into the voyage, the *Speedwell* was hit by storms. Martha's account becomes scanty and all but illegible at times because of the rolling of the ship. One can gather, however, that conditions were peculiarly horrible. The *Speedwell*, a smaller ship even than *Mayflower*, was thrown about like a leaf on the waves, and the 'tween decks where Martha and Mercy spent most of their time was often swilling and slippery with sea water which had come in through a thousand tiny leaks in the ship's sides. Martha and Mercy often took a hand at the pumps to prevent the ship from sinking altogether.

Captain Reynolds's log during this period is terse: *Heavy seas… The seamen discontented and anxious to make landfall… We are short of victuals and are like to starve if relief does not come soon.*

Then comes a more detailed series of entries, and it appears as if Reynolds is beginning to use his log more as a confessional than a record:

October 3rd. *High seas and contrary winds continue. Moreby comes to me and commands that I turn south. I reply that it would take us out of our way, and that our provisions and drinking water will last us but few days longer, so that we cannot alter course on pain of starvation and sickness. But Master Moreby tells me that this is his ship by right, and I must obey. Besides, he says, by turning south I must escape the tempest. I ask him how he knows this, for assuredly I do not, and I have been at sea many years longer than he, and he tells me that he knows and it its written in the stars, and he commands me to turn south. I must perforce obey, but all is not well about my heart.*

There have been murmurings from my men about some of the guests he has aboard, for they are very ill-favoured and speak often in strange tongues. But I must endure all this.

October 4th. *We had been travelling south for nigh on twenty hours, Master Moreby ever at my side when I am at the wheel, the weather never abating. Then, at about eleven in the forenoon, suddenly all is calm. The wind is hushed, the billows abate as if by some miracle, and a light mist descends. Barely a breeze stirs our sails, and yet we seem to be borne forward as if by a current. Moreby instructs me minutely where I must turn my ship. I ask him where we are – for I know not – and if we shall see land soon, but he says only that I must follow his instruction precisely, for he has guidance from the stars. I take this* to be mere whim wham, for we have seen little of the stars for many days, but I may not reason with him. On each occasion that I raise some complaint or objection, he gives me such a look that I dare not venture further.

He carries about him a great old book, about the size of a church Bible, which he consults most reverently and studiously, and yet methinks it is no Holy Book, for once, when I chanced to see into it, I beheld the image of a most blasphemous shape, a demon most like, with a heavy head and a most venemous hair and beard, like to a Medusa I have seen in an old carving, all serpents and writhing coils. And when Master Moreby espyed that I had seen it, he did shutt the book and commanded me on pain of Death never to look into his book againe.

October 5th. The mist clears a little, the sea staying calm and almost glassy, when shortly after two in the afternoon, Bates, one of my seamen, spies land from the crow's nest in the main mast. Master Moreby takes out a length of leather like a staff and puts it to his eye in the direction to which Bates pointed. I, greatly wondering, asked him what this signifyed, and he passed me the object and bade me look through it. At first I could make nothing of it, then I saw. This must be the new spying glass of which I heard tell in Holland last summer.

It was land of a sort that I saw, and, I guessed, an island, yet a very strange land indeed the like of which I had never yet beheld. It stood up out of the sea in great rocks and pillars of a green stone, yet with scarce any vegetation upon it, and all at angles as if shaped by a giant, or Cyclops. It mounted in steps and causeways up to a great summit, level at the top yet with one black stone upon it. It seemed to me – fanciful though it may sound – that I beheld not so much an island as the topmost excrescences of some great palace or monument, much of which must be sunk in the depths of the sea. The sight of it filled me with much amazement and terrour, but Moreby told me to steer towards it. There, he sayd, we would find sweet water and a safe haven in which to repair our battered vessell. I could scarce gainsay him for we were sorely in need of both, yet I had great misgivings.

I asked him if there might not be savage men and beasts dwelling on the isle who might do us harm, but he merely gave me the spying glass againe and bad me look to discern if there was any man or beast to be seen. I looked and there was not, and yet this very emptiness giveth me cause to fear. Who made these vast rocks to stand thus? For assuredly it is no work of Nature, so exact and sharp are the angles of their turrets, spires, terraces, and cloud-mantled pinnacles. And yet no men did neither, but only some race of giant and monstrous Daemons, Anthropophagi, Cyclopes, or some fell Ogre.

It must be from about this time that the last of Martha's account derives, though she gives no exact dates:

We are entered into calm waters, for which Christ in His mercy be thanked. Master Moreby came down to speak with the assembled company in the 'tween deck. He spoke of our being "very near our deliverance," and sayd that we should make land shortly. Then I asked what part of the New World we were coming to and when could I meet again my brothers and sisters in Christ. But he looked upon me with a strange smile and sayd that we were not there yet, and that it was not a New World but a very ancient one indeed. That talk of New Worlds was mere foolishness, for all worlds were indeed older *than God Himself, which I took to be blasphemy, but I held my tongue and restrained my daughter Mercy from crying out in righteous objection. The others in the company kept silent, but methought they understood more than I, for I heard much murmuring among them about "The Olde Ones" and of "Chtholhoo" [sic] which troubled me greatly. I am now most grievously assured that we are fallen among the Ungodly and may not escape the snares of the Evil One.*

That night, my Mercy had a dream which she told me of the following morning. For she dreamed she was on a high place surrounded by the sea, and she lay upon a bed of stone open to the heavens, and above her stood a great black pillar or monument, highly polish'd and carved with many curious figures and characters. On that pillar was crouched a beast, or demon, but like no demon she had ever seen in any cut or engraving in a book; for it had no horns, but only short leathern wings and its mouth parts were a mass of serpents. For the rest she would not tell me because it had so affrighted her. And all around her were gathered those who worshipped the beast upon the stone with great cries and wailings. And she looked for me in her terror but could not find me, and then she besought Christ of His great mercy to deliver her, but the company round about laughed her prayers to scorn. And looking up she saw a light from Heaven and Jesus in his infinite pity looking down upon her from a cloud all lit up from within by the glorious rays of the sun. Yet he was very far off and could not reach her, and as she pleaded for him to descend and rescue her she woke in fear and trembling, and with such a piteous cry that those who were about us in the 'tween decks did scold us for waking them from their slumbers.

That morning, it being calm and bright, we came on deck and beheld the Island where we were to make landfall. We gazed in wonder at its strangeness, for in the milky sunlight with which it was bathed we could see that it was all made of great green rocks, sharp and cut askew as if by some giant hand.

Then I asked Master Moreby if he knew the name of this place that we were coming to, and he replyed that he knew the name, but it was one that might not be spoken in common company, for it was a very holy place. So I asked if it was some shrine or temple where the Papists in their folly worshipped the bones of the Virgin or some such vanity. Then he sayd it was not like that at all, but that we should presently see its wonders when we came ashore with him. I sayd that neither I nor my daughter Mercy would care to set foot in this heathen and ungodly place, but Master Moreby sayd there was no choice in the matter, for all must go ashore. Then was I much affrighted, but of what I know not.

Here the testament of Martha Edwards ends abruptly. For the rest we must rely on the account of Captain Reynolds in his log book:

***October 6th.** On this day we made landfall at the Island which has no name and is not marked on any map. We found an inlet where we could drop anchor and enjoy shelter from the winds. There was but a small beach of grey-green stones where our boats could land, and from there I saw an ancient stepped causeway which wound upwards through the rocks into the centre of the Island. I was for going ashore, but Master Moreby prevented it. He sayd that I and my crew should remain aboard to conduct repairs, but that he would lead a party ashore from among the passengers who would presently bring back to the ship casks filled with fresh water, meat, provisions, and other necessary things for the completion of our voyage. I was much amazed at this, but knew better than to raise objection, for Master Moreby hath a way of looking at one that quells all protest. Among* *those who went ashore were Martha and Mercy Edwards, and I thought they went with an ill-grace, but I had little reason or power to prevent them.*

October 7th. *The party is returned from the Island, bringing with them our barrels filled with fresh water, and other provisions, including some herbs and roots, many great crabs gathered from the shore, and two carcasses of fresh meat. When I did ask from what animal came the carcasses, they replyed that they were piggs with which the isle abounded. On my remarking that I had never seen piggs of such length and leanness, Master Moreby sayd that these creatures were native to the Island and nowhere else to be found. Then I and all my men came ashore and made a fire on the beach, where we roasted the piggs on spits and made merry, for it was a long time since we had been able to feast with such abundance. The meat was very good and, especially that from the smaller of the two carcasses, most tender, sweet and flavoursome.*

But I noticed that Master Moreby held aloof and would eat nothing but a few pot herbs and dried fruit, and when I asked him the cause, he sayd that his needs were simple and that he made a practice at all times to live on little. Then I saw that Martha and Mercy Edwards were not of the company, and he told me that they were weary of the sea and had resolved to stay on the Island and convert the natives – if such there be – to the true religion of Christ and make it their home. But I did not altogether believe him, though I sayd naught, and was very troubled in my conscience at it.

October 7th (later). *This day I thought we might set sail, but Master Moreby came to me and sayd there was one thing most necessary to be done, and for this he required the strength and skills of myself and my men. He told me that at the top of the Island was a black stone which he wished to be removed and placed in the ship to take to the Americas. He sayd that it required the strength and skill of my men to transport this object by means of ropes and other devices. I protested most strongly that neither I nor my men were contracted to service the random desires of anyone aboard and that, besides, I knew not if my vessel would sustain the weight of such an object. Then Moreby stared at me and sayd that any disobedience to his commands would go very ill with me. He sayd, moreover, that if it were known widely that my men and I had tasted of forbidden flesh, I should suffer the hatred of all the world. Angrily I asked him what he meant, but he, remaining silent, eyed me as before, and I knew, to my everlasting shame, what he meant. I therefore gave instructions to my men, who were much astonished by my commands, but made no murmur of complaint. And so, with six of my crew, a quantity of rope, and other necessary accoutrement, I stepped ashore once again, accompanied by Master Moreby and a few of the more able-bodied passengers.*

I had had occasion to remark the strangeness of the Island, even on slight acquaintance; now, on venturing further in, I was struck most forcibly by the alien and unnatural quality of its features. The rocks of which it was chiefly composed were of a greenish hue, but not from moss or vegetation, but like the verdant marbles, so highly prized by the men of Italy. Yet I have never seen such stone in such abundance before, and it seemed to have been shaped by cunning hands. We followed a path of smooth flat stones, like the pavement of some great palace or temple, which led ever upwards between great clefts in the rock.

I noted but few plants growing there, and saw no creatures, not even so much as a sea bird, but nevertheless the isle was full of voices. Strange cries echoed among the surrounding stones, and yet not like the voice of any man or beast that I have heard before. It filled me and my men with a great dread, so that I asked Master Moreby what they might be. He replyed that they were not the cries of man or beast but were caused by the exhalation of air through holes and clefts in the rock, and that these exhalations came from very deep caverns beneath the Island. I could scarce credit his observation, but held my peace.

As we wound upwards, I began to see many curious signs and figures carved into the surrounding rocks. Again, in wonderment, I asked Moreby what these might be, and he told me that these were marks left by a very ancient people, but would not say aught further.

At length we arrived at the summit of the isle, where upon a kind of platform of stone stood a black rock, smooth and polish'd, carved into a conical pillar with its topmost part level and with many strange devices inscribed upon it. Upon the topmost part of this black stone was a carven figure which struck me with much confusion and terror, for it was very like the image that I had glanced in Master Moreby's great book. It was crouched upon a seat of alabaster, though it was composed of smooth stone of a dark green like the deep shade of a cypress tree. Its eyes were made of milk-white moon stones, and all manner of writhing serpents flowed from its hideous visage as if they were limbs. The skill and art of the limner had truly been put to the service of Hell itself on making that image.

Master Moreby commanded that this monstrous object be taken down from its pinnacle and transported most reverently to the ship. My men professed the greatest reluctance to have anything to do with the removal of this Hellish and Heathen idol, but Moreby was insistent and I promised goodly measures of strong drink to those who would aid us in this endeavour. My men obeyed, but with a very ill grace.

As the idol (as I may call it) was being taken down from its exalted post, I heard many murmurs and strange cries among those on our passage who had come up with us to this place. One of them, known to all as Mother Demdyke, a most pestilential ancient, lifted up her skirts and began to dance, cackling and keening as she did so. Few fouler spectacles have I ever beheld than that toothless crone capering on the summit of such a barren and accursed isle, but her other companions paid no heed.

The idol was lowered into a kind of wooden chariot our carpenter had devised for transporting it to the ship. When this was done, we must perforce handle the black stone itself and this, being heavier and greater in size than the idol, excited more complaint, yet we succeeded. One thing I noted as it was being removed was that, at its base, the stones round about it were darkened by a reddish substance, as it might be blood. I remarked on this to Master Moreby, but he told me in a very sharp voice to attend to my appointed task.

And so the thing was done, and those two stones were safely stowed aboard, but with much ado so that when it was done it was dawn of October 8th. At once Moreby commanded me to set a course, and gave me instructions as to which I had no choice but to submit to his demands.

October 8th. As the sun rose over the Island, we left our anchorage. It was a bright day with a fair wind and, as we came out into the open sea, I heard again those sounds that the Island gave out, like unto a mournful hollowing from its depths.

Then a most strange and astounding event happened. We were about a league from the Island when I looked back upon it and it appeared to me to be smaller than was just. I kept my eye upon it and saw that the whole Island was sinking beneath the waves. The beach where we had feasted but one day previous was gone completely under the waves, but this was no mere tide, for the isle was sinking fast. The sea began to close over cliffs and crags whither but yesterday we had climbed with much labour. As the land sank a mist was borne upwards, like a steam from the clefts in the rocks, and it was coloured grey and green. Presently, we could see only the topmost spire of that mysterious congery of rocks; then with a final exhalation of green smoke and what sounded like a melancholy sigh, the whole sank beneath the waves, which bubbled a while and then was still. All that was left of it was a wreath of greenish fog which hung, like some foul garland, above the place where the Island had been, before it was dissolved by the winds.

So astonished was I at this spectacle that for a full hour I could not speak, and issued commands to my men by gesture only. Yet I dared not ask Master Moreby what manner of place it was we had visited. I read once in an old book that there be certain mouths of Hell on this Earth such as at Hecla in Iceland, where the ghosts of dead men are familiarly seen, and sometimes talk with the living, and where lamentable screeches and howlings are continually heard, which strike a terror to the auditors; moreover, fiery chariots are commonly seen to bring in the souls of men in the likeness of crows, and devills ordinarily go in and out. This I truly believe was such a place. Yet, more like, it was not a mouth of Hell, but Hell itself that we had visited.

October 20th. I am once more aboard the Speedwell and must depart for England on the next tide. We made land but three days after we had left the Island, our progress being free and swift, as if by a miracle. We dropped anchor some sixty miles south west of Cape Cod to which we were destined in Narragansett Bay. I was for sailing for Cape Cod to join the Mayflower, but Master Moreby prevented it, saying we had a safe anchorage above Rhode Island.

It would appear that he knows the land, for after we had spent our first night in terra firma on Rhode Island, Master Moreby directed all those aboard that they should go across to make a settlement on the Providence River and sayd he would instruct them where to go. Moreover, he required myself and a party of my men to go with them, carrying the black stone into the country of the Pokanokets.

I did protest most strenuously at this, saying I was not contracted for such a task, but he overbore me, for he had complete mastery over the people he had brought with him on the voyage and they outnumbered us, though they were a foul and filthy congregation of persons.

Keeping the Providence River to the left of us, we moved upstream through dense woodland, my men carrying the black stone and Master Moreby's people the fearful idol of the strange Island in a cabinet which my carpenter, Bates, had made. At every moment I expected that the savages of those lands should set upon us, so that our men carried swords and muskets in addition to the stone monolith. Presently, we came to a clearing. Moreby pointed through the trees to a hill-top and declared that this was where the black stone was to be laid. My men, exhausted, set down their burden, upon which Master Moreby most peremptorily commanded the men to take it up again, for, sayd he, 'twas but a short league to the summit. I told Master Moreby that we must rest and he turned upon me, his eyes ablaze with anger, when from the trees came men, such as I had never seen before. They were naked, savage, and painted all over with patterns and devices all in red and black, and their faces were marked with black and white to look like the skulls of the dead. These were the Pokanokets of whom I had heard tell. All but one, who seemed their *king or commander, carried bows and arrows, and he, the king, wore a great cloak of feathers and carried a staff whose head was the head of a fish. His name, as I discovered, was Massakoit, a man with a fearful reputation. We prepared to defend ourselves, though we had little hope among so many.*

Striding forward, this Massakoit spake harsh words in his barbarous tongue, and his men made ready with their bows so as to kill us all. But Moreby seemed undaunted. He made a sign to Old Demdyke who, with others of her brood, uncovered the cabinet and brought out the idol. This they held aloft, uttering strange and hideous cries like to those of the Savage King.

All at once Massakoit drew back in amazement, and all his men put down their weapons and abased themselves before the idol which was an object of reverence and fear to them. And they seemed to call it "Koothoolu" or some such, in their barbarous tongue. Then King Massakoit also abased himself, and Master Moreby spake to him in his own language.

By nightfall, the Pokanokets had carried the black stone to the hill-top and set the idol upon it. Moreover, they had supplied all our folk with tents and bedding (of a sort) and plentiful supplies of food, so that that night, by the light of many fires, we feasted.

As these celebrations were concluding, Master Moreby came to me. He told me that my task here was completed and that I and my men might return to my ship, unless I wanted to join him in his venture in the New World. "For," sayd he, "from all you have seen and tasted, you are become, perforce, one of my Olde Fellowes."

I asked Moreby what were these "Olde Fellowes" of which he spake, and why were they so-called, to which he replyed that they were thus named for they were fellowes of the Olde Ones, and were their servants and ministers here on Earth, taking great powers thereby. Then I asked who were these "Olde Ones," and he answered that they were Great Beings who came from the Starrie Vault of Heaven. To which I sayd that assuredly these Olde Ones were nothing but Demons and Boggarts, enemies of Almighty God, and I would have none of them. At this Master Moreby looked at me with much fury and amazement, but he spake not a word, and presently he went away into his tent. Some time later he came to ask me what I and my men intended to do. I told him that I intended, once I was assured of my just recompense, to make sail with all speed for England.

Moreby then gave me a package of parchment, sealed with a great seal on which was the image of that accursed idol that they carried about. He instructed me that I was to deliver this budget to his cousin, Trismegistus Moreby, at his house near Bartonstone in the county of Morsetshire, and there I would receive full reward and remuneration for all that I and my men had done. But I sayd that this should not be, for I was to be payd in gold on completion of the voyage to the Americas. At this Moreby smiled and sayd that silver and gold had he none, but that what he had he gave me. He sayd that all my needs would be satisfied once I had delivered the parchment, which I was on no account to open, for it was sealed with an important seal.

Seeing that his people outnumbered mine and there was no help for it, I agreed with much reluctance, and the following morning I and my men left the encampment of these "Olde Fellowes". But at our parting, Master Moreby stood before me, and, making a strange sign with his left hand, spake these words:

"May the Olde Ones go with you."

To which I, in my great distemper, replyed: "A fart of my arse for your Old Ones!"

Then I and my men departed and saw him no more. We followed our path down the Providence River and reached the ship in two days, and have furnished ourselves as far as we can with fresh water and provision for the voyage home.

October 21st. *We set sail on the morning tide for England. Winds are favourable, and we are like to make a rapid crossing.*

October 25th. *Our voyage continues fair. This morning I found I could not contain my curiosity further. I went to my cabin and, by heating my poignard in a candle flame and putting it under the seal, endeavoured to open Master Moreby's parchment package without breaking the sayd seal. In this I partly succeeded. When I opened up the parchment a thin fragment of linen fell out, so light that it caught the breeze, for my cabin window was open. It seemed to have some strange writing on it, and I sought to seize hold of it, but it flew out of the window and was lost in the waves beyond.*

The documents within the parcel were written either in some cypher or a strange and barbarous tongue, and there were many signs and sigils upon them which I did not know. One paper only was written in plain English and read as followes:

> My Deare Cousin,
> The bearer of this budget is one Captain Reynolds, a most pernicious knave, a shit breeches, and a filthy fellowe. See to it that he doth not leave your house alive.
> In Nomine Magna Veterorum *[in the name of the Great Old Ones]*
> Your most humble and obdt kinsman
> T. Moreby, esq.

This put me in so great a rage that my men feared for my sanity. I tore or burned all documents that were in the budget and cast them over the side. The last of these to sink was the parchment on which was set the great seal in red wax. It settled on the water and seemed for a while to grow, sending out great sprays or tendrils of red from its centre so that it incarnadined the foam on which it rested before being enfolded by the billows.

It was a sight which filled all those who saw it with great amazement and terror.

October 26th. *Contrary winds. A strange fogg.*

After that, the log book of Captain Reynolds contains nothing but vague scratches and random, meaningless words. Only one last coherent sentence comes at the end of this document:

What hope have we? We are lost.

Attached to the log and the manuscript of Martha Edwards is a scrap of parchment on which the following has been written:

Memorandum for Amos Motherby, Secretary to their Lordships of the Admiralty by Jas Hooke, Captain of His Majesty's Ship, Centaur, *December 20th 1620.*
At about eleven of the forenoon on December 14th in this Year of Grace 1620, we were sailing in an Easterly direction some ten miles SSW of the Isles of Scilly when we saw a black vessell about fifty feet in length, lying low in the water and seemingly

adrift, its sails all flindered and awry. Coming within hailing distance, we bade the ship declare herself, but there being no replye, We came alongside her to board said vessell, which proved to be the Speedwell, last seen leaving Plymouth for the Americas some four months since.

We boarded her to find the decks strewn with dead or dying men. These latter, being only three in number, we tried most earnestly to revive, but received little for our pains but outlandish babblings. They appeared, insofar as their feeble bodies could permit them to shew, to be in a state of mortall terror. Of what, I could not tell for sure, but they spoke of great monsters from the deep, of vanishing islands, and other such foolishness. Surely hunger and thirst had robbed them of their wits, for there was no sign of provision, nor any drop to drink.

The ship itself was very low in the water, its hull leaking most grievously, and like to sink upon the instant. Nonetheless, I ventured below to enter the Captain's cabin in the stern of the ship. There I found Captain Reynolds (as I later discovered his name to be) hanging from the central beam of the cabin, having most impiously taken his own life. I guessed that he had been dead some time, for the stink from his corse was prodigious. Upon his table were some charts and documents, in addition to the ship's log, which I took up before leaving that awful place of Death.

I judged that the vessell was beyond redemption, so having removed those left alive, we fired our cannon into the side of the Black Ship (as I may call it), whereupon it sank rapidly beneath the waves. The three still living whom we had taken aboard the Centaur *and tended with much care, notwithstanding our ministrations, all perished before we had made landfall.*

I beg your Lordships of the Admiralty to receive the documents herewith appended and to judge for yourselves – for I have not read them – what manner of fate befell the Speedwell. Or you may dispose of these documents in whatever manner pleases your Lordships.

Jas Hooke, esq.

The Moon-Slave

Barry Pain

THE PRINCESS VIOLA had, even in her childhood, an inevitable submission to the dance; a rhythmical madness in her blood answered hotly to the dance music, swaying her, as the wind sways trees, to movements of perfect sympathy and grace.

For the rest, she had her beauty and her long hair, that reached to her knees, and was thought lovable; but she was never very fervent and vivid unless she was dancing; at other times there almost seemed to be a touch of lethargy upon her. Now, when she was sixteen years old, she was betrothed to the Prince Hugo. With others the betrothal was merely a question of state. With her it was merely a question of obedience to the wishes of authority; it had been arranged; Hugo was *comme ci, comme ça* – no god in her eyes; it did not matter. But with Hugo it was quite different – he loved her.

The betrothal was celebrated by a banquet, and afterwards by a dance in the great hall of the palace. From this dance the Princess soon made her escape, quite discontented, and went to the furthest part of the palace gardens, where she could no longer hear the music calling her.

"They are all right," she said to herself as she thought of the men she had left, "but they cannot dance. Mechanically they are all right; they have learned it and don't make childish mistakes; but they are only one-two-three machines. They haven't the inspiration of dancing. It is so different when I dance alone."

She wandered on until she reached an old forsaken maze. It had been planned by a former king. All round it was a high crumbling wall with foxgloves growing on it. The maze itself had all its paths bordered with high opaque hedges; in the very centre was a circular open space with tall pine-trees growing round it. Many years ago the clue to the maze had been lost; it was but rarely now that anyone entered it. Its gravel paths were green with weeds, and in some places the hedges, spreading beyond their borders, had made the way almost impassable.

For a moment or two Viola stood peering in at the gate – a narrow gate with curiously twisted bars of wrought iron surmounted by a heraldic device. Then the whim seized her to enter the maze and try to find the space in the centre. She opened the gate and went in.

Outside everything was uncannily visible in the light of the full moon, but here in the dark shaded alleys the night was conscious of itself. She soon forgot her purpose, and wandered about quite aimlessly, sometimes forcing her way where the brambles had flung a laced barrier across her path, and a dragging mass of convolvulus struck wet and cool upon her cheek. As chance would have it she suddenly found herself standing under the tall pines, and looking at the open space that formed the goal of the maze. She was pleased that she had got there. Here the ground was carpeted with sand, fine and, as it seemed, beaten hard. From the summer night sky immediately above, the moonlight, unobstructed here, streamed straight down upon the scene.

Viola began to think about dancing. Over the dry, smooth sand her little satin shoes moved easily, stepping and gliding, circling and stepping, as she hummed the tune to which they moved. In the centre of the space she paused, looked at the wall of dark trees all round, at the shining stretches of silvery sand and at the moon above.

"My beautiful, moonlit, lonely, old dancing-room, why did I never find you before?" she cried; "but," she added, "you need music – there must be music here."

In her fantastic mood she stretched her soft, clasped hands upwards towards the moon.

"Sweet moon," she said in a kind of mock prayer, "make your white light come down in music into my dancing-room here, and I will dance most deliciously for you to see." She flung her head backward and let her hands fall; her eyes were half closed, and her mouth was a kissing mouth. "Ah! Sweet moon," she whispered, "do this for me, and I will be your slave; I will be what you will."

Quite suddenly the air was filled with the sound of a grand invisible orchestra. Viola did not stop to wonder. To the music of a slow saraband she swayed and postured. In the music there was the regular beat of small drums and a perpetual drone. The air seemed to be filled with the perfume of some bitter spice. Viola could fancy almost that she saw a smouldering camp-fire and heard far off the roar of some desolate wild beast. She let her long hair fall, raising the heavy strands of it in either hand as she moved slowly to the laden music. Slowly her body swayed with drowsy grace, slowly her satin shoes slid over the silver sand.

The music ceased with a clash of cymbals. Viola rubbed her eyes. She fastened her hair up carefully again. Suddenly she looked up, almost imperiously.

"Music! More music!" she cried.

Once more the music came. This time it was a dance of caprice, pelting along over the violin-strings, leaping, laughing, wanton. Again an illusion seemed to cross her eyes. An old king was watching her, a king with the sordid history of the exhaustion of pleasure written on his flaccid face. A hook-nosed courtier by his side settled the ruffles at his wrists and mumbled, "Ravissant! Quel malheur que la vieillesse!" It was a strange illusion. Faster and faster she sped to the music, stepping, spinning, pirouetting; the dance was light as thistle-down, fierce as fire, smooth as a rapid stream.

The moment that the music ceased Viola became horribly afraid. She turned and fled away from the moonlit space, through the trees, down the dark alleys of the maze, not heeding in the least which turn she took, and yet she found herself soon at the outside iron gate. From thence she ran through the palace garden, hardly ever pausing to take breath, until she reached the palace itself. In the eastern sky the first signs of dawn were showing; in the palace the festivities were drawing to an end. As she stood alone in the outer hall Prince Hugo came towards her.

"Where have you been, Viola?" he said sternly. "What have you been doing?"

She stamped her little foot.

"I will not be questioned," she replied angrily.

"I have some right to question," he said.

She laughed a little.

"For the first time in my life," she said, "I have been dancing."

He turned away in hopeless silence.

* * *

The months passed away. Slowly a great fear came over Viola, a fear that would hardly ever leave her. For every month at the full moon, whether she would or no, she found herself driven to the maze, through its mysterious walks into that strange dancing-room. And when she was there the music began once more, and once more she danced most deliciously for the moon to see. The second time that this happened she had merely thought that it was a recurrence of her own whim, and that the music was but a trick that the imagination had chosen to repeat. The third time frightened her, and she knew that the force that sways the tides had strange power over her. The fear grew as the year fell, for each month the music went on for a longer time – each month some of the pleasure had gone from the dance. On bitter nights in winter the moon called her and she came, when the breath was vapour, and the trees that circled her dancing-room were black bare skeletons, and the frost was cruel. She dared not tell anyone, and yet it was with difficulty that she kept her secret. Somehow chance seemed to favour her, and she always found a way to return from her midnight dance to her own room without being observed. Each month the summons seemed to be more imperious and urgent. Once when she was alone on her knees before the lighted altar in the private chapel of the palace she suddenly felt that the words of the familiar Latin prayer had gone from her memory. She rose to her feet, she sobbed bitterly, but the call had come and she could not resist it. She passed out of the chapel and down the palace-gardens. How madly she danced that night!

She was to be married in the spring. She began to be more gentle with Hugo now. She had a blind hope that when they were married she might be able to tell him about it, and he might be able to protect her, for she had always known him to be fearless. She could not love him, but she tried to be good to him. One day he mentioned to her that he had tried to find his way to the centre of the maze, and had failed. She smiled faintly. If only she could fail! But she never did.

On the night before the wedding day, she had gone to bed and slept peacefully, thinking with her last waking moments of Hugo. Overhead the full moon came up the sky. Quite suddenly Viola was wakened with the impulse to fly to the dancing-room. It seemed to bid her hasten with breathless speed. She flung a cloak around her, slipped her naked feet into her dancing-shoes, and hurried forth. No one saw her or heard her – on the marble staircase of the palace, on down the terraces of the garden, she ran as fast as she could. A thorn-plant caught in her cloak, but she sped on, tearing it free; a sharp stone cut through the satin of one shoe, and her foot was wounded and bleeding, but she sped on. As the pebble that is flung from the cliff must fall until it reaches the sea, as the white ghost-moth must come in from cool hedges and scented darkness to a burning death in the lamp by which you sit so late – so Viola had no choice. The moon called her. The moon drew her to that circle of hard, bright sand and the pitiless music.

It was brilliant, rapid music tonight. Viola threw off her cloak and danced. As she did so, she saw that a shadow lay over a fragment of the moon's edge. It was the night of a total eclipse. She heeded it not. The intoxication of the dance was on her. She was all in white; even her face was pale in the moonlight. Every movement was full of poetry and grace.

The music would not stop. She had grown deathly weary. It seemed to her that she had been dancing for hours, and the shadow had nearly covered the moon's face, so that it was almost dark. She could hardly see the trees around her. She went on dancing, stepping, spinning, pirouetting, held by the merciless music.

It stopped at last, just when the shadow had quite covered the moon's face, and all was dark. But it stopped only for a moment, and then began again. This time it was a slow, passionate waltz. It was useless to resist; she began to dance once more. As she did so she uttered a sudden shrill scream of horror, for in the dead darkness a hot hand had caught her own and whirled her round, and she was no longer dancing alone.

* * *

The search for the missing Princess lasted during the whole of the following day. In the evening Prince Hugo, his face anxious and firmly set, passed in his search the iron gate of the maze, and noticed on the stones beside it the stain of a drop of blood. Within the gate was another stain. He followed this clue, which had been left by Viola's wounded foot, until he reached that open space in the centre that had served Viola for her dancing-room. It was quite empty. He noticed that the sand round the edges was all worn down, as though someone had danced there, round and round, for a long time. But no separate footprint was distinguishable there. Just outside this track, however, he saw two footprints clearly defined close together: one was the print of a tiny satin shoe; the other was the print of a large naked foot – a cloven foot.

Agon

Jason Parent

WHEN she pushed me off the cruise ship, I was at first fairly calm about the whole thing. Beyond the initial shock – not all that shocking, really, given the turn our marriage had taken these past few years – I didn't then have a true sense of the danger. An appreciation for the vast expanse of insolubility, the endless miles and unfathomable depths of poison water that surround the continents, eating at their edges to eventually consume all, sure, I had *that*. But I guess I figured someone, on a vessel as large as a continent itself, would have seen me fall, heard my shouts for help, thrown me a literal circle of life so that I might not become part of the figurative one.

As if I could escape it.

That was hours ago, back when the sun was high in the sky, now barely more than a pink lipstick stain on the horizon. I've gone through panic and rage, hysteria and denial, then through them again many times over. My tears and my tantrums, my curses and promises of revenge, have expunged much needed energy as I struggle vainly – nigh, hopelessly – to cling to life.

Without accounting for its toil upon my mind and soul, living is not so hard as one might think. I am an expert swimmer. The same chemical make-up that would leave me dehydrated despite an endless supply of drink also keeps me buoyant. My sneakers and jeans, and with them my wallet and sole means of identification should something happen to my fingers and teeth, have long since been discarded in favor of floatability. They lay somewhere far below, on an ocean floor unlikely to be otherwise touched by man – certainly not in my short lifetime. Perhaps they will be discovered by far-future explorers, from this world or beyond.

Or below.

My effects might end up in the belly of an ocean behemoth, clang against the great dome of Atlantis or some other lost civilization, or disturb the eons-old resting place of a sleeping god. I'll never know. I'll not likely wake with the dawn.

All I must do is close my eyes, lie back, relax, and let the waves carry me where they will. If only I could slow the rise and fall of my chest to match the ocean's swell. My mind is my first and foremost enemy; allowing it to fall into despair and madness is certain doom. I struggled against it for hours but have come to a fragile peace, insanity nevertheless lingering at the back of my skull, its tendrils searching for cracks through which to seep.

If I survive panic, then any number of deaths await me: drowning, dehydration, exhaustion, exposure… What is the word for being eaten alive? If given the choice, I'd rather be eaten dead. But it is thoughts like these that threaten to melt the glue keeping me whole.

For now, I float, easily and undisturbed as I stare up at the emerging stars, clinging to the smallest fraction of hope. I must be stranded in the path of another cruise ship or maybe in a shipping lane, though I have little knowledge of such things to be certain.

At least, I suspect I was. God only knows where the currents have taken me. And if I must die, then I hope these currents take me directly to Him.

If He'll have me.

Other beings have taken interest. Occasionally, an amphibious creature brushes against me, or a curious fin idles by, amorphous shapes in the dark. At most, their attention is fleeting, toying even. I've heard somewhere that sharks feed at night. Perhaps I need a little more marinating before I'm done.

If they are going to take me, I'd rather it be sooner than later. End this waiting. Kill the hope, for the hope is killing me. I am easy pickings, a dying fish floundering on the surface.

I picture my wife, sipping wine on our room's balcony, the same one she heaved me from, pleased with her crime and confident no fingers will point toward her. No body, no murder – at least that's what all those cop shows say. No one will ever find mine out here.

It's funny how much the night sky looks like an ocean. Puffy clouds roll over it like white caps. Stars twinkle like moonlight on dark water. As above, so below.

My ears underwater, I listen to whale songs and the deeper tones of lower things as my body rocks with the gentle ebb and flow of the tides. I watch as the moon, full and bright and far bigger than I'd ever seen it before, climbs into view as if rising out of the water itself, so close I can almost reach it. It looks like a giant eye, studying me as I study it, wondering what this strange growth might be on its ocean mistress. Its full orb fills the sky, open and aware. Are its phases just how long it takes for a god to blink?

I tread water and take in its unusual grandeur. Its many craters and canyons, with their own unknowable depths and darkness not unlike those below my feet, make strange striations in its surface. They do not appear random, instead more like runes or ancient symbols carved by hands beyond my mind's ability to conjure. The sheer scale of such a creature would erase all semblance of sanity, striking me dumb as a baby turning in the womb, terrified of what comes with light and enlightenment.

In an attempt to drive out these morbid thoughts – understandable given my rather morbid predicament – I view the moon in light of its eerie, almost mystical beauty. It may be the last thing of beauty I witness in this world, and the last thing to see me.

I am neither a good man nor a bad one. I am just a man. Perhaps, I could have been a better husband. I tried, but maybe not hard enough. My heart cannot contrive forgiveness; not yet, and perhaps not in life. Maybe someday she will have enough forgiveness for the both of us.

The moon's refracted light shines like a corridor that cuts across the water directly in front of me. The celestial sphere hangs in the sky just over the horizon, which, in that otherworldly radiance, doesn't seem so far away. If I swim hard enough and fast enough, I feel as though I truly could reach it. A part of me recognizes the absurdity of the notion, but other forces work upon me. The waves, for one, push me toward the moon as if urging me to try. Something unseen, something stronger than the inertia of the ocean itself, compels me toward that great eye in the sky. I am caught in its gravitational pull and see no cause to resist.

And so I swim, the glowing corridor my swim lane, the water growing ever stiller like the soft rush and fizzle of dying waves reaching the end of their roll. Still pushing on my back, but gently now, caressing. The soothing hand of a mother drawing circles on my skin to coax me to sleep.

Not only is the moonlight brighter now, but the water, too, seems alight. Neuron blasts illuminate the sea like lightning through a dark sky, the stars above matching their strobe-like effect as if the two surfaces are communicating in Morse code. I know my efforts will deplete my remaining reserves, but I must continue. The pull is too strong, the promise of the moon too enticing. Its song beckons me, and whether menace or madness, I must heed its call.

And as I race forward, kicking and slapping water with violence and haste, I touch something. My heart thuds in my chest as only it can when one realizes he is not alone in the darkness. But I do not stop, cannot stop. My hand makes contact again, swiping first through water then through a soft, semi-solid muck as it circles down and back.

Land? It can't be. Somewhere, perhaps a mile back, I must have died, or else I'm dreaming. I stop, make to tread water, but my toes collide with thick mud, sinking in before I can plant them and pitching me forward onto my knees. And there I stay for a moment, head and shoulders above water, a penitent man offering a prayer. *Please, God. Let this be real.*

On shaking legs, I rise. For the love of God, I'm standing!

But on what?

The ocean has gone quiet around me, unnaturally still and black as subterranean night. But it is still ocean, in all directions, as far as the eye can see. I must have found a sandbar, must be close to land, only it's too dark to see it. If I could just stay here, hold fast and survive the night, I may actually have a chance at life. Morning's light will reveal all.

I yank off my T-shirt and wring it out. Particles of light sparkle in the falling droplets. Others tingle on my skin. The moon seems so close now I feel as though I could lean forward and kiss it. I dare not for fear of its mistress's wrath. And something else causes my breath to hitch, an atmosphere growing cloudier and steamier, as if someone has poured water over the coals in a sauna. Or hot breath. The air is cloying, or maybe it is the tiny particles of luminescence on my body, droves of them swarming closer, filling the water with brilliance that acts like a lantern through the fog. They pile against my boxers, creating tiny sand-like drifts wherever they collect.

Two black obelisks protrude from the water, one almost directly in front of me, the other fifteen meters or so to its right. How I had not noticed them before causes only a moment's alarm, for surely they are more evidence of the land I seek. They can only be rocks, and yet they are oddly symmetrical: conical on their inner sides and arching like train tunnels on the outer sides, slightly curved toward me, rising out of murky depths like sacrificial altars to a lunar deity.

And they continue to rise. *I,* too, am rising.

I look down to see the water only inches high but lapping against my knees, the rest of my legs sunken in quagmire. The light critters form a circle around me. They slide with the muck upward over my thighs and belly, climbing. I gasp and swipe them away, managing to dislodge swaths of them while others, seemingly sensing my attack, disappear as if burrowing under my skin. And still they keep coming like an army of ants whose mound I have disturbed, but with no biting, no pain, but creating that impulse to be free of them, that sensation of wrongness that comes from skittering things on skin. Bigger things slither like eels across my legs and over my feet, and I am thankful I cannot see them under the mud.

All the movement stirs the ocean bed. Bubbles pop on the surface, releasing noxious gases that reek of dead fish, rotten meat, and the odor of catacombs breached after having been sealed for ages. The bones of unidentifiable creatures rise to the surface, fossils of beings that had been much larger than me but whose fate I now seem to share.

The ground continues to rise, and I continue to sink. The mud is at my thighs, the water gone, the light creatures creeping higher still like strangling vines. With every frantic swipe, more swaths emerge and others disappear, and although I do not feel them, I am certain they are inside me.

I cannot fathom what this place is, know only that I am where no man should ever be. I cannot move, my legs entrenched in slimy, abhorrent mire. Earth that I have disturbed and should have left alone. Earth that had never before been corrupted or maybe always had been.

The sparkling parasites continue their upward climb, worming their way up and into me. Comprising me. *Becoming* me.

A milky film forms on the outer side of the obelisk in front of me, now as tall as a house. My mind reels as I think of my grandmother's cataracts. A vertical slit in that film shifts forward. In it, I see the doorway to Hell. I laugh as tears squirm from the corners of my eyes. My broken mind again wonders how long it takes for a god to blink.

And yet I continue to look. God help me, I look. I see it, and it sees me. We share light and enlightenment, and my mind shatters with all that is exchanged. And as I open my mouth to scream, sparkling creatures pour down my throat.

* * *

I awake, floating in the water. How I survived falling asleep in the ocean is beyond me, for the monstrosity to which I bore witness surely could only have been the stuff of nightmares.

But no, I am… changed.

I hear a horn. A ship is approaching. Not just any ship – *my* cruise ship, its name emblazoned on the side. Someone must have seen me fall, after all. I am saved!

Or do I have something else to thank for my life? As I tread water, waiting for the lifeboat to approach, I sense I am not alone. And it is not the marine life in the water that causes me concern. A nagging in the back of my mind tells me I should dive down, the human part that yet remains, a mousy voice amid the screeching of the others.

In a matter of minutes, hands are pulling me from the water. A blanket drapes over my shoulders, smiling faces and mouths exclaiming miracles, disbelief that someone could possibly have survived a week in the water. I am offered food, told to drink. I want none of it, but I suppose I must keep up appearances.

For now.

My wife and her betrayal seem of no consequence now. The moon will be out in full again tonight, and I have the light of the stars to share.

The Facts in the Case of M. Valdemar

Edgar Allan Poe

OF COURSE I shall not pretend to consider it any matter for wonder, that the extraordinary case of M. Valdemar has excited discussion. It would have been a miracle had it not-especially under the circumstances. Through the desire of all parties concerned, to keep the affair from the public, at least for the present, or until we had farther opportunities for investigation – through our endeavors to effect this – a garbled or exaggerated account made its way into society, and became the source of many unpleasant misrepresentations, and, very naturally, of a great deal of disbelief.

It is now rendered necessary that I give the facts – as far as I comprehend them myself. They are, succinctly, these:

My attention, for the last three years, had been repeatedly drawn to the subject of Mesmerism; and, about nine months ago it occurred to me, quite suddenly, that in the series of experiments made hitherto, there had been a very remarkable and most unaccountable omission: no person had as yet been mesmerized in articulo mortis. It remained to be seen, first, whether, in such condition, there existed in the patient any susceptibility to the magnetic influence; secondly, whether, if any existed, it was impaired or increased by the condition; thirdly, to what extent, or for how long a period, the encroachments of Death might be arrested by the process. There were other points to be ascertained, but these most excited my curiosity – the last in especial, from the immensely important character of its consequences.

In looking around me for some subject by whose means I might test these particulars, I was brought to think of my friend, M. Ernest Valdemar, the well-known compiler of the *Bibliotheca Forensica*, and author (under the *nom de plume* of Issachar Marx) of the Polish versions of *Wallenstein* and *Gargantua*. M. Valdemar, who has resided principally at Harlaem, N.Y., since the year 1839, is (or was) particularly noticeable for the extreme spareness of his person – his lower limbs much resembling those of John Randolph; and, also, for the whiteness of his whiskers, in violent contrast to the blackness of his hair – the latter, in consequence, being very generally mistaken for a wig. His temperament was markedly nervous, and rendered him a good subject for mesmeric experiment. On two or three occasions I had put him to sleep with little difficulty, but was disappointed in other results which his peculiar constitution had naturally led me to anticipate. His will was at no period positively, or thoroughly, under my control, and in regard to clairvoyance, I could accomplish with him nothing to be relied upon. I always attributed my failure at these points to the disordered state of his health. For some months previous to my becoming acquainted with him, his physicians had declared him in a confirmed phthisis. It was his custom, indeed, to speak calmly of his approaching dissolution, as of a matter neither to be avoided nor regretted.

When the ideas to which I have alluded first occurred to me, it was of course very natural that I should think of M. Valdemar. I knew the steady philosophy of the man too well to apprehend any scruples from him; and he had no relatives in America who would be likely to interfere. I spoke to him frankly upon the subject; and, to my surprise, his interest seemed vividly excited. I say to my surprise, for, although he had always yielded his person freely to my experiments, he had never before given me any tokens of sympathy with what I did. His disease was if that character which would admit of exact calculation in respect to the epoch of its termination in death; and it was finally arranged between us that he would send for me about twenty-four hours before the period announced by his physicians as that of his decease.

It is now rather more than seven months since I received, from M. Valdemar himself, the subjoined note:

My Dear P—,
You may as well come now. D— and F— are agreed that I cannot hold out beyond
tomorrow midnight; and I think they have hit the time very nearly.
Valdemar

I received this note within half an hour after it was written, and in fifteen minutes more I was in the dying man's chamber. I had not seen him for ten days, and was appalled by the fearful alteration which the brief interval had wrought in him. His face wore a leaden hue; the eyes were utterly lustreless; and the emaciation was so extreme that the skin had been broken through by the cheek-bones. His expectoration was excessive. The pulse was barely perceptible. He retained, nevertheless, in a very remarkable manner, both his mental power and a certain degree of physical strength. He spoke with distinctness – took some palliative medicines without aid – and, when I entered the room, was occupied in penciling memoranda in a pocket-book. He was propped up in the bed by pillows. Doctors D— and F— were in attendance.

After pressing Valdemar's hand, I took these gentlemen aside, and obtained from them a minute account of the patient's condition. The left lung had been for eighteen months in a semi-osseous or cartilaginous state, and was, of course, entirely useless for all purposes of vitality. The right, in its upper portion, was also partially, if not thoroughly, ossified, while the lower region was merely a mass of purulent tubercles, running one into another. Several extensive perforations existed; and, at one point, permanent adhesion to the ribs had taken place. These appearances in the right lobe were of comparatively recent date. The ossification had proceeded with very unusual rapidity; no sign of it had discovered a month before, and the adhesion had only been observed during the three previous days. Independently of the phthisis, the patient was suspected of aneurism of the aorta; but on this point the osseous symptoms rendered an exact diagnosis impossible. It was the opinion of both physicians that M. Valdemar would die about midnight on the morrow (Sunday). It was then seven o'clock on Saturday evening.

On quitting the invalid's bed-side to hold conversation with myself, Doctors D— and F— had bidden him a final farewell. It had not been their intention to return; but, at my request, they agreed to look in upon the patient about ten the next night.

When they had gone, I spoke freely with M. Valdemar on the subject of his approaching dissolution, as well as, more particularly, of the experiment proposed. He still professed himself quite willing and even anxious to have it made, and urged me to commence it at once. A male and a female nurse were in attendance; but I did not feel myself altogether at liberty to engage in a task of this character with no more reliable witnesses than these people, in case of sudden accident, might prove. I therefore postponed operations until about eight the next night, when the arrival of a medical student with whom I had some acquaintance, (Mr. Theodore L—), relieved me from farther embarrassment. It had been my design, originally, to wait for the physicians; but I was induced to proceed, first, by the urgent entreaties of M. Valdemar, and secondly, by my conviction that I had not a moment to lose, as he was evidently sinking fast.

Mr. L— was so kind as to accede to my desire that he would take notes of all that occurred, and it is from his memoranda that what I now have to relate is, for the most part, either condensed or copied verbatim.

It wanted about five minutes of eight when, taking the patient's hand, I begged him to state, as distinctly as he could, to Mr. L—, whether he (M. Valdemar) was entirely willing that I should make the experiment of mesmerizing him in his then condition.

He replied feebly, yet quite audibly, "Yes, I wish to be. I fear you have mesmerized" – adding immediately afterwards, "deferred it too long."

While he spoke thus, I commenced the passes which I had already found most effectual in subduing him. He was evidently influenced with the first lateral stroke of my hand across his forehead; but although I exerted all my powers, no farther perceptible effect was induced until some minutes after ten o'clock, when Doctors D— and F— called, according to appointment. I explained to them, in a few words, what I designed, and as they opposed no objection, saying that the patient was already in the death agony, I proceeded without hesitation – exchanging, however, the lateral passes for downward ones, and directing my gaze entirely into the right eye of the sufferer.

By this time his pulse was imperceptible and his breathing was stertorous, and at intervals of half a minute.

This condition was nearly unaltered for a quarter of an hour. At the expiration of this period, however, a natural although a very deep sigh escaped the bosom of the dying man, and the stertorous breathing ceased – that is to say, its stertorousness was no longer apparent; the intervals were undiminished. The patient's extremities were of an icy coldness.

At five minutes before eleven I perceived unequivocal signs of the mesmeric influence. The glassy roll of the eye was changed for that expression of uneasy inward examination which is never seen except in cases of sleep-waking, and which it is quite impossible to mistake. With a few rapid lateral passes I made the lids quiver, as in incipient sleep, and with a few more I closed them altogether. I was not satisfied, however, with this, but continued the manipulations vigorously, and with the fullest exertion of the will, until I had completely stiffened the limbs of the slumberer, after placing them in a seemingly easy position. The legs were at full length; the arms were nearly so, and reposed on the bed at a moderate distance from the loin. The head was very slightly elevated.

When I had accomplished this, it was fully midnight, and I requested the gentlemen present to examine M. Valdemar's condition. After a few experiments, they admitted him to be an unusually perfect state of mesmeric trance. The curiosity of both the physicians was greatly excited. Dr. D— resolved at once to remain with the patient all night, while Dr. F— took leave with a promise to return at daybreak. Mr. L— and the nurses remained.

We left M. Valdemar entirely undisturbed until about three o'clock in the morning, when I approached him and found him in precisely the same condition as when Dr. F— went away – that is to say, he lay in the same position; the pulse was imperceptible; the breathing was gentle (scarcely noticeable, unless through the application of a mirror to the lips); the eyes were closed naturally; and the limbs were as rigid and as cold as marble. Still, the general appearance was certainly not that of death.

As I approached M. Valdemar I made a kind of half effort to influence his right arm into pursuit of my own, as I passed the latter gently to and fro above his person. In such experiments with this patient had never perfectly succeeded before, and assuredly I had little thought of succeeding now; but to my astonishment, his arm very readily, although feebly, followed every direction I assigned it with mine. I determined to hazard a few words of conversation.

"M. Valdemar," I said, "are you asleep?" He made no answer, but I perceived a tremor about the lips, and was thus induced to repeat the question, again and again. At its third repetition, his whole frame was agitated by a very slight shivering; the eyelids unclosed themselves so far as to display a white line of the ball; the lips moved sluggishly, and from between them, in a barely audible whisper, issued the words:

"Yes – asleep now. Do not wake me! – Let me die so!"

I here felt the limbs and found them as rigid as ever. The right arm, as before, obeyed the direction of my hand. I questioned the sleep-waker again:

"Do you still feel pain in the breast, M. Valdemar?"

The answer now was immediate, but even less audible than before: "No pain – I am dying."

I did not think it advisable to disturb him farther just then, and nothing more was said or done until the arrival of Dr. F—, who came a little before sunrise, and expressed unbounded astonishment at finding the patient still alive. After feeling the pulse and applying a mirror to the lips, he requested me to speak to the sleep-waker again. I did so, saying:

"M. Valdemar, do you still sleep?"

As before, some minutes elapsed ere a reply was made; and during the interval the dying man seemed to be collecting his energies to speak. At my fourth repetition of the question, he said very faintly, almost inaudibly:

"Yes; still asleep – dying."

It was now the opinion, or rather the wish, of the physicians, that M. Valdemar should be suffered to remain undisturbed in his present apparently tranquil condition, until death should supervene – and this, it was generally agreed, must now take place within a few minutes. I concluded, however, to speak to him once more, and merely repeated my previous question.

While I spoke, there came a marked change over the countenance of the sleep-waker. The eyes rolled themselves slowly open, the pupils disappearing upwardly; the skin generally assumed a cadaverous hue, resembling not so much parchment as white paper; and the circular hectic spots which, hitherto, had been strongly defined in the centre of each cheek, went out at once. I use this expression, because the suddenness of their departure put me in mind of nothing so much as the extinguishment of a candle by a puff of the breath. The upper lip, at the same time, writhed itself away from the teeth, which it had previously covered completely; while the lower jaw fell with an audible jerk, leaving the mouth widely extended, and disclosing in full view the swollen and blackened tongue. I presume that no member of the party then present had been unaccustomed to death-bed horrors; but so hideous beyond conception was the appearance of M. Valdemar at this moment, that there was a general shrinking back from the region of the bed.

I now feel that I have reached a point of this narrative at which every reader will be startled into positive disbelief. It is my business, however, simply to proceed.

There was no longer the faintest sign of vitality in M. Valdemar; and concluding him to be dead, we were consigning him to the charge of the nurses, when a strong vibratory motion was observable in the tongue. This continued for perhaps a minute. At the expiration of this period, there issued from the distended and motionless jaws a voice – such as it would be madness in me to attempt describing. There are, indeed, two or three epithets which might be considered as applicable to it in part; I might say, for example, that the sound was harsh, and broken and hollow; but the hideous whole is indescribable, for the simple reason that no similar sounds have ever jarred upon the ear of humanity. There were two particulars, nevertheless, which I thought then, and still think, might fairly be stated as characteristic of the intonation – as well adapted to convey some idea of its unearthly peculiarity. In the first place, the voice seemed to reach our ears – at least mine – from a vast distance, or from some deep cavern within the earth. In the second place, it impressed me (I fear, indeed, that it will be impossible to make myself comprehended) as gelatinous or glutinous matters impress the sense of touch.

I have spoken both of 'sound' and of 'voice', I mean to say that the sound was one of distinct – of even wonderfully, thrillingly distinct – syllabification. M. Valdemar spoke – obviously in reply to the question I had propounded to him a few minutes before. I had asked him, it will be remembered, if he still slept. He now said:

"Yes – no – I have been sleeping – and now – now – I am dead."

No person present even affected to deny, or attempted to repress, the unutterable, shuddering horror which these few words, thus uttered, were so well calculated to convey. Mr. L— (the student) swooned. The nurses immediately left the chamber, and could not be induced to return. My own impressions I would not pretend to render intelligible to the reader. For nearly an hour, we busied ourselves, silently – without the utterance of a word – in endeavors to revive Mr. L—. When he came to himself, we addressed ourselves again to an investigation of M. Valdemar's condition.

It remained in all respects as I have last described it, with the exception that the mirror no longer afforded evidence of respiration. An attempt to draw blood from the arm failed. I should mention, too, that this limb was no farther subject to my will. I endeavored in vain to make it follow the direction of my hand. The only real indication, indeed, of the mesmeric influence, was now found in the vibratory movement of the tongue, whenever I addressed M. Valdemar a question. He seemed to be making an effort to reply, but had no longer sufficient volition. To queries put to him by any other person than myself he seemed utterly insensible – although I endeavored to place each member of the company in mesmeric rapport with him. I believe that I have now related all that is necessary to an understanding of the sleep-waker's state at this epoch. Other nurses were procured; and at ten o'clock I left the house in company with the two physicians and Mr. L—

In the afternoon we all called again to see the patient. His condition remained precisely the same. We had now some discussion as to the propriety and feasibility of awakening him; but we had little difficulty in agreeing that no good purpose would be served by so doing. It was evident that, so far, death (or what is usually termed death) had been arrested by the mesmeric process. It seemed clear to us all that to awaken M. Valdemar would be merely to insure his instant, or at least his speedy dissolution.

From this period until the close of last week – an interval of nearly seven months – we continued to make daily calls at M. Valdemar's house, accompanied, now and then, by medical and other friends. All this time the sleeper-waker remained exactly as I have last described him. The nurses' attentions were continual.

It was on Friday last that we finally resolved to make the experiment of awakening or attempting to awaken him; and it is the (perhaps) unfortunate result of this latter experiment which has given rise to so much discussion in private circles – to so much of what I cannot help thinking unwarranted popular feeling.

For the purpose of relieving M. Valdemar from the mesmeric trance, I made use of the customary passes. These, for a time, were unsuccessful. The first indication of revival was afforded by a partial descent of the iris. It was observed, as especially remarkable, that this lowering of the pupil was accompanied by the profuse out-flowing of a yellowish ichor (from beneath the lids) of a pungent and highly offensive odor.

It was now suggested that I should attempt to influence the patient's arm, as heretofore. I made the attempt and failed. Dr. F— then intimated a desire to have me put a question. I did so, as follows:

"M. Valdemar, can you explain to us what are your feelings or wishes now?"

There was an instant return of the hectic circles on the cheeks; the tongue quivered, or rather rolled violently in the mouth (although the jaws and lips remained rigid as before); and at length the same hideous voice which I have already described, broke forth:

"For God's sake! – Quick! – Quick! – Put me to sleep – or, quick! – Waken me! – Quick! – I say to you that I am dead!"

I was thoroughly unnerved, and for an instant remained undecided what to do. At first I made an endeavor to re-compose the patient; but, failing in this through total abeyance of the will, I retraced my steps and as earnestly struggled to awaken him. In this attempt I soon saw that I should be successful – or at least I soon fancied that my success would be complete – and I am sure that all in the room were prepared to see the patient awaken.

For what really occurred, however, it is quite impossible that any human being could have been prepared.

As I rapidly made the mesmeric passes, amid ejaculations of "dead! dead!" absolutely bursting from the tongue and not from the lips of the sufferer, his whole frame at once – within the space of a single minute, or even less, shrunk – crumbled – absolutely rotted away beneath my hands. Upon the bed, before that whole company, there lay a nearly liquid mass of loathsome – of detestable putridity.

The Stones Move at Night

Bonnie Quinn

THE WALLS were built by the settlers. That was all they'd tell Jessica when her family moved to New England from Texas. They were left by the glaciers and dug out by the people clearing land for cattle and fields. They stacked them, only a few feet high, on the property lines.

No one seemed interested in the walls. Most of the people in town had lived here their entire lives and the stones were merely another fixture. But Jessica, who came from a planned subdivision with evenly divided lawns where everything was new and modern, was fascinated by them. They crisscrossed the woods in long, straight lines. Most enticingly, they ran beside Jessica's new house before tumbling down into the ravine cut by a tiny stream.

It wasn't much of a ravine. The sides were an easy slope of soft earth, perhaps fifteen feet on one side and a mere five feet on the other. The stream could be jumped with one long leap. But there was a fallen tree that created a bridge from side to side and the water ran through the stones to form gentle pools and rapids scarcely big enough to hold a leaf boat. Jessica had never seen anything like it.

The woods stretched on for some time on a level field, dotted by the occasional patch of undergrowth. Jessica liked to explore here, as sometimes she found strange things that were discarded in the woods. Broken pieces of furniture, rotting baskets. A ceramic flower pot in the shape of a swan that had split in two. She sometimes saw houses in the distance, if she walked far enough, and had to assume the trash came from them, though she wondered why they'd take so much effort to discard it so far into the woods.

Then one day, towards the end of the summer, Jessica found a statue.

It was a saint with long flowing robes and one hand lowered to clutch at something that had long ago broken off. The other arm was raised, its hand broken off at the wrist. Its head was missing. It stood propped at the doorway of what had once been a house.

Only two walls still stood and the other two were tumbled foundations, the stones falling over each other like the haphazard walls that crisscrossed the forest. It wasn't big. Her bedroom was larger than it. The roof had collapsed, covering most of the interior. The wooden shingles were rotting and covered with moss and the exposed beams were charred. A fire. The house had burned.

It had to be old, she thought. Maybe it was a storage shed. She couldn't imagine anyone living in something so small. She wanted to explore it, to climb inside and see what was hidden under the roof and leaves. However, she'd grown up in Texas, and learned that debris like this was where the snakes hid. The poisonous ones. Tentatively, Jessica scouted the edges, and seeing nothing of interest inside, returned to the doorway.

At least the statue was within reach. She decided to add it to her growing collection. The empty glass soda bottles would crowd around its base like candles. She carried it through the woods and set it on the biggest boulder that sat in the middle of the stream, the water parting on either side to flow around it. She found a round stone and set this on top of the broken neck. Maybe if she looked hard enough she could find the saint's head. For now this would have to do.

Whenever she found a pretty stone, she put it at the statue's base. Like an offering. And although she spent the rest of the summer searching, she never found its head.

* * *

School started. Her teacher didn't like her accent and would demand she repeat herself in class. Very soon, Jessica stopped speaking up at all. It grew hard to make friends, once the initial interest from the other students wore off and she retreated further into her silence. The lone person she felt she could talk to was the town librarian.

Her name was Miss Taylor. She was a little bit younger than Jessica's mother and ran the children's library. She wasn't married and didn't have any children. These were all things Jessica asked her when Miss Taylor was helping her pick out books. She found out that Miss Taylor lived close by. In fact, if she cut through the woods, her house wasn't that far at all.

Eventually Jessica worked up the courage to ask if she could come visit sometimes. She didn't have any friends at school, she admitted, and she didn't have anyone to talk to. When Jessica's mom came to pick her up, Miss Taylor spoke with her, and they worked out an arrangement. Jessica could visit on Sunday afternoons, when the library was closed. But if she stayed past sundown Miss Taylor would drive her home. It was too dangerous to be in the woods after dark.

On the first Sunday of being allowed to visit Miss Taylor, Jessica went down into the ravine. She paused by the statue that sat on the biggest rock in the river. The empty soda bottles shone behind it like pale bits of emerald and sapphires.

"I'm sorry," she told the statue. "I don't think I'll ever find your head."

She imagined the statue's response in her head. It's alright, he said. He didn't mind. Then he smiled at her.

The rock, she realized, looked a little bit like a face. Little chips of mica glinted like eyes and an indentation formed a mouth, turned slightly up like a smile.

Suddenly uneasy, Jessica backed away and hurried across the log bridge. She passed through the woods and climbed over the long stretch of rock wall that stood between her and Miss Taylor's house. She glanced at the stones as she clambered over them. One of them stared up at her, half-buried in the dirt, and two faint hollows reminded her of empty eye sockets.

Miss Taylor had iced tea ready when Jessica arrived. The librarian asked how her weekend had been and Jessica told her about rummaging through the forest. She was searching for a piece of a statue, she said. It looked like a saint, but she couldn't tell which one it was. She didn't know anything about saints.

"Where did you find it?" Miss Taylor asked.

"Outside an abandoned room," Jessica replied.

Miss Taylor frowned and Jessica rushed to explain. It was old, she said, and falling apart. The building was so small that she couldn't imagine anyone could have lived in it. None of this seemed to reassure Miss Taylor. If anything, she grew increasingly worried and then finally turned to go to the pantry to cover for her unease.

"That's the old chapel," Miss Taylor said. "You should stay out of it."

"I do. There might be snakes."

"Snakes? I was more worried about rusty nails."

"What kind of chapel was it?"

Miss Taylor brought back a package of cookies and thought for a moment. She wasn't quite sure, she said. The early settlers had different beliefs back then, ones that had since faded into obscurity. When she was a little girl, her mother warned her to stay out of the woods, lest she attract the attention of the wind father. The woods belonged to him and the old chapel was where he would marry his many earth wives. That was all her mother could ever say about it though. It was just something passed down from generation to generation and taught to every child who grew up here.

"It's just superstition," Miss Taylor finished. "But you should still stay out. Some of the older folks around here wouldn't be happy if someone was playing inside."

"Should I put the statue back?" Jessica asked nervously.

"No, I think that's fine. It was discarded, right? No one wants it anymore."

Jessica didn't mention how she'd found the statue sitting upright by the entrance. Like it'd been placed there long ago. She sipped guiltily at her tea. It was fine, she told herself. The statue was in a better spot now. It had other pretty stones and glass bottles for company. She'd even given it a new head.

One with eyes and a smile, no less.

* * *

Autumn came. The forest crackled with every step as the trees shed their leaves. She continued to go into the forest while there was still sunlight. Even at school, she spent her recess in the woods. None of the other students were interested, so often Jessica was out at the edge of the playground by herself, walking along the stone wall that ended abruptly where the grass began. If the teachers saw her, they'd yell at her, but they didn't pay attention most days.

Jessica was drawing pictures in the soft dirt with a stick when the wind picked up. It shook the branches above her head and she glanced up, startled. A shower of leaves cascaded down, falling across her back and covering up the drawing at her feet. The wind continued to grow stronger and Jessica's heart began to race, as the leaves around her were stirred into a gale. They whirled around her, curtaining off the rest of the forest. She coughed and squeezed her eyes shut against the grit.

Then as quickly as it'd started, the wind quieted. The trees above her still groaned, their branches heaving to and fro, but the wind had retreated for now.

A distant voice was screeching at her. Jessica flinched reflexively. Her homeroom teacher, the one who didn't like her accent, was yelling at her to get out of the woods. Guiltily, Jessica hurried back to the playground. The other students cast covert glances at her as she walked past them.

"What are you doing?" her teacher demanded once she was in range. "Didn't you see the wind?"

Her teacher jabbed one finger towards the forest. Obediently, Jessica looked where she pointed. The trees were moving. Their branches rustled, jostling each other and shedding their dry leaves.

"You stay out of the woods," the teacher said firmly, then she raised her voice. "All of you stay out! The wind is rising."

Then she spun on her heel and stalked away. Why, Jessica wondered, did their teacher sound so *afraid*?

That evening, there was a new stone by the wall. Jessica jumped over this part of the wall every day on her way to the ravine, so she noticed something was different right away. She stared at the stone, tucked down near the base of the others. It was a bit out of place. It wasn't quite part of the wall. Who would have left it here? She crouched and turned it around. Overhead, the branches groaned in the persistent wind like they were leaning in for a look.

On the other side was a face. It'd been worn away with time, but there were little round nubs for eyes, a stubby bulge for a nose, and a thin gouge for a mouth. She ran her thumb along the rough surface where the eyebrows would go. Then she hefted the stone and carefully placed it on top of the wall, securely nestled among the other stones with its face pointing out towards the forest.

"There you are," she said. "Now you have something to look at."

A few days later both the wind and the stone was gone.

After that, Jessica began to look for stones that were out of place. She walked the length of the rock wall every day, from the road all the way down to the ravine. They moved during the night, she decided. In the morning she'd leave the house early, giving herself time to check the wall before the bus came. Most of the time there was nothing amiss, but sometimes she found a round stone with strange features. Little bulges and dips, always arranged in the rough approximation of a face. A few days later they'd be gone.

Someone was moving the stones around.

Had someone else discovered her sanctuary? Were they playing pranks on her?

The forest seemed less welcoming now. She was quieter when she was among the trees and she watched her surroundings. Trying to see if she wasn't alone out there.

But the mysterious person only came at night. She never saw anyone else in the forest.

* * *

Soon the trees were bare. Frost covered the ground and the branches in the morning, painting all the sharp edges of the forest white. Jessica still went to visit Miss Taylor on Sundays. Miss Taylor told her a lot of things about the town. Jessica started to think of Miss Taylor as an aunt and perhaps Miss Taylor thought of her as a niece.

The wind came and went as the seasons changed. Jessica paid it no mind for the most part. She visited her saint less frequently as it got colder. His smile seemed strained now. Like he was annoyed at her absences, so she brought him a geode she bought from the store as an apology.

The wind returned on Sunday as she made her way through the forest to Miss Taylor's house. It felt like a storm was coming. Jessica picked up her pace as a gust of wind raked through her hair. Her teacher's warning from weeks ago ran through her head. Stay out of the woods.

She broke into a run. And the wind followed her, darting from tree to tree, making the branches creak in its wake. It stayed at her back as if it was *following* her and she ran as hard as she could, until her lungs burned. Up ahead the trees thinned. Miss Taylor's backyard. She burst through the last line of saplings and sprinted across the grass, slamming against the back door and pounding at it with one fist. Behind her, the wind remained in the forest, rocking the trunks and making the canopy ripple like the ocean tide.

"Jessica!" Miss Taylor exclaimed when she opened the door. "What happened? You're all out of breath!"

Jessica was quick to slip inside. Miss Taylor remained at the door a moment longer, staring at the forest. Then she shut it and locked the wind out.

"Did the wind scare you?" Miss Taylor asked, and Jessica nodded. "Well, it gets like this sometimes. Storms blow in from the coast. Nothing to worry about."

Jessica sat down, staring at the forest. The wind rushed out from between the trees, rippling the grass in Miss Taylor's yard like it was the ocean tide.

"I found something out about the old chapel for you," Miss Taylor said mischievously. "Want to hear?"

The old chapel, she said, was where the wind father married his earth wives. He, his betrothed, and the officiant were the only ones allowed inside. Everyone else would gather outside and wait for the wind father to emerge with his new wife. Symbolic marriages weren't uncommon in old folklore beliefs, Miss Taylor continued, but it seemed that long ago, something about this custom angered someone. It was a young man that set the building on fire. He was angry that his sister was selected to be an earth wife and burned the chapel before the ceremony could happen.

She supposed that was the end of the tradition, as the chapel was never rebuilt. As for the young man, well, the story said that the wind father was so angry that it caught him up and dashed him to pieces on the stones. His body was never found.

Jessica glanced out towards the forest. The sun was setting and the trees were already plunged into a thick darkness. She couldn't even see the individual tree trunks. It was like the world ended at the edge of the woods. Somewhere in Miss Taylor's house came the sharp crack of a branch being blown against a window and Jessica jumped in her seat.

"Sorry, was that too upsetting?" Miss Taylor asked. "It's just a story. Every town around here has them. We like our ghost stories."

Miss Taylor drove Jessica home. The wind shoved at the car the entire time and blew through Jessica's hair as she hurried up her front steps. Only once she was inside and the headlights of the librarian's car vanished did the wind calm down. The trees grew still. It had stopped entirely.

The wind wasn't following her, Jessica realized. It was following Miss Taylor.

* * *

Jessica rarely went into the ravine during the winter. She made a handful of visits to see the ice forming where the water was calm and how the water rushed beneath it, through tunnels between the rocks. But there were more exciting things to do in the winter. Her parents took her sledding on the hill behind the high school and she learned to ice skate. Then, after the first of the year, when the air was so cold that the entire world felt *sharp*, she visited her ravine. The snow was thick, almost up to the top of the rock walls. Jessica could no longer tell if the stones still moved at night.

However, down by the stream, the statue of the saint was gone. His congregation of stones were gathered listlessly around an empty space on the boulder. His head lay on the ice nearby, carelessly discarded by whoever had taken the statue.

Maybe someone had returned it to the chapel, Jessica thought desperately as she retrieved the stone from the stream. Maybe it was the same person who moved the stones around.

That was fine, Jessica told herself sadly. She loved visiting her unknown saint every day and leaving him shiny stones and empty glass bottles, but in the end he didn't belong to her. He was only something she'd found in the woods and perhaps he wasn't hers to take. Still, it made her sad that all the things she'd gathered for him were left here. He didn't even have his head on him anymore.

She put the stone with the face in her pocket. Then she gathered up as many of the bottles and his congregation as she could and started off through the woods. Her legs ached with the effort of trudging through the thick snow. She began to wonder if she could reach the chapel and be home before it got dark out. Still, she was almost there, so she pressed on.

The saint was indeed at the chapel. He stood in a different place than where Jessica had found him, a short distance away with his back to the building. There was an aisle in the trees, Jessica realized. A clear stretch with the trees evenly spaced to either side in a row. How had she not noticed this before? She stood on top of the rock wall that ran along the back of the chapel and peered at it curiously.

There was someone coming. He hadn't been there a moment before. Jessica dropped the stones and the bottles. They sank into the snow at her feet. She stumbled backwards and fell to her knees, crouching in the snow behind the wall. She could see through a narrow gap between two large stones and she peered through this, watching the aisle and the waiting saint statue.

A man was walking down the aisle. He appeared out of nothing, the wind coalescing on a single spot and him stepping out of it. The dry leaves rose up to greet him, circling around his body to form a luxurious cloak, trailing down his back and dragging along the ground as he walked towards the headless statue. His skin was formed of mist and his eyes were like stars. His hair was like the wind on the lake, rippling down his shoulders.

He carried Miss Taylor in his arms.

The wind father. The wind father and his earth wife.

Jessica covered her mouth with both hands. It was only the hammering of her heart and the horrible feeling of dread in her chest that kept her from calling out for Miss Taylor. The librarian looked terrified, her face pale and her eyes wide, but she seemed unable to do anything but fall limply to her knees when the wind father set her down. She was shaking, perhaps from the cold, perhaps from fear. She tried lifting a hand but it was like her muscles weren't responding anymore.

The wind father stood there at her side, solemn and silent. He stared down at the headless saint. It was a wedding, Jessica realized. When that young man burned the chapel, did he also destroy the saint's head? Was he determined to make sure no more weddings ever happened here? The ceremony was silent, for the officiant could no longer speak. It felt hollow. An empty rite, held at the feet of a desecrated chapel.

Then, the silent oration came to a conclusion. The wind father turned and bent over. He grabbed Miss Taylor's chin and lifted her head.

He kissed her.

And Miss Taylor's head simply rolled off her shoulders. It fell to the ground with a heavy thump. The rest of her body tilted sideways, toppled, and crumbled into dust.

Jessica screamed. The wind father's head snapped up and his eyes fell directly on her. He took a step towards her and she stumbled to her feet to run. Miss Taylor's head lay on the ground at his feet, almost buried in the snow.

Would he do the same to Jessica? But where could she run to? Her house was so far away and he was the wind itself. The trees around here were swaying to and fro, like ships in a gale. Desperately, Jessica looked around her for answers.

The old chapel. It was desecrated. Maybe he couldn't enter. Maybe this was why the ceremony was held outside. She vaulted the wall to the old chapel and fell through the rotting shingles, down into the cushion of leaves that caught her. She huddled under the charred beams as the wind slammed into the walls. It roared overhead, circling the building, and leaves formed a funnel around the foundations. Like this tiny building was in the eye of a hurricane. The remnants of the roof trembled like a sail cloth and Jessica was terrified that he'd simply bury her in debris.

There was a weight in her pocket. The stone. The stone she'd used as the saint's head. Jessica pulled it out with trembling hands. She stared into its face. It was no longer smiling and its eyes didn't twinkle with light. She felt tears trickle down her face, so cold it was like they'd turn to ice right on her cheeks.

The wind father and his earth wives. All those stones with features like faces.

"I'm sorry," she whispered.

And she threw the stone. She never heard it hit the ground. The wind caught it and with one last roar that snapped the branches of the trees, he left. He took the stone and left Jessica laying in the debris, utterly alone.

* * *

The stones still moved at night. Jessica stayed out of the woods now, so she no longer saw them as often. When she did, she'd hurriedly look away and continue on.

There was one stone that never moved. It stayed where she'd put it, on the rock wall closest to the edge of the forest. It was within eyeshot of Miss Taylor's garden, which was being maintained by the new owners of her house. On Sundays Jessica would make her way through the forest as quickly as she could, until she reached the wall where the stone sat waiting.

Then Jessica would get out her book, sit on the wall, and read to the stone with Miss Taylor's face.

The Blessed Affliction

Eric Reitan

IT STARTED as a pulsing heat, a thrum of fire that strengthened with each heartbeat. If the sensation had been on her skin, born of some external kindling, it would've been the kind of affliction that fire-and-brimstone preachers promised to the unbelievers and the whores.

But it came from within, and so it was pleasure.

Sometimes Phoenix wished it were more literal: fire in the manner of her namesake. She imagined the purity of it. No mess. Just ashes to brush away.

She pictured herself standing on a hillside, raising a hand to her shoulder and, with a wry smile, flicking off an ember.

A hillside more open than this one, because if it happened with real fire she'd need a space free of dead leaves and underbrush. But given the truths about her life, what she needed was the cover of trees and wild things to consume the aftermath.

Her brother Terrance watched her. He was trembling: sixteen but still young for his age. This was his first time to stand vigil.

"Phoenix?"

"Yes, Terry."

"It's soon, isn't it?"

She pointed to the reddening sky. "When the sunlight touches me."

"Is it terrible?"

"You can look away if you like."

"Does it hurt?"

"Only for a second."

Her hand caressed the swell of her abdomen. That was the hardest thing to hide. During the last week of each cycle she'd sequester herself in the family cabin to avoid the inevitable questions.

"What if someone comes?"

She glanced at him. He was too timid for this, but Father had insisted. She knew Father was thinking about the future, about his own mortality. But still. Terry wasn't ready.

"It's your job to keep them away," she said. "But no one will come."

"How do you know?"

"Because it's almost time." It burned, and she wanted to spread her arms and throw back her head and arch her back and roar. She might have done it if she'd had a sister or a mother to stand vigil.

"And when it's over?"

"We've been over this, Terry. Look at the sky."

"But—"

"You need to get back. It's time!"

Terry scrambled behind the nearest tree. Phoenix turned to face the dawn.

* * *

Red light, red blood in a spray across her vision. And then a crimson root, fleshy, worming into her from somewhere beyond the world's outer skin. She saw it more clearly than ever before, and she smelled it: a thick, mucosal stench. Not a root at all. An umbilical, pulsing with heat, pouring the viscous fire into her veins. And beyond it, something that hungered, something just out of sight.

"Stand firm."

Her aunt's voice, a voice silenced too soon.

"As you grow older, you will see more, and it will be harder to forget."

She thought of closing her eyes against it, but her old eyes had already burst and what she saw with now had no lids, nothing to block out the glimpse of what lay on the umbilical's far side.

Her scream was like a birthing cry.

* * *

She was on her back with no memory of falling. Terrance was sobbing not far away. She pushed herself up, ran a hand through the slick of her hair, and looked towards the sun to gauge how much time had passed. No more than five minutes.

Phoenix rose from the ruins of her old body, sloughing off a slurry of gore. "The towel," she said. "My clothes." She tried to say it gently, but it came out harsh.

Terry kept his gaze averted as he rummaged through the sack and tossed a bundle her way. She wiped herself clean and slipped into the dress.

The patch of earth in front of Terry was, it seemed, the most fascinating thing he'd ever seen.

"Terry."

"You do this every *month*."

"Yes."

Now, finally, he looked up and met her gaze. His eyes swam. "How do you *do* it?"

"I don't have a choice."

It wasn't true. Every month she chose. Chose not to rest, not to spend those few key nights alone. Chose to ignore the lure of normality – like the days she'd known as a girl, like the ones other women took for granted. One normal month and then darkness. When the fire came there'd be no rising from the ashes and the gore. Instead of eternal youth, eternal night.

The temptation was stronger than it had ever been, even though what she'd glimpsed in that moment before rebirth was already slipping away. Slipping free because it made no sense, because it was too strange and slick and terrible for her memory to find any purchase. What it offered up instead – the animal smell, the sticky liquid sound, a hundred thousand groping umbilicals uncoiling from the void – was not the truth of it any more than a slap was the truth about war.

She'd always known she was cursed. Never before had she thought she might be evil.

"Phoenix?" Terry stepped towards her despite his horror.

She swallowed bile and set her mouth into line. "C'mon," she said. "I need a shower."

* * *

He'd gotten his license weeks ago, but Phoenix did the driving. He didn't even offer, just sat there hugging himself.

Phoenix didn't mind. It gave her something to focus on: the feel of the plastic wheel, the rhythm of checking in the rearview and scanning the road ahead. By the time they pulled up the gravel drive, she could almost imagine that her rebirth had been like every one before: fire, anticipation and dread and the light of dawn; and then dislocation, a vision of blood and a coiling root. And then the aftermath.

"Now what?" Terry asked.

Phoenix put the car into park. Father's Volvo was gone. He'd already left for work. "You know what," she said.

"But I've never…" He shrugged.

"What do you need me to say, Terry?"

He answered with silence, but she saw what was in his eyes.

"What, Terry? If you have something to say, say it! Don't be a fucking coward."

He shriveled back as if afraid of her.

She slammed the car door, stamped into the house, and moved through her morning rituals with a fury she didn't wholly understand. She fought the urge to knock things off tables, tear down the shower curtain, fling the shampoo bottle into the mirror. Finally, standing in the shower, she forced herself to be still. At its hottest setting it hurt the way fire was supposed to hurt. She stood under it until the heat faded to a lukewarm stream. Finally the water ran cold, and she was shivering. She got out and rubbed her newborn skin with a ratty towel.

She dressed in a swishy cotton skirt and a peasant blouse scooped low enough to gesture towards sexy. The woman in the mirror was ambiguously poised between modesty and a gypsy recklessness. She pulled on a handful of bangles and gave her wrist an experimental twirl, trying to work up the mood for the days ahead. Trying to make it about something other than what she'd seen in Terry's eyes.

She found him on the living room sofa, staring at his tablet.

"Father said you were old enough to see it," she said. "Was he wrong?"

Terry wiped at his nose, shook his head, shrugged – as if trying out different responses. "It's who you are," he finally said.

She turned away and found herself staring at the picture of their mother: laughing and sun-splashed and wearing a yellow summer dress. Taken with an old-fashioned camera when she was twenty-five, before she was burdened with her eldest child. With that child's affliction.

"The blessed affliction," Aunt Millie called it. Men were the carriers, passing it to their daughters. But there were things she'd inherited from her mother, too, things you couldn't see in old photographs.

The thought of following her mother's path was a stronger temptation than it had ever been. As she envisioned doing it, the memory of what she'd encountered in the void came back to her, but this time as the sound of a thousand layered screams. She imagined the screams were voices, urging her to do it, to make an end of things.

Maybe Terry would approve.

He cleared his throat. "In high school you had a boyfriend." He fidgeted with the corner of a throw pillow. "Wouldn't that be…easier?"

Phoenix wanted to answer with something cruel, but nothing came to mind. And then the feeling vanished as she saw the little boy in Terry's features and remembered how she'd held him at their mother's funeral.

"Joe was different," she said.

Terry pulled his knees up. "How?"

"I don't want to talk about it."

"I fucking watched you *explode*. I have a right to—"

"Joe and I were together before it started, okay? We worked through it together. Aunt Millie was still alive and she walked us through what to expect and…" She closed her eyes. She wasn't going to let him see her cry. She took a breath and turned back to the picture of their mother. "I told Joe it was about life, every month it was about *life*. I…I thought that would make it special, not a burden."

When she glanced back at Terry his eyes had softened. He tipped his head back, blinking.

And then he laughed. He wiped his eyes and gave her one of his lopsided grins. "*Better knock up your girlfriend, or when she blows up at the end of the month she's dead!* Yeah, I can see how that'd make it hard to get it up."

Phoenix laughed, too, but it withered quickly. Her eyes raked the bookcase, pausing on the books of fairy tales. None of them got it right. "I swore I'd never make another guy go through that."

Terry gazed at the floor. "So this is better? Horny assholes at the blackjack table?"

"Don't use that kind of language, boy."

His laugh was a donkey-bray.

She picked up the picture of her mother and traced a finger along the silver frame. "I could stay home."

She felt the weight of Terry's silence. She wondered what it meant, but she didn't look at him. If she saw his face, she'd know.

And then she heard a slap: a hand striking the top of the coffee table. "Don't you dare, Phoenix." The anguish in his voice made her tremble. "Don't you fucking dare!"

She pivoted to meet his gaze. His eyes were brimming with tears.

Her fingers tightened on the picture frame. "I have better reasons than Mom."

He turned his gaze away, his tears catching the light from the window. "Do you?"

"That's how we die, you know. My kind. We don't grow old. We don't get sick. We die because we get tired."

"Like Aunt Millie."

Phoenix was silent. Millie had been gone for two years. Mom had been stolen away by suicide four years before that. Two days after it happened Terry had wandered into the silent kitchen, padding up to Phoenix and Father while they stared into their morning coffee. He'd wiped sleep from his eyes and announced he'd had a terrible dream. "I dreamt that Mama died."

Aunt Millie's death had been the same and not the same, at once less terrible and more so because of how it brought everything back, layered now with fresher loss.

"Sounds like the sort of thing Aunt Millie would say," Terry said into the silence. "*You die because you get tired.*"

"What she said to me…" Phoenix swallowed and blinked, forcing her way through it. "She said, 'In theory we could live forever. But we have to keep choosing it, over and over.'"

Her mother had said something too much like it when Phoenix was still a little girl: *Every morning I wake up and choose to live. Because of you.*

She hadn't understood what that meant, not until her own affliction woke in her blood, different from her mother's but similar enough for the meaning to grow clear: *Every morning it whispers to me how easy it would be. Every morning I seize the threads of love around me and will for them to be enough.*

And now this. This unfathomable something in the void. Aunt Millie had told her the visions grew clearer over time, but she never mentioned what she saw in that moment when the magma poured into her with the dawn.

It was always a secret truth lurking behind all the practical things she said, limning her words with hints of horror.

Now, at last, Phoenix knew what it was.

Every time, the monster grows more real.

Terry rose from the sofa and approached her. "I expect you to outlive me," he said. "I'm happy to stand vigil every month until I die."

"Terrance—"

"It's only once a month. I'm not losing anyone else to this thing."

Phoenix turned away. She set the photo of her mother back on the shelf. The frame left a crease in her palm. Her mother had to *act*: pour the water, empty the pills into her palm, put them in her mouth – maybe all at once, maybe one by one.

All Phoenix had to do was stay home. Stay in bed alone, let the crucial days slip past, and it would be done.

"I'm tired, Terry."

Terry took her hand. "We all get tired. We rest a bit and go on."

"I can't rest yet."

"That's right. I'm taking you to the city."

Phoenix took a breath. She pivoted, the bangles jangling on her wrist.

Terry's face was fierce. She hadn't expected that. She hadn't expected him to be fierce.

It was reason enough. "Today you take me," she said. "Tomorrow Dad will."

Terry nodded. He crossed to the entry and fished up the car keys. "You never go alone, do you?"

"I hate to go alone."

Terry tossed the keys from one hand to another as they stepped into the sunshine. "I'm sorry about earlier."

"I am, too."

"Not your fault."

"Even so."

She settled into the passenger seat and closed her eyes. It waited for her there, behind her lids: the monster, the thousand screams and the hundred thousand reaching worms, the stench of flesh and nameless fluids, all of it bound to her in a single meaty cord.

Terry started the car, flipped on the radio, and hummed out of tune as he backed over gravel. Phoenix opened her eyes. She looked at Terry's profile and felt a wave of tenderness. She snatched up his hand.

"What's that for?"

"Just seizing the threads of love."

"That sounds like one of Mama's phrases."

"Maybe," she said. "Or maybe it's something she made me think one day."

"I like it. You still feeling tired?"

"Nah," she said, but her eyes slid shut again and the thing was there, pink and huge and rushing towards her from a universe away. She blinked and held his hand. "This body's just an hour old."

Stray

Cody Schroeder

JACK STEPPED OUT of his car and stared at the big white truck parked beside him. It had a conservation department logo on the door.

He could count the number of times he'd seen conservation agents in the park on one hand and have a few fingers left over.

Stranger still, he recognized the man in uniform at the little gate separating the parking lot from the park.

"Morning, Mike," he said, approaching the gate, locking his car with his fob and slipping his keys into his pocket, his water bottle in his other hand, strapped to his wrist.

"Morning, Jack. Going for a run?"

"Every Tuesday and Thursday morning. Lyssa says I need to get more exercise. Too much time in a desk chair is bad for me, apparently."

"Jane and my doc been on me too."

Mike did have more of a gut than him. Probably weighed fifty-plus pounds more too.

He didn't mention any of that though. "What brings you out here so early?"

"Ugh." Mike groaned and waved behind him to the trees and trail. "Had some pets go missing here lately, maybe some homeless folks who camp near the trails and in the caves too. County wanted someone around to keep an eye on things, but couldn't spare a deputy or anything, so they begged us to send someone. Here I am."

He shrugged and grumbled some more. "Don't know what they expect me to do."

"Stand there, look important, keep people from coming to their offices and complaining to them."

"Right?"

They both laughed.

Jack passed him, clapped him on the shoulder, headed for the start of the trail he always ran on. "Don't work too hard."

Mike nodded, but turned to him. "Still, Jack, something's going on here. Be careful. Pay attention. Don't stray off the trails. May just be a loose bobcat or coyotes or something, but if people are going missing, it could be something bad. Don't you make me call Lyssa and tell her something happened to you. She'd kill me."

A rare serious moment from Mike.

He nodded. "I'll be careful, always am."

Mike turned back to the parking lot. Other runners and hikers to warn.

Besides, he'd run these trails dozens of times, never had any problems. Today wouldn't be any different.

He picked his usual trail and got started. A cool, breezy morning in early autumn, perfect for getting some exercise. The shade of the trees made it even cooler.

He jogged up the slope and into the woods, down the easier side of the hill where it joined another low rise. He took a deep breath of pure, fresh air. It stung his throat, but felt good, so clean.

The first half mile or so of the trail came and went with ease, his feet pounding against the ground and grass. Nobody else on the trail at this hour either. He had it all to himself.

No bobcats or coyotes either.

He shook his head and kept jogging.

Probably just a few people who let their pets get away from them trying to blame something else.

Poor Mike, standing there like a post all day. He must be bored out of his mind.

Easy money though.

About the halfway point, he stopped to rest where the trail crossed a small creek. A short wooden bridge ran over the sparkling clear water.

He knelt beside the creek, splashed some water over his face and head, cooling himself off and rinsing away the sweat.

He wiped at his face and leaned back against the bridge, sitting on a wide flat rock. Evidently, he wasn't the only one who favored this as a spot to rest. Water bottles, cigarette butts, a few beer cans, and plenty of other crap littered the banks of the creek, scattered among the rocks.

People could be such pigs. Could they not pick up after themselves? He took another drink from his own bottle, let it hang from his wrist.

"Enough rest." He rose with a groan and some popping joints and bones. Especially his knees.

Across the bridge and the path began to circle back. He'd come out on the east side of the parking lot.

Just a few more miles to go.

He chuckled, took another big deep breath, and took off again.

The hills were steeper and the woods thicker on this second half of the trail. It became much more of a hike than a jog. Really got his legs and heart – and everything else – working.

He skirted around a tree growing right into the path, twisting roots the perfect place to twist an ankle, and slowed.

His legs burned almost as bad as his sides. A boulder ahead would make for a good spot to stop and catch his breath again.

Moss covered the rock, along with a dusting of cedar needles and bird crap.

He leaned against it, taking care to avoid the crap, and took several deep, slow breaths. The cool breeze blowing through the woods helped a little too.

The car horn or alarm going off in the distance didn't.

"Doesn't sound like mine at least."

He brought his bottle to his lips and took a long drink.

Not much further now. Then, home to take a nice hot shower and see what sort of emails he'd get to start his day with.

He pushed off the boulder and stretched. More joints and bones popped.

Lyssa laughed in his head. The same way she chuckled when he grunted and groaned getting off the couch or out of bed.

"Getting old, Grandpa?" She'd asked a few times now.

To which he always reminded her she was three months older than him, which often earned him a playful smack.

Smirking to himself, he took another drink and stretched some more, ready to go again.

A long, low whimper came out of the woods to his left.

He stopped mid-step and turned toward the sound. A pair of thick old cedar trees shaded the woods and the side of the path, almost creating an archway deeper into the woods.

The sound came again, higher and louder this time. The sort of whimper or whine a puppy or kitten might make. It echoed through the trees.

He took a step toward the edge of the trail and Mike's warning about keeping to the path came back to him.

He stopped, still staring at the shaded space between the two cedar trees. Could this be someone or something trying to lure him away?

The most pitiful whimper yet, almost a cry, came through the trees. He stepped off the trail and into the brush. It sounded like a puppy crying.

"Poor thing."

The trail behind him was empty in both directions. No one else around.

"Oh what the hell..." He stomped deeper into the leaves and brush, raising a foot over a vine of thorns.

He'd never forgive himself if there was a puppy or something lost out here and he didn't at least try to help it. And if he went home and told Lyssa, she would demand they drive back and find it, make sure it was ok.

Another sharp little cry echoed through the trees as he ducked between the cedars and toward the sound.

The ground made a gentle slope up away from the trail. He pushed more cedar limbs out of his way, pulled his feet through more brush and thorns.

Another whimpering cry, a little louder. He had to be getting closer.

The trees and brush were thicker here, with nothing trimmed or maintained. He climbed over another huge rock crusted with moss. A washed-out gully snaked up the hill in front of him.

He sighed. "Great."

Maybe he should have stayed on the trail, heeded Mike's warning.

Another cry, the longest and most pathetic yet, banished any notion of turning around and heading back.

Whatever it was, it sounded like it was at the top of the hill. Close. Just a little further in.

"Grab it, get back to the trail, and get out," he whispered, scrabbling up the gully. Maybe leave the thing with Mike on the way out.

Probably just some poor stray.

Although...

Lyssa might want to keep it. They had talked about getting a dog before. Agreed that they would get a rescue too.

"Hold on. I'm coming."

Seconds later, he crawled onto the top of the hill, panting and sweating. Forget running or jogging, he needed to start climbing steep hills.

Another whimper. Something white flashed in the leaves on the other side of the hilltop. Definitely looked like a bigger puppy.

It flailed around, kicking up leaves and dirt everywhere. Hopefully, it wasn't trapped or caught in anything.

He took a couple deep breaths to calm himself and crept closer.

More thrashing in the leaves and another flash of white fur.

"Hey there." He put on his most gentle, soothing voice. "It's ok. I'm going to try to help you."

A series of short little whines. The leaves settled.

"That's it. That's it. Good puppy. Just calm down." He took another step closer, barely a yard away now.

Two more whines, short and sharp.

"Yeah, I know." He knelt down, more on its level. "It's ok. Come here."

He held out a hand, almost to the messy mound of leaves.

The leaves rustled, white front paws and chest appeared, though a few big oak leaves still covered the face.

It sneezed and shook its head, knocking the last of the leaves away.

"Wow, look at you."

Some kind of little shepherd or maybe a mix. Mostly white with patches of darker brown. Light gray-blue eyes.

He wiggled his fingers, trying to get it to come closer. "You are gorgeous. Come over here."

No collar or tags.

It eyed him and sniffed the air, its little nose going up.

Lyssa would love this little guy.

It took a hesitant step closer, watching him.

He didn't move, just kept his hand out. Didn't want to spook the poor thing.

"Yeah, come on. You want to come home with me?"

He reached forward a little more, almost brushed his fingertips on its black nose, but he slipped, fell forward, and landed hard on his right knee. Right on a rock or something hard and sharp.

"Ow, shit!"

The puppy yelped and jerked away. It scrambled through the leaves and down the other side of the hill.

He stumbled after it, probably not helping. "Wait. Come back. It's ok."

The puppy blundered through the leaves and brush across a small clearing.

His knee throbbed.

But he hurried down the hill after it. Couldn't just leave the little guy out here all alone. Especially if there was something after pets in these woods.

"Don't worry. Don't worry." He hobbled across the clearing after the puppy. "I'm not going to hurt you. Lyssa and me will take good care of you."

He found himself already thinking of names as he passed back into the trees.

Just had to hope it didn't belong to someone else. One of the pets who'd gone missing.

The ground sloped down again at the edge of the clearing. The puppy turned back to him at the top of the slope and let out a little bark, like it was playing with him.

He laughed. It was adorable. How could he not at least take it back out to Mike? See if it belonged to someone?

"I'm coming. I'm coming."

The puppy rolled in the leaves, some of them sticking to its fluff. It bounced back up and barked again, its tail whipping back and forth.

Breathing hard, he stopped a step away from it and knelt again, his knees popping. The one he fell on throbbed, a sharp hot pain.

No more jogging today.

He whistled.

The puppy's ears perked up and it turned its head at a curious angle.

"Come here, good boy. Come here." He wiggled his fingers again.

It sniffed the air and leaned closer to him, raising one front paw. Then it turned its head back, ears twitching, as if it heard something behind it.

"What is it? Huh? What'cha hear?"

It turned all the way around, butt and tail to him, its tail now still. It let out a low growl and its whole body vibrated.

He straightened up. "What is it?"

The puppy barked and barreled down the slope, bounding through the leaves.

"Ah hell." He stumbled after it, again.

At the bottom of the slope, it ran through a shallow stream, little more than a trickle of water, and into an opening in the hillside opposite this one.

A cave. One of the dozen or so in and around the park. No trail leading to this one either. It wasn't part of the actual park then. Never stopped people exploring them or squatting in them or using them to do drugs. At least once a year, rescue crews had to come in for some dumbass who got lost or stuck.

"Please don't let me be one of them."

He staggered down the slope to the opening. A dark narrow gash in the hillside, not much bigger than him. Roots and bits of dirt hung down over the opening.

Another high-pitched bark came out to him, echoing off the dirt and rock inside.

He leaned into the cool shade of the cave, breathing in the scents of damp earth, stone, and something stronger. A meaty, rotten stink.

Probably something dead.

A finger to his nose, he whistled again, the sound echoing off into the cave.

Another bark, smaller and more distant, came a second later.

"Come here, puppy. Come here, good boy."

Seconds dragged on to at least a minute, with no sign of the puppy.

God alone knew what could have happened to it, what it might have found.

He sighed, turned back to the daylight. He should go back, get Mike, or anyone else, to help him.

A faint whimper from the darkness.

"Son of a...I'm coming." He pushed his way into the cave, damp stone and dirt walls rubbing against him.

He reached into his pocket, took out his phone – no signal, of course – and turned its light on. The white light showed a winding narrow tunnel in front of him, moist and dripping walls.

"Please don't be very deep," he whispered, pushing on.

Small wonder this cave wasn't part of the park. He barely fit through. Anyone bigger than his – entirely average – size wouldn't fit at all.

The puppy whimpered again, long and low, a wavering little sound.

"I'm coming."

Sounded close, at least.

He pushed around a right-turning bend in the tunnel and moisture from the wall soaked through the back of his shirt.

"Ugh."

Warmer than he'd expected. More like stale sweat than water.

The air was warmer here too. Not the cool tickle against his skin from closer to the entrance. Didn't caves usually get cooler deeper in?

That stink from before came stronger too. Not the stone or earth, but that rotting, roadkill smell.

Must be something dead further ahead. Maybe that's what the puppy found? What brought it in here.

More warm moisture from the walls dripped on him, seeped through his clothes. It didn't feel like water at all.

Too thick, too sticky. It carried that foul, carrion stink too.

Just as his phone beeped to warn him about the low battery, the tunnel grew wider. The walls didn't press against him, tight on either side, anymore.

He stood straighter, walked normal.

But the stink grew worse, almost burning his nose.

A short sharp bark, right in front of him in the darkness.

He raised his phone, the light illuminating the puppy a few steps ahead. It wagged its tail and panted, happy as could be.

He sighed. "You took me on quite the journey, little guy. Let's get out of here."

The smell grew worse with every beat of his heart, almost more than he could take. His stomach threatened revolt, bile burning in his throat.

He wiped sweat and sticky wetness from his face. More sweat ran down his neck and back.

When had it gotten so hot? The air so thick?

He breathed deep, the air heavy, oppressive.

"Come on," his voice came lower, weaker, "let's go."

The puppy didn't move or make a sound.

He shone his light on the walls. They were wet, shining. More of that thick moisture oozing down them.

"What the hell?"

They moved.

Throbbing. Pulsing.

All around him, the walls moved. They were alive.

Even the floor seemed softer beneath his feet. Warmer too.

Not earth or stone, but…flesh.

He turned to leave. The door was gone. Now, just a flat wall, pulsing like the rest behind him.

His phone beeped again and the light flickered.

He kicked at the wall. His foot met soft, giving, warm tissue.

The puppy growled behind him. Far too big and deep a sound to come from so small a creature.

He turned to find it stalking toward him, three or four times the size it had been a moment ago.

Its body swelled and bulged in every direction, losing the luster and color of its fur. Now its whole body took on the color and texture of the fleshy walls around them.

It prowled toward him, still growling.

He backed away, against the wall where the tunnel had been.

The wall pushed back, nudging him toward the nightmare that had been a puppy seconds ago.

He slipped to the left against the wall to dodge the swelling monster, his heart ready to burst in his chest.

This couldn't be happening. This wasn't possible.

Another warning beep from his phone.

His back stuck to the wall, his ass and the back of his thighs too. He tried to push off with his arms and elbows, but they stuck to the soft wetness as well, pressing into the sticky flesh.

Like a rat in a glue trap.

In the flickering light of his phone, the bulging monster opened its mouth wide, dripping the same saliva that covered the walls, and smiled.

Its whole head split open in a horrible grin, and it lunged at him.

He screamed and dropped his phone, trying to shield himself, but his arms were stuck fast to the wall, useless.

The thing slammed against him, but didn't bite or claw. Its whole body hit his and fell apart, no bones or structure. It spread over him, thick and hot like tar, covering him, pressing him harder against the wall.

Into the wall.

He thrashed and struggled, to no avail at all.

It covered him. His stomach where it struck, down to his knees, to his toes, up over his chest, his arms, up to his neck. So thick and heavy and hot.

It burned through his shoes, his pants, his shirt, searing into the flesh beneath.

Dissolving him.

No. Digesting him.

It spread up his neck, to his chin and face.

His phone beeped one last time, and in its fading light, a glob of meaty flesh fell from the ceiling. It jerked and writhed on the floor, swelling and bulging as the puppy had.

As the spreading flesh covered his chin and climbed over his lips, the glob on the floor finished its change into a tiny kitten, mostly black with white paws, the tip of its tail white too.

It let out a little mew and toddled toward the wall where the tunnel had been, which opened to let it pass.

The light from his phone died as darkness and heat engulfed his eyes. He tried to scream again, but his lips were already burned away.

Another meow echoed in his ears before they were covered and everything went dark and silent.

The House of Sounds

M.P. Shiel

E caddi come l'uom cui sonno piglia.
Dante

A GOOD MANY YEARS AGO, when a young man, a student in Paris, I knew the great Carot, and witnessed by his side many of those cases of mind-malady, in the analysis of which he was such a master. I remember one little maid of the Marais who, until the age of nine, did not differ from her playmates; but one night, lying abed she whispered into her mother's ear: "Mama, can you not hear the sound of the world?" It appears that her geography had just taught her that our globe reels with an enormous velocity on an orbit about the sun; and this sound of the world of hers was merely a murmur in the ear, heard in the silence of night. Within six months she was as mad as a March-hare.

I mentioned the case to my friend, Haco Harfager, then occupying with me an old mansion in St. Germain, shut in by a wall and jungle of shrubbery. He listened with singular interest, and during a good while sat wrapped in gloom.

Another case which I gave made a great impression upon my friend: A young man, a toy-maker of St. Antoine, suffering from consumption – but sober, industrious – returning one gloaming to his garret, happened to purchase one of those factious journals which circulate by lamplight over the Boulevards. This simple act was the beginning of his doom. He had never been a reader: knew little of the reel and turmoil of the world. But the next night he purchased another journal. Soon he acquired a knowledge of politics, the huge movements, the tumult of life. And this interest grew absorbing. Till late into the night, every night, he lay poring over the roar of action, the printed passion. He would awake sick, but brisk in spirit – and bought a morning paper. And the more his teeth gnashed, the less they ate. He grew negligent, irregular at work, turning on his bed through the day. Rags overtook him. As the grand interest grew upon his frail soul so every lesser interest failed in him. There came a day when he no more cared for his own life; and another day when he tore the hairs from his head.

As to this man the great Carot said to me:

"Really, one does not know whether to chuckle or to weep over such a business. Observe, for one thing, how diversely men are made! There are minds precisely so sensitive as a thread of melted lead: every breath will fret and trouble them: and how about the hurricane? For such this scheme of things is clearly no fit habitation, but a Machine of Death, a baleful Immense. Too cruel to some is the rushing shriek of Being – they cannot stand the world. Let each look well to his own little shred of existence, I say, and leave the monstrous Automaton alone! Here in this poor toy-maker you have a case of the ear: it is only the neurosis, Oxyecoia. Grand was that Greek myth of 'the Harpies' – by them was this creature snatched away – or say, caught by a limb in the wheels of the universe, and so perished. It is quite a ravishing exit – translation in a chariot of flame! Only remember that the member first seized was the pinna he bent ear to the howl of the world, and ended by himself howling. Between chaos and our shoes swings, I assure you, the thinnest film!

I knew a man who had this aural peculiarity: that every sound brought him some knowledge of the matter causing the sound: a rod for instance, of mixed copper and tin striking upon a rod of mixed iron and lead, conveyed to him not merely the proportion of each metal in each rod, but some knowledge of the essential meaning and spirit, as it were, of copper, of tin, of iron and of lead. Him also did the Harpies snatch aloft!"

I have mentioned that I related some of these cases to my friend, Harfager: and I was astonished at the obvious pains which he gave himself to hide his interest, his gaping nostrils...

From first days when we happened to attend the same seminary in Stockholm an intimacy had sprung up between us. But it was not an intimacy accompanied by the ordinary signs of friendship. Harfager was the shyest, most isolated, of beings. Though our joint housekeeping (brought about by a chance meeting at a midnight séance) had now lasted some months, I knew nothing of his plans. Through the day we read together, he rapt back into the past, I engrossed with the present; late at night we reclined on sofas within the vast cave of a hearth-place Louis Onze, and smoked over the dying fire in silence. Occasionally a soirée or lecture might draw me from the house; except once, I never understood that Harfager left it. On that occasion I was hurrying through the Rue St. Honoré, where a rush of traffic rattles over the old pavers retained there, when I came upon him. In this tumult he stood in a listening attitude; and for a moment did not know me.

Even as a boy I had seen in my friend the genuine patrician – not that his personality gave any impression of loftiness or opulence: on the contrary. He did, however, suggest an incalculable ancientness; and I have known no nobleman who so bore in his expression the assurance of the essential Prince, whose pale blossom is of yesterday, and will perish tomorrow, but whose root shoots through the ages. This much I knew of Harfager; also that on one or other of his islands north of Zetland lived his mother and an aunt; that he was somewhat deaf; but liable to a thousand torments or delights at certain sounds, the whine of a door, the note of a bird...

He was somewhat under the middle height; and inclined to portliness. His nose rose highly aquiline from that sort of brow called 'the musical' – that is, with temples which incline outward to the cheek-bones, making breadth for the base of the brain; while the direction of the heavy-lidded eyes and of the eyebrows was a downward droop from the nose of their outer ends. He wore a thin chin-beard. But the feature of his face were the ears, which were nearly circular, very small and flat, without that outer curve called 'the helix'. I came to understand that this had long been a trait of his race. Over the whole wan face of my friend was engraved an air of woeful inability, utter gravity of sorrow: one said 'Sardanapalus', frail last of the race of Nimrod.

After a year I found it necessary to mention to Harfager my intention of leaving Paris, as we reclined one night in our nooks within the fireplace. He replied to my tidings with a polite "Indeed!" and continued to gloat over the grate: but after an hour turned to me and observed: "Well, it seems to be a hard world."

Truisms uttered in just such a tone of discovery I occasionally heard from him; but his earnest gaze, his despondency now, astonished me.

"Apropos of what?" I asked.

"My friend, do not leave me!" He spread his arms.

I learned that he was the object of a devilish malice; that he was the prey of a horrible temptation. That a lure, a becking hand, a lurking lust, which it was the effort of his life to escape (and to which he was especially liable in solitude) perpetually enticed him; and that so it had been almost from the day when, at the age of five, he had been sent by his father from his desolate home in the ocean.

And whose was this malice?

He told me his mother's and aunt's.

And what was this temptation?

He said it was the temptation to go back – to hurry with the very frenzy of hunger – back to that home.

I demanded with what motives, and in what way, the malice of his mother and aunt manifested itself. He answered that there was, he fancied, no definite motive, but only a fated malevolence; and that the respect in which it manifested itself was the prayers and commands with which they plagued him to go again to the hold of his ancestors.

All this I could not understand, and said so. In what consisted this magnetism, and this peril, of his home? To this Harfager did not reply, but rising from his seat, disappeared behind the hearth-curtains, and left the apartment. When he returned, it was with a quarto tome bound in hide, which proved to be Hugh Gascoigne's Chronicle of Norse Families in English black-letter. The passage to which he pointed I read as follows:

"Now of these two brothers the older, Harold, being of seemly personage and prowess, did go a pilgrimage into Danemark, wherefrom he repaired again home to Hjaltland (Zetland), and with him fetched the amiable Thronda for his wife, who was a daughter of the sank (blood) royal of Danemark. And his younger brother, Sweyn, that was sad and debonair, but far surpassed the other in cunning, received him with all good cheer.

"But eftsoons (soon after) fell Sweyn sick for all his love that he had of Thronda, his brother's wife. And while the worthy Harold ministered about the bed where Sweyn lay sick, lo, Sweyn fastened on him a violent stroke with a sword, and with no longer tarrying enclosed his hands in bonds, and cast him in the bottom of a deep hold. And because Harold would not deprive himself of the governance of Thronda his wife, Sweyn cut off both his ear(s), and put out one of his eyes, and after divers such torments was ready to slay him. But on a day the valiant Harold, breaking his bonds, and embracing his adversary, did by the sleight of wrestling overthrow him, and escaped. Notwithstanding, he faltered when he came to the Somburg Head, not far from the Castle, and, albeit that he was swift-foot, could no farther run, by reason that he was faint with the long plagues of his brother. And whilst he there lay in a swoon, did Sweyn come upon him, and when he had stricken him with a dart, cast him from Somburg Head into the sea.

"Not long hereafterward did the lady Thronda (though she knew not the manner of her lord's death, nor, verily, if he was dead or alive) receive Sweyn into favour, and with great gaudying and blowing of beamous (trumpets) did become his wife. And right soon they two went thence to sojourn in far parts.

"Now, it befell that Sweyn was minded by a dream to have built a great mansion in Hjaltland for the home-coming of the lady Thronda; wherefore he called to him a cunning Master-workman, and sent him to England to gather men for the building of this lusty House, while he himself remained with his lady at Rome. Then came this Architect to London, but passing thence to Hjaltland was drowned, he and his feers (mates), all and some.

"And after two years, which was the time assigned, Sweyn Harfager sent a letter to Hjaltland to understand how his great House did: for he knew not of the drowning of the Architect: and soon after he received answer that the House did well, and was building on the Isle of Rayba. But that was not the Isle where Sweyn had appointed the building to be: and he was afeard, and near fell down dead for dread, because, in the letter, he saw before him the manner of writing of his brother Harold. And he said in this form: 'Surely Harold is alive, else be this letter writ with ghostly hand.' And he was wo many days, seeing that this was a deadly stroke.

"Thereafter he took himself back to Hjaltland to know how the matter was, and there the old Castle on Somburg Head was break down to the earth. Then Sweyn was wode-wroth, and cried: 'Jhesu mercy, where is all the great house of my fathers gone? Alas! this wicked day of destiny!' And one of the people told him that a host of workmen from far parts had break it down. And he said: 'Who hath bid them?' but that could none answer. Then he said again: 'his (is not) my brother Harold alive? for I have behold his writing': and that, too, could none answer. So he went to Rayba, and saw there a great House stand, and when he looked on it, he said: 'This, sooth, was y-built by my brother Harold, be he dead or be he on-live.' And there he dwelt, and his lady, and his sons' sons until now: for that the House is ruthless and without pity; wherefore 'tis said that upon all who dwell there falleth a wicked madness and a lecherous anguish; and that by way of the ears do they drinck the cup of the furie of the earless Harold, till the time of the House be ended."

After I had read the narrative half-aloud, I smiled, saying: "This, Harfager, is very tolerable romance on the part of the good Gascoigne, but has the look of indifferent history."

"It is, nevertheless, history," he replied.

"You believe that?"

"The house stands solidly on Rayba."

"But you believe that mediaeval ghosts superintended the building of their family mansions?"

"Gascoigne nowhere says that," he answered: "for to be 'stricken with a darte', is not necessarily to die; nor, if he did say it, have I any knowledge on the subject."

"And what, Harfager, is the nature of that 'wicked madness', that 'lecherous anguish', of which Gascoigne speaks?"

"Do you ask me?" – he spread his arms – "what do I know? I know nothing! I was banished from the place at the age of five. Yet the cry of it still rings in my mind. And have I not told you of anguishes – even in myself – of inherited longing and loathing…"

Anyway, I had to go to Heidelberg just then: so I said I would compromise by making my absence short, and rejoin him in a few weeks. I took his moody silence to mean assent; and soon afterwards left him.

But I was detained: and when I got back to our old house found it empty. Harfager was gone.

It was only after twelve years that a letter was forwarded me – a rather wild letter, an awfully long one – in the writing of my friend. It was dated at Rayba. From the writing I understood that it had been dashed off with furious haste, so that I was the more astonished at the very trivial nature of the contents. On the first half page he spoke of our old friendship, and asked if I would see his mother, who was dying; the rest of the epistle consisted of an analysis of his mother's family-tree, the apparent aim being to show that she was a genuine Harfager, and a distant cousin of his father. He then went on to comment on the great prolificness of his race, stating that since the fourteenth century over four millions of its members had lived; three only of them, he believed, being now left. This settled, the letter ended.

Influenced by this, I travelled northward; reached Caithness; passed the stormy Orkneys; reached Lerwick; and from Unst, the most bleak and northerly of the Zetlands, contrived, by dint of bribes, to pit the weather-worthiness of a lug-sailed 'sixern' (identical with the 'langschips' of the Vikings) against a flowing sea and an ugly sky. The trip, I was told, was at such a season of some risk. It was the sombre December of those seas; and the weather, they said, although never cold, is seldom other than tempestuous. A mist now lay over the billows, enclosing our boat in a dome of doleful gloaming; and there was a ghostly something in the look of the silent sea and brooding sky which produced upon my nerves the mood of a journey out of nature, a cruise beyond the world. Occasionally, however, we ran past one of those 'skerries', or sea-stacks, whose craggy sea-walls, disintegrated by the struggles of the Gulf Stream with the North Sea, had a look of awful ruin and havoc. But I only noticed three of these: for before the dun day had well run half its course, sudden darkness was upon us; and with it one of those storms of which the winter of this semi-Arctic sea is one succession. During the haggard glimpses of the following day the rain did not stop; but before darkness had quite fallen, my skipper (who talked continuously to a mate of seal-maidens, and water-horses, and grülies), paused to point me out a mound of gloomier grey on the weather-bow, which, he said, should be Rayba.

Rayba, he said, was the centre of quite a nest of those rösts (eddies) and cross-currents which the tidal wave hurls with complicated swirlings among all the islands: but at Rayba they ran with more than usual angriness, owing to the row of sea-crags which garrisoned the land around; approach was therefore at all times difficult, and at night foolhardy. With a running sea, however, we came sufficiently close to see the mane of foam which railed round the coast-wall. Its shock, according to the captain, had often more than all the efficiency of artillery, tossing tons of rock to heights of six hundred feet upon the island.

When the sun next pried above the horizon, we had closely approached the coast; and it was then that for the first time the impression of some spinning motion of the island (due probably to the swirling movements of the water) was produced upon me. We affected a landing at a voe, or sea-arm, on the west coast – the east, though the point of my aim, was out of the question on account of the swell. Here I found in two skeoes (or sheds), thatched with feal, five or six seamen, who gained a livelihood by trading for the groceries of the great house on the east: and, taking one of them for a guide, I began the climb of the island.

Now, during the night in the boat, I had been aware of a booming in the ears for which even the roar of the sea round the coast seemed insufficient to account; and this now, as we went on, became immensely augmented – and with it, once more, that conviction within me of spinning motions. Rayba I found to be a land of precipices of granite and flaggy gneiss; at about the centre, however, we came upon a table-land, sloping from west to east, and covered by a lot of lochs, which sullenly flowed into one another. I could see no shore eastward to this chain of waters, and by dint of shouting to my leader, and bending ear to his shoutings, I came to know that there was no such shore – I say shout, for nothing less could have sounded through the steady bellowing as of ten thousand bisons that now resounded on every side. A certain trembling, too, of the earth became distinct. In vain, meantime, did the eye in its dreary survey seek a tree or shrub – for no kind of vegetation, save peat, could brave for a day the perennial tempest of this benighted island. Darkness, half an hour after noon, commenced to fall upon us: and it was soon afterwards that my guide, pointing down a defile near the east coast, hurriedly started back upon the way he had come. I bawled a question after him, as he went: but at this point the voice of mortals had ceased to be in the least audible.

Down this defile, with a sinking of the heart, and a singular sickness of giddiness, I passed; and, on reaching its end, emerged upon a ledge of rock which shuddered to the immediate onsets of the sea – though all this part of the island was, besides, in the grip of an ague not due to the great guns of the sea. Hugging a crag of cliff for steadiness from the gusts, I gazed forth upon a scene not less eerily dismal than some drear district of the dreams of Dante. Three 'skerries', flanked by stacks as fantastic and twisted as a witch's finger, and giving a home to hosts of osprey and scart, seal and walrus, lay at some fathoms distance; and from its rush among them, the sea in blanched, tumultuous, but inaudible wrath, like an army with banners, ranted toward the land. Letting go my crag, I staggered some distance to the left: and now all at once an amphitheatre opened before me, and there broke upon my view a panorama of such appalling majesty as had never entered my heart to fancy.

"An amphitheatre," I said: but it was rather the form of a Norman door that I saw. Fancy such a door, half a mile wide, flat on the ground, the rounded part farthest from the sea; and all round it let a wall of rock tower perpendicular forty yards: and now down this rounded door-shape, and over its whole extent, let a roaring ocean roll its tonnage in hoary fury – and the stupor with which I looked, and then the shrinking, and then the instinct of flight, will find comprehension.

This was the disemboguement of the lochs of Rayba.

And within the curve of this Norman cataract, robed in the world of its smokes and far-excursive surfs, stood a fabric of brass.

The last beam of the day had now nearly passed; but I could still see through the mist which bleakly nimbused it as in tears, that the building was low in proportion to the hugeness of its circumference; that it was roofed with a dome; and that round it ran two rows of Norman windows, the upper smaller than the lower. Certain indications led me to infer that the house had been founded upon a bed of rock which lay, circular and detached, within the curve of the cataract; but this nowhere emerged above the flood: for the whole floor which I had before me dashed one reeking deep river to the beachless sea – passage to the mansion being made possible by a massive causeway-bridge, with arches, all bearded with seaweed.

Descending from my ledge, I passed along it, now drenched in spray; and, as I came nearer, could see that the house, too, was to half its height more thickly bearded than an old hull with barnacles and every variety of bright seaweed; also – what was very surprising – that from many spots near the top of the brazen wall ponderous chains, dropping beards, reached out in rays: so that the fabric had the aspect of a many-anchored ark. But without pausing to look closely, I pushed forward, and rushing through the smooth waterfall which poured all round from the roof, by one of its many porches I entered the dwelling.

Darkness now was around me – and sound. I seemed to stand in the centre of some yelling planet, the row resembling the resounding of many thousands of cannon, punctuated by strange crashing and breaking uproars. And a sadness descended on me; I was near to tears. "Here," I said, "is the place of weeping; not elsewhere is the vale of sighing." However, I passed forward through a succession of halls, and was wondering where to go next, when a hideous figure, with a lamp in his hand, stamped towards me. I shrank from him! It seemed the skeleton of a lank man wrapped in a winding-sheet, till the light of one tiny eye, and a film of skin over a portion of the face reassured one. Of ears he showed no sign. His name, I afterwards learned, was Aith; and his appearance was explained by his pretence (true or false), that he had once suffered burning, almost to the cinder-stage, but had somehow recovered. With an expression of malice, and agitated gestures, he led the way to a chamber on the upper stage, where, having struck light to a taper, he made signs toward a spread table, and left me.

For a long time I sat in solitude, conscious of the shaking of the mansion, though every sense was swallowed up and confounded in the one impression of sound. Water, water, was the world – a nightmare on my breast, a desire to gasp for breath, a tingling on my nerves, a sense of being infinitely drowned and buried in boundless deluges; and when the feeling of giddiness, too, increased, I sprang up and paced – but suddenly stopped, angry, I scarce knew why, with myself. I had, in fact, caught myself walking with a certain hurry, not usual with me, not natural to me. So I forced myself to stand and take note of the hall. It was large, and damp with mists, so that its tattered, but rich, furniture looked lost in it, its centre occupied by a tomb bearing the name of a Harfager of the fourteenth century, and its walls old panels of oak. Having drearily seen these things, I waited on with an intolerable consciousness of solitude; but a little after midnight the tapestry parted, and Harfager with a rapid stalk walked in.

In twelve years my friend had grown old. He showed, it is true, a tendency to portliness: yet, to a knowing eye he was in reality tabid, ill-nourished. And his neck stuck forward from his chest; and the lower part of his back had quite a forward bend of age; and his hair floated about his face and shoulders in a wildness of awful whiteness, while a white chin-beard hung to his chest. His dress was a robe of bauge, which, as he went, waved aflaunt from his bare and hairy shins; and he was shod in those soft slippers called rivlins.

To my astonishment, he spoke. When I passionately shouted that I could gather no fragment of sound from his moving mouth, he clapped both his palms to his ears, and then anew besieged mine: but again without result: and now, with an angry throw of the hand, he caught up his taper, and walked from the apartment.

There was something strikingly unnatural in his manner – something which reminded me of the skeleton, Aith: an excess of zeal, a fever, a rage, a loudness, an eagerness of gait, a great extravagance of gesture. His hand constantly dashed wiffs of hair from a face which, though of the saffron of death, had red eyes – thick-lidded eyes, fixed in a downward and sidewards gaze. When he came back to me, it was with a leaf of ivory, and a piece of graphite, hanging from the cord tied round his garment; and he rapidly wrote a petition that, if not too tired, I would take part with him in the funeral of his mother.

I shouted assent.

Once more he clapped his palms to his ears; then wrote: "Do not shout: no whisper in any part of the building is inaudible to me."

I remembered that in early life he had been slightly deaf.

We passed together through many apartments, he shading the taper with his hand – a necessary action, for, as I quickly discovered, in no nook of the quivering building was the air in a state of rest, but was for ever commoved by a curious agitation, a faint windiness, like an echo of tempests, which communicated a universal nervousness to the curtains. Everywhere I met the same past grandeur, present raggedness and decay. In many of the rooms were tombs; one was a museum thronged with bronzes, but broken, grown with fungoids, dripping with moisture – it was as if the mansion, in ardour of travail, sweated; and a miasma of decomposition tainted all the air.

I followed Harfager through the maze of his way with some difficulty, for he went headlong – only once stopping, when with a face ungainly wild over the glare of the light, he tossed up his fingers, and gave out a single word: from the form of his lips I guessed the word "Hark!"

Presently we entered a very long chamber, in which, on chairs beside a bed, lay a coffin flanked by a file of candles. The coffin was very deep, and had this singularity – that the foot-piece was absent, so that the soles of the corpse could be seen as we approached. I saw, too, three upright rods secured to a side of the coffin, each rod fitted at its top with a little silver bell of the sort called morrice, pendent from a flexible spring. And at the head of the bed, Aith, with an air of irascibility, was stamping to and fro within a narrow area.

Harfager deposited the taper upon a stone table, and stood poring with a crazy intentness over the body. I, too, stood and looked at death so grim and rigorous as I think I never saw. The coffin looked angrily full of tangled grey locks, the lady being of great age, bony and hook-nosed; and her face shook with solemn constancy to the quivering of the building. I noticed that over the body had been fixed three bridges, like the bridge of a violin, their sides fitting into grooves in the coffin's sides, and their tops of a shape to fit the slope of the two coffin-lids when closed. One of these bridges passed over the knees of the dead lady; another bridged her stomach; the third her neck. In each of them was a hole, and across each of the three holes passed a string from the morrice-bell above it – the three holes being thus divided by the three tight strings into six semi-circles. Before I could guess the significance of all this, Harfager closed the folding coffin-lids, which had little holes for the passage of the three strings. He then turned the key in the lock, and uttered a word which I took to be "come."

Aith now took hold of the handle at the coffin's head; and out of the dark parts of the hall a lady in black walked forward. She was tall, pallid, of imposing aspect; and from the curvature of her nose, and her circular ears, I guessed her the lady Swertha, aunt of Harfager. Her eyes were quite red – if with crying I could not tell.

Harfager and I taking each a handle near the coffin-foot, and the lady bearing before us one of the black candlesticks, the obsequies began. When I got to the doorway, I noticed in a corner there two more coffins, engraved with the names Harfarger and his aunt. Thence we wound our way down a wide stairway winding to a lower floor; and descending thence still lower by narrow brass steps, came to a portal of metal, where the lady, depositing the candlestick, left us.

The chamber of death into which we now bore the body had for its outer wall the brazen outer wall of the whole house at a spot where this closely approached the cataract, and was no doubt profoundly drowned in the world of surge without: so that the earthquake there was urgent. On every side the place was piled with coffins, ranged high and wide upon shelves; and the huge rush and scampering which ensued on our entrance proved it the paradise of troops of rats. As it was inconceivable that these could have eaten a way through sixteen brazen feet – for even the floor here was brazen – I assumed that some fruitful pair must have found in the house, on its building, an ark from the waters. Even this guess, though, seemed wild; and Harfager afterwards confided to me his suspicion that they had for some reason been placed there by the original builder.

We deposited our load upon a stone bench in the centre; whereupon Aith made haste to be away. Harfager then repeatedly walked from end to end of the place, scrutinising with many a stoop and peer and upward stretch, the shelves and their props. Could he, I was led to wonder, have any doubts as to their soundness? Damp, in fact, and decay pervaded everything. A bit of timber which I touched crumbled to dust under my thumb.

He presently beckoned to me, and, with yet one halt and "Hark!" from him, we passed through the house to my chamber; where, left alone, I paced about, agitated with a vague anger; then tumbled to an agony of slumber.

In the far interior of the mansion even the bleared day of this land of bleakness never rose upon our gloom; but I was able to regulate my gettings-up by a clock which stood in my chamber; or I was called by Harfager, with whom in a short time I renewed more than all our former friendship. That I should say more is curious: but so it was: and this was proved by the fact that we grew to take, and to excuse, freedoms of speech and of manner which, as two persons of more than usual reserve, we had once never dreamed of permitting to ourselves in respect of each other. Once, for example, in our pacings of aimless haste down passages that vanished in shadow and length of perspective remoteness, he wrote that my step was very slow. I replied that it was just such a step as suited my then mood. He wrote: "You have developed a tendency to fret." I was very offended, and said: "Certainly, there are more fingers than one in the world which that ring will fit!"

Another day he was no less than rude to me for seeking to reveal to him the secret of the unhuman keenness of his hearing – and of mine! For I, too, to my dismay, began, as time passed, to catch hints of shouted sounds. The cause might be found, I asserted, in a fervour of the auditory nerve, which, if the cataract were absent, the roar of the ocean, and the row of the perpetual tempest round us, might by themselves be sufficient to bring about; his own ear-interior, I said, must be inflamed to an exquisite pitch of fever; and I named the disease to him as the 'Paracusis Wilisü'. When he frowned dissent, I, quite undeterred, proceeded to relate the case (that had occurred within my own experience) of a very deaf lady who could hear the drop of a pin in a railway-train[1]; and now he made me the reply: "Of ignorant people I am accustomed to consider the mere scientist the most ignorant!"

But I, for my part, regarded it as merely far-fetched that he should pretend to be in the dark as to the morbid state of his hearing! He himself, indeed, confessed to me his own, Aith's, and the lady Swertha's proneness to paroxysms of vertigo. I was startled! For I had myself shortly previously been roused out of sleep by feelings of reeling and nausea, and an assurance that the room furiously flew round with me. The impression passed away, and I attributed it, perhaps hastily, to some disturbance in the nerve-endings of 'the labyrinth', or inner ear. In Harfager, however, the conviction of whirling motions in the house, in the world, got to so horrible a degree of certainty, that its effects sometimes resembled those of lunacy or energumenal possession. Never, he said, was the sensation of giddiness altogether dead in him; seldom the sensation that he gazed with stretched-out arms over the brink of abysms which wooed his half-consenting foot. Once, as we walked, he was hurled as by unearthly powers to the ground, and there for an hour sprawled, bathed in sweat, with distraught bedazzlement and amaze in his stare, which watched the racing walls. He was constantly racked, moreover, with the consciousness of sounds so peculiar in their character, that I could account for them on no other supposition than that of a tinnitus infinitely sick. Through the roar there sometimes visited him, he told me, the lullaby of some bird, from the burden of whose song he had the consciousness that she derived from a very remote country, was of the whiteness of foam, and crested with a comb of mauve. Or else he knew of accumulated human tones, distant, yet articulate, busily contending in volubility, and in the end melting into a medley of musical movements. Or, anon, he was shocked by an infinite and imminent crashing, like the monstrous racket of the crackling of a cosmos of crockery round his ears. He told me, moreover, that he could frequently see, rather than hear, the particoloured wheels of a mazy sphere-music deep, deep within the black dark of the cataract's roar. These impressions, which I protested must be merely entotic had sometimes a pleasing effect upon him, and he would stand long to listen with a lifted hand to their seduction: others again inflamed him to a mad anger. I guessed that they were the cause of those "Harks!" that at intervals of about an hour did not fail to break from him. But in this I was wrong: and it was with a thrill of dismay that I soon came to know the truth.

For, as we were once passing by an iron door on the lower floor, he stopped, and for some minutes stood listening with a leer most keen and cunning. Presently the cry "Hark!" escaped him; and he then turned to me and wrote on the tablet: "Did you not hear?" I had heard nothing but the roar; and he howled into my ear in sounds now audible to me as an echo caught far off in dreams: "You shall see."

He took up the candlestick; produced from the pocket of his robe a key; unlocked the iron door; and we passed into a room very loftily domed in proportion to its area, and empty, save that a pair of steps lay against its wall, and that in the centre of its marble floor was a pool, like a Roman 'impluvium', only round like the room – a pool evidently profound in depth, full of a thick and inky fluid. I was very perturbed by its present aspect, for as the candle burned upon its surface, I observed that this had been quite recently disturbed, in a style for which the shivering of the house could not account, since ripples of slime were now rounding out from its middle to its brink. When I glanced at Harfager for explanation, he gave me a signal to wait; and now for about an hour, with his hands behind his back, paced the chamber; but then paused, and we two stood together by the pool's margin, gazing into the water. Suddenly his clutch tightened on my arm, and I saw, with a touch of horror, a tiny ball, probably of lead, but daubed blood-red by some chemical, fall from the roof, and sink into the middle of the pool. It hissed on contact with the water a whiff of mist.

"In the name of all that is sinister," I whispered, "what thing is this?"

Again he made me a busy and confident signal to wait, moved the ladder-steps toward the pool, handed me the taper. When I had mounted, holding high the light, I saw hanging out of the fogs in the dome a globe of old copper, lengthened into balloon-shape by a neck, at the end of which I could spy a tiny hole. Painted over the globe was barely visible in red print-letters:

HARFAGER-HOUS: 1389–188.

I was down quicker than I went up!

"But the meaning?" I panted.

"Did you see the writing?"

"Yes. The meaning?"

He wrote: "By comparing Gascoigne with Thrunster, I find that the house was built about 1389."

"But the last figures?"

"After the last 8," he replied, "there is another figure not quite obliterated by a tarnish-spot."

"What figure?" I asked.

"It cannot be read, but may be surmised. As the year 1888 is now all but passed, it can only be the figure 9."

"Oh, you are depraved in mind!" I cried, very irritated: "you assume – you state – in a manner which no mind trained to base its conclusions on facts can bear with patience."

"And you are irrational," he wrote. "You know, I suppose, the formula of Archimedes by which, the diameter of a globe being known, its volume also is known? Now, the diameter of that globe in the dome I know to be four and a half feet; and the diameter of the leaden balls about the third of an inch. Supposing, then, that 1389 was the year in which the globe was full of balls, you may readily calculate that not many fellows of the four million and odd which have since dropped at the rate of one an hour are now left within. The fall of the balls cannot persist another year. The figure 9 is therefore forced upon us."

"But you assume, Harfager!" I cried: "Oh, believe me, my friend, this is the very wantonness of wickedness! By what algebra of despair do you know that each ball represents one of the scions of your house, or that the last date was intended to correspond with the stoppage of the horologe. And, even if so, what is the significance of it? It can have no significance!"

"Do you want to madden me?" he shouted. Then furiously writing; "I swear that I know nothing of its significance! But it is not evident to you that the thing is a big hour-glass, intended to count the hours, not of a day, but of a cycle; and of a cycle of five hundred years?"

"But the whole contrivance," I passionately cried, "is a baleful phantasm of our brains! How is the fall of the balls regulated? Ah, my friend, you wander – your mind is debauched in this brawl of waters."

"I have not ascertained," he replied, "by what internal works, or clammy medium, or spiral coil, dependent probably for its action upon the liberation of the mansion, the balls are retarded in their fall: that was a matter well within the skill of the mediaeval mechanic, the inventor of the clock; but this at least is clear, that one element of their retardation is the smallness of the aperture through which they have to pass; that this element, by known laws of statics, will cease to operate when no more than three balls remain; and that, consequently, the last three will fall at almost the same instant."

"In Heaven's name!" I exclaimed, careless now what folly I poured out, "but your mother is dead, Harfager! Do you deny that there remain but you and the Lady Swertha?"

A glance of disdain was all the answer he then gave me as to this.

But he confessed to me a day later that the leaden drops were a constant sorrow to his ears; that from hour to hour his life was a keen waiting for their fall; that even from his brief sleeps he infallibly started awake at each descent; that in whatever region of the mansion he chanced to be, they found him out with a crashing loudness; and that each crash tweaked him with a twinge of anguish within the ear. I was therefore shocked at his declaration that these droppings had now become as the life of life to him; had acquired an entwining so close with the tone of his mind, that their ceasing might even mean for him the reeling of Reason: at which confession he sobbed, with his face buried, as he leant upon a column. When this paroxysm was past, I asked him if it was out of the question that he should once for all cast off the fascination of the horologe, and escape with me from the place. He wrote in mysterious reply: "A three-fold cord is not easily broken." I started, asking – "How three-fold?" He wrote with a bitter smile: "To be in love with pain – to pine after aching – is not that a wicked madness?" I stood astonished that he had unconsciously quoted Gascoigne! "A wicked madness!" "A lecherous anguish!" "You have seen my aunt's face," he proceeded; "your eyes were dim if you did not see in it an impious calm, the glee of a blasphemous patience, a grin behind her daring smile." He then spoke of a prospect at the terror of which his whole soul trembled, yet which sometimes laughed in his heart in the form of a hope. It was the prospect of any considerable increase in the volume of sound about his ears. At that, he said, the brain must totter. On the night of my arrival the noise of my boots, and, since then, my voice occasionally raised, had produced acute pain in him. To such an ear, I understood him to say, the luxury of torture involved in a large sound-increase around was an allurement from which no human virtue could turn: and when I said that I could not even conceive such an increase, much less the means by which it could be effected, he brought out from the archives of the mansion some annals kept by the heads of his family. From these it appeared that the tempests that ever lacerated the latitude of Rayba did not fail to give place, at intervals of some years, to one mammoth madness, one Samson among the merry men, and Sirius among the suns. At such periods the rains descended – and the floods came – even as in the first world-deluge; those rösts, or eddies, which ever encircled Rayba, spurning then the bands of lateral space, burst aloft into a whirl of water-spouts, to dance about the little land, upon which, converging, some of them discharged their waters: and the locks which flowed to the cataract thus redoubled their volume, and crashed with redoubled roar. Harfager said it was miraculous that for eighteen years no such grand event had transacted itself at Rayba.

"And what," I asked, "in addition to the dropping balls, and the prospect of an increase of sound, is the third strand of that 'three-fold cord' of which you have spoken."

For answer he led me to a circular hall which, he said, he had ascertained to be the centre of the circular mansion. It was a very large hall – so large as I think I never saw – so large that the amount of wall lighted at one time by the candle seemed nearly flat: and nearly the whole of its area, from floor to roof, was occupied by a column of brass, the space between the wall and column being only such as to admit of a stretched-out arm.

"This column," Harfager wrote, "goes up to the dome and passes beyond it; it goes down to the lower floor, and passes through that; it goes down thence to the brazen flooring of the vaults and passes through that into the bedrock. Under each floor it spreads out, helping to support the floor. What is the precise quality of the impression which I have made upon your mind by this description?"

"I do not know," I answered, turning from him: "ask me none of your enigmas, Harfager: I feel a giddiness…"

"But answer me," he said: "consider the strangeness of that brazen lowest floor, which I have discovered to be some six feet thick, and whose under-surface, I have reason to think, is somewhat above the bedrock; remember that the fabric is at no point fastened to the column; think of the chains which ray out from the outer wall, apparently anchoring the house to the ground. Tell me, what impression have I now made?"

"And is it for this you wait?" I cried. "Yet there may have been no malevolent intention! You jump at conclusions! Any fixed building in such a land and spot as this would at any time be liable to be broken up by some sovereign tempest! What if it was the intention of the builder that in such a case the chains should break, and the building, by yielding, be saved?"

"You have no lack of charity at least," he replied; and we then went back to the book we were reading together.

He had not wholly lost the old habit of study, although he could no longer get himself to sit to read; so with a volume (often tossed down) he would stamp about within the region of the lamplight; or I, unconscious of my voice, might read to him. By a whim of his mood the few books which now lay within the limits of his patience had all for their motive something of the picaresque, or the foppishly speculative: Quevedo's 'Tacaño'; or the system of Tycho Brahe; above all, George Hakewill's 'Power and Providence of God'. One day, however, as I read, he interrupted me with the sentence, apropos of nothing: "What I cannot understand is that you, a scientist, should believe that life ceases with the ceasing of breathing" – and from that moment the tone of our reading changed. For he led me to the crypts of the library in the lowest part of the building, and hour after hour, with a furore of triumph overwhelmed me with books proving the length of life after 'death'. What, he asked, was my opinion of Baron Verulam's account of the dead man who was heard to utter words of prayer? or of the bounding bowels of the dead convict? On my expressing unbelief, he seemed surprised, and reminded me of the writhing of dead cobras, of the long beating of a frog's heart after 'death'. "She is not dead," he quoted, "but sleepeth." The idea of Bacon and Paracelsus that the principle of life resides in a spirit or fluid was proof to him that such fluid could not, from its very nature, undergo any sudden annihilation, while the organs which it pervades remain. When I asked what limit he, then, set to the persistence of 'life' in the 'dead', he answered that when decay had so far advanced that the nerves could no longer be called nerves, or when the brain had been disconnected at the neck from the body, as by rats gnawing, then the king of terrors was king verily. With an indiscretion strange to me before my residence at Rayba, I now blurted out the question whether in all this he could be referring to his mother? For a while he stood thoughtful, then wrote: "Even if I had not had reason to believe that my own and Swertha's life in some way hung upon the final cessations of hers, I should still have taken precautions to ascertain the march of the destroyer on her frame: as it is, I shall not lack even the exactest information." He then explained that the rats which ran riot in the place of death would in time do their full work upon her; but would be unable to reach to the region of the throat without first gnawing their way through the three strings stretched across the holes of the bridges within the coffin, and thus, one by one, liberating the three morrisco-bells to tinklings.

The winter solstice had gone, another year began. I was sleeping a deep sleep by night when Harfager came into my chamber, and shook me. His face was ghastly in the taper's glare. A change within a short time had taken place upon him. He was hardly the same. He was like some poor wight into whose surprised eyes in the night have pried the eyes of Affright.

He said that he was aware of strainings and creakings, which gave him the feeling of being suspended in airy spaces by a thread which must break to his weight; and he begged me, for God's sake, to accompany him to the coffins. We passed together through the house, he craven, haggard, his gait now laggard, into the chamber of the dead, where he stole to and fro examining the shelves. Out of the footless coffin of the dowager trembling on its bench I saw a water-rat crawl; and as Harfager passed beneath one of the shortest of the shelves which bore one coffin, it suddenly dropped from a height to dust at his feet. He screamed the cry of a frightened creature; tottered to my support; and I bore him back to the upper parts of the palace.

He sat, with his face buried, in a corner of a small chamber, doddering, overtaken, as it were, with the extremity of age, no longer marking with his "Hark!" the fall of the leaden drops. To my remonstrances he responded only with the moan, "so soon!" Whenever I looked for him, I found him there, his manhood now collapsed in an ague. I do not think that during this time he slept.

On the second night, as I was approaching him, he sprang suddenly upright with the outcry: "The first bell is tinkling!"

And he had scarcely screamed it when, from some long way off, a faint wail, which at its origin must have been a fierce shriek, reached my now feverish ears. Harfager, for his part, clapped his palms to his ears, and dashed from his place, I following in hot chase through the black breadth of the mansion: till we came to a chamber containing a candelabrum, and arrased in faded red. On the floor in swoon lay the lady Swertha, her dark-grey hair in disarray wrapping her like an angry sea; tufts of it scattered, torn from the roots; and on her throat prints of strangling fingers. We bore her to her bed in an alcove; and, having discovered some tincture in a cabinet, I administered it between her fixed teeth. In her rapt countenance I saw that death was not; and, as I found something appalling in her aspect, shortly afterwards left her to Harfager.

When I next saw him his manner had undergone a kind of change which I can only describe as gruesome. It resembled the officious self-importance seen in a person of weak intellect who spurs himself with the thought, "to business! the time is short!" while his walk sickened me with a hint of ataxie locomotrice. When I asked him as to his aunt, as to the meaning of the marks of violence on her body, bending ear to his deep and unctuous tones, I could hear: "An attempt has been made upon her life by the skeleton, Aith."

He seemed not to share my astonishment at this thing! Nor could give me any clear answer as to his reason for retaining such a servant, or as to the origin of Aith's service. Aith, he told me, had been admitted into the palace during the period of his own absence in youth, and he knew little of him beyond the fact that he was extraordinarily strong. Whence he had come, or how, no person except the lady Swertha was aware: and she, it seems, feared, or at least persistently flinched from admitting him into the mystery. He added that, as a matter of fact, the lady, from the day of his coming back to Rayba, had with some object imposed upon herself a dumbness on all subjects, which he had never once known her to break through, except by an occasional note.

With an ataxic strenuousness, with the airs of a drunken man constraining himself to ordered action, Harfager now set himself to the doing of a host of trivial things: he collected chronicles and arranged them in order of date; he docketed or ticketed packets of documents; he insisted upon my assistance in turning the faces of paintings to the wall. He was, however, now constantly stopped by bursts of vertigo, six times in a single hour being hurled to the ground, while blood frequently guttered from his ears. He complained to me in a tone of piteous wail of the wooing of a silver piccolo that continually seduced him. As he bent, sweating, over his momentous nothings, his hands fluttered like aspen. I noted the movements of his whimpering lips, the rheum of his sunken eyes: sudden doting had come upon his youth.

On a day he threw it utterly off, and was young anew. He entered my room; roused me from dreams; I observed the lunacy of bliss in his eyes, heard his hiss in my ear:

"Up! The storm!"

Ah! I had known it – in the nightmare of the night. I felt it in the air of the room. It had come. I saw it lurid by the lamplight on the hell of Harfager's face.

A glee burst at once into birth within me, as I sprang from my couch, glancing at the clock: it was eight – in the morning. Harfager, with the naked stalk of some maniac prophet, had already taken himself away; and I started out after him. A deepening was clearly felt in the quivering of the edifice; anon for a second it stopped still, as if, breathlessly, to listen; its air was troubled with a vague gustiness. Occasionally there came to me as it were the noising of some far-off lamentation and voice in Ramah, but whether this was in my ear or the screaming of the gale I could not tell; or again I could hear one clear chord of an organ's vaunt. About noon I spied Harfager, lamp in hand, running along a corridor, with naked soles. As we met he looked at me, but hardly with recognition, and passed by; stopped, however, and ran back to howl into my ear the question: "Would you see?" He then beckoned before me, and I followed to a very small opening in the outer wall, closed with a slab of brass. As he lifted the latch, the slab dashed inward with instant impetuosity and tossed him a long way, while the breath of the tempest, braying through the brazen tube with a brutal bravura, caught and pinned me upon a corner of a wall, and all down the corridor a long crashing racket of crowds of pictures and couches followed. I nevertheless managed to push my way on the belly to the opening. Hence the sea should have been visible; but my senses were met by nothing but a vision of tumbled tenebrousness, and a general impression of the letter O. The sun of Rayba had gone out. In a moment of opportunity our two forces got the shutter shut again.

"Come!" – he had obtained a fresh glimmer, and beckoned before me – "let's go see how the dead fare in the great desolation": and we ran, but had hardly got to the middle of the stairway, when I was thrilled by the consciousness of some great shock, the bass of a dull thud, which nothing save the thumping to the floor of the whole lump of the coffins could have caused. I looked for Harfager, and for a moment only saw his heels skedaddling, panic-hounded, his ears stopped, his mouth round! Then, indeed, fear reached me – a tremor in the audacity of my heart, a thought that now at any rate I must desert him in his extremity, and work out my own salvation. Yet it was with hesitancy that I turned to search for him for the last farewell – a hesitancy which I felt to be not unselfish, but selfish, and unhealthy. I rambled through the night, seeking light, and having happened upon a lamp, proceeded to seek for Harfager. Several hours went by in this way, during which I could not doubt from the state of the air in the house that the violence about me was being wildly heightened. Sounds as of screams – unreal, like the shriekings of demons – now reached my ears. As the time of night came on, I began to detect in the greatly augmented baritone of the cataract a fresh character – a shrillness – the whistle of a rapture – a malice – the menace of a rabies blind and deaf. It must have been at about the hour of six that I found Harfager. He sat in an obscure room, with his brow bowed down, his hands on his knees, his face covered with hair, and with blood from the ears. The right sleeve of his robe had been rent away in some renewed attempt, I imagined, to manage a window; and the rather crushed arm hung lank from the shoulder. For some time I stood and eyed him mouthing his mumblings; but now that I had found him uttered nothing as to my departure. Presently he looked sharply up with the call "Hark!" – then with impatience, "Hark! Hark!" – then with a shout, "The second bell!" And again, in immediate sequence upon his shout, there sounded a wail, vague yet real, through the house. Harfager at the instant dropped reeling with giddiness; but I, snatching up a lamp, dashed out, shivering but eager. For some while the wild wailing went on (either actually, or by reflex action of my ear); and as I ran for the lady's apartment, I saw opposite to it the open door of an armoury, into which I passed, caught up a battle-axe, and was now about to dart in to her aid, when Aith, with a blazing eye, shied out of her chamber. I cast up my axe, and, shouting, dashed forward to down him: but by some chance the lamp fell from me, and before I knew anything more, the axe sprang from my grasp, and I was cast far backward by some most grim vigour. There was, however, enough light shining out of the chamber to show that the skeleton had darted into a door of the armoury, so I instantly slammed and locked the door near me by which I had procured the axe, and hurrying to the other, secured it, too. Aith was thus a prisoner. I then entered the lady's chamber. She lay over the bed in the alcove, and to my bent ear grossly croaked the ruckle of death. A glance at her mangled throat convincing me that her last moments were come, I settled her on the bed, curtained her within the loosened festoons of the hangings of black, and turned from the cursedness of her aspect. On an escritoire near I noticed a note, intended apparently for Harfager: "I mean to defy, and fly; not from fear, but for the delight of the defiance itself. Can you come?" Taking a flame from the candelabrum, I left her to her loneliness, and throes of her death.

I had passed some way backward when I was startled by a queer sound – a crash – resembling the crash of a tamboureen; and as I could hear it pretty clearly, and from a distance, this meant some prodigious energy. In two minutes it again broke out; and thenceforth at regular intervals – with an effect of pain upon me; and the conviction grew gradually within me that Aith had unhung two of the old brass shields from their pegs, and holding them by their handles, and dashing them viciously together, thus expressed the frenzy that had now overtaken him. When I found my way back to Harfager, very anguish was now stamping in him about the chamber; he shook his head like a tormented horse, brushing and barring from his hearing each crash of the brass shields. "Ah, when – when—" he hoarsely groaned into my ear, "will that ruckle cease in her throat? I will myself, I tell you – with my own hand – oh God…" Since the morning his auditory fever (as indeed my own also) appeared to have increased in steady proportion with the roaring and screeching chaos round; and the death-struggle in the lady's throat bitterly filled for him the intervals of the grisly cymbaling of Aith. He presently sent twinkling fingers into the air, and, with his arms cast out, darted into the darkness.

And again I sought him, and long again in vain. As the hours passed, and the day deepened toward its baleful midnight, the cry of the now redoubled cataract, mixed with the mass and majesty of the now climatic tempest, took on too intentional a shriek to be longer tolerable to any reason. My own mind escaped my sway, and went its way: for here in the hot-bed of fever I was fevered. I wandered from chamber to chamber, precipitate, dizzy on the upbuoyance of a joy. "As a man upon whom sleep seizes," so I had fallen. Even yet, as I passed near the region of the armoury, the rapturous shields of Aith did not fail to smash faintly upon my ear. Harfager I did not see, for he, too, was doubtless roaming a hurtling Ahasuerus round the world of the house. However, at about midnight, observing light shining from a door on the lower stage, I entered and saw him there – the chamber of the dropping horologe. He sat hugging himself on the ladder-steps, gazing at the gloomy pool. The final lights of the riot of the day seemed dying in his eyes; and he gave me no glance as I ran in. His hands, his bare arm, were all washed with new-shed blood; but of this, too, he looked unconscious; his mouth was hanging open to his pantings. As I eyed him, he suddenly leapt high, smiting his hands with the yell, "The last bell tinkling!" and ran out raving. He therefore did not see (though he may have understood by hearing) the thing which, with cowering awe, I now saw: for a ball slipped from the horologe with a hiss and mist of smoke into the pool; and while the clock once ticked another: and while the clock yet ticked, another! And the smoke of the first had not perfectly thinned, when the smoke of the third, mixing with it, floated toward the dome. Understanding that the sands of the mansion were run, I, too, throwing up my arm, rushed from the spot; but was suddenly stopped in my flight by the sense of some stupendous destiny emptying its vials upon the edifice; and was made aware by a crackling racket, like musketry, above, and the downpour of a world of waters, that some waterspout, in the waltz and whirl, had hurled its broken summit upon us, and burst through the dome. At that moment I beheld Harfager running toward me, his hands buried in his hair; and, as he raced past, I caught him, crying: "Harfager, save yourself! the very fountains, Harfager – by the grand God, man" – I hissed it into his inmost ear – "the very fountains of the Great Deep…!" He glared at me, and went on his way, while I, whisking myself into a room, closed the door. Here for some time with weak knees I waited; but the eagerness of my frenzy pressed me, and I again stepped out, to find the corridors everywhere thigh-deep with water; while rags of the storm, bragging through the hole in the dome, were now blustering about the house. My light was at once puffed out; but I was surprised by the presence of another light – most ghostly, gloomy, bluish – mild, yet wild – which now gloated everywhere through the house. I was standing in wonder at this when a gust of auguster passion galloped up the mansion; and, with it, I was made aware of the snap of something somewhere. There was a minute's infinite waiting – and then – quick – ever quicker – came the throb, snap, pop, in spacious succession, of the anchoring chains of the mansion before the hurried shoulder of the hurricane. And again a second of breathless stillness – and then – deliberately – its hour came – the house moved. My flesh worked like the flesh of worms which squirm. Slowly moved, and stopped – then there was a sweep – and a swirl – and a pause! then a swirl – and a sweep – and a pause! then steady labour on the brazen axis as the labourer tramps by the harrow; then a heightening of zest – then intensity – then the final light liveliness of flight. And now once again, as, staggering and plunging, I spun, the notion of escape for a moment came to me, but this time I shook an impious fist. "No, but, God, no, no," I gasped, "I will no more go from here: here let me waltzing pass in this carnival of the vortices, anarchy of the thunders!" – and I ran staggering. But memory gropes in a greyer gloaming as to all that followed. I struggled up the stairway, now flowing a river, and for a good while ran staggering and plunging, full of wild rantings, about, amid the downfall of roofs, and the ruins of walls. The air was thick with splashes, the whole roof now, save three rafters, having been snatched by the wind away; and in the blush of that bluish moonshine the tapestries were flapping and trailing wildly out after the flying place, like the streaming hair of some ranting fakir stung reeling by the tarantulas of distraction. At one point, where the largest of the porticoes protruded, the mansion began at every revolution to bump with grum shudderings against some obstruction: it bumped, and while the lips said one-two-three it three times bumped again. It was the maenadism of mass! Swift – still swifter – in an ague of flurry it raced, every portico a sail to the gale, racking its great frame to fragments. I, running by the door of a room littered with the ruins of a wall, saw through that livid moonlight Harfager sitting on a tomb – a drum by him, upon which, with a club in his bloody fist, he feebly, but persistently, beat. The speed of the leaning house had now attained the sleeping stage, that last pitch of the spinning-top; and now all at once Harfager dashed away the mat of hair which wrapped his face, sprang, stretched his arms, and began to spin – giddily – in the same direction as the mansion – nor less sleep-embathed, with lifted hair, with quivering cheeks… From such a sight I shied with retching; and staggering, plunging, presently found myself on the lower floor opposite a porch, where an outer door chancing to crash before me, the breath of the tempest smote freshly upon me. On this an impulse, partly of madness, more of sanity, spurred in my soul; and I spurted out of the doorway, to be whirled far out into the limbo without.

The river at once rushed me deep-drenched toward the sea – though even there, in that depth of whirlpool, a shrill din, like the splitting of a world, reached my ears. It had hardly passed when my body butted in its course upon one of the arches, cushioned with seaweed, of the not all demolished causeway. Nor had I utterly lost consciousness. A clutch freed my head from the drench; and in the end I heaved myself to the level of the summit. Hence to the ledge of rock by which I had come, the bridge being intact, I rowed myself on my face under the thumps of the wind, and under a rushing of rain, like a shimmering of silk through the air. Noticing the same wild shining about me which had blushed through the broken dome into the mansion, I glanced backward – and saw that the dwelling of the Harfagers was a memory of the past; then upward – and the whole north heaven, to the zenith, shone one ocean of variegated glories – the aurora borealis, which was being fairly brushed and flustered by the gale. At the augustness of which sight, I was touched to a gush of tears. And with them the dream broke! The infatuation passed! A palm seemed to skin back from my brain the films and media of delusion; and on my knees I threw my hands to heaven in thankfulness for the marvel of my rescue from all the temptation, the tribulation, and the breakage, of Rayba.

Footnotes for 'The House of Sounds'

1. Such cases are known to many medical men. The concussion on the deaf nerve is the cause of the acquired sensitiveness; nor is there any limit to that sensitiveness when the tumult is immensely augmented.

The Vaults of Yoh-Vombis

Clark Ashton Smith

IF THE DOCTORS are correct in their prognostication, I have only a few Martian hours of life remaining to me. In those hours I shall endeavor to relate, as a warning to others who might follow in our footsteps, the singular and frightful happenings that terminated our research among the ruins of Yoh-Vombis. If my story will only serve to prevent future explorations, the telling will not have been in vain.

There were eight of us, professional archaeologists with more or less terrene and interplanetary experience, who set forth with native guides from Ignarh, the commercial metropolis of Mars, to inspect that ancient, aeon-deserted city. Allan Octave, our official leader, held his primacy by knowing more about Martian archaeology than any other terrestrial on the planet; and others of the party, such as William Harper and Jonas Halgren, had been associated with him in many of his previous researches. I, Rodney Severn, was more of a newcomer, having spent but a few months on Mars; and the greater part of my own ultra-terrene delvings had been confined to Venus.

The nude, spongy-chested Aihais had spoken deterringly of vast deserts filled with ever-swirling sandstorms, through which we must pass to reach Yoh-Vombis; and in spite of our munificent offers of payment, it had been difficult to secure guides for the journey. Therefore we were surprised as well as pleased when we came to the ruins after seven hours of plodding across the flat, treeless, orange-yellow desolation to the southwest of Ignarh.

We beheld our destination, for the first time, in the setting of the small, remote sun. For a little, we thought that the domeless, three-angled towers and broken-down monoliths were those of some unlegended city, other than the one we sought. But the disposition of the ruins, which lay in a sort of arc for almost the entire extent of a low, gneissic, league-long elevation of bare, eroded stone, together with the type of architecture, soon convinced us that we had found our goal. No other ancient city on Mars had been laid out in that manner; and the strange, many-terraced buttresses, like the stairways of forgotten Anakim, were peculiar to the prehistoric race that built Yoh-Vombis.

I have seen the hoary, sky-confronting walls of Machu Picchu amid the desolate Andes; and the frozen, giant-builded battlements of Uogam on the glacial tundras of the nightward hemisphere of Venus. But these were as things of yesteryear compared to the walls upon which we gazed. The whole region was far from the life-giving canals beyond whose environs even the more noxious flora and fauna are seldom found; and we had seen no living thing since our departure from Ignarh. But here, in this place of petrified sterility, of eternal bareness and solitude, it seemed that life could never have been.

I think we all received the same impression as we stood staring in silence while the pale, sanies-like sunset fell on the dark and megalithic ruins. I remember gasping a little, in an air that seemed to have been touched by the irrespirable chill of death; and I heard the same sharp, laborious intake of breath from others of our party.

"That place is deader than an Egyptian morgue," observed Harper.

"Certainly it is far more ancient," Octave assented. "According to the most reliable legends, the Yorhis, who built Yoh-Vombis, were wiped out by the present ruling race at least forty thousand years ago."

"There's a story, isn't there," said Harper, "that the last remnant of the Yorhis was destroyed by some unknown agency – something too horrible and outré to be mentioned even in a myth?"

"Of course, I've heard that legend," agreed Octave. "Maybe we'll find evidence among the ruins to prove or disprove it. The Yorhis may have been cleaned out by some terrible epidemic, such as the Yashta pestilence, which was a kind of green mould that ate all the bones of the body, together with the teeth and nails. But we needn't be afraid of getting it, if there are any mummies in Yoh-Vombis – the bacteria will all be as dead as their victims, after so many cycles of planetary desiccation."

The sun had gone down with uncanny swiftness, as if it had disappeared through some sort of prestidigitation rather than the normal process of setting. We felt the instant chill of the blue-green twilight; and the ether above us was like a huge, transparent dome of sunless ice, shot with a million bleak sparklings that were the stars. We donned the coats and helmets of Martian fur, which must always be worn at night; and going on to westward of the walls, we established our camp in their lee, so that we might be sheltered a little from the *jaar*, that cruel desert wind that always blows from the east before dawn. Then, lighting the alcohol lamps that had been brought along for cooking purposes, we huddled around them while the evening meal was prepared and eaten.

Afterwards, for comfort rather than because of weariness, we retired early to our sleeping-bags; and the two Aihais, our guides, wrapped themselves in the cerement-like folds of *bassa*-cloth which are all the protection their leathery skins appear to require even in sub-zero temperatures.

Even in my thick, double-lined bag, I still felt the rigor of the night air; and I am sure it was this, rather than anything else, which kept me awake for a long while and rendered my eventual slumber somewhat restless and broken. At any rate, I was not troubled by even the least presentiment of alarm or danger; and I should have laughed at the idea that anything of peril could lurk in Yoh-Vombis, amid whose undreamable and stupefying antiquities the very phantoms of its dead must long since have faded into nothingness.

I must have drowsed again and again, with starts of semi-wakefulness. At last, in one of these, I knew vaguely that the small twin moons had risen and were making huge and far-flung shadows with the domeless towers; shadows that almost touched the glimmering, shrouded forms of my companions.

The whole scene was locked in a petrific stillness; and none of the sleepers stirred. Then, as my lids were about to close, I received an impression of movement in the frozen gloom; and it seemed to me that a portion of the foremost shadow had detached itself and was crawling toward Octave, who lay nearer to the ruins than we others.

Even through my heavy lethargy, I was disturbed by a warning of something unnatural and perhaps ominous. I started to sit up; and even as I moved, the shadowy object, whatever it was, drew back and became merged once more in the greater shadow. Its vanishment startled me into full wakefulness; and yet I could not be sure that I had actually seen the thing. In that brief, final glimpse, it had seemed like a roughly circular piece of cloth or leather, dark and crumpled, and twelve or fourteen inches in diameter, that ran along the ground with the doubling movement of an inchworm, causing it to fold and unfold in a startling manner as it went.

I did not go to sleep again for nearly an hour; and if it had not been for the extreme cold, I should doubtless have gotten up to investigate and make sure whether I had really beheld an object of such bizarre nature or had merely dreamt it. But more and more I began to convince myself that the thing was too unlikely and fantastical to have been anything but the figment of a dream. And at last I nodded off into light slumber.

The chill, demoniac sighing of the *jaar* across the jagged walls awoke me, and I saw that the faint moonlight had received the hueless accession of early dawn. We all arose, and prepared our breakfast with fingers that grew numb in spite of the spirit-lamps.

My queer visual experience during the night had taken on more than ever a phantasmagoric unreality; and I gave it no more than a passing thought and did not speak of it to the others. We were all eager to begin our explorations; and shortly after sunrise we started on a preliminary tour of examination.

Strangely, as it seemed, the two Martians refused to accompany us. Stolid and taciturn, they gave no explicit reason; but evidently nothing would induce them to enter Yoh-Vombis. Whether or not they were afraid of the ruins, we were unable to determine: their enigmatic faces, with the small oblique eyes and huge, flaring nostrils, betrayed neither fear nor any other emotion intelligible to man. In reply to our questions, they merely said that no Aihai had set foot among the ruins for ages. Apparently there was some mysterious taboo in connection with the place.

For equipment in that preliminary tour we took along only our electric torches and a crowbar. Our other tools, and some cartridges of high explosives, we left at our camp, to be used later if necessary, after we had surveyed the ground. One or two of us owned automatics; but these were also left behind; for it seemed absurd to imagine that any form of life would be encountered among the ruins.

Octave was visibly excited as we began our inspection, and maintained a running fire of exclamatory comment. The rest of us were subdued and silent: it was impossible to shake off the somber awe and wonder that fell upon us from those megalithic stones.

We went on for some distance among the triangular, terraced buildings, following the zigzag streets that conformed to this peculiar architecture. Most of the towers were more or less dilapidated; and everywhere we saw the deep erosion wrought by cycles of blowing wind and sand, which, in many cases, had worn into roundness the sharp angles of the mighty walls. We entered some of the towers, but found utter emptiness within. Whatever they had contained in the way of furnishings must long ago have crumbled into dust; and the dust had been blown away by the searching desert gales.

At length we came to the wall of a vast terrace, hewn from the plateau itself. On this terrace, the central buildings were grouped like a sort of acropolis. A flight of time-eaten steps, designed for longer limbs than those of men or even the gangling modern Martians, afforded access to the hewn summit.

Pausing, we decided to defer our investigation of the higher buildings, which, being more exposed than the others, were doubly ruinous and dilapidated, and in all likelihood would offer little for our trouble. Octave had begun to voice his disappointment over our failure to find anything in the nature of artifacts that would throw light on the history of Yoh-Vombis.

Then, a little to the right of the stairway, we perceived an entrance in the main wall, half-choked with ancient débris. Behind the heap of detritus, we found the beginning of a downward flight of steps. Darkness poured from the opening, musty with primordial stagnancies of decay; and we could see nothing below the first steps, which gave the appearance of being suspended over a black gulf.

Throwing his torch-beam into the abyss, Octave began to descend the stairs. His eager voice called us to follow.

At the bottom of the high, awkward steps, we found ourselves in a long and roomy vault, like a subterranean hallway. Its floor was deep with siftings of immemorial dust. The air was singularly heavy, as if the lees of an ancient atmosphere, less tenuous than that of Mars today, had settled down and remained in that stagnant darkness. It was harder to breathe than the outer air: it was filled with unknown effluvia; and the light dust arose before us at every step, diffusing a faintness of bygone corruption, like the dust of powdered mummies.

At the end of the vault, before a strait and lofty doorway, our torches revealed an immense shallow urn or pan, supported on short cube-shaped legs, and wrought from a dull, blackish-green material. In its bottom, we perceived a deposit of dark and cinder-like fragments, which gave off a slight but disagreeable pungence, like the phantom of some more powerful odor. Octave, bending over the rim, began to cough and sneeze as he inhaled it.

"That stuff, whatever it was, must have been a pretty powerful fumigant," he observed. "The people of Yoh-Vombis may have used it to disinfect the vaults."

The doorway beyond the shallow urn admitted us to a larger chamber, whose floor was comparatively free of dust. We found that the dark stone beneath our feet was marked off in multiform geometric patterns, traced with ochreous ore, amid which, as in Egyptian cartouches, hieroglyphics and highly formalized drawings were enclosed. We could make little from most of them; but the figures in many were doubtless designed to represent the Yorhis themselves. Like the Aihais, they were tall and angular, with great, bellows-like chests. The ears and nostrils, as far as we could judge, were not so huge and flaring as those of the modern Martians. All of these Yorhis were depicted as being nude; but in one of the cartouches, done in a far hastier style than the others, we perceived two figures whose high, conical craniums were wrapped in what seemed to be a sort of turban, which they were about to remove or adjust. The artist seemed to have laid a peculiar emphasis on the odd gesture with which the sinuous, four-jointed fingers were plucking at these head-dresses; and the whole posture was unexplainably contorted.

From the second vault, passages ramified in all directions, leading to a veritable warren of catacombs. Here, enormous pot-bellied urns of the same material as the fumigating-pan, but taller than a man's head and fitted with angular-handled stoppers, were ranged in solemn rows along the walls, leaving scant room for two of us to walk abreast. When we succeeded in removing one of the huge stoppers, we saw that the jar was filled to the rim with ashes and charred fragments of bone. Doubtless (as is still the Martian custom) the Yorhis had stored the cremated remains of whole families in single urns.

Even Octave became silent as we went on; and a sort of meditative awe seemed to replace his former excitement. We others, I think, were utterly weighed down to a man by the solid gloom of a concept-defying antiquity, into which it seemed that we were going further and further at every step.

The shadows fluttered before us like the monstrous and misshapen wings of phantom bats. There was nothing anywhere but the atom-like dust of ages, and the jars that held the ashes of a long-extinct people. But, clinging to the high roof in one of the further vaults, I saw a dark and corrugated patch of circular form, like a withered fungus. It was impossible to reach the thing; and we went on after peering at it with many futile conjectures. Oddly enough, I failed to remember at that moment the crumpled, shadowy object I had seen or dreamt of the night before.

I have no idea how far we had gone, when we came to the last vault; but it seemed that we had been wandering for ages in that forgotten underworld. The air was growing fouler and more irrespirable, with a thick, sodden quality, as if from a sediment of material rottenness; and we had about decided to turn back. Then, without warning, at the end of a long, urn-lined catacomb, we found ourselves confronted by a blank wall.

Here we came upon one of the strangest and most mystifying of our discoveries – a mummified and incredibly desiccated figure, standing erect against the wall. It was more than seven feet in height, of a brown, bituminous color, and was wholly nude except for a sort of black cowl that covered the upper head and drooped down at the side in wrinkled folds. From the size and general contour, it was plainly one of the ancient Yorhis – perhaps the sole member of this race whose body had remained intact.

We all felt an inexpressible thrill at the sheer age of this shrivelled thing, which, in the dry air of the vault, had endured through all the historic and geologic vicissitudes of the planet, to provide a visible link with lost cycles.

Then, as we peered closer with our torches, we saw why the mummy had maintained an upright position. At ankles, knees, waist, shoulders and neck it was shackled to the wall by heavy metal bands, so deeply eaten and embrowned with a sort of rust that we had failed to distinguish them at first sight in the shadow. The strange cowl on the head, when closelier studied, continued to baffle us, It was covered with a fine, mould-like pile, unclean and dusty as ancient cobwebs. Something about it, I knew not what, was abhorrent and revolting.

"By Jove! this is a real find!" ejaculated Octave, as he thrust his torch into the mummified face, where shadows moved like living things in the pit-deep hollows of the eyes and the huge triple nostrils and wide ears that flared upward beneath the cowl.

Still lifting the torch, he put out his free hand and touched the body very lightly. Tentative as the touch had been, the lower part of the barrel-like torso, the legs, the hands and forearms, all seemed to dissolve into powder, leaving the head and upper body and arms still hanging in their metal fetters. The progress of decay had been queerly unequal, for the remnant portions gave no sign of disintegration.

Octave cried out in dismay, and then began to cough and sneeze, as the cloud of brown powder, floating with an airy lightness, enveloped him. We others all stepped back to avoid the powder. Then, above the spreading cloud, I saw an unbelievable thing. The black cowl on the mummy's head began to curl and twitch upward at the corners, it writhed with a verminous motion, it fell from the withered cranium, seeming to enfold and unfold convulsively in mid-air as it fell. Then it dropped on the bare head of Octave who, in his disconcertment at the crumbling of the mummy, had remained standing close to the wall. At that instant, in a start of profound terror, I remembered the thing that had inched itself from the shadows of Yoh-Vombis in the light of the twin moons, and had drawn back like a figment of slumber at my first waking movement.

Cleaving closely as a tightened cloth, the thing enfolded Octave's hair and brow and eyes, and he shrieked wildly, with incoherent pleas for help, and tore with frantic fingers at the cowl, but failed to loosen it. Then his cries began to mount in a mad crescendo of agony, as if beneath some instrument of infernal torture; and he danced and capered blindly about the vault, eluding us with strange celerity as we all sprang forward in an effort to reach him and release him from his weird encumbrance. The whole happening was mysterious as a nightmare; but the thing that had fallen on his head was plainly some unclassified form of Martian life, which, contrary to all the known laws of science, had survived in those primordial catacombs. We must rescue him from its clutches if we could.

We tried to close in on the frenzied figure of our chief – which, in the far from roomy space between the last urns and the wall, should have been an easy matter. But, darting away, in a manner doubly incomprehensible because of his blindfolded condition, he circled about us and ran past, to disappear among the urns toward the outer labyrinth of intersecting catacombs.

"My God! What has happened to him?" cried Harper. "The man acts as if he were possessed."

There was obviously no time for a discussion of the enigma, and we all followed Octave as speedily as our astonishment would permit. We had lost sight of him in the darkness; and when we came to the first division of the vaults, we were doubtful as to which passage he had taken, till we heard a shrill scream, several times repeated, in a catacomb on the extreme left. There was a weird, unearthly quality in those screams, which may have been due to the long-stagnant air or the peculiar acoustics of the ramifying caverns. But somehow I could not imagine them as issuing from human lips – at least not from those of a living man. They seemed to contain a soulless, mechanical agony, as if they had been wrung from a devil-driven corpse.

Thrusting our torches before us into the lurching, fleeing shadows, we raced along between rows of mighty urns. The screaming had died away in sepulchral silence; but far off we heard the light and muffled thud of running feet. We followed in headlong pursuit; but, gasping painfully in the vitiated, miasmal air, we were soon compelled to slacken our pace without coming in sight of Octave. Very faintly, and further away than ever, like the tomb-swallowed steps of a phantom, we heard his vanishing footfalls. Then they ceased; and we heard nothing, except our own convulsive breathing, and the blood that throbbed in our temple-veins like steadily beaten drums of alarm.

We went on, dividing our party into three contingents when we came to a triple branching of the caverns. Harper and Halgren and I took the middle passage, and after we had gone on for an endless interval without finding any trace of Octave, and had threaded our way through recesses piled to the roof with colossal urns that must have held the ashes of a hundred generations, we came out in the huge chamber with the geometric floor-designs. Here, very shortly, we were joined by the other, who had likewise failed to locate our missing leader.

It would be useless to detail our renewed and hour-long search of the myriad vaults, many of which we had not hitherto explored. All were empty, as far as any sign of life was concerned. I remember passing once more through the vault in which I had seen the dark, rounded patch on the ceiling, and noting with a shudder that the patch was gone. It was a miracle that we did not lose ourselves in that underworld maze; but at last we came back again to the final catacomb, in which we had found the shackled mummy.

We heard a measured and recurrent clangor as we neared the place – a most alarming and mystifying sound under the circumstances. It was like the hammering of ghouls on some forgotten mausoleum. When we drew nearer, the beams of our torches revealed a sight that was no less unexplainable than unexpected. A human figure, with its back toward us and the head concealed by a swollen black object that had the size and form of a sofa cushion, was standing near the remains of the mummy and was striking at the wall with a pointed metal bar. How long Octave had been there, and where he had found the bar, we could not know. But the blank wall had crumbled away beneath his furious blows, leaving on the floor a pile of cement-like fragments; and a small, narrow door, of the same ambiguous material as the cinerary urns and the fumigating-pan, had been laid bare.

Amazed, uncertain, inexpressibly bewildered, we were all incapable of action or volition at that moment. The whole business was too fantastic and too horrifying, and it was plain that Octave had been overcome by some sort of madness. I, for one, felt the violent upsurge of sudden nausea when I had identified the loathsomely bloated thing that clung to Octave's head and drooped in obscene tumescence on his neck. I did not dare to surmise the causation of its bloating.

Before any of us could recover our faculties, Octave flung aside the metal bar and began to fumble for something in the wall. It must have been a hidden spring; though how he could have known its location or existence is beyond all legitimate conjecture. With a dull, hideous grating, the uncovered door swung inward, thick and ponderous as a mausoleum slab, leaving an aperture from which the nether midnight seemed to well like a flood of aeon-buried foulness. Somehow, at that instant, our electric torches flickered and grew dim; and we all breathed a suffocating fetor, like a draught from inner worlds of immemorial putrescence.

Octave had turned toward us now, and he stood in an idle posture before the open door, like one who has finished some ordained task. I was the first of our party to throw off the paralyzing spell; and pulling out a clasp-knife – the only semblance of a weapon which I carried – I ran over to him. He moved back, but not quickly enough to evade me, when I stabbed with the four-inch blade at the black, turgescent mass that enveloped his whole upper head and hung down upon his eyes.

What the thing was, I should prefer not to imagine – if it were possible to imagine. It was formless as a great slug, with neither head nor tail nor apparent organs – an unclean, puffy, leathery thing, covered with that fine, mould-like fur of which I have spoken. The knife tore into it as if through rotten parchment, making a long gash, and the horror appeared to collapse like a broken bladder. Out of it there gushed a sickening torrent of human blood, mingled with dark, filiated masses that may have been half-dissolved hair, and floating gelatinous lumps like molten bone, and shreds of a curdy white substance. At the same time Octave began to stagger, and went down at full length on the floor. Disturbed by his fall, the mummy-dust arose about him in a curling cloud, beneath which he lay mortally still.

Conquering my revulsion, and choking with the dust, I bent over him and tore the flaccid, oozing horror from his head. It came with unexpected ease, as if I had removed a limp rag, but I wish to God that I had let it remain. Beneath, there was no longer a human cranium, for all had been eaten away, even to the eyebrows, and the half-devoured brain was laid bare as I lifted the cowl-like object. I dropped the unnamable thing from fingers that had grown suddenly nerveless, and it turned over as it fell, revealing on the nether side many rows of pinkish suckers, arranged in circles about a pallid disk that was covered with nerve-like filaments, suggesting a sort of plexus.

My companions had pressed forward behind me; but, for an appreciable interval, no one spoke.

"How long do you suppose he has been dead?" It was Halgren who whispered the awful question, which we had all been asking ourselves. Apparently no one felt able or willing to answer it; and we could only stare in horrible, timeless fascination at Octave.

At length I made an effort to avert my gaze; and turning at random, I saw the remnants of the shackled mummy, and noted for the first time, with mechanical, unreal horror, the half-eaten condition of the withered head. From this, my gaze was diverted to the newly opened door at one side, without perceiving for a moment what had drawn my attention. Then, startled, I beheld beneath my torch, far down beyond the door, as if in some nether pit, a seething, multitudinous, worm-like movement of crawling shadows. They seemed to boil up in the darkness; and then, over the broad threshold of the vault, there poured the verminous vanguard of a countless army: things that were kindred to the monstrous diabolic leech I had torn from Octave's eaten head. Some were thin and flat, like writhing, doubling disks of cloth or leather, and others were more or less poddy, and crawled with gutted slowness. What they had found to feed on in the sealed, eternal midnight I do not know; and I pray that I never shall know.

I sprang back and away from them, electrified with terror, sick with loathing, and the black army inched itself unendingly with nightmare swiftness from the unsealed abyss, like the nauseous vomit of horror-sated hells. As it poured toward us, burying Octave's body from sight in a writhing wave, I saw a stir of life from the seemingly dead thing I had cast aside, and saw the loathly struggle which it made to right itself and join the others.

But neither I nor my companions could endure to look longer. We turned and ran between the mighty rows of urns, with the slithering mass of demon leeches close upon us, and scattered in blind panic when we came to the first division of the vaults. Heedless of each other or of anything but the urgency of flight, we plunged into the ramifying passages at random. Behind me, I heard someone stumble and go down, with a curse that mounted to an insane shrieking; but I knew that if I halted and went back, it would only be to invite the same baleful doom that had overtaken the hindmost of our party.

Still clutching the electric torch and my open clasp-knife, I ran along a minor passage which, I seemed to remember, would conduct with more or less directness upon the large outer vault with the painted floor. Here I found myself alone. The others had kept to the main catacombs; and I heard far off a muffled babel of mad cries, as if several of them had been seized by their pursuers.

It seemed that I must have been mistaken about the direction of the passage; for it turned and twisted in an unfamiliar manner, with many intersections, and I soon found that I was lost in the black labyrinth, where the dust had lain unstirred by living feet for inestimable generations. The cinerary warren had grown still once more; and I heard my own frenzied panting, loud and stertorous as that of a Titan in the dead silence.

Suddenly, as I went on, my torch disclosed a human figure coming toward me in the gloom. Before I could master my startlement, the figure had passed me with long, machine-like strides, as if returning to the inner vaults. I think it was Harper, since the height and build were about right for him; but I am not altogether sure, for the eyes and upper head were muffled by a dark, inflated cowl, and the pale lips were locked as if a silence of tetanic torture – or death. Whoever he was, he had dropped his torch; and he was running blindfolded, in utter darkness, beneath the impulsion of that unearthly vampirism, to seek the very fountainhead of the unloosed horror. I knew that he was beyond human help; and I did not even dream of trying to stop him.

Trembling violently, I resumed my flight, and was passed by two more of our party, stalking by with mechanical swiftness and sureness, and cowled with those Satanic leeches. The others must have returned by way of the main passages; for I did not meet them; and I was never to see them again.

The remainder of my flight is a blur of pandemonian terror. Once more, after thinking that I was near the outer cavern, I found myself astray, and fled through a ranged eternity of monstrous urns, in vaults that must have extended for an unknown distance beyond our explorations. It seemed that I had gone on for years; and my lungs were choking with the aeon-dead air, and my legs were ready to crumble beneath me, when I saw far-off a tiny point of blessed daylight. I ran toward it, with all the terrors of the alien darkness crowding behind me, and accursed shadows flittering before, and saw that the vault ended in a low, ruinous entrance, littered by rubble on which there fell an arc of thin sunshine.

It was another entrance than the one by which we had penetrated this lethal underworld. I was within a dozen feet of the opening when, without sound or other intimation, something dropped upon my head from the roof above, blinding me instantly and closing upon me like a tautened net. My brow and scalp, at the same time, were shot through with a million needle-like pangs – a manifold, ever-growing agony that seemed to pierce the very bone and converge from all sides upon my inmost brain.

The terror and suffering of that moment were worse than aught which the hells of earthly madness or delirium could ever contain. I felt the foul, vampiric clutch of an atrocious death – and of more than death.

I believe that I dropped the torch; but the fingers of my right hand had still retained the open knife. Instinctively – since I was hardly capable of conscious volition – I raised the knife and slashed blindly, again and again, many times, at the thing that had fastened its deadly folds upon me. The blade must have gone through and through the clinging monstrosity, to gash my own flesh in a score of places; but I did not feel the pain of those wounds in the million-throbbing torment that possessed me.

At last I saw light, and saw that a black strip, loosened from above my eyes and dripping with my own blood, was hanging down my cheek. It writhed a little, even as it hung, and I ripped it away, and ripped the other remnants of the thing, tatter by oozing, bloody tatter, from off my brow and head. Then I staggered toward the entrance; and the wan light turned to a far, receding, dancing flame before me as I lurched and fell outside the cavern – a flame that fled like the last star of creation above the yawning, sliding chaos and oblivion into which I descended...

I am told that my unconsciousness was of brief duration. I came to myself, with the cryptic faces of the two Martian guides bending over me. My head was full of lancinating pains, and half-remembered terrors closed upon my mind like the shadows of mustering harpies. I rolled over, and looked back toward the cavern-mouth, from which the Martians, after finding me, had seemingly dragged me for some little distance. The mouth was under the terraced angle of an outer building, and within sight of our camp.

I stared at the black opening with hideous fascination, and descried a shadowy stirring in the gloom – the writhing, verminous movement of things that pressed forward from the darkness but did not emerge into the light. Doubtless they could not endure the sun, those creatures of ultra-mundane night and cycle-sealed corruption.

It was then that the ultimate horror, the beginning madness, came upon me. Amid my crawling revulsion, my nausea-prompted desire to flee from that seething cavern-mouth, there rose an abhorrently conflicting impulse to return; to thread my backward way through all the catacombs, as the others had done; to go down where never men save they, the inconceivably doomed and accursed, had ever gone; to seek beneath that damnable compulsion a nether world that human thought can never picture. There was a black light, a soundless calling, in the vaults of my brain: the implanted summons of the Thing, like a permeating and sorcerous poison. It lured me to the subterranean door that was walled up by the dying people of Yoh-Vombis, to immure those hellish and immortal leeches, those dark parasites that engraft their own abominable life on the half-eaten brains of the dead. It called me to the depths beyond, where dwell the noisome, necromantic Ones, of whom the leeches, with all their powers of vampirism and diabolism, are but the merest minions...

It was only the two Aihais who prevented me from going back. I struggled, I fought them insanely as they strove to retard me with their spongy arms; but I must have been pretty thoroughly exhausted from all the superhuman adventures of the day; and I went down once more, after a little, into fathomless nothingness, from which I floated out at long intervals, to realize that I was being carried across the desert toward Ignarh.

Well, that is all my story. I have tried to tell it fully and coherently, at a cost that would be unimaginable to the sane...to tell it before the madness falls upon me again, as it will very soon – as it is doing now... Yes, I have told my story...and you have written it all out, haven't you? Now I must go back to Yoh-Vombis – back across the desert and down through all the catacombs to the vaster vaults beneath. Something is in my brain, that commands me and will direct me...I tell you, I must go...

Postscript

As an interne in the terrestrial hospital at Ignarh, I had charge of the singular case of Rodney Severn, the one surviving member of the Octave Expedition to Yoh-Vombis, and took down the above story from his dictation. Severn had been brought to the hospital by the Martian guides of the Expedition. He was suffering from a horribly lacerated and inflamed condition of the scalp and brow, and was wildly delirious part of the time and had to be held down in his bed during recurrent seizures of a mania whose violence was doubly inexplicable in view of his extreme debility.

The lacerations, as will have been learned from the story, were mainly self-inflicted. They were mingled with numerous small round wounds, easily distinguished from the knife-slashes, and arranged in regular circles, through which an unknown poison had been injected into Severn's scalp. The causation of these wounds was difficult to explain; unless one were to believe that Severn's story was true, and was no mere figment of his illness. Speaking for myself, in the light of what afterwards occurred, I feel that I have no other recourse than to believe it. There are strange things on the red planet; and I can only second the wish that was expressed by the doomed archaeologist in regard to future explorations.

The night after he had finished telling me his story, while another doctor than myself was supposedly on duty, Severn managed to escape from the hospital, doubtless in one of the strange seizures at which I have hinted: a most astonishing thing, for he had seemed weaker than ever after the long strain of his terrible narrative, and his demise had been hourly expected. More astonishing still, his bare footsteps were found in the desert, going toward Yoh-Vombis, till they vanished in the path of a light sandstorm; but no trace of Severn himself has yet been discovered.

While the Black Stars Burn

Lucy A. Snyder

CAROLINE tucked an unruly strand of coarse brown hair up under her pink knit cap, shrugged the strap of her black violin case back into place over her shoulder, and hurried up the music building stairs. Her skin felt both uncomfortably greasy and itched dryly under her heavy winter clothes; it had been seven days since the water heater broke in her tiny efficiency and the landlord wasn't answering his phone. Quick, chilly rag-baths were all she could stand, and she felt so self-conscious about the state of her hair that she kept it hidden under a hat whenever possible. She hoped that her violin professor Dr. Harroe wouldn't make her take her cap off.

Her foot slipped on a spot of dried salt on the stairs and she grabbed the chilly brass banister with her left hand to keep from pitching forward. The sharp, cold jolt made the puckered scar in her palm sharply ache, and the old memory returned fast and unbidden:

"Why aren't you practicing as I told you to?"

Her father scowled down at her. He was still in his orchestra conducting clothes: a gray blazer and black turtleneck. His fingers clenched a tumbler of Scotch over ice.

"M-my hand started to hurt." She shrank back against the hallway wall, hoping that she hadn't sounded whiny, hoping her explanation would suffice and he'd just send her to bed.

The smell of alcohol and sweat fogged the air around him, and that meant almost anything could happen. He wasn't always cruel. Not even usually. But talking to him when he'd been drinking was like putting a penny in a machine that sometimes dispensed glossy gumballs but other times a dozen stinging arachnids would swarm from the chute instead. And there was no way to know which she'd get, sweets or scorpions.

"Hurt?" he thundered down at her. "Nonsense! I'll show you what hurts!"

He grabbed her arm and dragged her to the fireplace in the music room. She tried to pull away, pleading, promising to practice all night if he wanted her to. But he was completely impassive as he drew a long dark poker from the rack and shoved it into the hottest part of the fire. He frowned down at the iron as the flames licked the shaft, seemingly deaf to her frantic mantra of *Please, no, Papa, I'll be good I swear please*.

The iron heated quickly, and in a series of motions as artful as any he'd performed on the orchestral podium he pulled it from the fire with one hand, squeezed her forearm hard to force her fingers open with the other, and jabbed the glowing red tip of the poker into her exposed palm.

The pain was astonishing. A part of her knew she was shrieking and had fallen to her knees on the fine Persian carpet, but the rest of her felt as though she'd been hurled through space and time toward the roaring hearts of a thousand black stars, cosmic furnaces that would consume not just her flesh and bone but her very soul. They would destroy her so completely that no one would remember that she had ever lived. The stars swirled around her, judging her, and she knew they found her lacking. She was too small, unripe, and they cast her back toward Earth. It was the first time and last time she'd ever been glad to be a disappointment in the eyes of the universe.

Tears blurred her vision and through them her father looked strange, distorted. In that instant she was sure that she knelt at the feet of a monstrous stranger who was wearing her father's pallid face as a mask.

"Now, that hurts I expect," the stranger observed cheerfully as her flesh sizzled beneath the red iron. "And so I don't expect I shall hear you whining about practice again, will I? Now, stop your little dog howling this instant or I'll burn the other one, too!"

She willed herself to bite back her screams, and he finally let her go just as she passed out from the agony.

When she woke up on the couch, she discovered that her father had fetched some snow from the porch and pressed a grapefruit-sized ball of it into her palm to numb her burn. Icy water dripped down her wrist and soaked her sweater sleeve. The air was filled with the odor of burned meat. Hers. It made her feel even sicker, and for the rest of her life the smell of grilling steaks and chops would make her want to vomit.

Her father gazed down at her, sad and sober.

"I would never hurt you, you understand?" He gently brushed the hair out of her face. "If anyone has hurt you in this world, it was not I."

He bundled her into the back of his Cadillac and took her to see a physician friend of his. Caroline remembered sitting in a chair in the hallway with a handkerchief full of ice in her hand, weeping quietly from the pain while the two men spoke behind a closed door.

"Will her playing be affected?" her father asked.

"Christ, Dunric!" The physician sounded horrified. "Is that your only concern for your own daughter?"

"Of course not!" her father huffed. "Nonetheless, it *is* a concern. So, if you would be so kind as to offer your professional opinion on the matter?"

"She's got a third degree burn; her palm is roasted through like a lamb fillet. I can't see how she could have held on to a live coal so long of her own accord. Are you sure no one else could have been involved? Perhaps a resentful servant?"

"Quite sure," he replied. "My daughter has some…mental peculiarities she regrettably inherited from her mother. You know how unstable sopranos are! Her mother often had a kind of petit mal seizure; I believe some pyromania compelled the girl to take hold of the coal and then a fit prevented her from dropping it as a sensible child would."

"That is unfortunate." The physician sounded unconvinced, and for a brief moment hope swelled in Caroline's heart: perhaps he would challenge her father, investigate further, discover the truth. And then perhaps she'd be sent to live with her mother's people in Boston. She'd only met them once – they were bankers or shoemakers or something else rather dull but they seemed decent enough.

But it was not to be. The physician continued: "Her tendons and ligaments are almost certainly affected. She may need surgery to regain full mobility in her fingers, and I fear that her hand may be permanently drawn due to scarring."

"Well, she only needs to curl it 'round the neck of her instrument, after all."

It took two surgeries to repair the tendons in her hand, and all her father's colleagues marveled at how brave and determined she was in her physical therapy and practice sessions afterward. Her father glowed at the praises they heaped on her, and while he never said as much, something in his smile told her that, should she cease to be so pleasingly dedicated to the musical arts, there were things in his world worse than hot metal.

Caroline traced the lines of her scar with her thumb. The doctor's knife had given it a strange, symbolic look. Some people claimed it resembled a Chinese or Arabic character, although nobody could say which one.

She flexed her hand and shook her head to try to banish the memories. There was no point in dwelling on any of it. Her father was long gone. Five years after he burned her, he'd flown into a rage at a negative review in the newspaper. He drove off in his Alfa Romeo with a bottle of Glenfiddich. Caroline suspected he'd gone to see a ballerina in the next city who enjoyed being tied up and tormented. But he never arrived. He lost control of his car in the foggy hills and his car overturned in a drainage ditch that was hidden from the road. Pinned, he lived for three days while hungry rats gnawed away the exposed flesh of his face, eyes and tongue.

At his funeral, she'd briefly considered quitting music just to spite his memory…but if she refused to be the Maestro's daughter, what was she? She knew nothing of gymnastics or any other sports, nor was she an exceptional student or a skilled painter. Her crabbed hand was nimble on a fingerboard but useful for little else. Worst of all, she knew – since she'd been repeatedly told so – that she was quite plain, good as a violinist but unremarkable as a woman. Her music was the only conceivable reason anyone would welcome her to a wedding. A thousand creditors had picked her father's estate as clean as the rodents had stripped his skull; if she abandoned the violin, what would she have left?

"Caroline, is that you?" Professor Harroe called after she knocked on the door to his office.

"Yes, sir."

"Do come in! I have a bit of a surprise for you today."

She suddenly felt apprehensive, but made herself smile at the professor as she opened the door and took her accustomed seat in the chair in front of his desk, which was stacked high with music theory papers, scores, and books. "What is it?"

He leaned back in his battered wooden swivel chair behind his desk and smiled at her in return. Her anxiety tightened; Harroe had been her music tutor since she was a teenager, and he almost *never* smiled, not at his colleagues' jokes nor at beautiful women nor at lovely music. She searched his face, trying to decipher his expression. He looked practically giddy, she finally decided, and it was a bit unsettling.

"Did you know that your father was working on a series of violin sonatas when he died?"

Her skin itched beneath her sweater. She rubbed at the scar again. "No, I did not."

"He was writing them for you, for when your playing would be mature enough to handle them. He told me he intended them to be a surprise for your twenty-first birthday. I think he realized his dalliance with drink might lead to disaster – as indeed it sadly did – so he arranged for his lawyer to send me the sonatas along with a formal request that I complete them in secret.

"I regret that I am not half the composer he was, but I am proud to say I have done as he asked. Six months late for your twenty-first, and for that I apologize, but at last his music is ready for you."

"I…oh my. I really don't know what to say. That was very…kind of you."

"I regret that kindness had nothing to do with it; as a composer I could not pass up the opportunity to co-author a work with the good Maestro. It was an extraordinary challenge, one that I am most pleased I was able to meet. I had to consult with…certain experts to complete the work, and one is here today, ready to listen to you perform the first sonata. If you do well – and I am sure that you will! – I believe that he is prepared to offer you a musical patronage that will ensure that you're taken care of for the rest of your life."

Caroline felt simultaneously numb with surprise and overwhelmed by dread. Was this truly an opportunity to escape her slide into poverty? Few students in her position ever saw salvation arriving before they'd even graduated. She *had* to rise to the occasion. But knowing her father was behind it all made her want nothing more than to go back to her cramped, drafty apartment and hide under the covers.

Her lips moved for a moment before she could get any words out. "That's amazing, but I couldn't possibly perform a piece I haven't even seen –"

"Nonsense!" His tone left her no room for demurral or negotiation. "You are a fine sight-reader, and after all this music is made for you. You'll be splendid."

* * *

Feeling supremely self-conscious about her dowdy thriftstore clothes and the unfashionable knit cap over her unwashed hair, Caroline took a deep breath, got a better grip on her violin case, lifted her chin, and strode out onto the small, brightly-lit recital stage. Her footsteps echoed hollowly off the curved walls. The theatre was small, just thirty seats, and she could sense rather than clearly see someone sitting in the back row on the left side. Normally having just one listener would bolster her confidence, but today, the emptiness of the room seemed eerie. She bowed crisply toward the dark figure, and then took her seat in a spotlighted wooden folding chair. The music stand held a hand-written musical booklet made from old-fashioned parchment. Her eyes scanned the cover sheet:

Into the Hands of the Living God
An Etude in G Minor for Violin
Composed by Dunric Cage-Satin with Dr. Alexander Harroe

Caroline frowned at the title. Was this some sort of religious music? As far as she knew, her father had been an ardent atheist his entire life. Ah well. There was nothing to do but struggle through as best she could. At worst she'd perform miserably, lose her mysterious patron, and be exactly as penniless as she'd been when she woke up that morning. She opened her violin case, pulled her instrument and bow from the padded blue velvet cutouts, carefully ran her rosin puck across the horsehair, flipped the cover page over to expose the unfamiliar music, and prepared to play.

The notes bore a cold, complex intelligence, and the tonality reminded her a little of Benjamin Britten. But there was something else here, something she'd neither heard nor played before, but nothing bound in stanzas was beyond the capacity of her instrument or her skills. She gave herself over to craft and educated reflex and the stark black notes transubstantiated into soaring music as nerves drove muscle, keratin mastered steel, and reverberation shook maple and spruce.

The stage fell away, and she found herself standing upon a high, barren cliff above a huge lake with driving waves. The air had an unhealthy taint to it, and in the sky there hung a trio of strange, misshapen moons, and opposite the setting twin suns three black stars rose, their bright coronas gleaming through the streaked clouds.

When the dark starlight touched her palm, her scar exploded, a nova made flesh. She fell to her knees on the lichen-covered rocks, unable to even take a breath to scream as the old lines glowed with a transcendent darkness, hot as any stellar cataclysm.

She heard footsteps and the rustling of robes, and through her tears she saw a regal iron boot beneath an ochre hem embroidered with the tiny white bones of birds and mice.

"You'll do," the figure said in a voice that made her want to drive spikes into her own brain. "Yes, you'll do."

She felt the terrible lord touch her head, and it was like being impaled on a sword, and suddenly she was falling—

—Caroline gasped and the bow slipped and screeched across her strings. Blinking in fear and confusion, it took her a half second to realize she was still onstage, still performing...or she had been until her mistake.

"I'm – I'm so, so sorry, I don't know what happened," she stammered, looking to her lone audience member in the back of the theatre. But all the seats were empty.

"It's quite all right." Professor Harroe hurried onstage from the wings, beaming. "You did wonderfully, just wonderfully."

"I...I did?" She blinked at him in disbelief. "But...I messed up, didn't I?"

"Oh, a mere sight-reading error...I'm sure you'll play straight through to the end next time! *And.* Your new benefactor has requested that you perform tomorrow evening at the St. Barnabus Church on Fifth Street. 6 p.m. sharp; don't be late!"

"Oh. Yes. Okay." She set her violin down on her lap, and the pain in her hand made her look at her palm. Her scar had split open during the performance, and her sleeve was wet with her own blood.

* * *

When Caroline tried to sleep on her narrow bed, she fell almost immediately into a suite of nightmares. She was onstage again, and the notes of her father's sonata turned to tiny hungry spiders that swarmed over her arms and chewed through her eyes and into her brain. Predatory black stars wheeled around her as she tumbled helplessly through airless, frigid outer space. And then she was back in the strange land with the twin suns, but now she was a tiny mouse pinned to a flat rock, and a masked man in yellow robes told her how he would flay her alive and take her spine.

She awoke sweating and weeping at 3 a.m., and in a moment of perfect clarity, she realized that she wanted no part of whatever was happening at St. Barnabus in fifteen hours. There was not enough money in the world. She quickly dressed in her dowdy second-hand pants and sweater, threw a few belongings into an overnight bag and grabbed her violin case. The Greyhound station was just a mile walk from her apartment building, and there would be a bus going somewhere far away. Maybe she could go to Boston, find her mother's people and learn to make shoes or whatever it was that they did. Shoes were good. People needed shoes.

But when she reached the pitchy street and started striding toward the station, she realized that the city was darker than usual. Tall buildings whose penthouses normally glowed with habitation were entirely black. She scanned the sky: no stars or moon, nothing but a seeming void.

And then, she saw something like a tattered black handkerchief flutter onto a nearby tall streetlamp, blotting it out. She stood very still for a moment, then slowly turned, beholding the uncanny night. Tattered shadows flapped all around. She started running, the violin case banging against her hip. The tatters moved faster, swarming around her on all sides. Soon she was sprinting headlong down the street, across the bridge...

...And realized the other side of the bridge was lost in the ragged blackness. No trace of light; it was as if that part of the world had ceased to exist, had been devoured by one of the stars from her nightmares.

She looked behind her. More utter darkness. The city was blotted out.

"I won't do it," she said, edging toward the bridge railing. She could hear the river rushing below. "I *won't.*"

The jagged darkness rapidly ate the bridge, surging toward her, and so she unslung her violin case and hurled her instrument over the edge into the murky water. The darkness came at her even faster, and she crouched down, covering her head with her arms—

—And found herself sitting in a metal folding chair in the nave of a strange church. In her hands was her old violin, the one she'd played as a child. Her father's sonata rested on the music stand before her, the notes black as the predatory stars.

"I won't," she whispered again, but she no longer ruled her own flesh. Her hands lifted her instrument to her shoulder and expertly drew the bow across the strings. The scabbed sign in her palm split open again, ruby blood spilling down her wrist, and she could see the marks starting to shine darkly as they had in the dream. Something planted in her long ago was seeking a way out.

Caroline found her eyes were still under her control, so she looked away from the music, looked out the window, hoping that blinding herself to the notes would stop the performance. But her hands and arms played on, her body swaying to keep time.

And there through the window she saw the glow of buildings on fire, and in the sky she saw a burning version of the symbol in her palm, and the air was rending, space and time separating, and as the firmament tore apart at the seams she could see the twin suns and black stars moving in from the world of her nightmares.

And she wanted to weep, but her body played on.

And the people in the city cried out in fear and madness, and still it played on.

And the winds from Carcosa blew the fires of apocalypse across the land, and still it played on.

The Moonstone Mass

Harriet Prescott Spofford

THERE WAS a certain weakness possessed by my ancestors, though in nowise peculiar to them, and of which, in common with other more or less undesirable traits, I have come into the inheritance.

It was the fear of dying in poverty. That, too, in the face of a goodly share of pelf stored in stocks, and lands, and copper-bottomed clippers, or what stood for copper-bottomed clippers, or rather sailed for them, in the clumsy commerce of their times.

There was one old fellow in particular – his portrait is hanging over the hall stove today, leaning forward, somewhat blistered by the profuse heat and wasted fuel there, and as if as long as such an outrageous expenditure of caloric was going on he meant to have the full benefit of it – who is said to have frequently shed tears over the probable price of his dinner, and on the next day to have sent home a silver dish to eat it from at a hundred times the cost. I find the inconsistencies of this individual constantly cropping out in myself; and although I could by no possibility be called a niggard, yet I confess that even now my prodigalities make me shiver.

Some years ago I was the proprietor of the old family estate, unencumbered by anything except timber, that is worth its weight in gold yet, as you might say; alone in the world, save for an unloved relative; and with a sufficiently comfortable income, as I have since discovered, to meet all reasonable wants. I had, moreover, promised me in marriage the hand of a woman without a peer, and which, I believe now, might have been mine on any day when I saw fit to claim it.

That I loved Eleanor tenderly and truly you cannot doubt; that I desired to bring her home, to see her flitting here and there in my dark old house, illuminating it with her youth and beauty, sitting at the head of my table that sparkled with its gold and silver heir-looms, making my days and nights like one delightful dream, was just as true.

And yet I hesitated. I looked over my bank-book – I cast up my accounts. I have enough for one, I said; I am not sure that it is enough for two. Eleanor, daintily nurtured, requires as dainty care for all time to come; moreover, it is not two alone to be considered, for should children come, there is their education, their maintenance, their future provision and portion to be found. All this would impoverish us, and unless we ended by becoming mere dependents, we had, to my excited vision, only the cold charity of the world and the work-house to which to look forward. I do not believe that Eleanor thought me right in so much of the matter as I saw fit to explain, but in maiden pride her lips perforce were sealed. She laughed though, when I confessed my work-house fear, and said that for her part she was thankful there was such a refuge at all, standing as it did on its knoll in the midst of green fields, and shaded by broad-limbed oaks – she had always envied the old women sitting there by their evening fireside, and mumbling over their small affairs to one another. But all her words seemed merely idle badinage – so I delayed. I said – when this ship sails in, when that dividend is declared, when I see how this speculation turns out – the days were long that added up the count of years, the nights were dreary; but I believed that I was actuated by principle, and took pride to myself for my strength and self-denial.

Moreover, old Paul, my great-uncle on my mother's side, and the millionaire of the family, was a bitter misogynist, and regarded women and marriage and household cares as the three remediless mistakes of an overruling Providence. He knew of my engagement to Eleanor, but so long as it remained in that stage he had nothing to say. Let me once marry, and my share of his million would be best represented by a cipher. However, he was not a man to adore, and he could not live forever.

Still, with all my own effort, I amassed wealth but slowly, according to my standard; my various ventures had various luck; and one day my old Uncle Paul, always intensely interested in the subject, both scientifically and from a commercial point of view, too old and feeble to go himself, but fain to send a proxy, and desirous of money in the family, made me an offer of that portion of his wealth on my return which would be mine on his demise, funded safely subject to my order, provided I made one of those who sought the discovery of the Northwest Passage.

I went to town, canvassed the matter with the experts – I had always an adventurous streak, as old Paul well knew – and having given many hours to the pursuit of the smaller sciences, had a turn for danger and discovery as well. And when the *Albatross* sailed – in spite of Eleanor's shivering remonstrance and prayers and tears, in spite of the grave looks of my friends – I was one of those that clustered on her deck, prepared for either fate. They – my companions – it is true, were led by nobler lights; but as for me, it was much as I told Eleanor – my affairs were so regulated that they would go on uninterruptedly in my absence; I should be no worse off for going, and if I returned, letting alone the renown of the thing, my Uncle Paul's donation was to be appropriated; everything then was assured, and we stood possessed of lucky lives. If I had any keen or eager desire of search, any purpose to aid the growth of the world or to penetrate the secrets of its formation, as indeed I think I must have had, I did not at that time know anything about it. But I was to learn that death and stillness have no kingdom on this globe, and that even in the extremest bitterness of cold and ice perpetual interchange and motion is taking place. So we went, all sails set on favorable winds, bounding over blue sea, skirting frowning coasts, and ever pushing our way up into the dark mystery of the North.

I shall not delay here to tell of Danish posts and the hospitality of summer settlements in their long afternoon of arctic daylight; nor will I weary you with any description of the succulence of the radishes that grew under the panes of glass in the Governor's scrap of moss and soil, scarcely of more size than a lady's parlor fernery, and which seemed to our dry mouths full of all the earth's cool juices – but advance, as we ourselves hastened to do, while that chill and crystalline sun shone, up into the ice-cased dens and caverns of the Pole. By the time that the long, blue twilight fell, when the rough and rasping cold sheathed all the atmosphere, and the great stars pricked themselves out on the heavens like spears' points, the *Albatross* was hauled up for winter-quarters, banked and boarded, heaved high on fields of ice; and all her inmates, during the wintry dark, led the life that prepared them for further exploits in higher latitudes the coming year, learning the dialects of the Esquimaux, the tricks of the seal and walrus, making long explorations with the dogs and Glipnu, their master, breaking ourselves in for business that had no play about it.

Then, at last, the August suns set us free again; inlets of tumultuous water traversed the great ice-floes; the *Albatross*, re-fitted, ruffled all her plumage and spread her wings once more for the North – for the secret that sat there domineering all its substance.

It was a year since we had heard from home; but who staid to think of that while our keel spurned into foam the sheets of steely seas, and day by day brought us nearer to the hidden things we sought? For myself I confess that, now so close to the end as it seemed, curiosity and research absorbed every other faculty; Eleanor might be mouldering back to the parent earth – I could not stay to meditate on such a possibility; my Uncle Paul's donation might enrich itself with gold-dust instead of the gathered dust of idle days – it was nothing to me. I had but one thought, one ambition, one desire in those days – the discovery of the clear seas and open passage. I endured all our hardships as if they had been luxuries: I made light of scurvy, banqueted off train-oil, and met that cold for which there is no language framed, and which might be a new element; or which, rather, had seemed in that long night like the vast void of ether beyond the uttermost star, where was neither air nor light nor heat, but only bitter negation and emptiness. I was hardly conscious of my body; I was only a concentrated search in myself.

The recent explorers had announced here, in the neighborhood of where our third summer at last found us, the existence of an immense space of clear water. One even declared that he had seen it.

My Uncle Paul had pronounced the declaration false, and the sight an impossibility. The North he believed to be the breeder of icebergs, an ever-welling fountain of cold; the great glaciers there forever form, forever fall; the ice-packs line the gorges from year to year unchanging; peaks of volcanic rock drop their frozen mantles like a scale only to display the fresher one beneath. The whole region, said he, is Plutonic, blasted by a primordial convulsion of the great forces of creation; and though it may be a few miles nearer to the central fires of the earth, allowing that there are such things, yet that would not in itself detract from the frigid power of its sunless solitudes, the more especially when it is remembered that the spinning of the earth, while in its first plastic material, which gave it greater circumference and thinness of shell at its equator, must have thickened the shell correspondingly at the poles; and the character of all the waste and wilderness there only signifies the impenetrable wall between its surface and centre, through which wall no heat could enter or escape. The great rivers, like the White and the Mackenzie, emptying to the north of the continents, so far from being enough in themselves to form any body of ever fresh and flowing water, can only pierce the opposing ice-fields in narrow streams and bays and inlets as they seek the Atlantic and the Pacific seas. And as for the theory of the currents of water heated in the tropics and carried by the rotary motion of the planet to the Pole, where they rise and melt the ice-floes into this great supposititious sea, it is simply an absurdity on the face of it, he argued, when you remember that warm water being in its nature specifically lighter than cold it would have risen to the surface long before it reached there. No, thought my Uncle Paul, who took nothing for granted; it is as I said, an absurdity on the face of it; my nephew shall prove it, and I stake half the earnings of my life upon it.

To tell the truth, I thought much the same as he did; and now that such a mere trifle of distance intervened, between me and the proof, I was full of a feverish impatience that almost amounted to insanity.

We had proceeded but a few days, coasting the crushing capes of rock that everywhere seemed to run out in a diablerie of tusks and horns to drive us from the region that they warded, now cruising through a runlet of blue water just wide enough for our keel, with silver reaches of frost stretching away into a ghastly horizon – now plunging upon tossing seas, the sun wheeling round and round, and never sinking from the strange, weird sky above us, when again to our look-out a glimmer in the low horizon told its awful tale – a sort of smoky lustre like that which might ascend from an army of spirits – the fierce and fatal spirits tented on the terrible field of the ice-floe.

We were alone, our single little ship speeding ever upward in the midst of that untraveled desolation. We spoke seldom to one another, oppressed with the sense of our situation. It was a loneliness that seemed more than a death in life, a solitude that was supernatural. Here and now it was clear water; ten hours later and we were caught in the teeth of the cold, wedged in the ice that had advanced upon us and surrounded us, fettered by another winter in latitudes where human life had never before been supported.

We found, before the hands of the dial had taught us the lapse of a week, that this would be something not to be endured. The sun sank lower every day behind the crags and silvery horns; the heavens grew to wear a hue of violet, almost black, and yet unbearably dazzling; as the notes of our voices fell upon the atmosphere they assumed a metallic tone, as if the air itself had become frozen from the beginning of the world and they tinkled against it; our sufferings had mounted in their intensity till they were too great to be resisted.

It was decided at length – when the one long day had given place to its answering night, and in the jet-black heavens the stars, like knobs of silver, sparkled so large and close upon us that we might have grasped them in our hands – that I should take a sledge with Glipnu and his dogs, and see if there were any path to the westward by which, if the *Albatross* were forsaken, those of her crew that remained might follow it, and find an escape to safety. Our path was on a frozen sea; if we discovered land we did not know that the foot of man had ever trodden it; we could hope to find no *caché* of snow-buried food – neither fish nor game lived in this desert of ice that was so devoid of life in any shape as to seem dead itself. But, well provisioned, furred to the eyes, and essaying to nurse some hopefulness of heart, we set out on our way through this Valley of Death, relieving one another, and traveling day and night.

Still night and day to the west rose the black coast, one interminable height; to the east extended the sheets of unbroken ice; sometimes a huge glacier hung pendulous from the precipice; once we saw, by the starlight, a white, foaming, rushing river arrested and transformed to ice in its flight down that steep. A south wind began to blow behind us; we traveled on the ice; three days, perhaps, as days are measured among men, had passed, when we found that we made double progress, for the ice traveled too; the whole field, carried by some northward-bearing current, was afloat; it began to be crossed and cut by a thousand crevasses; the cakes, an acre each, tilted up and down, and made wide waves with their ponderous plashing in the black body of the sea; we could hear them grinding distantly in the clear dark against the coast, against each other. There was no retreat – there was no advance; we were on the ice, and the ice was breaking up. Suddenly we rounded a tongue of the primeval rock, and recoiled before a narrow gulf – one sharp shadow, as deep as despair, as full of aguish fears. It was just wide enough for the sledge to span. Glipnu made the dogs leap; we could be no worse off if they drowned. They touched the opposite block; it careened; it went under; the sledge went with it; I was left alone where I had stood. Two dogs broke loose, and scrambled up beside me; Glipnu and the others I never saw again. I sank upon the ice; the dogs crouched beside me; sometimes I think they saved my brain from total ruin, for without them I could not have withstood the enormity of that loneliness, a loneliness that it was impossible should be broken – floating on and on with that vast journeying company of spectral ice. I had food enough to support life for several days to come, in the pouch at my belt; the dogs and I shared it – for, last as long as it would, when it should be gone there was only death before us – no reprieve – sooner or later that; as well sooner as later – the living terrors of this icy hell were all about us, and death could be no worse.

Still the south wind blew, the rapid current carried us, the dark skies grew deep and darker, the lanes and avenues between the stars were crowded with forebodings – for the air seemed full of a new power, a strange and invisible influence, as if a king of unknown terrors here held his awful state. Sometimes the dogs stood up and growled and bristled their shaggy hides; I, prostrate on the ice, in all my frame was stung with a universal tingle. I was no longer myself. At this moment my blood seemed to sing and bubble in my veins; I grew giddy with a sort of delirious and inexplicable ecstasy; with another moment unutterable horror seized me; I was plunged and weighed down with a black and suffocating load, while evil things seemed to flap their wings in my face, to breathe in my mouth, to draw my soul out of my body and carry it careering through the frozen realm of that murky heaven, to restore it with a shock of agony. Once as I lay there, still floating, floating northward, out of the dim dark rim of the water-world, a lance of piercing light shot up the zenith; it divided the heavens like a knife; they opened out in one blaze, and the fire fell sheetingly down before my face – cold fire, curdingly cold – light robbed of heat, and set free in a preternatural anarchy of the elements; its fringes swung to and fro before my face, pricked it with flaming spiculae, dissolving in a thousand colors that spread everywhere over the low field, flashing, flickering, creeping, reflecting, gathering again in one long serpentine line of glory that wavered in slow convolutions across the cuts and crevasses of the ice, wreathed ever nearer, and, lifting its head at last, became nothing in the darkness but two great eyes like glowing coals, with which it stared me to a stound, till I threw myself face down to hide me in the ice; and the whining, bristling dogs cowered backward, and were dead.

I should have supposed myself to be in the region of the magnetic pole of the sphere, if I did not know that I had long since left it behind me. My pocket-compass had become entirely useless, and every scrap of metal that I had about me had become a loadstone. The very ice, as if it were congealed from water that held large quantities of iron in solution; iron escaping from whatever solid land there was beneath or around, the Plutonic rock that such a region could have alone veined and seamed with metal. The very ice appeared to have a magnetic quality; it held me so that I changed my position upon it with difficulty, and, as if it established a battery by the aid of the singular atmosphere above it, frequently sent thrills quivering through and through me till my flesh seemed about to resolve into all the jarring atoms of its original constitution; and again soothed me, with a velvet touch, into a state which, if it were not sleep, was at least haunted by visions that I dare not believe to have been realities, and from which I always awoke with a start to find myself still floating, floating. My watch had long since ceased to beat. I felt an odd persuasion that I had died when that stood still, and only this slavery of the magnet, of the cold, this power that locked everything in invisible fetters and let nothing loose again, held my soul still in the bonds of my body. Another idea, also, took possession of me, for my mind was open to whatever visitant chose to enter, since utter despair of safety or release had left it vacant of a hope or fear. These enormous days and nights, swinging in their arc six months long, were the pendulum that dealt time in another measure than that dealt by the sunlight of lower zones; they told the time of what interminable years, the years of what vast generations far beyond the span that covered the age of the primeval men of Scripture – they measured time on this gigantic and enduring scale for what wonderful and mighty beings, old as the everlasting hills, as destitute as they of mortal sympathy, cold and inscrutable, handling the two-edged javelins of frost and magnetism, and served by all the unknown polar agencies. I fancied that I saw their far-reaching cohorts, marshaling and manoeuvring at times in the field of an horizon that was boundless, the glitter of their spears and casques, the sheen of their white banners; and again, sitting in fearful circle with their phantasmagoria they shut and hemmed me in and watched me writhe like a worm before them.

I had a fancy that the perpetual play of magnetic impulses here gradually disintegrated myself to any further fear, I cowered beneath the stare of those dead and icy eyes. Slowly we rounded, and ever rounded; the inside, on which my place was, moving less slowly than the outer circle of the sheeted mass in its viscid flow; and as we moved, by some fate my eye was caught by the substance on which this figure sat. It was no figure at all now, but a bare jag of rock rising in the centre of this solid whirlpool, and carrying on its summit something which held a light that not one of these icy freaks, pranking in the dress of gems and flowers, had found it possible to assume. It was a thing so real, so genuine, my breath became suspended; my heart ceased to beat; my brain, that had been a lump of ice, seemed to move in its skull; hope, that had deserted me, suddenly sprung up like a second life within me; the old passion was not dead, if I was. It rose stronger than life or death or than myself. If I could but snatch that mass of moonstone, that inestimable wealth! It was nothing deceptive, I declared to myself. What more natural home could it have than this region, thrown up here by the old Plutonic powers of the planet, as the same substance in smaller shape was thrown up on the peaks of the Mount St. Gothard, when the Alpine aiguilles first sprang into the day? There it rested, limpid with its milky pearl, casting out flakes of flame and azure, of red and leafgreen light, and holding yet a sparkle of silver in the reflections and refractions of its inner axis – the splendid Turk's-eye of the lapidaries, the cousin of the water-opal and the girasole, the precious essence of feldspar. Could I break it, I would find clusters of great hemitrope crystals. Could I obtain it, I should have a jewel in that mass of moonstone such as the world never saw! The throne of Jemschid could not cast a shadow beside it.

Then the bitterness of my fate overwhelmed me. Here, with this treasure of a kingdom, this jewel that could not be priced, this wealth beyond an Emperor's – and here only to die! My stolid apathy vanished, old thoughts dominated once more, old habits, old desires. I thought of Eleanor then in her warm, sunny home, the blossoms that bloomed around her, the birds that sang, the cheerful evening fires, the longing thoughts for one who never came, who never was to come. But I would! I cried, where human voice had never cried before. I would return! I would take this treasure with me! I would not be defrauded! Should not I, a man, conquer this inanimate blind matter? I reached out my hands to seize it. Slowly it receded – slowly, and less slowly; or was the motion of the ice still carrying me onward? Had we encircled this apex? and were we driving out into the open and uncovered North, and so down the seas and out to the open main of black water again? If so – if I could live through it – I must have this thing!

I rose, and as well as I could, with my cramped and stiffened limbs, I moved to go back for it. It was useless; the current that carried us was growing invincible, the gaping gulfs of the outer seas were sucking us toward them. I fell; I scrambled to my feet; I would still have gone back, but, as I attempted it, the ice whereon I was inclined ever so slightly, tipped more boldly, gave way, and rose in a billow, broke, and piled over on another mass beneath. Then the cavern was behind us, and I comprehended that this ice-stream, having doubled its central point, now in its outward movement encountered the still incoming body, and was to pile above and pass over it, the whole expanse bending, cracking, breaking, crowding, and compressing, till its rearing tumult made bergs more mountainous than the offshot glaciers of the Greenland continent, that should ride safely down to crumble in the surging seas below. As block after block of the rent ice rose in the air, lighted by the blue and bristling aurora-points, toppled and mounted higher, it seemed to me that now indeed I was battling with those elemental agencies in the dreadful fight I had desired – one man against the might of matter. I sprang from that block to another; I gained my balance on a third, climbing, shouldering, leaping, struggling, holding with my hands, catching with my feet, crawling, stumbling, tottering, rising high and higher with the mountain ever making underneath; a power unknown to my foes coming to my aid, a blessed rushing warmth that glowed on all the surface of my skin, that set the blood to racing in my veins, that made my heart beat with newer hope, sink with newer despair, rise buoyant with new determination. Except when the shaft of light pierced the shivering sky I could not see or guess the height that I had gained. I was vaguely aware of chasms that were bottomless, of precipices that opened on them, of pinnacles rising round me in aerial spires, when suddenly the shelf, on which I must have stood, yielded, as if it were pushed by great hands, swept down a steep incline like an avalanche, stopped halfway, but sent me flying on, sliding, glancing, like a shooting-star, down, down the slippery side, breathless, dizzy, smitten with blistering pain by awful winds that whistled by me, far out upon the level ice below that tilted up and down again with the great resonant plash of open water, and conscious for a moment that I lay at last upon a fragment that the mass behind urged on, I knew and I remembered nothing more.

Faces were bending over me when I opened my eyes again, rough, uncouth, and bearded faces, but no monsters of the pole. Whalemen rather, smelling richly of train-oil, but I could recall nothing in all my life one fraction so beautiful as they; the angels on whom I hope to open my eyes when Death has really taken me will scarcely seem sights more blest than did those rude whalers of the North Pacific Sea. The North Pacific Sea – for it was there that I was found, explain it how you may – whether the *Albatross* had pierced farther to the west than her sailing-master knew, and had lost her reckoning with a disordered compass-needle under new stars – or whether I had really been the sport of the demoniac beings of the ice, tossed by them from zone to zone in a dozen hours. The whalers, real creatures enough, had discovered me on a block of ice, they said; nor could I, in their opinion, have been many days undergoing my dreadful experience, for there was still food in my wallet when they opened it. They would never believe a word of my story, and so far from regarding me as one who had proved the Northwest Passage in my own person, they considered me a mere idle maniac, as uncomfortable a thing to have on shipboard as a ghost or a dead body, wrecked and unable to account for myself, and gladly transferred me to a homeward-bound Russian man-of-war, whose officers afforded me more polite but quite as decided skepticism. I have never to this day found anyone who believed my story when I told it – so you can take it for what it is worth. Even my Uncle Paul flouted it, and absolutely refused to surrender the sum on whose expectation I had taken ship; while my old ancestor, who hung peeling over the hall fire, dropped from his frame in disgust at the idea of one of his hard-cash descendants turning romancer. But all I know is that the *Albatross* never sailed into port again, and that if I open my knife today and lay it on the table it will wheel about till the tip of its blade points full at the North Star.

I have never found any one to believe me, did I say? Yes, there is one – Eleanor never doubted a word of my narration, never asked me if cold and suffering had not shaken my reason. But then, after the first recital, she has never been willing to hear another word about it, and if I ever allude to my lost treasure or the possibility of instituting search for it, she asks me if I need more lessons to be content with the treasure that I have, and gathers up her work and gently leaves the room. So that, now I speak of it so seldom, if I had not told the thing to you it might come to pass that I should forget altogether the existence of my mass of moonstone. My mass of moonshine, old Paul calls it. I let him have his say; he cannot have that nor anything else much longer; but when all is done I recall Galileo and I mutter to myself, "*Per si muove* – it *was* a mass of moonstone! With these eyes I saw it, with these hands I touched it, with this heart I longed for it, with this will I mean to have it yet!"

From Within

Richard Thomas

THE FIRST TIME they come to measure my son, he is only eleven years old. Two men knock on the door of our humble home that squats on the outskirts of Shell County, my boy and I eating Macaroni and Cheese, our eyes turned mid-spoon to the interruption. Outside the darkness is as black as pitch, matching their uniforms, their helmets slick, a measuring tape in each of their hands, dust devils spinning across the land – dirt and garbage lifting high up into the night.

They never say a word, simply walk inside and lift the boy from his seat, one of them holding him as the other measures height, then width, then depth. They never speak, only nod at each other, and then retreat into the night, the door left open, as silt slips inside, and over the floor. I blink, the boy shrugs, and we go back to our meal. These things happen when your overlords float over the cities, some as small as cows, the queen bees as large as blimps. The smaller ones are grey, like elephants, the largest translucent – colored organs in red and purple pumping from within. They are beautiful and horrific, having ruined all we know.

I work in one of the mines, as most of us do, out in the desert, certain ore that we previously thought of as common, essential to their life and continued development. Much like the stormtroopers, I dress in a jumpsuit, but mine is orange, my son's a shade of peach. We do not reside in the gothic mansions that line the pit, no, we are just workers, so little to live for, but each other. And most days, that is enough. Our shotgun shacks ring out around the pillared homes, porches wrapping around the dirty gothic structures, foremen with shotguns, their women in tattered dresses.

The boy works in a sorting facility, an expansive metal garage on the way to the Shell County mines. At night we reunite on the dirt path outside his building, holding up our hands to reveal the day's labor – his lavender and blue from the kyanite, as if dusted by fairies; mine rusty and muted from carts of mica, splinters of the fine ore leaving nicks upon my skin. If it weren't for the boy, one arm around him as we lumber home, exhausted, I certainly would have ended it by now. All up and down my arms are thin lines of mottled flesh, spider webs of dark promises I can't keep – unable to leave, unable to surrender. He finds a way to chirp and laugh, something they discovered inside a mineral today, some sort of ancient bug – these buried worms and larvae – trapped inside the rock, the highlight of his day. He holds his hand out to show me the wriggling creatures and my stomach turns over. They look prehistoric, with their pincers and feathered legs. I don't know if it's a beautiful thing, his discovery and excitement, or just another sad story in a long line of sad stories.

The second time they come to measure my son, I'm not nearly as receptive as the first. I ask them what they want, why they are here, and they simply push me aside and descend upon the boy. He is still so innocent, in this new world, never knowing the things I struggle to forget – free will, television, beer, football, movies, music, books, fine dining, travel – the list spirals out into the ether. He knows none of these pleasures, and never will. He stands up, his arms spread wide as they measure, and measure, and measure. I scream at them to get out, apoplectic with rage, my face flushing red, but they ignore me, simply nodding their heads – height, and width, and depth.

When I lay a hand on one of them he turns on me with an unforeseen speed, a baton extending out of his hand, pulled from a pocket or his belt, perhaps, his gloved hand lined with metal spikes, the rapid-fire beating faster than I can witness, simply a blur of metal and blood splatter, my eyes, my nose, my teeth – my vision lost in a mist of red, as I fall to the ground, my hands never even raised.

When they are gone, and I regain consciousness, the boy is dabbing at my face with a bloody washcloth, the cold water calming my hot flesh, his eyes full of tears, his lips bit and puckered in resolve, never saying a word. He understands his place, and his eyes implore me to remember mine.

I do not miss work, this is not allowed. So, beaten and bruised I make my way to the mines. The boy splits off at his juncture in the path, releasing my hand with reluctance. We have learned not to ask, when somebody disappears – no longer standing next us as we shovel, pick, and dig. We have learned to ignore the loss of fingers, the cuts and markings, changing in and out of our uniforms, backs covered in streaked lashings, weeping flesh, the whippings carried out in private, to keep us in constant fear. If the setting sun has no time of descent – no marked hour, or minute, or path – then how can we anticipate the darkness?

The third time they come it is not to measure my boy, but simply to take him. There are four guards this time, the first entering our filthy home with an electric cattle prod in front of him, pushing it into my raised hands, my strained chest, shock rippling over my flesh as I collapse to the floor, twitching while urine trickles down my shaking leg. And the boy never says a word as they extend their measuring tapes – height, and width, and depth. They nod to each other, jotting down a few notes, walking him out of the house as he tells me he loves me, tells me to be strong, to wait for him. They take him, leaving behind a small envelope with a few sentences about his new assignment. I do not know if he will return. He fits the mold for some strange new job, something about the health of the great ones, a bitter pill that the beasts must swallow – the medicine, somehow, my boy.

I know that I've taught him well, my son, even if I don't take my own advice. He has heard repeatedly that resistance is futile – my words slipping over his drooping eyes as he lies in bed, drifting off to sleep. I don't give him hope, when I tuck him in at night, because I can't give him something I don't have.

There are three great beasts that hover over our mine, their veiny skin transparent. I see them every day when I walk to work, and I hate their bluish tint, their waving tentacles, with all of my trembling heart. It's not like people haven't tried to rebel, to rise up. I've seen men rush out of the pits with rifles, blood on their hands, firing at the smaller grey ones, the great clear beasts in the sky rippling with puncture wounds. They pass right through them, holes made, certainly, but little changing. And as the smaller gray ones swarm closer, appendages descending, the men's screams are lost in the thick alien hides, ripped limb from limb as shots ring out, one or two of the elephantine creatures falling to the Earth, more vulnerable it seems, the hovering motherships unharmed.

It's all I can think about in the weeks to come, my boy, and his new job. There are whispers from the other men, no women down here in the mines, their work elsewhere in the pleasure districts of Moosejaw. My wife was dead of cancer long before any of this horror fell upon us, and I thank whatever gods are left that she never had to witness this decay. The boy has her quiet optimism, so I trudge back and forth to the mines, lost in the dust and noise, waiting to hear something – anything at all.

There are whispers at work, quiet conversations slipped between the spark of the pickaxe, the rattling thunder of jackhammers, sledges and shovels down here close to the veins of ore. I sidle up to two men who are bagging up mica, as overhead and in the distance great excavators rumble past, bulldozers and graders spanning out across the dirt. They speak of their boys, measured and taken, and I ask what they know. They shake their heads and scatter like cockroaches, but before they separate, I hear a few things. They are sick, the big ones, shedding scales of flesh that falls from the sky like graying snowflakes. I think of the sloughs of skin that have turned up over the past few weeks, great sheets of dry skin drifting about the dead land like tumbleweeds spinning in the wind. They hang lower in the sky, the men mumbled, and as I walk home from work, I scan the sky for confirmation. There are only two of them visible today – one as vibrant and glowing as ever; the second slightly lower, dull and hardly moving; the third falling onto a distant mountain range, its sickly skin like a dirty blanket draped over pristine snow.

The final knock at my door is nothing I expect – the boy standing there skinny and sick, his eyes shrunken, his face sallow – falling into my outstretched arms. He says that up close they are magnificent creatures, so very large, the quiet inside the floating bodies like nothing he's ever witnessed. I take him to his bed, and set him down gently, fetching him a glass of water, his eyes electric with stories. He wants to tell me everything, so I sit on his bed and listen.

He talks of the other boys, how they were to be fed to the beasts, wrapped in protective coatings, slick jumpsuits made of glossy materials, treated with certain chemicals to aid their healing treatment. The boy laughs, coughing up phlegm and blood, his eyes glazing over as he tries to finish his tale. Holding his bony right hand, I listen, as he smiles a crimson smile. A simple job, he says, swimming their way to the center of the monsters, against the vibrating cilia. Not just medicine, which the creatures can't swallow, skin too thin to inject, too tough for any spray, but specific instructions about hearts and valves, chambers and ventricles, how to remove any blockages, plaque, or disease.

But they had another plan, he says, grinning, holding out his left fist. When he spreads his fingers wide, it is the worm again, now grown, ten times its previous size, pincers snapping, as big as a mouse, eyes blood red, feathered legs twitching, wings now on its back, thin membranes lined with intricate patterns.

The boy is asleep now – his pulse slow, but steady. I take the worm, the caterpillar, whatever it is now, whatever it might become next – moth, or snake, or lizard – to the kitchen in search of a proper receptacle. I find a Mason jar, and drop it inside, an iridescence rippling over its skin, feelers probing the air, as I poke a few holes in the lid with a rusty old screwdriver, my stomach rippling with hope.

I go to the front door and swing it open, the sky filled with orange light as the sun sets in the distance. They are gone, the sky empty now – nothing hovering, a stream of men from the pits, gray skinned husks lying scattered over the earth, the worms devouring from within. The sickness has spread, the network of creatures like one long line of electrostatic shock, stilling their waving arms as they wither and die across the silent barren plains, our new home.

The Story of the Late Mr. Elvesham

H.G. Wells

I SET this story down, not expecting it will be believed, but, if possible, to prepare a way of escape for the next victim. He, perhaps, may profit by my misfortune. My own case, I know, is hopeless, and I am now in some measure prepared to meet my fate.

My name is Edward George Eden. I was born at Trentham, in Staffordshire, my father being employed in the gardens there. I lost my mother when I was three years old, and my father when I was five, my uncle, George Eden, then adopting me as his own son. He was a single man, self-educated, and well-known in Birmingham as an enterprising journalist; he educated me generously, fired my ambition to succeed in the world, and at his death, which happened four years ago, left me his entire fortune, a matter of about five hundred pounds after all outgoing charges were paid. I was then eighteen. He advised me in his will to expend the money in completing my education. I had already chosen the profession of medicine, and through his posthumous generosity and my good fortune in a scholarship competition, I became a medical student at University College, London. At the time of the beginning of my story I lodged at 11A University Street in a little upper room, very shabbily furnished and draughty, overlooking the back of Shoolbred's premises. I used this little room both to live in and sleep in, because I was anxious to eke out my means to the very last shillings-worth.

I was taking a pair of shoes to be mended at a shop in the Tottenham Court Road when I first encountered the little old man with the yellow face, with whom my life has now become so inextricably entangled. He was standing on the kerb, and staring at the number on the door in a doubtful way, as I opened it. His eyes – they were dull grey eyes, and reddish under the rims – fell to my face, and his countenance immediately assumed an expression of corrugated amiability.

"You come," he said, "apt to the moment. I had forgotten the number of your house. How do you do, Mr. Eden?"

I was a little astonished at his familiar address, for I had never set eyes on the man before. I was a little annoyed, too, at his catching me with my boots under my arm. He noticed my lack of cordiality.

"Wonder who the deuce I am, eh? A friend, let me assure you. I have seen you before, though you haven't seen me. Is there anywhere where I can talk to you?"

I hesitated. The shabbiness of my room upstairs was not a matter for every stranger. "Perhaps," said I, "we might walk down the street. I'm unfortunately prevented –" My gesture explained the sentence before I had spoken it.

"The very thing," he said, and faced this way, and then that. "The street? Which way shall we go?" I slipped my boots down in the passage. "Look here!" he said abruptly; "this business of mine is a rigmarole. Come and lunch with me, Mr. Eden. I'm an old man, a very old man, and not good at explanations, and what with my piping voice and the clatter of the traffic—"

He laid a persuasive skinny hand that trembled a little upon my arm.

I was not so old that an old man might not treat me to a lunch. Yet at the same time I was not altogether pleased by this abrupt invitation. "I had rather –" I began. "But I had rather," he said, catching me up, "and a certain civility is surely due to my grey hairs."

And so I consented, and went with him.

He took me to Blavitiski's; I had to walk slowly to accommodate myself to his paces; and over such a lunch as I had never tasted before, he fended off my leading question, and I took a better note of his appearance. His clean-shaven face was lean and wrinkled, his shrivelled lips fell over a set of false teeth, and his white hair was thin and rather long; he seemed small to me – though indeed, most people seemed small to me – and his shoulders were rounded and bent. And watching him, I could not help but observe that he too was taking note of me, running his eyes, with a curious touch of greed in them, over me, from my broad shoulders to my suntanned hands, and up to my freckled face again. "And now," said he, as we lit our cigarettes, "I must tell you of the business in hand.

"I must tell you, then, that I am an old man, a very old man." He paused momentarily. "And it happens that I have money that I must presently be leaving, and never a child have I to leave it to." I thought of the confidence trick, and resolved I would be on the alert for the vestiges of my five hundred pounds. He proceeded to enlarge on his loneliness, and the trouble he had to find a proper disposition of his money. "I have weighed this plan and that plan, charities, institutions, and scholarships, and libraries, and I have come to this conclusion at last," – he fixed his eyes on my face – "that I will find some young fellow, ambitious, pure-minded, and poor, healthy in body and healthy in mind, and, in short, make him my heir, give him all that I have." He repeated, "Give him all that I have. So that he will suddenly be lifted out of all the trouble and struggle in which his sympathies have been educated, to freedom and influence."

I tried to seem disinterested. With a transparent hypocrisy I said, "And you want my help, my professional services maybe, to find that person."

He smiled, and looked at me over his cigarette, and I laughed at his quiet exposure of my modest pretence.

"What a career such a man might have!" he said. "It fills me with envy to think how I have accumulated that another man may spend—

"But there are conditions, of course, burdens to be imposed. He must, for instance, take my name. You cannot expect everything without some return. And I must go into all the circumstances of his life before I can accept him. He *must* be sound. I must know his heredity, how his parents and grandparents died, have the strictest inquiries made into his private morals."

This modified my secret congratulations a little.

"And do I understand," said I, "that I—

"Yes," he said, almost fiercely. "You. You."

I answered never a word. My imagination was dancing wildly, my innate scepticism was useless to modify its transports. There was not a particle of gratitude in my mind – I did not know what to say nor how to say it. "But why me in particular?" I said at last.

He had chanced to hear of me from Professor Haslar; he said, as a typically sound and sane young man, and he wished, as far as possible, to leave his money where health and integrity were assured.

That was my first meeting with the little old man. He was mysterious about himself; he would not give his name yet, he said, and after I had answered some questions of his, he left me at the Blavitiski portal. I noticed that he drew a handful of gold coins from his pocket when it came to paying for the lunch. His insistence upon bodily health was curious. In accordance with an arrangement we had made I applied that day for a life policy in the Loyal Insurance Company for a large sum, and I was exhaustively overhauled by the medical advisers of that company in the subsequent week. Even that did not satisfy him, and he insisted I must be re-examined by the great Doctor Henderson.

It was Friday in Whitsun week before he came to a decision. He called me down, quite late in the evening – nearly nine it was – from cramming chemical equations for my Preliminary Scientific examination. He was standing in the passage under the feeble gas-lamp, and his face was a grotesque interplay of shadows. He seemed more bowed than when I had first seen him, and his cheeks had sunk in a little.

His voice shook with emotion. "Everything is satisfactory, Mr. Eden," he said. "Everything is quite, quite satisfactory. And this night of all nights, you must dine with me and celebrate your – accession." He was interrupted by a cough. "You won't have long to wait, either," he said, wiping his handkerchief across his lips, and gripping my hand with his long bony claw that was disengaged. "Certainly not very long to wait."

We went into the street and called a cab. I remember every incident of that drive vividly, the swift, easy motion, the vivid contrast of gas and oil and electric light, the crowds of people in the streets, the place in Regent Street to which we went, and the sumptuous dinner we were served with there. I was disconcerted at first by the well-dressed waiter's glances at my rough clothes, bothered by the stones of the olives, but as the champagne warmed my blood, my confidence revived. At first the old man talked of himself. He had already told me his name in the cab; he was Egbert Elvesham, the great philosopher, whose name I had known since I was a lad at school. It seemed incredible to me that this man, whose intelligence had so early dominated mine, this great abstraction, should suddenly realise itself as this decrepit, familiar figure. I daresay every young fellow who has suddenly fallen among celebrities has felt something of my disappointment. He told me now of the future that the feeble streams of his life would presently leave dry for me, houses, copyrights, investments; I had never suspected that philosophers were so rich. He watched me drink and eat with a touch of envy. "What a capacity for living you have!" he said; and then with a sigh, a sigh of relief I could have thought it, "it will not be long."

"Ay," said I, my head swimming now with champagne; "I have a future perhaps – of a passing agreeable sort, thanks to you. I shall now have the honour of your name. But you have a past. Such a past as is worth all my future."

He shook his head and smiled, as I thought, with half sad appreciation of my flattering admiration. "That future," he said, "would you in truth change it?" The waiter came with liqueurs. "You will not perhaps mind taking my name, taking my position, but would you indeed – willingly – take my years?"

"With your achievements," said I gallantly.

He smiled again. "Kummel – both," he said to the waiter, and turned his attention to a little paper packet he had taken from his pocket. "This hour," said he, "this after-dinner hour is the hour of small things. Here is a scrap of my unpublished wisdom." He opened the packet with his shaking yellow fingers, and showed a little pinkish powder on the paper. "This," said he – "well, you must guess what it is. But Kummel – put but a dash of this powder in it – is Himmel."

His large greyish eyes watched mine with an inscrutable expression.

It was a bit of a shock to me to find this great teacher gave his mind to the flavour of liqueurs. However, I feigned an interest in his weakness, for I was drunk enough for such small sycophancy.

He parted the powder between the little glasses, and, rising suddenly, with a strange unexpected dignity, held out his hand towards me. I imitated his action, and the glasses rang. "To a quick succession," said he, and raised his glass towards his lips.

"Not that," I said hastily. "Not that."

He paused with the liqueur at the level of his chin, and his eyes blazing into mine.

"To a long life," said I.

He hesitated. "To a long life," said he, with a sudden bark of laughter, and with eyes fixed on one another we tilted the little glasses. His eyes looked straight into mine, and as I drained the stuff off, I felt a curiously intense sensation. The first touch of it set my brain in a furious tumult; I seemed to feel an actual physical stirring in my skull, and a seething humming filled my ears. I did not notice the flavour in my mouth, the aroma that filled my throat; I saw only the grey intensity of his gaze that burnt into mine. The draught, the mental confusion, the noise and stirring in my head, seemed to last an interminable time. Curious vague impressions of half-forgotten things danced and vanished on the edge of my consciousness. At last he broke the spell. With a sudden explosive sigh he put down his glass.

"Well?" he said.

"It's glorious," said I, though I had not tasted the stuff.

My head was spinning. I sat down. My brain was chaos. Then my perception grew clear and minute as though I saw things in a concave mirror. His manner seemed to have changed into something nervous and hasty. He pulled out his watch and grimaced at it. "Eleven-seven! And tonight I must – Seven-twenty-five. Waterloo! I must go at once." He called for the bill, and struggled with his coat. Officious waiters came to our assistance. In another moment I was wishing him goodbye, over the apron of a cab, and still with an absurd feeling of minute distinctness, as though – how can I express it? – I not only saw but *felt* through an inverted opera-glass.

"That stuff," he said. He put his hand to his forehead. "I ought not to have given it to you. It will make your head split tomorrow. Wait a minute. Here." He handed me out a little flat thing like a seidlitz-powder. "Take that in water as you are going to bed. The other thing was a drug. Not till you're ready to go to bed, mind. It will clear your head. That's all. One more shake – Futurus!"

I gripped his shrivelled claw. "Goodbye," he said, and by the droop of his eyelids I judged he too was a little under the influence of that brain-twisting cordial.

He recollected something else with a start, felt in his breast-pocket, and produced another packet, this time a cylinder the size and shape of a shaving-stick. "Here," said he. "I'd almost forgotten. Don't open this until I come tomorrow – but take it now."

It was so heavy that I wellnigh dropped it. "All ri'!" said I, and he grinned at me through the cab window as the cabman flicked his horse into wakefulness. It was a white packet he had given me, with red seals at either end and along its edge. "If this isn't money," said I, "it's platinum or lead."

I stuck it with elaborate care into my pocket, and with a whirling brain walked home through the Regent Street loiterers and the dark back streets beyond Portland Road. I remember the sensations of that walk very vividly, strange as they were. I was still so far myself that I could notice my strange mental state, and wonder whether this stuff I had had was opium – a drug beyond my experience. It is hard now to describe the peculiarity of my mental strangeness – mental doubling vaguely expresses it. As I was walking up Regent Street I found in my mind a queer persuasion that it was Waterloo Station, and had an odd impulse to get into the Polytechnic as a man might get into a train. I put a knuckle in my eye, and it was Regent Street. How can I express it? You see a skilful actor looking quietly at you, he pulls a grimace, and lo! – Another person. Is it too extravagant if I tell you that it seemed to me as if Regent Street had, for the moment, done that? Then, being persuaded it was Regent Street again, I was oddly muddled about some fantastic reminiscences that cropped up. "Thirty years ago," thought I, "it was here that I quarrelled with my brother." Then I burst out laughing, to the astonishment and encouragement of a group of night prowlers. Thirty years ago I did not exist, and never in my life had I boasted a brother. The stuff was surely liquid folly, for the poignant regret for that lost brother still clung to me. Along

Portland Road the madness took another turn. I began to recall vanished shops, and to compare the street with what it used to be. Confused, troubled thinking is comprehensible enough after the drink I had taken, but what puzzled me were these curiously vivid phantasm memories that had crept into my mind, and not only the memories that had crept in, but also the memories that had slipped out. I stopped opposite Stevens', the natural history dealer's, and cudgelled my brains to think what he had to do with me. A bus went by, and sounded exactly like the rumbling of a train. I seemed to be dipping into some dark, remote pit for the recollection. "Of course," said I, at last, "he has promised me three frogs tomorrow. Odd I should have forgotten."

Do they still show children dissolving views? In those I remember one view would begin like a faint ghost, and grow and oust another. In just that way it seemed to me that a ghostly set of new sensations was struggling with those of my ordinary self.

I went on through Euston Road to Tottenham Court Road, puzzled, and a little frightened, and scarcely noticed the unusual way I was taking, for commonly I used to cut through the intervening network of back streets. I turned into University Street, to discover that I had forgotten my number. Only by a strong effort did I recall 11A, and even then it seemed to me that it was a thing some forgotten person had told me. I tried to steady my mind by recalling the incidents of the dinner, and for the life of me I could conjure up no picture of my host's face; I saw him only as a shadowy outline, as one might see oneself reflected in a window through which one was looking. In his place, however, I had a curious exterior vision of myself, sitting at a table, flushed, bright-eyed, and talkative.

"I must take this other powder," said I. "This is getting impossible."

I tried the wrong side of the hall for my candle and the matches, and had a doubt of which landing my room might be on. "I'm drunk," I said, "that's certain," and blundered needlessly on the staircase to sustain the proposition.

At the first glance my room seemed unfamiliar. "What rot!" I said, and stared about me. I seemed to bring myself back by the effort, and the odd phantasmal quality passed into the concrete familiar. There was the old glass still, with my notes on the albumens stuck in the corner of the frame, my old everyday suit of clothes pitched about the floor. And yet it was not so real after all. I felt an idiotic persuasion trying to creep into my mind, as it were, that I was in a railway carriage in a train just stopping, that I was peering out of the window at some unknown station. I gripped the bed-rail firmly to reassure myself. "It's clairvoyance, perhaps," I said. "I must write to the Psychical Research Society."

I put the rouleau on my dressing-table, sat on my bed, and began to take off my boots. It was as if the picture of my present sensations was painted over some other picture that was trying to show through. "Curse it!" said I; "my wits are going, or am I in two places at once?" Half-undressed, I tossed the powder into a glass and drank it off. It effervesced, and became a fluorescent amber colour. Before I was in bed my mind was already tranquillised. I felt the pillow at my cheek, and thereupon I must have fallen asleep.

* * *

I awoke abruptly out of a dream of strange beasts, and found myself lying on my back. Probably everyone knows that dismal, emotional dream from which one escapes, awake indeed, but strangely cowed. There was a curious taste in my mouth, a tired feeling in my limbs, a sense of cutaneous discomfort. I lay with my head motionless on my pillow, expecting that my feeling of strangeness and terror would pass away, and that I should then doze off again to sleep. But instead of that, my uncanny sensations increased. At first I could perceive nothing wrong about me. There was a faint light in the room, so faint that it was the very next thing to darkness, and the furniture stood out in it as vague blots of absolute darkness. I stared with my eyes just over the bedclothes.

It came into my mind that someone had entered the room to rob me of my rouleau of money, but after lying for some moments, breathing regularly to simulate sleep, I realised this was mere fancy. Nevertheless, the uneasy assurance of something wrong kept fast hold of me. With an effort I raised my head from the pillow, and peered about me at the dark. What it was I could not conceive. I looked at the dim shapes around me, the greater and lesser darknesses that indicated curtains, table, fireplace, bookshelves, and so forth. Then I began to perceive something unfamiliar in the forms of the darkness. Had the bed turned round? Yonder should be the bookshelves, and something shrouded and pallid rose there, something that would not answer to the bookshelves, however I looked at it. It was far too big to be my shirt thrown on a chair.

Overcoming a childish terror, I threw back the bedclothes and thrust my leg out of bed. Instead of coming out of my truckle-bed upon the floor, I found my foot scarcely reached the edge of the mattress. I made another step, as it were, and sat up on the edge of the bed. By the side of my bed should be the candle, and the matches upon the broken chair. I put out my hand and touched – nothing. I waved my hand in the darkness, and it came against some heavy hanging, soft and thick in texture, which gave a rustling noise at my touch. I grasped this and pulled it; it appeared to be a curtain suspended over the head of my bed.

I was now thoroughly awake, and beginning to realise that I was in a strange room. I was puzzled. I tried to recall the overnight circumstances, and I found them now, curiously enough, vivid in my memory: the supper, my reception of the little packages, my wonder whether I was intoxicated, my slow undressing, the coolness to my flushed face of my pillow. I felt a sudden distrust. Was that last night, or the night before? At any rate, this room was strange to me, and I could not imagine how I had got into it. The dim, pallid outline was growing paler, and I perceived it was a window, with the dark shape of an oval toilet-glass against the weak intimation of the dawn that filtered through the blind. I stood up, and was surprised by a curious feeling of weakness and unsteadiness. With trembling hands outstretched, I walked slowly towards the window, getting, nevertheless, a bruise on the knee from a chair by the way. I fumbled round the glass, which was large, with handsome brass sconces, to find the blind cord. I could not find any. By chance I took hold of the tassel, and with the click of a spring the blind ran up.

I found myself looking out upon a scene that was altogether strange to me. The night was overcast, and through the flocculent grey of the heaped clouds there filtered a faint half-light of dawn. Just at the edge of the sky the cloud-canopy had a blood-red rim. Below, everything was dark and indistinct, dim hills in the distance, a vague mass of buildings running up into pinnacles, trees like spilt ink, and below the window a tracery of black bushes and pale grey paths. It was so unfamiliar that for the moment I thought myself still dreaming. I felt the toilet-table; it appeared to be made of some polished wood, and was rather elaborately furnished – there were little cut-glass bottles and a brush upon it. There was also a queer little object, horse-shoe shape it felt, with smooth, hard projections, lying in a saucer. I could find no matches nor candlestick.

I turned my eyes to the room again. Now the blind was up, faint spectres of its furnishing came out of the darkness. There was a huge curtained bed, and the fireplace at its foot had a large white mantel with something of the shimmer of marble.

I leant against the toilet-table, shut my eyes and opened them again, and tried to think. The whole thing was far too real for dreaming. I was inclined to imagine there was still some hiatus in my memory, as a consequence of my draught of that strange liqueur; that I had come into my inheritance perhaps, and suddenly lost my recollection of everything since my good fortune had been announced. Perhaps if I waited a little, things would be clearer to me again.

Yet my dinner with old Elvesham was now singularly vivid and recent. The champagne, the observant waiters, the powder, and the liqueurs – I could have staked my soul it all happened a few hours ago.

And then occurred a thing so trivial and yet so terrible to me that I shiver now to think of that moment. I spoke aloud. I said, "How the devil did I get here?" ...*And the voice was not my own.*

It was not my own, it was thin, the articulation was slurred, the resonance of my facial bones was different. Then, to reassure myself I ran one hand over the other, and felt loose folds of skin, the bony laxity of age. "Surely," I said, in that horrible voice that had somehow established itself in my throat, "surely this thing is a dream!" Almost as quickly as if I did it involuntarily, I thrust my fingers into my mouth. My teeth had gone. My fingertips ran on the flaccid surface of an even row of shrivelled gums. I was sick with dismay and disgust.

I felt then a passionate desire to see myself, to realise at once in its full horror the ghastly change that had come upon me. I tottered to the mantel, and felt along it for matches. As I did so, a barking cough sprang up in my throat, and I clutched the thick flannel nightdress I found about me. There were no matches there, and I suddenly realised that my extremities were cold. Sniffing and coughing, whimpering a little, perhaps, I fumbled back to bed. "It is surely a dream," I whispered to myself as I clambered back, "surely a dream." It was a senile repetition. I pulled the bedclothes over my shoulders, over my ears, I thrust my withered hand under the pillow, and determined to compose myself to sleep. Of course it was a dream. In the morning the dream would be over, and I should wake up strong and vigorous again to my youth and studies. I shut my eyes, breathed regularly, and, finding myself wakeful, began to count slowly through the powers of three.

But the thing I desired would not come. I could not get to sleep. And the persuasion of the inexorable reality of the change that had happened to me grew steadily. Presently I found myself with my eyes wide open, the powers of three forgotten, and my skinny fingers upon my shrivelled gums, I was, indeed, suddenly and abruptly, an old man. I had in some unaccountable manner fallen through my life and come to old age, in some way I had been cheated of all the best of my life, of love, of struggle, of strength, and hope. I grovelled into the pillow and tried to persuade myself that such hallucination was possible. Imperceptibly, steadily, the dawn grew clearer.

At last, despairing of further sleep, I sat up in bed and looked about me. A chill twilight rendered the whole chamber visible. It was spacious and well-furnished, better furnished than any room I had ever slept in before. A candle and matches became dimly visible upon a little pedestal in a recess. I threw back the bedclothes, and, shivering with the rawness of the early morning, albeit it was summer-time, I got out and lit the candle. Then, trembling horribly, so that the extinguisher rattled on its spike, I tottered to the glass and saw – *Elvesham's* face! It was none the less horrible because I had already dimly feared as much. He had already seemed physically weak and pitiful to me, but seen now, dressed only in a coarse flannel nightdress, that fell apart and showed the stringy neck, seen now as my own body, I cannot describe its desolate decrepitude. The hollow cheeks, the straggling tail of dirty grey hair, the rheumy bleared eyes, the quivering, shrivelled lips, the lower displaying a gleam of the pink interior lining, and those horrible dark gums showing. You who are mind and body together, at your natural years, cannot imagine what this fiendish imprisonment meant to me. To be young and full of the desire and energy of youth, and to be caught, and presently to be crushed in this tottering ruin of a body...

But I wander from the course of my story. For some time I must have been stunned at this change that had come upon me. It was daylight when I did so far gather myself together as to think. In some inexplicable way I had been changed, though how, short of magic, the thing had been done, I could not say. And as I thought, the diabolical ingenuity of Elvesham came home to me. It seemed plain to me that as I found myself in his, so he must be in possession of *my* body, of my strength, that is, and my future. But how to prove it? Then, as I thought, the thing became so incredible, even to me, that my mind reeled, and I had to pinch myself, to feel my toothless gums, to see myself in the glass, and touch the things about me, before I could steady myself to face the facts again. Was all life hallucination? Was I indeed Elvesham, and he me? Had I been dreaming of Eden overnight? Was there any Eden? But if I was Elvesham, I should remember where I was on the previous morning, the name of the town in which I lived, what happened before the dream began. I struggled with my thoughts. I recalled the queer doubleness of my memories overnight. But now my mind was clear. Not the ghost of any memories but those proper to Eden could I raise.

"This way lies insanity!" I cried in my piping voice. I staggered to my feet, dragged my feeble, heavy limbs to the washhand-stand, and plunged my grey head into a basin of cold water. Then, towelling myself, I tried again. It was no good. I felt beyond all question that I was indeed Eden, not Elvesham. But Eden in Elvesham's body!

Had I been a man of any other age, I might have given myself up to my fate as one enchanted. But in these sceptical days miracles do not pass current. Here was some trick of psychology. What a drug and a steady stare could do, a drug and a steady stare, or some similar treatment, could surely undo. Men have lost their memories before. But to exchange memories as one does umbrellas! I laughed. Alas! not a healthy laugh, but a wheezing, senile titter. I could have fancied old Elvesham laughing at my plight, and a gust of petulant anger, unusual to me, swept across my feelings. I began dressing eagerly in the clothes I found lying about on the floor, and only realised when I was dressed that it was an evening suit I had assumed. I opened the wardrobe and found some more ordinary clothes, a pair of plaid trousers, and an old-fashioned dressing-gown. I put a venerable smoking-cap on my venerable head, and, coughing a little from my exertions, tottered out upon the landing.

It was then, perhaps, a quarter to six, and the blinds were closely drawn and the house quite silent. The landing was a spacious one, a broad, richly-carpeted staircase went down into the darkness of the hall below, and before me a door ajar showed me a writing-desk, a revolving bookcase, the back of a study chair, and a fine array of bound books, shelf upon shelf.

"My study," I mumbled, and walked across the landing. Then at the sound of my voice a thought struck me, and I went back to the bedroom and put in the set of false teeth. They slipped in with the ease of old habit. "That's better," said I, gnashing them, and so returned to the study.

The drawers of the writing-desk were locked. Its revolving top was also locked. I could see no indications of the keys, and there were none in the pockets of my trousers. I shuffled back at once to the bedroom, and went through the dress suit, and afterwards the pockets of all the garments I could find. I was very eager, and one might have imagined that burglars had been at work, to see my room when I had done. Not only were there no keys to be found, but not a coin, nor a scrap of paper – save only the receipted bill of the overnight dinner.

A curious weariness asserted itself. I sat down and stared at the garments flung here and there, their pockets turned inside out. My first frenzy had already flickered out. Every moment I was beginning to realise the immense intelligence of the plans of my enemy, to see more and more clearly the hopelessness of my position. With an effort I rose and hurried hobbling into the study again. On the staircase was a housemaid pulling up the blinds. She stared, I think, at the expression of my face. I shut the door of the study behind me, and, seizing a poker, began an attack upon the desk. That is how they found me. The cover of the desk was split, the lock smashed, the letters torn out of the pigeon-holes, and tossed about the room. In my senile rage

I had flung about the pens and other such light stationery, and overturned the ink. Moreover, a large vase upon the mantel had got broken – I do not know how. I could find no cheque-book, no money, no indications of the slightest use for the recovery of my body. I was battering madly at the drawers, when the butler, backed by two women-servants, intruded upon me.

* * *

That simply is the story of my change. No one will believe my frantic assertions. I am treated as one demented, and even at this moment I am under restraint. But I am sane, absolutely sane, and to prove it I have sat down to write this story minutely as the things happened to me. I appeal to the reader, whether there is any trace of insanity in the style or method, of the story he has been reading. I am a young man locked away in an old man's body. But the clear fact is incredible to everyone. Naturally I appear demented to those who will not believe this, naturally I do not know the names of my secretaries, of the doctors who come to see me, of my servants and neighbours, of this town (wherever it is) where I find myself. Naturally I lose myself in my own house, and suffer inconveniences of every sort. Naturally I ask the oddest questions. Naturally I weep and cry out, and have paroxysms of despair. I have no money and no cheque-book. The bank will not recognise my signature, for I suppose that, allowing for the feeble muscles I now have, my handwriting is still Eden's. These people about me will not let me go to the bank personally. It seems, indeed, that there is no bank in this town, and that I have an account in some part of London. It seems that Elvesham kept the name of his solicitor secret from all his household. I can ascertain nothing. Elvesham was, of course, a profound student of mental science, and all my declarations of the facts of the case merely confirm the theory that my insanity is the outcome of overmuch brooding upon psychology. Dreams of the personal identity indeed! Two days ago I was a healthy youngster, with all life before me; now I am a furious old man, unkempt, and desperate, and miserable, prowling about a great, luxurious, strange house, watched, feared, and avoided as a lunatic by everyone about me. And in London is Elvesham beginning life again in a vigorous body, and with all the accumulated knowledge and wisdom of threescore and ten. He has stolen my life.

What has happened I do not clearly know. In the study are volumes of manuscript notes referring chiefly to the psychology of memory, and parts of what may be either calculations or ciphers in symbols absolutely strange to me. In some passages there are indications that he was also occupied with the philosophy of mathematics. I take it he has transferred the whole of his memories, the accumulation that makes up his personality, from this old withered brain of his to mine, and, similarly, that he has transferred mine to his discarded tenement. Practically, that is, he has changed bodies. But how such a change may be possible is without the range of my philosophy. I have been a materialist for all my thinking life, but here, suddenly, is a clear case of man's detachability from matter.

One desperate experiment I am about to try. I sit writing here before putting the matter to issue. This morning, with the help of a table-knife that I had secreted at breakfast, I succeeded in breaking open a fairly obvious secret drawer in this wrecked writing-desk. I discovered nothing save a little green glass phial containing a white powder. Round the neck of the phial was a label, and thereon was written this one word, 'Release.' This may be – is most probably – poison. I can understand Elvesham placing poison in my way, and I should be sure that it was his intention so to get rid of the only living witness against him, were it not for this careful concealment. The man has practically solved the problem of immortality. Save for the spite of chance, he will live in my body until it has aged, and then, again, throwing that aside, he will assume some other victim's youth and strength. When one remembers his heartlessness, it is terrible to think of the ever-growing experience that… How long has he been leaping from body to body…? But I tire of writing. The powder appears to be soluble in water. The taste is not unpleasant.

* * *

There the narrative found upon Mr. Elvesham's desk ends. His dead body lay between the desk and the chair. The latter had been pushed back, probably by his last convulsions. The story was written in pencil and in a crazy hand, quite unlike his usual minute characters. There remain only two curious facts to record. Indisputably there was some connection between Eden and Elvesham, since the whole of Elvesham's property was bequeathed to the young man. But he never inherited. When Elvesham committed suicide, Eden was, strangely enough, already dead. Twenty-four hours before, he had been knocked down by a cab and killed instantly, at the crowded crossing at the intersection of Gower Street and Euston Road. So that the only human being who could have thrown light upon this fantastic narrative is beyond the reach of questions. Without further comment I leave this extraordinary matter to the reader's individual judgment.

Eternal Visions

Chris Wheatley

IF ONE is found among you who is cursed with the fear of his own likeness then he is to be put to death, rendered unto pieces and buried with no mark for his grave. All those with whom he consorted are to be immediately expelled from this land.

Translated from Sumerian Cuneiform found on a tablet in the ancient region of Sippar (modern day Iraq), on display in the British Museum

* * *

July, 1965

Dear Brendan,

Many thanks for your letter of the fourteenth. I am glad to hear your studies are progressing well and that you are also taking time to explore the delights which that wonderful old city has to offer!

In answer to your query, I can confirm that there was indeed trade between Sumer and Egypt, Upper Egypt especially. The ancient Mesopotamian societies were lacking in raw materials and developed a wide and sophisticated trading network.

I enclose a full list of recommended readings, together with, for your personal amusement, my own translation of a portion of the great Egyptian medical treatise, the Ebers Papyrus. It is a most fascinating document, particularly the portions which overlap my own pet-study, ancient attitudes to maladies of the mind and their treatment.

I believe you may derive some entertainment from the section on water, or 'bucket' madness. It seems, among these Nile-dwellers, a condition existed whose symptoms included an extreme aversion to one's own reflection. Unlike almost every other illness described in the papyrus, you will see that for this affliction there existed no known cure or treatment, save for the extreme action of immediate execution!

Yours in good health,

Uncle Terrence

* * *

Extract from 'A Crusader's Tale' – Robert De Payens, translated from the French by Jean Jacque Riems, Penguin Books, UK:
Be it known to all that in this, the year one thousand one hundred and seventy-seven years after the death of our lord and saviour Jesus Christ, I, Robert De Payens, Knight Hospitalier with five hundred of my brothers, did form part of the mighty and blessed Army of the Kingdom of Jerusalem under command of our holy leader, the leper-boy King Balwdin IV.

Be it also known that in the eleventh month of this year, we set forth en masse to do battle with the mighty infidel Vizier of Egypt, Saladin, the which was determined to take the Holy City itself. By this time we knew full well that our enemy numbered twenty-five thousand men all-told, these being

Mamluks, Ghulams, Qaraghulams and sundry auxiliaries. Of our own account, we numbered one thousand knights, some eighty being of the Order Templar, plus but four thousand infantry.

Nevertheless, with the sun at our backs, the King at our head and God in our hearts, we set forth in good order and with every belief in success. Marching hard, we pursued Saladin along the coast. The infidel left a trail of destruction in his wake. Too late we were to save Ramla, Lydda and Arsuf, yet the boy-King did not waver.

Much must be said of our leader's courage, fortitude and planning. Despite being but sixteen summers old and afflicted by the horror of the wasting disease, his hands wrapped and too painful to hold a horse's reins, the King was tireless in spirit and mind.

How could we lose! For we carried with us the holy relic of the True Cross and we good Christian men from toe to head. And God, indeed, smiled down upon us, for near Montgisard we came upon Saladin's baggage train, the which had been mired in deep mud and spread thin. The Vizier, believing us too insignificant a force, had allowed his men to roam wide, pillaging and looting. They were not at all prepared.

The King wasted no time. Holding the holy relic high, he prayed God for victory and every man among us cheered and every man among us felt the fire rise in our blood. It must be known to you now that the King fought as a lion. At each turn he was to be found in the very thickest of the fighting, laying about him with sword held high, though the pain in his ravaged body must have cost him dear.

Saladin and his barbarians took to the hills, fleeing for their lives before God and the sword. I believe this to be a victory unsurpassed in the history of our great crusades. Of those enemy left on the field, we sent they whose wounds were too severe to the mercy of the angels. We took a number of prisoners, many Egyptian levies, a small number of whom I took into my service as slaves.

Of curious note, one of these slaves, a man called Bithia, claimed to have been cursed by Saracen magics, so that he may not look upon his reflection without seeing something present so awful and so terrifying that this man could not put it into words.

We took him before the True Cross and had him kneel. The man was then compelled to turn his eyes toward a looking glass, whereupon he fell to the floor with such ungodly screams and cries that we despatched his soul there and then, the better to free him from Saladin's evil.

It was, I say again, a day for the annals which did much to further the glory of the One True God.

* * *

Taken from Hallam's Auctioneers Catalogue, Tudor Portrait Paintings of England, 2005:
Item #43 Portrait of Lady Helena Paignton-Smythe by Hans Holbeck the Younger of Heidelberg, circa 1585.

A fine characterization by the artist, probably completed during his first visit to England following successes in mainland Europe. Of particular interest is the subject. Lady Helena claimed direct descent from Robert De Payens, famous for his chronicles of the crusades. After returning from the Holy Land De Payens married English noblewoman Alice Parnell, taking ownership of her estate in South Yorkshire.

The Payens and their descendants suffered many well-documented misfortunes, leading to speculations of a family curse, which dogged the name for generations. Lady Helena's husband, Lord Alistair Paignton-Smythe, and her brother, Wilfred, both committed suicide within a few years of each other, the former having locked himself in his study for more than a year and, according to letters from family friend Godfrey Singleton, "...banished all mirrors, silver, cups, bowls and even polished wood from his presence."

Our guide price for this piece is £4000–£5000

* * *

From 'Signs and Signifiers of Witchcraft', John Fallows, 1673, facsimile by Brandon Press, UK:
The witch hath many nefarious devices with which to cloak her despicable and ungodly nature. Chief among these be her spells or glamours, whereupon, with the application of elixors, powders and such, worked in tandem with certain secret and sacrilegious signs, she may beguile those about her, or, in more severe cases, cause them harm by their own hand, the better to hide her heathen and unholy occupations.

Beware those who cannot stand their own image and seek to avoid it. This is as clear a sign of witchcraft as one might hope to discover. The unfortunate afflicted, as I have witnessed by mine own eyes, will undertake great spasms when presented with so simple an object as an hand mirror. They will thrash and froth and, if unable to flee, do great damage to themselves, up to and including inflicted mortal wounds upon their body.

Such a poor soul did I encounter at the hamlet of South Willow, this very Summer gone. It is a sight I shall not forget until my own body be lain cold into the open ground.

* * *

October, 1855

Dear Florence,

I hope this missive finds you in good health. It was very kind of you to enquire about your cousin George. There is not much new to tell. When George returned to Greenacres, your uncle insisted on summoning Dr. Michaels all the way from Harley Street. Oh, you would approve of Dr. Michaels! He is a fine figure of a man, upright and with the just the right level of sombreness. He informs me that George's condition is stable and has recommended we undertake to send him at once on an extended trip to Ahrenshoop to recuperate in the warmer climate of the Baltic peninsula.

Dr. Michaels is certain that spa treatment will do wonders for George's nervous condition. Truly, Florence, I have been much unnerved by your cousin's demeanour of late. He has not shaved or cut his hair in weeks and he keeps himself confined to his room with the curtains drawn. Dear Florence, I feel certain I can trust you not to divulge this to a soul!

I will write again once George has settled quarters in Ahrenshoop. Perhaps you would be darling enough to visit him there?

Yours Faithfully,
Deborah

* * *

From 'Conditions of the Psyche' by Dr. Gerhard Weber, translated from the German by Robert Klopp, Oxford University Press, 1937:
In one or two more extreme cases I have observed and catalogued a condition I shall find no better name for than *gegenteil narzissmus*. Symptoms of said malaise include, but are not limited to, an extreme fear of mirrors and reflective surfaces, lack of attention to personal hygiene and a general deterioration of the mental faculties. To date I can find no common denominator as to the preconditions of the arising of this state.

* * *

Internal communication from Hauptmann Dieter Fischer to Generalleutnant Hans Weber, 716th Infantry Division, 17th August, 1944 (translated):
Sir, it is with deepest regret that I must inform you of the sudden death this morning of Oberst Uwe Becker at our field headquarters outside Gensac, Bordeaux. As per regulations it falls to me to detail the exact circumstances of his passing. You will forgive me, I hope, my frankness. Oberst Becker was discovered in his room at 0900 hours deceased from a self-inflicted gunshot wound to the head. He held in one hand his service luger pistol, in the other, a fragment of mirror. It appears that he was in the process of shaving when the incident occurred. Sir, your brother will be deeply missed. I can assure you that no one outside of myself and Oberst's personal assistant are aware of the full circumstances of his passing.

* * *

Telegraph transmitted from US Army Base, Andrews Barracks, Berlin, Germany, 1954:
DEAR MOM AND POP – STOP – HAVE MET WONDERFUL WOMAN – STOP – HER NAME IS XIU YING – STOP – CHINESE EMBASSY ATTACHE – STOP – TRAVELLING TO SHANGHAI TO MEET FUTRE IN-LAWS EXCLAMATION POINT – STOP – LOVE FRANK

* * *

The Cambridge Herald, September 14th 1963, United States:
Millionaire Teen to Attend Harvard
Frank Schwarz Junior, heir to the Chinese-based Dongxiang Export Company millions is to attend Harvard University, starting next semester. Frank Schwarz Senior founded the company in Shanghai seven years ago after marrying into the wealthy Ying family. Since then, Dexco, as it became known, has gone from strength to strength, growing into a global giant with estimated assets totalling tens of millions in US dollars. Following the tragic death of Frank Senior (who, it is rumoured, committed suicide under mysterious circumstances) the company is being administered by his brother-in-law Zhang Ying and continues to trade strongly.

Schwarz Junior will be studying European Literature and hopes to make the baseball team in good time.

* * *

From 'Purple Prophets and Acid Saviours – a history of the beat generation' – by Richard Bartholomew, Future Press, New York, 2007:
If one were to choose a typical example from the Detroit scene in the mid-60s, one could hardly do better than to single out Robert 'Beatzy' Calhoun. Calhoun, a distant relation of the Dexco-Schwarz family, moved to the city from South Memphis sometime around 1959, and quickly fell in with counter-culture stalwarts such as Hal Joseph and Israel Banks, with whom he co-founded the radical underground publication 'Freedom Now'.

The following extract, taken from his only work published in book form, serves well to demonstrate Beatzy's somewhat derivative style:

From 'Beyond the Rainbow Door' by Beatzy Calhoun, Imaginarium Press, Detroit, 1967:
'Oh ye groovy brothers and ye freaky sisters, hear this! I have seen, my little cherubs and cherubin. Lo, I have beheld! I have passed through that great door, that beautiful sacred psychedelic

entrance that is the True Source of us all. I have seen, oh karmic wanderers and wonderers, I have visaged with my own two eyeballs the plane of perception beyond the concrete horizon.

And I tell you well, my children, it's a far - out - gas! All you cherry chicks and fab folks, you need to book fast from whatever it is that the man got you doing, whatever it is they got you slaving away at, and you got to take that ticket, children, you got to reach out and take that ticket. I'm talking Liquid Salvation Dippers, man! Yeah, you know what I mean.'

Amazingly Calhoun, who during late 1966 and early 1967 had been one of the foremost advocates of LSD was, by 1968, a staunch opponent of the drug, speaking out at a series of student meetings before retiring for good from the public eye.

According to Israel Banks, the change came after Calhoun experienced his first 'bad trip'. So severe was the change in Beatzy's character that he spent the last few years of his life in isolation, a sworn recluse, living in a tiny bedsit in Corktown. He did, however, rise from obscurity to declaim a series of increasingly bizarre announcements, before his death by his own hand in 1971.

Witness the following cryptic statement, which was issued through his publicist and appeared as a quarter-page advert in several regional and state-wide newspapers of the day:

LSD – A Warning! Listen my brothers and sisters. I urge you with all that remains of my soul to steer clear of this perfidious idol. Choose for yourself another path. The dangers are too great. Something evil lurks in the outskirts of the mind and it is my firm belief that it was my experiments with self-medication that invited it across to this world. Something opened the door, and, should my warning reach you too late, my only advice is destroy every mirror which you own. Cover any steel and have nothing polished in your house. Glass and reflective surfaces of any kind must become anathema to you. I hope, my friends, that by starving my unwanted companion in such a way I may be finally be free of this beast. Stay strong, stay true, Robert.

* * *

Taken from the San Francisco Chronicle, Obituaries, March 30th, 1987:
Frank Calhoun, 59
Astrologer and grandson of the beat-poet Robert 'Beatzy' Calhoun. According to family he died peacefully in his sleep at his home in Fremont. He is survived by two children and his wife.

* * *

Dear Shaun,

How are you? I am so sorry you had to hear about your Uncle Frank in the way that you did. Of course no one thinks the worse of you for not attending the funeral. It's a twelve-hour flight from the other side of the world and so expensive! I know Mary has told you a few details. I am in no way saying that you can't discuss this, however it's probably best, given the manner of Frank's death, if you keep certain things to yourself, for the sake of the family. I am sure that you understand.

I know you and he were very close. Mary tells me that you two spent much time together before you left. In fact, I believe you must be the last person he had any meaningful contact with before the end. I am sure that he appreciated your companionship.

Anyhow, unpleasantness aside, how is your work progressing? We are all so proud of you making a new life for yourself down there in Australia. Mary says to tell you that she and the kids miss you dearly. Please do tell us your news. Are you coming home for Christmas? Have you and Diane set a date for the wedding?

Regards,

Martha

* * *

From: Martin McGarrity <MartyM81@penn_state.com>
To: TotallyTina@ausie.com
Subject: woohoo!

Yo dudess! Is that you, Teeny? Hope I got the address right. As you can see, the college finally has email (!!!) so I'm trying it out on all of my friends. You are number 94 on my list (not really!). Life is good here. Hey, I'm a few months away from being Doctor McGarrity (fingers crossed)! Boy, am I going to lord it over you then! Won't say too much in case you never get this. If you do, let me know how things are back home, you droink. If this ends up somewhere else by mistake, please delete, unless you are a good-looking blonde in which case mail me back.

Word!

* * *

From: TotallyTina@ausie.com
To: Martin McGarrity <MartyM81@penn_state.com>
Subject: Re: woohoo!

You got me you phat jabend! Good to know you're not in the stone age any more (apart from sexually). How's it going? All is fine here in good old Oz. Our second cousin Jack (Jack Calhoun, not Jack McMinn) is ill, that's the only news. In fact, he'll be heading your way soon! Dad is sending him your way to recuperate with Larry and Janine, so he'll be just down the road from you. Don't ask me what's wrong with him. Lazyitus is my guess! Mum says he's been acting weird but let's face it – he's always acted weird! Talk soon, dork-face. — T

* * *

From ProntoNews.com 17th September, 2020:

The streaming platform GoView is under fire today after video of a man taking his own life which was uploaded onto the network somehow escaped censors and remained online for over three hours. The video, in which Martin McGarrity, a lecturer at Penn State, can be seen inflicting a gunshot wound to his own head, is believed to have been viewed and shared over twenty thousand times before GoView deleted the content. GoView have issued a full apology to the family, labelling the incident as 'highly regrettable'. The company say they will be reviewing procedures, however they maintain that such an occurrence is 'very rare'.

* * *

WhatsApp chat group 'friends4ever':

Martine: so sorry to hear about your father, Caz! How are you? Is there anything I can do?

Cassandra: Thanks Marty. Nothing seems real. Mom's freaking out. I have no idea what to do.

Rebecca: so sorry Caz! OMG. Sending so many hugs. Can I call?

Martine: We're here for you babes. Are you still at college?
Cassandra: No, I'm on my way home. Please come.

* * *

Vivo Talk Group 'sciencecohort24':
Cassandra: Hey dudes and dudesses, guess who landed the NASA job!!!!!!
Vivienne: What??!!! No way!!! That's stellar! (pun intended)
Cassandra: I'm going to be working on the rockets which will send humans to Mars!!!
Matthias: So many congratulations Caz. You toally deserve that job.
Karen: go girl! Hope you'll remember us little people!

* * *

ManFriday – Your Personally Tailored AI Assistant. For All Your Daily Needs:
Good morning Paul, here is your morning update. Don't forget your doctor's appointment at 15:30. Have a super fun day ;-)

Breaking News: *NASA Astronaut Henry Thompson confirmed for Mars One*
NASA have this morning confirmed that Henry Thompson *will* join the crew of Mars One, the first manned mission to the red planet, despite the tragic suicide of his fiancée, rocket engineer Cassandra McGarrity, who helped design the jet-propulsion system which will fuel the space-ship on its one-hundred-and-sixty-day journey. Cassandra McGarrity was found dead last Tuesday at the couple's home in Sacramento. The historic mission is due for launch this coming Saturday, at 10 a.m. EST.

* * *

Transcript of transmission from Mars One. Received 0900 NASA Headquarters, Washington DC:
This is Mission Commander Martin Daniels speaking from Mars Base One. It is with a sad and heavy heart that I have to report the death this morning of Geology Specialist Henry Thompson. Uh…this was no accident Houston. I don't mind telling you that we're all shaken up.

We'd like to send our condolences to his family and friends.

Thompson was part of a three-person team mapping the area South of the Zeus crater. According to Snow and Fielding Thompson seemed his normal self until he stopped to pick up a rock, one of those wind-polished sedimentary ones we showed you yesterday. Then he just…well he stared at it for some time. Snow and Fielding both asked Thompson what was wrong but didn't answer.

He opened his visor, Houston. It was quick and it was terminal and there was nothing Snow or Fielding could do.

Before unlocking his helmet-seals Henry said a few words that, well, frankly Houston they don't make a whole lot of sense. In fact they've got a few of us up here pretty spooked. We assume… That is, we can only think that some sort of mania or… Pardon me, Houston. I'm not feeling quite myself today.

Before unlocking his helmet seals Henry Thompson spoke the following words: "Oh my god. It's here. It's followed me here."

"It's followed me here."

Exogenous Cephalus Syndrome
A Case Report and Review of the Literature

Maria Wolfe

THE PATIENT is a 25-year-old female with no significant past medical history who presented to the General Surgery service as a referral from Internal Medicine with the complaint of a cephalic-type mass on her left shoulder. She asked that it be removed before "it gets me fired from my job."

Her symptoms began fourteen months prior to her presentation to this office. The patient first noticed a "tingling" sensation localized to her left shoulder, exclusively at the skin level. Over a week, the site became increasingly painful, described as an intense burning, as bad as a 5 to 8 on the 10-point visual analog scale. Direct pressure to the area worsened the pain, necessitating switching to a strapless bra and loose-fitting clothing; she was no longer able to sleep on her left side. There were no other exacerbating factors, including movement of her head, neck, or left shoulder. Both acetaminophen and the intermittent application of ice improved but did not eliminate the pain. She admitted to more fatigue than usual, which she attributed to the long hours she spent at her new job at a large marketing firm; her workload had expanded shortly after she started in her position, when a coworker in her department quit without notice and another unexpectedly died. No other symptoms, including fever, chills, shortness of breath, malaise, myalgias, bowel issues, unintentional weight loss/gain, or speaking in tongues.

Along with the pain, she reported a violaceous discoloration of the affected skin, starting as "tiny" but growing to approximately 3 centimeters in diameter, with a tuft of coarse black hair – unlike her ash-blond hair – in its center. Despite repeated shaving and chemical depilation, the hair returned within one to two days of removal. The patient had no previous dermatologic issues except "the usual teenage pimples." In particular, she denied any congenital or acquired skin lesions that identified her as a devil spawn, including tattoos created with unholy ink. Of note, one week before the onset of her symptoms, at a company potluck to celebrate new hires, she ate "some weird dessert that tasted awful, kind of like rancid meat mixed with fresh blood, only sweet"; to make a good first impression, she felt obligated to consume the item in its entirety, stating, "Mikey, a really nice guy in my department, baked it just for me from a special family recipe." She lived with her boyfriend of five years in an apartment professionally certified as "100% poltergeist-free," without any exotic pets or familiars. No foreign or trans-dimensional travel or encounters with registered practitioners of the dark arts. At age 18, she did attend what she thought was a Satanic Summoning Ceremony™ that involved an animal sacrifice, but, she conceded, it may have been fake. To her knowledge, she was not subject to any recent curses or demonic possessions. She had no sworn enemies. None of her first-degree relatives had been diagnosed with a genetic predisposition to supernatural phenomena.

She was seen by Internal Medicine two months after her symptom onset. At that time, several punch biopsies were performed of the lesion. The pathology was consistent with normal skin. There was no evidence of cancer or other abnormalities. A referral was made to General Surgery to discuss excision of the lesion with possible autologous skin grafting.

However, the patient was lost to follow-up during the next twelve months, citing "things got so crazy at work that I didn't have any time, and Mikey sure didn't help. I swear, it's like he wants me to quit or get fired." Over that period, her symptoms escalated despite her hopes that "it would just go away." She presented to this office for further workup and definitive treatment.

At her initial visit to this office, the patient complained of a mass on her left shoulder, at the site of the violaceous skin lesion. The burning pain had resolved approximately ten months ago, coincident with the mass appearing as a "small bump"; it reached its current size about two months later. Although no longer in pain, she described the mass as "a real pain in the ass" that she "absolutely cannot deal with anymore." She further stated: "It's driving me insane. Because of it, my boyfriend left *and* took my new air fryer with him. And, last month, I lost out on a big promotion to that jerk Mikey, who sure as hell didn't deserve it. That's when I scheduled this appointment." The patient repeatedly referred to the lesion as "Brian," which was also the name of her ex-boyfriend.

On examination, the patient was alert and oriented. She was in some distress, at times tearful during the visit, which she blamed on both Brians. Her hair was secured in a right-sided ponytail. A freshly bloodied bandage covered her left earlobe. Several scratches in varying stages of healing marked the left side of her face. The patient refused to tilt or turn her head to the left or to raise her left shoulder "because of Brian." Otherwise, she demonstrated a normal range of motion and strength of her head, neck, and upper extremities. A neat hole had been cut in the left shoulder of her dress, exposing the mass, because "Brian hates to be covered." For the past nine months, she had generally worn only off-shoulder, one-shoulder, or strapless tops.

The mass was located on the left shoulder, in the mid-clavicular line, but was not fixed to the underlying bone. Its range of motion on its 1-centimeter stalk was approximately 60° of flexion and extension; 45° of lateral flexion; and 80° of rotation. It measured approximately 5 centimeters in height, 3 centimeters in width, and 3 centimeters in depth and had the appearance of a wizened male humanoid head and neck with a violaceous complexion and with wiry black hair bristling over its scalp. Completion of the measurements was limited by the behavior of the mass, which hissed and attempted to bite this physician's hand with its many sharp fangs. "That's normal for Brian. He caused all this," the patient reported, gesturing to her face. "And, once, when Brian [the boyfriend] was kissing me, Brian [the mass] tore a big chunk off his right ear and spat it across the room." Its nose consisted of two holes above its mouth, a wide, featureless opening from which a short, bifurcated tongue regularly flicked. The right eye of the mass was dark and beady, similar to that of a rat; its left was missing and scarred over because the patient "stabbed Brian with a metal kebab skewer to get him to shut up." Of note, the patient reported experiencing pain as a result of the stabbing, described as initially sharp but ultimately fading to an intense ache that lasted for 24 hours, during which time the mass was silent. A sensory test confirmed that the patient and the mass had a common cutaneous innervation: on the mass itself, her two-point discrimination was 8 millimeters, and she was able to detect light touch and temperature variations. The mass had no evident external auditory apertures and, per the patient, "either doesn't hear me or never bothers to listen."

During the evaluation, the mass uttered a series of unintelligible sounds – primarily clicks and gurgles – amid its near-constant hissing. The patient claimed to understand this as a "language" and translated several of the phrases as the following:

> You are not smart.
> Your MBA is from a third-rate institution.
> You are bad at your job.
> Mikey deserved that promotion. Never you.
> You really should just quit in shame.
> No one likes you. No one.
> Brian [the boyfriend] should have left you years ago.
> You will never be loved.

"Brian never says anything complimentary," she commented. "It's like he's trying to make me feel bad." The frequency of the defamatory statements had gradually increased and, for the past month, had continued into the night-time hours, precluding a restful sleep. Additionally, due to the disruption caused to her co-workers at the office, three months ago, her employer had insisted that she work from home, a solution opposed by her co-worker (Mikey), who had advocated for her immediate dismissal from the firm. A prescription sleep medication mixed with wine as well as the sudden, forceful application of an old 1988 *Encyclopaedia Britannica* (Volume VIII: "Piranha to Scurfy") onto the mass, though painful, afforded some relief from the vocalizations. While the patient found industrial noise-canceling headphones effective, the mass chewed up the left muff of each one within a day or two of their purchase. Also, any material used as a gag was readily shredded by its fangs. Other interventions she attempted included exorcism, self-administered over-the-counter oral and topical holy water, and hot yoga, all without success.

The physical examination was otherwise unremarkable. No other skin lesions were present.

Bloodwork was ordered. Her complete blood count and comprehensive metabolic panel were within normal limits. However, her X-reactive protein was elevated, suggestive of recent exposure to the supernatural. Tissue from the punch biopsies was obtained and sent for special staining. A Gleason silver stain was positive, a finding consistent with Exogenous Cephalus Syndrome (ECS).

* * *

Exogenous Cephalus Syndrome is a rare disorder of supernatural origin first described by Ebenezer Aldersley in a contemporaneous 1613 English text.[1] Aldersley reported the case of a 31-year-old male, Jack Holingbery, who grew a "demon head" on his right shoulder. The condition was thought to have been caused by the witch Anne Butssey through an unspecified mechanism that she refused to divulge even under the standard vigorous torture. "Generalized witchy evil" was cited by Aldersley as her motive despite witness testimony in the trial transcriptions pointing to a feud arising from an ill-fated sheep trade.[2] The account established the classic signs of ECS: a violaceous skin lesion with a centralized tuft of black hair affecting

---

1   Aldersley, Ebenezer. *The Workes...Containing I. Chirurgicall Lectures of Supernatural Tumors and Otherworldly Ulcers. II. A Treatise of the First Part of Chirurgery and the Methodicall Doctrine of Witchcraft-Induced Wounds. III. A Treatise of the Second Part on the Treatment of those Afflicted by Generalized Witchy Evil. Published in his Lifetime in Several Treatises, and Now in One Volume, Corrected and Amended.* London: Printed by R.G. for William Thrale, and sold by Richard Reade, 1613. Print.

2   Altham, Preston. *The Wonderfull Discoverie of a Notorious Witch in the Countie of Cumberland. With the Arraignement and Triall at the Assizes and Generall Gaole, Holden at the Larger of the Two Public Houses of Cumberland, upon Munday, the Twelfth of July last, 1613.* London: Printed by W. Barnes for John Potts, 1614. Printed.

either shoulder that eventually develops into a humanoid head and neck. Holingbery suffered from localized pain that resolved once the mass reached its full size, melancholia, facial injuries, a loss of his livelihood as a sheepherder, and sleep disturbances. Furthermore, the patient claimed that the demon taunted him in a "devil language" that only he understood, driving him "nigh insane" with accusations of his unworthiness. Treatment involved burning the patient and the alleged witch on a shared pyre, which yielded a good result.

Since its initial description, only two additional case reports have been added to the medical literature. Both patients exhibited the same disease progression and symptoms as noted by Aldersley. The first case – of a 16-year-old female – was recorded in 1897 by Dr. Walter Gleason of Boston, Massachusetts.[3] Like Aldersley, Gleason identified the practitioner of magic who had caused the ECS in his patient. The mode of transmission was determined to be oral, via a "vile-tasting" potion secreted in a pastry. As the sorcerer had targeted not the girl but her great-uncle, a rival, he agreed to reverse the syndrome via a proprietary antidote. The remedy resulted in the self-decapitation of the exogenous head from her right shoulder. Afterward, the patient resumed her normal life, ultimately dying at the age of nineteen due to a childbed fever contracted after her third pregnancy. In the three-year interval since the reversal, there had been no recurrence of the mass. Gleason's subsequent gross and microscopic studies of the acellular gelatinous material that comprised the auto-amputated mass revealed the pathognomonic silver staining on histologic evaluation.

In 1951, Professor Dieter Bommer of Heidelberg, Germany detailed the case of a 55-year-old male patient with a left shoulder mass, present for 13 months.[4] The diagnosis was confirmed by the Gleason stain. Furthermore, Bommer discovered a link between ECS and an elevation of the X-reactive protein, a nonspecific but common marker of disorders of magical origin. As the identity of the practitioner responsible for the condition was unknown, Bommer undertook the surgical removal of the mass. However, during the dissection, he encountered an unexpected "network" of dilated blood vessels associated with the mass, the inadvertent injury of which led to massive intraoperative bleeding. An emergency median sternotomy was required to achieve vascular control. Despite maximal supportive care, the patient expired on postoperative day #1. An autopsy showed exuberant neo-vascularization arising from the subclavian artery, likely a consequence of the disorder and not a normal variant.

When assessing a patient with a cephalic-type mass, the more common Supernumerary Appendage Syndrome (SAS) must be considered in the differential diagnosis. Both ECS and SAS share an occult origin and feature tumors composed of an acellular gelatinous matrix. However, whereas ECS is transmitted via an oral route in the form of a potion, SAS relies on an aural delivery mechanism, i.e., spellcasting.[5] Of the 2,344 cases of SAS documented in the medical literature since 1751, there have been two instances of patients with a cephalic-type

3   Gleason, Walter. *An Unusual Case of an Exogenous Cephalus of Occult Origin in a Sixteen-Year-Old Woman.* Med Chir Trans. 1897; 73:377-430.

4   Bommer, Dieter. *Exogenous Cephalus Syndrome-Associated Neo-Vascularization Resulting in Massive Intra-Operative Bleeding: Report of a Case.* J Occult Surg. 1951 Jan; 13(1):73-5.

5   The International Society of Magical Practitioners (ISMP) holds the copyright to the spell responsible for SAS. Multiple attempts by a fellow of the Supernatural Medical Association (SMA) to obtain the text have been consistently rebuffed by the ISMP despite written assurances that it would solely be used to produce a countermeasure for medical purposes. In retaliation, that SMA researcher is believed to have been transformed into a small mammal, likely a beaver, and spirited away to a location somewhere in Central Asia. When questioned on the matter, an ISMP spokesperson denied the involvement of their membership in the alleged Metamorphosis and Kidnapping.

mass, one growing from the right thigh and the other from the abdominal wall; the masses, both male in appearance, were described as "quite attractive, all things considered."[6,7] The remaining cases involved a duplicate upper limb (56%), lower limb (40%), and "other" (4%), which presented on the upper torso (80%), lower torso (10%), and "other site" (10%). Unlike the masses of ECS, in SAS, the duplicate appendages – in particular, the two "heads" – were nonfunctional although anecdotal reports of working upper limbs exist. Since both syndromes are associated with an elevated X-reactive protein, a definitive diagnosis of ECS in a patient with a cephalic-type mass is based on clinical findings as well as a positive Gleason silver stain.

Centuries of experience with SAS have provided some insight into the management of ECS. In the absence of a reverse-engineered counter-spell, the sole treatment of SAS is simple amputation of the extra appendage. Yet, in the medical literature, three patients with SAS, all male, elected to retain their appendage – classified as "other" – for unspecified reasons without any known impact on their health. Due to their minimal vascular supply, smaller appendages may be easily removed in the office setting while those that are full-size or overgrown may benefit from formal excision in the operating room. Overall, the rate of local recurrence is 35%, with the status of the margins and the size of the appendage having no bearing on the incidence. Given the rarity of ECS, the recurrence rate following a successful operative excision is unknown. However, strategies for improving the recurrence rate in patients with SAS have been investigated. A recent prospective, randomized, double-blind, placebo-controlled study of 228 patients with SAS revealed a statistically significant reduction in the rate of recurrence if the excision site is irrigated with sterile holy water while a priest performs an exorcism: 11.3% versus 40% in the placebo group (p=0.0001); in contrast, treatment with sterile holy water or exorcism alone did not reach statistical significance (p=0.01).[8,9] In the event of a SAS recurrence, a re-excision may be safely performed.

* * *

The patient was advised of her diagnosis of Exogenous Cephalus Syndrome. Its supernatural etiology was discussed as were its management options: immolation, reversal by the culpable magical practitioner, and surgical excision. The possibility of no intervention was raised but dismissed by the patient as the natural history of ECS is unknown but likely includes insanity and/or an unnatural death. After Mikey – the suspect – threatened to "go to HR" when the patient asked him for the reversal potion, she chose surgical excision. The risks and benefits of the procedure were reviewed – most notably bleeding, infection, pain, damage to adjacent structures, recurrence, and death – and the patient signed the consent form. Of note, during the conversation, the mass became more agitated and violent, which the patient attributed to "Brian just being an asshole as usual, not because he knows what's going on."

6   Heymann, IA, Lichtenstein GR. *Supernumerary Appendage Syndrome Presenting as a Cephalic-Shaped Mass: An Unusual Case.* J SMA. 1978 October 6; 240(15):465-513.

7   Hongo S, Miyata AL, Wuepper JE. *A Handsome and Silent Male Head Appearing on the Abdomen of a Middle-Aged Female Patient.* J Supernatural Med. 1935 July 31;62(2):229-44.

8   Fox-Morales Y, Wansbrough-Herieka E, et.al. *Effects of Exorcism and Sterile Holy Water versus Placebo on Recurrence Among Patients with Supernumerary Appendage Syndrome Following Standard Surgical Excision: A Randomized Controlled Trial.* J Supernatural Med. 2016; 308(4):353-361.

9   The study arm of the trial exclusively used Exorcism #36 – "Non revertetur ad hoc humerum" ("Do not return to this shoulder") – from *The Big Book of Exorcisms for the Medical Setting.* Somerset, 1835.

Shortly after her arrival at the hospital, the patient was given a dose of the sedative midazolam to calm the mass, which had bit a nurse and the anesthesiologist. The patient was first seen by Interventional Radiology for mapping and embolization of any mass-associated blood vessels, to avoid massive intra-operative bleeding. She was then taken to the operating room for the procedure and placed on the OR table. Adequate intravenous sedation was administered, and the patient was intubated. Before proceeding, the mass was poked with a long-handled scalpel to confirm it was fully unconscious. The left shoulder and neck were widely prepped and draped in the standard surgical fashion, as was the chest in the event a median sternotomy would be needed for vascular control. A 5-centimeter elliptical incision was made at the base of the lesion, which was removed with a 1-centimeter gross margin, without resection of the clavicle. Following its separation from the shoulder, once it was clear that it was not faking its death, the mass was sent for pathologic evaluation. Bleeding was minimal, and no blood products were transfused. Prior to closure, the wound was irrigated with sterile holy water while a gowned-and-gloved priest performed the recommended exorcism. The incision was closed in two layers with absorbable suture. The skin was cleaned and dried and dressed with sterile gauze secured with silk tape. The patient tolerated the procedure well and was taken to the post-operative area in good condition. She was discharged home on postoperative day #2.

At her two-week follow-up appointment, the patient had no complaints. "But, without Brian around to insult me, it's weird how quiet my apartment is," she commented. Her wound was healing well without evidence of infection. On repeat bloodwork, her X-reactive protein level had fallen to "undetectable." The pathology corroborating the diagnosis of ECS was reviewed.

Three months later, she returned to the office for a routine re-assessment. The patient reported no recurrence of her symptoms nor of the mass and had resumed her normal activities of daily living. "I feel a lot more self-confident now," she said. An examination of the surgical site revealed a completely healed incision. She demonstrated full range of motion of her left shoulder, head, and neck. The patient noted that she still worked with "that asshole Mikey," who, since the mysterious disappearance of their supervisor, "now runs the entire department." She admitted to several new hobbies: studying the dark arts, crocheting, and seeking revenge.

Biographies & Sources

Louisa May Alcott

Lost in a Pyramid (or, The Mummy's Curse)

(Originally Published in *The New World*, 1869)

Born in Philadelphia, the second of four daughters, Louisa May Alcott (1832–88) had intellectuals for parents, friends of Ralph Waldo Emerson (1803–82) and adherents of his Transcendentalist movement. They were by no means wealthy, though, and Louisa had quite early to start working – as a seamstress and schoolteacher. She started supplementing her income with bits of writing. Most famously, the semi-autobiographical *Little Women* (1868), but across a wide range, from detective fiction and humour to horror and sensation. She became increasingly active as an abolitionist and temperance campaigner and feminist, speaking out for women's suffrage and women's education.

Mike Ashley

Foreword: Weird Horror Short Stories

Mike Ashley has been a writer, editor and researcher for over fifty years, specialising in science fiction, fantasy, the supernatural and crime fiction. Amongst his 140 or so books are the biography of writer Algernon Blackwood, *The Starlight Man*, a *Who's Who in Horror & Fantasy Fiction*, a study of science fiction *Out of This World* and a five-volume history of the science-fiction magazines. He received the Pilgrim Award in 2002 for a lifetime contribution to science fiction and fantasy scholarship. He lives with a collection of over 30,000 books and magazines and a remarkably tolerant wife.

Gertrude Atherton

The Striding Place

(Originally Published as 'The Twins' in *The Speaker*, 1896)

Gertrude Atherton (1857–1948), who also wrote under the pseudonyms 'Frank Lin' and 'Asmodeus', was born in California. She wrote her first novel while living with her husband in the Atherton Mansion in San Francisco. Her family disapproved of her writing, which often featured independent, driven women. After her husband died at sea she moved to New York, and travelled in Europe. Her novel *Black Oxen* (1923) was made into a silent film, and her other horror tales include 'The Foghorn', 'Death and the Woman' and 'The Bell in the Fog'.

E.F. Benson

Negotium Perambulans

(Originally Published in *Hutchinson's Magazine*, 1922)

Edward Frederic ('E.F.') Benson (1867–1940) was born at Wellington College in Berkshire, England, where his father, the future Archbishop of Canterbury Edward White Benson, was headmaster. Benson is widely known for being a writer of reminiscences, fiction, satirical novels, biographies and autobiographical studies. His first published novel, *Dodo*, initiated his success, followed by a series of comic novels such as *Queen Lucia* and *Trouble for Lucia*. Later in life, Benson moved to Rye where he was elected mayor. It was here that he was inspired to write several macabre ghost story and supernatural collections and novels, including *Paying Guests* and *Mrs. Ames*.

Algernon Blackwood

The Willows

(Originally Published in *The Listener and Other Stories*, 1907)

Algernon Henry Blackwood (1869–1951) was a writer who crafted his tales with extraordinary vision. Born in Kent but working at numerous careers in America and Canada in his youth, he eventually settled back in England in his thirties. He wrote many novels and short stories including 'The Willows', which was rated by Lovecraft as one of his favourite stories, and he is credited by many scholars as a real master of imagery who wrote at a consistently high standard.

Robert Bloch

The Secret in the Tomb

(Originally Published in *Weird Tales*, May 1935. All Rights Reserved. © Robert Bloch 1935. Reprinted with Permission.)

Robert Bloch (1917–94) was born in Chicago, Illinois. At sixteen years old he wrote a fan letter to H.P. Lovecraft, whose encouraging response led Bloch to become a prolific author in his own right. Bloch's earlier stories mirror the cosmic horror of Lovecraft, whom he greatly admired; though he later turned to writing more in the psychological horror and crime genres. He is perhaps most famous for writing the book *Psycho*, on which Hitchcock's movie is based.

Ramsey Campbell

The Place of Revelation

(Originally Published in *13 Horrors*, ed. Brian A. Hopkins. © 2003 by Ramsey Campbell.)

Ramsey Campbell has been given more awards than any other writer in the field, including the Grand Master Award of the World Horror Convention, the Lifetime Achievement Award of the Horror Writers Association, the Living Legend Award of the International Horror Guild and the World Fantasy Lifetime Achievement Award. In 2015 he was made an Honorary Fellow of Liverpool John Moores University for outstanding services to literature. Among his novels available from Flame Tree Press are *Thirteen Days by Sunset Beach, The Wise Friend, Somebody's Voice*, and his *Three Births of Daoloth* trilogy: *The Searching Dead, Born to the Dark* and *The Way of the Worm*.

Daniel Carpenter

Flotsam

(Originally Published in *The Shadow Booth*, 2017)

Daniel Carpenter is a writer and critic from Manchester. His stories have been published by *Black Static, The Lonely Crowd, Unsung Stories* and in a number of *Year's Best* anthologies including *Year's Best Weird Fiction* and *Year's Best Dark Fantasy and Horror*. He is a book critic for *Horrified Magazine, Sublime Horror*, and *Black Static* amongst others and lives in London with his family. He tweets at @dancarpenter85.

Micah Castle

The Things from the Woods

(First Publication)

Micah Castle is a weird fiction and horror writer. His stories have appeared in various magazines, websites, and anthologies, and he has three collections currently out. While away from the keyboard, he enjoys spending time with his wife, spending hours hiking through the woods, playing with his six animals, and can typically be found reading a book somewhere in his Pennsylvania home.

Robert W. Chambers
The Mask
(Originally Published in *The King in Yellow*, 1895)
Robert William Chambers (1865–1933) was born in Brooklyn, New York. He started his career publishing illustrations in magazines like *Life*, *Truth* and *Vogue* before abruptly turning his attention strictly to fiction. He produced works in numerous genres including historical, romance, fantasy, science fiction and horror. Everett Franklin Bleiler (1920–2010), a respected scholar of science fiction and fantasy literature, described *The King in Yellow* as one of the most important works of American supernatural fiction.

Lucy Clifford
The New Mother
(Originally Published in *The Anyhow Stories, Moral and Otherwise*, 1882)
Left unprovided-for after the death of her distinguished but unworldly mathematician husband William Kingdon Clifford (1845–79), Lucy Clifford (1846–1929) turned to writing as a source of income. She found success with plays and novels as well as with short stories. Much of her work was distinctly grown-up in tone – her most famous novel, *Mrs. Keith's Crime* (1885), was about euthanasia – but she also wrote (admittedly sometimes dark and daring) tales for children. 'The New Mother' was one of these, and proved a strong influence on Neil Gaiman for his dark fantasy novella *Coraline* (2002).

Arthur Conan Doyle
The Terror of Blue John Gap
(Originally Published in *The Strand Magazine*, 1910)
Arthur Conan Doyle (1859–1930) was born in Edinburgh, Scotland. As a medical student Doyle was so impressed by his professor's powers of deduction that he was inspired to create the much-loved figure Sherlock Holmes. However, he became increasingly interested in spiritualism and the supernatural, leaving him keen to explore fantastical elements in his stories.

H.D. Everett
The Next Heir
(Originally Published in *The Death-Mask and Other Ghosts*, 1920)
Born in Gillingham, Kent, Henrietta Dorothy Everett (1851–1923) married a Staffordshire solicitor in 1869 and only turned to writing in her forties. Publishing under the pen name Theo Douglas, she produced over twenty books, including several novels as well as an abundance of short stories. Whilst these included a number of historical romances, she really made her reputation with her tales of mystery and the supernatural, which were to be recommended by H.P. Lovecraft and M.R. James.

Francis Flagg
The Distortion out of Space
(Originally Published in *Weird Tales*, August 1934)
George Henry Weiss (1898–1946), who wrote under the name Francis Flagg, was born in Halifax, Nova Scotia. At the age of twenty, however, he moved to the United States, where he eventually made his home in Arizona. He made a splash with his debut-story, 'The Machine Man of Ardathia', which appeared in *Amazing Stories*, 1927. Most of his work was to be in this same sci-fi genre, but he was a great admirer of H.P. Lovecraft.

Kevin M. Folliard
White Noise
(Originally Published in *Hinnom Magazine #6*, © 2018)
Kevin M. Folliard is a Chicagoland writer whose fiction has been collected by The Horror Tree, The Dread Machine, Demain Publishing, and more. His recent publications include his horror anthology *The Misery King's Closet*, his YA fantasy adventure novel *Grayson North: Frost-Keeper of the Windy City*, and his 2022 dinosaur adventure novel *Carnivore Keepers*. Kevin currently resides in the western suburbs of Chicago, IL, where he enjoys his day job in academia and membership in the La Grange and Brookfield Writers Groups.

Anastasia Garcia
Dark Skies
(First Publication)
Anastasia Garcia is a writer of horror and speculative fiction. Anastasia's writing was recently featured in *Shadow Atlas: Dark Landscapes of the Americas*, an anthology of speculative fiction from Hex Publishers; the Lunatics Radio Hour Podcast; *The Deep*, a horror anthology from Ghost Orchid Press; and the *Nottingham Horror Collective* magazine. Anastasia was named a recipient of the Ladies of Horror Fiction writer's grant. Originally from Texas, Anastasia now works at Instagram and lives in New York City with her partner and her cats. Follow her writing journey on Instagram @anastasiawrites, on Twitter @agarcia_writes, or at anastasiawrites.com.

R. Murray Gilchrist
The Crimson Weaver
(Originally Published in *The Yellow Book Quarterly, Vol. VI*, 1895)
Horror fiction was a sideline for the Sheffield-born writer Robert Murray Gilchrist (1867–1917), who made his name as the author of over twenty novels – many of them set in the nearby Peak District, where he made his home. But his short stories commanded considerable respect, and a great many of those dealt in horror and the macabre. Never simply sensationalist, though, they were works of real literary ambition.

Timothy Granville
The Animal King
(First Publication)
Timothy Granville was born in the New Forest, England, and now lives in rural Wiltshire with his wife, daughter, and many weird and horrific books. His stories have appeared in magazines and anthologies such as *Nightscript*, *Supernatural Tales*, *Dark Lane Anthology*, *The Ghastling*, *Oculus Sinister* (Chthonic Mater), and *Crooked Houses* (Egaeus Press). In addition to reading and writing, he enjoys eerie megaliths, mushrooming, and obscure electronic music, occasionally combining all three. His website is timothygranville.com.

Steve Hanson
Isle of the Dead
(First Publication)
Steve Hanson is an author, aspiring screenwriter, and cognitive scientist in training whose work draws from a number of different sources in horror and speculative fiction. Some of Steve's major influences include speculative authors H.P. Lovecraft, M.R. James, and E.F. Benson, as well as more 'literary' authors such as Vladimir Nabokov and Jorge Luis Borges. In addition to

his burgeoning writing career, Steve is pursuing a Ph.D. in cognitive science, with a focus on the intersection of human cognition and language. A native of Pittsburgh, Pennsylvania, Steve currently divides his time between Vienna, Austria and Washington, DC.

Maria Haskins
The Brightest Lights of Heaven
(Originally Published in *Fireside Fiction #69,* July 2019)
Maria Haskins is a Swedish-Canadian writer and reviewer of speculative fiction. She currently lives just outside Vancouver with a husband, two kids, a snake, several birds, and a very large black dog. Her short story collection *Six Dreams About the Train* was published in 2021 by Trepidatio Publishing. Maria's work has appeared in *The Best Horror of the Year Volume 13, Black Static, Interzone, Fireside, Beneath Ceaseless Skies, Mythic Delirium, Shimmer, PseudoPod,* and elsewhere. Find out more on her website, mariahaskins.com, or follow her on Twitter, @mariahaskins.

Nathaniel Hawthorne
Rappaccini's Daughter
(Originally Published in *The United States Magazine and Democratic Review in New York*, 1844)
The prominent American writer Nathaniel Hawthorne (1804–64) was born in Salem, Massachusetts. His most famous novel *The Scarlet Letter* helped him become established as a writer in the 1850s. Most of his works were influenced by his friends Ralph Waldo Emerson and Herman Melville, as well as by his extended financial struggles. Hawthorne's works often incorporated a dark romanticism that focused on the evil and sin of humanity. Some of his most famous works detailed supernatural presences or occurrences.

William Hope Hodgson
The Hog
(Originally Published in *Weird Tales*, January 1947)
William Hope Hodgson (1877–1918) was born in Essex, England, but moved several times with his family, including living for some time in County Galway, Ireland – a setting that would later inspire *The House on the Borderland*. Hodgson made several unsuccessful attempts to run away to sea, until his uncle secured him some work in the Merchant Marine. This association with the ocean would unfold later in his many sea stories. After some initial rejections of his writing, Hodgson managed to become a full-time writer of both novels and short stories, which form a fantastic legacy of adventure, mystery and horror fiction.

Carl Jacobi
Mive
(Originally Published in *Weird Tales*, January 1932. Copyright © 1928, 1956 by Carl Jacobi; reprinted by permission of Wildside Press and the Virginia Kidd Agency, Inc.)
Born in Minneapolis, Carl Jacobi (1908–97) was an enthusiastic writer from his boyhood and grew up to enrol as a literature student at his hometown university. He started writing more seriously then, his earliest stories appearing in the *Minnesota Quarterly* while he was still a student. 'Mive' was something of a breakthrough-work, winning a university competition judged by the best-selling horror writer Margaret Culkin Banning (1891–1982).

M.R. James
The Diary of Mr. Poynter
(Originally Published in *A Thin Ghost and Others*, 1919)
Montague Rhodes James (1862–1936), whose works are regarded as being at the forefront of the ghost story genre, was born in Kent, England. James dispensed with the traditional, predictable techniques of ghost story construction, instead using realistic contemporary settings for his works. He was also a British medieval scholar, so his stories tended to incorporate antiquarian elements. His stories often reflect his childhood in Suffolk and his talented acting career, which both seem to have assisted in the build-up of tension and horror in his works.

Nyx Kain
He Led
(First Publication)
Nyx Kain is a writer with roots deep in both the Canadian prairies and a fascination with the power of belief. From velveteen rabbits to ghost stories that give more life to their subjects with each fascinated retelling, their passion is to celebrate and affirm how the feelings we share through fiction themselves create something new and real – whether that is a friendship with someone fascinated by the same story, a call to action, or something as small and tenacious as a memory that only breathes when a wind in the right season blows across it.

Shona Kinsella
The Call of El Tunche
(First Publication)
Shona Kinsella is the author of epic fantasy, *The Vessel of KalaDene* series, dark Scottish fantasy *Petra MacDonald and the Queen of the Fae* and British Fantasy Award shortlisted industrial fantasy *The Flame and the Flood* as well as the non-fiction *Outlander and the Real Jacobites: Scotland's Fight for Freedom*. She was editor of the British Fantasy Society's fiction publication *BFS Horizons* for four years and is now Chair of the British Fantasy Society.

Fritz Leiber
The Hill and the Hole
(Originally Published in *Unknown Worlds*, August 1942. Copyright © 1942 by Fritz Leiber. Reprinted with permission.)
His parents Shakespearean actors who ran their own touring company, Chicago-born Fritz Leiber (1910–92) was raised in a world of theatre, fantasy and myth. He grew up ideally equipped imaginatively to write, and to pioneer the genre he himself dubbed 'sword and sorcery'. Despite his humanities-orientated background, though, he took a step sideways into science at the University of Chicago, studying psychology and biology. He started writing fiction as a graduate student in philosophy. He only came into contact with H.P. Lovecraft in the last year or so of the older author's life, but they corresponded closely until he died.

H.P. Lovecraft
The Whisperer in Darkness
(Originally Published in *Weird Tales*, August 1931)
Master of weird fiction Howard Phillips Lovecraft (1890–1937) was born in Providence, Rhode Island. Featuring unknown and otherworldly creatures, his stories were one of the first to

mix science fiction with horror. Plagued by nightmares from an early age, he was inspired to write his dark and strange fantasy tales; the isolation he must have experienced from suffering frequent illnesses can be felt as a prominent theme in his work. Lovecraft inspired many other authors, and his most famous story 'The Call of Cthulhu' has influenced many aspects of popular culture.

Arthur Machen
Novel of the White Powder
(Originally Published in *The Three Imposters; or, The Transmutations*, 1895)
Arthur Machen (1863–1947) was born in Monmouthshire, Wales. Machen was an author of horror, supernatural and fantasy fiction. A key figure of the horror genre, his early novella *The Great God Pan* cultivated a reputation as an iconic classic. Casting his net wide, Machen was also an accomplished journalist and actor. His literary forays into fantasy and supernatural realms led to interesting works such as *The Three Impostors* (1895) and *The Hill of Dreams* (1907). In his essay 'Supernatural Horror in Literature', Lovecraft praised Machen highly, describing his stories as those 'in which the elements of hidden horror and brooding fright attain an almost incomparable substance and realistic acuteness.'

Lena Ng
Lola
(First Publication)
Lena Ng lives in Toronto, Canada, and is a member of the Horror Writers Association. She has short stories in seventy publications including *Amazing Stories* and the anthology *We Shall Be Monsters*, which was a finalist for the 2019 Prix Aurora Award. *Under an Autumn Moon* is her short story collection. She is currently seeking a publisher for her novel, *Darkness Beckons*, a Gothic romance. Her characters in her short story 'Lola' were inspired by the strange upper-class New Yorkers in the movie *Rosemary's Baby*.

Reggie Oliver
The Black Ship
(Originally Published in *The Lovecraft Squad – Dreaming*, Pegasus Books, 2018)
Reggie Oliver is an actor, director, playwright, illustrator and award-winning author of fiction. Published work includes six plays, three novels, an illustrated children's book *The Hauntings at Tankerton Park* (Zagava 2016), nine volumes of short stories, including *Mrs. Midnight* (2011 winner of Children of the Night Award for best work of supernatural fiction), and, the biography of the writer Stella Gibbons, *Out of the Woodshed* (Bloomsbury 1998). His stories have appeared in over one hundred different anthologies and three 'selected' editions of them have been published, the latest being *Stages of Fear* (Black Shuck Books 2020). His ninth volume of tales *A Maze for the Minotaur* was published by Tartarus Press in 2021.

Barry Pain
The Moon-Slave
(Originally Published in *Stories in the Dark*, 1901)
A regular contributor to *Punch* and other magazines, Cambridge-born Barry Pain (1864–1928) was renowned first and foremost as a comic writer. Like his friend and fellow-humourist Jerome K. Jerome (1859–1927), however, he had a longstanding interest in the

supernatural and the gothic. His mad-scientist shocker *The Octave of Claudius* (1897) was to become a pioneering Hollywood Horror movie, in the form of *A Blind Bargain*, with Lon Chaney and Raymond McKee, in 1922.

Jason Parent
Agon
(First Publication)
Jason Parent is an author of horror, thrillers, mysteries, science fiction and dark humour, though his many novels, novellas, and short stories tend to blur the boundaries between genres. From his EPIC and eFestival Independent Book Award finalist first novel, *What Hides Within*, to his widely applauded police procedural/supernatural thriller, *Seeing Evil*, to his fast and furious sci-fi horror, *The Apocalypse Strain* (Flame Tree Press), Jason's work has won him praise from both critics and fans of diverse genres alike. He currently lives in Rhode Island, surrounded by chewed furniture thanks to his corgi and mini Aussie pups.

Edgar Allan Poe
The Facts in the Case of M. Valdemar
(Originally Published in *American Review*, December 1845)
The versatile writer Edgar Allan Poe (1809–49) was born in Boston, Massachusetts. He is well known as an influential author, poet, editor and literary critic who wrote during the American Romantic Movement. Poe is generally considered the inventor of the detective fiction genre, and his works are famously filled with terror, mystery, death and hauntings. Some of his better-known works include his poems 'The Raven' and 'Annabel Lee', and the short stories 'The Tell Tale Heart' and 'The Fall of the House of Usher'. The dark, mystifying characters of his tales have captured the public's imagination and reflect the struggling, poverty-stricken lifestyle he lived his whole life.

Bonnie Quinn
The Stones Move at Night
(First Publication)
Bonnie Quinn is a programmer currently residing in Ohio with her three cats and one dog. She enjoys writing in her free time and her most notable work is the online horror series, *How to Survive Camping*. She draws inspiration from folklore and with 'The Stones Move at Night', sought to combine stories of forest spirits with her New England childhood, where she spent most of her time exploring the forest and playing along the stone walls.

Eric Reitan
The Blessed Affliction
(First Publication)
Eric Reitan, a philosophy professor and violinist, has had stories published in venues such as *The Magazine of Fantasy and Science Fiction*, *Gamut*, *Deciduous Tales*, and the *Alien Invasion* anthology from Flame Tree Publishing. He is also the winner of numerous writing awards, including fourth place in the Writer's Digest Annual Short Story Competition and the Crème-de-la-Crème award of the Oklahoma Writers' Federation, Inc. His non-fiction books include the 2009 Choice Outstanding Academic Title, *Is God a Delusion?* and, most recently, *The Triumph of Love: Same-Sex Marriage and the Christian Love Ethic*.

Cody Schroeder
Stray
(First Publication)
Cody Schroeder lives in Missouri, USA, surrounded by books. He spends unreasonable amounts of time reading and writing about all manner of creepy, macabre, and fantastic things. He can be found on Twitter @LordVoltrex, where he tweets about whatever happens to be distracting him. His published works include a short story, 'Clouds over Lichen Spire', in *The Literary Hatchet Issue 14*, 'Tracks in the Snow' in the *Supernatural Horror Short Stories* collection from Flame Tree Publishing, 'Storm Stones' published in *Occult Detective Quarterly Issue #5*, and 'Hunting the Howler' published in *Footsteps in the Dark Short Stories* also by Flame Tree.

M.P. Shiel
The House of Sounds
(Originally Published in *The Pale Ape and Other Pulses*, 1911, as a rewrite of 'Vaila')
Matthew Phipps Shiel (1865–1947) was born in Montserrat, West Indies. Upon his arrival in Britain in 1885, Shiel had been educated in Barbados at Harrison College. He wrote numerous science fiction, supernatural, horror and, later in his career, romance stories. Praised at length by H.G. Wells and H.P. Lovecraft, *The Purple Cloud* remains Shiel's best known and most often reprinted novel. A story of the last man on Earth slowly descending into madness, it is believed to have begun the future history genre.

Clark Ashton Smith
The Vaults of Yoh-Vombis
(Originally Published in *Weird Tales*, May 1932. Published with permission of CASiana Enterprises, the Literary Estate of Clark Ashton Smith.)
Clark Ashton Smith (1893–1961) was born in Long Valley, California. He is well regarded as both a poet and a writer of horror, fantasy and science fiction stories. Along with H.P. Lovecraft and Robert E. Howard, he was a prolific contributor to the magazine *Weird Tales*. His stories are full of dark and imaginative creations, and glimpses into the worlds beyond. His unique writing style and incredible vision have led to many of his stories influencing later fantasy writers.

Lucy A. Snyder
While the Black Stars Burn
(Originally Published in *Cassilda's Song*, 2015)
Lucy A. Snyder is the Shirley Jackson Award-nominated and five-time Bram Stoker Award-winning author of over 100 published short stories and 15 books. Her most recent books are the collections *Halloween Season* and *Exposed Nerves* and the forthcoming novel *Sister, Maiden, Monster*. Her writing has appeared in publications such as *Asimov's Science Fiction*, *Apex Magazine*, *Nightmare Magazine*, *Pseudopod*, *Strange Horizons*, and *Best Horror of the Year*. She lives near Columbus, Ohio. You can learn more about her at lucysnyder.com and you can follow her on Twitter @LucyASnyder.

Harriet Prescott Spofford
The Moonstone Mass
(Originally Published in *Harper's Monthly*, October 1868)
Harriet Prescott Spofford (1835–1921) was born in Maine, with the family moving to Massachusetts during her early life. From the age of seventeen she supported her family with

her early published stories: her mother was an invalid and her father, one of the California Gold Rush Pioneers and a founder of Oregon City, suffered from paralysis. Spofford published over one hundred stories in the next few years, but it was her 1858 publication of 'In a Cellar' in *The Atlantic Monthly* that elevated her reputation and secured her future as a widely successful author.

Richard Thomas
From Within
(Originally Published in *Slave Stories: Scenes from the Slave State*, April 2015)
Richard Thomas is the award-winning author of eight books – *Disintegration and Breaker* (Alibi), *Transubstantiate, Herniated Roots, Staring into the Abyss, Tribulations, Spontaneous Human Combustion* (Turner Publishing), and *The Soul Standard* (Dzanc Books). He has been nominated for the Bram Stoker, Shirley Jackson, and Thriller awards. His over-165 stories in print encompass the venues *The Best Horror of the Year* (Volume Eleven), *Behold!: Oddities, Curiosities and Undefinable Wonders* (Bram Stoker winner), *Cemetery Dance* (twice), *Weird Fiction Review, Shallow Creek, The Seven Deadliest, Gutted: Beautiful Horror Stories, Qualia Nous, Chiral Mad* (numbers 2-4), *PRISMS*, and *Shivers VI*. Visit whatdoesnotkillme.com for more information.

H.G. Wells
The Story of the Late Mr. Elvesham
(Originally Published in *The Idler*, May 1896)
Herbert George Wells (1866–1946) was born in Kent, England. Novelist, journalist, social reformer and historian, Wells is one of the greatest ever science fiction writers and, along with Jules Verne, is sometimes referred to as a 'founding father' of the genre. With Aldous Huxley and, later, George Orwell, he defined the adventurous, social concern of early speculative fiction where the human condition was played out on a greater stage. Wells created over fifty novels, including his famous works *The Time Machine, The Invisible Man, The Island of Dr. Moreau* and *The War of the Worlds,* as well as a fantastic array of gothic short stories.

Chris Wheatley
Eternal Visions
(First Publication)
Chris Wheatley is a writer and music journalist from Oxford, UK. He grew up on a diet of classic science fiction, fantasy and horror literature. His short stories have appeared in several anthologies and magazines and his debut novel, *The Vorticist*, was released in 2021. 'Eternal Visions' arose from a desire to create a piece entirely constructed from letters, emails, book extracts and text messages. Chris has too many records, too many guitars and not enough cats.

Maria Wolfe
Exogenous Cephalus Syndrome: A Case Report and Review of the Literature
(First Publication)
Maria Wolfe's stories have appeared in *The Examined Life Journal, Please See Me*, and *Coffin Bell*. She lives and writes in northeast Ohio, where she practised as a surgical specialist. Before earning a medical degree, she studied English and French literature, Russian language, and biology. Her interests include art history, German language, and running. Maria is currently working on a novel. She can occasionally be found on Twitter @realMariaWolfe.

FLAME TREE PUBLISHING
Epic, Dark, Thrilling & Gothic
New & Classic Writing

Flame Tree's Gothic Fantasy books offer a carefully curated series of new titles, each with combinations of original and classic writing:

*Chilling Horror • Chilling Ghost • Asian Ghost • Science Fiction • Murder Mayhem
Crime & Mystery • Swords & Steam • Dystopia Utopia • Supernatural Horror
Lost Worlds • Time Travel • Heroic Fantasy • Pirates & Ghosts • Agents & Spies
Endless Apocalypse • Alien Invasion • Robots & AI • Lost Souls • Haunted House
Cosy Crime • American Gothic • Urban Crime • Epic Fantasy • Detective Mysteries
Detective Thrillers • A Dying Planet • Footsteps in the Dark • Bodies in the Library
Strange Lands • Weird Horror • Lost Atlantis • Lovecraft Mythos • Terrifying Ghosts
Black Sci-Fi • Chilling Crime • Compelling Science Fiction • Christmas Gothic
First Peoples Shared Stories • Alternate History • Hidden Realms
Immigrant Sci-Fi • Spirits & Ghouls*

Also, new companion titles offer rich collections of classic fiction, myths and tales in the gothic fantasy tradition:

*Charles Dickens Supernatural • George Orwell Visions of Dystopia • H.G. Wells
Sherlock Holmes • Edgar Allan Poe • Bram Stoker Horror • Mary Shelley Horror
Lovecraft • M.R. James Ghost Stories • Algernon Blackwood Horror Stories
Robert Louis Stevenson Collection • The Divine Comedy • The Age of Queen Victoria
Brothers Grimm Fairy Tales • Hans Christian Andersen Fairy Tales • Moby Dick
Alice's Adventures in Wonderland • King Arthur & The Knights of the Round Table
The Wonderful Wizard of Oz • Ramayana • The Odyssey and the Iliad • The Aeneid
Paradise Lost • The Decameron • One Thousand and One Arabian Nights
Persian Myths & Tales • African Myths & Tales • Celtic Myths & Tales
Greek Myths & Tales • Norse Myths & Tales • Chinese Myths & Tales • Japanese Myths & Tales
Native American Myths & Tales • Aztec Myths & Tales • Egyptian Myths & Tales
Irish Fairy Tales • Scottish Folk & Fairy Tales • Viking Folk & Fairy Tales
Heroes & Heroines Myths & Tales • Gods & Monsters Myths & Tales
Beasts & Creatures Myths & Tales • Witches, Wizards, Seers & Healers Myths & Tales*

Available from all good bookstores, worldwide, and online at
flametreepublishing.com

See our new fiction imprint
FLAME TREE PRESS | FICTION WITHOUT FRONTIERS
New and original writing in Horror, Crime, SF and Fantasy

And join our monthly newsletter with offers and more stories:
FLAME TREE FICTION NEWSLETTER
flametreepress.com

GOTHIC FANTASY

For our books, calendars, blog
and latest special offers please see:
flametreepublishing.com